McPEEVISH IN MOFFATLAND

& Other Stories

By
Roger Leslie Paige

Ann,

With all my
love & prayers,
Roger

Spire Publishing - August 2011

First published in Canada and the UK 2011
by Spire Publishing Ltd.

*A cataloguing record for this book is available from the Library and Archives Canada.
Visit www.collectionscanada.ca/amicus/index-e.html*

Designed by Spire Publishing Ltd
in Salt Spring, Canada

www.spirepublishing.com

Printed and bound in the USA or the UK
by Lightning Source Ltd.

ISBN: 978-1-926635-62-0

Spire
Publishing
www.spirepublishing.com

*"We know nothing for certain.
And there is nothing to be known beyond that which,
in one way or another, is represented outwardly in actions.
Within is torment and weariness"*

Pirandello

CONTENTS

Hellzafreezin, Ontario

The Bull Moose was the only creature in sight as Father Andrew Manwell drew near to the building in which the morning service was to be held.

It has come to a pretty fine pass when only the local wildlife comes to hear me, he thought.

He was not surprised when the moose, finding nothing of interest in the garbage pail, emptied its bowels and sauntered off into the early dawn. By the time he opened the main door with the old key the moose's droppings- a gift or insult- had frozen. Some of the locals might use the lumps later as a puck on a makeshift rink. The thermometer on the wall read minus fifteen degrees; but then it was broken, like so much else he thought.

Apart from the interior the church was like any other building in the small township. Father Manwell went through his preparations, all the time wanting to have a quick snort from the hip flask he always carried. The flask was legendary in the area. Many a sinner it had revived and- this was the amazing thing- it had never been known to be found empty. Father Manwell had suffered the indignity of being mugged once on a visit to the large city to the west. Why he had gone there was at first a mystery to the locals- the truth initially had been known only to Father Manwell and the Bishop. Whoever had mugged the Father hadn't known he was a Father, seeing only a well-wrapped up late middle-aged easy meat customer. Father Manwell hadn't even realised that he'd been mugged, so quickly did it all happen: a shove in the back and a sprawl in the road, a quick frisking while threats not to move were growled, the removal of his wallet and then footsteps thundering down the icy sidewalk. The blessing was that his hip flask remained and he gratefully drank from it once he'd risen to his feet. The wallet, stripped of the little cash he had had, was handed in to the police station some days later, his various personal papers being intact. A badly scrawled note apologised for the mugging and requested that the Father offer a prayer for his assailant (who did not sign his name). The hip flask had been with him since his early days training in the seminary and had seen more service than his breviary.

Father Manwell had been in Hellzafreezin for more years than he could remember. Sometimes it felt as though he had been there forever, like the ice and snow and the cold. At times he thought that he had simply been posted there and conveniently forgotten. Apart from that summons to see the new Bishop he had not left the township in twenty five years or more, nor had he wished to do so. It was a town in which everyone seemed to be waiting for someone else to die first. The smart money, so Father Manwell was told, was on him. The odds had been fifty to one the week he arrived and had shortened as the years passed, the slate being kept on the wall at 'Bilcox's Bar'. The original proprietor of the bar had been named Wilcox but the sign writer of the time had an aversion to W. Father Manwell was reliably told by one of his confidants- Injun Jake who had lost an ear when it froze to the ground- that he was down to two to one on and that he should have got his bet in years ago as he'd be a rich man when dead: now he'd just be dead.

Without undue haste he said the Mass to the empty room. It had been like that for some time now. Most of the Native American residents- the Ojibway- had returned to their own beliefs. In some ways now he was no different from many of the businesses in the short main street. How they got by was impossible to say. Me likewise, Father Manwell would think as he locked the outer door. Mostly this time of year if they weren't out hunting or making ice sculptures, people stayed indoors, played cards and did all the usual things that people do. Sometimes someone would amble up the road, just to make sure all the buildings were there; and then they'd amble back to where they had emerged from to report that not much had changed since the last fall of snow.

Mostly wherever you look and whenever you care to look it's wilderness; the kind of wilderness that gives you pause and makes you check your ticket and think maybe you got on the wrong sled back aways. Stand anywhere you like and look in any direction you care to crick your neck and you'll see a lot of snow. You can't have too much snow some folks feel, usually while looking at it from inside through a window. That's considered to be the best way to see snow. Step outside and it's mighty pretty but it's mighty cold as well. There's a lot of wisdom in snow if you care to dig a bit. There may be some trees poking through it too and some boulders looking like lumpy pillows, perhaps there's even a frozen lake with a name which tests your teeth and tongue; and there sure is plenty of sky. There's so much sky you start to wonder if anywhere else has got any sky at all. Maybe you'll catch sight of a bear or hear a wolf howl. What you won't see is another living soul. Oh there are plenty of them hereabouts but they need plenty of elbow room in 'Bilcox's Bar'. If you do catch sight of another living soul then don't forget to mention it when you reach 'Bilcox's Bar'. The book is open on a sighting and the odds are pretty high so there's a fair pile of Beaverskin tokens to be had. Of course, you can't just claim to have seen another living soul out there in the wilderness: that other living soul has to claim that they've seen you: 'confirmation' that's what they call it and they're hot on that in Hellzafreezin.

As he made his way from the church up the main street- if it ever had any other name than "Street" nobody had ever mentioned it- Father Manwell stopped to study the ice sculptures which were scattered about. They were like miniature totem poles for the most part, immaculately made and sparkling in the low sunlight. Nobody could say when the custom had started, but it went on throughout the winter. In the summer the sculptures were replaced by blocks of wood, usually carved in the shape of a bear or lynx. It was the sort of scene tourists would have snapped avidly with their digital cameras, that is if a tourist could make it to Hellzafreezin. If you asked one of the locals what the purpose of those ice sculptures was you'd most likely get the answer 'Yep' and the local would move on at that steady pace which could only end in 'Bilcox's Bar'. There were some more loquacious residents in 'Bilcox's' who might embroider things for a price, but that would be a load of hokum or hooey, depending on the speaker.

Father Manwell went into the bar where he would eat his breakfast. Heads nodded as he entered and he nodded back. Nodding was an art in Hellzafreezin, one which the good Father had mastered early and well. If you couldn't nod in Hellzafreezin then you squandered a lot of energy which could have been put to better use. Behind the bar, which was shaped like an L, Estelle Shave was already piling bacon and eggs on the plate for him. He remembered baptising her when she was born, probably one of his first acts in the town; and he remembered more vividly unbaptising her along with the rest of the villagers. Unlike most bars you might go into in the northern territories 'Bilcox's' had no jukebox, no fruit machines and no beer. The only beverage served there was the local tonic called *Zhoom*. It was made by Long-tongue Johansson somewhere out in the wooded area by the lake and ferried into town daily by sledge. A local ordinance banned the use of snowmobiles anywhere in the surrounding you-name-it-we-cover-it-by-snowshoe region. The thing about *Zhoomiwaadizi* tonic was that it was non-alcoholic and non-hallucinogenic; but it put wool on your chest and banished the cold. It also added depth and vivacity to discussions about the performance of the Thunder Bay hockey team, the solitary object of betting officially sanctioned by the town council. There were those who swore by it as a hair-restorer and others who used it to light fires. During May and June it dealt death to blackfly and mosquito alike. Each year when the pressing was done Father Manwell would lead 'the blessing of the pressing'- it sounded better in Ojibway, it was true- and that guaranteed 'the proof' of the vintage.

The large mug of black coffee was there beside the plate when Father Manwell sat down. Estelle knew what he would order and when he would walk into the bar. Estelle knew the names and orders of everyone in the bar. If you listened carefully- and not much was being said it was true- you would seldom hear anyone's name mentioned in the bar. Conversation, when it took place, was directed at all and sundry; but you knew if it was meant for you by the kind of inflexion that a visitor would miss.

The last visitor to Hellzafreezin had been Father Manwell and he had stayed. There had seemed to be no other choice. As he'd stood there that morning, fresh off the sled and terrified as well as coated with a thin veneer of ice, his one thought had been- well, there were no thoughts until he had been warmed up a little with an infusion of local tonic (both poured down his throat and sprayed over his body after a polite 'Excuse me, Father'). The tongues of a dozen huskies had licked the ice from his body. Can eyeballs freeze? That, he remembered, had been the first conscious thought he had once he'd 'come around', though he was aware of every jolting second of the journey through the snow and forests. Then he thought about fleeing, but the dog team had disappeared as had the sled; and he was being introduced to a plate of delicious reindeer steak (which he thought was prime Texas beef) and a baked potato into the skin of which he wished he could curl and fall asleep. The clincher had been the glass of *Zhoom* which he had swallowed in one gulp. This instinctual response was the only correct way for the very first glass of it to be swallowed; thereafter you could sip it or tip it, whichever served your purpose. Somehow everything about Hellzafreezin had looked different after that. Besides, if he went back, Father Manwell recalled, he would only have to deal with whatever it was that he had volunteered to come here to get away from. Local speculation had early fixed upon that being unrequited love of a woman; but once the locals got to know him opinions veered between 'debts to the Mob' and unpaid bar bills. Sometimes, it was conceded, people came to the wilderness to find themselves; but the intellectuals in Hellzafreezin reckoned that Father Manwell couldn't find an axe in a block of wood; and if a man was daft enough not to know who and where he was, well, he might well find himself stuck in Hellzafreezin for the duration. Even the Ottawa government wouldn't come to Hellzafreezin to collect taxes and that suited everyone just fine, since they weren't going to Ottawa anyhow.

There had been some surprise, even concern, when Father Manwell received that letter from the Bishop a short time- some twenty years- after he had arrived. Not that letters were that rare. Most folk could read especially if it was an IOU or a ten dollar bill; after that they might lose interest it was true. The fact that everyone in Hellzafreezin knew that the good Father had received a letter from the Bishop could be explained by the insignia of the diocese being there in plain sight on the envelope which was handed round to everyone in town, along with Chief Stand-back's pair of spectacles, before it was dropped through Father Manwell's letter-box. When he booked the sled to the railroad halt some dozen miles south then some of the nods given over breakfast were more wondering and Estelle doubled the number of rashers she served him. When he'd gone the betting was high that he'd not be returning as the woman would want him to 'do the right thing', whatever that was away from Hellzafreezin. Medicine Hat Joe, wise beyond his thirteen years, put his family's money on the good Father returning within a week. Estelle said that her extra helping of rashers would have 'done the trick' and she went with Medicine Hat. When Father Manwell returned two days later, clean-shaved and whistling, some slates were wiped clean while others had the losses added to them. The nods he received that morning were respectful. It was reckoned that any feller who could sort that kind of business out in two days, get a shave and whistle like that was worth his salt and a muskrat tail. The next Mass he gave on Sunday was packed out, even though they'd all been unbaptized for years, the book being open on some sort of confession during the sermon. If Father Manwell had been surprised by the unexpected turn out he had given no sign. There were those amongst the older residents who said that they'd never seen him swinging the thurible so sweetly and vigorously.

In Hellzafreezin it was reckoned that there was always a defining moment in a person's life. Such moments could knit you or split you. Once they had become familiar with the good Father's ways and had quietly weaned him off them and adjusted him so that he was more accommodating to theirs, the townsfolk felt easy with the idea of him taking part in the annual lacrosse match with their neighbours from Loco Township. The match had been going on for as long as the towns had existed, and before that probably. Composing epics about each match kept some of the crabbier Elders busy. As a courtesy Father Manwell had been invited to participate that first summer. Nobody had expected him to accept the invitation, reckoning that he'd be good for a blessing and then could watch from the side-lines. When he did accept (feeling he would be insulting his parishioners if he declined) there had been much hasty re-shuffling of the line-up to accommodate him. For a week before the game, always held at the summer solstice, efforts had been made to familiarise the good Father with the rules- or, in the case of this local variety of lacrosse, the non-rules. This was not the game with which Saint Jean de Brébeuf would have been familiar. The object was to carry the ball across the town boundary of the opposing team. A certain chicanery had been practised in the distant past over the definition of 'boundary'; but nowadays, since hatchets had become unfashionable and lawsuits more numerous, the 'boundary' had to be clearly marked on the outskirts of each town. Both Chiefs had to inspect and confirm that the boundaries were there and properly marked with skunk extract. The teams would assemble midway between the two towns, a distance of ten miles either way. The Chief of the losing team the previous year would lob the ball into the massed ranks of the teams and, well, all hell broke loose. Part of the problem, though the participants saw it as fun, was that there was no way of controlling the huskies which got free from the grip of the spectators. There were also those more unscrupulous onlookers who would 'loose the husky' at vital moments, causing players to be tripped, licked incessantly or bowled over when in full flight. If a husky got the ball then play had to be stopped until the husky was brought to heel and surrendered the ball. Mischievous onlookers would coat the ball with bacon fat and there are few things more difficult on this earth than parting a husky from a bacon-fat greased ball. To do so often a blow with a wooden mallet between the eyes was called for. It was believed- and not without some evidence- that the harder skulled huskies looked forward to this as a sign of affection, or at least not indifference, from their owners.

The carrier of the ball (huskies aside) would run as far as he could towards the opponent's boundary. He would be escorted and protected by his team-mates, forming a phalanx around him which was akin to the Roman 'turtle' (minus the shields). The opposition would attempt to break through the phalanx and steal the ball from its possessor. For much of the afternoon the good Father with his soutane flapping like the wings of an eagle was peripheral to the action. Neither side came closer than five miles to the opponent's boundary. The moment of truth came as the twilight was gathering and the spectators were lighting the torches which would enable play to continue into the night. The only problem then would be the low flying owls which often made off with the ball. A melee of gigantic proportions, involving players, huskies and a passing moose in heat, developed. The ball squirted loose and Father Manwell scooped it up with his net. The moose, as locals would know, is a short-sighted animal, quite peaceably minded as long as it could chew some sphagnum moss; but the male in heat has other things on its mind. Catching sight of Father Manwell's flapping soutane, the moose let out a bellow which would have summoned cows from the depths of the tundra and it raced towards the priest. Choice is a funny thing,

Father Manwell thought as he gripped the hem of his soutane and began to exercise his legs. The moose has four and the human only two. Whether or not this is an advantage or disadvantage in the snow and over ice rather than in the mud, only scientists would be able to say. What was the case was that the good Father found gear after gear as the pair flew towards the outskirts of Loco. Huskies streamed after them, pulling spectators on sleds, all hollering encouragement, some for the good Father and others for the moose. At the seminary Father Manwell had been proficient at the long distance running- proficient but not necessarily excellent. However, there are few better stimulants to improvement than a single-minded bull moose in hot pursuit. It is difficult to say what might have happened had not fate taken a hand. The boundary was in sight; the moose was gaining and was within snapping distance of the flapping soutane; Father Manwell held the ball aloft like the host at mass; the smell of skunk suffused the night air. A female moose meandered into sight, uttered a summoning snort and the bull moose veered off to the left, crashing into the shrubs in pursuit. Father Manwell, unaware of what had developed behind him, crossed the boundary and was only brought to a halt when he ran into the side of a house. From that day on he was referred to (in hushed tones) as "*inini aweni gagwejikazh*"- or at least that's what Father Manwell thought he heard being chanted as he was chaired back to Hellzafreezin in triumph.

*

- Bugarach is getting crowded, said No-Drum Tom.

Now it's a peculiar thing in 'Bilcox's Bar' that, at any time of day, whenever No-Drum Tom started to give one of his up-to-date reports on what was really happening outside the snow zone, the flies, which normally hung around the light bulbs, took wing for the window at the far end of the bar and beat on it   until it shook. The behaviour of those customers seated around No-Drum Tom would have emulated the flies except that nobody had any wings and, as the passage of time had shown, they were quite safe where they were; whereas on the window the flies would be swatted when Estelle reached that end of the bar. That was where the beaver tail fly-swat was hung. You would have thought the flies would have known that by now, but none lived to tell the tale to the next generation of larvae, Estelle having inherited her mother's keen eye and strong wrist (amongst other things which needn't detain us here though they may later).

No-Drum Tom had one of those sizeable satellite dishes which city folk are so proud of they hang them outside their homes in clusters like trophy *moominensan* (dingle berries). He'd picked it up in a trade for some mink furs a while back, reckoning he'd got the better end of the deal since hanging any number of mink furs outside your cabin brought nothing but trouble. For a time people in Hellzafreezin thought it might be some kind of giant outdoor spittoon or a rink for birds to skate on. It took them a few months to get used to the idea that they had an immediate direct link to Thunder Bay that didn't involve huskies and the train. Friday nights as soon as Estelle threw them all out- and nobody made the first move until she reached down the beaver tail and slapped it on the counter- they would mooch on over to No-Drum Tom's cabin to catch the live game action on his big plasma screen. Sometimes the picture broke up when the geese were flying in any or every direction. Whoever was nearest the door would step outside and fire a blast of bullets into the night sky: that usually got the picture back.

No-Drum Tom said that folks in Thunder Bay could get hundreds of those sky images for something called a subscription fee. Folk in Hellzafreezin had little time for subscription fees it has to be said, them being too similar to a tribe of irrational fleas in your pants. One thing you can't do is shoot fleas in your pants; they were all agreed on that. Just how No-Drum Tom got the hockey game and news channel without paying a subscription had folk scratching their heads until they recalled that his nephew worked as a computer engineer in the city and knew a load of stuff about computer script and signal decoding.

Watching an inquisitive gaze run from one customer to another in 'Bilcox's Bar' was a pleasure to be savoured. There wasn't much they didn't know about snow and moose and bear crap and how to set a trap and how to paddle a chemanis; but that gaze travelled the length of the bar and round again before Too-Slow Luke- the best moose-caller in the place who was seated beside No-Drum Tom- gathered it and raised an eyebrow which saved everyone else the expenditure of energy needed to do so.

Nuance and subtlety were like a second skin to the customers in 'Bilcox's Bar'. The 'hereabouts' of Hellzafreezin were known to every man and woman of the village from birth and probably the womb. Nobody hereabouts ended up lost, not even when they had to go to Lost, which was as seldom as they might wish to go to Unreachable Creek. Everyone knew those places and others like Itchy Flats, Can't Climb Hill and Dead End Pass. But that eyebrow might as well have been a klaxon bellowing: 'Where in blazes is Bugarach?'

The answer, which No-Drum Tom had off pat, didn't significantly lower Too-Slow Luke's eyebrow. After another gaze rippled around the bar the question had to be put: 'Where in blazes is France or Langue D'Oc?'

A sudden "tick" drew every eye to the clock on the wall; but it was a false alarm: Tadpole was merely scratching at a mouse hole.

Paddles-Zigzag Harold gave it out as his opinion that there was little below Highway 666 which needed remembering or visiting and to go outside was a waste of good trapping time. Little Moose-Nose said that when he'd reached the Bay he'd given it the once over and decided there wasn't much to it except drift-pan, which they had plenty of on the Boogijise river back in Hellzafreezin. He did admit that the Northern Lights looked pretty enough but the shower curtain his squaw Shake-Tent had made for their cabin looked much nicer and served a more useful purpose. Folk were generally agreed that if there was such a place as France it was too far away to worry about: an angry bear in your cabin, now that was something to worry about. As for Bugarach, if 'hippies' and 'new worlders' wanted to drag their sandals and ponchos there and wait to dance the Apo-cal-ypso then leastwise they weren't leaving footprints in the snow around Hellzafreezin and taking up valuable elbow-room in the bar. It was generally agreed that the Apo-cal-ypso- which the good Father Manwell knew about even if he couldn't dance unless someone put a chickaree up his cassock- wasn't something that need concern them, not tonight anyhow and certainly not on a Friday night. Since tomorrow also would be a tonight then they needn't worry about it at all. Someone nodded and suggested another round. Estelle uncapped the bottles and that was it settled with a comforting unanimity. If there was one thing the folk in the bar wanted, apart from not slipping off the stool or being caught around the ear with a swinging beaver tail, it was unanimity. Nobody had every hooked one or trapped one but they knew it when they were in it, just like they knew what a snowdrift was, in or out of one.

Behind the racks of bottles the mirror- the only one in the territory- reflected everything in the room and some things which weren't. That mirror had been the pride and joy of the original Wilcox, the *waabishkiiwe* (white man) who had first set up the trading post. The wall-length mirror was purported to be either the one in which the drinkers in Deadwood's 'Number 10 Saloon' saw Wild Bill Hickok being shot or that of 'The Last Chance' saloon in Dawson City where 'Klondike' Kate Rockwell had danced and sung. The ancestors of the good folk seated at the bar gazed tolerantly out of the mirror at their descendants, who sometimes gazed meditatively back at them. Seeing yourself in that mirror was the equivalent of having your picture taken.

The day Wilcox had brought the mirror into the small village there had been a blizzard in the making. The mirror had been crated and hauled on a couple of double-teamed sleds tied together. The villagers watched as Wilcox dismantled the mirror to set it in the cabin. The rest of the story about Wilcox- his first name had never been known- was easy to tell: he had come to the village to make his fortune selling *ishkodewaabo* (whiskey) to the natives and *toot-sweet* had left strapped to a sled. Estelle's great-granny had been the one who strapped Wilcox to the sled and had stuck the icicle up the backside of the lead dog to encourage the team. Her last words to Wilcox as the snow flew from wildly pedalling paws- the words still used by the women of the village on those occasions when a line needed to be drawn in the snow for the menfolk - were 'Bugger off, *moosh koosh*!'. Whenever a blizzard arose from the south it was said that the sled was still heading full steam in that direction. Sometimes if you stared into the mirror long enough while sipping your *Zhoom* you could see the blizzard blooming just like back then.

Whistles-Badly Pete checked the number of his teeth in the mirror. He swore that he had had twenty when he came in but those around him told him he was mistaken: it had been eighteen. This was the part of the morning that once a month drove Estelle into the back room to check the slop-pail. No one would be buying *Zhoom* while they all checked their teeth; and the sight of her uncles removing their *wiibidikaanan* (dentures) and handing them to the Chief for counting was a performance she had seen once too often. Inevitably they would start to call out for her to come back and sort out which dentures went into whose mouth. She'd end up scolding Whistles-Badly Pete for causing the confusion and he'd grin happily with his full set of teeth and whistle that tune which teased the yellowjacks from their hives. For days afterwards she would have customers complaining to her about their dental furniture, blaming her for popping the wrong set back into the wrong mouth. She knew from her aunts that they'd swop dentures before coming into the bar the next day just to keep her on her toes. These are devious men, her aunts would warn her; never marry a man if you can help it: a wolf's teeth are kinder.

Time has this way of slipping by, standing still or recurring in 'Bilcox's Bar', all at the same time and never at once. Each customer upon entering would salute his ancestor in the mirror and greet Estelle with a nod. Some blamed the mischievous behaviour of time on the light which the mirror would catch and shine back into the room and your eyes. Some felt the ventilation could have been improved, while others (a minority) felt it was all to do with the height of the bar stools. Others thought it was the way Long-Tongue Johansson had prepared the tonic for that day. The customers swore that no two bottles were the same. One day they were convinced that the tonic had a hint of bunchberry in it. The next day all were sure that Johansson had slipped in some birch bark. At one time they were all in favour of bringing in one of those *connoisseurs* No-Drum had told them about. If there was one thing Hellzafreezin lacked and could make use of at such times of friendly disagreement, it was a *connoisseur*. The problem was that nobody knew what one looked like or what kind of bait to use. It was agreed that maybe Father Manwell, who had been in a seminary sometime and knew about things from outside might be in the best position to advise them; so the whole idea was shelved until he next came in. By the time Father Manwell next came in- let's be generous and say it was twenty four hours later- time had moved on- or back- and other more pressing issues (such as the performance last night of Thunder Bay's goalie) had risen to the top of the agenda.

That was another thing they could thank No-Drum for, Estelle thought. Before he started tuning into the sky Hellzafreezin had somehow stumbled along without an agenda; the most they had had was a menu on which pride of place on a Sunday went to roast muffle. You don't miss some things if you haven't got them; but once you knew you hadn't got them then didn't you start to itch? Take the crab louse for example, Whistles-Badly Pete said one morning- that made everyone sit up straight and look like they wanted to scratch some. Estelle frowned slightly and moved down the bar so that she couldn't overhear what was clearly going to be some 'men's talk'. It wasn't that she found it offensive but that it bored her antlerless. Most of them wouldn't know a crab louse if it walked up and tapped them on the shoulder. Some of them (so her aunts said) knew more about the contents of an *amikwiish* (beaver lodge) than they did about what was in their pants. Estelle was concerned about all these new ideas and words No-Drum would casually drop into the conversation. They were harmless enough but you never knew what ideas would do to her uncles who were more at home walking through the snow and talking to their dog teams.

Her aunts reckoned the uncles and men in general didn't have a brain cell between them and had the memory capacity of sphagnum moss but Estelle wasn't so sure. Maybe, she mused as she emptied the slop-pail, I should get married and find out for myself. If my aunts could hear me thinking like that they'd be scowling, Estelle thought with a smile. At other times- usually once a new litter of any kind of creature had been born- her aunts would start to wax lyrical about the manliness of one or other of the unmarried young men and encourage Estelle to 'get into his canoe and paddle'. Estelle decided they were each as crazy as the other, her aunts and uncles alike.

When she got back Tadpole had both paws stuck up the mouse hole and was mewling for help. The customers had paused in their philosophical speculations and were wondering how best to intervene or whether to let nature take its course (which often equated with doing nothing at all). Much bearberry was being puffed as the problem was being chewed over. Some were advocating enlarging the hole and wondering what tool would be the best to use; others were all for pushing Tadpole through the existing one. All felt in need of some more *Zhoom* to help them resolve this sudden conundrum which felt as slippery as drift-ice. No-Drum Tom put on his longest face feeling left out.

Men, Estelle thought as she reached down and pulled Tadpole free. With her she brought an old pair of dentures which had been put down as a mouse-trap. Tadpole stalked off to recover her feline dignity.

Hawk-Feather Maurice swiftly reached down to retrieve this old pair of teeth. For years- with the discretion of a seal moving amongst polar bears- he had been collecting cast off dentures, building up a collection second to none in the province. Each month Swift-foot-No-noise on his postal run would deliver a specialised collectors' magazine to Hawk-Feather's cabin. There was much speculation as to what this magazine could be- 'Husky', 'Snowshoe Monthly' and 'Playboy' carried a lot of bets- and the truth remained known only to Hawk-Feather and *Postes Canada*.

When Father Manwell made his appearance, after the obligatory time required for a new customer to settle and tune in it was generally wondered what this Apo-cal-ypso dance was all about and could the good Father enlighten the company. Father Manwell, not wishing to put the wind up anyone, said that he believe in the Corbières mountains- which were full of holes being limestone, which was porous unlike the fine solid stuff under the snow and ice they lived on- it was a dance associated with a hat-making festival and involved a lot of hopping on first one foot then the other, the inhabitants of that region near Carcassonne having the minimum number of lower limbs necessary for such a dancing style. Estelle caught his quick wink (as did everyone else in the mirror) and responded to his nod by placing the correct number of bottles of *Zhoom* on the bar.

This explanation seemed to all to have a satisfactory cohesiveness about it, never mind the confirmatory arrival of the *Zhoom*. Some were of the opinion that the dance sounded like the jingle dance while others thought it was like the snowshoe dance. Twelve-Toes (who spoke seldom and often made less sense) said he'd danced like that when crossing the path of a tribe of ants.

The reference to hats gave rise to considerable discussion as to what kind of hats they might be. Now the only member of the clan who had a hat- albeit for ceremonial purposes- was Chief Stand-back. The hat he had- well, it was the clan's hat but as Chief only he could wear it- was a *Chapeaux en peau de castor*, though whether it was of the Regent, D'Orsay or Paris Beau style was not something about which anyone lost much sleep. There were those who said it was the very hat worn by President Lincoln when he gave the Gettysburg address; but then there were those who would have talked through their hat (if they had had one). Others swore that it was the very Beaver hat over which Sir John MacDonald and Alexander Mackenzie fought when leaving the Ottawa Curling Club. You can still see the thumb and stretch marks on the brim; but whose teeth marks they were had never been established. Whenever any celebrity might pass through Hellzafreezin Chief Stand-back would be ready to don the hat and wait to greet them. There was often prolonged debate at the bar as to who might be visiting and who would qualify as a celebrity. There was general agreement that Gretzky was worth the Chief donning the hat; after that there was no agreement whatsoever. It had to be admitted that it was seldom that a celebrity happened to be passing; in fact it had never happened. But they had the hat just in case. To make sure it didn't lose its shape, and to keep the Chief's head the correct size, it had been agreed at a meeting many melts ago that the hat would be worn on less august occasions. These usually coincided with someone with a long memory saying: Ain't seen the hat for a while, Chief; whereupon with due ceremony (which did *not* include the playing of the clan's copy of the old 78rpm Cadman's '*The Ojibway Canoe Song*' as sung by Elsie Baker) Chief Stand-back would enter 'Bilcox's Bar' bearing upon his skull the hat from the band of which sprouted a freshly plucked owl feather (or a chicken feather if his great-great grandson had been up to his tricks the night before).

It was thought most unlike that the bullet hole in the hat had come from Davy Crockett's rifle. No-Drum Tom, whose one visit to Thunder Bay to collect the satellite dish was bearing unexpected fruit and broadening the minds of those in the bar, was of the opinion that the hat ought to be subjected to a ballistic test, to settle the question as to what bullet could have made that hole once and for all. Now folk in Hellzafreezin quite liked not knowing some things (though they often weren't sure what they were until someone brought it up and they found out that they didn't know that but now they did). They also quite liked knowing other things. They'd like to know, just for example, what the magazine was that Hawk-Feather Maurice took each month so that they could close that book and the lucky winner could use his pay-out to buy a round; but they knew better than to ask Swift-foot-No-noise to sneak a peek by ripping the plain brown covering a little,

Poste Canada frowning on that kind of thing.

No-Drum Tom said there were all kinds of tests folk outside could take-paternity tests, new-clear tests, IQ tests, lie detector tests and so on. There was general agreement that folk from outside were best left where they were to test what they liked and the folk in Hellzafreezin would keep on with their hunting, fishing and *Zhoomiwaadizi* and baby making. It was agreed that they found out most things by-the-by and if they didn't, well the ice would melt anyhow.

Now and then Twelve-Toes would descend from his stool and go outside to check his huskies. Of all the teams in the village Twelve-Toes's were the craftiest, always playing jokes on their owner. They all looked the same, having come from the one litter, and would answer to each other's names whenever he called them. In his cabin they were always hiding his boots and mittens, moving things about in drawers and generally keeping him on his toes.

When the rasping of fingers on chins reached a certain pitch and Tadpole began to yowl in tune, Estelle went into the small back room to wheel out the barber's chair. She placed this by the back window, through which the afternoon sun shone, and eyed the men at the bar.

-Who's first? she called.

Each man contemplatively stroked his chin, an act which involved more muscles and brain time than one would have thought possible or necessary. Stroking the chin was not something to be done casually and haphazardly. You never knew what might happen if you rubbed your bristles the wrong way. Was it time for a shave or would an extra day's growth prove manageable? Shaving was one of those things which needed thought and preparation. It was one thing to be shaved while you were courting, quite another to bare the throat too readily to one's wife. Estelle was known by her many aunts to have a steady hand and a sharp razor; and with the only mirror in the village the menfolk were guaranteed to return from a session in 'Bilcox's Bar' sober and neat after the coon tail had lathered their faces. Her aunts might murmur to each other: If only Estelle could do brain surgery as well. But their natural desire to see her happily wedded off was counterbalanced by their investment in her ability to shave their husbands. If ever Estelle was found to have shaved an unmarried man there'd be trouble, they were sure of that.

Goes-way-back Henry would tell anyone who would listen- and even those who'd heard it all before would respectfully listen to the oldest inhabitant of Hellzafreezin, just to make sure he told it right- about the day the map-makers came to the town and tried to put the town on a map. Now you look at any map of the county, any map at all, and all you'll see so much of that it makes you want to blink and exchange your eyeballs is whiteness and emptiness. You'd as well try to map the tracks of animals as pin down Hellzafreezin. Those who know how to get there get there and those who don't can't, it's as simple as that.

Pinned to the wall they call the 'Map-wall' (or *akii-mazini'igan aasamisagoon* for those who got no other way of using their tongue) is a large map of the Province. Now there are plenty of bugs squashed on it but nobody pays them any mind except Tadpole the cat. She likes to sit and count the smudges and meow for her grub when she's done. Estelle is the only one can feed the cat; anyone else tries he gets a clawing from Estelle. Here and there on the map-wall you might see the stain of tobacco juice where someone's aim was off and they missed the spittoon. If the spittoon looks like a wolf skull to you well you're right, it is: costs you a nickel if you miss it and a dime for Estelle when she wipes the spit off the map. You look at that map and you see plenty of places with names- Dead Horse Falls, Snakepiss, No Trees Forest, Scratchass and such like. Names don't mean too much and most of them look like somewhere else that you can't quite remember.

'So,' says Goes-way-back Henry warming to his tale, 'the door opens and in comes this young feller saying he's from the guv-er-ment and he's gonna put us on the map. In those days, way back, we didn't have a map, not like we do today. (At this point in the telling everyone looks at the Map-wall and nods. They're proud of that map, prouder still that it doesn't show Hellzafreezin.) What we had then was a blizzard; but not like the blizzards we had when I was a kid. My pa would tell me about some he had to dig himself out of with his bare hands. Biggest pair of hands I've ever seen (and here Goes-way-back Henry would demonstrate the size of his father's hands by holding his not very small hands side by side.) If snow was cents we'd be rich, he was always saying. Sometimes the blizzard would last so long, he'd tell me, you'd forget how to count. He comes out of one blizzard and I'd been born and grown three foot high. Says it was a surprise 'cause when she started to blow and snow he was single, but that's how funny the mind gets. (Everyone would nod, having been in blizzards which had turned you round the corner and holed your kayak.) This young feller-called himself Samuel-something-or-other- he had all kinds of e-quip-ment with him- telescope, compass, chain, and something called a theod-o-lite which walked on three legs and had us all walking around it crazywise.

Most folks round here then didn't go in for e-quip-ment. No call for it, I guess. Anyone here got any e-quip-ment?'

At this people in the bar checked their pockets and inside their boots and looked around to see if they could see any lying around. The huskies might drag anything in, if they were in the mood. But all agreed there was no e-quip-ment to hand that morning. Father Manwell's hip flask they didn't count as such but as an e-ssen-tial.

'So we gets Samuel-something-or-other sat down, right where you are Father, and we listens to him while Estelle's great-granny One-tooth-smile poured him some *Zhoom*. Feller was lost, that was for sure, and he had a touch of snow-blindness never mind all the rest. We reckoned the best thing was to get him bedded down in the sweat lodge and get that fever out of him. That blizzard just kept on blowing. I must've whittled a thousand pipes before it stopped blowing. By then we'd got right friendly with Samuel-something-or-other. He was good with co-ordinates, though none of us had seen one fly. We helped him put some places on the map- Many-Bugs-Bite, Too-Deep-Bog, Loon Haunt them's some of ours. (And here folk would look at the map with pride and pick out the names of the places their forefathers had put on the map, places no man had ever been to and if he passed through their co-ordinates would wonder where they were.) I guess we forgot to give him the co-ordinates of hereabouts but by then he was right friendly with my sister Make-Sun-Shine. She had that look women get sometimes- begging your pardon, Estelle- and she took him away on a long sled with his e-quip-ment once the blizzard had blown herself out. Haven't had a blizzard like that since then; no need I guess.'

Estelle banged a full glass of *Zhoom* down in front of Goes-way-back Henry to signal the end of the story. There was more, of course, much more; but if you let Goes-way-back Henry get up a real head of steam then, hell, the moon would bump shoulders with the winter sun and nothing would get done in Hellzafreezin. Not that anyone minded nothing getting done; it's just that they liked the easy feeling of being able to get something done should they turn their mind to it. There was always something that ought to be got done, but maybe not right now since there was a blizzard coming and the huskies needed a run. If the huskies didn't get their run, well, forget about sleeping tonight because they'd be howling fit to make a dead moose shit. Besides, Estelle's grandmother would be waiting for Goes-way-back Henry to get home with the box of matches he came out for six hours ago.

But Goes-way-back Henry isn't budging till he's had his fill. He's not left his seat of his own volition for more than fifty years- probably longer, if there was anyone older than that to remember. Blame the clock over the bar, which he swears by. It's been ten o'clock since it was knocked off the wall in the last indoor fist fight in Hellzafreezin thirty years ago. Everyone has tried to fix it but it won't tick and it won't tock. Now and then they all look at it in the hope that it will, though the odds are getting longer by the no-tick-no-tock. Everyone else is settled and waiting to see if Estelle's grandmother will come in like she always does and bat Goes-way-back Henry round the head with a dead pike. The betting favours a bear's paw this morning, though some of the clientele fancy the beaver's tail. One thing's certain, though: sure as hell he'll get it round the left ear. Estelle's grandmother comes in swinging and Goes-way-back Henry always turns his good ear to the door when it bangs open. The sight of his feet being dragged through the door means it's time for a smoke and out will come the pipes and tobacco pouches. Whoever calls it right- dead pike, bear paw or beaver's tail- gets a free glass of *Zhoom* from Estelle. Most days nobody wins, but that's fine as there's always a one day carry-over.

Estelle leans across the counter and tells Father Manwell that Tadpole has given birth again and would he do the baptising. Of course, he replies. All Tadpole's litters- and she keeps dropping kittens once Sneaky the stray has got at her- have been baptised and it's a tradition the good Father gladly keeps up. Somehow it takes the wildness out of them, at least that's what Estelle says. The next infant born in the town will also be baptised and then unbaptized before the shaman takes over. Father Manwell and the shaman have their systems synchronised so that everyone is happy (except the Bishop who isn't interested in Catholic kittens). Today it's the good Father's turn to go first; tomorrow it will the shaman's turn. Everyone is agreed that this division of labour thing is good news. Everyone at the bar feels fine and dandy about the fact that someone somewhere is doing something, just as they are. The most important thing they are doing, they will explain once they've meandered back home to face the music, is preparing themselves for doing something. By sharing their wisdom, the say, they're improving their prospects. The wives are unimpressed and many a beaver's tail is swung in private.

*

Father Manwell had a dilemma. He has told no one since he knows that the solution- if there is a solution- is down to him and him alone ('begging your pardon, Lord', he adds as an afterthought). The Bishop had been direct with him. He was one of the new school, was Bishop Burden, the kind who expects results and compare statistics with other statistics in the belief that the resulting statistics will reveal something statistically significant. He had all kinds of documents on his desk and while Father Manwell patiently waited seated before that desk, the Bishop read them and sighed. His sighs were more than punctuation or those of a weary man longing for spiritual rest. They were interspersed with sharp glances up at the good Father who would have fidgeted except he knew that would not do in such august company. Finally, when he had read enough, or there was no more to be read, Bishop Burden leant back in his chair and steepled his fingers and sighed. Alas this last sigh tipped the scales, he over-balanced and fell backwards. The good Father hastened to help the Bishop rise, not without having been shocked by the colourful expression which Bishop Burden emitted. Once his derangement was seen to he waved Father Manwell back to the other side of the desk and tried on several frowns until he found the right one, mixing gravity with injured dignity. This, he said, will not do at all. Father Manwell awaited clarification but none came. He heard mutterings about 'kittens' and 'wasted time' and 'godlessness'. Then Bishop Burden said that he felt Father Manwell had been 'in the wilderness' too long, had 'gone native', and needed to be 'refreshed' in the ways of the priesthood. To this end the Bishop was going to move him to another, inner city parish and send Father Lenfer of the *Rigorós Ordre Déu Meu* to bring some spiritual discipline and orthodoxy to these 'savages'. Father Manwell was to return to this 'backwater' and ready himself for the summons. That would be all; good day.

Once Father Manwell had left the Bishop rang for his secretary to take a letter which was to be sent off that very day.

Since the next train back to the halt near Hellzafreezin wasn't until the following day, Father Manwell decided to get himself a good shave and pass the evening pleasantly at the *Magnus Theatre* watching a performance of 'The Marine Excursion of the Knights of Pythias' based on Stephen Leacock's short stories- manna to a tired priest!

News travels fast when it's cold enough for the eagle to fly with one beat of its wings. The train from Thunder Bay slowed and stopped at the halt and Father Manwell descended whistling and clean-shaved to be whisked away by Swift-foot-No-noise and his team of huskies. Father Manwell was deep in thought throughout the journey and didn't notice that it took twice as long as it normally would. One birch tree looks pretty much like another when you're whizzing along strapped to a sled with billows of snow curtaining your eyes and the rumps of slavering huskies before you. Some customers of Swift-foot-No-Noise's have asked for the mallet to be applied before they've been conveyed wherever they wanted to go. Father Manwell cheerfully endured the sights and sounds as the sled wove from hillock to hillock and past birch wood stands galore.

Chief Stand-back had called the Pow-Wow to order in 'Bilcox's Bar'. He asked Estelle Shave to report to the community the news she had received from her cousin in Thunder Bay that very evening. Everyone had seen the eagle arrive at her chimney. All forty-seven inhabitants, huskies, Tadpole and Sneaky listened intently as Estelle relayed the news. It was agreed, with one of those Hellzafreezin nods, that it was not good news. The question was: what to do? It was the shaman who, from her close business acquaintance with Father Manwell, had thought of the solution. There were nods of agreement. The only thing left to decide was who was to write the letter? It was agreed that Ink-finger Charlie had the necessary handwriting skills for a letter such as this, even if he couldn't tell a cormorant from a lynx. There was a comfort break of an hour while *Zhoom* was served and Chief Stand-back, Estelle and Ink-finger Charlie worked on the wording. It met with approving nods when the Chief read it to the meeting and sped on its way within minutes of the meeting being closed. It still being early and the bar being open there was general agreement (even from Estelle's granny) that people might just as well stay where they were and do a bit of dancing and powerful medicine making, howling with the huskies. Maybe some babies would be made as well; it was a full moon after all.

Father Manwell knew nothing of this as he sipped his coffee and marvelled at the accuracy of Estelle's grandmother's swing. There were four men, including himself, sitting on that short side of the bar and she picked out Goes-way-back Henry with the accuracy of a magnet. The good Father has often wondered why Henry doesn't duck; but then why does a husky like the mallet? Some questions in Hellzafreezin were just too profound for even the likes of Saint Thomas Aquinas, he decided.

A few days later the eagle returned to Estelle's chimney. Father Manwell, who had received an urgent call to baptise a new child in the distant settlement of Lost, noticed the 'Closed' sign on the door of 'Bilcox's Bar' as the sled sped him out of town. To his knowledge this was the first time he had ever seen that sign. Even when the Thunder Bay Eagles had lost in the Northern Territories Senior Cup (sponsored by 'Chilly' ice cream makers) and many bets had sunk without trace the bar had remained defiantly open. It was another one of those journeys when Swift-foot-No-noise and his huskies seemed to meander to their destination. When he arrived at the small building all on its own by a frozen lake Father Manwell found that it was a false alarm; it was the family's pet wolf which was whelping. The family stood by respectfully as he went through the ritual and sprinkled the water. The wolf licked his hand in gratitude. After such a long journey he was thankful for the meal he was offered and staying the night was agreeable too. The *Zhoom* they all shared had a particularly piquant Maplewood bouquet.

As the weeks went by Father Manwell had wondered when the promised letter would arrive. He still remembers the day it did. The snow fell as it had been doing since the first logs of the first cabin in the town were slotted together a century or more ago. Under his feet the snow crackled like a gleeful child. His Mass that morning had been as usual a lonely one, apart from the moose by the door. As he made his entrance to 'Bilcox's' he saw that though the bar was packed his stool was free. Estelle was already shovelling the necessary victuals on to a plate which seemed the size of a snowshoe- in fact it was a snowshoe over which had been wrapped some caribou hide and foil. Unusually early for Christmas, the good Father thought. On his stool he saw a letter. He exchanged nods with all and sundry. Odd that Chief Stand-back should be in so early, Father Manwell thought. The Chief usually went through four or five pipes while getting in the mood for thinking in the morning and hit the bar around noon. Estelle's grandmother was here as well: now that was unusual! Goes-way-back Henry was sitting demurely by her side, his ear-flaps down. The conversation had paused as the good Father entered and now all eyes were upon him as he took the letter and slid on to his seat. The platter was placed in front of him, the coffee by his elbow; and then Estelle stood back to watch. Something told Father Manwell that everyone was waiting for him to open and read the letter. It bore the Bishop's insignia. This is it, Father Manwell thought. Had the clock been able to tick or tock- even hiccough or cry 'whoopsy!'- it would have found plenty of elbow room in that watchful silence. Father Manwell was not the kind to hesitate, certainly not when forty-seven pairs of eyes were on him and he had a plateful of bacon and eggs- and was that Estelle's famous blue corn and oatmeal pudding? Can't be Easter, I'd've noticed, Father Manwell thought as he slid a finger under the flap of the envelope.

As he read the letter a broad grin began to spread over his face; and as it spread over his face so it spread over the faces of all the townsfolk in the bar. Even Tadpole was grinning.

Folk don't rush in Hellzafreezin, there being no need to. If you rush it'll be just as cold over there as it was over here. The snow will be just as deep, maybe deeper. Just as much as nodding so settling down to the business in hand is one thing you've got to learn in Hellzafreezin if you're going to sleep easy at night and not forever be checking the traps. There are priorities in Hellzafreezin and when someone is sitting at the counter in 'Bilcox's Bar', even with forty-seven folk and a cat grinning at you, the first matter of business is the contents of the plate in front of you. Father Manwell set the letter to one side and addressed the plate. He didn't rush: the bacon and eggs weren't going anywhere except his belly. The silence all around him was one of those respectful, anticipatory silences which bound people together and kept them in good shape for that dead pike around the ear or the unexpected beaver's tail of fate. Only once he'd cleaned the entire plate, mopping up the yolk with the pudding, did Father Manwell nod his appreciation to Estelle and reach for his coffee with one hand and the letter with the other. Chief Stand-back unbidden and silently passed over his spectacles. Father Manwell, who could see perfectly well without any such artificial assistance, perched them on the very tip of his nose and studied the letter. You could have heard a fly fart.

'This letter', Father Manwell said, 'it's from the new Bishop, the new one that is who has just replaced Bishop Burden.' He looked at the grinning faces, his own face as solemn as if he was exorcising a demon. 'The *new* Bishop says that the Holy Father has called the previous Bishop to Rome for some "vitally important work"- that'll have to do with paper, I guess. The new Bishop says that the Holy Father is pleased with the incumbent priest's diligence and confirms his position in that parish.'

Father Manwell looked around at all his friends and returned the spectacles to Chief Stand-back. He nodded and everyone went about their daily business. Estelle's grandmother caught Goes-way-back Henry by the ear-flap and dragged him (not so unwillingly today, Father Manwell noted) out the door.

The Nothing That Is

The steam locomotive is maintaining a steady seventy-five miles per hour as it makes its way across the continent. A few miles per hour less and what is happening may not have happened.

*

Whilst travelling between Toronto and Vancouver James Thomson, who was reading '*Die Legende vom Heiligen Trinker*' by Joseph Roth, glanced out of the window. He was seated on the right hand side of the carriage in which he was travelling (having been assigned the seat by an automated service). As the train approached Savant Lake he saw, or thought he saw (it being much the same thing), al-Masih ad-Majjal. There were doubtlessly dozens of other travellers on that particular train who at the same moment as Thomson had his vision saw only a black bear, perhaps another offspring of the mother whose abandoned cub Harry Colebourn had bought for fourteen dollars in August of 1914.

He could not help thinking of that moment in 'Simon's' nightclub in '*Un Flic*' when Alain Delon plays '*When you and I were young, Maggie*' on the piano and Catherine Deneuve (his favourite actress) glances at him from the wings of the stage. She is smiling secretively to herself, her lips starting to curl at the corners as some memory of intimacy flickers through her mind; and it is then, as though he shared the same moment (for they are lovers in the film and perhaps in fact), that Delon looks up. On his face is likewise a slight smile of fond remembrance. Thomson has seen that moment a dozen times. It is because of that smile that the policeman Delon plays does not arrest her when she appears at the end of the film to drive the night club owner Simon away. There are many ways of smiling, Thomson thinks. I have never smiled at anyone like that; and nobody has ever smiled at me like Deneuve smiles at Delon. There is fondness in that smile, mischief and a knowledge that goes beyond what the onlooker- the staff in the club preparing it for the night's business or the patron in the cinema- can comprehend. As Commissaire Edouard Coleman (Alain Delon) caresses the keys of the piano smoke from his Gauloise Disque Bleu twists upward like a corkscrew. He plays the piano well and is intent as he leans into the tune, easing it from the heart of the upright piano as though he was making love to it. He knows she has been watching him for some moments. He was playing the tune in order to draw her out of the office at the back of the club. Later he will visit her in her flat and she will playfully take his gun away from him before they kiss. Such moments stick in the memory and pause time whilst events are still unfolding in time.

Thomson had seen the film on a television channel whilst staying in the Royal York Hotel just minutes away from Union Station, where he had boarded this train. His room had overlooked the lake and he had made liberal use of the courtesy bar. The story Thomson had been reading as he fell asleep that last night in Toronto concerned the volcanic eruptions of Mount Hibok-Hibok in the Philippines, Villarica in Chile, Mount Tarawera in New Zealand and Cerro Negro in Nicaragua. It was only by chance that he knew of the other eruptions – Hekla in Iceland, Nikafo'ou in Tonga and Popocatépetl in Mexico- but they did not figure in the story by Joshua Chikowski (who came from White River but now lived in Montréal). Some critics thought that they should have done and regarded the story as incomplete. Those who criticised Chikowski's move to Quebec knew nothing of the pressures of being gay and Jewish in the northern backwaters of Ontario.

Thomson was resigned to having such visions. He recognised that they were projections of his inner fantasies, perhaps even his inner desires. There was little wrong with his eyesight, as his optician assured him while running his credit card through the payment machine. There had been times, if Thomson was being honest with himself, when he had welcomed such diversions from the drabness of ordinary affairs. The appearance of a caped (or uncaped) Woland at cocktail parties usually livened things up no end.

We are never nearer to the truth than when we fall into error, Thomson thought listlessly as he entered the dining car to have his lunch.

In the paper he would read about the undefeated Calgary Stampeders, lead by their quarterback Keith Spaith, and their famous victory over the Ottawa Roughriders at Varsity Stadium in the Grey Cup final. There was something about the score- twelve points to seven- which he found pleasing. Some of those also taking luncheon had been spectators at the match- or would be spectators at the match, depending upon how fate played its hand. How many of them would know that Norman Kwong, the first Chinese Canadian to play in the CFL, would become Lieutenant Governor of Alberta; or that Woody Strode would fight as a gladiator with Kirk Douglas in '*Spartacus*'? How many of them would eat at Pete Thodos's brother's Victoria diner '*The*

Only Café'? How many had enjoyed a pancake breakfast on the steps of Toronto's City Hall the morning after the victory, or had ridden a horse into the lobby of the Royal York?

As he chewed his steak Thomson recalled once again the whispered words Bismarck addressed to Kaiser Wilhelm the Second in 1890: '*Ihr fliegt werden rückgängig gemacht, Hoheit.*' In his head, as he reached for his glass of wine- a '*Quail's Gate*' Chasselas from the Okanogan Valley in British Columbia- he could hear the words of George Washington Johnson of Hamilton being sung by John McCormack. *Clickety-clack, Maggie.* Those arrayed around about him in the dining car he noticed were also drinking a white wine, perhaps the same type as he was sipping happily. What words or thoughts they were having he did not know; nor did he care to know for he was happy with his own, as he was with his choice of wine.

Making his way back to his seat he could have fallen asleep dreaming of Alan Ladd and Loretta Young in '*And Now Tomorrow*', scripted by Raymond Chandler and showing that week at the '*Fox*' theatre at the Beach. However, he remained awake watching the train pulling out of Union Station before it reached that point on the line, somewhere outside Savant Lake, where he had his vision. As good there as anywhere, he thought. Had he been assigned the seat he had wished he might not have seen it.

Thomson glanced to his left and weighed up the passenger he saw seated there, where he should have been: an ordinary man in a suit, as he was a man in an ordinary suit. The man had been in the dining car lunching a few tables down from him, facing the other way so that Thomson had a clear view of his jaw as he masticated his meal. For some reason Thomson couldn't understand, now that is that he could see his profile, he had thought the man was Alan Ladd. But what would the film star be doing on a train touching the westernmost corner of Ontario? Was it likely that Ladd had ever been to the Province? Perhaps the nearest he had come to this point on Thomson's journey, the point when he sees al-Masih ad-Majjal, was when he was in Banff National Park making '*Saskatchewan*' with Shelley Winters. Who was to know then that he would commit suicide when his good looks and mental stability were being eroded by his heavy reliance on alcohol?

If you are ever to write this story you have to look out a different window, Thomson thought.

He was not fond of travelling, though when he had to travel (as was the case that day, the day he saw what he saw) he found he enjoyed the railway journey. He had decided early in his life never to own an automobile.

This decision was not ethically motivated, for example through a desire to spare the environment further pollution. He knew nothing significant about 'pollution': who did in those days? He preferred the rhythm of the train's wheels on the metal track to the irritating susurrus of vulcanised 'Goodyear' rubber on concrete or tarmac. *Aesthetics, dear boy, aesthetics,* as Noel Coward had once purred in his unresponsive ear.

No, Thomson thought; the fellow sitting where I should have been sitting doesn't look like Noel Coward either. If there are any celebrities on this train they are in hiding and who can blame them.

This train will never cease leaving Union Station and it will never arrive, he thought.

From his room in the hotel he had watched the train leaving several days in a row, always at the same time. Once he had gone down to the platform to watch it beginning to draw out. He had carefully studied the windows of the coaches as they slowly slid past, looking for himself.

As the train had left the station earlier this day Thomson had scanned the platform for a sight of himself. Was he watching *this* train pulling out? Did he really want to catch sight of himself standing there watching himself being driven away by some force he did not comprehend?

When an attendant was passing he asked for a coffee and smoked a Carreras *'Black Cat'* cigarette as he sipped the hot liquid. The man seated adjacent to him across the aisle was also sipping a coffee and reflectively smoking an unknown brand of cigarette, his head turned towards the window so that he was watching the scenery as it flashed past.

Thomson counted the cigarettes left in the packet. There were nineteen. He could not remember when he had bought the packet: perhaps it was when he had gone to the cinema? Yet he could remember smoking a cigarette that morning as he waited on the platform for the train.

There was a passage he recalled in the book (*Nemožnost času* by Jaroslav Smrti) he had reviewed recently for a literary magazine in which the hero- Ivan Poláček- whilst waiting to catch a train and escape from the Nazis similarly lights a cigarette. But it is because of this that he is noticed by a Gestapo agent and arrested. Thomson wondered if he had lit his own cigarette as an unconscious echo of that scene.

From the window of the carriage in which he sits Thomson watches himself on the platform lighting a cigarette. All the little mannerisms which he inhabits are there on display for him to see as others might see him. He is tilting his head to the left as he holds the struck match and its flame up to the cigarette which is thrust into the left side of his mouth: always the left side, never the centre or the right. His eyes are fixed on the flame, the core of the flame, until the tip of the cigarette glows and his head moves back to the almost vertical and he flicks the match out with one swift, short gesture. Then the dead match is put carefully back into the box.

When, later, Thomson looks inside the match box he will find half a dozen used matches, all neatly bedded down in the reverse direction to those which are still usable. It is impossible to tell, even had he wanted to, which of those half dozen used matches was the one with which he lit his cigarette on the platform.

On the platform he became aware that someone was watching him with considerable interest. Why he should be picked out for such scrutiny when there were dozens of others milling around on the platform he could not say. He settled his fedora slightly and then looked to see where the nearest door was so that he could board the train. He could feel the eyes of the person watching him following him.

As Thomson enters the carriage and makes his way to his assigned seat he sees- or thinks he sees- someone move from that seat and cross the aisle. When he takes his seat he is aware of the man at the other window looking out with evident boredom on the empty tracks.

When he travels by train on such a long journey Thomson always takes plenty to read. He does not always read it all but he knows he has plenty should the journey prove tedious. Such journeys never do, however. He will read a paper, read a magazine, read a book, or gaze out of the window and daydream (which is sometimes even better than watching a film). Occasionally he will write, jot down notes (as he is doing now) which he can elaborate later. Sometimes he wonders what if there was no later; but there always has been and he sees no reason why there should not be a later after this journey.

He does not, as some people do, deliberately get into conversation with those around him, although he will be polite should someone pass a remark. It is seldom that he is recognised and he has never yet met anyone he knows on such a journey. The people he knows- or, rather, those who know him- do not make such journeys.

When Ivan Poláček reached the station in Prague he had with him a small, rather battered suitcase. There was nothing in it, nothing of value that is. He needed to have such a suitcase with him, he believed, so that he did not stand out in the crowd. He believed, rightly or wrongly, that the authorities were more likely to stop and question someone who did not have some luggage with them. What he did not know was that by lighting a cigarette he would draw attention to himself.

Had Poláček not taken a suitcase perhaps he would not have been caught and perhaps he would have been able to finish the book he had been writing (*Hněvu a odpuštění*). Had he not struck the match which lit the cigarette which he never got to finish perhaps the Gestapo agent would not have focussed on him and asked to see his papers.

We do not need a Judas for thus do we betray ourselves, Thomson thought. We try to make ourselves inconspicuous but somehow we are found out.

For lunch he would have a glass of white wine with his meal. He will not drink too much, having indulged himself somewhat in the days before this journey. But a meal without a glass of wine would be unbearable. He thought of Smrti who, like Roth, had been a heavy drinker and had died much too young because of that habit. Whereas Roth's body and organs had given out, Smrti had died in a car crash, on his way across the border as he fled Prague in 1969. He had been drinking heavily before making his failed dash for freedom. But then perhaps he had not failed after all.

Did I nod off? Thomson wondered as he watched al-Masih ad-Majjal transforming the desolation of a far corner of Ontario into something nightmarishly familiar.

Poláček knew the moment that the Gestapo agent accosted him that he was lost. His papers were in order; that was not the problem. The problem was that he reeked of guilt -*Schuld* - and the agent could smell it. They will take me to an office somewhere, he thought, and they will go through my suitcase. They will frown at the bundle of rags in it, will scrutinise me closely and then, with that casual indifference to humanity they have, they will have me locked up while they decide what to do with me. It did not matter what I might say- that I'm on my way to see my family at Kralupy nad Vltavou, that I'm going on holiday to the Krkonoše Mountains or that I'm travelling to look for work in Vrútky - it will be enough to condemn me that they can smell the guilt oozing off me. What I might be guilty of they will not care. None of us are innocent; it is just that some of us escape by chance, good fortune or the grace of God, take your pick. It would do no good to run: they'd shoot me down without a thought. None of these people milling around on the platform will come to my aid; they will just be glad that I have been apprehended rather than them.

I will never travel over the Negrelli Viaduct again, Poláček thought as he was being marched away between two German soldiers.

Had he caught a later train perhaps Poláček would have been safe, Thomson thought.

Had Smrti not been drinking perhaps he would have been able to get across the border into Austria.

Had Pete Karpuk not fumbled a lateral pass and hesitated over the ball believing the whistle to have been blown perhaps Calgary would not have scored their second and winning try.

And if I had not had that cigarette on the platform, what then?

In the main hall at Union Station Thomson had seen the headline and bought a paper from the dispenser. The derailment, he read, had happened somewhere between Jasper and Valemont in British Columbia. Thirty people had been killed. There was a blurry photograph of rescuers at the scene. He could not make out the numbers on the carriages which lay on their sides like discarded toys. He gave a dollar to a three-fingered vagrant begging outside on Front Street.

Chikowski in his story about the series of volcanic eruptions that year had described the growing cult of end-of-the-worlders in Youbou, British Columbia. Their leader was one Pastor Zachariah Cutter, a wealthy tycoon who had made his money through logging. After the failure of his fourth marriage he had become a virtual recluse and had taken to reading as much as he could about prophecies of the end of time. Cutter, in the story, is killed at precisely the time he had predicted that the world would end.

He got it right for himself then, Thomson thought as he closed the paperback. Too bad about everyone else; we could all do with a break.

Just because one volcano erupts and then another; or because you light a cigarette on a railway platform in Prague doesn't mean that the world is going to end. But then maybe it does; who knows? When Poláček got up that morning did he think he would make it out of the city? He had read the signs after the Anschluss and the subsequent annexation of his own country, had surmised what was going to happen and had tried to escape. What if he had gotten away? How would that alter the career of the Gestapo agent? Would he arrest someone else on the platform that morning?

Thomson's invitation to the literary festival had been unexpected. His work though published had never been that highly rated. He did not make a living out of it and spent a lot of time washing up in kitchens, filling boxes in factories or sweeping office floors. Then suddenly he was being taught on courses in universities and his old works were being re-issued and praised as 'ground-breaking' and 'modern literary classics'. Some director wanted to make a film based on one of his books. Agents wanted him to hire them when once they wouldn't give him ashtray space for his cigarette in their offices. He could afford to stay in hotels such as the Royal York instead of Queen Street flop houses. He could afford to buy suits. Doors were held open for him even when he didn't want to go through them.

Chikowski was murdered in an alley somewhere in Montréal; at least that's what Thomson read in the paper. It didn't name the alley, perhaps to discourage ghoulish sightseers who sometimes flocked to the scenes of such tragedies. Thomson thought that dying in a nameless alley was hardly the way to go, not if you had to choose. Why was Chikowski in the alley? The police thought he had been looking for some action, presumably of the deviant sexual kind. But he could have been trying to rescue a mewling cat. He might have been lost. Thomson thought of Pasolini, run over on the beach at Ostia by his own car driven by a hustler.

People were waving to family or friends on the platform as the train slowly began to draw out of the station. Those on the platform were waving back. Thomson watched himself waving from the platform. Do I wave back? What if it's not me that I'm waving to? So because everyone else was doing it Thomson waved as the platform slowly disappeared from sight. They pass the roundhouse and light glints off the neck of a bottle from which a man is drinking. Thomson waved at him as well. The points clicked and clacked under them like the intro to some jazz extemporisation by Oscar Peterson.

One of Smrti's lecturers had been Dr. Bohan Skovajsa. He had encouraged the young man to write. They would meet in the older man's flat and discuss the renaissance that was happening culturally in their country. It is likely that Smrti flirted with Skovajsa's daughter, who was very attractive and responsive to such blandishments. She was, however, a devout Communist and it is possible that she was the one who denounced the pair of them. Skovajsa was subsequently arrested and died in jail while awaiting trial. He had been going to join Smrti on his dash for freedom but was apprehended before he could do so. Smrti did not know the reason for his friend's non-appearance and drank as he drove himself along innumerable back roads trying to decide which the best way out of the country was. Perhaps death was the best way for him. We shall never know since he died alone in the car, which collided at full speed with the fountain in the town square of Kaplice near the Austrian border. The route he and Dr. Skovajsa had decided on was in another direction. It would have taken less time and there were no memorial fountains of any kind on it. The petrol tank of the car was almost empty when it crashed so there was no fire. Smrti was killed 'at once', though how anyone can tell that is beyond comprehension.

Although the festival organisers were willing to pay Thomson's air fare to Vancouver, he had told them in his last telegram that he would take the train. This would mean leaving a few days earlier but he would enjoy the trip. It would also give him some time to finalise the address he would be giving about the influence of middle European literature on his work.

Pastor Cutter had been convinced that the Antichrist would appear in the north and that this would coincide with the onset of another ice age. Had he lived to see the melting ice caps and tornadoes and erupting Icelandic volcanoes perhaps he would have revised his theories, Thomson thought. But then what am I to make of al-Masih ad-Majjal popping up outside Savant Lake and whirling the snow around as everything froze and shattered?

Someone had shoved a religious tract under the door of his hotel suite on the first night of his stay. Thomson had a fondness for such unexpected things. Most people threw such literature straight in the waste paper bin. But he would accept flyers from people in the street and would read them carefully. Those which intrigued him- and some did whilst others did not- he would file away for future reference in his apartment. Quite often he would never read most of them again, though he might recall that he had been given such and such a flyer. Many of them were advertising store bargains or public meetings about theosophy and suchlike. The tract under his hotel door had been about 'the end of the world' and was published by some organisation calling itself 'Trumpets of the Eschaton'. While he lay on his double bed reading the tract, which made him drowsy- or perhaps that was the Scotch he was sipping as he read with one eye and tried to follow the hockey on the muted television with his other eye- Thomson was also listening to *'The World Tomorrow'* on the bedside wireless. He wondered what Garner Ted would make of his 'Trumpet' rivals. He lost interest in all that when Toronto scored their second goal. At the same time he fell asleep and only woke up when, having neglected to pull the curtains shut, the bright sunlight hit his eyelids like a puck entering the net.

The person who pushed the tract under Thomson's door- a young part-cleaner who had been hired only a week previously and would soon lose his job when one of the guests (not Thomson) complained about the tract- was a relative of Bill Wusyk, the Calgary flying wing who had been the first recipient of the Jeff Nicklin Memorial trophy two years previously. Nicklin had played for the Blue Bombers and died during the Allied advance into Europe. Whether or not his being sacked had any impact on the young man's beliefs is not certain. He may well have gone on to have a distinguished career in the diplomatic service.

The person who complained about the tract and cost the young man his job- 'We can't have guests being upset about the world ending while they are staying in this hotel; they are here to relax' the young man had been told as he was handed his outstanding pay- was also a passenger on the train (but only as far as Saskatoon) which Thomson was travelling on to his festival in Vancouver. Thomson may well have seen him getting off the train at Saskatoon, but he would have had no way of knowing that this was the man who had cost the young man his job. No way of knowing that is unless it was part of the story he was telling himself as he tried to overcome the occasional fit of boredom which tugged at him like a beggar in an Indian bazaar.

In his book- *Hněvu a odpuštění* (Anger and Forgiveness) - Poláček (that is Smrti, if we are to believe his biographers) has a section about the Antichrist. Roth also wrote a book entitled '*Der Antichrist*' but it is unlikely that Smrti had read this. Poláček's version of the Antichrist is a bumbling, corrupt bureaucrat, who would seem almost Kafkaesque were it not for his pitiless vengefulness and corrosive powerfulness. Thomson thought of SS *Obersturmbannführer* Eichmann in his office routeing the extermination wagons with their human cargo to the awaiting gas chambers and ovens.

As he switches through the channels in his hotel room, searching for some late-night entertainment, Thomson comes across a film he has partially seen a few times before. It's a black and white foreign language film and is badly dubbed into English. Whenever he has come across the film, which he recognises from two of the characters and the scene now on the screen, Thomson has always missed the opening. He does not know the name of the film, but in his mind refers to it as 'That Film'. Each time he catches a snippet of it he tells himself that he will watch it to the end; but he always falls asleep and so sometimes thinks of 'That Film' as 'My Soporific'. What he likes about the film is the way so much of it is set on a train. This gives the story, which he cannot make head or tail of, a disconcerting menace and sense of claustrophobia. It would be a relief if someone were to hurl themselves out of the train. Perhaps in the segment of the film he has not seen, and possibly never will see, someone does do this. The story takes place in the inter-war years and such dialogue as there is may well be better, more meaningful, in the original language. It could be Romanian or Hungarian for all he knows, perhaps even Czech. The odd phrase in German he can understand but without the context it is like the jabbering of a baboon in a zoo cage. In fact, one section is set in a large zoo and he wonders if the city is Berlin. Never having been to Berlin Thomson cannot say with any certainty. He is unable to say why he is convinced that the film is scripted by Jaroslav Smrti. If he was able to remain awake long enough perhaps he would be able to prove that this was or wasn't the case. He wonders sometimes if knowing for certain would affect the film's ability t

As Chikowski emerges from the alley which he has taken as a short-cut to the inn where he is to meet his friends he sees a cat dashing across the road and being hit by a car. He wonders when was the last day that he had gone through without either seeing some such death or reading about death in the newspapers.

'La mort rôde dans les rues' is the title of the pot-boiler he has just had published. Such works pay the rent and he smiles each time he sees one of his at a supermarket check-out. One of Alan Ladd's lesser known never finished films was based on a screenplay by Chikowski of that pot-boiler. Somewhere in the vaults of one of the film companies are the few reels that were shot of the film before it was cancelled. It is only later that he reads in the final edition of the local *'Montréal Journal'* that someone has been mugged in the very same alley. He promises himself that he will never take short cuts again. It will be hard to stick to this and maybe one day, in Buenos Aires say, he will disappear down an alley and never emerge.

The Gestapo agent is called Günter Jäger. He watches as the man lights a cigarette. There is something about him which makes the German wrinkle his nose. At that precise moment the train- a 345.7 steam locomotive- pulls into the station. The German is waiting to meet someone who is on that train and he loses interest in the man lighting the cigarette as he sees his friend stepping down from one of the carriages. They will leave the station and go to a café where they can drink and carouse and reminisce. When the war is over Jäger will make his way with the help of the 'Red Cross' from the displacement camps under a false name and papers to Canada. By this time he will have a scar on his back where he was hit by shrapnel and was burnt during the bombing of Dresden. His service record will have been destroyed and he will be able to become whoever he wishes to become. He is still young, only thirty years old, and there are opportunities in Canada for those who work hard. Nobody recognises him. He did not work in the camps and all those he might have arrested were killed swiftly. He likes to forget who he was as though he no longer is that person, at least not publicly. He sits at the window of the train and gazes with disinterest at the countryside as it flashes past. He can see reflected in the window the figure of the man sitting across the aisle from him, a man whose seat he had almost taken in error.

Poláček heaves a sigh of relief and boards the train. There are many hurdles still to overcome but he feels lucky. At the end of the journey he decides to abandon the suitcase, believing that it (rather than the cigarette) had drawn attention to him. The suitcase will be found by one of the cleaners once the train is out of service and it will be taken to the left luggage office. Nobody will collect it. When the war is over it will still be in the locked office waiting to be found. Smrti had wondered about the 'symbolism' of that suitcase. How could he make it simply an artefact again once it had become a symbol? His death in the car crash did not solve the dilemma. Poláček's solution- abandoning the suitcase- may be the best one. There are those, critics especially, who would like to delve into the suitcase, to unlock it and display its grubby insides to their scrutiny. But does it matter what kind of socks and underwear a fictional character wore?

Jäger when he arrived in Halifax had little more than the clothes he stood up in and the required documentation. Now- of course, he is not called by his real name any more- he has hand-made Italian suits by the dozen and sports a silver tiepin. The scar is still on his back but no one has ever seen it. He has no intimate and when he needs sexual relief he hires expensive prostitutes whom he blindfolds. Poláček never knew his name but believed that they would meet again. Such a thought never crossed the German's mind, however.

The divorce settlement that Pastor Cutter's fourth wife received was deemed excessive by a court of appeal, though the reduction to ten million dollars still worked out at two hundred thousand dollars for every day they had been married. Whilst the Pastor went into his shell his former wife was escorted to a variety of sports events and galas by a series of muscular athletic young men, many from Eastern European countries and skilled at skating and hitting a piece of vulcanised rubber into a net. One of these young men was the grandson of Ivan Poláček, though his name was Peter (originally Petr) Ashcroft as a result of his mother's marriage to the man of that name. Peter knew nothing about his grandfather's life since once Ivan had slipped out of Europe he chose to forget the past and to re-build his life in the United States where he had landed one Spring morning in mid- 1939. How events in Ivan's life would have turned out had Smrti not lost control of the steering wheel when he nodded off as the Tatra T77 raced across the square it is impossible to say. After the crash locals looted what belongings there were in the wreck before the local police arrived. Among the items taken was the unpublished manuscript of Smrti's magnum opus. Some years later it was sold privately for five thousand korunas and was donated to a museum in Tennessee.

Once he had finished the draft of his speech Thomson returned to the book he had been reading. Before he opened it he ran his fingertips over the colourful cover, letting his fingers caress the letters of the title and author as though he was depressing keys on a piano. He had read the book many times before, taking comfort in its familiarity the way one does with an old sweater. At times as he read he would close his eyes and ignore the printed words, letting the images spool in his mind as though upon a cinema screen. The work had been translated from the Czech but the paperback copy Thomson had was a dual language one. He enjoyed reading the original Czech and then making his own mental translation, which differed at various points from the printed text. Little by little the story would change from what it seemed to be to something quite different. It was like watching some strange bird moult and become a different bird, an angel perhaps, adorned with beautiful and colourful feathers where previously there had been dowdy down. The other passengers would know nothing about this as it was all taking place in his head. What they might see, if they bothered to look, would be a slightly enigmatic curl to his lips (similar to that of Deneuve in the nightclub) as he enjoyed the story. What he liked particularly was the way he could turn back through the pages and images and follow a different track, or interpose another scene. For some reason this story alone of all those he had brought with him on the journey, afforded him this kind of opportunity, this freedom to ravel and unravel it as though it was a ball of knitting wool, without destroying the original story and its characters. The conclusion would still be the same though the route by which it was reached might differ.

Chikowski was on the run. Here he is cutting down an alley in Paris. There is a railway station up ahead. Behind him he can hear the heavy breathing of the police as they chase him. The Pastor has betrayed him. If the police don't catch him the Nazis will. He thinks of the night club singer and the rose she gave him. What was that tune being played on the piano? The train seemed to be taking forever to draw into the station.

The train seemed to be taking forever to be leaving the station. In the cabin of the engine the fireman was shovelling fuel into the furnace. The engineer was watching the signals and adjusting the speed as they navigated the points which would send them out of the city and to the north-west. He had worked for the company for a dozen years. His name was Jan Šipek and he had escaped from Europe as the war was breaking out. He had driven locomotives in the snuffed out Czechoslovakian Republic and had been hired by the railway in Canada. Being a chess player he had a reasonable grasp of English already and was a quick learner. Each day before he came on the shift he would copy out positions by problem composers such as Ladislav Prokeš or Karel Traxler. As the locomotive followed the rails through the wilderness he would try to solve them, usually succeeding before they reached their destination.

Thomson studied the crossword and occasionally wrote in a word. He enjoyed solving them but curiously never finished one. There is no doubt that he could have finished any of the hundreds he had worked on over the years; but as some people will leave a few scraps on their plates 'for the gods', so Thomson would leave at least one but often two or more clues unsolved. He could not remember when he had first taken an interest in solving crosswords. It was possibly during that time now referred to as 'the Great Depression' when like thousands of others in the Province he was unemployed. He would spend as long as he could in public libraries keeping warm and reading the papers from first page to last. He would memorise the crossword- he had always had a good memory- and recreate it on a piece of paper and try to solve it while tramping around the city. In those days he would never fill in the squares of the puzzle thus enabling himself to re-solve each of them whenever he liked. Once he had money coming in he could afford to buy a daily paper- the '*Star*' or '*Telegram*' for preference, but any paper from any city would do, as long as it had a crossword puzzle in it. He would never smoke whilst solving the puzzle, reserving that pleasure for after he had succeeded in doing so. It was seldom that he failed. Today's puzzle diverted him as the train passed through McKee's Camp, Felix and Ruel. Then he laid the paper aside and thought about lunch which would be served in a couple of hours. He had eaten a light breakfast before leaving the hotel, anticipating the meal on the train. Now that he was in his early fifties Thomson felt he had to watch his diet since he was conscious of his tendency to put on weight quickly. When he was younger and life was harder he had been as thin as a rake. Those who knew him then when they met him now would remark on how much he had changed. Sometimes that was painful to hear since Thomson felt he had changed not at all, or only in that he was now successful rather than anonymous and a failure.

As he chewed his steak the man who had been Günter Jäger and was now known as Bernard Edison studied the man dining a few tables away from him. Why does this man seem familiar to me? Edison thought. His face has been troubling me since I saw him on the platform searching for the car in which his seat would be booked. Jäger-Edison had always had the dual ability of recognising those who reeked of guilt and forgetting instantly his victims. His defeated business rivals spoke about him with both envy and awe. But he was certain he had had no such commercial dealings with this stranger who seemed to have ordered the same meal as him and to be drinking the same wine. Jäger-Edison had kept the same svelte look, the same aesthete's face and build, as he had had before the war. Anyone from those times would have recognised him; but there was nobody from those times to do so. He had been small fry, as they say nowadays, merely a local agent winkling out Jews and traitors and saboteurs. He had been used to dining in the finest restaurants then as well. He remembered once sending for the chef in the '*Café Louvre*' to compliment him and then having the fellow shot. Was it not Brillat-Savarin in '*La Physiologie du goût*' who said 'After a good dinner body and soul enjoy a peculiar happiness'?

Pascal, the waiter who had taken the man's order, said there was something *désagréables* about the man. Pascal could not define it more precisely than that. There had been *quelque chose de mal* about the man though: the way he had stared at Pascal as he stood politely to take the order; the way the man had spoken- politely, yes- but as though Pascal were some *espèces inférieures* rather than a free man doing a necessary, valuable and skilled job. It was not everyone who could balance plates on his forearms and move in a cramped space whilst the floor shifted underneath one's feet! Pascal and the chef were lovers, though none of their colleagues knew this. It was not something about which you could talk too openly. When Pascal, waiting patiently by the hatch to receive the plates, had told that little snippet his lover- not knowing why he is doing it- carefully spits into the sauce which will be ladled on to the vegetables for the diner at table trois.

As the engineer driving the train smoked a cigarette he bantered with the fireman. They had crewed together many times. They knew the names of each other's wives and children and parents and relatives several generations deep. The fireman as a young man had been in the Royal Canadian Air Force. He had been a navigator on the raid which had destroyed Dresden. Whenever he opened the door of the boiler and shovelled in the coal he saw again the brightness flaring below as the bombs fell. Sometimes, overcome by the heat and the memory of that firestorm, he would have to sit down and then the engineer would tell him about the beauty of Prague and the countryside. He would recite poetry to him- Karel Hynek Mácha's '*May*'- or regale him with the exploits of *Jára Cimrman* until his nerves had settled and he had recovered his normal good humour and strength. Such moments of weakness were few and the two men kept them to themselves, not wishing the company doctors to learn about it. Neither could imagine himself working with another, so ably did they complement each other in the cabin of the locomotive they fondly referred to as '*Smokey Drak*'.

'The Trumpets of the Eschaton' tracts were printed by 'The Loon Press', a small company that had also printed some of James Thomson's early works. When he picked up the tract he had noticed the name but hadn't recalled the part that press had played at the start of his career. Original copies of those works sell for considerable sums in antique book auctions. Collectors buy them not for the content but for the value of the item itself. His original manuscripts of those works, unlike that of Smrti found in the wreck of his car, have long been lost, abandoned during one of his frequent moves. Some were used as fire lighters during the cold winters he had endured in poorly insulated lodgings.

The tract urged Thomson to repent and to prepare himself for the coming of the Lamb. There was nothing original about the tract though he thought some of the line drawings showed promise. Whoever was doing their art work was clearly gifted. Thomson had heard religion being described as being as useful as a pair of socks: they kept your feet warm but had to be thrown away when the holes could no longer be darned. His parents had been Presbyterians but Thomson had long since deserted that and all the other camps. He wouldn't style himself an atheist or an agnostic. He preferred to regard himself as shunted into a siding somewhere waiting for the points to change. He enjoyed standing in the street listening to the Salvation Army band and singers, but that was about as far as he would go in accommodating himself to ritual. If the Lamb turned up- and so far He hadn't, which showed remarkable perspicacity on His part- then Thomson doubtlessly would be for the high jump, or the long drop, or short shrift, whichever it was. Not that I have lived a bad life, he thought as he watched al-Masih ad-Majjal wreak havoc beyond the window. I have simply done what I could to survive without causing too much trouble to others.

Across the aisle Bernard Edison was quietly paring his nails. He always carried a manicure kit in a dark leather case. It was one of the few items he retained which he had had whilst in Europe. Other things he had discarded without thought or regret, the copy of '*Mein Kampf*' for example. It had belonged to Reinhard Heydrich and had borne his signature on the flyleaf. Jäger had abandoned it reluctantly but he knew he could not turn up in a displaced person's camp with such an item. A manicure set, yes; but Nazi propaganda, no. Edison took particular care with the half-moons of his cuticles. He despised those who bit their nails, like that perverted person who had waited on him at lunch. That one's nails had been bitten to the quick. Edison had felt like complaining but then he had controlled his revulsion and ignored the creature.

The CPR transcontinental line was completed in November 1885. There is a historic photograph of Lord Strathcona hammering in the last spike. In fact his Lordship only posed with the sledge hammer poised on the spike; it was an anonymous Irish navvy who actually hammered it home. Among the unnamed onlookers is Ednam Thomson, the father of the James whose eyelids are drooping now and then as the stripped barrenness of northern Ontario flashes past his window. Ednam had immigrated to Canada from Glasgow and had made his way westward working on the railway. He had married the daughter of an orchard owner in British Columbia but had abandoned her and the infant James, returning to the itinerant life he had been leading. They never heard from him again. When his mother re-married James was sent to a boarding school in Toronto. He ran away to begin his own life of wandering, sometimes imagining that he might meet his own father. Thomson had not seen his mother since the day he'd last left for boarding school. She had seen him to the door of their house but had left him to be taken to the station by the nanny. When Thomson thought about Upper Canada College it was without pleasure. He had felt abandoned and could remember the ritualised bullying. If ever I have a son, he thought, and that is highly unlikely, I would never abandon him to such a place. His mother had hired a private detective to trace him on one occasion during the late thirties. When located and asked if he had any message for his mother he said to tell her that he was 'fine and dandy'. It is likely that his grandfather excluded him from his will since his mother subsequently bore two other children who took up the family business when they came of age. James would now and then see their photographs in the papers. One of his step-brothers owned a string of race horses and often would pose with his winning jockey and horse at Hastings race track, with its backdrop of Burrard Inlet, or Woodbine by the Lake.

Now, Thomson thought sleepily, I am heading back to Vancouver for the first time in almost forty years and whether any of my family will know of my return I neither know nor care. It's unlikely they will have read anything I've written; though if they had he wondered if they would recognise themselves in some of the characters. *Would I recognise my mother*, he thought, *after having created a fiction out of the memory?*

Why Chikowski had chosen those series of volcanic eruptions as symbols in his story was hard to say. Thomson could understand much better how Pastor Cutter had interpreted that chain of natural catastrophes as portends of 'The End'. It was unlikely that Cutter ever read the story; he did not strike Thomson as the kind of man who would subscribe to 'Pandora's Box' literary magazine, even though it was printed by 'The Loon Press', which Cutter owned shares in. A volcano was a potent symbol, Thomson thought, though his own preference was for snowstorms. One critic during a radio interview with him had commented that in all of Thomson's mature œuvre there were always blizzards and he had wondered about the significance of that. Thomson's reply was 'Oh dear, are there?' which seemed to nonplus the critic. Thomson wondered if, during their run through the Rockies, the train would pass any Dr. Bohan Skovajsa's daughter Lenka climbed up the local and then national Communist hierarchy rapidly. She was an expert linguist and can often be seen in contemporary photographs and newsreels beside ministers translating for them. Amongst the languages she spoke fluently were Chinese, Turkish, Russian, German, Finnish, French, English and Spanish. She still lived in the apartment which she and her father had shared in Prague, though her daughter (Šarlota) now used her bedroom while she has moved into her father's. Šarlota knows nothing about her grandfather for she was born several years after his arrest and death. All photographs of him have been removed from the apartment. Her own father, who she quickly learnt to despise because of his artificiality and soullessness, was one of those middle apparatiks with whom Lenka slept both in order to help her career and to give herself some erotic stimulation. None of the men she took as short-term lovers in any way captivated her or satisfied her sexually or intellectually. Most of them were time-servers who would have been dustmen in another kind of society. Their creativity was nil. But they were useful rungs in her climb upwards. She forgot their names as soon as they were no longer of use to her. They doubtlessly found solace elsewhere as such men do.

A ladder works both ways, Thomson thought as he considered what he had just read.

Šarlota, a talented young pianist, fled to the West and her mother's career climb came to a halt. There survived in the daughter that independent and creative spark which her mother had not inherited from her father. Throughout her teenage years Charlotte (as she now called herself) had given the impression of being the perfect Communist child. But early on, perhaps having come across some hidden pamphlet in her grandfather's old study- now overlaid with Party literature and Soviet realist works by the likes of Sholokhov, Ostrovsky and Gladkov- and intrigued by the world of free thought, she had secretly dreamt of making a dash for freedom. Unlike her grandfather she shared none of this with her mother, or her college friends. Informers were everywhere. She planned carefully and finally smuggled herself on to the Prague- Vienna train while her mother was attending a conference in Moscow. Charlotte sought asylum once she arrived in Austria. She made her way to Montréal where she studied at the 'Schulich School of Music'. She is on her way to give a concert recital in Vancouver and sits on the same side of the train as Thomson, but in the next carriage. She is thinking about her repertoire and has decided: she would play Janáček's 'On an Overgrown Path' and Suk's 'Things Loved and Dreamt'. Thomson knows neither of these works though he adores the music of Dvorak. The Orpheum Theatre where Šarlota will give her recital is barely ten minutes walk away from the hall where Thomson will give his address to whoever turns up. The two events do not clash, for his is at lunch-time while hers is in the early evening. Thomson has not given any thought to what he will do with the time he will have on his hands both before and after his address.

It has been many years since Thomson last looked at a woman with any interest or longing. It was enough of a challenge to survive without becoming emotionally and physically entangled. You are scarred enough by the cold and lack of a job and hunger without needing further lacerations. Some in the literary world think he is gay but this is not the case. Nor is he one of those sexless, androgynous beings that float around like seahorses. Unlike the man across the aisle (who at that moment is having lascivious thoughts about a young woman he has seen in the coach ahead of the one he is travelling in) Thomson does not pay for prostitutes or otherwise seek sexual relief. He has poured himself into his writing for some years now, once he realised that he could secure his living by doing so. Critics point out the lack of female characters in his works; Thomson points out the lack of dwarves or mulattos. In the world he has lived in, the world he writes about, women were hardly to be seen, except in the same way as they are seen in Henry Miller's world, and he does not see the point in writing about them like that, as convenient sexual objects. Maybe, he once told an interviewer, he will write a memoir one day and in it he will talk about his mother. For the moment, however, it is his father he inadvertently follows with his writing, that absent man of whom he has no memory whatsoever.

It was snowing when Charlotte last saw Prague. She had feared that her footprints would somehow betray her as she walked through the clogged streets towards the station. But whenever she gazed back she would see that more snow had already fallen and her footprints were as anonymous as anyone else's. But these are the fears and fantasies which can trouble a mind. Ivan Poláček had not been troubled by snow but by the smoke of a cigarette. Bernard Edison watched the falling snow with indifference; it was fire which held a fascination for him- the flare of a match even in this carriage made him glance quizzically at the smoker. James Thomson could remember many nights when he was trudging through the snow-shrouded streets of Toronto looking for shelter. He did not remember making snow balls as a child and flinging them at someone else, though he had seen children doing just that. Snow was beautiful but it killed in so many different ways. Thomson thought of George Mallory buried and preserved somewhere near the summit of Everest and of Captain Oates frozen somewhere in the vastness of Antarctica. He thought of the sixty-two men buried under an avalanche in Rogers Pass.

Chikowski's fascination with volcanoes began when, as a child, he read in an encyclopaedia about the eruption of Mount Vesuvius which engulfed Pompeii and Heracleum with ash. He has never seen a volcano or been to Italy. He was fascinated by the ash fluttering down on people and preserving their bodies. If the world was to end he imagined that this was how it would end, with clouds of ash blotting out the sun and suffocating all life. Chikowski's favourite book when he was growing up was '*The Scarlet Plague*' by Jack London. He cannot recall how he came by it but he remembers that he read it again and again, there being little else to read in their household other than the Bible and Eaton's catalogue. If he read it now he would shudder with embarrassment and wonder what there had been about it which absorbed him- perhaps only the words. He had never realised that words could be used in so many different ways and mean so many different things. Now he traded in words as his father had done in furs. As he stood on the edge of the volcano and looked down into the fundament of the world Chikowski wondered what words he would find to say.

As he made his way to the washroom, the sight of a group of four men- undoubtedly supporters of the Stampeders on their way home- playing cards made Edison grimace. In the displaced persons' camps he had had to play thirty-six card Trappola with others. He had never played cards in his life until that moment, perhaps not wishing to taint his fingers with the germs that others may have left on the pack. But if he was to escape he needed to fit in and compromise was essential. What infuriated him, though he could not show it, was that he would be easy to beat, so much so that others would laugh at him in a good natured way. He would play up to this unwelcome image of a loser ('*Verlierer*') and answered to that nickname for a while. He would swallow the humiliation he felt and his anger at being unable to respond as he wished to and once would have done. He deliberately kept contact with some of those in the camps who also came to North America and took a sweet delight in blighting their lives in whatever way he could.

Charlotte watched the man pass her a second time. The first time, returning from lunch, he had seemed to pause for a moment beside her seat and she thought he might be about to speak to her. It was not that she minded strangers exchanging pleasantries with her, or fans asking for her autograph (a rare but happy experience); but since her childhood she had had an acute sense of danger where people were concerned and this man, she felt, was dangerous to know. Her mother, she had soon realised was dangerous, the more so for being her mother; as such she was naturally within some of the social defences Charlotte could use to distance her peers. She had always been kind to Charlotte but there had been strictness behind that kindness. She had wished that her daughter become a miniature version of her and any sign of individuality had had to be suppressed. Whenever as a teenager she was made to accompany her mother to some formal Party occasion Charlotte would grow tired of hearing them described as '*dvě sestry*' (two sisters). Her mother had always made sure that her hair was cropped short and that she wore it straight, just as she had hers. Charlotte never kept a written diary but in her own mind would refer to this haircut as her '*přilba*' (helmet). Now that she was an independent and successful young woman- a celebrated pianist as well- Charlotte wore her hair long and had it styled however she wished. In fact, one of the first things she had done when she reached Montréal was to go into a salon and ask for something to be done about her hair. It was the hair which had attracted Edison. He would have spoken that second time but he had noticed a slight change in the way she was sitting, a certain sudden defensiveness, and he had decided not to bother. His charm would not work on that one, he thought; a shame as the game would have spiced up the long journey.

In the Costume and Wardrobe department working on '*Un Flic*' was a young man called Kryl Zdeněk. He had been responsible for ensuring that Alain Delon's clothes were maintained in pristine condition between takes. Unnoticed by others he would collect the numerous stubs of the cigarettes that Delon smoked, keeping them at home in a porcelain jar. When he moved to Canada he took the jar and its contents along with his other effects. Zdeněk worked in the movie industry in Montréal and saw Chikowski for the first time at an Alouette game in July against Calgary in Olympic Stadium. He was struck by how ruggedly handsome Chikowski was but they did not speak or meet, merely passing as they took their seats in the same row. By the time they watched the Alouettes beat the Edmonton Eskimos forty-one to six later in November, thus winning the Grey Cup, they were lovers. They had met the second time on the set of the making of '*La colère et le pardon*', based on Chikowski's translation of Smrti's original book. The police searched their apartment after Chikowski's death, having learnt of an argument on the set between the two men. Chikowski's lover had by then disappeared. A police constable found the old cigarette stubs in the jar but nothing that was incriminating. The murder remained unsolved after Zdeněk eventually reappeared and was questioned. When the film was released it was dedicated to Chikowski's memory. Zdeněk would weep each time he saw it because in one scene there appeared that jar and its treasured contents. He was not sure if he was weeping for his lost lover or the cigarette stubs- perhaps both, Thomson thought.

Poláček did not believe his eyes when he saw Jäger playing cards with the others. He had been lighting his cigarette and had just glanced into the dormitory to make sure he had all his few belongings. Despite the passage of five or six years he recognised the man. What should I do? If he reported Jäger his own departure would be delayed and he desperately wanted to get away to America. Perhaps he was wrong. Surely someone like that wouldn't have been able to burrow his way into a place like this? In the end, having hesitated for less than a minute, his need for motion overcame his shock and fear. Poláček made his way silently towards the exit and the awaiting bus. Jäger had not once looked up; but out of the corner of his eye he had recognised the way the match had flared and the half profile he had seen. Jäger felt an iciness grip his insides; and then he relaxed as the man disappeared from sight, responding to the call for those departing to hurry to the bus.

The 'Montréal Locomotive Works' employs hundreds of men and from its facilities in the Pointe-Saint-Charles and Angus districts turns out many of the locomotives still in use in Canada. Ednam Thomson worked there as an unskilled labourer for a few years though he no longer does. He lost an eye in an accident and at the same time lost two fingers on his right hand. Once discharged from hospital he was last seen walking towards the St. Lawrence River. Some believe he jumped in while others say he was going to fish. Sometimes people just sit and watch a river flow and that can be a most calming and soothing way of passing the time. Those who knew Ednam Thomson did not feel that he would be able to sit by any river, no matter how pleasantly it might flow, for more than two minutes. One of his drinking companions offered the opinion that Ednam had 'the itchiest feet I ever knew'. But whether Ednam jumped or simply wandered across the bridge what is certain is that he disappeared. He had disappeared before. Some people only disappear the once; some disappear bit by bit; Ednam disappeared and re-appeared then disappeared again. It was during one of these brief surfacings that he worked in the Locomotive Works. The war was raging in Europe and the yards were churning out tanks and armoured vehicles as well as trains. Whether or not he could re-appear again anywhere is a moot point; sometimes your luck does run out, Thomson thought.

In the mail car near the baggage car and the caboose all was quiet. The guard was snoring softly on his seat with his feet up on a pile a mail bags. In one of the bags is a letter written by a Miss Blaise of Victoria to her fiancé in Kelowna. The letter has been in the bag for a dozen or more years, having become caught in a fold that has never been properly shaken out. The couple are now married and are travelling on the train back to their home in Vancouver after attending the funeral of her mother in Gatineau. Perhaps on this occasion the errant letter will be delivered and they will wonder and laugh at its appearance.

As the bombs fell on the city on Ash Wednesday Günter Jäger took shelter where he could in the cellar of the local Gestapo office. It was one of the few whose original thick walls had not been taken down and replaced with thinner partitions. He was part of the section which had sent letters to the remaining Jewish residents to report to *Zeughausstrasse 1*; from there they would be marched to a 'work camp', which was Theresienstadt, the Czech transfer point to extermination camps.

Rank and status no longer matter when the bombs are falling; all that matters is the security of the place where you shelter. Jäger cursed his luck for in another couple of hours at dawn he would have been on a train heading elsewhere to safety, or so he hoped. He had already decided to use his knowledge and make for Switzerland and vanish. For a pragmatist like Jäger loyalty to the cause was one thing; suicide was another. His primary goal had always been to survive. Any fool could see that the war was lost and that what was now happening was madness. There were rumours that the Führer was drugged and insane. During the recent flurry of typing and filing for the letters he had been removing all his own records so that nothing would remain to incriminate him once the Allies or Russians eventually arrived.

Snow suffocates slowly.

Thomson woke in his hotel room and felt the dream disappearing as rapidly as the storm which had invaded him. He had been dreaming of his favourite jazz group 'The Trumpets of the Eschaton' as they played *'Kaiser's Last Break'* in a set at the *'Palaise Royale'* on Lakeshore. He wasn't sure if he was in the Hotel Vancouver or Toronto. A peek out the window didn't enlighten him. Snow was falling outside as well. There was snow everywhere, he thought: in my dreams and in wherever I am. The room was warm, however. The bedclothes were on the floor. He must have kicked them off as he struggled to reach the surface. There was some kind of avalanche swamping him in his dream. One minute there had been brightness and lots of interested eyes focussed on him as he addressed the literary gathering; then black musicians in tuxedos were blowing out a hot rhythm; and the next thing he knew he was fighting his way through a driving blizzard while the music seemed to turn into the shrieking of the wind.

He read the time from the bedside clock: it was three in the morning.

We tether ourselves by time, he thought. What was it the doctors would write as they assessed your sanity: orientated in time and place? Sometimes I think I am only 'located' in "me", Thomson thought.

He couldn't remember how much he had had to drink. I don't drink anymore, he thought. It's been a dozen years or more since I gave it up. There is no bottle lying on the floor, pointing in the only direction an empty bottle can. If I'm not drunk then what am I? Thomson asked himself.

He took a shower. The hot water revived him. He dressed, finding fresh clothes neatly laid out in the drawers of the wardrobe in the room. He must have unpacked carefully He sat down and read through his notes for the address, wondering if he had already given it. He looked at his watch to see what the date was but the watch had stopped years ago. Sometimes someone would ask him why he continued to wear a broken watch. He would shrug as though to reply 'Why not?' What he did not tell them about was the inscription on the back. I'll go down to the lobby, he thought and see if there's a paper around. But for a while before he did that and found out where he was and what the day was he sat and watched the snow falling endlessly outside. If there was a city out there it was hidden, buried. He found himself falling asleep again and didn't resist.

Snow seduces scurries silently.

Charlotte smiles fondly as she watches the flakes falling outside. The train seems to be burrowing into unknown depths of silence. She recalls her feelings as she travelled from Prague to Vienna those several years ago. Whereas now in her mind she skips through excerpts from Tchaikovsky's '*The Snow Maiden*' or Liszt's '*Chasse-neige*', then in silent fear and shivering with cold she had kept herself mute and alert by mentally composing a work which she was later to entitle '*Uprchnout v zimě'(Flight in Winter)*. Hidden in the cramped, uninsulated space as though trapped in a sterile womb, it had been all that she could do to remain still and silent. Never had she so vividly visualised musical notes. They had come alive like small, friendly creatures- ants sometimes- which had busily skipped or scrambled up and down the scale, tinkling inside her like iciles in the wind. She had felt at times as though she was in a delirium but the warmth of the internal music as it shaped itself in response to her remarkable will-to-survive kept her safe. It was that piece of music, when fully formed and first presented to her teachers in Montréal, that had established her reputation. Her proudest moment had been when, that first time she returned to Prague after the Velvet Revolution, she had performed her composition in the Smetana Hall to rapturous applause. If her mother had been in the audience she did not see her; nor was she at the reception afterwards.

The dining car is crowded. When Thomson takes his seat for dinner the waiter asks if he minds that another passenger, '*Cette mademoiselle*', be placed at the same table. The choice Pascal has was between Thomson's table and that of Edison and he had not thought long about whom to approach. Thomson nods his head agreeably and Pascal seats Charlotte opposite him. They smile at each other, neither knowing the other, and Thomson offers his hand as he briefly introduces himself. His name means nothing to Charlotte. She notices how delicately boned his hand is, how soft it is within hers. Many men engulf a woman's hand, as though taking possession; but Thomson's hand nestled comfortably within her hand like the pet rabbit she had once had. Thomson, who likewise does not recognise her name- she does not use her professional surname but her real one- is struck by the strength of her handshake and the slenderness and length of her well-manicured fingers. She brings with her a delicate perfume- L'Air du Temps- which lifts Thomson's weariness. They talk the way two strangers on a train might talk. She finds him attaractive in a way which surprises her. Many paramours have laid seige to her but her dedication to her music and her instant awareness of their manifold faults- in this one arrogance, in that one insincerity and so on- had soon persuaded them that they were wasting their time. She was always charming but firm in her rejection. She did not keep flowers or gifts she was given. She did not engage in any protracted correspondence. Her 'No' meant no. There was something *odlišný* (different) about this man Thomson, she felt. His eyes had a gentleness about them, unlike the predatory gaze of so many men she had met. She could sense that he had suffered as she had suffered and that he had dealt creatively with that suffering rather than succumbed to it . She did not know any of his personal history- that is not the kind of thing strangers on a train talk about- but sometimes one's life history is written on one, in the eyes and on the hands and face. The tone of a voice, one's stance, how one says something- all this gives a clue to the other person, if you have the ear and eye for it. That was how Charlotte had survived her childhood and adolesence: by being acutely aware of what her mother- or those she met through her mother- said or did. She recalled the time her mother had introduced her to Pavel, clearly hoping that this young Party member would become her intimate. But when she wanted to go ice skating he would want to sit and discuss marxist ideology. His body odour, which nobody else seemed to notice, repelled her. For a month after Charlotte had sent him packing her mother was in a Thomson was struck by the fact that ordering from the menu separately they had ordered the same items. They had both smiled as they rearranged the setting so that the knife and fork were now laid for a left-handed person. He told her that he was travelling all the way to Vancouver to give a talk to a literary group. So, she asked, you are a writer? Yes, he replied; but not a Hemingway. It was then that she told him about her music. As she spoke Thomson knew that he would be going to see her performance at the Orpheum Theatre.

Edison was watching the young woman speaking so freely with the middle-aged man. He had seen how the waiter had swiftly looked from this table to that and had approached that other man. Edison recalled how he had been swept across crowded rooms to the best tables in countless restaurants in this city and that in Europe all those years ago. No one would have dared to act as that creature had. There had been artistes, nobility and bankers sitting opposite him in those days, all of them hanging on his every word while they tried to shield from him the fear he read so easily in their eyes. The waiter had looked at him with disgust and Edison wished for a brief moment that they were back in time and he could act as he once would have. Perhaps I can get the creature fired, he thought as he sipped his soup.

It had been many years since Vojtech Capek had been in his homeland. He remembered his last time in Prague, as he waited on the platform for a train and watched the Gestapo man arresting someone. Vojtech had felt a shiver run down his spine as he saw the man being marched away between two soldiers while the Gestapo agent strolled behind them, like some big game hunter watching his prize being carried back to camp. There have been many things that have happened to me since that day, Vojtech thought as he laid down another card. It is odd that I should remember such a brief incident. The train was drawing up at the platform; there were faces at the windows as passengers waited to descend; I am sweating at the thought of a sudden tap on the shoulder and a demand to see my papers; and this stranger was being marched away under escort. What could I have done? Capek thought as he considered the cards remaining in his hand. The other three players, his friends from Radisson Heights who had travelled with him to watch the Grey Cup final in Toronto, waited patiently for him to pick his card. I recall little of the train journey. Everything passed in a blur as though I was inside a block of ice. After that it was even more of a timeless kaleidoscope of places and faces until I reached Halifax and safety.

He played a card and lit a cigarette. He sits and watches them, listening as they describe the heroics of 'Sugarfoot' Anderson and Red Pantages and how Wilmot kicked those two conversions without fuss. Capek smiles and laughs along with them but his mind is almost a decade in the past as he draws on his cigarette. Something had disturbed him and he was frowning. When his friends asked if he'd like another hand he said no, it must be dyspepsia and he'd go for a stroll up the train. Capek was a big man, barrel-chested and with long legs. He was a carpenter. As a teenager back home (for he still thought of the Republic in that way though he had become a Canadian citizen shortly after the war) he had trained under Sekora and played rugby, though it wasn't as popular then as it gradually became. He had quickly developed a liking for the Canadian version of football and had turned out for a local amateur team for a few years until he started courting his wife.

This is a strange journey, he thought. I am happy because we won and I am with friends who know nothing about what happened in Europe all those years ago, and yet I am dredging through those times as though trying to find a sprat among the weeds. I look out the window where there is a blizzard building and I see not my new homeland but my old land. The face I see reflected in the glass is me as I now am but the thoughts inside are me as I was then.

Chikowski and Kryl are in Mar del Plata for the film festival. The film Kryl had been working on and for which Chikowski had done the script-

'*Dead Man's Switch*'- was showing in one of the competitions. Kryl was excited at the thought of the event as one of the judges was Alain Delon. Of course Delon will not remember him, Kryl thinks and wonders whether he should risk talking to   him. A few words in French, what harm could that do? Once the festival was over Chikowski wants to take a trip to see the Aracar volcano on the edge of the Puna de Atacama plateau. Kryl has no interest in volcanoes and prefers to spend his time attending parties. Despite their disagreement over how to spend the remainder of their time in Argentina Kryl is happy as he has been able to add two more stubs to his Delon 'collection'. Chikowski, promising to return in a couple of weeks, sets off on his journey without his companion. He is happy at the thought of finally being able to see a volcano. Chikowski's guide to the volcano was called Juan Luis Savater. If I'm lucky, Chikowski thinks, maybe it will erupt while I'm there. What is also possible is that Savater will cut his throat while he sleeps and disappear into the night.

Jaroslav Smrti is surprised but glad that he has survived the crash in Kaplice. The shock of the impact woke him. The hitchhiker he had picked up along the way lies on the road, his neck twisted and his face an unrecognisable mess after its impact with the shattering windscreen. It must be because I was relaxed that I've survived, he thinks as he limps into the shadow of an alley. It's early morning, the town is not yet awake, but soon enough someone will look out a window to find out what the noise was. With his haversack and his manuscript in it Smrti vanishes before he is noticed. The hitchhiker will be mistaken for him. He will become a non-person, a ghost, and as such he will be able to survive.

Lenka is surprised at the tears she sheds when she learns that Smrti is dead. Perhaps she had not intended that her father and Smrti should die as a result of her betrayal. Perhaps she did not see it as a betrayal but as an attempt to bring them to their senses. She identifies the body as that of Smrti, though she avoids looking at the mangled face. It is the things found in the wreck which mislead her into believing that the body is that of Smrti. He is already safely over the border to Austria in any case. He will seek asylum but under the name of the hitchhiker whose identity papers he carries. The 'Smrti' who is cremated is not the Smrti who fled.

'*Film beze jména*' (Film with no name) won critical approval at Karlovy Vary film festival just after the war. No copies of it existed until a film enthusiast found some decaying 35mm rolls in a stack of canisters in a storeroom in a Prague building scheduled for demolition. The film was carefully preserved and restored so that copies could be made. Thomson watched a showing of the film in the Toronto Film Festival and it is parts of this film which keep recurring in his dreams. He only needs to be waking up, having fallen asleep in front of the television in a hotel room somewhere, and he sees a scene from that movie. It is not that movie but something which his imagination must conjure up from the disparate elements of whatever is on the screen at that precise moment. A zoo: yes, there is a scene set in a zoo in that film and should Thomson wake up and see a zoo on the screen he will believe that he is watching that film again. Of course, he may well be watching that film again, but he will doze off and when he wakes up the television will be a blur of white snow, just like the scene he is gazing at now through the window of the speeding train.

When Lenka opens the door to Charlotte she is surprised at how much her mother has changed. Lenka says nothing as she holds the door open to permit Charlotte to enter. This is not the house in which she grew up, Charlotte knows, for that had been taken away from her mother in the wake of Charlotte's defection. This is one of those standard, soulless utilitarian blocks in which the socialism miracle was delivered to the masses. Lenka leads her through the narrow, dark hall into the main room where, with a gesture, she invites her daughter to sit. She offers her some tea and disappears into the small kitchen while Charlotte takes in her surroundings. The room is small, not much more than a cell, and the two windows are narrow looking out on to a wide, deserted street down which the trams do not run. There are no pictures on the walls or low tables. Charlotte recognises none of the furnishings, which are worn in a way which suggests some grinding stone has been invisibly working on them. She concludes that even those belongings had been taken from her mother as a punishment. As her mother re-joins her and seats herself silently opposite her Charlotte thinks that her mother has been stripped of even more than the externals. The almost feverish glow in her eyes of those days, her enthusiasm for 'the cause', has disappeared. Now the eyes are dull, lifeless, those of a whipped animal. Her expressionless face might well have been eroded by the same invisible stone. She wonders what her mother must see as she looks at her well-dressed daughter. As she sips her tea Charlotte seems to remember all the 'conversations' the two of them used to have, if you could call them 'conversations'. Her mother would chose the subject and deliver her opinion and Charlotte would be expected to remember and repeat what she had heard. There was never any 'small talk' or idle chatter. As a child she would have to have that with her doll and pet rabbit. It was only when she began to excel at the piano that Charlotte found conversations with that instrument taking place and that what she said and felt mattered. Now it seemed her mother had nothing to say, not even 'welcome' or 'how are you?' or even bitter words of reproach like 'do you see what your betrayal has done to me?' She just sat and looked at her daughter, her eyes not roving over the person she saw but latched on to her face. So Charlotte simply told her about her music and her life in the 'new world' and about the concert that evening. Her mother nodded and sipped her tea and said softly that Charlotte (she called her *Šarlota* as of old) had done well. Afterwards, as she walked back to the hotel through the old familiar streets Charlotte found herself beginning to hear within herself a melody which became more insistent, just as had the melody which her fearful mind had clung onto when she fled the country. As soon as she was back in her suite she wrote down the beginning of the work that was to become *Návrat domů* (Homecoming).

The incidental music for '*Film beze jména*' was composed by Mateju Slavický, the pseudonym of an unknown musician. Many of those who worked on the film, including the director and producer, used false names to avoid persecution or prosecution. It is likely that none of them imagined that their serio-comic farce, which subtly criticised the Communist government of Gustáv Husák, would be shown outside of secret radical clubs and groups. It was only when the authorities, who had initially approved the film, realised its true import that the perpetrators were sought and the film suppressed. None of the actors, who were all amateurs, students and other young people, had ever been caught or imprisoned. None had pursued careers in films though several of them might have been able to do so. The screenplay- though much of the dialogue was improvised there was an underlying structure- was attributed to one 'Josef Kafka', whom some (including the half-awake Thomson) believed to have been Jaroslav Smrti. This has never been proved or disproved. Smrti himself has never laid claim to authorship. Many of the street scenes, shot with a hand-held *Arriflex* 35mm camera, show various literary, sporting and artistic Czech personalities of the time. Their unintentional and peripheral involvement in the film lead to some of them being harassed by the repressive government which took over from that of Alexander Dubček. Much of the dialogue is spoof philosophy, some of it condensed from '*Sur la logique et la theorie de la science*' by Jean Cavaillès and '*Paradoxien des Unendlichen*' (*The Paradoxes of the Infinite*) by Bernard Balzano. A popular coffee house pastime for a few months after the film's release was to try to identify snippets of other works in the at times hilarious interchanges.

In his jacket's breast pocket Thomson can feel the folded leaflet that had been pushed under his hotel door. He wonders if anyone else on the train, some of whom may well have been staying at the Royal York, have a similar leaflet in their possession. He likes the name of the organisation and wonders how they acquired it. In that film, some scenes of which he has been replaying in his head as he dozes, Thomson remembers the silent clown who goes around the zoo handing out printed leaflets to passers-by. Some of the leaflets are blank and some of them contain quite meaningless or partial messages and sayings. Whoever had designed those leaflets had taken as much care as 'Trumpets of the Eschaton'. To which message should you listen, the one warning you of the coming of 'The End' or the one which bewilders you because it seems meaningless?

Vojtech Capek's pacing along the length of the train did not ease his discomfort. He was not suffering from dyspepsia but from something less easily identifiable. Something was nagging at the fringes of his mind, like one of those parasites the egg of which is laid in a living host and then eats its way through it. Capek was the kind of person who was not content until he had put his finger on whatever it was that might be bothering him. Nothing pleased him more than to encounter some problem in his work which needed original thinking to overcome. He did not just bang things with a hammer or saw a bit off an end to force a fit. When a shred of meat caught between his teeth he would work his tongue at it for however long was necessary to dislodge it. If one stroll down the length of the train to the entry forbidden sign of the mail van did not bring forth a solution then he would stroll back and continue his contemplation.

The suitcase did not stand out among the many similar items stacked in the left luggage office in Prague. Some would be reclaimed very quickly. This one, a small brown suitcase which could have belonged to anyone, had already gathered more dust than most of the items stored there. The clerk responsible for the office had been replaced a week after this suitcase had turned up and his ledger entry never made. So unlike the other umbrellas and hats and gloves and suitcases and coats and books- all manner of things, in fact- this suitcase did not draw attention to itself. No clerk when he looked through the log for items that had remained unclaimed for more than a month put a star against its entry since there was no entry. Other items which went unclaimed for the maximum time that they would be kept were eventually sold and the money received deposited in the account especially set up for such receipts. At the time of the outbreak of war there were four hundred and ninety-five crowns in the account. When the war finished the account was empty. Nobody could say where the money went to. Of all the items on the shelves in the drab storeroom the battered brown leather suitcase remained unnoticed. Other suitcases, many of superior make and design, came and went. Then one evening, the year doesn't matter though it was during another troubled period in the country's history, the clerk then working in the office needed a suitcase for himself as he was going on holiday. It was not unusual for clerks to 'borrow' items (especially raincoats or umbrellas) and to bring them back the following day. An unofficial system of notating the original log entry had grown up so that the items could be accounted for even when they were 'out on loan'. We know that the clerk could not find any entry for the suitcase- in any event the log books for that period in the thirties had been lost- so he simply took the case home. As he walked through the darkened streets he swung the suitcase gently beside himself much as Ivan Poláček had done more than thirty years ago. (Of course he had been walking to the railway station rather than away from it.) When he opened the suitcase the clerk was surprised at what he found.

Thomson's sole piece of luggage was in the baggage car. He always travelled light. The books he took with him were kept in a casual shoulder bag; his clothes were in the small brown suitcase. He had found it under the bed in one of those cheap hotels he had stayed in before fame had found him. It did not have the appearance of an item which someone would return to claim. 'Finders keepers' the desk clerk had said when Thomson had asked his advice. Although nowadays Thomson could afford to buy Louis Vuitton or any superior make of travelling bag he rather liked carrying around with him that undistinguished, mysterious suitcase. Each time he opened it in a new hotel room he wondered what he might find in it irrespective of what he might have put in it. '*La valise magique*' was a story only someone like the late lamented Joshua Chikowski could write, Thomson thought.

Jäger looked around the interior of the church of Sainte Marie des Batignolles with indifference. He did not see a place of worship but a place with little that could be looted- a grand organ and the colourful stained glass window were both too much trouble to plunder when there were paintings galore hanging on gallery and private apartment walls all around the city. His only concession to the purpose of the building was to have extinguished his cigarette before entering. He would not have bothered to do that had he been here on official business rather than his own. While we are withdrawing from the city, he thought, the crazy French are playing pétanque in the square outside. A priest came out of the confessional, saw him and discreetly beckoned him to follow. Jäger was not there for confession, but was already making plans for escape. This retreat is the beginning of the end, he thought. The priest would give him information on the escape network which he could use when it became necessary. As they passed into the small back room where vestments were donned and removed, the bell on the towerless roof chimed the hour.

Edison had never been back to Paris but the information the priest had given him had been invaluable when he disappeared from Dresden. Strange, he thought, that I have made a small fortune through finding and selling religious artefacts- icons and the like. The superstitions of others have turned into profit and comfort for me. Nowadays he made more from what had essentially been a hobby to start with than he did from his main job.

In the newspaper Thomson was reading in his hotel room he saw the advertisement for Pastor Cutter's rally at the 'Capilano Stadium'. The photograph of the Pastor could have been of a car or fuller brush salesman. There seemed to be nothing exceptional about the Pastor's appearance; perhaps his oratory was more inspiring. Thomson had heard on the radio plugs for the rally. He wondered if it was worth going to see the man. Entrance was free. Would there be a choir? According to the tract he had read in Toronto there was even the possibility that 'The End' would occur during the rally! If it did then it certainly wouldn't be in tomorrow's newspapers, Thomson thought, since there won't be any newspapers or any tomorrow.

The distance between Toronto and Vancouver by rail is two thousand seven hundred and seventy odd miles, Thomson read. The train has a maximum speed of seventy-five miles per hour. Going flat out all the time it would take only thirty seven hours to reach the west coast. But the train slows and speeds up; it stops at stations and takes on water and coal; there are inclines and mountains, bends and bridges. It will take the better part of three days. Thomson tried to remember when he had been in anyone's company for that length of time, let alone a collection of strangers such as surrounded him Ednam Thomson looks at the dollar bill he has just been given. He has been pan-handling around downtown for a few hours. Until that well-dressed stranger coming out on to Front Street had put the dollar in his hand he had managed to scrape together less than thirty cents. Most people ignored you. Why not, since you ignored them most of the time. When you've got a bottle and you've got a spot then to hell with the rest of the world. Ednam had a nice spot by the John Street roundhouse. That was the thing about knowing railroad ways, he thought. You can always find somewhere dry to shelter. But this dollar, now, that made a difference. He wondered why the man, who had seemed no different from the dozens of others issuing out of the swing doors, had given him a buck like that. He remembered how the man had paused as he came out, had reached inside his jacket for his wallet and had taken out the dollar bill. Ednam had imagined the man heading for the hot dog stand but instead with a quick smile he had thrust the dollar into Ednam's hand. Well it's my lucky day then, he thought. Ednam will sit in his hiding place and tip the bottle in celebration. He will see the train leaving the station and continuing its long journey across the country to the ocean. It is just another train, just another train, just another train: he has seen thousands of them, going in all directions. He no longer rides on trains. There is no longer anywhere to go, or any reason to go anywhere.

It's unlikely that Dr. Bohan Skovasja knew it was his daughter who had betrayed him. He had turned up at the university as normal that morning and two men wearing hats and belted raincoats had called at his office to take him for questioning. It had all been done very publicly, quite deliberately of course. That was how they warned others by showing quite openly what could happen. As his colleagues watched him being put into the car he knew that they would not be wondering what he had done but worrying about what they might be doing. During the questioning though Dr. Skovasja was treated with some courtesy he was also treated as though his guilt was in no doubt. Dr. Skovasja could not imagine his daughter betraying him. He assumed (wrongly, as we know) that Smrti had been indiscreet when drinking, perhaps even bragging about his intention to defect, and that the authorities had heard about this and acted swiftly. When his daughter did not come to visit him he assumed it was because the authorities were forbidding it. When he died he was alone in his prison cell and had just recited Erben's *Zlatý kolovrat* (The Golden Spinning Wheel) to himself, it being Lenka's favourite poem. When his guard found him the next morning Dr. Skovasja was still smiling and his eyes were fixed on a point somewhere beyond the windowless cell. A laudatory biography of his mentor, which Smrti was to write some years later when teaching Czech literary studies at Brown University in Providence, Rhode Island contained none of these inconsequential details.

It is the train segment in the '*Film beze jména*' which Thomson remembers most vividly. As he sits in this car watching the snow whirl and dance outside he visualises a similar scene in that film. It wasn't snowing but raining. The camera moved up and down the carriage showing the passengers travelling between two unnamed places- anonymous, poorly lit stations are rushed through their names blurred and unreadable. The train had stopped only once at a small halt, somewhere in the countryside- it could have been anywhere in middle Europe but presumably was in the Czech Republic. One person was shown getting off the train and another getting on. All the while this monologue in faux philosophical terms, intermixed with jokes that perhaps lose something in the translation, is carrying on in the background. It seems to be happening in the head of one particular passenger, who sits alone at the rear of the carriage. Though he looks out the windows on either side as the train progresses through what seem to be several days and nights- or it could just be a series of tunnels and brightly lit panoramas outside which become repetitive so similar are they- the man is also taking in the antics and conversations of those in the carriage with him. Perhaps he is meant to be the camera that moves up and down the aisle, focussing now on one couple or group and now on another. One of the groups, workmen by their clothing, are playing a silent version of paper-rock-scissors. Another solitary man is reading a newspaper which, if you watch closely, changes from scene to scene. One frame shows it as one day and date with one particular headline and then it is something else, and so on, never repeating itself the several times the man is the focus of the camera. Inter-cut with the train episode is a lecture being given at some educational institution. In the background of the packed lecture room can be seen the darkened shapes of armed soldiers. These may simply be statues for they never move; but there is something menacing about them. The face of the lecturer is also in shadow, possibly veiled as a bee-keeper might be and his voice is incessantly haranguing the audience who are shown hooting with laughter rather than quivering with fear. The train never seems to arrive at its destination, but nobody seems distressed by this. Through the window at times can be seen other trains all heading in the same direction, though they vanish within seconds of being seen. Thomson can make neither head nor tail of it. What is the meaning of the signs which every now and then you see hanging around this person's neck and then that person's? The words are translated in the subtitles but that doesn't help much. One group of passengers seem to be rehearsing a play- they all have printed scripts- and they invite some of their fellow passengers to join in, but not all at once and not everybody. The solitary man at the far end of the carriage is studiously ignored by everyone. Suddenly the carriage is crowded with people, some in uniform and others naked. Moments later the carriage is shown totally empty and the train seems to be motionless in a siding as a crowded seemingly endless train howls past.

The hitchhiker felt glad to be alive as he crawled out of the wrecked car. The driver was impaled upon the steering wheel. What Smrti had not known- and would never know now- was that the man he had picked up was a 'fugitive from justice'. Smrti had been too, though he was unaware of that as well. What crime the hitchhiker had committed is a matter of conjecture. In fact Stepanek Tuxen- that was the chap's name- was nothing more than a petty thief. He may well have been a 'subversive influence'- the exact expression which was written on an official warrant issued a few days prior to his disappearance from his digs. What his political leanings were we do not know, though the State would have ear-marked him as an 'imperialist lackey' or given him some such label. It is true that he liked listening to western music and knew several beatnik poets from San Francisco (by reputation only). He was once heard calling the President a 'shitbag' but to any liberal-minded person that was a fairly accurate description and much worse could have been said. The authorities didn't discriminate in those early days and their dragnet would haul in big fry as well as minnows. *Se želva* (be a turtle) was advice often given at that time. Stepanek, when he got wind of the State's less than benevolent interest in him, decided to take to his heels, though he had no plan in mind other than to disappear. He had been on the road for five hours, was wet and hungry and wondering if it wouldn't be simplest just to turn himself in (for at least that way he'd get a meal and dry off) when Smrti pulled up and offered him a lift. Stepanek only hesitated briefly when he saw the half-empty bottle of vodka on the passenger's seat; but a lift was a lift. Smrti had not been talkative but that suited Stepanek fine: he just wanted to rest his feet, get some warmth into his body and relax. Smrti hadn't even asked where he was headed, had just opened the door and called 'Want a lift?' Within ten minutes Stepanek had fallen asleep and so he wasn't aware of Smrti's steady drinking and increasingly erratic steering. Though it had long stopped raining Smrti still had the wipers going and he was peering uncertainly through the windscreen even though he maintained his high speed. It was habit which made the hitchhiker rapidly check Smrti's pockets and remove his wallet and the bag which had been lying on the back seat. He put his identity papers in Smrti's pocket and slipped quietly into the still darkened streets of the village. With his 'new identity' he felt safe, not knowing that he was still a wanted man!

A blizzard is a blizzard is a blizzard, thought Thomson as the train remained stopped at the small halt. Snow drifts were blocking the line ahead and it was being cleared; they would be underway soon, a voice reassured the passengers. As he nodded off Thomson was trying to decide whether Alan Ladd or Alain Delon would play the villain in his imaginary movie based on the Czech novel he had been reading.

Not much happens in Savant Lake if it can help it. There's the wildlife, of course, the creatures such as the moose and black bears that flit around just out of your sight. They had it pretty good until people started shooting at them. There are fish, plenty of walleye, northern trout and pike in the lake. Some are pretty savvy about hooks and lures and give them a wide berth, sticking to grubs and real bugs. Then there are the biting bugs as well, mean as hell and liking to swarm. Some have no finesse and saw right through your skin to get at the blood inside. Whatever made the Antichrist decide to put in an appearance there? Thomson wondered. You'd've thought that he'd've preferred a better, more moderate climate, somewhere sunny like the Sahara for example. But there he was, his white robes swirling about him, flattening and burying everything indiscriminately. Maybe this was a trial run, Thomson thought wearily.

It was on his third journey through the cars as they stood motionless in the blizzard that Capek came to realise what it was that had been gnawing away at him. He had passed from his car into the one behind it and was making his way down the aisle when he saw a man glaring at him. Capek could see himself on the platform and the same fierce eyes focussed on the waiting passenger who had just lit a cigarette. Capek strode past the seated man and found himself shivering with fear. Jesus Christ! Capek thought.

What am I to make of the 'interrogation' scene? Thomson wondered. It begins the film- rather it is set a few minutes after the opening titles beyond which you see a train rushing across an open tract of wilderness. The two men are seated in a café, across a table from each other. They are both looking directly into the camera and then, as though given a signal, they begin to ask each other questions. Some of these questions are quite trivial and some are direct quotes from well-known scientists and other sources. It is as though the two men are dancing around each other verbally. Throughout the film this scene, less and less well lit, occurs. The questioners change places and at one point they are seen to change 'scripts' (or what Thomson assumes are scripts). The questioning becomes faster and faster until, towards the end of the film, without the two men being on the screen their two howling voices can be heard over other images- the lecturer in the auditorium, a woman with a child in a pram looking up at some public sculpture (perhaps Wenceslas on his plinth) and so on. The silence with which the film ends is almost like a slap in the face, Thomson thinks.

James Thomson's mother's second husband was named Oppenheimer, one of the sons of a wealthy wholesale grocer. Her father deemed him to be a much more suitable match for his daughter than 'that man' as he chose to refer to Ednam in absentia. The daughter's first marriage had been one of love rather than the socially and financially acceptable kind her father had been hoping to negotiate for her. It had been his incessant belittling of Ednam, who was a practical man rather than a wheeler-and-dealer like his father-in-law, which had driven Ednam away. He never wavered in his love for his wife but there was no way he was going to put up with the old paterfamilias's constant needling and undermining. It was hard enough wearing a suit and shaving every day. James's mother was devastated by Ednam's disappearance- he left behind a semi-literate note explaining why he was running away but the old man found it before his daughter did and destroyed it, leaving his daughter to believe the malign stories he told her about Ednam. He had already lined up the replacement and worked on his daughter subtly over the next year or two. When it was clear that Ednam was not coming back and had had no contact, 'for the sake of the child' she had agreed to the second marriage. Once that business was settled and she had quickly given birth to two more sons, her father concluded his scheming by ensuring the removal to a distant boarding school of 'that man's spawn' as he privately referred to James. He had detested the boy from the first, believing that no son of 'that man' could amount to anything more than railroad trash. None of this did he say to his daughter but he would discuss it openly with his associates over brandy and a cigar at the Vancouver Club on West Hastings Street. That he had started out as a lumberjack he chose to forget.

Grace Blaise, whose letter breaking off her engagement with Ethan Oppenheimer, one of James's step-brothers, was still lodged in a mail bag, had been surprised when that young man had shown up at the family's front door acting as if all was well between them. She had not had the heart to turn him away, about which her mother was secretly pleased since she had disagreed with her daughter's ending of the engagement. The fact was that Grace was soft on a local lad who made her laugh in a way that Ethan never could-or would. Looking back now, as she gazed out into the blizzard and waited for the train to edge forward, she had to admit that she had enjoyed a good life. Ethan, if uninspired in his love-making and somewhat dull in his conversation, had been steadfast in looking after the family they raised. She got on well with her husband's mother who treated her like the daughter she had never had. She knew all about Ethan's whores, of course, but now that he and she had their own rooms and he no longer required sexual services of her, she didn't concern herself with that side of his life. Had she married her local lad she would have been poor, for he still worked in the same factory he had been in when they used to go dancing together. He had never married and had come home from the war something of a hero. She had kept the cuttings from the newspapers in which the story of his exploits was told. If she passed him in the street she kept her eyes firmly to the front though her heart would beat just a little faster. *Perhaps everyone needs a regret in their life as some people need worry-beads*, Thomson thought.

As he catnaps waiting for the snow on the line to be cleared Jan Šipek visualises a chess problem. It starts out as the famous one by Suk called 'závěje'; but the pieces keep changing and just when he thinks he has discovered the key he finds himself staring at a completely different composition. It is tiredness, he tells himself. Once we are underway again it will settle down inside. Charlotte is quietly moving notes around in her head as she works on the musical piece she has been creating for some weeks. The lack of motion fits in very nicely, she tells herself. Edison is staring fiercely out into the blizzard wanting to shout orders at someone. He waits badly, he knows, as he recalls the cellar in which he was buried as the bombs fell. Some of his comrades ran out into the street trying to seek a safer refuge but they were engulfed by the firestorm. When he had crawled clear of the rubble in the morning a rescue team found him and took him to a makeshift hospital so that his wounds could be dressed. All the while he lay bandaged he raged inside at his immobility and impotence. It was only later that he discovered that his impotence had become all too physical.

It is two in the morning and the victory celebration in 'The House of Hambourg' shows no sign of stopping. The house band, 'Trumpets of the Eschaton', is playing *'Preachin' Blues'* with as much vigour as when they first took the spotlight. They go on to play *'What a Dream'* and later *'Jelly Roll'*. Outside the snow is falling. Somewhere the train will be making its way towards the city. In his hotel room overlooking the lake Thomson has been trying to sleep but now sits at the window in the dark watching the whiteness slowly covering everything like dust sheets settling over furniture in a deserted mansion. When he has such dreams it is always his childhood home he sees. There are no figures in it and the rooms seem countless. His bedroom was on the second floor, looking out over water- a pond or lake or the ocean itself he cannot recall. He recalls how he would sit there and watch as the snow fell and wait for his father to come home. When he had left the tavern in Wellesley Street it had been snowing lightly. In his dream or dreams it never seems to snow; unless that is he forgets those dreams. Did I ever build a snowman? Thomson thinks as he watched two drunken Calgary supporters rolling a large ball of snow along the sidewalk. He gave them a hand as they tried to lift the second ball onto the base. With his head down and his hat clasped to it Thomson struggles down Yonge through the snow back to the hotel. Here and there, like silent sentinels, he passes other misshapen snowmen, some left incomplete. By the time he reaches the hotel he is a snowman himself. The doorman helps him to dust off the snow before he enters the lobby and finds the lift. He watches the dial indicating the floors as they pass. In some dreams (not this one) the lift seems to rise forever until he is in the attic where he used to play. His two favourite places in that old mansion, his home, were the attic and the basement. He would watch the snow from the attic window, as he is now watching through the hotel window as the snow is falling. From high up how different the world looks, he thinks. The silence that wraps itself around him was as mysterious then as it is now. When he fell asleep as a child- or perhaps only in those dreams- he would wake to a pristine world.

What kind of world will I wake to now? Thomson thinks- but he has to fall asleep first.

Thomson reads about the death aged ninety-six of 'the Honourable Lancelot Chatham' in Victoria some days ago. It is the name which has caught his eye and the photograph of the woman standing with the two men and their wives outside the house that he dreams about, for he can recognise that place. She has to be my mother, he thinks, though he would not have recognised her had they passed in the street. In his dream his mother is always turning away and just glimpsed, like his father: a presence felt rather than seen. His grandfather had been a self-made man (according to the obituary) who had arrived in the Province before the turn of the century and worked as a lumberjack, gradually building up his own small logging company. He had shown considerable business acumen and began to acquire tracts of land which were used as orchards. His businesses flourished, his wealth grew and he became one of the richest and most powerful men in the area. He had a reputation for ruthlessness. Thomson reads about his grandfather's career, his political affiliations and ambitions, his support for this and that charity and his passion for hunting wild animals. He has read hundreds of such obituaries about such men who were strangers to him. This man is also a stranger to him. He wants to hurry on to the sports pages or the crossword puzzle but his eye keeps straying to that family portrait. On either side of his mother, this woman called Mrs Oppenheimer he does not recognise, are two middle aged men. These are named as her sons Ethan and Joseph. Flanking them are two women- a Grace and an Amelia- their wives. He notes the date of the funeral. All of this was news to Thomson who gazes at the photograph without recognition. Somewhere in the back of his memory lurks an image of a man's face which may have been that of his father, though it could just as well have been a servant. But this older man, with his severe looks and mutton-chop whiskers, his high collar and indomitable stance, he could be anyone.

He reads about the man discovered dead on a train. The cause of death was a heart attack. In his luggage they found dozens of rare Byzantine icons. He came from Ottawa and was an art dealer. He had no known family. People die all the time anywhere and anyhow, Thomson thought. You don't have to leap into a volcano or jump out of a moving train: just stay where you are, do what you're doing, and death will come to you, eventually.

The fireman is thinking about his wife while the engineer is solving another chess puzzle in his head. The tail-end crew are playing *Mille* in the caboose while sipping some coffee. Pascal has tidied up the dining car and will shortly be setting the tables for the next meal. The chef is having a cigarette while his assistant is replacing the washed pots and pans. Many of the passengers have nodded off, soothed by the rythmn of the wheels beneath them. Snow is falling outside. Thomson watches the storm unfolding.

Charlotte will usually choose to miss the series of cocktail parties that would follow one of her performances. At the most she would go to the first night one but turn down all other invitations. The reception arranged at the consulate is one she is pleased to attend. For it she will choose an evening gown by Jeanne Lanvin. The design shows off her delicate figure in an unostentatious manner. She never wears jewellery. She knows that she cannot compete with all the socialites wearing the latest Parisian fashions and showing off their sculpted and tanned bodies. Charlotte will only drink one small glass of white wine. She will sip at it so lightly that the liquid will barely wet her upper lip. There are dozens of people wanting to meet her. Often they will ask the same questions. She sometimes thinks that it is easier to play '*Gaspard de la Nuit*' or Rachmaninov's '*Second Piano Sonata*' than to maintain a polite look on her face as she responds to such prattle. Someone will ask her to play- they always do- and for ten minutes or so she may give a little recital. It is as though she has to prove to these strangers that, yes, she was the one on the platform a few hours ago. As she glances around the crowded room she will see the man from the train and feel a sense of relief and excitement.

Despatches From Moffat
[Articles reprinted courtesy of "The Moffat Messenger"]
智慧是一個鼻子袋充滿燕麥
才能成為糞土。
Wisdom is a nose-bag full of oats
before it becomes dung.
Lao-Tse-It (5th century B.C. Chinese)

Got the cork out of the bottle but not being able to get it back in had to empty the damned thing. Not to worry- there's plenty more on the shelf. Saturday 16th at Kelso races should be a cracker, what with human pantomime horses taking the field for the first race.

In Moffat where the race track is shaped like a pretzel and wanders through back-gardens, privies and china shops, this Saturday's big race is between the spring lambs. Last year's winner, alas, is now chops in the window of 'McMince the Butcher'. Just goes to show you shouldn't beat the favourite.

I've managed to persuade McFleece, the local bookie (when he's not in uniform directing traffic), to accept a bet- I thought a pony on a lambkin named 'Little Miss Moffat' was a steal at 1000-1. The fact that it's wearing blinkers and wellies means it's got a good chance of running in a straight line. With my winnings I plan on retiring from retirement and serving my country; that is once I've emptied this bottle of Glen Moffat. 25 years it's been in there waiting to get out!

If it rains at Kelso next weekend I shall watch the gee gees from the member's room while flipping beer mats and carousing with the whelk millionaires who're buying up all the property from the Arabs down here. Weather surprisingly fine for yachting. More once the race is over and the cork is removed.

McPeevish

***

The only malt distillery in the Borders is hidden away in Moffat.

Why, I want to know, do you have to wrap yourself in sheepskin for the tour? And why, as the contents of the bottle diminish, does the world seem a vaster place? In no other distillery that I have visited in the course of my travels have sheep been actively employed in the fermenting process. In fact the entire process, from mashing the malt to bottling has been fully "sheepomated" in Moffat. Mind you, they give you a good measure down here. Never mind the gill- girlish name I've always thought. Down here you get the full 'Bleat'. This is the one measure Brussels have been unable to stamp out with their silly metric nonsense. If God had meant us to count in 10s then sheep would have not had four good legs. Off to the races next Saturday. McPeevish.

***

Trying to learn every word for sheep in Gaelic- '*uan*' is one! It's a great way to stimulate the synapses and the tongue should the malt be temporarily corked. While they're struggling with trams in the capital down here Ram-wrestling is a popular sport as you can imagine. Two falls, one submission and you've got your Sunday joint. Best not dwell on what happens if *you* hit the canvas! I've never seen so many women in jodhpurs! And as for their habit of cracking the whip (I say "cracking the whip") against a shapely thigh...

A philosophical dilemma: which would one rather be, the whip or the thigh? Many a night has been spent debating this and other profundities in '*The Caoraich & Mint Julep*', the local thankfully unadorned with jukebox or muzak! The old reivers game of "toss the maiden on the ram's horn" has its own league and Moffat rule supreme- quite understandable when a glance at the local telephone directory reveals that more than half the male inhabitants are named Hogg...More from Kelso later.

McPeevish o' the Kirree

***

There's a peculiar way they ride horses in Scotland and this way everyone's a winner! '*Scottish Enterprise*' has invested a lot of money in training horses to run backwards. A naked stable lad with the bag of oats is chased by the horses. Unlike greyhounds (which seldom are really grey) chasing a mechanical hare, should the stallions catch the stable boy...well, centaurs don't come into it. Now for the card...

Saturday October 16th 2010 (Going: Good to Firm in places: J= Jockey)

Kelso 14:30 Clifford Firth Memorial 'National Hunt' Maiden Hurdle £3600.00 added, 4yo plus, 2m 110y, Class 4, 35 runners… (Form: PP0PPP) That's All Right J= Brian Toomey

Kelso 15:05 Edinburgh City F.C. Novices' Handicap Chase £4500.00 added, 4yo plus, 2m 6f 110y, Class 4, 15 runners… (Form: 4532F4-)Young Buddy J= J.M.Jefferson

Kelso 15:35 Tourmaline Novices' Hurdle £4000.00 added, 4yo plus, 2m 6f 110y, Class 4, 20 runners… (Form: P-424) <u>Rain Stops Play</u> J=F.Davis

Kelso 16:05 Peter Doyle Handicap Hurdle £4000.00 added, 4yo plus, 2m 110y, Class 4, 25 runners… (Form: 641-445) <u>Heavenly Chorus</u> J= J.Reveley

Kelso 16:40 Lapis Handicap Chase (For the Marshall Trophy) £8000.00 added, 4yo plus, 3m 1f, Class 3, 14 runners… (Form: 435653) <u>Stagecoach Amber</u>

Kelso 17:15 Chrysolite Novices' Handicap Chase £4500.00 added, 4yo plus, 2m 1f, Class 4 19 runners… (Form: 44/06-63) <u>Best Horse</u> J= G.Lee

Kelso 17:50 Betfair Training Series Conditional Jockeys' Handicap Hurdle £3600.00 added, 4yo plus, 2m 6f 110y, Class 4, 20 runners…<u>Young Buddy</u> (Form: *Fontwell Principle*)

Blacksheep (our tipster) gives his picks above. You'll follow the logic of them: Elvis's first record was *'That's All Right'*; Buddy Holly naturally; anything ridden by a dead snooker player has to ghost it home; Elvis, of course, sings in the heavenly chorus; Elvis rode in a stagecoach in a movie; 'Best Horse' couldn't be clearer!

Form is no guide in Kelso, not with flocks of sheep being driven at random around the track by specially bribed sheep-dogs. Anticipating much merriment in the *'Dewlap and Midden'* in Kelso once the dung has been shovelled from the course. More once the jockeys' silks are re-starched.

McPeevish o' the Cloch

***

Where's *Blacksheep?* Where's my gutting hook? Looked at the <u>declared</u> runners this morning and only **one** of the picks is bothering to leave its stables! Too much hay and oats if you ask me; stable lads need a good thrashing. All that planning and fore-thought goes for nought…

-Remain calm, dear. Just use a pin like before.

The blessed voice of reason and calm from the beloved one!

McPeevish's (adjusted) tips:

2.30 pm…*Mr. Jay Dee*   3.05 pm *More Equity*   3.35 pm…*Sam Hall*
4.05 pm…*Gwyre*   4.40 pm…*Soubriquet*   5.15 pm…*Best Horse*
5.50 pm…*Desert Soul*

You'll notice there's no rhyme or reason to this selection. Desperate tactics old man, a bit like *Zulu*- form a circle, hide the women, throw Bibles at the darkies and drink lots of whisky. Never fails…

-Where's the car, dear?

I've got to drive? But I've got to study the form!

I'll wear the hat then. Might as well travel obligato. Nobody will recognise me in these parts anyhow will they?

It's on TV you say! My God, what if my presence leaks to the press?!

They can't possibly change the cards *again*, can they?

What do you mean: the coalition can do anything they bloody want?

We'll try an on-course bookie then, since *Blacksheep* won't answer the phone. This chap McSkinnue, he sounds an honest sort of chap.

Well that's the engine started…must dash. Hope the grass is green and all that

McPeevish o' the Clootie.

***

You'll've seen the pictures, you'll've read the police reports…Yes, it was me…the hat was a dead give-away…

Headed straight for the hospitality tent, grabbed some bubbly- that was the first mistake!

Always wise to be easy after the event…pardon… not got the old monocle screwed in properly. How was I to know? I'm not a country boy- you'd've spotted it right away…

After they threw me out of the haddock…sorry, paddock where I was toasting the horses, it was straight to the stand and lean on the rail and consider the odds. Boy, were there some odds, few evens. The odd squelchy bit, you know the countryside…dead leaves everywhere, manure that kind of thing.

Top up? Don't mind if I do…

Leave it to me, dear, I know how to talk to these men; you just keep hold of that shooting stick…

Are these my feet? Oh yes, that's how they work. I'll get a top-up on the way back…

The bookies were eyeing me the way a Roman consul would a Nubian galley slave. They liked the colour of my money. They took it readily and gave me little strips of paper which they swore I could redeem if I could run fast enough.

It all started so well. In the 2.30 *Magio* led them over the first flight anti-clockwise. But my horse, smart feller, knew the short-cut clockwise and wouldn't you know I've got a winner! 3 to 1. That'll do nicely. Carry on like this and it's Dubai and sand, sand and more sand! We're on a roll, baby, the oyster's ours and have a cigar!

Now just take a look at these silks: that will tell you- there's not a **spot** anywhere!

Mr. Jay Dee…WON! Fontwell Park here I come!

More Equity…Second (closing fast)

Sam Hall…Fourth (with a belated rush, once rid of the cart)

Gwyre… (Last seen grazing under the trees)

Soubriquet… (Fades at the final fence into the distance and joins Gwyre for a cud or two)

Best Horse… (A likely "soubriquet": best for what? Another grazer…)

Desert Soul…There's only 5 in this race so they can hardly get in each other's way, can they? But this specimen FALLS over its horseshoes…If only they'd've cut the grass closer…

I should've heeded the warning but no, I plunged heedlessly on, bit between my teeth, spur up me bum, eyes blinkered to the signs and by the time Desert Soul fell I'd said good-bye to my only button-down collar shirt…

Don't mention stud to me! What's all this about bloodlines and stock and form? Isn't a pin any good for the ex-working man anymore?

Is there no balm in Gilead? Is there whisky in the jar? Who let the dogs out? Where is Tammy Wynette when you need her?

I never did like that shirt anyhow. It's sackcloth and ashes for me now, mate. I've learnt my lesson…

Now this meeting in November; gotta plan properly for *that*. Study the form. Consult the runes. Carve the odd calves' liver or two. Stake out the stables. Get the gen from the inside, straight from the gee-gees mouth. Check the silks for spots- only spots will do! I'm polishing the pommel from now on, I'll tell you.

What's this for? Oh, it goes under the bed…

Thank you, dear. Just put the light out…

McSkint

***

McPeevish o' the Peedgie here.

Whilst thumbing through an old copy of Joad's '*Sheep-dip & Illicit Stills around Moffat*'- bound in lambskin and beautifully illuminated by the monks of Melrose Abbey- I chanced across this little-known Border Ballad:

The Moffat ram
Was in a jam

While hunting for a ewe;
In Amsterdam
He found his lamb
Swimming in a stew.

Anon, quoted in *'Oatmeal and its 101 uses on the Sabbath as agreed by the Elders of the Kirk o' Grimshanks'* as translated by the Ettrick Marinader.

We still await, with poised pen, the runners at Kelso on Saturday.

More will follow. We may call upon the Scottish Executive for soil analysis and they could well be receiving samples of turf cut from the course in the next few days.

McPeevish

***

TALES FROM THE BORDERS 2

The world's first sheep dip was invented and produced by George Wilson of Coldstream, Scotland in 1830. That dip was based on arsenic powder and was exported by Package Steamer from nearby Berwick-upon-Tweed. A local group are organising a petition to have a statue, carved from a special block of Moffat marl, erected in his honour. A famous local sculptor, Francis Punchett, has already won the competition for designing this memorable work, which it is hoped will adorn the site of the now abandoned Moffat sheep-dippery.

It is a sad fact that many *State employees* are still being subjected to the age old training ritual of "sheep dipping". This is a process by which employees are "refreshed", "cleansed" and "re-invigorated" by ensuring they attend set training courses or, perhaps, are placed on the ubiquitous "refresher" course. This refresher course is necessary because most employees immediately forget what they have learned on similar courses that they had been on. This is quite unlike sheep which, once they've had their first dipping, come back enthusiastically for more once the dogs catch them.

Companies just love "the sheep dip". It's easy to create, easy to administer and can cut costs. Simply get your Training Department to devise a list of courses that link to the company's priority capability areas (PCAs); decide who needs that training; tell which employees to go on what course, and then give everyone a "big pat on the back" for achieving the Training and Development Plan (TDP). Easy!

'Sheep dip' is also:

(a) Country <u>slang</u> for whisky. To avoid taxes farmers hid 'home made' whisky in barrels marked 'sheep dip'. Farmers' merchants continued the tradition by entering cases of whisky as 'sheep dip' on farmers' bills. Farmers' daughters on their wedding night would lose their maidenhood (if they had not lost it already, being a rather forgetful lot those country girls) in the sheep-dip bed of the local hotel ("*The Plough and Furrow*").

(b) A half filled bath of hot soapy water shared amongst friends, used to wash off the post clubbing or boozing dirt before everyone crashes out on the sofa and floor

MOFFAT'S famous *"Hogg"* Distillery

It is unknown when, where and by whom Whisky was discovered, though the Murphy brothers have been mentioned. This is as it should be for something that, like manna, is a '*bhronntanas ó na déithe*' (= a gift from the gods). Distilling has been going on in Scotland and Ireland for at least 1500 years, often in illicit stills disguised as places in which sheep are bathed. It is claimed by the Irish that they invented it, calling it *Uisce Beatha* which means the Water of Life; but then the Irish also claim to have invented the shovel and the potato sack. The English anglicised the *Uisce* to Whisky, having trouble with diphthongs, close back rounded vowels, semiotic waws, uncials and unicycles.

The local distillery was rebuilt in the 1880s after a period of use as a nunnery and then a candle factory. The distillery manager, then one W.J.McPeist, reputedly fed his prize-winning Aberdeen Angus cattle on the spent grain. Their dung was much sought after by rose growers of the district, who used it to stuff the pillows of those caught cuckolding another's wife. A Sheriff sitting in Edinburgh once fined an entire herd- the *herd*, not the drover- being driven through the Flodden city gate on their way to the Tollcross slaughterhouse, for being 'drunk, excessively flatulent, and uncattle-like': that judgement is sometimes quoted when local football hooligans riot.

The *"Hogg"* is the only remaining malt whisky distillery close to Edinburgh. The quality of this lowland malt is considered second to none. It is much sought after. The secret, of course, is in the home grown 'bleat', which thrives only in the hills above Moffat. The distillery offers tours of the facility, which includes a ritual 'dipping' for authenticity.

Of course, nowadays they do not use such dangerous substances as arsenic but good old natural organophosphorus compounds and synthetic pyrethoids which grow in abundance around this idyllic Borders town. The used dip is often then bottled and sold to unwary Arabian gentlemen who seldom return to trouble the golf course again.

McPeevish (quoting an article by *Wolfgang McTottle, Town archivist*)

***

Our selections, sniffed out by Syd Spyv, the local seer where horseflesh is concerned and often to be found in the snug at Moffat's *'Marmoset and Manatee'* (opening hours flexible to suit, likewise the barmaid), are made. Several are without jockeys. This is not regarded as a handicap and Syd swears the horses know their way around the course like the back of his hand. One's doubts are silenced by this piece of Borders wisdom. Money has changed hands. Quite why he took his suitcase and where Syd has gone to place the bet I'm not sure.

Others may consult the form book, test the wind, bribe the blacksmith, squeeze the horse's gonads or force feed the jockey puff pastry. We believe our principle of selection is sound: *spots and only spots*! There are those short-sighted pundits who believe that there is no difference in the aerodynamic resistance of spotted silks and others, but they are an unwashed minority. Many underhand tricks have been tried in the Borders- giant magnets set by the rails to drag the weighted saddles off the horse's back; or wind farm fans diverted to blow across the course causing mayhem to the members' hattery and horses with Vaseline smeared on their hooves to skid uncontrollably.

The Reverend Anthrax Cleet will bless the course prior to the first race. He is taking as his text an obscure verse from Zechariah 10v5 (*'Riders on horses shall be confounded...'*). We understand that he is a *stripes* man and shall watch him closely at the nosebags.

More once the bandages are off,

McPeevish o' the Trate.

***

We have identified another *spot* running in the **1:00pm SHIP INN, DALKEITH NOVICE'S HANDICAP CHASE** and have advised our representative Syd Spyv (currently reachable only by an illegible *Poste Restante* number in Belize) to pile the shekels on this *silk* and to expunge all outlay pledged to *Isla Pearl Fisher*. We understand that Mr. Graham Lee is such a skilled jockey that he is actually riding several horses in many of the races.

Keep your radio tuned to Radio Moffat for advisories on gull-snatching, turf-tossing and nose-bag interference. We are currently combing the course for grass above the height of 10mm to ensure that none of our balletic horses trip. They are also being fitted with a special tool, similar to a lawn-mower or tunnel drill, which will help them through the hurdles. Punters are advised to remain behind the white-painted rails (large birds with twisted beaks and an eye for oysters,).

I shall leave you with this item culled from the Moffat Museum of Merriment:

Ballad of the Pommel
O Pommel! Bra' Pommel!
I gummle and chirple
Like yon yaffle
As I hargle-bargle.

O Pommel! Bra' Pommel!
Fowk may marvel
Tat I'm sae bruckle
And aye ma hoddle,
A sneevling jevel
As I hargle-bargle.

O Pommel! Bra' Pommel!
Upo this saidle
By yon vangel
Let me no daidle
O spek mair twaddle
As I hargle-bargle.

(Attrib: Mattie Onhing, known as 'The Gawkie', *fl* 1795 near Moffat)

Recently discovered and published by Professor Frandie Fulyie in his treatise "*The pommel in history: Who sat on What and Why*" (published by Killogie University).

This work elucidates the pros and cons of the high and low pommel and focuses on the preferences of three famous women- Boudicca, Wu Zetian (Tang Dynasty) and Catherine the Great- each of whom had a "penchant" for elaborate pommels. Those of the latter are on display in the Hermitage, St. Petersburg. Boudicca is known to have been interned with hers, as X-rays of the recently discovered burial chamber have revealed. Her burial barrow has become the site of Sapphic revels with platinum pommels come the new moon of each Leap Year. The pommels of the Chinese Empress are kept in the Qianling Museum on top of Liang Mountain and are as revered as the terracotta army who guard them.

We trust this information is of use to you.

McPeevish o' the Blait

***

-Now don't be a silly boy, darling. Take your head out of the bag.

-Yes, I know it's a shame and that everyone is laughing at you, but they're laughing at everybody else who lost as well.

-I'm sure they appreciate the fact that you don't wear a suit and tie every day of the year, only on special occasions. Yes it was a special occasion, dear. Just think of all those corks you popped.

-Yes, I know it's cold and it's damp but we'll soon be in the pub.

-You did get one winner, dear. Yes, I know the others kept falling or throwing their riders. It's such a shame for Lucinda. She tries so hard, you know,

-No, I don't think the grass was to blame. It's always been green around here and the horses are used to that.

-Yes, I'm sure you & that Plato chap are right, spots are best.

-How much did you say you'd lost? Well, that's not so bad when compared to the national debt…

-No, dear, I'm not trivialising the matter. I know it's your pension but you did want to have a good time and you did say to hell with the consequences.

-Yes, of course I still love you; I'm driving us home, aren't I?

-No I didn't think it was a good idea to lock you in with the horses… or the jockeys…

-I didn't know Lucinda could swear like that either. She certainly didn't know those kinds of words when we were at school together. I'm not sure what it means, but that stable lad and horse did.

-No I don't think it would have helped putting a broom handle up the jockey's backside. I think there are rules against that. The horse wouldn't take kindly to it either.

-I'm not sure how boycotting porridge is going to help, dear. You'll feel better in the morning.

-I'm sure if you'd had a tricycle as a child it would have helped you to empathise, dear. But horses have four legs…Not the kind you back?

It's not often you see a miniature camel humping the leg of the chairman of the Stewards' committee, McPeevish thought savagely as he sought to blot out all trace of this latest humiliation as a pundit. It had been quite a scene in the unsaddling enclosure: that Sheikh from Birmingham with his entourage all wearing their sheets and quoits and the local Pictish fraternity with their pit-bull turn-up tuggers. When accepting the prize as the best dressed trainer unfortunately Lucinda used several uncommon Gaelic words which, to a camel, were the equivalent of 'Fetch!' and other less savoury commands. The enclosure had become a maelstrom of swinging fists and artificial limbs- surprising how many prosthetics there were in the Borders, McPeevish had thought- and still did think. Toupees were sent flying in all directions, which naturally set off the hunting dogs in pursuit, for what toupee doesn't look like a low flying grouse in the half-light of a partly clouded wintry November afternoon in the Borders? Gaiters were graiped, waistcoats wasted and top hats astaired. It had become an absolute houbrabra of brouhaha until the tinny Tannoy had announced that "They" were "off". All eyes swivelled to the young lady with the pet tamandua and bosoms who was with the Sheikh but then the horses thundered past and order was restored. 'A camel without sand is like a lighthouse without a horse' one old sage whispered as Lady Cumshortleigh carried off the distressed camel. We understand that it now happily resides at her manorial home adding spice to the 'one hump or two' conversations on wet Thursday afternoons. The cleaning bill for the Sheikh and his entourage enabled the local Chinese laundry owner Gung-Hau to retire to his native Paisley where he spends his time bathing in the natural starch spa…

What I don't understand, McPeevish muttered to himself, is how a tried and trusted system based upon the rubric 'spots and only spots' could have come amiss so drastically. The whole raison d'être of sentient life itself was under threat. Were we witnessing the breakdown of the universe? Would E still equal mc^2 in the morning? Was Kelso the equivalent of a portal in time, a point of weakness in the fabric of existence, a kind of astronomical ley line? If spots couldn't be trusted then where were we…?

-On the way back to Moffat, dear.

Ah, he thought, that sweet, kind woman! Nothing seemed to shake her. So wise in the ways of the countryside! At ease in the paddock with the horses while he tiptoed around on the *qui vive* for dung. The way she could handle a fetlock…

He shuddered with the passion such a vision engendered and caught her knowing glance as she twisted the wheel and stepped on the accelerator.

How was it though, he wondered, that he should come away feeling like a sheep newly fleeced whereas she seemed to have a handbag twice the size of when they arrived.

He squinted casually across the darkened interior of the car at her strong profile. How could she pick the winners without a system?

-Yes, I was rather lucky, dear. Lucinda was never much good at Maths and could never make the spit-ball stick to the ceiling. They are nice horses she looks after but I remember that her hamster was always coming second to my turtle when we raced them in the scullery. Mother never knew, of course.

-I doubt even if they'd've saddled you or the turtle that things would have gone any better. You need too much of the whip, you know dear.

-Horses aren't a bit like hamsters, I know dear; but it's Lucinda I'm talking about. She and Peter- *Scuddy* we call him- run such a lovely stables at Arlary near Loch Leven but I'm afraid their horses are dog meat.

-I'm sure she won't serve *that* when they have us up for the meal, dear.

-Yes I'm sure you will have tweaked the system for the next meeting, dear. A glass of Moffat's finest malt, a romp in the hayloft, and you'll be a new man.

What if Sting was right about Tantric sex? McPeevish mused. Could the horses pick up the aura? What about the horseshoes? Were they imprinted with magic symbols, like Egyptian hieroglyphics? Did the Uzbek rather than the Romany nosebag make all the difference?

Suddenly McPeevish felt his spirits rising. He wasn't beaten yet! The secrets of the turf would reveal themselves to him before he was done! He rolled down the window.

-You'll feel much better now that's out, dear. It was the last glass of bubbly, I fear. They do say you should always leave the bottom half for the *sìthiche*.

-Bless you too, dear. Here we are…

Ah! The lights of Moffat! A quick dram in the "*Mink and Membrane*" then the bliss of the pillow! Perhaps it was all a dream after all.

McPeevish o' the Figmaleerie

***

The racing this Sunday at Kelso
reminds me of something art nouveau:
I'm not quite sure what
perhaps a kumquat
as painted by Pablo Picasso.

'A nosebag?' sweet Lucinda cries

and casts her eyes to the skies;
she's not very keen
on jockeys who're lean,
preferring the ampler size.

The bookies are raking it in;
the Vicar is preaching of sin-
he considers the whip,
then gives it a flip
while downing a bottle of gin.

Forget chevrons and ink-blots,
those bows and granny knots;
don't bet on a stripe:
Ignore all the hype;
you're better off betting on spots!

©*McPeevish Bard o' the Ferintosh*

The horses are all at the start
The favourite's dying to fart;
O dearie me!
He's started to pee-
Would anyone like some jam tart?

The grass *is* a nice shade of green
The stable's immaculately clean;
But just *entre nous*
I do like it *blue*
I'm sure you get what I mean.

They're passing the winning post
The favourite looks like a ghost
He's stuck at the rear
And I must say I fear
We'll have him for Sunday's pot roast.

© *McPeevish Bard o' the Cludgie*

Remember: "Spots are the ticket!" as Plato wisely said counting his winnings. There's a kiddie who should know about the Tote and other such kit. Don't waste a dime, drachma or shekel on a diamond, slash or hoop. Just put your wad on anything odd that's covered in spots.

***

"Out damned spot! Out, I say!"

-Yes, dearest, Shakespeare knew about spots too. 'With a spot I damn him'- *Julius Caesar*, I believe. We did that for the Boswell Society a few years ago when I had a walk on part in the crowd that viewed the body…

-I'm not sure why you say it's *entirely* your brother's fault…

-How long ago was it that the spotted silk won? …55 years? Goodness!

-I'm not sure that joining the Foreign Legion is a good idea, sweetness. You don't really like sand, do you?

-Yes, I did think you looked majestic clearing that last hurdle, dear. I'm sure your horse would have found it in any case…

-I know you were upset at being stigmatised, dear heart, but that Sergeant was *most* understanding when I told him you were just out from Dingleton for the afternoon and in my care…

-Yes, I'm sure the photographer won't publish the picture he took, dear. I did mention to him that his wife, who I know through the malt-mashing club, might be interested in what the stable lasses could tell her about his flash photography…

-That sounds very clever, dear heart, but I'm not sure the bookies are ready for retrospective betting yet…

-There's really no secret, bless you; if they've got strong hind-quarters that's good enough for me…*Of course* I don't think of you like that, dearest!…

-Yes French is a lovely language to swear in…

Was he wrong to be inconsolable? McPeevish gazed glumly into the darkness as the car sped back towards Moffat. Seven bummers! Seven! Could he have been so wrong all these years? Why had spots so calamitously let him down? Where was the flaw? A system that had worked so perfectly 55 years ago surely couldn't have been changed by the insignificant passage of so little time? Was Einstein's theory to be consigned to the scrap heap? No, he exhorted himself as his breath misted on the window. This was a test, a trial. Look at Jean Seberg as Joan of Arc. The hours she spent agonising over that hair-cut was worth it when you saw the blissful look as she roasted at the stake. He who wavers falls off the rope- was that Shakespeare?

-No, my love, I think it was Del-Boy…

The woman was a miracle-worker. In the end the Sergeant was apologising to *him*! How she kept her composure while counting her winnings was beyond him. And with the drizzle and the cold, the mud underfoot, she remained as immaculate as a mannequin in a store window. What was it in the way she held the umbrella, that delicate turn of the wrist as the shaft rested lightly on her collar bone, which sent a premonitionary shiver through his cortex?

He caught the affectionate, teasing glance she threw at him as, with the sureness of Hannay in '*The 39 Steps*', she steered the vehicle through the rain-swept one lane hill road. The headlights were like the flared nostrils of Svaðilfari or some other rampaging priapic mythological equine.

Mustn't think like that, McPeevish. Later, not now in this confined space. Hannay would never have…

Could pockets really be so empty? Yet he felt strangely replete. That would be the hamper. Not much left in there. The odd half-gnawed chicken wing, a few autographed corks…

-Would they really sell on eBay, dear? You know more about that sort of thing, of course; but I'm not sure anyone much cares for jockey-autographed corks…

Probably right. He had no head for business, whereas she…Best stick to what you're good at, McPeevish. There'll be something you're good at…

-I do think you're too hard on yourself dear. You've had a very successful career and now you're just enjoying your retirement…

He wondered what those Spanish saints who drove nails into their feet and hands would have said to that.

-I'm sure they had a reason for what they did, dear. It takes all sorts.

The question was: could he find the flaw and repair the system before December 5th? One more shot at it before Xmas, that's all he had. Perhaps he'd forgotten his golden rule: Keep it simple. What was it she'd said about hind-quarters?

-Lucinda told me about that, dear. It's the sign of a good jumper. Plenty of push and whoosh…you know.

Again that intriguing, inviting glance as the wheel was twirled as delicately as the shaft of the umbrella…*Mustn't think like that McPeevish.*

-It's the finishing straight that's the most exciting part of the race, don't you think dear heart?

Her eyes gleamed in the mirror at him.

By Jove! The lights of Moffat! They were sailing straight past the "*Corn-*

cob and Cucumber"! The promise was on!

***

$$(a+b)^3 = \sum_{k=0}^{3} \binom{3}{k} a^{3-k} b^k$$

$$= \binom{3}{0} a^{3-0} b^0 + \binom{3}{1} a^{3-1} b^1 + \binom{3}{2} a^{3-2} b^2 + \binom{3}{3} a^{3-3} b^3$$

$$= 1 \cdot a^3 b^0 + 3 \cdot a^2 b^1 + 3 \cdot a^1 b^2 + 1 \cdot a^0 b^3$$

$$= a^3 + 3a^2 b + 3ab^2 + b^3$$

We would not have you believe that our selections are entirely random nor based solely on the simple mantra "*spots are all*"; nor is the colour "red" a casually introduced factor.

The above illustration makes everything clear.

To reach our conclusions, which are ineffably sound, we have considered the following factors:

1. The SIZE of the field (in acres)
2. Whether the horse prefers to run CLOCKWISE or ANTICLOCKWISE
3. The STATE of the GOING (we are not interested in the "coming")
4. The TIME of the race
5. The WEIGHT of the bookmaker's satchel
6. Previous FORM (circular, triangular, square etc)
7. The JOCKEY and the shape of his ears (n.b. flattened ears indicate an unhappy jockey- and horse)
8. The LENGTH of the race (in metres, yards and the Border's measure of 'sheep-skip')
9. The OWNER, the state of his/her tan and size/model/year of his/her car
10. The INNARDS of a freshly slaughtered cockroach

By using the above formula and the Hadron Collider deep in the bowels of Cern- we would have used Moffat's own sheep-driven 'RAM' (Random Antimatter Mangler) but it was otherwise in service- which we run on a torch battery in the garden shed, we have come up with our selections.

Syd Spyv, back from his recent holiday in Belize- and I must say his tan looks immaculate- has personally guaranteed that none of these gee-gees will trip, slip or flip. I have utter confidence in him. Any man who can break out of the 12 toughest prisons in Europe and retain his licence to trade has my backing. I believe he is to be Moffat's Conservative parliamentary candidate at the next election.

But I digress. I have raised enough cash from my 'Pudsey Bear' nosebag scam operation to fund the weekend's jaunt at Kelso. I shall be wearing my new red long-johns, embossed with the insignia of this fine municipality. I shall not be out of place despite the absence of a suit and titfer since I'm being smuggled in by milady with a supply of chickens looking for somewhere to roost. Subterfuge is necessary: if the bookies get wind that it is McPeevish who is laying down some heavy bets then the odds will shrivel to the size of a rooster's reproductive apparatus.

By 5pm tomorrow I'll be rolling in oysters, setting light to Euro-notes by the barrow-full, spreading canapé on my corns and littering the living-room with designer luggage as I prepare for a round-the-world trip with SAGA (Syd's Aged Group Away-days)

McPeevish o' the Jundie

***

bordertelegraph

SUNDAY 5th DECEMBER (John Smith's Scottish Borders National Day) ABANDONED DUE TO SNOW

Kelso Stewards abandon richest meeting six days early after 24 inches of snow.

Arctic conditions are still causing havoc with the racing programme in Britain, and Kelso have already given up hope of hosting Sunday's fixture because the Borders track is covered in 36 inches of snow.

Officials at Kelso have acted early, calling off the lucrative meeting six days early without the need of an inspection. Clerk of the course Anthea Mumbleton said: "There's no hope at all. We've got three feet of snow on the track and temperatures are below freezing, even during the day. The forecast remains the same - there's further snow all week - and it's just not going to stop in time. It's very bleak."

Sunday's meeting had prize money totalling £80,000 and was due to be Kelso's richest meeting of the season, with the *John Smiths Scottish Borders National* as the main feature race. Although yet to be confirmed managing director Roderic Leanalot hopes to negotiate a re-staging of the Scottish Borders National on Wednesday 29th December, a new fixture to the Kelso calendar between Christmas and New Year.

Despite the disappointment this has occasioned to horse racing enthusiasts, the Borders Sheep Snowmobile Club have stepped in to fill the gap. They will be staging a Gala of special Sheep slaloming and snow-boarding races, followed by the *First Annual Sheep Snowmobile Championship*. Entries are graded and there are prizes for the 2 year old maiden stakes (if any are to be found). Riders will be subject to inspection by sniffer dogs specially trained to detect mint sauce. The judge is the well-known landowner and bon viveur Lord Ramsbottom who will present the tup to the winners.

From our Special Correspondent 'Julian Fleece' [aka McPeevish].

"The Dangling Dirk Inn", Moffat

-Evening McPeevish…Some weather, eh?

-…Brr!

-Didn't catch that…

-Brrff!

-Call this cold? Worse last year. Even the sheep carried hot water bottles…

-Brrrrykn!!!

-Can't say I have seen the Yukon…What d'you fancy?

-Mmmmt…

-Nice malt, eh? Got a shelf full of 'em. Take your pick…

-Rdbgrrrr

-Ardbeg? Fine malt...Oops! Bit heavy with the thumb. Get that down you...

-BrrrrrBrbbbh!

-Better?

-Mmmmch…

-Freezes the birds in flight, this kind of wind, never mind the vowels…

-Smgn…Bnnhbhn…rrr

-Bunnahabhain it is…Minus seven last night…Old Bill the shepherd said the sheep were building igloos in the hills…Crafty buggers: no council tax on igloos in Scotland…

-Ssmmggnn…Brchlddchrrr!

-And how's the good lady? Not with you tonight?...

-Wbrmmhhzzph…

-Ah! Just coming along…You'll be upstairs for the Bridge night I expect…

-Jjbbhxx!

-Another? Same again?

-Cccl!

-Caol Ila…fine malt...

Give him his due, McPeevish thought; he was liberal with the thumb. Whenever he motioned for another, the landlord correctly interpreting the glottal sound he emitted from within the scarf and balaclava.

-Ah! Here she is. Evening Miss...

-Evening Jim. He still got lockjaw?

-McPeevish? Seemed in fine oratorical form to me. Malt will get past anything…The usual Horse's Gaskin for you?

-Mmmm. How many of those has he had?

-Those? Just the one.

McPeevish noticed how her eyebrow arched just a notch, hardly recordable on any of Stevens' scales of measurement: nominal, ordinal, interval or ratio. He must re-read Thurstone's *'The Vectors of the Mind'*. Come to that he must have a haircut soon.

James gave a weak grin and nodded at the shelf behind him.

-And one of those and that and them as well. Seems he plans on drinking himself through the alphabet of malts.

F's a bit of a bugger though, McPeevish thought.

-We'll take these up with us, shall we darling?

McPeevish acknowledged the landlord with a nod.

He followed her up to the room where the Bridge tables were set out. He found himself desperately trying to distinguish a Phoney Stayman from a Reverse Drury; or was that a Fishbein? No that was Mrs. Crowhurst's Maltese Terrier. Yappy little thing, especially when she bid one No Trump. Was that a Brozel? No, that was the kettle for tea at the break. And what the hell was a Rystra, some kind of West Indian music fanatic? Somewhere in his memory floated a Sputnik and a Flannery and a Gerber and an Ogust and a …

How the dear one did it McPeevish had no idea as he stumbled to the table and sat. She was elegance personified, greeting all about her with cheerfulness and a smile. If he moved a muscle he knew his face would crack like a skim of ice on a lake.

He looked at the cards he had been dealt, trying to remember the protocol of royalty, the order of numbers, the ability to feel. Where was his drink? Safely on the table, thank God. He arranged the pieces of card into reasonably pretty patterns.

Now everyone was looking enquiringly at him: what had he done? Couldn't be his flies. Had he started to dribble? Dementia was similar to the tram project in the capital: by the time it was due to be finished you'd forgotten about it. Something stirred in the cellar of his memory. Speak-bid.

-Pss.

That seemed to relieve the tension and the eyes swivelled to the person to his left. Remember that one, McPeevish he told himself. Might come in useful again.

Oh Lord, now they're all looking at me again, he thought. Should I be paying more attention? Drift off like that all the time. The cold, dulls the brain, like Scott of the Antarctic.

-Pss.

Worked again! he thought with delight, or at least the frozen embryo of delight. Easier than I thought, if I could think.

As relief edged through his autonomous nervous system, what little of it was still functioning after the teeth of the easterly had sawn through it, McPeevish considered the contents of his glass. Someone's been at it, he thought. Short thoughts he could manage; the longer ones fell over the precipice of oblivion. Good word that, oblivion. He looked around, using his eyes rather than chancing swivelling his neck and breaking it- nasty shock to all if his head rolled around the carpet. McPeevish eyed the Maltese Terrier speculatively as it eyed him evaluatively. If it made a move towards his leg…

My, he thought, it has a long tongue. Why do dogs lick their undercarriage like that?

They were looking at him again.

McPeevish stared at the table. Oh Lord, there were cards strewn on it. They were waiting for him to play. Would his digits work? He desperately plucked a card from the fanned collection which clung to his fingers like a frozen bouquet.

There, now someone else has the problem, McPeevish thought. He felt a trickle of sweat running down the back of his neck. The open fire was thawing him out. How long would it take, he wondered, before it was safe to remove the scarf and balaclava?

The eyes were on him again. There, take that, he thought as he propelled another card on to the green cloth. The eyes moved on around the table. McPeevish wondered what his eyes were doing. At least they were still in his head. The internal mechanism for shifting them seemed reasonably intact, the channels of communication with his central sponge likewise. They found the glass; dare he take another sip? Life was full of conundrums and half-empty glasses and dogs that licked their unmentionables with glee…

-Well played, partner; a nice finesse.

McPeevish blinked. They were going down the stairs, her arm though his.

-One for the road? The landlord called as McPeevish and consort reappeared in the lounge bar.

-Oh I think so, the beloved voice said.

McPeevish fumbled through the vague imprints of the snow-banks of his recent memory. Finesse?

He looked around, noting that each person present seemed constitutionally correct and intact. No sheep had infiltrated the company. The beloved one was deep in conversation with those others from upstairs who had likewise mastered the ability to descend. Probably talking about horses and the prospects for Kelso on Sunday, McPeevish decided.

Finesse.

McPeevish glanced at the landlord, who stood receptively and attentive to every nod and wink.

Nod or wink? McPeevish thought. I'm not a nodder or a winker.

Finesse.

That did it. Some of the old skill was still there, McPeevish. A glass, nicely filled with a light amber restorative that promised bliss seemed to materialise in his hand, which remained attached to his wrist and arm. Some things hadn't changed, despite the cold. Now, could he raise it to his lips, parting the scarf carefully so as not to expose too much flesh?

Done. Bliss.

-A fedora's not much use in a blizzard, is it dear?

-Hwfrtg?

-It was kind of the Colonel and his wife to ask us over tomorrow night.

-Nmm?

-Oh you poor dear, the sinuses must be gummed up too.

McPeevish's head had always been the problem, he thought. They struggled against the howling blizzard which raked the High Street like Stukas on the rampage. He knew no Colonel, let alone this chap's wife. God, how much snow was coming down from Siberia? Couldn't they keep their house in order there? Snow-nets, everyone knew you needed snow-nets or it blew all over the blace. Blace? His synapses were seizing up. He was moments away from Nirvana and he didn't mean the pop group. Think warm thoughts.

His arm was squeezed in reply.

-Almost there, darling.

He knew that voice; he knew that tone. There was a strange tingling feeling…

-This should take away the chill, she was saying as he sank into the armchair. I thought all those Canadian winters you told me about would have toughened you up for a little blow like that.

McPeevish considered that cat. The cat considered him. They agreed: little blow outside it was not.

His feet were still there, thank God. How he'd not lost them during that interminable trek through mountains of snow he had no idea. Best not to think about it, McPeevish. Remember Scott, Robert Falcon not Walter Sir.

His hand clung to the glass she had put in it. His spirit clung to his body. What his body clung to he wasn't sure.

A mere hundred yards? What did she mean, mere? Men like he and Scott of the Antarctic knew that yardage was nothing where snow was concerned. Snow had this way of erasing all meaning. You never caught sheep nipping down to their local for a snort or two and a hand of bridge on an evening like tonight. Snuggle up to a bottle of Moffat malt, that was the sensible answer to weather like this.

-We'll take a bottle of wine over tomorrow, shall we dear?

If there was a tomorrow, McPeevish thought glumly. After all that stuff about Global Warming, this could be the final, apocalyptic snow to end all snows, the *capo di tutti capi* of snows, the Grandfather of the Godfather of the *capo di tutti frutti capi* of snows...

Then again, McPeevish thought as his glance caught that of the dear one in the armchair on the other side of the fire, if there *was* a tomorrow then, by the miracle of logical deduction, there *had to be* a tonight! He could see the flames reflected in her eyes and he rapidly gulped the remains of the malt...

*

The full moon shone on the mother-of-pearl snow-covered lawn.

-What a lovely bird bath.

-He's cheating, McPeevish muttered through clenched teeth.

He felt her hand tighten on his arm.

-Good Lord, dear heart, surely not here in Moffat!

-The buttons on his cardigan, McPeevish whispered.

-I thought he was just a bit fidgety.

The Colonel was at it, all right, McPeevish thought as they circumnavigated the Stupa by the garden shed. It was the way the Colonel fingered the buttons before and during the bidding. Everything had been tried now, McPeevish thought despairingly, wondering at the depravity of a man who could involve buttons in his perfidious schemes.

There's obviously some kind of rudimentary coding system, a bit like Schapiro and Reese using their fingers to signal Hearts held, McPeevish thought. The Italian pair Facchini and Zucchelli had been more direct, playing footsie under the table. Others held their cards high or low, held them in peculiar portions, or coughed and sniffed to signal to their partner. There was even one inventive pair who hummed and whistled excerpts from operas!

-Why on earth would he stoop to that? her beloved voice floated to his ear. He's such a good player he's really no need to do that to win.

How 'superior' did one have to feel oneself to be? McPeevish supposed that, wiser in the ways of devious and scheming men, he might make a stab at trying to fathom the Colonel's motives; but was it worth the effort?

-What are we to do? Shall I have a headache?

How typically sweet of her to offer to be the victim, McPeevish thought.

Why do I have to be so damned observant?

-That must be why Clarrisa advised me that we shouldn't play Bridge with them after supper tonight.

This is fiendish! They must have done it to other couples from the club, McPeevish thought grimly. I was the new boy so the Colonel decides it was our turn. For him it must be like branding strays.

Their hostess's voice announcing that the coffee was ready floated from the open French windows like an escaping moth.

I'll be damned if he's going to get away with this, McPeevish thought determination stiffening his resolve. It took a lot to do that to McPeevish. If there was a way to avoid it, whatever it was, he'd head for that channel with all paddles flapping. The man's probably not even a Colonel, just like Elvis's manager wasn't. What unit did he say he served in out in India, the King's Own What? Surely it had been the 6th Field regiment out there? Even the 4th Indian, the Red Eagles, had fought with the 8th Army through Africa and Europe. Maybe like Adolf in the Great War the Colonel just ran messages from gin hole to snooker table. Was that really a Cobra bite on his wrist? Having Sabu's autograph on the brochure of the premiere of *'Elephant Boy'* didn't prove anything other than the gullibility of the on-line buyer. Quoting *'Gunga Din'* carried no weight; nor did having jars and jars of Kopili Assam and Nilgiri Black and Darjeeling Green or Kashmiri Chai teas. Nowadays the local *'Spar'* catered to your every taste.

--I'll try to think of something, McPeevish whispered as they neared the windows. If I do I'll start talking about pony trekking in Tibet.

-Oh darling, not that!

-When I do, if I do- when and if I do- just have a wobbly, you know, come over all flushed or something, women's stuff and get their attention for a moment. Then just say 'Pass' when it comes to the bidding.

-Be careful, dear heart.

Thus it had been with Hannay, so it must be with McPeevish, McPeevish thought.

As they stepped back into the deceitful warmth of the drawing room with its walls hung with souvenir paintings of *Ratnasambhava* and *kha-dens* from the Himalayas, McPeevish felt as though a mantle had fallen upon his shoulders. But it was only her hand gently brushing dust, loose hairs and drops of snow from his sweater. Thus did the women in ancient Greece prepare their men-folk for battle with the Persians, McPeevish thought approvingly. Fortunately she wasn't given to the wailing and gnashing of teeth, the pot smashing and foul Attic oaths which also accompanied the men-folk decamping for a good randan.

In his childhood he had once shoved tadpoles in his brother's ears. That had been enough to prove conclusively that it could be done. Whether it had been a *wise* thing to have done was another matter. Wisdom and boldness sit uncomfortably together- who said that?

-Alan Sugar, I'm afraid dear, she whispered back.

Oh well; at least my name's not an anagram of '*a glar anus*', McPeevish thought.

The bruises his brother had inflicted upon him had soon healed. If the gods of the card table were with him- and so far this evening they were sneering disdainfully at his efforts to trump, finesse, overcall and show that he had a modicum of savvy- then perhaps he, McPeevish, would be able to teach the Colonel something. As long as it wasn't 'There's always another sucker who comes along'- was that W.C.Fields? It certainly wasn't Saint Augustine.

As their hostess poured the coffee the Colonel offered to pour the special Indian liqueur he had had sent over from Mumbai. It tasted suspiciously like Cointreau to McPeevish, with something not un-akin to 'Quink' added to it. He blinked as the Colonel asserted that it was an 'expensive' Arrack whose ingredients included cardamom and blueberries. When McPeevish said he preferred the Mangalore with its flavour of the coast of Malabar, the cinnamon and cardamom being blended to smooth out the pepper, the Colonel suggested they resume play. McPeevish glanced knowingly at his beloved who had been discussing croquet grips; she had heard the exchange and caught his raised eyebrow, acknowledging the sub-text: the man *is* a fraud. Perhaps I can unnerve him a bit, McPeevish thought, letting drop that his mother came from the foothills of the Hindu Kush and had grown up on the sub-continent. She used to croodle to him in Hindi as he lay in his cot. He excused himself to use the facilities as the others edged their way towards the table, his eye having been caught by the very thing he'd hoped to see on a desk in the hall.

*

The cards were running better for them after the break, McPeevish thought. Maybe he had rattled the Colonel a bit. Damage limitation was all he and his wife could muster for a run of several hands until McPeevish and partner equalised the score and sent it into a final game for the rubber.

How many hands had they played now?

Not that any of their successful rear-guard action could be put down to

McPeevish. He was playing like a berserker intent on reaching Valhalla at all costs. His bidding, never the most seasoned part of his game, stank to high heaven, ranging from the unimaginable to the gorblimey. It was only by the heroic and Herculean efforts of the dear one that they avoided being despatched time and time again.

She reads me like a book, McPeevish thought as yet again she interpreted his bizarre play and found the rescuing card, the route that avoided loss of game.

McPeevish could see that the strain was beginning to tell on the Colonel. There were no more generous chuckles and words of consolation, no more sparkling repartee and witty remarks to his soul-mate and aide-de-camp. They were well past the stage when slippers would have been welcome. There was that set look about the Colonel's mouth that McPeevish had once seen on John Wayne's face as he despatched an injured horse. Perhaps the Colonel had seen the same film? He had long given up responding to McPeevish's puerile and dislocated remarks and questions. Now and then McPeevish caught a look of contempt on the Colonel's face as with the luck of the devil and the dear one's skill yet again they drew back from the abyss. They had eased their way through the drinks trolley, McPeevish carefully sticking to the rather inferior (and probably watered) whisky, leaving the much touted Indian liqueur to the Colonel.

There is a heavy cobalt tinge about his gills now, thought McPeevish, the kind of colouration known as '*Calcutta Shadow*'.

That remark almost made the Colonel snarl; but hosts don't snarl. Perhaps aware that some primordial test was nearing its culmination and mindful of her best china and ornaments, his wife was mechanically playing her cards. She seemed hypnotised by her husband's button fiddling, which at times had a Wagnerian frenzy about it.

The cotton thread will be wearing thin by now, McPeevish thought. A few more tugs and twists and he'll lose number three. I'm sure that button number four shows acute signs of wear as well. Will he twiddle his shirt buttons next? His belly button? He's close to cracking, that's for sure.

But McPeevish was concerned about his partner. Throughout the proceedings he had kept a close eye on her. Uncomplaining she had taken up the slack as he had seemed to disintegrate under the effects of the alcohol and that rich dessert of *Makhana Kheer*. A wisp of hair, like a silent question mark, had come loose from her coiffeuse. It seemed such a frail, slender thing as it trembled against her temple, wherein he could discern the pulse of a delicate blue vein. He longed to reach over and...

The clock struck eleven.

The mechanical figure of Shiva as Nataraja with his unkempt hair within the fiery circle emerged and began his ritual dance.

McPeevish, whose deal it was, reached for the cards and began to shuffle.

-D'you know, once when I was pony trekking in Nepal…

The dear one seemed to snort and whinny, then let out a scream that Bette Davis would have given her soul for. She fell sideways in her seat, twitching and mewling. The next moments were a whirl of activity as their hostess leapt to comfort her and the Colonel poured her a stiff medicinal brandy from the reserve supply in his ivory golfing hip flask with its tiger skin covering.

-I am *so* sorry, the dear one said fanning herself as she gulped down the brandy. The curtains…when the clock struck…Nepal…that anecdote of yours at supper, Colonel…I thought I saw… those demons Rahu and Shesha…

With a vigorous bracing of her shoulders she regained her composure, smiling weakly in thanks as their hostess patted her hand. The loose strands were neatly tucked into place. Everyone settled.

It had been a rather dark story the Colonel had told as they'd dined, McPeevish mused. You couldn't call him a bore, whatever else you might call him. The tale certainly ranked with the best of Rider Haggard. In fact it *was* Rider Haggard! The Colonel had subtly stripped it from its nineteenth century setting and brought it into the nineteen forties, making himself rather than Allan Quatermain the hero. Few people knew of '*The Jewel Stone of Shambhala*' these days, McPeevish sighed inwardly. Perhaps I should have spoken up then, cut the whole thing short. But when you are a guest you're rather on the back foot, at the mercy of those who are entertaining and feeding you. What was that story about the couple who would never let their guests leave? Was it by Edgar Allan Poe or Marie Louise Ramé?

McPeevish finished dealing. He tried to focus on his hand as he fumbled the cards into some semblance of order. The Colonel noticed the trembling in McPeevish's voice as he croaked out his bid:

-Err…One Spade thingy…

-One No Trump, the Colonel barked.

Scenting the coup de grace he permitted himself a final *Godfrey Philips* cigar. Clearly his posture now said: I am a man of patience, a determined man, a man not to be gainsaid. McPeevish couldn't recall if he had ever gainsaid anyone in his life. It didn't sound a pleasant thing to do, rather like gutting a trout. Not that he'd gutted a trout either. Gainsaying and gutting were two things, without deliberately avoiding them, he had never done and never would. Never. Yes, the Colonel had the air of a man who had been mightily tested, mightily, but who now was about to reap the reward of his patience as Sinatra prepared to sing '*My Way*'.

The others passed.

You could hear a cymbal drop, McPeevish thought as he screwed up his eyes, screwed up his courage and seemed to screw up altogether.

-Umm…two Clubs.

The Colonel upped his bid, eyeing his wife confidently as he twiddled a button.

Pass once more echoed around the table. McPeevish seemed hell bent on hurling himself over the barricade as he found voice afresh:

-Ahhh…three Hearts? his voice quivered querulously.

There was to be no relief for Lucknow tonight, the Colonel's blood-shot eyes seemed to be saying.

The Colonel once more raised his bid.

There's more passing going on than during the Melrose Sevens, McPeevish thought as once more the Greek chorus that foretold his doom rang out crystal clear- the lyric soprano of the dear one and the contralto tessitura of the hostess: P-ASS.

McPeevish sat back, studied his hand, looked at the clock, looked for the exit sign and seeing none assumed the air of Sydney Carton mounting the scaffold.

-Seven diamonds, McPeevish said with what might have been his last breath.

-Double, the Colonel snapped.

Both ladies passed and for a brief moment all that could be heard was the creak of a hempen rope somewhere out in the dark night.

That'll be the bird feeder, McPeevish thought.

The Colonel ran his eyes over his cards. He looked pitying at McPeevish who seemed aghast at the shore to which he had drifted. The Colonel let his gaze wander deliciously over to the cabinet in which were displayed his collection of antique knives. He seemed to be trying to decide which one to select for the final thrust- a katar? A kukri? The kila which had belonged to Vajrakilaya? Finally he led the Ace of Spades and dummy lay down her hand.

-'Roger, thou, unskilled in art must, surer bound, go through thy part,' McPeevish muttered.

What the devil is the fool on about? the Colonel thought. He was now sure that McPeevish had completely taken leave of his senses.

Whistling can have an odd effect on some people. Dolphins may take to their heels at a certain pitch, horses bolt and kangaroos dive in each other's pouch. Whistling, like a persistent wasp or midge, can drive maiden aunts to profanity. There are tales told about Saint Simon Stylites…but this is hardly the place to go into that.

McPeevish was emitting a sound that could have been the punctured boiler of the 'Flying Scotsman' as it wheezed its last. There were many useless skills he had not mastered and whistling or blowing bubbles with chewing gum were two of which he was particularly proud. Give him a yo-yo and ask him to make it 'walk-the-dog' and he'd benumb his toes with each failed effort. Let him loose on a Border hillside with a whistle like that and sheep would flock to him while sheep dogs bolted for the horizon. Men would dive down mines should they hear a whistle like that, thinking that a doodle-bug was about to land.

-Well there's a stroke of luck, McPeevish said as he trumped the Ace with *The Curse of Scotland*. Wasn't the nine of diamonds the card used by Sir John Dalrymple to authorise the Glencoe Massacre, my sweet?

-I do believe it was, she said smiling across the battlefield at him.

*

McPeevish had noted with joy the uneasy expression that began to flit like a grave-robber across the Colonel's face. The latter had shifted more and more uncomfortably in his seat, as though prodded somewhere delicate by Shiva's trishula. As the play had unfolded the Colonel watched with all the reluctance of a man obliged to lick a leprous toad. The buttons popped one by one. As he won the last trick completing the grand slam McPeevish had smiled at his beloved and sighed:

-'Such are the fortunes of the game, and those who play should stop the same by wholesome laws.'

They had bid their hostess goodnight thanking her for the wonderful meal and delightful evening. She had seemed distracted beyond conversation, aware of the strangled growling noise coming from the sitting room. The Colonel had been too busy folding the table, picking up the scattered cards and pieces of the broken glasses to see the couple out.

-McPeevish, the dear one said much later; you are the only man who can make me snort and whinny without feeling like a complete nincompoop.

-And you, beloved, are the only woman who can…

She silenced his mouth with a kiss.

And she did.

The Ruby of Kathmandu

McPeevish was on the horns of a dilemma. This was a machine akin to a bucking bronco which, according to the club's publicity brochure, would 'shake the weight' from your hips after that festive indulgence.

What he knew for certain was that one more buck and his breakfast would be in the public domain.

The stop button came in handy.

He surveyed the company.

I am, he thought, a mature man; a man in his mid-sixties. Don't be coy, McPeevish, he chided himself- a good chiding never did a salad any harm, he thought (a subsidiary thought). Don't be coy, man- he looked around for the echo- you're on the doormat of seventy if you're a day: none of this "mid-sixties" nonsense. You're stretching out your hand to the biblical threescore and ten and the Angel of Doom is reaching out to grasp it. Most of these spring chickens weren't even born when you were learning to grease your hair and comb a ducktail.

The gym throbbed to the sound of modern music. He wondered if it was Grunge or Garage, perhaps even Gabber or Grime. Whatever it was it throbbed, as did various parts of the *Lycra*^{T} encased bodies scattered about the gym.

McPeevish dismounted with the grace of Tom Three Persons at the *Calgary Stampede*. He held on to the saddle momentarily as he found his balance where he had left it. A rough sea this morning, he thought. The gym seemed like a Shaky Castle at the Christmas Carnival.

With a manly stride he moved towards the rowing machine. He was diverted by the water cooler around which some young ladies were collected. They moved aside with sweet smiles.

It is fortunate, he thought, that I am spoken for; a man of rectitude and probity, virtue and principle. Just what the principle was, McPeevish couldn't quite articulate to himself as he watched the ladies move like graceful grazing gazelles towards the array of rowing machines. Sweat did that to you, he decided; it addled the synapses, dissolved rectitude and rusted probity. He noted that they had left one machine vacant.

Oh well, he thought; it's better than the lion's den.

The secret, he thought, as he pulled at the substitute oar, was not to try to compete. All around him muscles rippled and wheels whirled. Just imagine you're on Canoe Lake, paddling casually amongst the ducks, weeds and plastic bottles. This isn't the Henley Regatta.

The air was rife with pheromones.

I must be at the shore by now, McPeevish thought.

He shipped oars, spliced his main brace, stowed the tackle and dismounted-rather, stepped ashore.

Another wobble- was that a minor earthquake? They had been known in the region, but usually were associated with closing time. Behind him the young ladies heaved as though each was hauling a whale ashore.

McPeevish made it to the water cooler.

Best piece of equipment in here, he thought. No stress, no strain, just a quick push of the button and voilà.

He stared at his wet foot.

Ought to be a sign: Remember the plastic cup. One of the young ladies- where had they come from - passed him a cup. Must be the pheromones, he thought. Not in here ten minutes, McPeevish, and you're creating havoc with the totty. Must remember I'm a man of virtue, principle...whatever.

The treadmill was aptly named, McPeevish thought. No self-respecting mouse would get on one of these without being bribed with a very large piece of cheese. Here am I on the road to nowhere- ah! *Talking Heads*! That's more like it!

Must concentrate, McPeevish chided himself again as he wobbled. The young ladies were glancing at him. Probably wondering if the old dodderer is going to crash land, he thought.

Whoops! Who turned it up? The track beneath his feet had started to spin more quickly.

A friendly hand- quite a shapely wrist, McPeevish noted- reached over from one side and pressed a button, slowing the machine down.

-Sorry, a breathy voice said near his ear; I left it on 'run'.

McPeevish settled down into the kind of amble which took him from A to B down the High Street, a newspaper under his arm, without ruffling his hair. Not that there is much left to ruffle, he thought ruefully. He'd noticed the beloved one inspecting her fingers after she'd run them through his hair to straighten it. Was she considering a manicure or counting the strands that had come away? Perhaps a hairnet was in order? No, McPeevish, he thought; there's nothing artificial about you. Apart from the glasses, he reminded himself; and the rebuilt front tooth; and the prosthetic leg and penal implant...

You must stop running yourself down, McPeevish.

Was he chiding himself now or what- reprimanding, castigating, and exprobating? How far had he gone: only half a kilometre? The machine must be broken. Surely he'd shed more weight than one calorie? This was just like stocks and shares: high investment and low return. McPeevish set his face to grim and strode purposefully towards the future.

That's enough of that, he thought as he disentangled himself from the control panel. The problem was the trainers, usually named Grant or Cheryl, showed you how everything worked- buttons, switches, that kind of complicated stuff- and then expected you to remember it all. The instruction panel was always in some kind of code: little ideograms; whatever happened to words? I'm a published Arthur- make that Author- he thought and here I am having to learn some hieroglyphic code more obscure than Ugaritic just in order to operate this machine.

What was next on the circuit? Ah yes, the water cooler. The young ladies seemed to have mastered that one as well.

Yes, McPeevish said, this is my first time in the club. Well thank you, that's kind of you to say so. I've just retired actually. Moved down here from Edinburgh. Still got a flat there.

Like bees around a honey pot, McPeevish thought. Never mind that *'Lynx'* advert these pheromones were pretty powerful! Mind you, he inhaled; with my useless nostrils I'm lucky if I can smell a curry.

What's the time now? He glanced around for the clock.

Everything's a blur, McPeevish thought. It's all moved too far away. He casually sauntered nearer the wall and made out the hands of the clock. It was either ten past eight or twenty to one. As it was still dark outside he opted for the former. That can't be right, McPeevish thought. Only ten minutes? Surely I've been at it longer? It must be the pheromones. They got everywhere: interfered with the machinery and time and misted the windows.

McPeevish decided to pump a little iron. He found he couldn't move the handles of the press-up machine. His biceps, deltoids and trapezius whatsits had gone AWOL. What he needed was a good foot pump or an Archimedean lever. A good length of rope and a team of four Shire horses would do.

-Let me adjust that for you, the young lady said.

Pheromones again, McPeevish thought as he lifted the one ten kilogramme weight without difficulty. That's the trouble with being as blat as a bind- make that blind as a bat. Mind you, it's quite a little fan club you're building up here, McPeevish, he thought.

He pumped iron for a while, where 'pumped' equals gently eased from position A to position B. The secret in this exercise, McPeevish concluded, was to pick a spot as high on the opposite wall as possible (thus avoiding staring at the demoiselles ranged opposite you) and to think of England- or any other country that took your fancy and didn't involve too many consonants. Mind you, five out of seven was a pretty high percentage for one country, he thought. You'd have to go some to beat Egypt and Cyprus, however, McPeevish thought. And there weren't many like dear old Canada with three vowels all the same! Niue only has...

Time for the water cooler again, McPeevish decided. He could feel something somewhere but he wasn't about to send a thought to locate it and bring back the result.

As he swallowed gratefully McPeevish was doubly thankful that there were no neck exercises he had to do. He'd specified a routine that would 'tone him up' rather than turn him into a Schwarzenegger or Rambo. He was confident that when he once again smelt the pheromone free air of Moffat- give or take the odd dose of carbon monoxide and sheep expelations- at least that part of him would not ache.

He eyed the cross-trainer with apprehension, then stiffened his back and mounted it.

- I did that once too, a soft angelic voice said as hands gently eased McPeevish upwards and disentangled him from the foot-trays. It's best not to press the 'start' button until you've both feet in the trays.

No, nothing was injured, he assured the crowd of charming helpers. I'm just a bit clumsy with the new equipment, he added. I was the same with my first pencil at school.

What a delight it was to hear them laughing as they went back to their exercises, McPeevish thought. People in the countryside are so kind. He'd seen a farmer with a smile on his face shoot a crow just the other day.

McPeevish decided he wanted 'manual' and set the machine for a low, slow performance. Once confident he could up his pace, if he had any up left. He'd seen those Nordic cross-country skiers and this was rather like that; except there was no snow, no rifle slung across your shoulders, no teeming herds of reindeer crashing through the forests after you; nothing but the whitewashed wall with its posters and slogans urging you to go for the burn or reduce yourself to a puddle of candle melt in the pursuit of a better, trimmer figure. There was nothing there on the wall about pheromones or about Korean ideograms.

Once McPeevish found he could not remember which was his right and which was his left- right or left of anything because he'd forgotten that too- he decided-insofar as he could decide, there being little left with which to decide- that 'enough is enough'. Had he had to think of another word instead-'is' taxed him to the limit- then he would have confessed himself beaten. 'Enough' would do nicely. He had sat on *enough* saddles. He had spun *enough* wheels. He had pushed and pulled *enough*. He had worked the water cooler like a bee might a pollen bearing bush. He had learnt the names of half a dozen young ladies and had begun to wonder what accident might happen to him next. He had eyed the large bouncy ball with suspicion; a suspicion which had proved well founded when he discovered himself sliding down one side of it. Do balls have sides? McPeevish thought as he hit the mat on the floor. He was beginning to recognise the nails and fingers of the hands as they reached down to help him up again- Nancy, Marjorie, and Morag. Weren't there rings on those fingers before? McPeevish wondered.

One of the ladies- how they'd decided he hadn't a clue- helped him to find his card on which to enter the details of what he'd done that morning. I can't read a thing without my glasses, McPeevish had said.

The final challenge had to be remembering the code to get back into the male changing room. There were nine numbers on the keypad; only four were needed, in the correct sequence of course. It was the work of barely a quarter an hour before someone inside came out and thus let him in.

McPeevish found there were two more challenges: how to turn the shower off and how to open his locker.

*

-Did you have a good time at '*Beechgrove*', dear? the beloved one asked.

They were sitting in the *Café Ariete* and McPeevish was looking untrustingly at the cup with its handle. Devices like that, he thought, had it in for him.

-I must say it's put a glow in your cheeks, she said gazing appreciatively at McPeevish over the rim of her cup.

It had only been brute force, not the guile of his intellect, that had wrenched the locker open, McPeevish remembered. Perhaps after all we were closer to the animals than we thought.

- I was speaking with Lucille and Mathilde on the way over and they said Corinne said that you'd made quite a hit in the club this morning.

McPeevish gazed awe-struck at the beloved one. The bush telegraph and internet had nothing on the ladies of Moffat for instant communication. He wondered what had been said.

- I wouldn't have thought a punch bag was so hard to locate, she said with a twinkle in her eye. Don't they just hang from the ceiling like bats?

If she only knew what it was to live without glasses. She could spot a midge at two thousand yards and hit it with a twelve bore blast before it got within biting distance. The waters of Moffat, in mediaeval times were reputed to work miracles akin to Lourdes; perhaps that was why the natives, especially the females, seemed so keen-eyed.

- I'll just go and see what Miriam wants, the beloved one said waving at a distant blur across the tea room.

McPeevish wiped the thumb print off his glasses. No wonder he'd been bumping into things. It had been difficult getting out of the gym; there had been several people, himself and the ladies, all trying to exit at the same time and a certain amount of *entanglement* had been inevitable. As a gentleman he had stood aside, but the ladies, perhaps acknowledging the precedence of age had likewise stood aside. Entanglement. What was surprising was that nobody seemed to be in a hurry to *dis*entangle. The ways of the countryside were still novel to him, McPeevish acknowledged. For several minutes they had all been nose to tail, so to speak, like sheep eagerly waiting at the gate.

Pheromones, McPeevish sighed. You don't see them on the menu here but they're all around.

He thought he recognised the beloved's laugh across the room. It had a certain timbre and swoop, like some exotic wind instrument being played. It was that cheerful sound which could stop brawls on the pitch at the Melrose

Sevens ten times out of ten. There was nothing finer than to see a dozen muddied and surprised bloodied faces peering up from a mass of tangled limbs trying to identify from whence were coming the hoots of laughter. That the beloved one was able to remain anonymous despite the telling scrutiny of rugby players said much for her composure and skill at voice-throw.

McPeevish looked at the crumbs on his plate then glanced around. Nobody was in sight. Had he really eaten that pastry? He looked at his fingertips: licked clean and not a dog in the place.

That laughter again: what could they be talking about? He carefully poured himself some more tea. The pot, though delicate and patterned bone china, unlike those dinky silvery ones did not drip from the lid. He wondered if he might risk another of the delicious frosted pastries. Surely he had combusted enough calories this morning to have a second? Oh to hell with it, McPeevish thought and swooped on the display tray set in the centre of the table.

The beloved glanced at the icing that still powdered his lips. She moves with such a light tread, McPeevish thought. Fortunately his mouth was full so he could only signal his apologies for sudden gluttony with the doleful look in his eyes.

- Dear one, you look just like poor Billabong before I shot him.

Pastry flew everywhere. Fortunately the beloved one had not sat down so the full force of it hit her chair. With a quick flick of her napkin she cleared the debris while McPeevish gulped down some tea to clear his air passage.

-I have told you about that poor dog, haven't I? she asked sweetly.

Thank god, McPeevish thought; it was a 'dog' story. He looked enquiringly at her.

-No? Oh dear, you must have thought I meant something else.

His eyes narrowed thoughtfully as he caught just a hint of a wicked twinkle in her eye.

- Shall I pay? Miriam was just saying that several of the machines weren't in proper working order this morning, the beloved one said as she opened her handbag to extract her purse. I'm sure they'll all be sorted for tomorrow morning.

Tomorrow morning? McPeevish thought. Was there to be no rest for the wicked? Didn't she know that every bone in his body- what was left of his body- felt as though it had been on Torquemada's rack? How she could remain so fit and slender with just that dance class, the croquet club and hill-walking he didn't know. Perhaps women had different metabolisms to men, he thought. What was all that stuff about bio-rhythms? Were they anything like those clubs the young women were whirling around their heads at the far end of the gym? He thought that had been some kind of local semaphore class. When he'd tried it the club had almost pulled his arm out of its socket. The last time he'd seen clubs like that was at the end of the bowling alley in the *Duddingston Inn.*

McPeevish rose with as much dignity as his aching body would permit. I mustn't look *too* much like Billabong, he cautioned himself.

-And she says everyone in the Culture Club is looking forward to hearing your talk tomorrow evening.

Talk? Tomorrow evening? McPeevish desperately tried to think what he had forgotten. Well, it wasn't that he had *forgotten*, just that he couldn't *remember*. The distinction- active/passive- was a neat one he would remember if he didn't forget it the minute they exited the tearoom. Mnemonics, that's what he needed, a good system of ABC which prompted XYZ- or something like that. What was it with the Greeks and Mn?

-I'm quite looking forward to hearing what you have to say myself, the beloved one said as she took his elbow and slipped him into gear. Lady Glenda Gelding will be chairing the meeting as Lord Cumshortleigh caught his foot in a badger's sett and triggered off his gout again. Myself I think he'd been at the port and tried to kick the cat- he's always doing that, according to his wife. She puts it down to his time in the Far East. He has too many convenient hunting accidents. In the summer when he was due to open the bazaar- or was it the fête- he said he was bowled over by a pack of hounds when we all know the scullery maid blackened his eye when he tried it on before luncheon. After luncheon might have been all right, I suppose- the ways of the landed gentry have always escaped me. You do know how to open the door, don't you dear heart? It's one that twist and turns, not a push and pull type...

*

Moffat, like many Borders towns, had dozens of clubs and societies. Once you were through rounding up sheep or counting them, or reeling in trout and throwing them back again, the jaded palate wanted some stimulation of an evening. There were the Lawnmowers club; the Croquet and Crumpet club; the Toffee club; the Hare and Hound club; the Bridge and Gin club; and countless others (including a Traditional Counting club). There were clubs for those who knitted and those who didn't. There were clubs for those who bred sheep and those who ate them. There were clubs for those who drank and those who abstained. There were clubs for those who juggled and clubs for those who jiggled. But, McPeevish now knew, the Moffat Culture Club would hardly be the place for his juvenile memories of prowess with the willow on the playing fields of Pompey. Whilst there might be some mileage in his story about becoming trapped in a turnstile at Lords and the number of firemen it took to extract him, he hardly thought this was "culture".

His mind was a blank. Whilst there was nothing wrong with the old *tabla rasa* in the general course of his life, McPeevish felt the clammy hand of panic gripping his nether parts...

He woke up and realised he'd spilt his afternoon tea down his trousers. Thank goodness the beloved one was visiting the sick and dying, or whatever it was she said she was away to do. He really ought to have a blackboard and chalk, or chisel and block of stone so that he could note important stuff down. Forgetfulness was all very well when he wanted to whatever it was that he wanted to...McPeevish clutched like a drowning man at the wisp of a thought and felt himself....

Nodded off again, McPeevish he admonished himself. This was a decidedly comfortable armchair and that was a decidedly stunning view through the windows and he felt awfully comfortable and...

McPeevish rose from the decidedly comfortable armchair with the determination of a man about to do something. That's right, he remembered: change my trousers. This achieved he was convinced everything else would fall into place. Well, hopefully not *fall* but perhaps *slot*. Yes slot was a nice word; in fact it was the very fit for that last damned crossword clue that had been eluding him. Did things, he wondered as he climbed the stairs, elude him? Was he really the sort of person who should be eluded?

He'd left their bedroom door open so that he and the door knob didn't have another altercation. The last time the beloved one had come home and found him outside the closed bedroom door on his knees with a collection of screwdrivers, tin of oil, and various other picks and pries, her laughter had lasted for what seemed like hours. Once again she had to explain to him the difference between "push" and "pull". McPeevish yearned for the old days when doors sprung open magically at the press of a switch, or the white-gloved flick of a doorman's wrist.

Trousers, he thought. You want to change your trousers, McPeevish. In order to do this you need to locate another pair of trousers.

There were some, McPeevish knew, who carefully and religiously hung their trousers on coat-hangers in wardrobes or closets. This had always struck him- as indeed did the coat-hangers when they got into the swing of things- as a rather *American* custom and one which, unlike driving on the right hand side of the road, he had always resisted. His father had always stored trousers in a drawer, a habit which had caused his mother much soul-searching; and if a drawer was good enough for his father, McPeevish thought, then a drawer it shall be for me. The problem was: which drawer?

In the bedroom McPeevish was confronted, as had been Aladdin in the cave, with a multiplicity of drawers. There was a his and hers dressing table, hers with a mirror and his (as befits a man in need of little grooming) without. This difference allowed McPeevish to narrow his quest down to the one piece of furniture.

That is my dressing table, he said to himself. Even had there been anyone else in the bedroom it was unlikely that he would have said the same to them. What would they care whose dressing table was whose? Unless they were a burglar, of course, and after the jewels...

Trousers, McPeevish, he reminded himself, not jewels; that's what you're after. And you're not a burglar, though if you were you knew where the jewels...

Trousers. Top drawer? Middle drawer? Bottom drawer? Was that an extra drawer? My god, McPeevish thought; don't tell me the drawers are starting to multiply! Surely there must be something that is stable in this universe!

Rather than rush in where angels and all that- he had learnt something from his encounter with the locker that morning, though it had not been how to re-arrange a coat-hanger after you'd straightened it- McPeevish took a long, cool and calculating look at his dressing table.

Oak, probably, he thought, though that gave him no clue as to in which drawer he had so neatly placed his trousers.

Certainly not mahogany, he thought again. Didn't mahogany have a certain...?

Trousers, McPeevish; trousers. First rule of the bedroom: trousers, on or off. If off then dispose of them in...a drawer. Or hang them over the back of the chair if they are to be re-introduced to your legs in the morning.

The back of the chair was clear of trousers. They were on his legs, the front still damp with tea, though drying off nicely.

Though it could be pine, McPeevish conceded.

Furniture had never been his strong point, McPeevish acknowledged to himself. He could never tell a *Louis Quatorze* from a *B&Q*. The same with birds, McPeevish thought. In fact, now that the thought was in train across his mind- a short journey but a necessary one for any thought- McPeevish granted himself that his ability to recognise most things specifically rather than generally was limited. Bird, yes; pigeon or penguin, yes he could manage that; but peewit or bunting? Was this some deficiency in his brain, a limitation perhaps caused by the absence of some vital mineral in his diet during the war; or was he blessed in that he was thus spared all that specific information which must clutter up the minds of bird-watchers and anglers and plane spotters? As a philosopher of life was it a handicap to live in the general rather than the particular, Moffat as opposed to *'Chez Nous'*?

Trousers- was this the mnemonic he had sought all his life?

Mantra, McPeevish, mantra not mnemonic. Trousers as a mantra: could that be the title of his next book? He could see it at the 'Waitrose' check-out being eagerly snapped up by the hands of the likes of Nancy, Marjorie and Morag.

The dumb, closed lips of the drawers gave him no clue as to their contents.

Did he, McPeevish asked himself, within the drawers reproduce or even mirror life as he saw it and lived it *outwith* the drawers? Not that he'd ever been *in* a drawer. Perhaps had he taken up amateur dramatics he might have found himself in a drawer- McPeevish felt sure that some playwright, probably Georges Feydeau, must have written a play in which someone secreted themselves in a drawer. But even if he had replicated within the drawers the state of his life outside the drawers, the problem still remained: in which drawer were the trousers?

He could open each in turn. McPeevish acknowledged, and that way locate the trousers eventually- unless they were in the first drawer he opened...And that would be?

He carefully counted again: yes, there was now *another* drawer! And a mirror! And some fiendish figure reflected in it!

Steady, McPeevish: wrong dressing table.

Philosophy was all very well, McPeevish thought as he approached his dressing table, but it doesn't open any drawers.

As he expected, but could not prevent happening, the trousers- as many pairs of them as he could have wished to have- were in the *last* drawer he opened.

Had I opened that drawer first, McPeevish told himself, they would not have been there. It's the "Find-the-Lady" trick in another medium, McPeevish thought.

-Darling, are you having trouble with the door-handle again?

The beloved's voice floated up the stairwell and snapped McPeevish back into the bedroom. Not that he had left the bedroom though his mind, as was its wont, was elsewhere, adrift like some ancient explorer seeking new worlds.

Trousers, and be quick about it, McPeevish told himself. He unzipped and tugged.

Belt, undo the belt.

He tugged.

Shoes, remove the shoes.

-I've put the kettle on, dear one.

Thank god, McPeevish thought. He had time to work this out. Undo the laces. Knots, how to untie knots. Was it left over right and through or right over left and through? That was tie knots, McPeevish; you want undo. Scissors. No scissors. Have to do this the old way...

McPeevish managed to wriggle and kick his shoes off. Alas he tried to don a clean pair of trousers before he had removed the others. For a moment he sat on the bed bewildered. Entanglement. Then that old McPeevish survival instinct snapped into play. Off with the new then off with the old and *then* on with the new! A Rubik's cube was child's play after this, McPeevish thought triumphantly as he proceeded calmly down the stairs.

-Where are your shoes, dear heart? the beloved asked as she poured the tea.

McPeevish looked at his feet as though admiring his toes which were wriggling within the socks like trapped sprats.

- Is there any particular reason why you're wearing Plus Fours, my love?

McPeevish's eyes moved upwards from his toes and considered the tweeds that now encased his lower limbs.

- They do look rather smart on you but you really didn't need to dress for tea, the beloved one smiled as she stirred.

McPeevish decided that a slice of cake would fortify them both and headed for the kitchen.

When he returned he glimpsed the headline of the '*Moffat Messenger*': FITNESS GYM FLOODED. The dear one glanced over her shoulder at him and in her eyes there was that *knowing* look.

*

The upper room of '*The Dangling Dirk Inn*' was packed. Sardines would have felt right at home.

They must have bussed people in from Unthank, Beattock and Johnstonebridge, McPeevish thought, as he gazed out from the cloakroom upon the heaving mass. In fact, he wouldn't be surprised if they hadn't done a Gogol and dug up long dead residents and brought them along.

Maybe they imagined he was W.H.Auden. Waiting was the worst part; once the oil started boiling at least he could scream. He thought of Rollo Martins in '*The Third Man*'. He wrote pulp Westerns under the pseudonym of Bruce Dexter and mistaken for the more famous B. Dexter was invited to address a book club. McPeevish treasured in his memory Joseph Cotten's speech and its effect in the film. He also hoped to draw inspiration from Robert Donat as Richard Hannay giving an impromptu speech to a local political meeting in the film of *'The 39 Steps'*. If Hannay had escaped his pursuers then perhaps so could McPeevish.

When the Vicar had first suggested McPeevish might give a talk to the Club he hadn't been aware that the slight twitch of his head- a nervous tick left over from childhood when he had to dodge spitballs in class- had been taken as tacit assent. Episcopalians were big on 'tacit assent': if you didn't say you were out you were in; and if you didn't say you were in you were in. Even if you said you were out, well, were you really sure and we'd count you as in just to be on the safe side. Would that elections were so simple.

-We may not be the *'Forest Club'* or the *'Poker Club'*, the Reverend Cleikum had smiled; but neither are we the *'Hellfire Club'*.

It had snowballed from there. When the snow had fallen and even the sheep had to snowboard everywhere, McPeevish had felt certain that the event would be off; or that only a few hardy Antarctic veterans would make it to the meeting. They'd go anywhere to sit around a roaring peat fire and reminisce about blizzards they had known.

- Quite a turn out for you, my dear, the beloved one's voice at his elbow said.

McPeevish wondered what hand she might have had in this. Hard was the heart- and unwise too- that could resist her persuasive tongue. He noticed the tip of it was poking slightly between her teeth as she gazed innocently at him.

- I believe reporters from the *'Dumfries Despatch'*, the *'Castle Douglas Clarion'* and the *'Newton Wamphray News'* are out there.

She straightened his tie.

-It goes under the Adam's apple, she whispered, not over it. You don't want to strangle yourself, dear heart.

Who knew how the frantic, frenzied mind thought, McPeevish's frantic and frenzied mind thought. Who knew when he had last worn a tie? When she had approached him in the bedroom with this length of cloth stretched firmly between her outspread hands, McPeevish had thought of Hitchcock's *'Frenzy'* and had given his soul up for a gonner. Useless to fight, old boy, he had sobbed within himself as she had encircled his throat with the loop. He knew it had been too good to last, this late flowering romance. Had he pumped enough iron, he wondered, to press up daisies?

-There, she had smiled as she finished the Windsor knot. That looks very good on you.

A glance in the mirror had confirmed his worst fears: he wasn't dead, he was wearing a tie. He gazed at her mournfully, his entreaty unspoken.

She was unrelenting.

- Yes, dear heart, I'm afraid it is absolutely necessary. One of the rules of the club: gentlemen must wear a tie or a horse's halter. I'm sure you'll be much more comfortable with the tie.

McPeevish inspected the pattern and weave: a Rollo Ancient tartan, he thought.

-It's all the '*Oxfam*' shop had, she said and he was heartened to hear just a trace of apology in her voice. Well, there was another one but it was some regimental thing and I knew you'd not submit to that. Besides, some of the pukka wallahs in the audience would have started muttering that you never were with the Bengal Lancers or whatever. They're very hot on that sort of thing in the Borders.

McPeevish cast his eyes desperately towards the curtained window. Behind it he knew the window was barred to avoid break-ins. Could he make a dash for the emergency fire exit? But this was futile; he knew that the moment he set foot in the room applause would break out. What would Hannay do?

- There's Lady Gelding now, the dear one whispered. We'd best go in.

Too late for anything but the music, McPeevish. Chin up.

- I don't think you should bring the hat-stand with you, darling, the beloved whispered as he tried to camouflage himself.

-...Welcome you all to this evening's monthly gathering of the Moffat Cultural Club, Lady Gelding was booming from behind a table.

She was a fine boomer and an impressive woman, McPeevish thought, well suited to tweed, both the cloth and the river. She knew more about fish and horses than horses and fish themselves. Around the walls of her manor's sitting room, affixed to decorative boards, were hung all manner of dead and stuffed fish, mouths agape in stunned surprise, the last expression on their faces before the club struck. It was rumoured that she'd spent her wedding night in the stables familiarising herself with her favourite stallion's bodily geography before entering the marriage chamber. Lord Gelding, well, he wasn't around for long once she got over her disappointment but received a splendid funeral. The son Lady Gelding subsequently bore was often seen galloping around the countryside, mouth agape like a browsing trout. Exactly what he was chasing had always been a mystery. Foxes would sit by the roadside combing their tails and watch him whizzing past shouting 'Tally-ho!' and other useful phrases that horses seemed to enjoy. The hounds would veer after the scent but the young Lord Gelding seemed to be pursuing some phantom of his own. It was bound to become the stuff of legends and folk were already foretelling a nasty end for him in one of the many bogs past which he would hurtle.

-Tonight, Lady Gelding boomed on, we are privileged to have as our special guest and speaker a gentleman writer who has just moved to our town. I am delighted to welcome...

McPeevish hadn't really needed the little pat on the back and gentle shove the beloved had given him. He would have launched himself once he'd weighed anchor. As polite applause rippled around the room he strode in his best Ronald Colman manner towards the guillotine...

His attempt to climb on to the table had at least raised a laugh, McPeevish thought. Someone had dimmed the lights so that the spotlight fell on him. Lady Gelding had moved to one side, seating herself on what might have been a howdah but was in fact an upholstered high-backed chair. It had been McPeevish's experience that there was always one such chair- not that chair in particular but one such as it...

The silence was pregnant...

McPeevish called to mind all those wise words about silence: how Cato the Elder thought silence was a virtue and Horace wished to be favoured by it. Carlyle (Thomas, not the railway station) thought it was more eloquent than words and as deep as eternity; and Schiller believed that great souls endured in silence...But then they had never stood in front of an eager, receptive, anticipatory room full of folk from Moffat. Some of these folk had sheared sheep. Others owned and knew how to use pitchforks. He'd seen elderly ladies using knitting needles to ward off the attentions of drunks in the park. These folk had left the warmth of their home and hearth, the drama of 'Eastenders' and 'Coronation Street' to listen to him. McPeevish felt humbled. He embraced the silence, he drew it into himself and knew he must utter.

And utter he did.

A great actor knows just how long to hold the gaze of those in a crowd- consider Marlon Brando in 'Julius Caesar'; learn from Olivier in 'Henry the Nth'. One moment more and it's a lynch mob. Not quite long enough and they're off for lunch and swapping cigarette cards or exchanging cooking tips. If there was one thing worse than talking to the back of a dozen or more heads it was being lynched by the village postman, baker and cobbler. When to utter was the key.

- Once, when I was pony-trekking in Nepal..., McPeevish began.

From the back of the room, the very darkest recess, he thought he heard a muffled, familiar sound. But with elegant and well-practiced ease (and, it has to be acknowledged, the chemical support of the several discreet snorts of Moffat Malt he had managed whilst pretending to cling to the hat-stand) McPeevish began to weave his web of words.

*

- But how on earth did you manage to smuggle the sacred ruby of Kathmandu out of the city?

- Is it true that the hair of the *Yet-teh* if woven into a cloak by a virgin can make you invisible?

- Had that snow leopard not found you and carried you to safety how would you have escaped?

- Would you autograph this for me?

He recognised those fingers: had they not helped him from the floor what seemed a lifetime ago? Still no wedding ring, he noticed. Never mind that it was an old copy of '*Women's Own*', McPeevish thought as he basked and twiddled the Biro. It's all over now. The mesmerised crowd milled around the room holding glasses of wine and nattering like cockatoos in a cage.

Maybe, McPeevish thought uncharitably, it was the free wine- a rather nice 'Chardonnay', if he wasn't mistaken- that had drawn such a large attendance.

-Lady Gelding told me she hadn't laughed so much since her wedding night, McPeevish overheard someone say.

She had been most effusive with her thanks in the closing speech, he thought. He had caught that glitter in her eye which he suspected any stallion worth its stud fee would have recognised. Good Lord, then it was true: she was wearing spurs! She meant business. He must find...

-You should have warned me, the voice of the dear one said.

McPeevish permitted himself a self-effacing smile as she slipped her arm through his.

- I think we can make it to the stairs while she's diverted by that rather charming cub reporter, the beloved whispered, steering McPeevish with practiced ease towards the exit.

-This one is of the push variety, she prompted.

Ah, doors, McPeevish thought as he dealt with the hazard.

- We'll give the hat-stand a miss this time round, shall we dear? she said.

Truly, the All-Seeing Eye of the Ruby of Kathmandu has met its match, McPeevish thought. A sense of joy and relief welled up in his heart- no it was acid reflux: 'Chardonnay' always does that to me, he thought.

-And this is one of the pull variety.

Outside in the moonlight I shall kiss her, McPeevish thought- and he did.

In the chequered shade

Oh dear, thought McPeevish as he sipped his glass of wine; here comes Hortense.

It wasn't that she was a bore- though Hortense Madrigal could bore with the best of the Teredo shipworm family-but that she had a 'thing' for McPeevish despite his clear and unshakeable attachment to the beloved. He could see the beloved across the crowded room as Hortense, eyes aglow and who knew what else afire, cleaved her way towards him like the '*Scharnhorst*' dashing through the English Channel to the fjords of Norway.

'Hortense' was a name which was redolent of fog-horns or thorns on roses. McPeevish knew of only a few women named Hortense- Napoleon I's step-daughter, Charles II's mistress and Cézanne's wife. Miss Madrigal-yes, it was true, she was unspoken for- was unlike any of these. They had in common the fact that they were long dead: she was not. Neither was Miss Madrigal like the young widow in Gilles Bazin's '*Abregé de l'histoire des insectes pour servir de suite à l'histoire des abeilles*', Lady Dedlock's maid in '*Bleak House*' or the old woman in Maupassant's '*La Reine Hortense*': they were fictional; she was real, and in the room.

The thing that McPeevish had found with Miss Madrigal was that nothing worked. There was no escape. Once in an attempt to avoid being noticed he had stepped into a large urn with a potted palm. She had parted the fronds with her bare hands and said jollily 'There you are, you silly boy. Playing hard to get?' On another occasion he had impersonated a traffic cone but to no avail. Short of opening a vein he knew he was cornered and would have to suffer. He was deciding which vein it would be when Hortense sailed straight past him and latched on to someone who was wearing a purple cravat.

McPeevish gave silent thanks to the beloved's sensible advice on attire as they were dressing.

- Your throat is much too nice to hide behind something like that, she had said. It is an informal affair and Adam's Apples may be shown.

Perhaps I should move from the immediate vicinity of the danger, McPeevish advised himself. A purple cravat may have limited appeal.

He eased himself between a large aspidistra and the grand piano, propping open its lid and studying the insides with feigned interest.

- Do you play? a husky voice asked.

A young woman of ample and quite visible proportions was manoeuvring herself between him and any route of escape. The champagne in the glass in her hand didn't ripple at all and McPeevish could count every one of the two bubbles.

As an author he knew that he had to endure the kind of trials and tribulations which an evening at Dame Hilary's inevitably involved. Despite his eschewing such aids as male deodorant and gold-plated neck chains, McPeevish knew that there was that about him- analyse it at your peril, McPeevish, he would warn himself- which drew such creatures as this young woman to him. He was long past the stage of fooling himself that it was his brains, wit and charm which were the attraction. Young women of a certain age and precocity tended to gaze at men of his age and experience and edge towards them with unambiguous intent.

McPeevish, who could gibber like an idiot with the best of them, admitted with as much depreciation as he could muster, that he had been known to 'tickle the ivories'. It was clear from the young woman's widening eyes that he had chosen the wrong metaphor despite the presence of a large grand piano.

- I'd love to hear you play, she said in a voice which would have tamed a ravenous pride of lions or halted in its tracks the charge of an enraged rhinoceros.

McPeevish found himself sitting at the keyboard and wondering where the keys had gone.

A most delicate wrist with five well-manicured fingers attached lifted the lid to reveal the black and white ivories he had been looking for.

Well I never, McPeevish thought; a *'Steingraeber and Söhne'* and eighty-eight keys.

He'd hardly expected a *Hollein Bösendorfer* Imperial Grand or a hand-painted *Pleyel* autographed by Georges Meunier, but this was very stylish. He looked around for the handle and monkey.

Come along, McPeevish, he chivvied himself- or was he admonishing himself- get on with it, the young lady is waiting.

McPeevish remembered with delight the time he had seen Victor Borge in concert in Boston. Music could be fun as much as it could be inspirational. As his fingers strayed over the keys, now black now white, chords and single notes- F B flat F C B flat- McPeevish found himself in that familiar dream world to which music could take him. There were those, he knew, who thought that the pianist should simply play what the composer wrote, interpreting or imposing one's own personality as little as possible. Others threw themselves into the playing wrist, elbow, shoulder and torso.

As he concluded his brief display he smiled apologetically and quickly counted his fingers.

The young lady seemed to have wandered away- shame, he thought; I was just getting in the groove. Perhaps Richard Penniman's *'Tutti Frutti'* was a trifle raucous for such a 'clavicembalo col piano e forte'. Maybe she had been expecting Rossini's *'Soirées Musicales'* or Poulenc's *'Les Soirées de Nazelles'*.

I know few of the people here, he thought. These are not the people who one would find in the snug at *'The Dirk'*. It is unlikely that anyone here other than the dear one and himself had crossed that threshold, McPeevish thought. But duty was duty and the dear one, as chairperson of the theatrical committee had been invited to hob with these knobs. McPeevish, as a sort of partner-cum-adjunct-cum-supportive-person had accompanied her willingly. Willingly in the sense that he would go through hell and high water with the beloved, not wishing her to face the horrors she so bravely volunteered to face without him. Knowing of his previous experience of a 'soirée' with its pebroch-playing and cart-wheeling host in a semi-deserted flat in Portobello, the dear one had said she would attend tonight alone.

I am not a brave man, McPeevish acknowledged to himself. I do not seek conflict or welcome it. But I cannot stand by and watch the one I love venture into the lions' den alone. It will not, the dear one advised him, be on a par with the evenings hosted by the Comtesse Élizabeth Greffulhe who together with the Comtesse Adhéaume de Chevigné (a descendant of the Marquis de Sade) was Proust's inspiration for the *Princesse de Guermantes*. The people who attend will own yachts, not support local football teams, possess portfolios, know other people who know people like themselves and be inclined not to whistle. Some will be hyphenated. McPeevish had always considered himself to be more a pint, pie and peas person than a port and polo pony one.

Curtains were important at a soirée, McPeevish felt as he edged his way around the main room eavesdropping on conversations. Windows that were stark naked offered nowhere to hide. You could tell a lot about the household, McPeevish felt, by the way curtains were hung. Not that he was an expert in this field; but he felt it was one which warranted his fuller attention at some other time.

As he gently circulated, like a random piece of flotsam on the tide's fringe, McPeevish noticed how the company- a far from homogenous mass and yet mobile without being disparate- managed to keep a certain distance between itself and him, or himself and it. Some curious glances passed over him the way the beam of an unattended lighthouse might sweep the sea.

- What do you do?

McPeevish considered the question. As little as possible was the answer but he knew there was a skill to surviving such evenings and that his burst of boogie-woogie earlier had already disgraced him in the eyes of some. Dame Hilary had probably already branded him as uncouth, unwashed and uninvited but inevitable.

McPeevish thought it would be better to say that he was in socks.

- Socks? his interlocutor echoed.

McPeevish confirmed this by elevating a foot and exposing part of his calf, just enough to penetrate the fog of bewilderment in the other guest's eyes.

- Oh hosiery; you're a salesman!

An opening was an opening to McPeevish. It was not often that he had the chance to entertain someone with his reminiscences of the sock industry and the next fifteen minutes passed sweetly enough for him. It was amazing how little other people seemed to know about socks. It was also amazing how much they wished they didn't know what they then knew once McPeevish had passed on wholesale his acquired knowledge. The exposition itself, his follow-up researches had confirmed to him, was indelibly imprinted on the mind of the listener. As he moved away he wondered if anyone would be able to tell the difference between the aspidistra and the semi-comatose victim he had just left.

Some people circulate to the left and some to the right at soirées, McPeevish had noticed. Perhaps one should not generalise from such limited experience as he had had, he acknowledged; but if Plato could do it so could he. There are also those, he was aware, who shot off at tangents, not circulating at all, but rather like the ball in a pin-ball machine, bouncing off the buffers. Here comes one now, McPeevish warned himself.

- Hello, I don't think we've met. I'm Gadfly, Godfrey Gadfly.

McPeevish could confirm that they hadn't met as he hadn't met anyone named Gadfly in his life- until now. His previous experience, which was "Gadfly-less", in no way prepared him for his experience of encountering his first Gadfly. It was only when one has shot oneself in the foot that one may think 'I shouldn't have done that'. One may think it beforehand but one usually doesn't think that one would shoot oneself in the foot. McPeevish considered shooting Gadfly, Godfrey, in the foot but was stopped from doing this by the lack of a gun. When he checked Gadfly's mouth was still moving and sounds were coming out of it. Sounds also come out of a cement mixer, McPeevish thought. Five minutes have passed and he hasn't given me space to say my name. Not that McPeevish particularly wanted Gadfly, Godfrey, to know his name. The thought of Gadfly saying to someone else in the room 'I was just talking to that chap McPeevish' didn't fill him with any joy at all.

What is needed here, McPeevish decided, was the full soil analysis discourse. He found the correct gear and shifted into overdrive. At first- and McPeevish had found that this was a common reaction- Gadfly had continued with whatever it was he was saying, secure in the belief that he was being listened to. But then the steady barrage of words coming in the opposite direction made him falter and wonder if he wasn't talking into an echo-chamber or empty room. Bewilderment was replaced by annoyance, as though one was being dive-bombed by a, well, gadfly; and then the look of horror gradually spread in a manner which would have perked up Edgar Allan Poe no end if he hadn't been dead.

As McPeevish detached himself from the husk that was Godfrey Gadfly he felt confirmed in his belief that the soil analysis monologue was the most lethal weapon known to man and that it was safe only in his hands.

- You've made an impression, the dear one whispered as their trajectories intersected. Who are the zombies?

McPeevish permitted himself a wicked smile and then saw the beloved being swept away by Dame Hilary to meet someone else who doubtlessly had money to spare. It wasn't that Dame Hilary wanted those of her friends who had money to spare to spare it for someone like the beloved; just that she wanted people who didn't know that there were people with money to spare and that Dame Hilary knew lots of them to know this.

McPeevish gravitated towards the table on which were spread all the edibles. It was an impressive display of goodies. McPeevish thought Damien Hirst would have been proud of it. All manner of beast had been slaughtered and sliced and diced. Plates and bowls were stacked so that one could help oneself. He doubted that the redoubtable Dame Hilary had stood in her kitchen wearing an apron all yesterday slicing things and buttering things and mixing and stirring. She would have dialled the number of the local outside caterers and they would have produced the works. That way she would have avoided having to wear an apron.

- Can I help you find anything? a voice asked.

McPeevish wondered if there was any jellied eel but settled for the cucumber sandwiches. Had the triangle not been invented by Pythagoras or his uncle, he thought, the Earl of Sandwich's invention would have failed miserably to catch on. McPeevish wondered whether it was best to cut the sandwich diagonally or across the middle. Certain schools of philosophy could argue the case compellingly for either method: upon such things did one's position in society depend, as Gulliver's travels attested.

There was a skill in eating cucumber sandwiches. Some simply bared their teeth and devoured the sandwich in as few bites as possible. Others nibbled around the edges, using the front teeth the way a mouse might. A lot might depend on the consistence and type of the bread and how long the cucumber has been resting within its embrace. There were those who believed that cucumber should crunch as one masticated it; others felt it should surrender itself soundlessly. Swallowing, in polite society, should be as discreet as possible. The Czar of Russia- which one McPeevish was not sure- it was said could eat a cucumber sandwich without moving his lips. How necessary this was to being the ruler of all Russia and a lot of snow wasn't clear to McPeevish. Likewise he was as yet unclear as to the link between how one ate a cucumber sandwich and one's personal destiny. Could one be ostracised for eating a cucumber sandwich the wrong way? Who decided what was the wrong or the right way? Should local Polytechnics offer free evening classes in the proper way to consume a cucumber sandwich?

There was much about all this, as there was about the drape and hang of the curtains, which bemused McPeevish. To free himself of such cares- if they were cares- McPeevish decided to see what the room looked like when he circulated on the perimeter in the reverse direction, humming '*La Cumparsita*' as he did so.

*

Shayla purred contentedly on his lap.

The problem with many people, she thought, was that they wouldn't hold still properly and let you settle for a good nap. This one, this McPeevish the mistress had found wandering somewhere like a poor lost soul in Hades, had needed considerable training, but now he was well house-broken. As that French chap Montaigne he was sometimes quoting suspected, Shayla could amuse herself with him when she felt like it. You could get him to open the fridge door and fork out the fish with the minimum of fuss. You could leave him on his own for long stretches of time and he didn't wander or misbehave. Not that Shayla knew too much about how a human might misbehave. She might be tuned into all the ancient wisdom of Egypt and beyond, but in the ways of men- a most peculiar bunch- she was still acquiring knowledge. Until this McPeevish was brought into the household the mistress had kept her well protected from such influences.

Shayla could barely remember when she had been a kitten, though sometimes in her dreams memories of that time would flicker through her like a malevolent flea. It was only when the human now her mistress had heard her mewling and picked her out of the bushes where she had been dumped that life had seemed possible. There was a difference, Shayla knew, between being tuned in to the millennia of Catdom and having access to her own personal life. It was not something that could be explained in the odd purr or two. She was heartened and amused by the fact that this McPeevish seemed willing to try to understand such secrets. Of course, Shayla knew that she could never pass on to him the full wisdom, but only give him glimpses. He was a decent enough chap, easily trained and generally well behaved, so he deserved at least a peek or two into the wisdom of Catdom. But the human mind, as Shayla understood it, was a feeble thing and incapable of grasping the fullness of such ancient wisdom. Yet there was something about this McPeevish which made Shayla think that somewhere within his lineage there might have been a beneficial feline influence.

But for the moment she was content to be curled up on his lap, being stroked and digesting the sprats which he had given her.

There were likely to be a good few hours of this, Shayla thought. He's had that distant look in his eyes for some time now. When he's like that he'll bump into things, if he's moving about, and leave things lying here when they were meant to be there. He'll be ruminating, looking inward and trying to come up with something he can sit at the computer and type about.

Shayla would often watch him while she perched on the desk beside him. He thought she was fascinated by the light and flickering on the screen. Sometimes he would explain to her- or thought he was explaining to her- what he was typing. She could see all that; but what she was wondering was why he was taking so long about it. A cat sees things in an instant; but humans seem to take ages to see and they use all these words until they reach the full stop of understanding. What he really needed to do was to plug himself into reality and stop relying on artificial aids like computers and books. Cats had gone beyond that phase centuries ago. Cats had simplified language to its essentials, though humans could only comprehend the smallest bit of it, the purr. The higher stuff, to use McPeevish's language, was quite beyond them. It was like the energy humans made travel through wires or invisibly; they needed intermediary devices to hook into that, whereas a cat had direct access to it.

As McPeevish might say, Shayla thought: I am both in the lap of McPeevish and in the lap of Ankh-khepery-Re.

Whereas humans like to curl up with a good book, Shayla liked nothing better as a cat than to curl up on a good human.

There was nothing worse than a fidgety bum, Shayla thought. McPeevish, once she caught him in the right mood, certainly wasn't that. She often wondered what it was that he was thinking when he went into those trances. Doubtlessly she would find out once he had one of those other phases, the ones when he seemed to lock himself on to the keyboard and pound out word after word until he had emptied into the computer the entire rearranged Oxford English Dictionary the way bin men empty the trash into those snarling machines which prowl the street in the early morning. Once she was older, Shayla knew from her own heritage as a cat, she would be able to at least peer into the relative void that was the human mind- only a mature cat, with ultimate mind control, could safely do this, she knew. To attempt such a feat now if not expressly forbidden was dangerous, for the human mind could be a maelstrom of contraries and dangerous storms for a cat.

Besides, as long as the sprats kept coming her way why change things? Shayla thought with a yawn and a stretch.

*

What's he up to now? Shayla wondered as she came in from the garden.

She paused and sat to watch developments. Cats had this wonderful repertoire when confronted with anything novel. They could turn tail, of course, and either walk away in haughty disdain or run like the blazes and head up a tree. Neither of these two methods seemed necessary in the current circumstances, Shayla decided, though they were the default options permanently held in reserve. A haughty cat stalking away with its tail held high was the most devastating comment imaginable on any human activity. Pharaohs had stepped down from thrones and Emperors had fallen on the sword because of this gesture.

McPeevish had scattered pieces of cut paper on the living-room carpet. This in itself Shayla thought was boring enough. He had marked each piece of paper with those symbols which humans used to convey numbers and abbreviations. It was clearly some form of game or puzzle. Shayla watched as McPeevish held a book in front of him and then, without much grace she thought, proceeded to step or hop from one piece of paper to another.

Cats only scratch their head if they itch and want to get rid of fleas. Shayla metaphorically scratched her head in bemusement as she watched these strange antics. Somewhere in her ancestral past she recalled similar, paperless situations in vast stone built halls. The movements were quite different and in that earlier performance, Shayla recalled, there had been echoing sounds, the kind of human-wailing which drove cats into the garden (or desert as it had been in that case). At least I'm spared that, Shayla thought.

Had it been a mouse or bird summoning ritual then perhaps Shayla might have been more interested; but though she waited a while no mice or avians appeared. A glance over her shoulder told her that it wasn't raining in the garden so that kind of ritual also was out.

Maybe he's just gone plain bonkers, Shayla thought.

It had always been on the cards, in her opinion. From that first time when he'd run away from the electric lawnmower, which had been rampaging through the flower bed, Shayla had guessed that McPeevish lacked organisational ability and stability. Put him on a fence, she thought, and he'd fall off ten times out of ten- that is if he could climb on to a fence. He'd never shown the least inclination to do that, although she'd demonstrated the technique countless times. Not that this prejudiced her against McPeevish. As long as he kept opening the fridge he could go as bonkers as he liked.

The best thing to do, she decided, was to curl up in the mistress's armchair and chase mice in her dreams.

Over the next several days Shayla came across McPeevish engaged in this strange performance. If he was trying to perfect it- as she tried to perfect catching her tail when she had a spare moment and was temporarily at a loss as to what cat thing to do next- then Shayla could see that he was no better than he had been when she had first clapped eyes on him enacting the ritual.

Being an intelligent cat she was able to conclude that the performance didn't depend on what might be called external circumstances- the weather, the time of day, what he'd had for lunch and so on. But there was one invariable: the ritual took place only when the mistress was out. Shayla concluded, at least temporarily, that this was a secret ritual, a male thing like the trimming of facial hair she had watched McPeevish doing on several occasions. That seemed an unnecessary affectation to her and it would certainly impede his hunting ability at night when whiskers came into their own. But since McPeevish bumped into things even when it was bright daylight, Shayla concluded that he was more the stay-at-home species of human than the night roaming kind. Those occasions when he (and the mistress) did go out at night to hunt Shayla was disappointed when they'd return without a sack full of field mice, though they did seem to be in convivial mood. It was on nights such as those that she would find the bedroom door firmly closed and no amount of meowing would make it open. Even her rattling of the fridge door-handle failed to evoke any response.

When McPeevish wandered away from the living-room, perhaps distracted by the telephone ringing or his need to write, Shayla would trot over to the carpet and study the pieces of paper. She'd flick them with a paw or dive under them to see if anything was hidden there. But in the end she'd conclude they were inedible and of no interest to a cat. What was of interest, however- and best watched from the outside of the living-room window sill- was the performance McPeevish would give should he return, pick up the book he had to hold in his hand, and then start to move from one piece of paper to another. On such occasions Shayla noticed that McPeevish was often bumping into himself. He would tangle his feet and fall repeatedly. After a while he'd sit on the carpet, scratch his head, look at the book, turn a few pages...and then look across to the window sill. At such a moment, Shayla instinctively knew, it was best to head rapidly for the far side of the garden fence and inspect the bushes there.

*

The Town Hall was packed as the charity *Dance-athon* was about to start. It had been a sell-out for weeks.

McSwindel had published the official form book and guide to the odds.

The band members were all sober for a change. Instruments were tuned and polished until they were sparkling. Ken Klippert, the conductor, tested the wind resistance of his Mollard Rosewood tulip handled baton one last time. It sliced silently through the air like the wings of an angel. In a moment he and his orchestra would enter the hall and take their seats on the stage. The tension would have broken the strings on lesser violins than those in the hands of the Goutherfow twins. The conductor ran his eyes approvingly over the assembled group as thirty seconds was announced and Murdo Hobbleshaw, the compère for the evening made his way on to the stage. This was it; there was no going back.

- We're on!

...And they were off.

McPeevish had never seen so many people in the town willing to shake a leg, that is their own leg. Clearly the closets of Moffat held many mysteries, not least of all the tuxedos and gowns of secret ballroom dancers. Bruce Forsyth had a lot to answer for, McPeevish thought. Those who couldn't dance watched; those who couldn't watch drank at the bar; those who couldn't drink at the bar drank out the back. Some watched those who drank more than they watched those who danced.

Overhead the glittering crystal ball- specially repaired and mounted by Willie 'All-trades' Tregullion- spun and sparkled, adding that touch of authenticity to the night's proceedings.

The judges, under the chairmanship of Lord Gelding, were seated at a table to one side of the hall. They were: Mrs. Jirgle, matron of the local hospital; Father Xavier, lecturer in Terpsichore at Drygrange; and retired ballet instructor Perchance Feeth. Each of them had taken and passed the Royal Scottish Academy of Dancing and Drama Nureyev Test. None had any relative who could dance, perhaps in itself a remarkable curiosity but not something which should detain our attention here. For the duration of the contest they would be abstaining from hard liquor, so that their critical faculties remained unimpaired. This period of abstinence was water off a duck's back to Mrs. Jirgle, for she was a life-long abstainer. All that is known about 'Mr. Jirgle' (and there were those who doubted that there had been such a person) is that he had 'walked out' one morning to get the paper and never returned. No one knew which paper it was. Father Xavier, though used to temptation, found the going slightly harder as he was also used to his medicinal intake of 'the water of life'. He took solace in the fact the evening would not last forever and that there was a very late licence on the bar. Perchance Feeth was a relative newcomer to the community but was familiar with feet, calves and thighs from his work in the ballet. Though retired he still offered private lessons at a reasonable fee. It was, however, the case that there were few aspiring Billy Elliott's among the sheep-orientated families of the town. Nevertheless, his impromptu *jetés*, *pas de basque* and *tours en l'air* in the butcher's queue were welcome divertissements for those who found the grind of everyday life dulling to the senses.

The preliminary dances saw the floor crowded with couples. Only as the second dance was ending would the three judges finalise their decisions and the elimination begin.

-Very well done, sweetheart, the beloved whispered as they took a breather while awaiting the second stage of the competition. I thought we'd be gone. Have you been practising?

McPeevish smiled knowingly, pleased that Shayla hadn't given the game away. The evenings when the dear one would come home and comment that the furniture seemed to have been moved around again and the carpet was spotless, had been testing times for McPeevish; but Shayla had sat there blinking wisely and saying nothing. It was amazing what sprats and salmon could do. The odd piece of squid had certainly helped his standing with Shayla, McPeevish thought. It was a moot moral point as to whether or not you could bribe an animal: he would have to re-read Kant to clarify the matter.

With more space on the floor the remaining sixteen couples could show off their individual skills. McPeevish was of the firm opinion that what mattered at this stage of the competition was to put in a solid, workmanlike performance. All the flashy stuff- if there was to be any flashy stuff- could safely be left to a later round. The beloved was, as one would expect from a woman who had excelled on the hockey fields in her youth and still wielded a mean croquet mallet and badminton racquet, limber and lithe and had excellent footwork. It was McPeevish who might have proved the donkey, had he not decided to brush up his technique.

Like so much else in life, McPeevish thought, real dancing was a marriage of the technical physical ability and the mental. You had to be able to 'dance in the mind' (मन में नृत्य), as the Zen master said, before you could dance with the body. Mind you, if you had two left feet- or two right feet, for that matter- and if you had no sense of rhythm, then no amount of dancing in the mind would suffice.

- Here we go again, dear heart, the beloved whispered as the compère called the couples to the floor for the next round.

As the band struck up '*Sylvia ou la nymphe de Diane*' by Delibes, McPeevish could feel his feet waltz into action; and by the time the last notes of Johann Strauss's '*Fruhlingstimmen*' had faded his toes were really twinkling. They were in the last eight.

The surviving competitors were given a break and the floor was swamped with those who wanted some general dancing to the swing numbers the band pumped out. Here and there a cummerbund was popped and the odd high heeled shoe flew through the air, but otherwise there was little wreckage and plenty of enjoyment.

Then it was the quarter final and the orchestra struck up '*Jungle Rhythm*' followed by '*Steppin' out with my baby*'.

-Oh my, this is bliss! the dear one said as the music faded and the judges pondered.

Down to the last four now, McPeevish thought, watching the floor fill again as there was a break for the competitors. Throughout the dancing he had paid no attention to any of the others, following the patterns engraved in his memory. It's the socks, he told himself at times, these special socks. Who could resist a brand called 'Astaire's' and only £4.99 for two pairs?

And then they were in the final.

The crowd were at fever pitch. McSwindel was seen to be sweating as he chalked his board. McPeevish and beloved showed at 5/1 now, having come in from 100/1 at the off. The early bets on them had been sentimental, perhaps, but now those punters stood to win a handsome bundle as long as the couple didn't fall. Still the favourites were Sylvester Proop and his partner Marigold Slughan. McPeevish recognised them from Dame Hilary's soirée. He had been struck then by the amount of hair oil it must have taken Sylvester to slick his hair down- a North Sea oil rig's monthly barrel output, he calculated. McPeevish had been fascinated by it, the fact that even the light had slid off it unable to find a purchase. Miss Slughan he likewise recognised: she had been the young lady at the piano. It was a close thing between the percentage of her that was in   the gown and the percentage that was out of it.

- Darling, the dear one sighed; if we don't win I don't care. This is so much fun and you're wonderful.

Her eyes glowed with all the light from the orb spinning above the floor.

Of course McPeevish knew that winning was not the main thing. Dancing was all about expressing oneself, the joy of being and all that. He had astonished himself that they had come so far. All that time spent studying Fred and Ginger in 'Swing Time' and 'Top Hat' and those hours spent re-reading Jane Austen had paid off handsomely. Yet somehow he felt there was something more at stake here, something intangible but somehow vital. For himself perhaps he wouldn't mind not winning; he was familiar with things overwhelming him. But this is not just about you, McPeevish, he thought as he studied the happy glow on the beloved's cheeks and saw the joy and amusement on the faces of their friends in the crowd. Knowing that the entire clientele of 'The Dangling Dirk' had availed themselves of the 100/1 odds and stood to make a killing were a spur to a higher destiny.

A McPeevish did not disappoint his friends, McPeevish thought. The Zen master said: *To dance step on stars* (सतिारों पर कदम न॒त्य) so let's do it!

For once Shayla found the door unlocked. She jumped happily on to the bed and did her little dance to the cat goddess Bast before settling down at their feet.

The Moffat Mug

This, thought McPeevish, is the life. If it wasn't then he would complain to the Management and get a refund.

He lay back on the river bank, eyes closed, his interior senses tuned to the great Infinite. The great Infinite was usually on a different wavelength but today it deigned to spread a sunbeam or two on his brow. He felt warm, comfortable and replete. Somewhere nearby was a hamper in which lay the shreds of a picnic. Somewhere nearby also must be the dear one who had filled the hamper before they had emptied it.

McPeevish listened to the sounds of the birds calling to each other. Perhaps, he thought lazily, that could be his next project: a study of bird-call- those chirps, chirrups, chiks and caws; those tsips, tweets and twitterings which skipped and cascaded around about him now. There was a skill which would enthral a crowded elevator, he thought. McPeevish had never progressed further than that discreet cough meant to alert strangers that they were standing on his foot. Not much good in the wilds, of course, but it served its purpose.

His mind drifted like a leaf floating down the Tweed. If he raised an eyelid he might even see such an object; but why bother when the image could be satisfactorily projected upon the inner screen? A leaf, the empty canoe of Kwasind or '*Le Bateau Ivre*', Huckleberry Finn and Jim, the Lady of Shalott, and 'the Nelumbo bud that floats for ever with Indian Cupid down the holy river...' all bobbing along the watery flow while he, digesting, lay on the river's bank taking his ease.

Something tugged his toe.

Eastern mystics who have conquered whatever it is that they conquer before they return to tell you about it in sayings that were as obscure as the instructions on IKEA packs; Eastern mystics- and for all McPeevish knew their Western brethren: Eastern and Western mystics (he continued with deliberation) would have said that what he experienced as a 'tug' on his toe was nothing more than a yearning to return to the temporal and all that pain and suffering from which he had freed himself through the imbibing of a fine vintage Sauvignon and the better part of a quartered spicy chicken. When you were under the Bo tree- well, in this case a good Scottish oak- contemplating the profundity of it all, whatever it was, then you did not bother with mundane things such as a tug on your toe. It was merely the external world reminding him that it was still there, though Bishop Berkley might have put in his tuppence worth in an attempt to disprove that.

The tug on his toe was more insistent.

McPeevish wondered how the Buddha had dealt with that sort of thing. 'To tug the toe of the Buddha' (बुद्ध के पैर की अंगुली करने के लिए खींच) was a well-known saying in the *Buddhavacana*; or at least McPeevish thought it was. He must browse through the pertinent texts again, if he could be bothered to open his eyes.

-I think you have a bite, a voice said somewhere in the exterior world.

I have a bite, McPeevish thought dreamily. Not 'I have bitten' or even 'I have been bitten', but 'I have a bite'.

McPeevish sat up with a sudden jerk, just in time to catch his Hardy rod and reel as it began whizzing towards the water attached to some unseen marine creature.

The line went slack.

-That was a pity, dear heart, the voice said. It looked like quite a big trout.

He gazed around like a recently landed alien on a strange planet. The voice had come from a large straw hat that lay on the grass a short distance away. The hat was not dissimilar to a flying saucer. The beloved one was nowhere to be seen. Had she been abducted whilst he was on the higher astral plane?

McPeevish studied the implement in his hands. From the end of it dangled a length of silken line the purpose of which his semi-comatose mind was unable to grasp.

-Yes, the straw hat said; the river's teeming with them. They usually keep to the other side of the stream; that one must have strayed from the straight and narrow.

McPeevish considered the straw hat carefully. He was a broad-minded chap, when all was said and done. He had nothing against talking hats, straw or otherwise. A touch of the Alice in Wonderland's never did anybody any harm. All the same he thought it might be best if he just edged away a yard or two from this apparition. He was not particularly fleet of foot and you never knew the velocity at which these aliens could move, so the bigger the head-start he manufactured the better.

Good lord! McPeevish thought as a hand holding a fluted glass appeared and waved lazily in the air.

-Is there anymore of that chilled wine, my sweet?

What to do? McPeevish felt caught in a ghastly dilemma. It wasn't like this in the interior world. There it was all stillness and light, apart from the dark bits. He looked around and noticed a bottle protruding from a hamper. He crawled hesitantly towards the hamper, ready to bolt should the hat start to follow him. Yes, it was a bottle of wine, half empty and half full. They were better full and ready to be emptied than empty, McPeevish thought; but half empty would have to do. He seized the bottle and turned to haul his external being towards the hat, like a pilgrim prostrated and approaching a holy site. He poured some of the wine into the flute which then vanished into the hat.

- Thank you sweetheart, the hat said after a moment or two.

McPeevish resumed his crouch against the bole of the tree. He studied the branches above. A red squirrel gazed down at him, ready to repel any attempt by McPeevish to climb up there. He wondered if a grey one would have been as uninviting.

Indolence overcame him. Clutching the bottle to his breast he gazed out across the water and studied the clouds as they bounced over the distant hilltops. He could hear Percy Edwards emitting Messiaen's *'Réveil des Oiseaux'* from a bush; no, it might have been Ronnie Ronalde giving voice to Respighi's *'Gil Uccelli'*. You really couldn't tell them apart. An evening listening to Charles Kellogg recordings wasn't high on his list of priorities at the moment, though he had recently snapped up in the Saturday morning market an almost pristine poster of *'Alexandre, Imitateur de Chants d'Oiseaux'*.

Perhaps if he tried chattering to the squirrel in the branches above? No, that wouldn't work: his tail wasn't bushy enough. If you were going to try to fool a squirrel, red or grey, you needed the bushy tail.

As he was musing McPeevish found close beside him a fluted glass of his own and he filled it with the remaining contents of the bottle of wine.

I'm just in the mood, he thought as he took a sip, to get to grips with Nikolaj Chernyshevsky and the Philosophy of Realism. However, not having a copy to hand, McPeevish brought into his line of sight a well-thumbed copy of Maupassant's short stories. Before he had entered the interior world he had been reading about M. Morissot and M. Sauvage who had gone fishing for gudgeon on the island of Marante. The hat had said it had been a trout that had tugged at his toe. McPeevish wondered how a trout differed from a gudgeon. There are more fish in the river, dear Holzhammer, McPeevish thought as he tried to focus. He wondered if being a poor swimmer was the reason why he had no real affinity with fish, fish of any description or creed. He had never kept goldfish as a child: he couldn't stand the sight of them staring at him as they endlessly circled a bowl. He had no fondness for aquariums- was it um or a?

He began to count clouds, always a good idea when thought pressed. The problem there was that what he thought was one cloud might be made up of two or three or even more all clustering together. The effect of the perspective- he had gradually slid down the bole of the tree and now lay flat on his back- was a factor which influenced the count.

He closed his eyes. That was much better.

It was a shame about the two friends shot by the Prussians, McPeevish thought; but the story wasn't really about angling as such. If you wanted angling as such then Big Ernie was your man. Not that he was fond of those descriptions of Nick Adams fishing in '*Big Two-Hearted River*' in the wilds of Michigan. Somehow McPeevish felt there was more to this angling lark than simply describing it.

McPeevish, when first they had come down to the river to find a spot for their picnic, had wondered about the fish in the water. Did they wonder about the likes of him staring down into their world as they might be staring up into his? We cannot live in each others world, he thought sadly. If we men invent tales of mercreatures do the fish invent their stories of terra-creatures? What was that impulse which drove us up from the water, McPeevish mused, all those millennia (or was it –um) ago? Why do these fish stubbornly cling to the waters rather than wade ashore anew? He watched as a Kingfisher struck and bore aloft the wriggling victim. Nature red in tooth and claw, he thought remembering some Tennyson.

His thoughts were like the colourful cloth the beloved one spread upon the grass for their picnic. McPeevish had sat with her and they had toasted each other and the birds and fish and other wildlife-seen and unseen- round about them. How can such a beautiful setting evoke so many thoughts? But then how could it not? The cutlery and plates- not paper or plastic but those from which they always ate- were set upon the cloth. Wax-paper wrapped packages were opened and the profusion of their repast laid bare to the sky. They ate in silence, gazing happily into each others eyes as into the river, or looking about contented in the act of seeing itself. Trees were friendly sentinels. Happiness was in the silence as much as the being together. The trill and plectrum of the Tweed upon the stones over which it ran fleet-footed were a harmony that would have done credit to Mozart. It was the kind of idyllic setting which Seurat might have painted with a brush made from the feathers of an angel's wings...

*

As he donned the pads McPeevish thought back to that enchanting day beside the Tweed. Now here am I, he thought, in a strange school playing field. How manifold are the twists and turns of fate! All I have to do is sit in a folding canvas deck-chair and wait until it's my turn to have someone precipitate a hard ball at me. He wondered what sort of games fish played. Surely their lot couldn't just be one of sex, spawn and swallow (or be swallowed)? Perhaps gulping down mayflies and mosquito larvae was their version of bobbing for apples, McPeevish thought.

Beside him, her delicate frame curved into another striped deck-chair, was the beloved one. She was reading a book while out in the sun on the green field men sweated and ran or stood and cursed. She caught his eye as he gazed contentedly at her. She smiled *that* smile and then continued her reading. The book, McPeevish thought, was possibly a romance- something by Jane Austen, Barbara Cartland or Jean MacLeod. Women of a certain age retreated into such soggy handkerchief territory when the men folk put on white and threw and hit balls. There was no reason why a woman should understand cricket; indeed, to be a woman it was almost imperative that one did not understand cricket. For that matter McPeevish did not understand cricket. It was one of those male peer group bonding rituals which, thankfully, his education overseas had spared him. If you were going to throw a ball, McPeevish thought, you should throw it straight, not bounce it on the ground. All that bouncing only ruined the nap of the sward. No, any decent chap would hurl the ball straight at you; and anyone worth his salt would swing athwart the shoulders not up and under as was the custom in cricket.

Perhaps, McPeevish thought idly, fish play volleyball with plankton.

It was the highlight of the season, the annual *'Dangling Dirk Inn'* Eleven versus *'The Colic Coffin-makers'* Eleven. The prize was the 'Moffat Mug', a silver trophy reputedly the work of Hugh Ross of Tain. It was first fought over by the two coaching inns in the eighteenth century. Then they had used swords and muskets; once cricket seeped into the Borders as a manly way of resolving differences and allowing one to drink beer and fart discreetly in open spaces, the scars and duelling death toll in the region declined exponentially. For the last several years the mug had remained behind the bar in *'The Colic'* as *'The Dirk'* had been unable to raise the eleventh man.

As the fates would have it McPeevish was number eleven.

McPeevish himself preferred round numbers: twelve, for example, or ten. The Sumerians, McPeevish recalled, only counted up to eight; which meant they had to go without their 'elevenses' when building those ziggurats. The Romans never did get the hang of numbers and chiselled large capital Ms and Ds and Cs all over their public buildings. The occasional X, L or V and

I only added to the confusion. The first thing Alaric was reputed to have shouted when he and his Visigoth mates sacked Rome was: *Lassen Sie uns ein paar anständige Zahlen hier*!

There was nothing *wrong* with eleven, McPeevish could concede. For some psychics eleven was the doorway, the bridge of our vitality and oneness. It was a 'Master' number, a 'Lucas' number. Written upside down it stayed the same, though you might find the blood rushing to your head. But it lacked that essential roundness which suggested fruition and completion.

McPeevish always found himself wanting to run and join something whenever anyone said eleven. There was undoubtedly an explanation for that but he was stumped regarding it. Some people liked to ride on buses sporting a certain livery; others would not enter one if the driver was left-handed. Fish seemed to live perfectly happy lives without the need to count, McPeevish thought. The debate as to when a school was not a school never arose amongst them. They'd flip fins with any old number of like-minded fish.

McPeevish glanced at the score-board. This, of necessity, had to be improvised, the school not having one. It was here that the Reverend Cleikum had come to the fore. A staunch '*Dirks*' man, he had volunteered the use of the church hymn display boards. He had also volunteered the use of the spinster Miss Bevel whose task it was to insert the numbers in the slots. That she did not understand the method of scoring, and had left her earpiece at home in her excitement that afternoon, meant that the Reverend Cleikum, a recent widower, had to be on hand to assist her. The method he used was ingenious but simple: he would call out hymn titles from the general hymnal and Miss Bevel would post them with meticulous accuracy all the while continuing to knit a scarf for the minister. The Episcopalians in the crowd would find themselves humming unexpectedly. Some would be humming 'The God whom earth and sea and sky' ('*Hymns Ancient and Modern*' 1861-1874); others would be humming 'O Wondrous type! O vision fair!' ('*Hymns Ancient and Modern*' 1904); and others would be humming 'The God of Abraham praise' ('*Anglican Hymn Book*' 1965). Not a dog moved, not a pigeon flew till the humming was over.

It was clear to McPeevish that things were not going well. After the ceremonial coin had been inspected (both sides of it) the well-practised thumb of the Reverend flipped it towards the heavens, which briefly gave it a glance and judged it acceptable. '*The Colic*' had batted first, having won the toss. The outfield still bore the marks of the grazing sheep that had had to be manoeuvred off it that morning. The Corgis which had been pressed into rounding-up service had been slow but deliberate. The sheep had been bewildered by their breed and acted more amenably than was their wont. The heavy roller- a gravel-filled cask from the local distillery- had seen off the fresh mole hills in the pitch. In their fifty overs *'The Colic'* had amassed two hundred and forty nine runs. The forty nine were extras. In response *'The Dirk'* were now a beggarly one hundred and thirty for six (no extras). The light was excellent; the sky was clear of clouds, the storm gods staying their hand. Unless the tail wagged the result seemed inevitable. McPeevish could sense the gloom spreading amongst his fellows. Loin girding was called for.

The denizen of *'The Dirk'* if they were one thing it was that to a man they were stubborn to a degree that exceeds the national norm. Bull dogs have given up the boot in a tug-of-war with them. Sheriffs on the bench have wept when faced yet again with the Monday morning regulars who litter the High Street of a Sunday morning after a Saturday night in *'The Dirk'*. Local by-laws have been amended to take into account this intractable stubbornness, given the absence nowadays of Australia as a convenient place to send miscreants. McPeevish watched with pride as the tail enders, if not exactly wagging, proved as difficult to dig out as a dandelion root. But now the inevitable had happened: the grim click of broken bones announced the fall of another wicket. It was his turn to bat and they remained forty nine runs in arrears.

McPeevish yawned and stood.

-You'll need this, dear heart, the beloved's voice said.

She was holding out to him an oddly shaped piece of willow which, bandaged, had seen better days.

What on earth do I want with a walking stick? he thought.

-You wave it at the ball- that's the round thing- as it flies past you, she smiled.

McPeevish chided himself: I really should have read up on the mechanics of this sport. Sitting in the sun, his weak eyes unable to make out more than whitened blurs on the horizon, it had all seemed like an alchemist's convention to him.

-And this might be of some help, the dear one added.

She was handing him the book she had been reading.

McPeevish glanced at the cover: *'Wittgenstein at the Wicket: Analytic Philosophy: the Deconstructionist's Dilemma'* by Jules Perceval. McPeevish remembered reading one of the author's racy Chick-Lit westerns. The man could turn his hand to everything; but would McPeevish have time to read the tome whilst at the crease? He raised an eyebrow in her direction.

Without hesitation the beloved one seized the book from his engloved hands and firmly, decisively shoved it down the front of his trousers. She would have patted it but something in his embarrassed look made her forgo that affectionate gesture.

-Do come back in one piece, she urged him.

Awaiting McPeevish in the middle- a glance around himself with a calculating eye told McPeevish that it was more off centre than middle, but then he didn't make the rules- was the captain of '*The Dirk*'.

An amazing transformation came over the young Lord Gelding once he was off a horse and held in his hand the magical willow. Gone was the trout mouth and tendency to utter cries which drove all wild life back to its burrows and nests. In its place was a young, engaging fellow with a piece of carved wood in his hands and an air of authority. It was all a matter of colour, McPeevish thought. White suited his lordship; whereas that gaudy red colour he wore whilst on a horse completely scrambled his personality. But you've no time to develop your philosophy of colour, McPeevish, he cautioned himself; there's work to do.

- Damned awkward situation we have here, McPeevish, his lordship said. D'you know how to use that thing? It's this way up. Do the best you can, old man. I'll try to keep strike as long as possible. At least we've made them work for the Mug.

McPeevish noted the tears in the young man's eyes. The Geldings, for all their foolishness, were a proud line. It had been their ancestors who had had the Mug cast, a wedding present for the Lord of the time. The Mug had been stolen by a rival clan whilst on its way to Moffat and thus had started the internecine battle for possession. Local legend had it that the Mug would be returned in perpetuity to the family if honourably won in battle by a Lord Gelding of the time. This had never happened, neither in the skirmishing with claymores nor the more peaceable battles with the willow and cork and leather. The current Lord, due to marry the delightful Lavinia Loople, an old school friend of the beloved's, had hoped to have the Mug as their loving cup.

McPeevish cast his eyes towards the crowd of onlookers beyond the boundary marked with up-turned milk crates. In that undifferentiated mass of colours McPeevish knew sat the beloved, trusting that he would return intact, and Lady Gelding, cheer-leading for her son with all the pride and hope a mother could have for a son. As she had watched his white-clad body move about the grounds that afternoon perhaps she had repented of the day she had ever set him on a horse. McPeevish knew what he had to do.

Lord Gelding played out the over he had to face with that grim solidity which marked the Scottish aristocrat and serviceman at his best. He called for a quick single on the last ball, but McPeevish held up his hand in refusal noting the rapid swoop of mid-on to collect the ball. Besides, McPeevish thought, running only made one sweaty. Lord Gelding acknowledged with a nod that his call had been unwise, if well meant.

The Colonel had waited for months to have his revenge. Since that night when he had lost at Bridge he had deserted 'The Dirk' and taken his trade to 'The Colic'. He already had more than a brace of wickets. His side's best fast bowler he had been saved for the last overs once it became clear that 'The Dirk' were resisting with might and main. The Colonel had snatched the ball from his captain and his eyes gleamed with undisguised malice as he looked at McPeevish.

"'The insane root that takes the reason prisoner'", McPeevish thought catching that glance. He might well trawl through 'Macbeth' for other pithy epigrammes when he had more time; and he must re-familiarise himself with Macaulay's poem of the Romans on the bridge: dear old Horatius Cocles, with his mates Spurius Lartius and Titus Herminius!

McPeevish watched as the Colonel seemed to walk off the ground. At least in baseball, McPeevish thought, you knew where the pitcher was. Now there was a game he understood, its shape and its purpose. There was no other way it was possible to sell hotdogs, he thought.

Hello! Be on your guard, McPeevish, the Colonel's florid face and pumping arms were coming into focus!

The Colonel, despite his age, had worked up a head of steam that would have seen the 'Royal Scotsman' up the slope at Beattock with barely a puff or two out of its smoke-stack. His arm turned over and he released the ball at a velocity which may well have broken the grip of gravity had it been vertical rather than horizontal.

McPeevish swatted as at a fly and watched as the re-directed ball rose in a Bézier curve towards the distant on-lookers.

The Colonel's thunderous approach was only halted by the buffers of the wicket-keeper.

McPeevish sauntered down the wicket to exchange pleasantries with his captain.

-Fine shot, McPeevish, Lord Gelding said. A few more of those and we're home and dry.

On his way back to his crease McPeevish did a spot of gardening. A mole withdrew its head and went about its subterranean business, leaving the surface to the titans who bestrode it.

Here came the Colonel again. His face, if anything, had become more engorged with rudescence and might well have been the light atop a speeding police cruiser. Or were they blue? McPeevish never could remember.

Swat: another fly; they seemed to be swarming out here, probably because of the sweat. This time the curve of the ascending ball was more akin to the top of a blancmange, McPeevish thought. A man had been placed on the boundary at the spot where his previous blow had settled, but the arc of this ball went in the opposite direction.

Fine piece of timber, McPeevish thought. To his ears came cheering and laughter from the crowd. The Colonel seemed to be wheezing a bit; hope there's a medical chap to hand, McPeevish thought.

-Your luck is about to change, McPeevish, a voice like a clogged meat grinder snarled in his ear.

McPeevish watched as the Colonel, rubbing the ball on his buttocks, strode once more towards the haze of the distance. I wonder, McPeevish thought, how the man had become so dyspeptic.

As the Colonel ran in this time McPeevish noted there was a more settled rhythm to him. He means business, McPeevish thought. Brute force having not done the trick he's turning to guile. Two beamers to soften me up and now this one will bounce. Look for the mole's head, McPeevish advised himself. Moles are a good guide to most things.

The Colonel flung the ball down the wicket with the venom and velocity of a Frank Tyson and Larwood combined. There was heat in this delivery.

The mole ducked; McPeevish swatted.

Countless eyes, including those of the thankful mole, watched as the ball describe a serene double helix on its way to some unpatrolled part of the boundary. McPeevish inspected his piece of timber for any unsightly marks, aware of the noise level having increased somewhat in the distance. Lord Gelding marched down the wicket to pat him on the shoulder. No words were necessary between the two men, thought McPeevish.

He held up his hand to the umpire and a pause took place. McPeevish removed Wittgenstein from its lodging and flicked though the first few pages, his mind suddenly teased by some philosophical nicety which only Ludwig could resolve. Once reassured- the work of a few moments during which the grass grew taller- he returned Wittgenstein to its place of honour.

The Colonel meanwhile had scarred indelibly parts of the distant fields with the studs of his boots.

Here he comes again, noted McPeevish. By Jove, he's coming round the wicket!

Another mole had just come up to see what all the commotion was about.

One look and it popped back below where considerable discussion was going on in mole language about the noisy neighbours upstairs.

The ball bounced and lunged towards McPeevish like a crazed cobra. Swat.

Now that, McPeevish thought shouldering the timber and following the rise of the ball keenly, was a Nephroid curve if ever I saw one.

The Colonel, hands on his knees and panting like a Pantomime Panda, was glaring at McPeevish with eyes that could rivet metal. McPeevish noted that two or three moles had popped their heads out to watch the goings on. Then there went the Colonel again, back to the distance to recommence his run in.

As the fifth ball was released a voice called out 'No Ball!' McPeevish would have argued the point- any philosopher would- but he felt duty bound to swat first and ask questions afterwards. So: swat.

All heads turned skyward to watch the magnificence of a Césaro curve unfolding on its way to an uncharted part of the boundary.

The Colonel, McPeevish noticed, was deep in animated discussion with the umpire who had made the call. McPeevish knew better than to trot over and offer his services as adjudicator. Somehow he felt that references to Immanuel Kant and Husserl on the subject of the reality of the ball qua ball might not be helpful. Best mind your own business, McPeevish, he told himself. Arguments about phenomenological reality can be thorny bushes at the best of times without sparking them into the burning variety.

The Colonel approached the crease afresh and whirled his arm like a distressed Dutch windmill.

'No ball!' was again called. McPeevish swatted with impunity. A parabola of some artistic delicacy was carved by the ball, the outer covering of which fell away in its flight to another desolate spot on the boundary. The umpire quelled all argument by pointing decisively at the boot mark over the line, which only McPeevish's keen eye had spotted being made by another diving mole.

Play was held up while a new ball was sought. This took some time. It was not the lack of balls but rather their make which caused the delay. The match ball had been an old, well used one manufactured by T. Ives and Son of Tonbridge. The Reverend Cleikum, President of '*The Dirk*' and rather traditionalist in his theology, argued that like should be replaced by like. But as the holders of the Mug '*The Colic*' insisted on the use of a '*Kookaburra*' ball. Once it had been 'roughed up' so as to resemble, as far as possible, the previous game ball, the Colonel seized it with renewed enthusiasm.

Throughout this pause the Episcopalians, augmented by their Church of

Scotland brethren and sisters, glissaded through 'Great God, what do I see and hear?' and 'Set thine house in order' from the *'Universal Hymn Book'* of 1905. Miss Bevel added another stripe to the scarf that would now have wound around the neck of a giant.

The Colonel as a young man had been very found of jazz and had learnt all about swing and reverse swing whilst serving in India. Having perfected 'the Delhi grip' many years ago he liked nothing more than to regale unwary listeners with the story of how he had once dismissed the great Iftikhar Ali Khan, the Nawab of Pataudi, for a duck. If pressed the Colonel would produce the very ball- autographed by the Nawab- with which he had done the deed. The 'Delhi grip' was, the Colonel added, his own patent. He was not at liberty to demonstrate it since he had sworn a solemn oath never to reveal the grip. The secret had been conveyed to him by an old fakir from the foothills of the Hindu Kush. Only an initiate into the mysteries of the hashish thuggees could flex and twist his fingers around the ball to give it maximum velocity, maximum swing, maximum everything. The Nawab, the Colonel swore, had been shaken by the experience and vowed never to play cricket again.

McPeevish prepared himself yet again as the Colonel moved in with the stealth of Rudolph Valentino slipping into a maiden's tent. As the ball left the Colonel's hand it could have been mistaken for a Kansas tornado. McPeevish, of necessity, swatted *'encore une fois'*.

One may live for a century and not see the Aurora Borealis or lemmings vaulting over a cliff; and it is rare in nature to glimpse the *folium of Descartes* in its purest form. As the Kookaburra ball described in the skies above Moffat that philosopher's miracle, the entire crowd burst into a spontaneous verse of 'To Thee, O God, we fly' ('*The book of Common Praise*' 1908). The Nawab would have smiled; Duleepsinji would have applauded; and Ranjitsinghj would have doffed his cap. Had he been able to distinguish individuals in the mass on the boundary McPeevish would have seen strangers embracing and Miss Bevel's needles flashing like Ali Baba's scimitar.

Hubris, McPeevish cautioned himself. There's many a slip twixt and all that. In the battle between good and evil the latter sometimes held the trumps. Do not count chickens before the toast is ready, he told himself.

As the Colonel turned and raced in to bowl the final ball of the over, McPeevish crouched à la Babe Ruth and narrowed his eyes. If the gods were going to play him false then he would go down swinging. Who had said that: Ned Kelly? Remember *Devon Loch*, he urged himself.

The Colonel prepared to hurl the ball towards McPeevish like Captain

Ahab had hurled the harpoon at the Great White Whale. Harpoons are long and have a point at the end; a Kookaburra ball is circular, rather like a small cannon ball. There are universal laws of thermodynamics and trajectory, the temperature at which various materials melt or combust, which cannot be denied by sinner or saint. There are laws which define which object must give- shatter or disintegrate- when two objects of varied shape and material collide. There are moments in time when Goliath meets David and flattens him with a mallet before the slingshot can whirl. There are times when it seems that time itself has stopped and everything is waiting to take on a new shape or significance. There are times when the gods, bored beyond belief, call for the dancing girls.

This was not one of them.

As the ball soared gracefully towards the boundary the crowd broke into 'Ain't that good news!' and 'Zekiel saw the wheel'.

*

This, thought McPeevish with more than a touch of déjà vu, is the life.

He was in the arms of the beloved as they shuffled around the dance floor. The Moffat Mug sat in its long vacant spot on the mantelpiece in the hall of *Gearran Manor*. Somewhere amongst the crowd of couples who likewise drifted aimlessly across the floor were the young Lord and Lavinia, his bride to be, both having been the first to taste the victory champagne from the cup. The Reverend Cleikum, enswathed in an endless scarf, coaxed Miss Bevel through the intricacies of the steps. Time had emancipated her from tonality and any sense of rhythm; but that was part of her charm. Lady Gelding had thrown open the manor to all after the famous victory - magnanimously including the adherents of the beaten ' *Colic'*- and celebrations were now well past midnight. Even in the stables, to which her ladyship would slip out now and then, there was a festive atmosphere amongst the piles of hay and ornate nose-bags.

-Trout are best tickled, the dear one had said.

There goes my mind again, thought McPeevish. It's just like an escaped balloon; one puff of wind or spark of memory and it's off, flying out the window. McPeevish's mind replayed that moment when the hymn displayed became 250 ('If there be that skills to reckon' from '*The English Hymnal*' of 1906). The young Lord Gelding had hoisted a surprised McPeevish on to his shoulders and bore him in triumph from the field.

But she was right: where hook, line and toe had failed the nimble, knowing fingers of the dear one had come up trumps. McPeevish savoured the moment when, lying beside his beloved and gazing down into the waters of the Tweed, she had tickled a trout and flipped it on to the river bank.

'Left foot then right,' a gentle voice corrected.

With his eyes shut or even with them wide open, McPeevish on the dance floor was all at sea.

-Now reverse, sweetheart; don't bother with the clutch.

If I had had a driving instructor like her, McPeevish thought, it would not have taken me nine times...

-Ten, the dreamy voice corrected.

She remembered better than he did, McPeevish acknowledged. I was forgetting about that time in Lower Wallop...

-Upper Jallop, the beloved amended lovingly.

The territories of middle England were so confusing, McPeevish mused. So long since I've been there. Ah well, I'm here and this is bliss...Moffat, he corrected himself.

The band ended the waltz and permitted the couples enough time to disentangle and sip refreshment at the hastily arranged but fully provisioned bar. The cellars of both inns had been emptied by willing volunteers and there was no danger of any shortage. Many speculated around the bar, now as crowded as the dance floor had been, what the text of the Reverend Cleikum's sermon would be that coming Sunday. Bets were being placed discreetly. Strongly fancied were *Psalm 149*[4], *Proverbs 20*[22] and *Leviticus 19*[17ff]. McPeevish, feeling lucky since horses weren't involved, had put a fiver on *2 Chronicles 15*[7] ('But as for you, be strong and do not give up, for your work will be rewarded').

With a whoop and a whistle the band plunged into the *'Gay Gordon'*. From a safe vantage point McPeevish watched as the beloved one whirled and twirled amongst those up to scratch with the steps. He knew his limits. Not for him the intricacies of the *'Sausage Machine'*, *'Strip the Willow'*, *'Highland Schottische'* and *'Moffat Mowing'*.

At some hour best left unrecorded McPeevish and the beloved strolled homeward. Behind them the manor still emanated a glow of sound and lights as the celebrants got their second and third winds. They had decided to go when, during a lull in the proceedings, Lady Gelding had ridden into the ballroom on her favourite stallion calling for hay and oats for the animal and a man of spirit for herself. McPeevish, still overawed by the clatter of hoofs, couldn't swear that it hadn't been the other way round. One of the duties of a son is to care for his mother. As the negotiations were protracted- Lady Gelding clung to the pommel as filial hands tried to ease her from the saddle- McPeevish had glanced at the beloved and she had given him the nod. A horse on the dance floor was one thing; dung was another.

-I never knew you were good at cricket, my love, the beloved said.

If she only knew, McPeevish smiled. It's just that he was good at swatting flies. I must get her to teach me how to tickle trout, McPeevish thought.

- Of course, dear heart. There's one proviso.

Perhaps this 'trout tickling' business was more difficult than he realised. Experts made their chosen skill look like falling off a log -which of course a Canadian lumberjack would never do; so find another metaphor, McPeevish. Take all that leaping and skipping on the dance floor; had I been there, McPeevish thought, it would have been like traffic snarling up in Bologna. Not that I've been to Bologna. It's just a place where I assume, it being Italian, traffic snarls up. That's the thing about horses: they don't snarl up. Drop dung where they will- field, dance floor, parade ground- but no snarling up.

McPeevish wondered what it could be this qualification. It was rather unlike the beloved to enter a proviso.

-Wittgenstein will have to go, she said squeezing his arm.

Sometimes, McPeevish thought a few hours later, philosophy simply has to be put to one side so that trout may be tickled.

The Niblick

*'There was nothing in that clear, calm day, with its blue
sky and its flooding sunshine to suggest in the slightest
degree the awful tragedy so close at hand...'*
Chester K. Steele "The Golf Course Mystery"

McPeevish's reflection considered him as he considered it.

He tried out the expression 'handsome devil' but agreed with his reflection that the hat didn't fit. When he thought of 'handsome devil', McPeevish thought- and assumed his reflection (now with hands in pockets and fedora more awry) also thought- then to mind came the images of Errol Flynn, Douglas Fairbanks (father or son) and Cary Grant. McPeevish knew that he was not in their league, no matter how he might groom himself or apply scents specifically designed to bring out the essence of his masculinity. His thoughts ranged briefly over the shelves in 'Boots' in the High Street laden with '*L'Homme*', '*Ossession*', '*SRY*' and '*Musque*', all of which brought him out in a rash and attracted cohorts of cleggs from every corner of the Borders. To them such potions were like salad cream.

No, McPeevish thought, you cannot deny the gulf between yourself and those matinee idols. For one thing they are dead and you, though somewhat crocked here and there, a mite frayed and creased, a trifle concave and convex, a *soupçon* um and er: you, McPeevish, are very much alive. For another you have no tan, perma or otherwise. Some- and here he called to mind the inevitable Jess Conrad- are more 'tan than tone' [©] [RAS]. Alas, McPeevish, you are a freckler. When abroad in the sun, on a beach in Biarritz, say- not that I've been to Biarritz, McPeevish corrected himself, so Bournemouth will do: when abroad in the sun in Bournemouth, where it is true the sun shines less often than it does in Biarritz -or Bahrain, for that matter- and there are fewer yachts and film stars promenading; when out in the sun, McPeevish doggedly persisted, I have to be greased to the gills with maximum strength nut free sun block. It's either that or a burnous. Perhaps, he subsumed, one attraction of Bournemouth was that there were no yappy poodles or athletic Afghan hounds galloping along the front. He wondered idly, as he practiced his grip on the umbrella he held reversed in his hands and chipped another hard boiled egg into the wastepaper bin, what such hounds hunted: possibly poodles, unless they were disguised as hedges.

Not a 'handsome devil' then, McPeevish, he conceded. But perhaps distinguished? When he thought of *distingué* McPeevish called to mind Charles Boyer and Alain Delon. No, McPeevish, he thought, you lack that certain *'je ne sais quoi'*, that *beaucoup de chic*, that *zut alors sang-froid* and *s'il vous plaît élan* which ooze off the French rake. Decidedly, McPeevish, you are neither an oozer nor a rake more a colander.

A little less elbow, perhaps, McPeevish advised himself as an egg shattered against the wall. He'd have that for his lunch along with the half-dozen others he'd hastily de-shelled and put with the lettuce in the kitchen. Fortunately the wallpaper was of a pattern and colour that the mark wouldn't show, unless one inspected the spot with a Sherlock Holmes type magnifying glass.

He glanced out the window as he noticed a rumbling sound akin to that produced by an Aveling and Porter two-gear single-engine road roller. If he had to guess McPeevish thought it might be *'Wymeswold'* of 1884 vintage.

Odd for the council to be bringing their steam-rollers up this way, he thought. But to neither left nor right, as he gazed out of the bay window giving on to the front lawn, could McPeevish see a steam-roller. Must de-wax the ears, he thought. It seemed that these days he was having to re-bore, polish or clean out every niche and cranny in his bodily apparatus. 'Grooming' no longer covered it; this was major reconstruction work that occasionally he put out to tender with a chiropodist or masseuse. The magical fingers of the beloved could only do so much to his twisted and aching neck muscles.

Well, McPeevish thought as he ran out of eggs, if not 'handsome devil' or 'distinguished' then certainly not extinguished! There's life in the old dog yet!

Dogs again, McPeevish thought.

McPeevish glanced at Shayla the cat. She had been watching him carefully in that calm, considered manner felines have before they bite the head off a mouse. Could cats tell when you were thinking about dogs? McPeevish thought. Was there a 'woof' factor which cats could pick up on their radar? Perhaps if I think sardines, McPeevish thought. But the thought of thinking sardines as opposed to the thought of sardines was clearly insufficient, for the cat yawned and resumed its sleep.

He noticed that a remote control lay on the pouffe over which he had been chipping the eggs.

Of course, McPeevish reminded himself, there's racing on at Kelso! I wonder how Lucinda's doing. He flicked the switch and looked at the screen. Nothing happened. Batteries must be kaput, he thought.

There's that rumbling sound again, McPeevish thought.

He looked around, out the window, all the while flicking the switch on the remote control, yearning for the days when a television was all valves and coils and warmed up with a contented hum.

The rumbling sound had now become a snarl and whine.

Shayla opened her eyes with alarm, stared into the kitchen and bolted for the cat flap.

McPeevish glanced towards the kitchen and bolted for the cat flap. He was at an inherent disadvantage: the cat was faster.

Trapped! McPeevish thought as he turned to confront the horror he had glimpsed in the kitchen. Defenceless, like Hannay at bay before Professor Jordan!

Ah! McPeevish thought as it all became clear. He sensibly placed the washing machine's remote control on the kitchen counter. Strewn across the floor was the load of laundry the dear one had asked him to tend to whilst she was on her usual Monday round of her friends in the town.

No time to lose; mop and bucket, McPeevish, and snappy about it.

Apparently he needed to perfect his grip, stance and swing.

Until now he had never doubted his ability to grip and (metaphorically, unlike Hannay) had clung to many a cliff edge with the grim determination of a man waiting for the last bus. His stance- well, he thought he had perfected that whilst maintaining his balance on the ferry crossing to the Isle of Wight; but that was many long years ago and a few tips and a brief refresher course wouldn't go amiss. As to his swing- he glanced around the room somewhat embarrassed- he didn't see that this was anyone's business except his own and the beloved's.

As McPeevish delved further into the intricacies of this arcane art he realised that he was making fundamental mistakes. For one thing he was holding the book upside down. For another he was adapting too literal approach. But the real error was that there was no tea in his cup and this must be put right at once or the whole matter would crumble and civilisation as we know it would crash. Or something like that.

Unlike the old feather balls a soggy tea bag doesn't carry very far, McPeevish acknowledged as he began to vacuum the lawn where the remains of a chip shot had scattered.

Naturally it was a windless day. But these are the handicaps one must overcome. It said 'handicap' somewhere in one of the books. Did this mean that when he went around the course there would be extra lead weights in his plus fours? It was difficult enough recovering the foot- either foot-from those bogs. Anyhow, weren't the blind and infirm encouraged to call themselves 'differently gifted' nowadays? McPeevish didn't feel himself to be 'differently gifted', though at times he did feel a bit slack here and there, a bit tight elsewhere and somewhat short-changed in this or that department. But essentially he wouldn't alter either this or that; though it would be nice if he could...but then perhaps there was a down side to that, as Casanova might have found leaping from high windows.

Clear the mind, McPeevish. Concentrate on the essentials.

McPeevish cleared his mind. He began to concentrate. Everything was gone, the whole job lot- the props, the actors, the whole stage set and theatre and the kitchen sink: '*den Inhalt des Geistes*', *Empfindung, Gefühl, Gestälten, Weltganze*, ; not a thought was in sight, essential or otherwise. A new broom couldn't have swept his mind cleaner.

Not a skill everyone has, he reminded himself as he threshed about groping for words. For most people the mind is like the attic, full of junk, rocking horses and banjos and that sort of thing. There are no banjos in my mind, he assured himself.

Somewhere he heard something twanging.

Banjos in Moffat?

Ah; one of the armchair's springs had gone. A bit of repair work called for.

At some stage in life every one has to learn not to hammer a spring. Late is as good as never, thought McPeevish as he licked the wound on his thumb.

Focus, McPeevish, he chided himself, wondering exactly what it was he was doing. Was chiding similar to salt and peppering, he wondered? Or was it salting and peppering?

Grip, McPeevish, grip; get a grip.

He got a grip.

Now I can't let go, he thought as he looked around for something with which to pry it off his hand. Why is the sticky side always up?

A few minutes in the woodshed and McPeevish emerged dusting his hands and whistling '*Last night's fun*'. Those who knew him well- and the beloved was paramount among those- would immediately have gone into the woodshed (giving him a wide berth, in case he was contagious) to find what it was that had lead to this onset of whistling. McPeevish was not a whistler. Some people are. Some people whistle while they work; others whistle while reading the newspaper; still others (it is reported in those surveys so popular with the tabloids) whistle while having sex. McPeevish was doing none of these things, but here he was emerging in rather jovial and self-satisfied fashion from a woodshed which, up to that point, he had seldom visited. Ipso facto, something was up-or, more accurately, hidden in the woodshed.

But in the absence of the beloved there was no one to hear his whistling, except the birds. They were more interested in the seed in the feeder. Exactly what had happened in the woodshed must remain a matter of conjecture.

McPeevish continued his extemporised gripping, though now he was rather more circumspect about what he might grip.

Then he realised that this type of gripping was folly! Of course: it was all in the mind! How could he 'grip' that which was not? Dear old Buddha, champion of the was not, to the rescue again! McPeevish would have clapped him on the back, except Buddha was not present and hadn't been for some thousand or more years.

Even that was not, was it not?

McPeevish cautioned himself. Perhaps one can have too much of this was not business.

Get a grip, McPeevish. Move on to stance.

McPeevish moved on to stance, studying the diagrams carefully.

A milkman chanced to be passing the front garden when McPeevish took up a stance, perhaps that of Diagram 13.

Now in Moffat as well as anywhere else in the Borders, but perhaps more discreetly, many people- politicians especially- are taking a stance. This is very popular with those who have time on their hands but do not wish to be gainfully employed. Sociologists, for want of anything better to do, have produced voluminous works on 'stance'. There was, so McPeevish had learnt, a stance for everything. If you held a certain stance for long enough, so the proverb went, a ferret would run up your leg. Plus fours, in these circumstances, were an eminently sensible precaution, thought McPeevish.

The milkman- let it not be forgotten- was passing in his float when McPeevish took up his stance. There is little that is wrong with retired gentlemen taking up a stance in the privacy of their own front garden. However, the stance that McPeevish foolishly took caused the milkman to utter a cry of disbelief. He whipped up his horse. There was no response as it was an electric float. For everyone's sake the hedge intervened. McPeevish was totally unaware of the shock he had given and certainly can't be held responsible for the curdled milk subsequently delivered.

There's only so much one can do with a stance. A stance is a stance for all that, as one might say. Once you've taken a stance, McPeevish mused, could one continue to call it a stance? When did a stance become a position? He considered the garden statuary. This was made somewhat harder by the fact that there was none; but had there been, he prompted himself, could one say that the statues were taking a stance? Or were they merely posed?

There seemed a lot to be said for staying in motion, McPeevish felt; which brought him neatly on to swing.

He strode purposefully back into the house and drew the curtains.

*

It had all started, as these things often do, with the ringing of the phone. McPeevish had been at his post in the garden, sprawled in a deck-chair contemplating the dance of the leaves on the trees. Was it a conga or a black mamba? he mused as the bees buzzed. The dear one had been in the house freshening up the lemonade pitcher and doing all those other secret things of the feminine toilette which seemed to keep her so cool looking despite the heat. McPeevish had been trying to remove his thumbs from between the pages of the book ('*Trent's Own Case*' by E. Clerihew Bentley). When he had momentarily nodded off, lulled by the enchanting murmur of the breeze and the hypnotic sway of the leaves, McPeevish had left his thumbs in the book to mark his place; that is he had not so much left them there as had fallen asleep without removing them. Upon awakening he had become aware of being handcuffed, shackled, and had gazed with bemusement at the device constricting his hands. Fiendishly inventive, McPeevish thought as, without causing alarm to the birds on the feeder, he sought to free his hands. Hannay, he remembered, had been handcuffed to Madeleine Carroll in the film of '*The 39 Steps*'. Many an author would have gone for a round figure, McPeevish thought; but hats off to Buchan, he'd stuck with that *Stømer* number which was the sum of five consecutive primes. A glance had told McPeevish that it was no good trying to loop his hands under his feet and wriggle that way; all he'd do would be to knot himself tighter. A calm, rational approach was called for here, he thought coolly and rationally. Perhaps he could whistle and entice the birds from the feeder and have them peck him free? Could he chew his way through the book? He was reluctant to do this as it was a 1936 first edition which he'd found in the 'Moffat Book Exchange' and he didn't want to ruin his appetite for tea

He yawned and stretched and, miraculously, his thumbs were free. He retrieved the book from the lawn, his place lost.

-Tsk, the beloved one said as she rejoined him.

McPeevish took the frosted glass of lemonade she handed him and raised an eyebrow. Tsk! he thought. Something had agitated the dear one if she was driven to uttering sounds without vowels! He wondered what the reason for this was.

- It's Hamish, she said.

Hamish? wondered McPeevish. Was that the chap with the lop-sided moustache and tendency to quack when excited? No, that was someone named Dalgleish.

- He can't partner me in the match next month. Some crisis in the financial world requires his immediate flight to Hong Kong. We'll have to scratch.

McPeevish gave this some thought. He knew that when he itched he scratched. He knew that Hong Kong was round the other side of the sphere on which gravity held them all captive and that no amount of wishful thinking would bring it nearer. He knew that on a distant Sunday the beloved one was due to play golf at the club. He knew that he was her partner in life and that he wouldn't be in Hong Kong and that he didn't itch. He knew that golf involved shouting an even number occasionally and much bending of knees and waist. He felt he was getting close to the nub of the matter. The solution was simple.

- That's very kind of you, my sweet, the beloved one said with a warm smile. I know how any game with a ball in it can confuse you.

It's the way they bounce, McPeevish thought as he basked in the glow of her smile. Balls qua balls, spheres of any kind, large or small, hovering or at rest, do not distress me. It's when they bounce that I feel the other side of the fence is the place to be. He recalled the incident of the meatballs in the restaurant in Paris. For months afterwards he had been unable to look at a tin of meatballs in the supermarket without wanting to slink in shame from the store. The waiter had been consideration personified, swiftly erecting a screen around their table to shield them from the laughter of the other diners. The beloved had had to retreat to the ladies room to compose herself and repair her makeup which tears of laughter had damaged. Before he would deign to leave their hotel room the next morning McPeevish had scanned the complete selection of local papers to ensure that there were no reports of the event. For the remainder of their week in Paris he had worn dark glasses, slouched as much as possible, used his left as opposed to his right hand when drinking café au lait and parted his hair on the other side. One or all of these subtle changes to his appearance and behaviour seemed to do the trick. Several people came up to him shyly in the Boulevards and bistros to ask if he was Peter Falk and he graciously gave them his autograph. Once even the dear one failed to recognise him; this may have been because he had a brown paper bag over his head as he soaked in the bath. She later remarked that it wasn't 'Columbo' he resembled.

*

It was Saturday, the day before the golf match.

McPeevish had set aside his natural prejudice against a game known to be the refuge of villains. Hannay, while keeping watch on Trafalgar Lodge, had seen a man on a bicycle with a set of golf clubs. The man was on his way back from the Kingsgate golf course and was one of the conspirators. It surely was no coincidence that Hannay himself did not play golf.

Never mind 'What's it all about, Alfie?' he was done training. He had browsed through a copy of *'Propositiones ad Acuendos Juvenes'* and Fibonacci's *'Liber Abaci'*; and then had moved on to Cardan's *'De Subtililate'* and the Rhind papyrus before dabbling in some Kakuro and Sudoku puzzles. That should get the old brain seething, he thought.

Golf is a sport of the mind as much as of the body, McPeevish thought. When a warrior prepares himself for battle many and varied are the rituals that are performed. The Dakota Indians toss a handful of dust into the air. The Spartans slaughtered a goat, oiled their own bodies and combed each others' hair. The Maori *peruperu* dance sees grown men grimacing as though at stool and shouting *'Tika tonu mai'* at their opponents. Others beat drums, scar themselves, sweat and bathe, or pray long and hard. The Englishman- and despite his lengthy sojourn in the north, McPeevish was still this at heart- enjoyed a nice cup of tea and a good book.

McPeevish had browsed the boxes and shelves of second-hand books on display at the 'Antique Fayre' in the town hall during the intervening weeks. He had driven to the Springwell Park Showground by Kelso to see what he could find. He had left the side of the beloved to spend a few days in Edinburgh visiting the auctions at 'Lyon and Turnbull' and he had popped into West Register House. Beside his armchair in the living-room were stacked some of the fruits of his expeditions.

Despite the beloved one's assurance that the result didn't matter McPeevish knew that it behoved him to do his utmost. There were few occasions, he mused as he flipped through the faded pages of Sir W.G. Simpson's *'The Art of Golf'*, when he behoved, let alone reached for his utmost. McPeevish preferred that gentle drift and wafting through life which, despite the odd bump or two- well, three or four, perhaps several at a pinch- had served him well.

Had he wished to McPeevish could have summoned from the dungeon depths of his memory, countless examples of his struggle against the universal laws of motion, dynamics and chance. Even when he did not wish to remember them, the ghosts of contretemps past would parade before him derisively. Why did he always put some object of immense value in the pocket with the hole? Doubtlessly there was a Germanic sounding name for the law which governed McPeevish's life trajectory:

gemachteindurcheinandervondingenwieder would do at a pinch. At times he felt like one of those balls in a pinball machine bouncing between buffers. Recently there had been that nasty business with the car jack, of course. Why did cars always break down on slopes? Who invented grease? How many wing nuts were there on the average wheel? Why did spare tyres roll so far downhill? How was it that there was always a bull in the very field in which a spare tyre landed? Why was it that cursing under one's breath always drew flocks of sheep from the furthermost hills to stand at a fence and watch a grown man sweat? Didn't they know that he worked best when unobserved? How could the dear one remain so calm and besport herself on the roadside bank in the sun maintaining, despite all the evidence to the contrary, that she knew he would manage eventually? And why was it that, just as the whole jigsaw puzzle of wheel and axle had been reunited, someone came along and asked if you needed any help? No good looking up to the heavens, McPeevish; they're all at the seaside for the day.

It was a perfect evening: the sun was setting with that leisureliness peculiar to the Borders; the sheep were grazing in the distance and the beloved one was by his side- well, was by his side until he inadvertently encountered a bit of boggy stuff. He watched as she strolled on, sure and dry-footed enjoying the scenery of the hills all around them. What had started out as a gentle *après dîner* stroll had turned into a Himalayan expedition. McPeevish looked around for the Sherpas but there was nobody else in sight. Down below like Shangri-La lay Moffat. McPeevish wondered if they were twinned. He couldn't recall that many sheep wondering about in Shangri-La but then there weren't that many Buddhist monks wandering around in Moffat. Those that were came once a week in a SUV four-wheel drive from Eskdalemuir and bought whole foods by the crate load.

- That's the golf club down there, the dear one called. I'll walk you round the course so you get the lie of the land.

Had Custer followed this mandatory procedure before the Battle of Little Big Horn, McPeevish mused, perhaps he would have avoided ending up in a dead-end street and dead to boot. He wondered if the Sioux were any good at golf.

The regulation eighteen holes were laid out on moorland, hence the squelching. All around him McPeevish could envisage wild birds desperately trying to hatch stray golf balls.

- It's best to avoid the hazards, if you can, the dear one called over her shoulder; but I know you enjoy a challenge.

The whole course is a hazard, McPeevish thought despairingly as he pulled another waterlogged shoe from a bog-hole. The expression 'terra firma' didn't apply up here. The secret, McPeevish thought was to embrace all contretemps with an open mind. Wellington boots would have come in handy as well.

-The weather is going to be a bit blowier tomorrow, she called as McPeevish wrestled with an invisible adversary who was trying to tear his clothes off. The hair McPeevish didn't bother to dispute about.

Scattered around the course he could see figures swinging their arms like pendulums and heard the crack of iron striking the ball. He noticed the absence of birds in flight. Perhaps it was an ignoble fate for a bird to be downed by a golf ball.

The golf club was both exclusive and inclusive, complying with the kind of legislation which flies from the flagpole in the kingdom these days. It included those who wanted to be in and excluded those who those who were in didn't want to be in. As well as those who really didn't care about being in or out, those who weren't in often included those who wanted to be in but couldn't be because they were not the right sort. Not being the right sort was a problem since it wasn't clear to the wrong sort what the right sort was, mused McPeevish. Am I the right sort? Do I want to be the sort who is the right sort in these circumstances? As a philosopher of life the definition of terms was his forte. Well, if not his forte then one of his foibles or interests; that is if something so vague could be defined as an interest let alone a foible. He often wondered how many foibles one was allowed before they became a handicap or some kind of blemish, like a wart.

It was usually at this juncture in his cogitation that he wondered what was for supper.

McPeevish wondered what was for supper. He had a good idea; but having a good idea was not the same as knowing.

This train of thought is going nowhere, McPeevish decided and headed for the junction. There were many of those within his mind, he acknowledged, but in the circumstances one was as good as another. Let's follow the beloved and see what happens, McPeevish prompted himself.

*

Their opponents were the Chudleighs. Horace Chudleigh was wealthy. He was something big in the city; not a skyscraper but a CEO, which was bigger. People when they said that usually assumed a knowing look, the kind of look once assumed when one talked about highwaymen or sea bandits. 'Finance' like fencing- epée and range- was a closed world to McPeevish.

He was familiar with money, of course, having samples of it in various pockets and bank accounts; but he knew that 'finance' was something different. It happened out of sight, a bit like smoking behind the cycle shed in his schooldays. The problem with 'finance', McPeevish thought, was that it leads to a certain kind of diet, a certain kind of waistcoat and a certain kind of facial expression. The Chudleighs had it in spades, diamonds and clubs but not in hearts, McPeevish decided after only five minutes in the same room with them.

Before play began there were speeches. Those who spoke were those who weren't playing. It gave them something to do, McPeevish decided. They were not the kind of speeches which were listened to, certainly not by a McPeevish. They filled the air the way the droning of wasps would. People nodded their heads and some heads fell off. People clapped and muttered encouraging words in a variety of languages none of which McPeevish understood. Then more heads nodded and fell off. If anyone noticed they'd bend down and pick one up and screw it back on, hopefully to the correct neck. A large silverware trophy was exhibited. It was for this that they were playing, McPeevish knew. With it went honour, praise and a rather large annual bill for polishing it. McPeevish couldn't quite visualise it on the beloved's living-room mantelpiece but thought it would look grand in the woodshed.

*

On the first tee the honour of driving off went to the Chudleighs. They both played off a four handicap. The beloved was a six handicap; and, of course, McPeevish thought, I am my own handicap.

He had taken care with his equipment and attire. His clubs were original Arnaud Massy Hickory shafted clubs, the very set with which he won the '*Grand Championat Omnium*' (the first French Open) at La Boulie in 1906. His plus fours, jacket and flat cap were modelled on those worn by Harry Vardon in 1911 when he beat Massy in a play-off for the British Open at Royal St. Georges, Sandwich.

McPeevish knew he could do nothing about the external elements. The gusting wind one moment blew in your face and the next booted you up the back, or swiped you from either side. Likewise the grass and the composition of the soil- hard or boggy- was as it was. Conscious only of the beloved one by his side as they walked, McPeevish knew that to win he must master himself: he must become a *Zen* golfer.

There are those who maintain that the game is won or lost on the first tee;

others would have you believe that it is only on the final green. There are those who say it depends on how well you play the wind, or if you have the wind after a fine luncheon. Others point to your putter and ask if it dribbles or stutters. As the tension mounts do you twitch and pull and slice the way others dice carrots or peel spuds? Are you good in the sand with your wedge and can you keep it on the fairway once it gets loose? Can you read the greens? Do you eat your greens?

McPeevish knew it was easy to become confused. Should your shoulder be up or down, the elbow in or out? Can you do the Hokey-Cokey? Which foot should be where and when? Should you pivot at the knee and rupture a kneecap or swivel at the hips and put your back out?

But the *Zen* golfer has no such dilemmas. He floats as on a cloud, except there are no clouds. The *Zen* golfer remains balanced and centred, there being no right or left. To the *Zen* golfer the hole is all, all is the hole. Yardage schmardage: the ball is in the hole before the ball is hit- Om!

Halved hole followed halved hole. Can you truly halve a hole? McPeevish pondered, leaning idly on his driver. When does a hole become half a hole? Surely, he thought, as he chipped from a bunker, a hole is always a hole. Profundities lay all around, like clumps of gorse. Om...

The tension mounted- in the gallery, in the Chudleighs, but not in McPeevish or the dear one. We are as One, McPeevish thought. We radiate calm and consistency. One putt or two, never three. Shot follows shot- down the fairway go the drives; down the driveways go the fairs...

Om! Concentrate, McPeevish. No time for nonsense now, man. This is serious; there's silverware at stake. Put the iron on the green in regulation; go get the shirt and...

Om! Steady man. Thank goodness you're playing alternate shots: time to recompose yourself: Om!

The final hole was a par four. From the tee there was a sudden drop to the fairway and along it lurked footpad clumps of low gorse and wind wrecked trees. The Camelot of the distant putting green was protected by a burn and two deep bunkers. Whoever designed this course was a fiend in the class of Fu Manchu, McPeevish thought. He might as well be playing in the great Grimpen Mire. The words of "Dartmoor Days" by E.W.L.Davis 1863 sprang to mind: '*A dreary shroud is o'er his head, A yawning swamp around him spread; Spell-bound and lost he ventures on, One fatal step - and all is done; Hopeless he struggles, vain his throes, Deeper and deeper down he goes!*' Then the words sprang right out again.

It was his turn to drive off.

McPeevish composed himself with the Memphis Mantra '*Tutti frutti, oh Rudy, Wop-bop-a-loom-a-blop-bam-boom*'.

He watched as the ball settled in the middle of the fairway. Om...

The Chudleigh's ball was on the green in three and like the tiger's head 'four feet from its tail' (Donegan): a likely par. The dear one's second shot had landed just short of the burn in front of the raised putting surface. A wall of sand seemed to stand between McPeevish and the flag.

There are moments of decision in history- John Wayne at the Alamo and Michael Caine at Rorke's Drift. There are moments when the close is hushed, breaths are bated and the midnight train leaves for Alabam...

We'll give them that, thought McPeevish.

The beloved one strode on to the green, picked up the Chudleigh's ball without a word and handed it to them.

The gallery gasped in unison. A wall of faces ringed the final green. Even the sheep had put down their knitting and ambled over to join in the fun. Sundays in Moffatland were a bit of a drag, they thought, so any spectator sport made them flock.

Some folk take the biscuit; some take the Mickey: I'll take the niblick, McPeevish decided.

From where he stood he could just see the top of the beloved's head and the fluttering flag.

For a brief moment McPeevish's interior was flooded with thoughts of curves- dragon curves, transcendental curves, space curves, skew curves, Devil's curves.

Clear the mind, McPeevish. *Bama lama, bama loo, bama lama, bama loo, Bama lama, bama loo, bama lama, bama loo.*

This is where those hours spent in his armchair reading Sir Walter Scott's 'Chronicles of the Canongate' (1824), 'The Golfer's Manual' (by H.B.Farnie, 1857), 'Le Golf' (by Arnaud Massy, 1911) and 'The Bunker at the Fifth' (by Marcus Dods, 1925) either paid off or went *phut*! Through McPeevish's mind flashed images of Vardon's stance and grip as he addressed the ball. He thought of Samuel Beckett's little known prose piece, cut from 'More Pricks than Kicks', on mobile immobility whilst playing the course at the Royal Dublin on Bull Island. Om...

As he began to draw the niblick back a light reflected from the Colonel's fob watch dazzled his eyes.

McPeevish cleared his mind for the last time: *Boom...Ping...Ya ta ta ta*!

*

It was the Colonel who thrust the blade in just as the beloved one was about to receive the cup from the club President.

- Hang on, the Colonel cried. Only members can hold the trophy. He's not a member!

A chill to equal that in the hut where they found Scott of the Antarctic crept through the clubhouse. Clammy hands clutched at throats. Eyes popped out of sockets. Stays didn't. Wallets tightened.

McPeevish realised that the Colonel's finger was pointing at *him*. All eyes were looking at *him*. Yep, he thought; it's definitely me he's meaning.

I will always remember, McPeevish thought, the sorrowful look on the dear one's face.

The Colonel was quoting from the club rules, paragraph this and section that, note whatever, page somewhere. He brandished the book of club rules with the fervour of Moses exhibiting the Tablets of Stone at the foot of Mount Sinai. His eyes glowed with the same exultant light that must have shone in those of many a heathen god as the sacrifice was shovelled into its maw.

- I'm frightfully sorry, my dear, the President said once he'd consulted sub-paragraph and section and footnote and amendment and so on. The Colonel is quite right. A terrible oversight, I'm afraid. Guests may play *hors de combat* but cannot receive any prize.

Horace Chudleigh stepped smartly forward with the ease of a man used to such last-minute takeovers.

-Well actually..., McPeevish said.

*

- I wondered why you brought that copy of your birth certificate, the dear one murmured contentedly in McPeevish's ear much later.

They clinked glasses again and gazed at the trophy on the shelf just above the sacks of lawn fertiliser.

-I will always remember that look on the Colonel's face, the dear one said. I've seen its like only once before, when Shayla vomited up a vole.

It is common knowledge that the '*Gentlemen Golfers of Leith*' in 1744 drew up the first recognised rules of golf. What began to choke the Colonel was the lesser known fact, supported by McPeevish's photocopied documentation, that the original members of the club at that time '*et germen eorum in perpetuum*' (and their offspring in perpetuity) were to enjoy full convivial and reciprocated membership with all golf clubs '*tamen esse ponenda*' or '*existente tamen formari*' (current and yet to be formed) throughout the land, and '*vice versa*' (the other way round). It remained only for McPeevish to then exhibit the various photocopied birth and marriage certificates he had obtained from the National Archives in Edinburgh recently. These proved that he was a direct descendant of the Honourable James Leslie who had played in that first five round tournament on Leith Links.

Tableau: exit Chudleighs and collapse of Colonel, last seen sucking his ruined thumb.

McPeevish realised that he needed to practice his swing and the beloved one decided she needed to work on her grip. The happy couple withdrew from the lawn to assume a more comfortable stance.

The Theatre of Mysteries

McPeevish felt a hand clutching his throat and choking him.

-It's almost over, he heard the dear one whisper.

He released his grip on his throat and felt the blessed air surge down into his lungs.

Was that a curtain falling or was he fainting?

McPeevish was first to the bar and had gulped down a large malt before the applause stopped and another foot had touched the aisle.

-I thought you were very brave, sweetness, the beloved one said as she reached his side.

McPeevish waved the barman over and received a second dose of medication while a large gin materialised in the beloved's hand. She smiled at him and patted his arm.

-I'll just go and say hello to Hilary backstage.

No, McPeevish thought, I'll just stay here if it's all the same to you.

- Of course, the dear one smiled. I know how she brings you out in a cold sweat. You just stay here where I can find you.

He watched her making her way through the crowd. What a brave woman, McPeevish thought. I must have another drink before someone asks my opinion and I risk imprisonment.

The '*Moffat Amateur Dramatic Society*'- MADS to its patrons- had just staged in the Town Hall, originally the Bath Hall for the Spa, its annual tribute to the little known French dramatist Madame Elisa Adam- Boisgontier. She was a distant, long dead relative of Dame Hilary Bonchaffe, the leading light of the dramatic society.

Not dead long enough or distant enough, McPeevish thought uncharitably. Barge poles didn't come in the requisite size these days.

Her Dame-ship had a stranglehold on the Dramatic Society's output that would have delighted the thuggees. It was her position and influence with the Arts Council, she never ceased reminding her cowering subjects, which brought in the grant. Mister Dame Sir Benedict Bonchaffe, her husband, sat on that council. McPeevish assumed the man had to sit somewhere; it got rather tedious standing for this and that office all the time. He had been variously Chairman of the Community Council, the Town Hall Redevelopment Council, the Urban Grants Council, the Sewage Treatment

Improvement Council, the Justice and Legislative Council, the Heritage Council, the By-Pass Council, the Kite-flying council- no, McPeevish acknowledged to himself, I made that last one up. The Monopolies Committee, if they had a spare hour or two, ought to look into the matter of who sat on what. Personally, McPeevish preferred a bar stool.

McPeevish had had dealings with Madame EAB before when doing research for one of his short stories. The beloved had found him hiding inside the woodshed and it had taken all her persuasive powers to coax him out. She had known there was nothing she could promise him that would overcome his sheer terror at the thought of seeing one of Madame's plays. How she had managed it was beyond McPeevish's comprehension. A Nazi with thumbscrews, hammer and dental pick would have had no chance. Perhaps it was *that* look in her eyes as she'd gazed through the barricaded door spotting him amongst the flower pots and empty sacks which had somehow softened McPeevish's resolve to remain where he was come hell or high water. She had said not a word- *not a word*! No sigh of disappointment, no reminder of vows shared, destinies entwined and troughs plighted- nothing! Just those large, enthralling, luminous, beseeching, deep emerald eyes which made him feel protective and loving despite his aversion to suffering unnecessarily. So what was an hour and a half of sheer unmitigated artistic misery and agony apart from an hour and a half of sheer unmitigated artistic misery and agony when weighed up against that look which she bestowed *only* on him? It was the look that Helen of Troy must have bestowed upon the Greek chappie. What would Hannay have done, McPeevish? he chided himself. Be a man; don't funk it. As he had started to emerge, hesitantly, the look in the dear one's eyes had grown brighter. He had felt the strength which had been flushed from his limbs the moment she had shown him the season's programme returning to him. He threw aside the pitchfork with which he had been prepared to defend himself to the death, removed the bucket from his head and stepped almost gaily, giddily, into her arms...

McPeevish gazed around himself at his fellow theatre-goers.

Was this a re-enactment of 'Invasion of the Body Snatchers'? Was he the only one with a stunned expression on his face?

He checked his appearance in the mirror behind the bar: two eyes, two ears, two heads- no, somebody standing beside him. He whistled up a replacement medicament for the one which had evaporated so rapidly. Is it really over eighty degrees Celsius in here? he thought as he fanned himself with a drinks list. Heat does funny things to liquids, apparently. How on earth are all these people looking so normal? Don't they know what they have just experienced? Would they allow such cruelty to happen to their herds and flocks? Where were the Health and Safety people when you really needed them?

Good Lord, was that the price of a malt? McPeevish gestured commandingly for another one. This should give the local economy a boost, he thought.

At what point could it be said, McPeevish mused, that he was feeling better? Ten minutes ago he was as close to demented as he would ever wish to be. If there had been a closing chorus in the play- play!- he would have throttled every song bird on the stage. Whose mad idea had it been to offer, in return for ten pounds sponsorship and your name in the programme, stage space to every pet owner's tame chirping budgie, bulbul, fairy-bluebird, oriole, peppershrike and parrot? There had been life-forms in cages on the stage which he swore were not to be found even in the depths of the Amazonian rain-forest, the swamps of Venus and labyrinths of Pellucidar.

Better, of course, he told himself consolingly, was a relative concept. After the opening five minutes of the play McPeevish had known that the only thing worse would have been being run over v-e-r-y-s-l-o-w-l-y by an uninsured steam engine whose wheels bore spikes and razor-sharp studs. It's very difficult in a crowded theatre to seek alternative forms of death. He realised too late that he should have taken the precaution of bringing along with himself a means of self-despatch. He'd forgotten to pocket his cyanide capsules on the one occasion when they would have come in handy: a packet of Tic-Tac mints was no substitute. The beloved had merely shaken her head when he discreetly asked if he might borrow her high heels to stab himself with. There were no sockets to hand into which he could stick his tongue. McPeevish would have tried stuffing into his mouth the toupee of the gentleman in front of him but that would have drawn attention to the hairpiece. Gentlemen who wear toupees to the provincial theatre should be able to do so without fear of exposure, McPeevish thought. There was probably a by-law about uncovering a Justice of the Peace's bald head in any event, let alone a fiasco such as the one through which he had just sat. Revolvers were in short supply, except on the stage; and there the wrong people were being shot: they all should have been shot. No hissing cobra came readily to hand. Herds of wildebeests refused to stampede through the auditorium, though one of the actresses pointed some out as they cavorted off stage left. The ground did not conveniently open up and swallow him. No oriental assassin obligingly plunged a curved dagger into his back- had one done so McPeevish would have urged him to get up on the stage and have some fun. No heavy weight fell from the ceiling and crushed him beneath its bulk. No vampire sucked the life out of his neck. No bomb was slipped into his pocket in the form of a chocolate bon-bon. He had to sit there and watch unfolding before him something that promised death but refused to deliver it.

How on earth did that glass empty itself? McPeevish wondered.

By now the simple raising of McPeevish's eyebrow (either) was sufficient for the barman, who remained conveniently stationed nearby, to tip into the glass some more elixir.

McPeevish thought of those mystics who underwent torments by the devils. They had it easy; this had been worse, he knew it beyond a doubt. Saint Sebastian would have relished the arrows and called out for more had he been in the seat beside me, McPeevish thought. Being buried up to your neck in a termite hill would be Paradise compared to those ninety minutes. Having your beating heart ripped from your chest by a drug-crazed Aztec priest would have been the bliss that Dante felt when contemplating Beatrice. How was it that time became so elastic, so interminable?

No need to waste energy on raising the eyebrows, McPeevish found now; a simple glance, a swivel of the old ocular equipment and there it was, a full glass. Perhaps he should suggest for the lead role in the next production this barman. He had poise, he had grace, he had a neat turn of the wrist; but above all he said nothing: he simply poured.

There was more than a touch of Ionescu about the drama in which McPeevish felt himself participating as he sat at the bar. Perhaps it was time I turned my hand- he looked at it splayed on the bar and turned it- perhaps I should turn my hand to writing a play, McPeevish thought. There was material all around; I have only to delve, to transform, to create- an absurdist farce, a neo-romantic whatever, a dark Ibsenist thingy, a Beckettian impasse.

The man's a mind reader, McPeevish thought thankfully as his glass was replenished. He recognises a suffering soul when he sees one. Mercy is not strained it is poured full measure into a glass such as this I see before me.

I hope the beloved one is all right, McPeevish suddenly thought.

Could it have been a trap, the inviting of her backstage? Would Hannay have let her go so unthinkingly to her doom? Who knew what awful fate awaited her in that dressing room? This could be 'The Three Hostages' all over again.

-Sorry I was so long, the dear one said as she slipped on to the stool beside him. Has he been behaving himself? she asked the barman.

McPeevish blinked.

- I asked the barman- Tony- to keep an eye on you, dear heart, she smiled.

McPeevish looked at her, looked at the barman- Tony- looked at his glass. Suddenly it all became clear: he knew he'd seen the barman's face before.

'Marvello the Magician' from the annual summer fair! That's who he was!

The barman smiled almost apologetically and demonstrated the sleight of hand by which he had purloined and replaced McPeevish's glass.

McPeevish looked at the dear one in awe. He was an open book. He was as sober as when he'd arrived.

- I think just one more before we go, don't you? the beloved said. Hilary wants me to be in her next production.

Tony discreetly wiped the spray from the bar's mirror as the dear one patted McPeevish's back.

- That must have gone down the wrong way, she said sympathetically.

Shayla had greeted them as they arrived home. A contented cat is a cat that has not been to the theatre, McPeevish thought. Shayla lead them proudly through to the living room where lay the remains of some poor creature that had dared to venture into her domain. She had separated as many bits from each other as possible with the precision of Sushruta, the father of surgery. McPeevish momentarily considered bringing the cat with him next time he went to the theatre, a thought which gave the expression 'to set the cat among the cockatoos' a certain resonance. He reluctantly dismissed the idea since the logistics- smuggling in a cat box under a cape would hardly go unnoticed- seemed insurmountable. While McPeevish dealt with the corpse the beloved uncorked the malt and poured them both a large one. This, thought McPeevish, is a sign that something more gruesome than the disembowelled remains of vermin was on the cards. He wondered why pet food manufacturers churned out all that 'savoury' stuff when any real cat, red in tooth and claw, wanted mouse meat, neat and unseasoned.

- And Hilary would like you to do the script, the beloved said before she handed McPeevish his drink.

Had he had it in his hand as she uttered those words McPeevish knew that it would have been all over- all over the carpet, all over the curtains and all over the cat.

Shayla, astute at reading the signs, had taken up fall-back position B behind the settee from which she watched with concern the developments. Could this be the end of her access to the sprats and sardines McPeevish brought her on the sly?

He gulped down what must have been a hogshead of restorative and mutely held out the glass. The beloved was way ahead of him, clearly having anticipated what could become a medical emergency.

- She has this idea of using Buchan's unpublished work on Hannay, the dear one continued.

McPeevish was glad that she remained standing and close by, the bottle poised as she considered his condition. A nurse with a warmed bedpan could not have been more welcome.

When she judged it to be the right moment, the dear one sat in her chair and sipped her drink decorously.

- I told Hilary that I'd only do the part if you wrote the script, the dear one explained. She was rather reluctant to agree; you know how she likes to keep a firm grip on everything.

McPeevish did indeed; he'd seen that couple's progeny and had often wondered about his Dame-ship's reproductive responsibilities.

- In the end she agreed, the beloved said. She had wanted to use one of those Boisgontier things...

The bottle was passed without a word and McPeevish left to self-medicate.

- I talked her out of that- it's easy when she's struggling with her corsets and you're holding the stays, she added.

McPeevish wondered if Mister Dame-ship would pay handsomely for knowing this secret.

- I know you've been working on that Buchan story so I suggested that. Hilary could see the potential- her eyes always light up at the prospect of cash and a Chair in contemporary literature at the university.

God forfend, McPeevish thought.

He could see the dear one eyeing him speculatively. He returned the bottle and she corked it. The danger must be passed, McPeevish thought. The worst was over.

He noticed Shayla emerge and saunter across to the beloved and clamber into her lap, from which only the appearance of another rodent would draw her.

- I told her I'd put it to you and you would decide whether your timetable gave you space to do it.

Well now, McPeevish thought. I've got my sock drawer to re-organise. There's yesterday's 'Scotsman' crossword to complete. I'm still not certain how many blades of grass there are in the lawn. I rather wanted to learn to play the comb and paper. That light in the fridge needs to be changed. I'm sure I need to sharpen my pencils. There are a million things which right now need tending to, but at a pinch I might...

- That's wonderful, dear, she smiled.

Yes, McPeevish thought later as his head rested on the pillow and the dear one's head rested on his shoulder, and Shayla rested at their feet; perhaps I owe it to Buchan to finish that abandoned work. Hannay has stood by me through thick and thin, so it's only fair dos that McPeevish should stick by him. And if the dear one was playing the heroine then there was scope enough for feelings and action. Yes, I'm glad I thought of this, he thought as sleep drew him beneath the covers and he felt the beloved's breath softly fanning his cheek.

*

Buchan's many works are well known to scholars and the general reading public, McPeevish knew. Yet '*The Mystery of Broughton Tower*' was an unfinished piece of the Richard Hannay canon which had only recently come to light. McPeevish's visit to Elsfield Manor, where Buchan had lived before moving to Canada, had uncovered in the library the handwritten draft which now resided in the National Library in Edinburgh. It was this work, sequentially following on from '*The Thirty-Nine Steps*', which McPeevish was reworking into the play in which the beloved took the role of the heroine Charlotte Hulme. The role of Hannay remained to be cast.

Not shy regarding publicity Dame Hilary had already alerted the press to the impending unique 'world first' production. The media, like hordes of midges, were descending on the town seeking to interview anyone remotely connected with the play. Road blocks of stray sheep along the main roads merely constricted rather than choked off the flow of newspaper and television people. Dame Hilary, of course, made herself permanently available to the media. She exhibited a new hair style for each appearance on television, no matter how brief. The hair driers in 'Carmen's Coiffeuse' Hair Salon were red hot and supplies of scissors and curling tongs had to be couriered in from Sheffield.

If McPeevish's profile had been any lower he would have been subterranean. He came to a mutually beneficial arrangement with Matty Dewspit, the local ne'er-do-well who played Santa Claus in the annual Christmas celebrations. Matty could turn his hand to anything, which often saw him resuming acquaintance with Sheriff Pomple at the local courthouse. All parties appreciated Matty's ability and willingness to pay the invariable and inevitable fine on the spot. McPeevish's instructions were quite simple: Matty was to make himself available to the press and media in his stead- in his raincoat and fedora as well. He advised a pipe and lots of foul smelling smoke for that authentic, authorial look. He provided several pocket-sized prompt cards on which he'd typed quotes from great playwrights of the past. The rest he left Matty to extemporise. Matty said he'd just make things up. McPeevish said that would do nicely as long as he offered no address (other than '*The Dirk*') and did not mention the dear one. Matty could keep whatever he charged for any likenesses taken of him (his left side profile being best). What profit it a man indeed, thought McPeevish.

McPeevish would gaze with simple pleasure at pictures of 'the author' taken standing beneath the Ram or in some corner of '*The Dirk*'. Matty had even sub-contracted out some of the deception. What pleased McPeevish most was that nobody blew the gaffe; and Dame Hilary was too busy to notice.

It's the simplicity and quietness of life in the countryside I like most, McPeevish thought as he watched another production team setting up their cameras in the town square. This one seemed to be from Swedish television. People can go about their business unhindered, he thought as he stumbled over another television cable. He watched as a passing dog sniffed at it while a pair of determined Great Spotted Woodpeckers went at it like a couple of navvies with road drills.

McPeevish felt he had by now learnt all the body swerves known to a Welsh fly half as he weaved his way through the mingle of microphones. I didn't realise how many types of microphones there were, McPeevish thought, dodging a small-diaphragm condenser, shotgun and Blimp covered Shure SM57. He watched from the butcher's shop with fascination as Matty once more explained how he had found the manuscript, a tale to equal anything Indiana Jones could come up with.

The man's a genius, McPeevish thought. He's absolutely right for the part of Hannay. Somehow he must dissuade Dame Hilary from manoeuvring her son, 'Dame' Jeremy, into the part.

- Here's your pork chops, Mister McPeevish, the butcher said.

It was a line he'd have to work into the script.

*

...Hannay was trapped, bound hand and foot with more rope than had held down Gulliver. He could see the stars through a hole in the sack. Down there in the dank hold of the trawler where he had been tossed amongst the smelt and smells, Hannay could hear the chugging of the engine as the boat made its way out to sea. He heard the guttural laughter of the leader of the gang, Count Blingdorf of Schnitzel- or was it Schnitzorf of Blingdel? Too late to worry about that, Hannay, you're for the long, cold bath unless you can wriggle your way out of this one...

No, thought McPeevish as he stroked Shayla; we'll never get a big enough tank of water on the stage.

All around him lay balls of scattered dialogue. Shayla had spent a fitful few minutes playing with the screwed up paper as McPeevish tossed it over his shoulder. She knew there were sprats in the offing and was indulging his whim until such time as he opened the fridge and liberated them. The things a cat had to do, she might have been thinking, McPeevish thought.

-There's a cup of tea down here for you, darling, the beloved called from below.

Abandoning Hannay seemed callous but McPeevish desperately needed the tea. Shayla, scenting sprats, took the stairs in the minimum required number of bounds and stood patiently awaiting McPeevish by the fridge door.

-What are we having for dinner, dear heart? the beloved asked him.

McPeevish stirred his tea distractedly.

- I'm not sure Shayla can manage that chop.

McPeevish glanced into the kitchen and realised exactly how Hannay could pull it off.

The beloved one sighed and watched as McPeevish hastened back upstairs.

*

It simply isn't true, McPeevish thought as he sat in a quiet corner of '*The Dirk*' playing dominoes, that the media lot are hard drinkers. Most of the time they seem to be keeled over in corners snoring.

Every spare room in the town was taken for a week before the play's opening. He would fall asleep listening to the beloved one reciting her lines as she lay beside him. His occasional unnecessary prompt drew either a nudge in the ribs or a giggle, depending on the scene.

She had been absolutely right about blackmailing Dame Hilary into giving Matty the part, he thought. McPeevish, a weak male with morals, had been all for the direct, honest approach. Your son, he would have said, lacks gravitas, has no voice projection, can't remember his name let alone the words of another, has as much expressiveness as a block of unseasoned wood, and will insist in making every other word 'yah'. Wet paper bags are perfectly safe is his company. The only part he can safely play is the role he is in now: that of the simpering, moronic scion of an overbearing and domineering bully of a mother. Such an approach, the dear one had suggested, was likely to rouse the protective mother instinct in the Dame, as well as lead to a possible lawsuit for defamation, slander, whatever.

The subtle, blackmailing approach, on the other hand, had worked a treat. Family secrets were no proof against the hair dryer, the dear one had maintained. A few visits to the various salons in the town had soon netted the dear one all the information she had needed and the next day the art sections of a dozen papers announced that "the author" would himself be playing Hannay opposite the ravishing et cetera. McPeevish longed to know what choice titbit had been the key to the Dame's personality change, but he knew that the secrecy and sanctity of the hair dryer outweighed that of the confessional.

He had finished the script after a monumental tussle with Shayla for the remaining chop. How the cat had opened the fridge McPeevish did not know. The secrets of the evolutionary process were beyond him. Perhaps Shayla had learnt to mimic. Apparently chimpanzees could now drive Toyotas and wore suits with the same panache as board room geezers.

It's not often, McPeevish thought, that I put two words with double-ees in one sentence. I must try this more often.

Matty, as McPeevish had hoped, was masterly. The town was going to have to find another Santa Claus this Christmas, McPeevish thought. Maybe Robert Carlyle or Ewan McGregor would be available; but they had nothing comparable to Matty's interpretive skill and range of expressions, well practised before the beak. Matty had charisma; he had the patter; he had that star quality which cried 'mint me'. Perhaps, McPeevish thought, he will think fondly of me as he lounges by his luxury swimming pool out in LA while I dream my dreams in M. As his star rises and mine wanes, perhaps I will be asked to give interviews to 'Hello', 'Maybe' and 'Good-bye' magazines about the day I discovered him.

Highly unlikely scenario, McPeevish; Matty's never been ten miles in any direction from his home town and would miss the sheep.

*

Tickets sold like hot cakes. In fact, '*Crumbles*' the baker sold tickets with their cakes. Enough tickets seemed to have been sold for the week of performances to fill the amphitheatres of Uthina, Pozzuoli, Jardin des Plantes and the great Flavian amphitheatre. Mister Dame Sir Benedict was all for forming a company- he'd be the chairman- whose remit – if there was a board, McPeevish had found, there was often a remit (which he assumed to be some kind of furry mascot)- would be to capitalise the capital that was being coined. The words 'non-profit making' were as foreign to Sir Benedict as '*Danke*', '*Hvala*' and '*Merci*'. They would make him frown and wave his hands around as though fending off wasps. McPeevish didn't mind the butcher, the baker and even the candle-sticker maker in Moffat making a bob or two out of the bonanza the play was bringing in; but he thought that Sir Benedict and his ilk (probably a non-furry animal, McPeevish thought) had more than enough money and should be kept out of things. One evening McPeevish innocently mentioned Sir Benedict's aspirations and the beloved one said she'd be taking tea with the Dame-ship the following morning. Sir Benedict seemed subsequently to develop a passion for non-profit making charitable trusts which was commendable in such a public minded citizen as he.

But McPeevish's nomination for a people's gong still went to the lollipop lady.

*

McPeevish felt at a loose end. There are those who believe that one end is as good as another. There are those who believe that no end is the absolute and utter end. There are those for whom the end, loose or otherwise, can't come quickly enough. Some skip through life without bothering about loose ends, be they in one's hair, the rigging or the plot. McPeevish quarried his mind for pithy sayings- Norwegian would do at a pinch- about 'loose ends'. He kept dredging up sayings about ties and artichokes, which left him unsatisfied if amused.

It was final dress rehearsal day and the beloved one had been gone since dawn. 'Gawn since dahn!' McPeevish moaned to Shayla, who was curled comfortably in the dear one's armchair.

How could a cat sleep through such withdrawal symptoms as he was experiencing, McPeevish wondered. Just when you needed companionship, comfort, a cuddle, you were deserted. No good hiding in the woodshed, McPeevish. Nobody will find you. You've done your job and now you're cast off like a burnt out candle or a holed Wellington boot. No good standing at the fridge door and rattling the handle: the sprats are all gone.

You're on your own, old chap. Left to your own devices.

McPeevish looked around for a few devices- the Hand of Fate, the Sword of Damocles, Talos and synchysis, stuff like that. He saw only the unstarted crossword puzzle, pen and empty tea cup. This was torture. Surtur, Rotwang or Count Fosco could not have devised anything more dastardly. String me up by chains on a wall, McPeevish pleaded; at least I'll serve some decorative purpose. Anything but this, this interminable waiting, this...

He ran to the door to catch the letter popped through the flap by the postman before it hit the mat. A bill: nothing from the beloved; no billet-doux, no scrawled line in invisible ink or code for him to come to rescue her.

How long had she been gone? McPeevish stared at the clock: half an hour. This was worse than the death by a thousand and one strokes of the feather; death by the tickling fingers of a thousand Thai virgins; death by a thousand purring Persian pussies...

McPeevish became aware of Shayla's stare.

He closed his eyes. Quite right, he thought emulating the cat. It's the only way, McPeevish: cat nap for two...

All around him birds were merrily singing and squirrels were gathering nuts and playing cards or dice. McPeevish had walked up the hill to clear his head and draw inspiration from nature as one might water from a burn.

He rested his elbows on the crossbar of the kissing gate and gazed out over the landscape. Beautiful, idyllic, empty.

Turning he gazed out over some more of the same landscape.

He was trapped.

Getting into the gate had been easy. So was it for a fly to enter a Venus Fly Trap, McPeevish thought. Getting out was a different matter. Reverse gear was no good; forward had its problems; the only way seemed to be up, since he didn't have a shovel.

McPeevish scrambled up and over. For a moment he wasn't sure if he'd exited on the correct side of the gate. All grass looked the same to him.

Short-term memory's gone, McPeevish, he told himself. McPeevish, who he?

Fortunately he forgot what he was thinking the instant he thought it. McPeevish strode briskly onward. It was a path he knew well from his evening walks with the beloved. She had pointed out the sheep marking the way and now he duly followed those he saw until he was thoroughly lost. He could feel the sheep smirking.

Back-up, McPeevish, he told himself. Either that or he wasn't alone. He looked sharply around: nobody in sight, so I'm talking to myself.

Reassured, McPeevish began to stride purposefully in what he hoped, lacking a compass or sense of direction, was the reverse direction. Relief swept through him when he saw a kissing gate. Of course, being an educated kind of fellow, McPeevish knew that kissing gates littered the hillside like turnstiles into every field; but this one looked familiar, mainly because he'd inadvertently left his jacket hooked to an overhanging branch as he'd climbed out of the trap.

With increasing confidence McPeevish headed down towards the town. He felt refreshed; he felt invigorated; but he was none the wiser as to how to resolve his creative dilemma. His short-term memory came to the rescue, however: he forgot all about it.

The beloved one found him in reflective mood when she finally returned from the dress rehearsal.

-Did you have a good time at the school, dearest? she called as she entered. Kirstie said the children loved your story.

Children are as keen judges of character as are cats or Borders sheep. McPeevish had felt himself being eyed carefully as he entered the classroom.

-Class, say good morning to Mister McPeevish, the teacher had instructed.

- Good morning Mister McPeevish, two dozen voices chorused as one.

McPeevish had said good morning mister McPeevish back and the class giggled. That was silly of me, wasn't it, he thought; or, rather, he found he had said, for the class giggled again.

- Mister McPeevish has come this morning to tell us one of his stories, the teacher said.

Ah, thought McPeevish; that clears that up.

Soon he had them entranced with his tale of 'The Ginger Gang', the bears and kittens who lived in a big house in the countryside. They had amazing adventures with the most ordinary of things- like spoons, string and bouncing balls. The Gang liked to sleep a lot, but that wasn't because they were lazy just that they liked to dream. When they dreamt they dreamt of being pirates or Reivers, not ballroom dancers or bankers. They had lots of friends just like the children in the class and had fun rearranging things in the dressing tables of the grown-ups with whom they lived. The kittens purred a lot and the bears growled gently. The grown-ups would wonder who'd made paw prints in the butter and who'd been at the milk in the fridge. They never guessed because 'The Ginger Gang' looked just like stuffed toys as they lay there on the baby's bed.

This is hard work, McPeevish had told himself as he fielded another question from a seven year old. These kids ought to be at Holyrood. How do bears and kittens live together? If you make the rules for them, who makes the rules for you? Where did the bears come from? (How to tell a child that Gregor was made of the dear one's old tights stuffed inside a knitted body, or that Elsa was found in a skip in the High Street?) They've got more understanding about tolerance and civic responsibilities than all the elected members: that lot parrot; these kids practice. And when they drew pictures of the Gang they'd never seen but had only heard about from him, McPeevish's heart was gladdened by the variety of images and wonderful nature of their pictures.

*

The first performance was packed.

Students from the local technical college as part of their scholarship project would be filming and recording the production. The national media were permitted to film the crowd outside and inside before and after but not during the performance. Interviews with audience members and the cast afterwards were permitted (though a fee might be charged). Two reporters from a tabloid newspaper were set adrift on a raft on the Annan when they were found trying to smuggle recording devices into the town hall that evening. The sniffer sheep were infallible and put the drug squad's dogs to shame. Their only fault, the sheep that is, was that they also sniffed out chocolate bars and would wolf those down before the handler could intervene. A brisk trade was being done at the confectionery stall inside the hall. McPeevish dismissed from his mind the idea of the sheep handlers receiving kick-backs.

Anyone who was anybody and a few somebodies who weren't anything in particular, had turned out for the opening night. There were those who always turned out for any opening night. There were those who hadn't been seen for so long in public that everyone else had thought they were dead, or had immigrated. There were those who had come to see what the fuss was about and those who wanted to be fussed about. There were bigwigs and little wigs and baldies. There were those who knew someone and those who didn't even know themselves.

The best seats were not necessarily the seats nearest the front of the stage. The seats nearest the front of the stage had only this in their favour: they were away from any draught coming through the doors at the back of the hall. The best seats were those which didn't collapse, and these had been imported from the Episcopal Church. If there was one thing the Episcopalians prided themselves on (not in the sinful sense, one understood, but in the sense that they made damned sure it worked) it was chairs, or seats, that did not collapse. They were mindful of the tendency nowadays of the offended in congregations to sue for the veriest trifle. The inferior seats (in the sense that they might collapse; but not in the sense that those who sat in them were inferior since we have all fallen short and are equal, if recumbent on our backsides, in the sight of the Lord); the inferior seats, McPeevish was aware, were Free Church of Scotland. This may have been because they put more trust in the unseen, the spiritual, than the seen, the material, in contrast to the Episcopalians, who much preferred a bird in the hand. Not that the Episcopalians were unspiritual: it's just that all the joiners in town happened to belong to that congregation. Other religious groups and atheists were also among the audience, but their attitude towards seats was not known to McPeevish. He would have canvassed opinions on this in other circumstances but found himself too nervous to do anything but grin inanely from the secluded corner he had located for himself at the back of the hall.

Here I am safe, he thought; here I can make a speedy exit should the need arise.

As the hall lights dimmed McPeevish clutched his heart.

This is it, he thought; my Maker calls. I've had a good innings, though a few more runs would have been nice. I repent the fact that I've not repented enough. I trust I am not found wanting: at least my underclothes are fresh on tonight.

The lights went out.

*

- What a simply superb idea to set the dénouement at a Burns Night Supper! And how Hannay defused that haggis was a stroke of genius. Was it one of 'Wallace Brothers' d'you think?

- It was so symbolic when Hannay said 'It was when I heard the butcher being asked for two pork chops that the answer came to me'. Until that moment I couldn't for the life of me see how he'd broken the code.

- The scene with the lake in the background as they took Hannay off to what looked like certain death- I mean, how did they get a water tank that size on the stage?

- That scene in the classroom with those spooky kids when he was on the run, that really made my hair stand on end. It reminded me of '*The Village of the Damned*'.

- When Charlotte wrestled with Frau Rampenlicht that was so realistic I thought Constable Alexander was going to jump up on the stage.

The gathering in '*The Dangling Dirk*' was by invitation only- cast and stage crew, partners and sponsors. All the interviews were over and the late licence had just kicked in. McPeevish found his niche by the bar and Jim saw to his requirements promptly. The beloved one eased her way through the congratulatory crowd to his side.

Hollywood next, McPeevish thought.

- A week of this will be *quite* enough for me, she said downing her gin with the kind of quick backhand flip which had seen her through to the Scottish Ladies Badminton Finals (Borders Section) for half a dozen straight years.

- That scene with Dame Hilary was *awfully* good, Jim said leaning forward with interest and mischief in his eyes. It got quite a cheer.

McPeevish had thought so as well. At the time he couldn't recall that bit of the script; but there had been so many late revisions it's probably just my faltering synapses, he thought.

- Yes, well, the dear one said with some heat. She was only meant to have a walk on part, like Hitchcock on the music hall stage at the end of '*The 39 Steps*'. But she was determined to hog the limelight for a few minutes and started improvising a monologue. I decided to heave her off.

-My Dad said he'd not seen a cross-buttock throw like that since the days of dear old G.E. Mitchell wrestling in Glasgow! Jim said as he moved to tend to other customers.

McPeevish had been about to say that he had, but caught *that* glance from the beloved and refrained from further comment.

- The backstage crew had to hold her down, the beloved added once she'd been refuelled. If she'd put foot on the stage again it would have been the full body-slam.

McPeevish inspected the optics behind the bar, a smile playing around his lips. '*Now clear the ring for hand to hand the manly wrestlers take their stand,*' he thought. No wonder Dame Hilary hadn't shown for the party.

-Now if I could just have your attention, the voice of Lady Gelding boomed.

All ears and eyes turned to her, like the Early Warning antennae on the moors above.

- We've had an absolutely splendid evening and all of the cast and crew are to be congratulated for their performance. But none of this would have been possible without the efforts of our scriptwriter. So please raise your glasses to the man who brought us bountiful Buchan and revived heroic Hannay!

McPeevish had the grace to blush as the dear one kissed him and the assembly burst into cheers.

Limbo

['Così andammo infinio alla lumera,
parlando cose che 'l tacere è bello,
sì com'era 'l parlar colà dov'era.'
Dante: Inferno Canto IV]*

The vacuum cleaner was fighting back.

McPeevish found himself being manoeuvred into a corner. Shayla had already seen the way things were going and had bolted into the garden.

I've done everything right, McPeevish thought desperately as his foot was seized and he struggled to avoid losing a shoe. The machine gave another bestial snarl and sucked up half the carpet. He was sure that ornaments used to be on that windowsill.

With a sudden wheeze the monster expired as the plug came out of the wall. McPeevish collapsed in his armchair surveying the wreckage that had once been the living room. A fifteen minute's invasion by a herd of stampeding wildebeest could not have wrought more havoc, he thought. Even the pictures on the wall hung awry, if they were hanging at all.

The next half hour, which should have been devoted to sipping tea, he grimly set about the chore of rebuilding the furniture, removing from the maw of the monster such items as had not been devoured, and then unzipping its belly to retrieve other bits and pieces. Vast clouds of dust escaped and McPeevish coughed and spluttered as he fought his way out into the fresh air.

Shayla watched him from the far end of the garden. The birds perched on the fence seemed like vultures on the walls of the Parsee's Tower of Silence in Bombay.

When it seemed safe McPeevish returned and, with brush and dust pan spent the next hour on his hands and knees as patiently as Howard Carter in Tutankhamen's tomb sifting debris until the colour of the carpet could once more be seen.

He spent the afternoon translating the vacuum cleaner's instructions from the original Croatian, too late discovering that there was an adjustable suction switch (*'podesive usisne prekidač'*). Nowadays, he thought, the instructions which came with a fork would make eating difficult. Were the benefits of universality outweighed by the difficulty inherent in reading poorly printed instruction manuals in every tongue but your natural one?

I am a better person, McPeevish thought, for this humiliation. I think that I have mastered the universe and then I am taught this lesson. One can become arrogant and too casual, thinking that you understand the switch when it really controls you. Zen was everywhere, if you looked in the right way.

At the moment, however, McPeevish thought, I am more interested in boiling the kettle and having a cup of tea.

He noticed that Shayla had followed him into the kitchen, ignoring the hastily concealed signs of the storm that had struck the living room. She sat patiently by the fridge, emanating thought waves until McPeevish was convinced that he had to open the fridge and replenish her bowl with handfuls of sprats.

That, he thought, was the epitome of Zen: get someone else to do it for you.

He reached for the phone and rang a number he found in the 'Yellow Pages'. A friendly voice said yes, they could come tomorrow and do the job. The throaty chuckle at the end made McPeevish suspect that they had been forewarned...

McPeevish consulted the book. Yes, he thought, that was definitely a weed. It had a weedy look about it. He wielded the trowel without mercy. One less weed, he thought.

As his eyes ranged over the flower bed he could see the ranks of weeds watching him carefully. They knew he had their number. Their only chance was to remain as still as possible and hope that he overlooked them. Another hope they had was that they were so numerous that they would overwhelm him. Some of them perhaps hoped that their prickly bits would dissuade him from touching them; but that's where the gloves come in.

When a McPeevish sets about any task, McPeevish thought, he comes prepared. This gardening business wasn't as simple as it looked. Things grew, all kinds of things, but the secret was to have only those you wanted to be growing where you wanted them to grow. Weeds had this habit of growing where they wanted to grow, and that was more often than not exactly where you didn't want them to grow.

This was a bit like the tiny hair which insisted on growing out of the middle of his nose, McPeevish thought.

He realised that he and hair had a difficult relationship. In his youth the hair on his head, which had been plentiful (the hair, not his head, which was singular), had had a mind of its own when it came to being parted. Rather like the Red Sea it had insisted on being parted in the middle, despite the fact that he would wield the comb deliberately to the left and part his hair there. He might turn away from the mirror with his hair so parted- on the left, that is- but the next time he caught sight of himself, for example in another mirror, his hair would be parted in the middle. Now McPeevish had nothing against hair which was parted in the middle, or on the right, as long as it wasn't his hair. His hair had to be parted on the left; but that's where he and his hair parted company: it insisted on being equidistance from either ear. Throughout his teens McPeevish had struggled with what a barber might call 'unruly hair syndrome'. There were those individuals who revelled in unruly hair, but McPeevish was not one of them. In his twenties he gave up the unequal struggle and acceded to his hair's stubborn mind. But hair is a funny thing, McPeevish decided; once you give it its own head- and the head in this instance was his- hair shows its contrary nature.

His decided that it wanted to move on to pastures new. For whatever reason hair had decided to take flight from certain parts of his body, mainly the top of his head where it was needed (and not just for ornamental purposes) and to set up camp on other parts of his body, for example the middle of his nose or the insides of his ears, where it was unwelcome and a hindrance rather than a help. The hair on the middle of his nose at first had timidly, but then with greater determination, appeared in his later life, which he was now living in a 'reduced hair state'. Of all the hairs on his head- and they were fewer and fewer each day, McPeevish recognised, disappearing so rapidly that he had no time to tell them good-bye- the one which seemed the most vigorous, the one which thrived while all else withered and vanished, was the one in the middle of his nose. There were times when he thought this must be the "Ur-hair".

I need a defoliant, McPeevish told himself each morning as he stared at his face. You rub hair restorer on your bonce and nothing grows there; but, like some weed with a mind of its own, this hair grows on your nose. It's like all those weeds: in the morning when you look at the garden there are dozens of the little buggers all nodding their heads and smiling. They wait until you're asleep and then over the wall they parachute. With all the space available on the hill sides and river banks why do weeds seem so set on taking root in your garden? McPeevish thought.

The Reverend Cleikum had a clear line on weeds, McPeevish was heartened to note. They might spring up, as the tares did among the wheat, but they should be rooted out. We're agreed on that, McPeevish thought; but the 'how' was the problem, be it physical or spiritual.

Maybe it is time for me to brush up on the Desert Fathers, McPeevish thought. If knowledge was transferable then maybe they could give me a few tips that would be helpful both in the garden and with regard to the hair on the nose.

Doubtlessly there was a Zen answer to this dilemma, a chant he might use; but what he really wanted was a good weed-killer.

Maybe if I put weed-killer on my nose? No, McPeevish, he told himself; your nose is a precious and delicate piece of equipment, useful for picking up scents should you ever be on the trail of something like an escaped Danish Blue cheese. The nose would not take kindly to being doused with some acidic compound designed to wither the roots of a dandelion.

Maybe if I keep the sun off it and wear some kind of cover over the nose, à la Lee Marvin in '*Cat Ballou*', McPeevish thought. Maybe that will persuade it to take its business elsewhere.

But then he thought of mushrooms thriving under cover and feared that the solitary hair might be joined by others under the sunshade such as he envisaged.

No, McPeevish told himself- it being his nose and there being nobody else in the room with him except Shayla; and she was decidedly more interested in the sprats than the hair on his nose- no, I have to resign myself to the thankless daily task of shaving the hair in the sure knowledge that it will spring up again like a daisy on the lawn.

*

Choice was a bewildering thing, McPeevish thought as he surveyed the shelves laden with tins of beans.

He considered his list. Beans were definitely on it, but which kind was left for him to choose. The field of choice might be narrowed somewhat by the fact that it was baked beans that he was after but this didn't solve the problem. There were several varieties, each in different liveried tins, each priced attractively.

He was not a connoisseur of beans, McPeevish admitted silently. Presented with several dishes of different makes of baked beans, blindfolded and permitted to sample them all, McPeevish knew he would flunk any question then asked, be it 'Which was the tastiest?' or 'Which was this brand and which was that brand?'

The Reverend Cleikum could wax lyrical about the vast variety of life and how it reflected the bounteousness of the Lord; but this was of no use to McPeevish as his eyes ranged over the stacks of beans. He could agree that there was a bounteous selection of beans on display- or, rather, beans in tins, for one had to trust that the contents were indeed baked beans and not dandelions or some other weed.

I am actually choosing tins, McPeevish thought.

The dilemma of choice was made more complicated by this realisation, for which he could thank Wittgenstein, if not his maiden aunt who had encouraged him to be precise in all things. For example, she had exhorted him never to marry a Norwegian, though she had never said why he should not. Perhaps, he thought (whenever he thought about his aunt), she had had some unfortunate experience with a Norwegian sailor and had developed a prejudice. Or perhaps, being a school mistress, she was merely using this as a pedagogic example, rather than intending it as a grim warning about the Nordic character.

I have not come here, McPeevish thought, to choose tins but to choose beans. Had I wanted tins I would have made such an entry on my shopping list.

He looked around himself in dismay. There was nothing for it: he grabbed the nearest tin and dumped it unceremoniously in his cart.

- Excuse me sir, the young lady said; we're carrying out a survey on consumer choice and I wonder if I might ask you a few questions? It will only take a few moments of your time and you'll receive this voucher for money off several items.

McPeevish always had time for attractive young women who were devoting their lives to scientific research. Why had he chosen this brand of beans? How did he decide what was 'value for money' when each item cost the same? Was he swayed by brand preference? Did he suffer from brand fatigue? Could he calculate how much each bean had cost in terms of human effort? If the beans weren't in a tin would he be able to recognise them? What was his attitude to mixed beans? Did he have anything against naked beans? Should beans be in tins or vacuum-packed bags? Was he shopping just for himself or a group? How many dependants did he have? What kind of cat was it?

- Thank you for your time, sir.

McPeevish moved briskly down another aisle, feeling satisfied that his contribution would help inform whatever the research was in aid of.

He spent several minutes trying to find something on the voucher which he might need. Not a word about beans anywhere, he noticed. What did they know that he didn't? He looked at the tin in his cart suspiciously. He moved decisively back to the array of beans and swapped the tin for another brand.

That's better, McPeevish thought. Choice with regard to eternal matters, as the Reverend Cleikum would say, might be forever; but choice when it came to beans was mutable.

*

- They're at it again. I see, Jim the barman said.

McPeevish, who had been admiring the way Jim was cleaning the glasses, couldn't have agreed more. As beavers in the wild felt compelled to gnaw trees and build dams, so the council was compelled to dig holes in the road.

What McPeevish admired most about the way Jim was cleaning the glasses was the casual, practiced manner that he twisted each glass in the tea towel. Two twists seemed to do the trick, McPeevish saw. Many might have been tempted to twist and twist, wasting energy and leaving the glass no cleaner than it had been after two twists.

McPeevish, passing on from the way one might clean glasses with the minimum of energy, realised that he had never refined any theory about roads, let alone holes in roads. It was not that he was unaware of what a road was and what it was for. In his comings and goings he had trod many a road, not always the same road but a road nevertheless. All roads might well lead to Rome but those he had ventured to set foot on didn't. Often they would lead nowhere in particular. Not that they might be so signposted; though on his few excursions into the Principality of Cymru he had to admit that some of the signposts might well have read 'Unman-yn-Arbennig'.

He contemplated the malt in his glass, estimating its depth and wondering what it would be like to swim in it. The beauty of malt, he thought, was that no matter how much or how little there was left in the glass- any glass- it always had the same reassuring glow and warming taste. It always promised. It always put everything else in life into perspective. Malt in the bottle, then malt in the glass and malt down the old gullet equals outlook on life better and more charitable, McPeevish subsumed for himself. Wisdom, he found, should this indeed be wisdom, needed to be subsumed. Malt consumed: wisdom subsumed. Either way round might well do, of course, though the malt must perforce be in the glass.

McPeevish decided- by what exact mechanism he could not be sure but he was sure that he had decided- that it was time he came down from the fence and took a clear stand on roads. I am for them, he thought. Without roads Crosby and Hope would have been lost, Judy Garland would never have reached Emerald City and Kerouac would have stayed at home. Without roads the Romans would have had to find other ways of conquering the known world. Straight lines might even not have been invented! What use was the roundabout without roads?

The Minister for Irrelevancy being interviewed on the news programme had just said "infrastructure" for the fourth timeMcPeevish glanced at Jim, who nodded and refilled the glass. In some establishments McPeevish had visited during his journeys testing the roads and comparing the heights of bars or styles of beer mats used, he had noticed a servile attitude towards Weights and Measures legislation. McPeevish was not against weighing or measuring per se, or in any Shire or county. He had nothing particularly against the London Quart, or the Hedon, the hogshead or the Maund. He did not object to small thimble containers- be they of silver alloy or baser metal- by which liquids might be measured. They might be called Gill or Gail for all he cared. But he admired the free spirit of '*The Dirk*', the skill exhibited by Jim's wrist and eye and sense of fair play as, without the aid of arbitrary measuring implements, he hosed the malt into the glass. Malt should be poured freely, McPeevish felt, rather than dribbled into an intermediary before arriving in his glass. The quantity was also more pleasing to the palate and wallet.

- What's the record? Jim asked meditatively.

McPeevish gave this the consideration it deserved as he eyed the almost overflowing glass and kept one of his two ears tuned to the far from melodious tones being emitted by the television. The Minister of Fuzzy-things, he recalled, had hit nine during an interview with Jeremy Paxton. However, the Minister of Inconsequentialities had certainly hit twelve during '*Any Questions*' with David Dimbleby rather off form that evening. There was- and the caveat must be raised- general agreement in '*The Dirk*' that wintry evening that two had been mere slips of the tongue occasioned by a sudden bout of hiccoughing as a member of the audience heckled.

- Good lady back tomorrow, isn't she? Jim asked.

It hasn't taken him long, McPeevish thought, to get to the nub of the matter! Four malts and he has arrived without any outside guidance or help at the very fact which has occasioned my presence in his establishment this evening.

A week wasn't that long a time, McPeevish reassured himself as he re-counted the optics and bottles on the shelves. Their number remained the same as it had been ten minutes ago; when it had been identical with what it had been when he had previously computed the total ten minutes before that; and before that. You can depend on bottles and glasses not to absent themselves from shelves unless there's a very good reason, McPeevish thought. I had washed my own socks for forty years or more- not the same socks, of course, he corrected himself since his hosiery wore out just like the next man's; though this evening there was no 'next man' since McPeevish was alone in the bar with Jim (who was likewise alone with McPeevish, by an odd quirk of circumstance) - I had washed my own socks before my destiny became entwined with the beloved's. Now our linge and other items of apparel flirt and tumble in the washing machine like lambs gambolling in the springtime.

That's a lot of socks, McPeevish thought as he tried to calculate how many he might have worn and washed over the past forty years. By and large they were of the navy blue variety, or brown; but never striped or polka dotted. A sock, in his opinion, should be a solid colour. His feet and shoes would reject anything else.

-..."regenerating the infrastructure...," the Minister of Pointless Repetitions said without so much as blinking.

Jim shrugged helplessly, uncorked and refilled McPeevish's glass.

It's like taking sweets from a child, McPeevish thought. Fortunately they had agreed a limit of half a dozen.

A slow night in 'The Dirk' was as rare as a perm on a sheep, McPeevish thought. The unexpected holes in the road outside had caught out several regulars over the last few days. If you're not expecting holes you don't see holes, McPeevish concluded. Wittgenstein might have put it more elegantly, perhaps even colourfully and possibly in German, but McPeevish had no doubt that dear old Ludwig would have agreed. The council, to meet their legal obligations and avoid costly lawsuits for negligence, might have put up safety barriers around the newly dug holes; but barriers had never stopped anyone who frequented 'The Dirk' from heading by the shortest and most familiar route to its welcoming doors. This directness of approach which typified the 'Dirkers' was, in this particular instance, the downfall of several. The statistics for the town in terms of broken or sprained ankles quadrupled overnight and the local NHS Trust bureaucrats were unable to explain, despite their slide rules and handbooks on quantum theory, why this should be so. Like many another unexplained occurrence in statistics, this was regarded as a 'rogue' one. What was incontrovertible, McPeevish knew, was that the darts and domino teams had been decimated, handing walk-over victories to the 'Strumpet and Sackbut' of Hawick and the 'The Baillie of Bafuff' of Jedburgh. Black crêpe had been spread over the pool table in the back room. It had been bad enough when smoking had been banned; but without the cheery clicking of balls- a noise like that made by the Ju'hoansi San people of the South African veldt, or crickets courting in the corn- many of the regulars who had made it through the landmines and barbed wire were disorientated and their thirsts much reduced for several days. Those regulars who got through, such as McPeevish, felt like survivors of convoys that had dodged the U-boats.

The heavy weather hadn't helped trade either, it had to be said. Since it had to be said Jim had said it. For the best part of a week it had been raining, thus increasing the statistical count of cats and dogs wandering the streets should an animal census have been taken. The rivers had risen, being in sympathy with the rain, and banks had been burst. McPeevish wondered if a burst bank could be counted as a bust bank and whether the local river bank qualified for a government bail out or subsidy.

Roads, tricky enough at the best of times, McPeevish felt, especially since few in the town wanted to go to Rome, roads had been flooded; which made the holes in the road more difficult to see. A flooded hole is still a hole; and such holes, courtesy of Archimedes's principle, still have space for the human body. It was not unusual, therefore, during this period of inclement weather, to see the odd denizen of '*The Dirk*' bobbing about in the road, confused by their sudden fall from grace. Various methods were devised to extract those unfortunate enough to fall into a flooded hole. These ranged from the simple shepherd's crook to the improvised life-belt. Roadside bollards were soon discarded as unhelpful in this capacity. Several volunteers used a standard foot pump to try to drain the flooded holes; but as the water kept falling from the sky in quantities far superior to those which were being pumped out (and which extracted water naturally flowed straight back in again, the street being flooded and there being no capacity within the drains to absorb it), the foot-pump (or stirrup pump) was likewise discarded as a means of assistance to those fallen in the flooded holes. But the townsfolk of Moffat are ever inventive and soon a fleet of gondolas, left over from a Gilbert and Sullivan opera, were plying their trade up and down the High Street, rescuing those in peril for a small fee.

Finally the council had conceded that the holes they had dug were surplus to requirements and hadn't 'enhanced the infrastructure' of the town. It was also the case McPeevish knew from his Lordship that the environmental agency had misread tea stains on a planning map and had dug holes where none were intended. The monsoons had stopped; the lagoons were gone; the gondolas returned to the shed behind the town hall.

If the heavy weather was a hindrance- and it could be put stronger than that- then spirits had been even more dampened by the delivery drivers' strike at every large brewery in the country. It struck McPeevish that people were striking in the same way that some suffered from Tourette's syndrome. The delivery drivers' strike had been settled by the simple expedient of giving them more money in return for guaranteed 'efficiency savings'. 'Efficiency savings' McPeevish knew was in the same litany as 'infrastructure'.

He studied himself, his reflection, in the mirror behind the bar. The skin-coloured Band-Aid on his nose was barely visible in this light. He would soak it off tomorrow morning and hope that the slight scar would have healed. His hair was rather bedraggled but this was a look that couldn't be cultivated and film stars spent fortunes on trying to copy. The cravat at his throat was settled in such a way as to suggest casual but classy. His eyebrows remained steady and there was a sparkle in his eyes.

-...."modernising the infrastructure", the Minister for Insomnia intoned with the solemnity of a church bell falling from its tower.

- Game, set and match, McPeevish, Jim conceded with a smile as he uncorked the bottle and passed it across the bar.

McPeevish poured, but graciously erred on the side of caution. Another wayfarer might pass this way, he thought as he handed the bottle back to Jim, and be in need of this elixir. As he sipped his reward he felt that warming glow familiar to any prophet who was sinking his sixth fine malt without having had to part with a shekel. If only it were this simple at the Kelso races, McPeevish thought as he shifted his weight on the barstool.

Captain Stinkle and his daughter Virtue of the 'Salvation Army' came in with the 'War Cry', which ranked with Garner Ted's 'The World Tomorrow' as McPeevish's favourite reading when in a liquid reflective mood. McPeevish had a soft spot for the Captain. He had helped many a fallen 'Dirker' negotiate his way home of a night. Many of the regulars in the 'Dirk' had a soft spot for the Captain's daughter. If anyone could convert the fallen she could. Lachie said her eyes reminded him of the sheep when they were pining for the ram.

The Reverend Cleikum in the pulpit was a different kettle of fish, McPeevish thought. He looked down upon his flock with as kindly an eye as Lachie must do to his in the hills. The Reverend's job was to get his flock on the train and to keep them there as they chugged and chuffed their way to the terminus. People always wanted to jump off at the wrong spot. There were some preachers, McPeevish knew, who spouted fire and brimstone and waxed lyrical about the fate backsliders would receive when the train reached the next station- if the Inspector even let you get on, that is. That was not the Reverend Cleikum's way. He would enthral you with the scenery along the route and the goodies to be found in the dining car. This train was no British Rail chugger but a first class express, this train...

- All ready for her return tomorrow then, are you McPeevish? Jim asked.

McPeevish allowed that he was. The cupboards were stocked with the requisite tins and packets. The house was neat and tidy. All signs of the wildebeest invasion had been erased by Gleitham's house-cleaning service. Whatever weeds might be foolish enough to spring up overnight would be ruthlessly dealt with in the morning before the dear one's arrival. The table had been booked at 'Itham's' for eight, which would give them just enough time to reacquaint themselves with each other before driving over.

The telephone behind the bar rang and Jim answered it. McPeevish noticed the way he turned his back and lowered his voice as he spoke into the receiver. Then Jim turned and held the receiver out to him.

-It's for you, Jim grinned.

Ah! McPeevish thought as he took the instrument.

- I thought I'd ring there first, dear heart, the dear one said. Jim was just telling me about the floods.

He wondered whether she meant the rainfall or the malt.

Yes, McPeevish said, he had been eating sensibly. Just the one smoked sausage supper...

Jim had said it was three, had he? He's probably right, McPeevish acknowledged; you know how I am with figures.

Yes, Shayla is being fed...

Best not mention it's salmon, McPeevish thought...

Of course it's not salmon, dear heart, he said with a gay laugh that would have been taken for hysteria in an early Hitchcock thriller.

How could he be so easily dominated by a cat? McPeevish asked himself. He could remember the very first time he had been introduced to Shayla. It had been more like an audience being granted and he was the grantee rather than the granter. Shayla had conveyed in the minimum of glances and blinks- this was before McPeevish had been allowed to be on petting terms, for which his reward would be purrs, though the exchange rate seemed to be unbalanced, he thought- that though McPeevish may have the key to the beloved's heart and limitless egress to her boudoir, there was only one boss in the place and it sure wasn't him. There was, as is the case with cats, no discussion and no negotiation. The terms were simple: surrender the contents of the fridge as and when required and you may occasionally be permitted to stroke my fur.

Sprats and salmon, furtively supplied, had slightly weakened Shayla's stance, but their supply had to be guaranteed before her heart could be won. It had been easier going with the dear one, McPeevish thought: a glance, a shared malt, a few words and laughter and he was putty in her hands. Well, perhaps not all that different then, McPeevish conceded, discounting the malt.

How was the writing going?

McPeevish felt Jim's amused eye upon him from the far end of the bar, to which he had withdrawn to allow McPeevish some privacy. I don't know what for, McPeevish thought; he's already spilled the beans and is just watching me squirm. Maybe I should have poured more from the bottle.

Well, yes, McPeevish told her, you know how it is when you hit a dry patch.

- Some dry patch, the beloved laughed.

Yes, she said, her friend Galietta was recovering nicely from the broken leg. That would teach her to go skateboarding at her age; fifty-five was no age to take up sports like that. Yes she was missing him and was looking forward to returning tomorrow and trying that new restaurant near Beattock.

McPeevish held out the receiver to Jim as the call ended.

- All well in the Highlands? Jim asked innocently.

McPeevish nodded and eyed his glass. He weighed up Jim's inscrutable expression. What instructions had he been given? McPeevish wondered. Was one for the road too much to ask?

There must have been something heart-wrenching in the look I gave him, McPeevish thought, as he watched Jim top up the glass. But there was no mistaking the finality with which Jim placed the bottle back amongst its fellows. The road it would have to be after this.

It is not easy, McPeevish thought, tracking down every corpse scattered throughout the house.

Shayla was sitting in the beloved's chair watching with what McPeevish thought was some amusement as he located another mauled mouse body beneath the dining table.

It was one thing to perform your duties as a cat punctiliously and thoroughly, McPeevish thought; but it was quite another to treat the disposal of the corpses as a gruesome game of hide-and-seek. Since his return from 'The Dirk' he had located four of the half dozen he knew Shayla would have left scattered around the house. As soon as the beloved one had driven away that Saturday morning Shayla had started the game. He could acknowledge that she played fair: none were buried under cushions or hidden behind skirting boards. But when I am in a rather mellow state, McPeevish thought; and the need to think at all is hard, searching a large house like this- he swore that while he had been gone several extra rooms had been grafted on- is the last thing I need.

Once the game was finished Shayla would present herself at the fridge door and wait to be rewarded. If he expected her to catch the mice, she seemed to be saying, then he'd best be prepared to unlock the fridge. It went without saying that she would sleep on the beloved's side of the bed.

McPeevish strongly suspected that as much as Jim had been left his instructions by the dear one so had Shayla.

*

Before the beloved one and McPeevish drove to the restaurant they strolled around the garden, enjoying the mildness of the early evening. Shayla sat patiently under the bird bath looking upwards.

- I see you've cleared away the *Floribus Pulcherrima* I planted, sweetness, the dear one said. Did you put it somewhere else?

Ah...a slight touch of Vavilovian mimicry perhaps, McPeevish thought

He suggested that they move smartly towards the car as they didn't want to be late.

Wedding Fever

It was a big decision, McPeevish knew; but he had to be man enough to make it. Some men delegated such decisions; some fudged them; others simply did not see them even as the car rushed over the cliff. McPeevish knew he was not that kind of man.

He set his face to determined and stared into the mirror with a look the man behind him could tell was made of steel or some other body centred cubic crystalline structured metal.

- Take the beard off.

The words were as clipped as McPeevish's hair.

-Off? Dougal the barber asked, it being his custom to always check with the customer whenever anything outlandish, such as a Mohican cut or tonsure, was requested.

-Off.

McPeevish felt no shudder of remorse or regret as he repeated that decisive word. He sat back in the Koken chair that was all well-worn leather and firmness and bared his throat to the world. There could be no turning back: the Rubicon was a distant sight.

-Lather up, Dougal and be done with it, he said as the face behind him nodded that he understood.

There are times in a man's life- his spiritual life as well as his material- McPeevish thought meditatively as he heard the gurgle and stirring noises off left, when the road forks, the path emerges from the woods, and the mist lifts and all is clear. As he gazed into the mirror, which was now becoming as steamed up as the main window of the barber shop, McPeevish sensed- nay, he *knew*- that this was a moment when it all changed. His life flashed in front of him- that is it spooled rapidly through his interior viewing room- and he tried to think of a comparable act, some similar rite of passage which had left its mark on him. He blushed and hastily suppressed that memory for later scrutiny, the barber shop being hardly the proper place for so intimate a matter.

Whatever you do now, McPeevish, he told himself, don't shake your head: the blade was at his throat after the lather had been daubed on his face. He could see Dougal hesitating, catching his eye through the steamed mirror.

-Mwuff, McPeevish confirmed as lather filled his mouth.

Dougal worked with the delicacy and skill of a master of the art. He moved around the elevated and tilted chair like Modigliani in his studio or Nureyev at the Bolshoi. From his lips sprang some operatic air which McPeevish, to divert himself as he sat there, tried to identify. Dougal loved the opera and his family were originally from Pisa- hence the angle of the striped pole outside his shop. On the wall was a sign proclaiming that any customer who could successfully identify the aria he was humming would receive a fifty percent discount. Many had tried, McPeevish knew, but none had succeeded. Opera buffs were few and far between in Moffat and if it wasn't from '*Lucia di Lammermoor*' then most customers were stumped. The '*Largo al factotum*' from '*Il Barbiere di Siviglia*' was too obvious as was Cornelius's '*Bin Akademiker*' from '*Der Barbier von Bagdad*'. Many had fallen into that trap. As the razor was stropped and then slid through the foam McPeevish also discounted '*Come un bel dì di maggio*' from '*Andrea Chénier*' by Umberto Giordano and '*Mamma, quel vino è generoso*' from '*Cavalleria Rusticana*' by Pietro Mascagni.

Dougal, razor raised, stood back and surveyed his handiwork; and plunged in afresh.

Then came the hot towel and the cooling unguent lotions.

As McPeevish crossed to the till where Dougal stood ready to ring up the price, he offered his opinion: '*Fantaisie aux divins mensonges*' from '*Lakimé*' by Leo Delibes. Dougal beamed with delight, bowed and rang up half price. McPeevish tipped lavishly.

A new man, cheeks agleam, strode out into the High Street. People wondered who *Uomo senza nome* was and gave him not a second thought. Cats arched their backs and slunk away; dogs didn't bark; vultures overhead turned tail and fled. McPeevish squinted and looked around for an undertaker.

He was meeting the beloved at noon in 'The Lime Tree'. The 'Ariete' was temporarily closed for re-decoration. She was spending the morning in leotards at her yoga class, wrenching her ankles around her ears. Personally, McPeevish could see the sense of putting his hands in his pockets but not his feet around his neck. The one occasion on which he had tried yoga- this was in the years before he had met the dear one- McPeevish had had to be prised open by a couple of instructors when bits that weren't meant to know each other became entangled with bits that really shouldn't be tampered with. The class had been adjourned for what was politely called 'a laughter break'. McPeevish regarded the ten pounds fee as money well spent on a useful lesson. Since that day his legs had never strayed anywhere above the waistline.

McPeevish saw the beloved seated at a table in the middle of the room and he sat down opposite her. She gazed at him blankly. Then, to his horror, she jumped up.

-McPeevish, dear heart! she cried out and rushed up to a complete, bearded stranger just coming through the door. She flung her arms around him as McPeevish watched his mouth agape and eyes some distance outside their sockets.

A light flashed. Laughter engulfed the room.

-Oh McPeevish, the dear one said as she returned to the table. You should have seen your face!

She turned to the waitresses lined up behind the serving counter.

-What do you think, ladies? she asked.

In turn they each held up a menu on which was written- 5.5, 5, 6, 4.5 and 3.

- Not very good marks, my dear, the dear one smiled.

She patted his hand sympathetically and called over his shoulder.

- Thanks, Charlie.

The man with the beard- a false beard, McPeevish now noticed- waved and left the tea-room.

-The cakes are on me, my love.

As he stirred his tea McPeevish wondered about the flash.

-Digital camera, the dear one said. The photo's half way round the town as we speak. But don't look so despondent; it's all in a good cause.

Indeed it was, McPeevish knew. I'm man enough to survive this humiliation, he told himself. Today was the official "Beardless" day in Moffat. The local 'Co-operative' bank was donating ten pounds for every bearded male who shaved his beard off that day. The students of the Academy were out and about in the streets with their cameras and buckets for cash donations, encouraging the bearded to be shaved. The proceeds were to go to the local children's centre. Should there be not a beard to be found in the town centre by six o'clock that evening the bank would add another five hundred pounds to whatever was collected. Business was booming for Dougal.

*

McPeevish studied his face in the mirror. To shave or not to shave, that was the question. Twenty four hours had passed since his ritual offering and now on his cheeks there was a slight stubble as on a freshly mown barley field. For twenty years or more no blade, whether Gillette or Wilkinson, had touched his skin until that Thiers- Issard Olivewood handle straight razor wielded with finesse by Dougal. He could get away without shaving for another day, given the lightness of the stubble, but thereafter he either shaved or accepted the re-growth of his beard.

He considered the matter. Unlike Samson he had suffered no sudden loss of strength. It was true that there had been a sudden revival in his 'Jules Perceval' persona and that yesterday afternoon, once they had returned from the tea-room, McPeevish had for the first time in over a year poured out the beginnings of a story of romance, intrigue and unquenched passion in the 'Chick-noir' series that had brought him considerable financial rewards. When, exhausted by that creative burst, he had stumbled back down to the dear one in the living-room, she had straightaway seen how matters stood and whisked him away to bed.

He felt refreshed and restored and made his decision.

- I'm so glad you're growing the beard again, dear, the beloved said as she poured their coffee. It would be terrible to have to be throwing myself at strangers all the time.

He could see the devilment in her eyes. If only she knew what alter ego Jules was going to get up to she would have run the lawnmower over his face. Not that McPeevish knew what Jules was going to write this morning. That was how it was with him when in the creative grip of Jules; he was like some spiritual medium responding to prompts which came from he knew not where. Perhaps at such times he was flushing his subconscious. Was there such a thing as oneiric irrigation?

His publisher would be pleased. They had been harassing him for months for a follow-up to Jules's last block-buster '*The Virgin and the Fallen Tower*'. Petitions by readers had been forwarded to him. Fans suffering from withdrawal symptoms had appeared on the 'Richard and Judy' television show pleading for more. He felt like a Frankenstein who had created a monster. 'The Ginger Gang' for children, written under his other pseudonym, had sold by the truck load to young parents; but it wasn't what those other fans wanted.

*

People stood on corners and talked. In the cafés and bars they chewed it over. Wherever you looked there were posters. The '*Moffat Messenger's*' readers' letters page struggled to cope with the collective outpouring of views and opinions. The two hot topics of conversation were the forthcoming wedding of Lord Gelding to Miss Loople and the local council elections.

Small sub-groups, it is true, continued to discuss the going at Kelso and the chances of the local rugby team scoring a try, let alone fielding a fully sober team. Here and there you might find a sub-sub-group who worried about the floral display in the grounds of Cantilever House, or how much curtains might swish before you had to call it swash. Petitions were still raised about the need to educate citizens in the proper use of pelican and zebra crossings- was it a cardinal sin to step on the black stripes or the white? Miss Potter (Maude) was still to be found handing out white feathers to handsome young men and urging them to volunteer. If you had any sense you took the feather and hurried away. Those who tried to reason with her received a severe beating from her umbrella which, remarkably, remained undented after fifty years of vigorous service. It was only when her twin maiden sister Miss Potter (Mildred) appeared to take her back indoors that calm could be restored to the High Street. Fortunately it was not every day that Miss Potter (Maude) managed to slip out of the house; it was only when the knitting wool ran out and her needles fell silent that the urge came upon her. 'Moffat Millinery Supplies' continued to try to find ways to meet the demand and supply of a hand-combed, hand-drawn, hand-twisted and hand-spun type of Moffat bred sheep's' wool that had long fallen out of general use.

McPeevish would listen intently to the ebb and flow of discussion and debate as he went about his daily shopping chores. He had elevated the act of standing in a queue to a high art form. His lively eye would be caught by posters advertising the various council candidates. He especially liked the variety of moustaches drawn on their faces. These ranged from the Pencil, through the Toothbrush to the Walrus. Whoever the anonymous person was who snuck around in the dead of night to make such additions, McPeevish felt he or she showed the promise of a Dali. There were few artists, he thought, who twirled the moustache with such vivacity as Salvador. It might seem easy to scrawl such an appendage to a face, but these moustaches all varied. They had all been chosen with care, McPeevish thought, so as to bring out and highlight some feature in the candidate's platform. Here there was a Zapata, there a Stalin or a Hitler and another à la Souvarov. As quickly as the defaced posters were removed and a fresh one stuck up so too did another moustache appear overnight. Special anti-graffiti patrols by Constables Dripstone and Glendale were authorised and torches supplied, all to no avail. The Chief Constable suspected that many of the general public were aiding and abetting the vandal, and in this he was not far wrong. To the townsfolk it was a matter of joy to encounter a new moustache each morning. Local art historian Sir Jasper Nonesuch was of the opinion that the streets where the defaced posters were displayed should be designated as mobile open air galleries and taxed accordingly. The following day a second moustache appeared on his face in the poster advertising his evening address to the local history society.

To McPeevish, who preferred simplicity in all things, there seemed to be as many candidates as there were sheep on the hills. As well as the usual suspects (après Ronald Colman: '*Casablanca*') - the Scottish Conservative and Unionist Party; the Scottish Labour Party; the Scottish Liberal Democrat Party; the Scottish National Party; and the Scottish Independent Party- there were the more exotic candidates from the Scottish Sheep Party; the Scottish Greens Party; the Scottish Scottish Party; the Scottish Haggis Party; the Scottish Potty Party; the Scottish 'Let's-Have-a-Party' Party; the Scottish Free-Porridge-for All-Party (revised); the Scottish 'We're-All-Doomed' Party; the Scottish 'Say-No-to-Yes' Party.

He was looking forward to Friday night when the public debate in the Town Hall promised to revive the lapsed tradition of local wrestling bouts. The compère for the evening- McPeevish thought that 'referee' was a more accurate term as he read the poster (moustache-less for the moment)- was a well-known political commentator from the capital, one Brian Leash. McPeevish wondered what kind of moustache would grow overnight on his face. Perhaps a scimitar; definitely not a Poirot.

*

The dear one was much caught up in bridal wear these days, McPeevish thought as he gazed out into the garden.

He focussed his Swarovski binoculars on the bird feeder. Several species of bird sat there watching him, though none was using binoculars. I shan't go out just now, he thought; there may be a shortage of worms.

Yes, bridal wear magazines littered the low table by the beloved's armchair. When they had first begun to appear McPeevish had to confess that his heart had given a slight flip, as had his stomach and various other unspecified internal organs. He had tiptoed around the house for days, hoping that he'd be mistaken for a paranormal occurrence, until the dear one had mentioned that Miss Loople had asked her advice on trousseau. McPeevish had wondered what a dead Canadian politician had to do with anything until the beloved had shown him a sampling of wedding dresses. The one thing you could say about McPeevish, apart from the fact that his hearing was poor and he was absent minded and his grip was going and he sometimes left the light on in the loo; the one thing you could say for certain about him, he thought, was that he was quick on the uptake when there was any slack to be taken up. It wasn't that he thought, he thought, that he was "off the hook"; for he knew that the beloved did not see the necessity of having him on a hook. If she could tickle fish from the Tweed then there was no doubt...

But this question of bridal wear, McPeevish thought. It was an entire new world to him. He was like Samuel de Champlain standing on the shores of Lake Ontario and contemplating the unseen vastness of Canada. Not that bridal wear would have been a problem to Champlain, McPeevish thought. They did things differently then. Buckskin was more à la mode, he thought.

From what McPeevish understood- and he had to admit that he had been listening with only one ear and that his impaired one- Lady Gelding had offered Miss Loople her trousseau. This had only been used once, as any decent trousseau should be, and had been carefully preserved in some chest in Gearran Manor house since that distant day when the soon-to-be Lady Gelding (originally the Honourable Philippa Capall) had galloped happily up the aisle of Saint John the Evangelist's church in Moffat. Those present- the Reverend Cleikum wasn't then the incumbent but had heard the story- still remembered the difficulty the vergers had in removing the horse, which had become inordinately fond of the soon-to-be Lady Gelding. The roses of many in the congregation benefited from the droppings shovelled up in haste before the newly wed couple came back down the aisle in more seemly fashion.

It was this same horse- sixteen hands high- which had been the cause of Lord Gelding's sad demise the very day after the consummation of their union- that is of Lord and Lady Gelding's union. His lordship (so the story goes, but it's all second hand reportage via a rather inebriated stable lad and a tenant farmer) had set out that morning in somewhat of a temper. He was looking for someone or something to horse-whip or pummel, or generally grind into the ground.

His mistake was in entering the stable. There was a commotion which woke the stable boy in the loft. He saw, or thought he saw, the stallion covering his Lordship. He definitely saw his Lordship bolt out of the stable hotly pursued by the stallion.

The tenant farmer in a field some distance from the Manor was testing the worth of a pitchfork by leaning on it. He was also testing the malleability of some plant's stem by chewing it. He admitted that his eyes had been at rest behind their eyelids for a moment or two. He explained that he had been calculating the potential yield of the field in which he stood and working out its value on the market per bushel and a peck. 'An honest man doing an honest day's work' was how the '*Moffat Messenger*' put it when reporting the case. 'Lazing about as usual', was the farmer's wife's verdict. But it was what he saw that was the key to the matter, not the value of ungrown wheat on the market. His Lordship, he said, was running like the clappers pursued by the stallion which every now and then would nudge his Lordship with its nose. 'It were like it were a game to the beast', the tenant farmer said. His Lordship was making the best of his condition: he wasn't in his prime, that had to be said, and having his trousers concertinaed around his ankles shortened his stride. The stallion, on the contrary, was in perfect condition. As his Lordship reached the hedge he tried to leap over it. He would have cleared it handsomely, the farmer swore, had it not been for his dangling braces. These caught in a branch and at first his Lordship's momentum carried him over the hedge. At this point in his evidence the tenant farmer needed to drink several glasses of water and receive brief medical treatment. He swore that he heard his Lordship's last cry of premature triumph as he thought he had escaped: 'Bugger you, dobbin'. But the braces- sometimes called 'suspenders' in other parts of the world- were of superior quality (as one would expect with the attire of a noble) and their elasticity came into play. Lord Gelding shot back over the hedge as though fired from a catapult and his neck was broken as he landed. The stallion it was which brought the sad news to Lady Gelding as she was taking her morning tea in bed. It is said that she did not spill a drop but rang for her maid and asked for a top-up.

There were those who blamed the horse and there were those who blamed the braces. A verdict of 'accidental death' was recorded and the stallion put out to pasture where it contentedly grazed until called to the great round-up in the sky.

In the matter of the trousseau, however, Miss Lavinia proved to be of her own mind. Whilst thanking her prospective mother-in-law for the offer she desired to choose her own wedding attire. This secretly pleased Lady Gelding who admired the young woman's independent mind. She felt this augured well for the marriage, having recognised that her son needed a firm hand on the pommel as it were.

It was also the case that, upon inspection, the trousseau would not have fitted Miss Lavinia. She was a slender girl, willowy, the kind who swayed at the least light gust of wind on a balcony or patio; which is not to say that she was brittle but resilient. Lady Gelding had been- and still was- a muscular woman, well used to hauling hogs to the ground or ejecting bulls from china shops by gripping their horns. Men were easy meat, should she decide to tame one. During one period, while her son was at boarding school being bored, Lady Gelding had fought in the wrestling ring under the soubriquet of '*Moffat Meg, La Dama de Hierro*" (The Iron Maiden) wearing a full-body stocking and horse-head mask. She retired with a perfect record and a more than comprehensive understanding of the weaker points of the male anatomy. Pirated DVDs of some of her more refined battles exchange hands over discreet internet sites for considerable sums.

*

The Town Hall was crowded as McPeevish and the dear one squeezed in. Many of those who had turned up had come to see who else had turned up. Others had come because they enjoyed shouting catcalls at the candidates and blowing raspberries. In the interests of democracy no tomatoes could be thrown. Events such as these, McPeevish knew, converted hardly anybody but gave everyone a chance to blow off steam.

What was delightful, he thought, was that everyone in the audience was wearing a false moustache. The '*Messenger*' had published a supplement consisting of a series of cardboard press-out silhouettes of moustaches which could be clipped to the nose. It had encouraged its readers to wear them should they attend. As the main candidates filed on to the stage, under the chairmanship of the man from the capital, McPeevish took note of their level of discomfort. All save one seemed ill-at-ease as they caught sight of the sea of moustaches: that one was Lord Gelding, who sported such a mock moustache. McPeevish estimated this had won him a considerable number of votes without having to utter a word.

Beside him the beloved fidgeted with her moustache, a bushy marvel that would have not looked out of place on an Austrian Emperor.

After the microphone had been tested one-two-three the clean-shaven Mr. Leash explained to the audience, most of whom had brought plastic bottles of fizzy pop and an adequate supply of chocolate to see them through the tedium, the rules of engagement. He did mention that each candidate would make a five minute address to the audience before questions would be taken. Questions could be either for all candidates or for a particular candidate. He would be the sole arbiter regarding time allowed for the response and would cut short any candidate who rambled. A wireless microphone would be passed to the member of the audience who wished to ask a question. There would please be no shouting and no abusive language.

Apparently, McPeevish thought, eye-gouging and crotch-kneeing were not expressly forbidden, since he did not mention them. This ought to be rich!

With a sigh McPeevish put down the morning's '*Messenger*' and sipped his tea.

A family newspaper of necessity has to be impartial, readable, and responsible. What was admirable about the brief summary in the paper- 'Our correspondent reports that there were lively exchanges of views at the prematurely abandoned meeting with five council candidates in the Town Hall last night'- was that it succinctly conveyed the essence of what had happened; more or less, give or take an incident or two.

Anyone reading that would turn the page without a qualm, confirmed in their belief that Pax Britannica held firm.

Anyone who had been there would marvel and consider ringing their doctor to check that they weren't hallucinating.

It probably hadn't helped, McPeevish thought, when Matty shouted out 'Man overboard!' and someone in the milling crowd had thrown the fire hose through the window in the belief that it was a life belt.

He had been impressed with how compact the Episcopalian scrum was as, braced by chants of '*Gainst what foeman art thou rushing*' (number 157, Anglican Hymnal, 1868), they bore down on the Selkirk Reds who had infiltrated the meeting and chosen their moment for a volley of chants of Lenin's favourite slogans. If the Moffat club needed a hooker then they need look no further than Hamish Pardeep whose heel played havoc with the shins of more than a few interlopers.

Long after the other four candidates had been whisked to safety by Sergeant Sandpiper (off duty) Lord Gelding, moustache impeccably in place, had been directing play with shouts in Gaelic and the ancient shepherd's semaphore which is known only to those in the area around Moffat. This put the Selkirk Reds at an acute disadvantage and the Moffat faithful made the most of that.

The proceedings broke up at ten as the janitor wanted to close the Hall and there was only an hour's drinking time left in '*The Dirk*' and similar hostelries.

McPeevish had trouble remembering the initial addresses by four-fifths of the candidates. The Conservative standing was one Cyril Birskett. He had an impressive CV. He also had an MBE and part-owned MTV. McPeevish decided there was something shifty about the man despite his hale-fellow-well-met manner. The Labour candidate was one Newcastle Cloch, whose voice grated like a sack full of coals tumbling down a chute. He wore a red tie and clearly had no dress sense. The SNP prospect, Sandy Donsie, either had a terrible cold or his bronchial tubes needed re-boring quickly. Those sitting in the front row edged noticeably backwards whenever he spoke. The SDLP candidate was Lionel Hagberry whose entire attire seemed to have been crafted from a sunbeam. The Independent standing was, of course, the young Lord Gelding. He had declined the overtures of the Conservative party on the basis that the needs of the people of Moffat would be best served by someone who wasn't caught in an ideological strait-jacket. McPeevish had been impressed by the fact that the young man could make the word 'ideological' sound ridiculous, rather like a piece of mouldy cheese being handed back by a disgruntled mouse.

Five minutes in the hands of a great orator can work wonders. At Gettysburg in November 1863 the Honourable Edward Everett gave a two hour oration at the dedication of the Soldiers' National Cemetery. Nobody remembered a word he'd said. Abraham Lincoln spoke for two minutes and every American schoolchild knows by heart the 'Four score and seven years ago...' speech. Mr. Birskett had clearly studied at the Everett school and Brian Leash had to use the guillotine. Mr. Cloch threw words at the audience, who noticeably flinched and dodged. Mr. Donsie was like a puppy eager to grip your leg and hump and he too had to be reined in by Mr. Leash. Mr. Hagberry dazzled like the broken mirror of a clapped out Ford Anglia. Lord Gelding spoke for ninety seconds and the audience sighed with relief. More points to his Lordship, McPeevish smiled.

It was during the question and answer session that things had begun to hum. The seat, even prior to recent re-organisation- sitting governments love to re-draw boundaries as it gives them something to do and leaves an indelible mark on the historical landscape- the seat had been a safe Conservative one for decades. A time-traveller from the eighteenth century- or a very, very, very old person- would have recognised much of the Borders' landscape, political and physical. 'Grass is grass' is a gnomic saying often uttered by the shepherds as they go about the daily chase, following naughty sheep over this and that brow of a hill. Rabbie Burns would have felt comfortable in '*The Black Bull*'.

-What about the wind farm? Lachie Stirrit asked.

Up to that point thirty minutes in, McPeevish thought, proceedings had run smoothly. The townsfolk were in mellow mood. The rugby club had, the previous evening, notched up their tenth consecutive loss but had scored a try. A thousand pounds had been collected for the children's centre.

Earlier in the week the ladies croquet team had once again brought back the 'Moffat Mallet' after triumphing in the national finals. McPeevish had personally witnessed on television the beloved's winning blow, recognising the delicacy in the wrist movement. A hen's night of epic proportions had ensued. It was seldom that McPeevish had to carry the loved one home over his shoulder, a feat made especially difficult by her insistence on swinging her mallet at every circular shadow as they marched up the High Street. McPeevish had not paid much attention to the shape of shadows throughout his life, but that evening he had had to manoeuvre with skill. Preparations were well in hand for the marriage on the Saturday after polling day at the Manor and the entire town was eager for the nuptial knees-up.

Capitalism, McPeevish mused, is a double-edged sword, or a two-faced mask. It both feeds and bites the hand that feeds. It's both a demon and the tooth fairy.

The townsfolk appreciated wind. It was free and friendly, but also wild and wicked. Duality lurked in the hills, as the Ettrick Shepherd could attest. But what the townsfolk frowned upon was the thought of somebody getting their grubby hands on that which was free for all and making it their possession alone. It was bad enough that most of the land was owned by someone other than themselves. It was bad enough that you couldn't pull trout and salmon from the river without a license. It was bad enough that you paid tax on what you earnt and where you lived.

Wind farm? What wind farm? McPeevish could see the ears appearing from under hats and beneath collars and through perms like crocuses popping up through the melting snow.

He could feel the dear one's eyes upon him, asking unspoken questions. McPeevish turned upon her a gaze of such pristine innocence that the light in her eyes told him that she knew. The gentle nudge she gave him said it all: This is your doing, McPeevish!

It was the chance sighting of the Colonel cosily ensconced with Mr. Birskett in the Tempus Bar of the '*George Hotel*' in Edinburgh which had made him curious, McPeevish acknowledged. He had drifted in there whilst in the city doing his research at the National Archive. Unobserved, he had briefly studied the Colonel and the politician. Based upon his understanding of body-language and facial expressions he had decided that they were up to no good.

Hello, McPeevish, he had thought; skulduggery is afoot. When skulduggery was afoot McPeevish could feel the steadying hand of Hannay upon the tiller of his destiny.

He slipped unseen from the restaurant and regained the street. The question was how to proceed. If the Colonel was hob-knobbing with a politician of the colour of Cyril, McPeevish thought, whatever was in the offing needed a large spanner thrown into it, for you could bet that it wasn't in anyone's interest but their own. If it couldn't be voiced openly in the High Street then it augured ill for all. In Leith there is the expression 'Follow the smell', commonplace to those who live in Seafield. Any detective worth his salt will follow the money and that is what I shall do, thought McPeevish.

Mr. Cyril Birskett seems to have enriched himself at ever step up the ladder he took, McPeevish told himself as he ploughed his way through details garnered from a wide range of sources. Whilst none of the business deals he invested in were illegal the morality of most of them was dubious. The nett result of them all was that he had more money than he started with and others around him had both less money and fewer shirts on their backs. As his wealth had expanded so had his political ambitions and he found a natural home within the Conservative Party- though there are rogues everywhere, McPeevish knew.

Having found what he wanted McPeevish considered how best to deal with the problem. The one thing he knew that the forces of darkness did not like was light being shone on their schemes.

-There is no wind farm, Mr. Birskett snapped. Next question.

McPeevish had been watching the Colonel's back. He had taken a prominent seat in the front row from which he had vigorously applauded Mr. Birskett's address. At Lachie's question the Colonel's back had stiffened and McPeevish thought he saw some colour suffusing the nape of his neck.

Lachie was one of 'The Dirk's' men. He was either in the hills tending the sheep or in 'The Dirk' recouping his losses. At dominoes there was no one better. At tracking down a lost lamb it was said he had no match save The Good Shepherd. He seemed ageless and there were those who swore that the inn had been built around him. His great gift was his doggedness and Mr. Birskett's curt dismissal cut no ice with him.

- Is it no right then that you're a major share-holder with 'Vapour Industries'?

- My investments are none of this meeting's business. Next question.

Mr. Birskett looked at Mr. Leash for intervention; but something seemed to tell the latter that getting between Lachie and an answer would be like getting between a mother lion and her cubs.

-An' is it no the case then that 'Vapour Industries' are seeking to become the preferred bidder for the Colonel's patch o' moorland next the golf club?

- This is quite beside the point, Mr. Birskett blustered.

McPeevish noted that the back of the Colonel's neck was now three quarter's aglow.

- And is it no the case that ye both wined and dined the minister o' Renewable Energy just the other day there?

McPeevish noticed sweat appearing on Mr. Birskett's upper lip and brow. Every eye in the room was fixed on him, every ear tuned to pick up his answer. The owl which lived in the rafters had come out to view the meeting, attracted by the rhythm of Lachie's voice and the prospect of some rich pickings.

- And perhaps you could correct me if I'm off beam here but is it no the case that a memorandum has been circulated by the minister to say that 'Vapour Industries' offer best value and should be considered for the job o' building any future wind farm on said site?

Lachie's grasp of fine detail and bureaucratic phraseology did him credit, McPeevish thought. His hours of tutoring in *'The Dirk'* were paying off handsomely.

McPeevish noticed that the Colonel had been neatly boxed in by his neighbours.

- I didnae notice anything about wind farm above Moffat in yer manifesto, Lachie rumbled on remorselessly. I'm no aware that there's been any change of use granted and the sheep havnae been asked their view, let alone the tax payers of this toon. Have there been studies done to ascertain the effect of said hypothetical wind farm on the drives off the fifth tee? Ye seem to have gone awful pale and quiet, Mr. Birskett. I'm sure it's no just me as would like an answer. A plain "It's no' true" would do fine.

McPeevish knew the damage had been done: the prospect of a series of 'War of the Worlds' wind turbines looming over the town would hardly enhance its attractiveness to tourists. Solar panels already discreetly adorned the rooftops of many dwellings. Whatever benefits a wind farm might bring to the pockets of the likes of Mr. Birskett and the Colonel it would clearly not bring to the majority of those who lived in the town.

It was perhaps not the best moment for the Selkirk Reds to choose to begin their chanting. The response was immediate and gloriously effective. A vibrant burst of *'The call to arms is sounding'* (number 537 in Hymns Ancient and Modern, 1904) brought the Episcopalians to their feet. In the ensuing mayhem McPeevish noted that the Colonel's trousers had been lost and Lachie's shepherd's crook held him fast as his lower limbs were coated with Moffat toffee. The only known way to remove this was for it to be licked off by sheep. For a spasm of a millisecond, but no longer, McPeevish pitied the Colonel.

The dear one gripped McPeevish's arm as a mass of bodies swarmed about them. A hunting horn was blown and a swathe of biblical proportions was cut through the unholy hordes of the Reds by the Church of Scotland irregulars to the words of '*Onward Christian Soldiers*'. Bible bashing took on a new meaning and the voluminous collected works of Lenin proved too unwieldy to counter this.

Before he and the beloved slid out a side door the last McPeevish saw of the Colonel was him being borne aloft towards the town's historic horse trough and adjoining stocks. The owl perched on his head was hooting triumphantly.

The '*Messenger's*' photographer is not wanting for material, McPeevish thought.

*

Now it all seemed like a dream.

McPeevish basked in the afterglow like a contented seal on a rock.

Movie stars often smoked a cigarette at such moments, he thought. Heroines gazed adoringly at handsome hunks who glistened with the sweat of their manly efforts. Cats purred; coyotes howled; chimpanzees- well, he wasn't quite sure what they might do but it probably involved some kind of noise, a banana or scratching.

The election results were the banner headline in the '*Moffat Messenger*' the morning of the wedding.

It was only the second such election using the Single Transferable Vote system introduced in 2004. The problem with the old 'first past the post' system- locally called the Kelso System- was that it took all the fun and uncertainty out of the election night count. If you were going to spend all day and night from seven in the morning suffering from election fever then you might as well have fun.

The STV was a system devised by bored bureaucrats to confuse as many voters as possible. The principles on which it was based were simplicity itself and a ten month old baby with a cot full of abacuses and quipus could have worked out the winners and losers. Key to the whole system was the location or voting place. This had to be an obscure sheep pen as far up a hill as possible; failing that a leaky and depressing church hall would do, one with only a single and narrow entrance (which must also serve as the exit).

Guidance to officials is clear and succinct as the following extract from the Annandale and Eskdale constituency brochure will make clear:

"It is imperative that all pencils be unsharpened stubs and tethered to the voting booth by lengths of string which make them impossible to be used unless the voter (here a diagram of a voter would be useful but not absolutely necessary) is flat on his or her back (but not someone else's back). It is imperative that all instructions be muffled (if vocal) or blurred (if printed). Queues should be allowed to form the way icicles form, slowly and at length. There is no set size for any queue, but long is preferred by most election officers. It helps if buckets of freezing water could be periodically thrown over queues. Incontinent dogs are encouraged at such times to prowl the pavements. If the corporation street cleaning vehicle could disinfect the pavements at the same time, using maximum spray, this would help the general humour of those in queues. All movements by the voting place officers (VPOs) should be slow and considered. Prior to election day teams should practice their movements in darkened rooms in pairs. The voting card of each voter (diagram) should be scrutinised thoroughly (both sides). It should then be looked at more closely (inside and out). After the hand and eye inspection it should be run over with a magnifying glass (standard issue). The details on the card should be compared closely with the Electoral List (EL) which itself should be compared with the menu of the local Bengali restaurant. Once the voting place officer (still a VPO) is completely satisfied he should pass the card on to a colleague who will confirm his analysis- if he/she disagrees a third member of the team should arbitrate. If the card is folded it should be unfolded as per local authority unfolding regulations; if it isn't folded it should be treated with scorn. The voting paper before it is issued should be stamped- the foot will not do, though voting place officers are encouraged to stamp their feet if they need to keep warm- stamped with the official seal. No fish are required for this seal which is a metal implement (standard issue). Once the voting paper has been given to the voter (same diagram) he or she should be waved away with a dismissive hand. Note the time it takes any one voter to find a booth in which to vote- these should be concealed in the darker corners of the hall. Make a note of this time and feel free to enter that figure in the lottery for longest time a voter is wandering between table and cubicle. (Voters may not participate). Once the voter has concluded his or her business he or she must put the voting paper (now called a used voting paper: UVP) in the box. The box need not be a box but must have a lid. It could be, for example, a piggy bank or a refurbished dustbin. Voting place officers are encouraged to be creative in this respect; but they should also comply with the laws of hygiene at all times. The placement of the box (we will use this expression to cover all varieties of containers for brevity's sake) is a matter for the PVPO's (principal voting place officer's) discretion. By law the box has to be in the same room where the voting takes place and it must be within the line of sight of the VPO (we will now be using this abbreviation as often as possible with a view to annoying as many as possible). This is to avoid voters, who are notoriously fickle and devious, stuffing the box. 'Stuffing the box' is illegal in some constituencies unless it is accompanied by the transfer of money from voter to official. This should be done discreetly and a supply of brown paper envelopes (all sizes) is provided for this purpose and this purpose alone. The box may be placed at any height in the room though a ladder (its state of repair is immaterial, though it must have at least four rungs) has to be provided by law. Camouflage is permissible as long as it doesn't obscure the box completely- a landslide, for example, is not permissible as camouflage. Regulations as to the size of the slit through which the UVP should be passed are set by Brussels, which has little else to do when it's not regulating the shape of sausages..."

The voters of Moffat are a hardy breed, thought McPeevish with a smile as he put down the paper.

Despite the sudden flurry of council works which involved digging up streets, re-naming streets and vanishing streets altogether, on the Thursday of the election the voters had turned out in force, over two thousand of them in the North Annandale ward. McPeevish and the dear one had been among the first into the Town Hall to vote. They had spent the morning ferrying the likes of the Misses Potter (Maude and Mildred) to the voting station.

There was that air of determination about people which typified the Borders inhabitants when the raiders came up from England in the good old days. Lachie herded his charges into the Hall and back out within the time permitted, taking the prize for best regulated flock. Dougal's repertoire of arias brought smiles to the faces of those who had to queue. While he serenaded those in the Hall and gave a quick free trim to those who felt too shaggy to vote, Matty and his jug band kept the feet of those in the street outside skipping. Hot pies were distributed at noon courtesy of 'Crumbles'. Even the Colonel in the stocks (where he had been graciously provided with an umbrella and fly swat by the local 'Salvation Army') was given a pie. His vote had gone in by proxy some weeks before, but the paper was found to be 'spoiled' by the nibbling of sheep's' teeth.

At eleven that evening 'The Dirk' emptied and its denizen joined the spectators in the Hall for the count. The count involved fingers- nimble fingers, nicotine stained fingers, manicured fingers, any type of fingers.

Tellers from 'McSwindel's' the local betting shop lead the race for a while, but the steady flicking of the fingers of the 'Co-operative Bank' staff gradually overtook them. The Post Office kept pace with that grim determination typical of a public body. The dealers of the Moffat Bridge Club were not to be outdone and, despite their lack of formal training, they more than held their own. Holding someone else's was not appropriate behaviour during a count. The occasional call of 'two no trumps' would be met with a brisk 'double' and paper would be shifted at a rate which risked it catching fire.

When the Returning Officer (RO) announced the result there was a quiet sigh of satisfaction, not an unseemly rioting and excess of noise. In surfing parlance it was a wipe-out. Lord James (Jimmy to his friends) Gelding had secured two thousand four hundred and ninety five votes (2,495 votes). The remaining five (5) in the ward were shared by the SSP, the SGP, the SPP, the SHP and the SWADP. The STVs had gone equally to the Sheep Party, the Potty Party and We're-All-Doomed Party who would take their seats on the council with pride. Lord Gelding gave a speech of thanks which was clocked at sixty seconds, though there were those who swore it had been fifty eight and not a second more. McSwindel issued a statement that he would pay out on all bets between fifty-five and sixty and cancel his holiday this year. The citizens of Moffat, knowing that they had elected the right person, retired to their beds content. All were tucked up by midnight, even the Colonel who was released as an act of clemency, much to the disgust of the attendant sheep who were having a lot of fun and enjoyed the toffee. Sheep never would understand humans, McPeevish thought.

- You look the picture of elegance, sweetheart, the beloved said as they arrived at the Manor.

McPeevish fidgeted. He felt like a bit player in an *'Adam Adamant'* episode. If it isn't bad enough that I'm wearing a tie for the second time in six months, he thought, then the fact that I'm wearing a made-to-measure suit adds injury to insult.

McPeevish was one of those men who liked space. The clothes that he chose to wear were commodious- not baggy or unsightly, but full of ample space for movement and crosswinds and those tectonic shifts which the human body is liable to make in the course of any day.

But here I am, he thought, in broad daylight in a MTM suit that pinches just a trifle despite my explicit instructions to Giovanni to cut *generously*! Giovanni Greis, whose family came originally from the Abruzzo area in Italy, had his small bespoke tailoring premises in the Southside of Edinburgh and it was he who had equipped McPeevish. In his less 'pinched' moments McPeevish would concede that it was a fine looking suit. The pinching was caused by matters beyond any competent tailor's control.

The beloved had ruled out the wearing of a kilt since she said- meaning it in the kindest possible way- McPeevish's knees were not fit for general viewing. There would be single ladies present and undoubtedly sheep would muscle in as they usually did, so he had best wear trousers. Besides which, she pointed out, the McPeevish tartan would clash with her outfit.

Although no expense had been spared for the nuptials, the wedding was a simple and dignified affair, in the main.

Lord Gelding was of the Episcopal variety whilst dear Lavinia came from the Church of Scotland team. A marriage made in heaven, some of the single matrons sighed as they clutched their Order of Service cards and discreetly evaluated the single men in the congregation. McPeevish stayed by the beloved's side for safety's sake.

Lady Gelding had hired in several of her ex-wrestling acquaintances to act as stewards. McPeevish was surprised at their agility, given their muscularity. Between them all he could spot not one neck.

It would take a JCB of serious power to unlock a couple of them if ever they grappled, McPeevish thought.

Unlike pugilists, he noted that their facial features were not squashed or dented. Whether their teeth were their own he did not wish to pass close enough to enquire. Though friendly, their expressions ranged from 'Go Away' to 'Stay Away'. He wondered how their rather nicely perfumed male deodorants managed to adhere to them.

The Reverend Cleikum conducted the service with decorum and despatch. The object of a wedding ceremony in his view was to bring couples together not to hold them apart for extended periods of time. The sooner the bridal garter was let slip the better.

For the ceremony Miss Loople was dressed in an imperial cloak of crimson velvet with gold stitching. The long train was carried by four ladies in waiting-Aileen, Murdina, Murdann and Raghnaid. Their fervent hope was that they wouldn't be waiting long. Under the cloak Miss Lavinia wore a creation by the renowned dressmaker Vitale Vasquine. He had made his name as an arbiter of female elegance during the Sixties and was patronised by royalty (major and minor), pop stars (atonal and melodious), and the nouveau and aristocratic rich. The outfit was a magnificent dress made from silver tulle netting, embroidered with pearls and lamé. The high waist dominated the long, flowing dress and the whole outfit hugged Lavinia's slender figure. Her blond locks were covered by a veil in Alençon lace, held in place by a simple diadem. On her feet she wore white satin slippers, embroidered with silver Celtic fertility symbols.

As the bride on the arm of her father processed up the aisle- well, actually, the main path in the sunken garden maze, in the central clearing of which the ceremony was held- the choir sang '*Una vergine, un` angel di Dio*' from Gaetano Donizetti's opera 'La Favorita'. This was followed by '*L'amour est un oiseau rebelle*' from Georges Bizet's 'Carmen'.

Those guests who couldn't fit into the central clearing were able to look down on the spectacle from the upper lawn. They followed with interest the progress of the bride as her father, not having been initiated into the mysteries of the maze, took wrong turn after wrong turn. It was clear to the onlookers, but not to her father, that they were heading towards one of the many dead ends in the maze.

It was the faithful old gardener Norrie Ramshoe, having led a blameless life for eighty years in the service of the Geldings, who saved the day. Being somewhat deaf- stones had better hearing, so it was whispered- he had been unaware of the day's significance and so had gone out into the maze to trim and prune as usual. Just as the bride was guided by her father into a cul-de-sac Norrie's shears cut a perfect arch through the ten foot high wall of privet, leaving a clear run (slightly at an angle, it has to be said, but an angle that was certainly well under forty-five degrees) in to the altar. As the bride passed he saluted her, thinking it was her Ladyship, and presented her with a nosegay of freshly cut privet.

All this was unknown at the time to those who were privileged to be at the centre of the maze. It only became more general knowledge when Oliphant Dulbert, second cousin to Lavinia through a strange quirk of fate which need not concern us here, let slip that he had won the widespread betting on whether or not the bride would negotiate the maze and make it through in time. McSwindel for the second time in weeks was magnanimous and let the payout stand despite the illegal use of shears.

After the ceremony and once the company had managed to make their way out of the maze by routes diverse and means wonderful- these included hopping and collie-buckies – there were the usual libations, toasts and general entertainments.

It was fortunate, McPeevish thought, that the newly weds were whisked away early in a horse and carriage to some secret location for their honeymoon. They were thus spared the spectacle of Lady Gelding (the mother) once more entering the ring for a charity challenge match against all comers.

No son, McPeevish thought, and certainly not a newly wed one, should have to watch his mother hurling beefcake in swimming trunks across a standard sized wrestling ring. Her perm remained immaculate. Ortera, Penthesilea and Hippolyte could not have been more victorious. Finally tiring of the sport, as all mothers must, Lady Gelding took herself and a bottle of fine red wine to the stables.

Her place in the ring was taken by Calum Catham, one of the stewards. For fifty pence you could fight him; and anyone who could throw him from the ring or hold him down for a count of three won ten pounds. A steady stream of by now slightly pixilated regulars from the inns of Moffat pitted their strength against Calum, who was watched by his mates the other stewards. Their duties discharged they were just part of the general celebration.

McPeevish remembered fair Phoebe from the fitness club, having seen her ringless fingers many times from a horizontal position. He watched with interest as she approached Calum who looked almost apologetic as he reached forward to seize her and toss her as gently as possible from the ring.

Calum picked himself up and looked with interest at the woman who had just flipped him like a playing card. The couple approached each other again and this time McPeevish knew, from the look on Calum's face, that there could only be one outcome.

Yup, McPeevish thought as Calum picked himself up again. When it comes to the mating ritual of the ladies from Moffat there's only one winner.

Calum signalled 'Respect' in that secret wrestling code gesture known only to aficionados of the sport, and used his weight and height and enormous strength as he bore down on the lady opposing him.

That didn't help the roses one little bit, McPeevish thought as Calum extracted himself from the flower bed. He watched with some interest as the couple sauntered arm in arm towards the distant boat-house.

A glance over his shoulder told him that Calum's mates- Fionnlagh Fusker, Nebbie Neid, Iain Eallach and Lafach Limmer- were stripping off their dark suits and preparing to enter the ring. The misses Aileen, Murdina, Murdann and Raghnaid were already laying their fifty pence down and girding up. There could only be one outcome, thought McPeevish as he wandered away in search of the beloved.

All the maidens of Moffat, McPeevish concluded, must be taught that distinctive cross-buttock throw from childhood.

*

Turning his gaze from the inside of his eyelids McPeevish re-focussed on the form of the dear one seated with her legs up on the settee opposite him. He had only nodded off for a moment after putting the paper down but she was exactly as he remembered her. He wondered what it was that she was studying.

- Those sketches I drew of Lavinia and Jimmy's wedding, the beloved said.

She patted the settee beside herself and McPeevish was by her side in an instant. Space meant nothing where they were concerned, McPeevish knew. As a philosopher he recognised that space was just, well, space. Doubtlessly it was filled with molecules and things like that, unless you were familiar with dear old Gautama's teachings. Space to the Zen master did not exist. Throw the word out the window- but open the window first: was that one of Buddha's sayings? Perhaps it was the one about baby and bath-water. But McPeevish had the general gist of it: space wasn't space qua space, rather an absence of anything, an emptiness, such as there was in his glass at the moment.

- The bottle's on the table, the dear one said.

For the purposes of re-filling his glass McPeevish was prepared to accept the objectivity of that proposition. Students of Wittgenstein might quibble and maintain that the table was under the bottle. What mattered to McPeevish, he recognised, was that the contents of the bottle- a rather fine Merlot- were transferred immediately to his glass and that of the beloved (which had materialised under his nose).

The beloved laid her head back against McPeevish's shoulder and together they looked at her drawings.

McPeevish had to admit that they were fine sketches, capturing the gaiety and happiness of the day and the couple. Others had taken their snaps with SLRs and digital cameras; but the beloved, having completed her evening class in life studies, had wanted to document that day in a more personal way.

I am no art critic, McPeevish acknowledged, but these are very fine. The trees look like trees, the gardens look like gardens and the people look like people. Here and there he noticed a sheep or two. On the day he could not remember having seen any.

-Oh they were there all right, the dear one said. Lachie had them under control most of the time but one or two of the more curious strayed away. They'd always come back when he whistled. This pair wanted to see Lavinia and Jimmy off. This pair were curious about the boat-house and had to be shooed away.

Ah, the boat-house, McPeevish thought.

He sipped his wine as the beloved turned the page. There he was in profile.

- It was when Lafach was balancing those four ladies on his shoulders. You were very still.

Ah yes, McPeevish thought. Lafach managed five if he remembered aright. Then the barn owl dive bombed him and the pyramid collapsed. He didn't seem to mind being at the bottom of it. The owl made off with one of the lady's hats, under the impression that it was a dormouse. It had brought it back when it realised its mistake. Such are the ways of the countryside.

- You don't need to see the rest, the dear one said self-depreciatingly.

McPeevish was already turning the page.

What he saw made him gasp with surprise.

The dear one suppressed a giggle.

He looked at her with new eyes and undisguised admiration.

The studies were unmistakable: he had found the phantom moustache drawer.

Their laughter filled the room and Shayla woke on the windowsill wondering what they were up to now.

Oh that, she thought and closed her eyes again.

"The Passion of Beatrice Beal"
(By Jules Perceval)

The beloved sat demurely beside him.

- Mr. McPeevish, at your age, such an accident can happen, said the smiling young female doctor.

McPeevish felt like a naughty schoolboy caught with his pants down in the cycle shed. Their laughter was still ringing in his ears; or was that his tinnitus? The words "at your age" were like a lance thrust through his reins.

-He does have a very inventive turn of mind, the dear one said.

- It is important to keep one's mind active in retirement, Doctor Gaily agreed with a smile. And the body, she added as an afterthought.

There they go again, McPeevish thought as the two women dissolved into fits of the giggles, like schoolgirls in a biology class. At least they weren't laughing at him but because of him. Keep a tight grip on the mantra, McPeevish he told himself. Oms bounced off his inner walls like coloured balls at Friday night's Bingo down the 'Odeon'.

If only you'd kept a firm grip on the headboard, McPeevish, he chided himself. What were you thinking of? You're not *Plasticman*, you know.

- Now, the doctor said, struggling to control her voice; I can give you a booklet of exercises to help once you're unlocked.

They're off again, McPeevish thought miserably. This is like a Brian Rix farce. Dignity in adversity, McPeevish, he counselled. If only you hadn't slipped. Too late now. What's done is done.

Now look at them. They've gone through a box of tissues and started on a second one! Who is the patient here? Grown women rolling about like that while here he is suffering unimaginable pain: would Florence Nightingale, Mary Seacole or Clara Barton have behaved like that? Where in the Hippocratic Oath does it say doctors were to laugh themselves silly when confronted by the woes of mankind? What good's a poultice when everyone's in hysterics with laughter? How could two grown women- one a qualified professional with a score of years experience in dealing with the ailing and miserable; the other his intimate who professed only the night before to love him with an ardour that mere earthly things could not assuage (if he had interpreted her cries of pleasure correctly) - how could two such women be so heartless?

-...lots of rest, the doctor struggled to continue.

Rest? McPeevish thought; what I want to be is unconscious and unwound, please.

-... and no vigorous activity...Oh dear...

Apart from playing at blowing bubbles, McPeevish thought, I'm hardly likely to be doing anything else, am I? How can a chap who makes Richard Crookback look like a straight-edged ruler indulge in any kind of vigorous activity?

He had only made it to the surgery because of the dear one's insistence and assistance. Left to his own devices he would have joined the mushrooms in the potting shed and waited to seed.

-You can't stay locked up like that, my love, the dear one had said in the morning. You must see the doctor. I'll come with you. If anyone saw you making your own way through the streets like that they'd think you were Charles Laughton as Quasimodo.

Then she was off again, clutching her sides and crying out 'The Bells! The Bells!' Some people had no mercy. His suggestion that she ply him with malt whisky and run the rolling pin over his spine was met with an indulgent smile.

McPeevish wondered if he would be being mocked so heartily if he had been wounded in war.

-You poor man, Doctor Gaily had said only ten minutes earlier when the dear one had virtually rolled his corkscrewed body through the door.

For a moment the two women had looked from the chairs to McPeevish and then at each other.

- Perhaps, Doctor Gaily had said with a swift grasp of the problem and its geometrical consequences; perhaps we'd best poise you on the couch, Mister   McPeevish.

A shade better than hanging me on the wall, McPeevish thought miserably.

It took both women to manoeuvre him on to the couch and make sure he didn't roll off.

It was the word 'poise' and the sight of McPeevish once 'poised' which had ignited the slow fuse of the first fit of giggles in the beloved. Doctor Gaily, who until then McPeevish had seen in the charitable, haloed light of his saviour, had glanced at the beloved. By that inexplicable telepathy that exists between members of the opposite sex (that is, the sex opposite to the sex which McPeevish was), a telepathy which is an excluded zone to members of the male sex, McPeevish could tell that she *knew*. There was no need to consult the thick volumes arranged in her office's small bookcase; no need to struggle with long Latin or Germanic tags and definitions; no need to scratch her head and its attractive bun of red hair. As the two women's eyes locked, excluding the miserable sight of the comma which was McPeevish, they both began to giggle. The sound may well have evoked thoughts of spring mornings and birds dancing delicately on the lawn in their quest for worms; but to McPeevish it was like the dagger of Macbeth thrust again and again into his contorted flesh.

Woe, he thought, when he wasn't thinking Om. For what seemed an eternity he was left 'poised'. Woe, Om and thrice woe- or Om, if that's any better: but they were still giggling and chewing tissues by the handful.

It was all very well, McPeevish thought, to agree with Rabelais that '*Rire est le propre de l'homme*', but how long can one laugh? McPeevish assumed there must be a point at which the muscles seize up, or some other bit packs in and the shoulders stop heaving and the tear ducts run dry.

Where are you now, Buddha? he thought. So if it's all an illusion why does my back hurt like Billy-o? This amount of pain would have had even Saint Theresa whatsit flipping her habit.

- He's locked and we can't find the key, the dear one spluttered.

Any passing hyena would have been spooked by the howls coming from the surgery, McPeevish thought.

Om bloody Om.

- Now I'm going to give you a shot of painkiller and muscle relaxant, Doctor Gaily eventually said. It will make you less kyphotic. I'll give you a prescription for some painkillers and you should take them every four hours. The important thing is to keep mobile as much as possible.

At least, McPeevish thought, the ride back from the surgery in the wheelbarrow was less painful.

The beloved one, having seen him settled in his armchair, propped up with cushions and all he needed within easy arms reach, left McPeevish to go to her morning gossip meeting with the ladies in the new tea-room.

It'll be all over the town by midday, McPeevish thought. It had been bad enough enduring the curious looks he'd received as he lay curled up like a hose-pipe in the wheelbarrow. The beloved had greeted everyone with that friendly, candid tone of voice which suggested that this was a perfectly ordinary occurrence in her daily existence. But once the full details were in circulation- and McPeevish felt certain that the full details would not be withheld- he would have to alter his appearance. Perhaps he could order a disguise kit on-line. I'll become a recluse like Howard Hughes and live in the attic, he thought; but then realised that he'd not be able to climb the ladder.

Shayla, he noticed, was giving him a wide berth. He was surprised she hadn't moved in for the kill; but then there were still some sprats in the fridge. All the same, he thought, I'd best keep my eye on her. If she comes over the back of the chair I've no defence, he thought.

Being an invalid is a drag, McPeevish thought once the glamour of battle wore off. There had already been several phone calls from friends who had received his e-mail about his fall and injury. A garden accident, he had said. A slip as I was putting some plants in. Nothing serious; soon be line-dancing again. No, no need to visit; the painkillers make me drowsy and I'd not be much company- in a few days maybe.

Each time the phone clicked once they'd said their good-byes McPeevish knew from their chuckles that his feeble story had already been rendered redundant. Word had spread like wild-fire, probably from the moment he had been wheeled out of the surgery. All the curious faces of those in the waiting room when he'd been wheeled in were now mysteriously hidden by newspapers, month old magazines and handkerchiefs the size of pillowcases. In place of that regulation silence which if broken, even by a snivelling child, would bring forth synchronised, collective frowning; in place of that etherising silence McPeevish had heard coughs and splutters and moans such as the rigging of a distressed vessel at sea in a huge storm might make. Symptoms which quarter an hour ago had been rendering life borderline and unbearable in half a dozen people had been miraculously banished by the peels of laughter which must have filtered out from the consulting room. By the time the dear one had pushed him to the end of the High Street even the shepherds deep in the hills, via their 'Blackberrys', would have heard the news of how McPeevish had been crocked.

This is all Jules Perceval's fault, McPeevish thought.

His agent had been on the phone yesterday morning, he recalled. What a glorious morning that had been- bright sun, no clouds in the sky, the beloved humming melodiously as she chopped wood on the patio...

...And now this gulag of misery, this unbearable sense of impotence and immobility.

After the usual enquiries about how McPeevish was doing and how he was enjoying the tranquillity of the countryside, his agent had asked how work on the book was going. The knowledge that he still had much to do had driven McPeevish to a burst of activity at the word processor which had left him feeling, well, elevated. Primed, if one may call it that, he had retired to the Elysian fields of the boudoir only to meet the calamity which had gripped him and left him unable to flex.

You don't complain when the cheque goes in the bank account, Jules said.

True, McPeevish thought gazing out into the garden. If it wasn't for Jules's oeuvre I wouldn't be sitting here at all.

The problem is, he thought, I am insufficiently disciplined.

Surely that's my department? Jules responded, raising a carefully groomed eyebrow.

You misunderstand me, McPeevish thought. I meant only that it is wrong for me to stray into your territory.

Stray in as much as you like, my dear fellow; but you'll need to watch that back of yours, Jules said.

To distract himself from the need to distract himself from his anticipation of the return of the pain, which by the process of creative imagination he could already feel, McPeevish tried to decide about Heisenberg's uncertainty principle. He was uncertain what it was, but felt that was a good start in deciding anything. Was he sure, in any case, what was certain or what was uncertain? If he was, did that matter? These were deep, murky waters, McPeevish decided.

Om became Um...

He decided instead to put on some music.

It was not, he accepted reluctantly, the day for Chubby Checker and '*The Twist*', or for Elvis and '*Jailhouse Rock*'.

Mock on, Voltaire, he thought. Chopin was the music he would play when he was creating qua McPeevish, that is himself. Of that he was certain and bugger Heisenberg, he thought.

On a day such as this- from the point of view of the weather it was fair, calm, and spring-like; but there was much tragedy embedded in it, angst and all kinds of jagged Germanic words he dare not pronounce for fear of puncturing his lips- yes, McPeevish thought, it is a day for opera, for caterwauling and histrionics that will have the ravens folding the wings over their ears. Today is definitely a day for Italian to be bawled across the lawn and to hell with the nesting sparrows.

Anaesthetise me, he thought and drive from me all cares and woe; or thrust the dagger deep and gorge yourself on blood. It probably sounded better in Italian: '*Spinta il pugnale e profonda gola te sul sangue*'.

He became aware of Shayla taking a sudden interest in his movements as he flicked through the compact discs. He extracted Donizetti's recently re-discovered and recorded opera '*La Vendetta di Montezuma*'. McPeevish preferred this to Vivaldi's '*Motezuma*' as there was more pain and suffering, more wailing and woe-ing in it. Out of the corner of his eye McPeevish saw Shayla making a dash for the woodshed. Smart cat, he thought; she knows what is coming.

Grasping the stout walking stick the beloved had given to him, McPeevish rose carefully and, via the fridge, he made his way out into the garden, leaving the stereo on auto-play. He had two minutes to make it across the lawn. The 'Mission: Impossible' team would have appreciated the timing. Doctor Gaily had said the muscle relaxant would last five or six hours and that he was to move about ('but not *vigorously*' she'd managed to say before howling with laughter once again) every twenty minutes or so. He doubted that Jules would follow him into the garden; he was an interior creature, preferring the shadows to the bright sunlight of a Borders' late morning.

Here I can commune with my natural side, McPeevish thought. Here I can consider the lilies- if there were lilies- and the glorious cut and thrust of nature.

A creature hopped across the path.

Toad or frog? McPeevish thought. It's the Spring Fair in a fortnight and there's no chance of me making the Three-Legged Race.

He doubted that he'd ever walk a straight line again as he weaved slowly across the lawn towards the woodshed to join Shayla. Shakespeare must have said something profound about man's progress through life, if not across lawns; the way one's horizons expand and contract, the way here becomes there and there becomes here, that sort of thing.

He also said something about old codgers hobbling around on three legs when the end was nigh- or was that Sinatra? McPeevish thought.

That Shakespeare wallah, as they called him in certain parts of Stratford, said something about most things. No wonder Mistress Hathaway used to shoo him out of the house early and not let him back in till late. If you're going to rabbit on and say that sort of thing in blank verse all the time, she said, then you can do it outdoors, William. What a way to treat England's greatest playwright! If she but knew! He spent as much time outdoors as it took him to amble along to the '*White Lion Inn*', where his cronies were rattling dice, sluicing down juice and crossing quill pens as they vied in composing dirty ditties and odd odes.

Shayla was waiting patiently at the woodshed door for McPeevish. He opened the door and admitted them both. He removed the top from the golf trophy and reached in to take out the bottle of malt.

Ah, McPeevish thought as he saw the label tied to the bottle's neck.

The label bore just one word in capitals: McPEEVISH! He noticed the pencil mark on the label. The beloved had found his stash. He gazed mournfully at Shayla. She gazed expectantly at McPeevish. He poured himself just the one slug- on the generous side but it had to last- which the label limited him to. He seated himself on the two-person bench beside the shed and began to feed sprats to the appreciative Shayla.

As the opera burst into life the birds on the feeder took flight, the ants raced back to their holes in the ground, the grass pulled its roots in tight and flight plans overhead were altered dramatically. McPeevish sighed contentedly: there were others worse off than himself. If there was one thing those Spanish Conquistadors were good at it was slaughtering- and pillaging; don't forget the pillaging. There's no point in slaughtering if you don't pillage afterwards.

He listened to the magnificent voices of Vincenzo Rumoroso, the tenor playing the role of the doomed Montezuma; of Giuseppe Brontolare, the baritone playing Hernán Cortez; of Benedetta Stridulo, the contralto playing Monte's wife, Princess Teotlalco; and of Lucrezia Polmoni, the soprano playing Tecuichpotzin, Monte's daughter.

'*Dove si trova l'oro? Dateci l'oro e si può vivere*' sang Brontolare; '*Uno spagnolo sa rispettare coraggio.*'

'*Mi stai uccidendo ingiustamente,*' sang Rumoroso;'*Che Dio la penitenza domanda da voi.*'

McPeevish felt comforted by the company of the cat. Alas, once the sprats ran out- and sprats must of necessity run out when they come in bags rather than oceans- Shayla gave him a strange look and went off to put some distance between herself and the tortured noise coming from a choir as Aztecs were butchered by the cartload.

*

McPeevish had never seen so many chamber pots in his life.

It seemed that everyone in this particular queue carried a chamber pot. One or two, he thought, might have been soup tureens, but he wasn't an expert. It was unlikely, McPeevish thought, that any of the hopefuls queuing with their chamber pots (or tureens) would have anything as rare as the silver Charles II guzunda made by Marmaduke Best of York recently come to light. And it was not everyday that one might chance upon Rousseau's pot from Madame Boy's house in Môtiers; or that rarest of the rare, Alcofribas Nasier's gargantuan French pot with its left hand thread.

At best what most were carrying, wrapped in a variety of newspapers (mainly 'El Sol' he was heartened to see) or proudly exposed to the elements, was their great grandfather's chamber pot. Such pots might be the work of W. Adams and Sons; or Powell, Bishop and Stonier; or J. and G. Meakin; or the Johnson Brothers. There were Spode pots and Royal Staffordshire pots and Doulton pots and Wedgewood pots. There were

Regency pots and Edwardian pots and Victorian pots. Some were decorated with floral patterns, others with scenic designs- Italian ruins or the husks of English abbeys were much favoured; or panoramas and nursery characters. Whoever had made them and whenever they had been made, and however they had been decorated, they had one thing in common.

The dear one was elsewhere in the grounds looking for bargains, watching and listening, sketching when she saw something of interest. Croquet mallets seemed to be the latest object of interest. In the grand mansion behind the lawns on which the tables had been set out McPeevish knew there was a fine collection of pall maille mallets.

For the first time in over a week I am walking without artificial aids, McPeevish thought. Never had ambulation felt so delightful. I am like a new born babe, toddling carefully in a world in which others stroll, stride and skip. I shall make certain that I can walk before I run. Nothing *vigorous*, he told himself.

The dihydrocodeine helped, of course, he acknowledged. It was not unpleasant seeing everything through a kind of gauze mist, McPeevish thought. It was amazing the concessions one made just in order to feel human. Fortunately the course of painkillers finished in a day or two. After that, so Dr. Gaily had told him, he should manage any residual pain normally.

Residual pain, McPeevish thought, glancing around as though expecting to see it bounding up to him like a playful dog.

He wandered into the mansion and made his way to the cool quietness of the large library deep in the bowels of the building. Just to gaze on all those leather bound old volumes was a pleasure. He wondered when they had last been read by their owner as he gazed at the bust of Sir Walter on the desk. Probably before he snuffed it, McPeevish guessed with some certainty.

There he had sat and composed all those works, McPeevish thought. What would he have made of the word processor with its cut and paste and save and delete? What would his quill fetch on eBay?

Back outside in the sunlight McPeevish browsed the stalls where second hand books were on sale. It's unlikely you'll find another copy of Hortense Allart's '*Settimia*' anywhere in the kingdom, he thought, and certainly not so stylishly juxtapositioned between used paperback copies of '*Le Diable de Dijon*' and '*Le Boudoir de Mademoiselle Marguerite*' by Jules Perceval. He felt insulted by the price pencilled inside the covers; but then, he sighed to himself as he moved away, they weren't autographed leather-bound first editions. That would have at least doubled their value.

What would the ideal attic contain? McPeevish mused as he sat on a bench overlooking the gardens. Behind him the throng still shuffled with their offerings from attics suburban and provincial to be valued by the experts.

-Dust, Jules suggested.

Ah, thought McPeevish; glad you could come.

- How are you doing with the book? Jules asked wickedly.

That's your department, McPeevish thought dismissively. I'm just enjoying the ambience.

- You should be garnering information, ducky, Jules retorted. This place is a gold mine! You could set the action of the bodice ripper here!

Bodice ripper: is that the level to which I have fallen? McPeevish thought.

- Come along, McPeevish, Jules sneered. Let's face it; you're washed up, a has-been. The march of modernity has left you behind, old dear. You're redundant, obsolete, *so* last week! I didn't see any of *your* books in the remnant section.

You forgot passé, McPeevish suggested.

McPeevish glanced about himself. Is it wise, he thought, to have this kind of debate publicly? At any moment he expected to see the butterfly nets descending. Don't forget, he warned himself; Dingleton is but a short drive away.

*

I don't know how I let myself be talked into it, McPeevish thought miserably. All I signed up for was a quiet life: a book, a pouffe, a fine Islay malt by my side that would suit me. The beloved one as well, McPeevish added hastily. The whole point of coming to the countryside was to enjoy my retirement, not jump on to another treadmill and perform.

He was dreading the impending recording of an appearance on 'Spotlight', the television arts programme which his publisher had persuaded him to go on to publicise the new book.

But it's Jules Perceval they want, McPeevish had protested. They don't want me.

- You should have thought of that when you chose to write under a pseudonym, McPeevish, his agent had retorted.

McPeevish wondered what the difference was between a retort and a reply. There had to be a difference. Everything was different from everything else. Even Shayla knew that Schrödinger's cat wasn't a real pussy, whether it was alive or dead in the box. McPeevish was different to Jules Perceval. Jules Perceval didn't exist, of that McPeevish was certain. For one thing, if empirical proof was needed, Jules couldn't whistle '*Dixie*'.

- Well that's an unkind thing to say, Jules complained. I suppose all that money in your bank doesn't exist either.

There were times. McPeevish thought, when a pseudonym could be exasperating.

- Do I complain about you? Jules demanded to know. Do I wish that I existed and that you didn't?

Never mind all that, McPeevish thought, furrowing his brow.

Lord, he thought, it's nothing but dilemmas for me these days. I must check the mirror and see exactly how much I'm furrowing it. When is a furrow a frown? Now, come on McPeevish: focus; in a couple of hours you'll be in the studio under the lights.

- What do you think I should wear, sweetheart? the dear one called down the stairs.

He didn't know how women did it. One minute there was nothing to wear and the next there was such a choice that an arbiter was called for. Gone are your baggy pullover days, McPeevish; Gone that casual, ragamuffin look which endeared you to the ladies of CND in your youth. Now you have responsibilities, an "image" to live up to! A published Arthur- make that author- can't just flop around in flip-flops...or is it flip around in flop-flips? Get used to the world of Armani and Chardin, McPeevish; this gets more complicated by the minute.

Jules laughed unhelpfully. Who'd be an author? Being a figment of the imagination beat that every time.

Of course, McPeevish thought later as he sat in the car which the dear one was driving to Edinburgh, such a question is rhetorical. What should *I* wear? McPeevish thought was more to the point.

- You do look rather fetching, my love, the dear one said, her eyes never leaving the road as she whipped past another lorry in the overtaking lane.

She has never really lost that rally driving urge, McPeevish thought as he lifted his head from between his knees and opened his eyes. You don't navigate when the beloved is at the wheel and has her foot on the accelerator: you pray to survive. There must be saints of any hue one can invoke from the cockpit of a car, McPeevish thought. He wondered what Buddha would have made of belting down the A701 in a 1934 Austin 7 Ruby at maximum velocity.

Ommmmmmm.....

*

If I stay at the very back of the pub, McPeevish thought, then maybe they'll forget it's about me.

No such luck, of course. As nine o'clock approached the dear one was seated at the bar, surrounded by the '*Dirk's*' denizen who had been primed. Their chants of 'Arthur! Arthur!' unnerved him to the extent that he had to go to the bar for refreshment. Once there the gang had closed ranks, the beloved had patted the bar stool beside her, and McPeevish had complied *faux de meilleur*. He'd always wanted to do that, was never sure when he had done it, and wondered what it was in any case.

-There's an Old Firm derby on the other side, he offered hopefully.

No takers. Nobody was interested in the programme about polar bears on the 'Discovery' channel, or the van Damme action movie, or the celebrity cooking programme, or the fracas on 'Coronation Street' and 'Eastenders', or the Prime Minister's speech about the economic crisis-or was it a boom? What they and probably most of the sentient adult population of Moffat wanted to see was their local author on the tele.

- Just in case you get any silly ideas, McPeevish, Jim smiled; I've got an emergency back-up system for the electricity that cuts in automatically. Have another malt and relax.

It must have been like this in the tumbrel on the way to Madame Guillotine, McPeevish thought. I must read again '*Un episode sous le Terreur*' by Balzac.

The titles rolled and then the camera was focussed on the smiling face of Mervyn Begg, the host of the programme.

"No other author deserves the title of 'the Bonk King' more than the author of '*The Passion of Beatrice Beal*' does," Mervyn Begg said in those tones which have sold everything from chocolate to condoms. "This is the latest and ninth adventure of the feisty, sexually ambiguous investigative journalist, compared by some critics to Orithyia, Queen of the Amazons. She started as a bespectacled 'is-she-isn't-she' librarian in Barnsley in '*No ticket to Ryde*' and still has her reader's card. Beatrice sets out to track down the story behind the most famous chamber pot in history: that of Ekaterina Alexeeva who in 1763 was crowned and subsequently known in history as Catherine the Great. The bejewelled chamber pot had been stolen from the Hermitage Museum during the break-up of the Soviet Union. The action ranges from Saint Petersburg to Paris, to 'The Fleece' in Farsley' and Stratford-on-Avon; with the dénouement in a small town in the Scottish Borders. The story swings from the here and now to the where and when, from the twenty-first century to the eighteenth. It slips in and out of English, French, demotic Greek, Russian and Esperanto as smoothly as does a waif-like concubine to and from the desert tent of an Arabian sheikh. Along the way are name-checked authors such as Bonaventure des Périers ('*Nouvelles Récréations et Joyeux Devis*'), Marie-Aglaé Despans de Cubières ('*Léonore de Biran*') and Madame la Comtesse Nathalie ('*La Villa Galietta*'). Celebrities have queued up to 'appear' in these books, as a fashion statement, a declaration of hip-ness and right-on-ness. The real, if simply bemused, Surintendant de la Police Simone Sylvestrine of the Sûreté Escouade Spéciale, makes a surprise appearance in the subterranean 'Sapphic Sisterhood' nightclub scene. Briefly mentioned because of her many moles is Gill Bates, founder and owner of the world dominating company 'Fflysio Limited'. Naomi Campbell, who has never been mentioned in any of the previous eight books and isn't in this one, went to court to try to force the author to mention her. She was unsuccessful and is currently doing an unspecified number of hours community service somewhere that is not Sidcup for throwing the gavel at the presiding Judge. It is rumoured that Steven Spielberg is negotiating to buy the rights of the series and that 'Dildo Delight' wish to sponsor the author in the New York marathon. Countryside lovers may be offended by the casual disregard of the feelings of the ovines mentioned in the book. 'You're a kebab!' is an insult which springs all too readily to the heroine's lips; though some of the recipes mentioned are quite tasty. If you like a good romp through the upper and lower reaches of mysticism and existentialism; if you have plenty of Vaseline in the bathroom cabinet; if you know what a splage-nobblet is used for; if you want to be treated to a good adult read which leaves you bent backwards, drained and satisfied, then this is the book for you. It's best read with a partner, or in a troilism in a troika that's not moving too fast. But please, don't take it on holiday to Alabama where some of the practices mentioned are still banned and don't read it near a naked old flame. Let me finish..."

- Is it really a wig? Gillie Gritstone whispered.

A dozen voices shushed him.

"...by introducing tonight's guest the well-known "chick-lit" author Jules Perceval and his Native American Indian familiar and muse Achachak," Mervyn said as he ended his introduction.

The camera cut to where the beloved sat demurely beside McPeevish.

The '*Dirk*' was rent asunder with a storm of laughter that would have startled Gargantua.

Constable Herdwick who was passing on his beat was so alarmed at the racket that, truncheon drawn for the first time in his short policing career, he rushed into the lounge bar. He was rendered unfit to submit a report by the contagiousness of the laughter which infiltrated his blue uniform and tickled his ribs. He only emerged ten minutes later when he had been revived by an infusion of mid-priced whisky. The smile on his face was enough to dissuade potential burglars from lifting a jemmy that night.

"Your new book '*The Passion of Beatrice Beal*', where did the idea come from, Jules?" Mervyn asked.

- Well, Mister Begg, the dear one replied in her deepest voice, I was ploughing through '*Tableau de l'amour conjugal*' by Nicolas Venette when it suddenly came to me serendipitously.

It often happens like that, McPeevish thought. The only way out of a corner is a touch of *Les Trois Mousquetaires*: One for all and all for one; up 'em and at 'em; keep 'em guessing- that sort of thing.

When he had reached the top of the stairs and had seen the beloved wearing the leather jacket, bicycle chain necklace, pencilled moustache, stud through her nose and pirate bandana headscarf he knew he was home dry. What chap wouldn't sacrifice his own image when he had such a game loved one by his side?

On with the eye-liner, mascara, lipstick...

- I think the Revlon Fire and Ice, don't you dear heart?

And the Hiawatha buckskin outfit was an absolute trump, McPeevish thought. It had been snapped up at the Road Show outing for a fiver. A few alterations and it fitted McPeevish like a tourniquet.

- Miss Achachak, Mervyn began uncertainly, perhaps unnerved by a bearded squaw, perhaps bending the knee to Heisenberg.

- She communicates through me, the dear one interjected. Just ask me the question and I'll transfer it to her and she'll transfer the answer to me, won't you dear heart?

Achachak blinked. Her long, dark lashes fluttered like the webs of tree spiders in the tropical rain forests of the Amazon.

- That means yes, the dear one explained.

None the wiser after a few minutes Mervyn asked:

- How did you find your muse, Jules?

- I didn't find her, the dear one replied; she found me. It was serendipity.

There was unanimous agreement in '*The Dirk*' that there was a lot of it about, whatever it was.

The Great Beyond

As far as McPeevish could see the sky was full of stars. This didn't surprise him. What did surprise him was that he was standing in the cold night air on Plotcock's Hill above Moffat peering through a telescope at it. Nearby the large ancient standing stone the locals called Juttie's Javelin seemed plunged into the earth. Courting couples often came up here to gaze at the moon.

The beloved one sat beside him reading Jeanne Dumée's *'Discusion da opinion de Copérnico sobre o movemento da Terra'* by the light of the lamp tastefully attached to her headdress. Beside her was a thermos flask full of hot tea.

- That should be Jupiter over there, she said.

How she knew these things was beyond him. In fact McPeevish felt that the stars where beyond him. As he looked upwards at them he had the uneasy feeling that millions of eyes, hopefully in a variety of bodies but possibly in just the one, were staring down at him; though for them they too would be looking up, would they not?

It's enough to make your head whirl, McPeevish thought, his head whirling.

He sat down and blinked.

- Eyes gone funny? the dear one asked sympathetically. Have some tea, dear heart.

Why are we here? McPeevish wondered as he sipped.

- To see the meteor shower, the dear one replied.

Mankind's purpose summed up in a nutshell, McPeevish thought.

It was a clear night, ideal for watching meteors. It was ideal for many things, McPeevish thought. Sleeping came high on his list; in fact, it was the only item on his list.

Dotted around them on other hill tops were other amateur astronomers watching for the same shower. Not that I'm an amateur astronomer, thought McPeevish. This isn't even a hobby. In fact, I'm not entirely sure how I've ended up here. Things happen to me like this, he told himself. One minute I've got my feet up and I'm reading Voltaire's *'Plato's dream'* (or was it Lucian of Samosata's *'True History'*?) and the next minute I'm on a hill in the dark waiting for meteors to whiz past. It's the in-between bit which puzzles me.

Ever since Billy Brecknock and Charlie Closewool had reported seeing a UFO over the hills the Moffat branch of the nationwide 'UFO Watch' had gone into overdrive.

McPeevish suspected that the intake of alcohol the two shepherds had had that night at '*The Dirk*'accounted for the phenomena. The police Alco-meter read zero when they were tested and several of their flock supported their story. The police were naturally reluctant to breathalyse so many sheep.

McPeevish quite coincidentally had been considering the space above his head. Whilst the terrain under his feet was relatively familiar territory, albeit uneven at times, the space above his head remained unexplored. Did it, he wondered as he fiddled with his credit card, mirror the space within his head? That was familiar, if confused territory, much like an unplumbed well. He decided that the purchase of a *Skyhawk 1145P SynScan*™ *AZ GOTO* 114mm 4.5inch computerised parabolic Newtonian Reflector telescope was warranted by his wondering and that it was a good investment. If there were going to be any spare UFOs whizzing around the hills then McPeevish, as a published author, wanted to be at the forefront of whatever the front was for. If there were no UFOs to be found then he could study rooftops and chimneys to his heart's content. If all else failed he could put the telescope in the woodshed with the golf trophy and treat it as a mobile sculpture.

- Look! Over there, darling, the dear one said.

McPeevish looked over there.

It was dark over there. It was dark everywhere. Everything was so far away. He couldn't see anything, not even the hand in front of his face. Perhaps he couldn't see anything because of the hand in front of his face.

He peeked through his fingers.

- Use the telescope, the dear one suggested.

He banged his eye with the end of it. Then he had to focus. This was more complicated than he would have wished.

A huge bug with multiple legs and of indeterminate sex crawled across the lens at the other end. It was staring down at him. It looked hungry.

McPeevish shuddered and turned his head away.

*

From his lounger on the lawn McPeevish gazed contentedly up at the sky. It was blue, had fluffy white bits to it, like froth on coffee- which McPeevish knew wasn't blue, but the principle was the same- and there were no stars in it. There were no stars in coffee, either, unless you got one of those continental blends. If pushed- and this was unlikely to happen as he was alone on the lawn- McPeevish would not have been able to name any kind of coffee bean. This fact caused him no distress; neither did the fact that he had never seen a fig tree.

According to the forecast, McPeevish read, it was going to be fine all day and all week. That was fine with him. When things were fine and settled, then McPeevish had noticed that he was fine and settled. It was seldom nowadays that he was unsettled; but when he was he had noticed that he was not fine, not fine at all.

He turned the page.

Hello, Jupiter was in the ascendance.

McPeevish looked skyward. All was blue, serene, and not a sign of Jupiter or any other god.

Maybe he's ascended so far that he's out of the sight of mortals, McPeevish thought. That was the thing with the gods, the Greek variety anyhow; they kept out of sight until they decided they wanted to meddle a bit because life was getting boring on Olympus. Then they could make it rain cats and dogs (and fish, if the mood so took them) or blow like the dickens (or any other author- Strindberg was particularly foul weather).

It was an awful long way to come to Scotland, McPeevish thought. I'd've thought they had enough to do tinkering with daily life around the Aegean without wandering over here. He wondered how Thor and the other Nordic gods felt about the Greeks muscling in on their territory. You never read about that in the newspapers, he thought; more's the pity.

Might as well run the old eye over the horoscope, McPeevish suggested to himself.

You can never consider a paper read until you'd gone over every word of it. All that political gibberish taxed the patience a bit, as did the sports pages; and he wasn't too fond of the business pages with their beaming CEOs and balance sheets and forecasts of doom and gloom for everyone on the planet except the millionaires.

Thankfully, McPeevish thought, all my wealth is in buttons. First thing I look at in the stocks and shares columns is how 'James Grove and Sons Buttons' are doing. Mind you, this Velcro stuff seems to be catching on.

But in the boudoir, certainly of world cinema, McPeevish had noticed the button (and zipper) still ruled supreme. There was little that was erotic about the ripping of Velcro, according to those Italian film directors like Antonioni, Bertolucci and Zeffirelli who knew their buttons and zippers.

Sagittarians are 'mutable', he read, and 'adaptable' philosophically. Glad to know that whatever it means, McPeevish thought; but what good is this nonsense to me? Give me the winner in the three-thirty at Thirsk tomorrow, mate, and then you get my vote. What's this now: 'Not known for their reliability...Attention tends to be scattered'? Whoever wrote this is a charlatan! Hmm, it's a 'fire' sign- I have been feeling a trifle feverish, but I don't take the sun well. 'Partial to the great outdoors'...well, I like the lawn, I must say. Perhaps I misjudged this chap. What's this bit: 'Ardent, sincere and straightforward in love...normally conventional and in control of their sexual...' let's leave that shall we? What's on at the 'Odeon'?

His horoscope said nothing about falling asleep, which he did once he'd read it.

McPeevish surfaced with a start.

Now and then a bird flapped its way across his field of vision, looked down at him, and flew on. Birds were always going somewhere, he thought. You don't see them lying in a lounger considering the vastness of the sky. Maybe they considered the solidness of the earth as they enjoyed the vastness of the sky.

On the lawn beside him where it had fallen from his slack hands as he fell asleep- a brief lapse in consciousness never did anyone any harm, he thought once he'd roused himself- on the lawn lay the paper. It was going nowhere. Had it started to move McPeevish would have moved smartly and decisively in the opposite direction. Newspapers were supposed to lie where they had been dropped, not shift about.

I wonder what I was reading, McPeevish thought.

One of the delights of his day- any day of the seven in any week- was to try to remember what it was that he had been doing, or thinking, prior to his trying to remember what it was he had forgotten he was doing, or thinking. He felt sure that the dear one had given him instructions before she had left to visit her friend. It was merely a matter of relaxing the mind, of clearing the path, of closing the eyes and...

Another bird, or possibly the same one making another surveillance flight, flew overhead. Perhaps it was a game they played, McPeevish thought. They'd sit on a branch in that tree there, for example- an oak, if I'm not mistaken, he thought squinting into the brightness- and one would flap overhead while the others watched. Spot the species- a crow, perhaps- or something like that.

Now McPeevish, he told himself, focus. You were supposed to do something.

He stared at his feet. They were mute and no help at all. He wriggled his toes within his shoes to ensure that they were all there. All present and correct.

So it was nothing to do with toes, McPeevish concluded.

The best approach was perhaps the process of elimination approach, McPeevish thought. There were other approaches, he knew. At times he was partial to the random approach, plucking things from thin or thick air. He'd tried lateral thinking but found he was always falling off the ladder. As a child he had been partial to the open-the-box method and the chuck-it-in-the-air approach; but you are an adult now, McPeevish, he reminded himself and childish things have been set to one side. Mind you, they looked awfully attractive at times, especially when he was baffled by the sheer complexity of the universe. Shoe-laces, for example, had always managed to defy him, whatever their length or colour. How did the knots get in there? How do you get the knots out? Once they were out where did they go?

I work best, he thought, when I am organised. As a rational creature, one capable to creativity and processing data, I should make a list in an orderly fashion and proceed to eliminate whatever it is that I chose to eliminate as I proceed in a deliberate and...

Nodded off again, McPeevish. Is that the same bird or one of its mates? Perhaps I should keep count. Let's say that is one. One. Now you're getting the hang of it, McPeevish.

He could distinctly remember the loved one pulling on her gloves as she stood by the open door giving him instructions. He had nodded- and here he nodded in the hope that this would jog his memory- and muttered words which had confirmed that he understood. Then the beloved had kissed his cheek- left or right, he couldn't quite recall which- and she had exited left- or perhaps right; anyhow, out the door, which closed behind her.

At that point, McPeevish had to concede, it became a bit blurry. Was it something to do with the door having been closed? Was he supposed to open the door? No, she could manage that herself as she had a key. Forget the door, McPeevish; the door is a red herring.

He considered the door as a red herring for a moment.

Two or perhaps it was one again? The bird was travelling in the same direction and its flap looked awfully familiar. Best call that one to be on the safe side. One: that's better.

Now we're getting somewhere, he thought.

This lounger is very comfortable, McPeevish. This is the kind of lounger in which a chap like Einstein could come up with a theory like Einstein's theory. Perhaps I could come up with McPeevish's theory: if I did what would it be? Lots of people have got their own theories. The Greeks were particularly good at theories. There's that Pythagoras bloke with his triangles. Look at old Archimedes: a fine theory that. And don't forget Euclid with his geometrical theories and Aristarchus who first formulated the theory that the Earth went around the sun.

Process of elimination, McPeevish: retrace your steps; that's the way to do it. Think of it as a treasure hunt. This is the map- he rustled the paper now in his hand.

I must have picked it up, he thought. When did I do that? Perhaps I never dropped it? Then what was that white thing on the lawn a moment ago.

McPeevish looked sharply at the lawn. Green and empty, apart from the lounger and whatever wildlife paraded around hidden by the grass. Best not to poke around down there, McPeevish; remember the bug on the telescope. Brrr!

I was reading the newspaper- this one, unless a substitution has been made. But who would substitute a newspaper for the one I was reading? What was in that one that I wasn't meant to read? Perhaps there's a clue in this one.

Focus, McPeevish, he admonished himself.

Things have come to a pretty pass when you have to admonish yourself, he admonished himself. Best start again.

He shook himself as he woke.

That's better, McPeevish thought, watching a bird flying happily overhead. Is that a worm in its beak or has the worm learnt to fly? Evolution had always puzzled him. One moment he was in the house, the door was being closed, his cheek was still tingling from the beloved's kiss, and the next he was on the lawn in the sun watching a bird fly with a worm in its beak. Amazing!

He rustled the newspaper, folding it and unfolding it as he tried to find whatever it was he had been reading- or wasn't meant to be reading.

He frowned.

I could almost swear I heard the echo of some words, McPeevish thought. Some instructions to do something. Yes, that's right; as she went out the door the dear one had said...

There's that bird again- no it's a plane.

Ah! McPeevish thought as he noticed that someone had been doing the crossword. Now you're on to something, McPeevish. You recognise that handwriting. This could be important, a clue of some kind. 'Pole with chain got the bird': seven letters.

A second bird- no, it could be the same bird on its way overhead again- passed overhead, or passed overhead again.

McPeevish yawned. Maybe I've been drugged, he thought. Wouldn't put it past them. Who's them? Best watch your step, McPeevish, he cautioned himself. Better check inside the house to see if anyone's lurking.

McPeevish struggled to his feet, wrestling with the lounger which seemed to have enfolded him like a Venus-Fly-Trap. Fiendish invention, he thought;

could do some damage with one of those.

He approached the house with care but also casually, hands in his pockets and whistling some tuneless ditty he had picked up in his travels. Odd things stick to me, he acknowledged, inconsequential bits of information or images. They might come in useful, I must think, if I think at such moments, and they stick. Other things just fly past and leave no imprint at all.

Best that way, McPeevish, he told himself. Don't want to become cluttered up.

I could give anyone lessons in sauntering, McPeevish thought as he sauntered through the open French windows. Not that I've quite mastered the art, but I must be a pretty high dan. Not just anyone can saunter, he told himself with modest pride as he put the kettle on; you have to have an aptitude for it. He looked around his body for his aptitude. It's the bending of the knees and the swaying of the hips which are the key to the saunter, he smiled as the kettle boiled. The hands in the pockets is the final touch. Some try to saunter with just the one hand in a pocket- left or right- but this is at best casual rather than the full saunter.

McPeevish casually carried the cup with his tea in it back to the lounger. He thought well, he thought, when he was sipping tea. He thought better when he was sipping tea whilst stretched out comfortably on a lounger, this one for example. He thought best once he had sipped his tea and emptied his cup and lay back with a smile of satisfaction on his face and had closed his eyes to block out all external clutter.

Pheidippides has a lot to answer for, McPeevish thought as he stripped off his track suit and handed it to the beloved. He felt a chill sweep up his antipodes and jogged on the spot, any spot.

Here I am, about to run in the 'Moffat Marathon' and all because this ancient Greek soldier ran from the battlefield of Marathon, where the Persians had been defeated, to Athens. Why did Plutarch have to quote from the lost book of Heraclides Ponticus in his '*On the Glory of Greece*'? Why not leave it as lost? Why could he not have said the Athenians sent a pigeon? Pigeons are good at that sort of thing, McPeevish thought.

All around him, under the watchful eye of the Ram Statue, men and women were milling awaiting the start of the race. They came from all kinds of running clubs- the Border Harriers, the Teviotdale Harriers, the Moorfoot Harriers, the Gala Harriers. There was a lot of it went on in the hills of the Borders, McPeevish acknowledged! He noted that the Sheep-Strike-Back Club had also entered. He'd keep a close eye on them in case of any substitution along the way.

On his tee-shirt (McPeevish's not the Greek's who'd run the piffling distance in full battle armour) was a transfer of an image of Pheidippides and the sponsor's legend: this was the mothers and toddlers group, threatened by Draconian government spending cuts. If there was one thing McPeevish disliked- and he acknowledged there were many things he disliked but few he could do anything about: for example, he disliked the fact that his hair was falling out when he wasn't looking- if there was one thing above all else he disliked, or disliked almost above all else, since he disliked colonic irrigation quite a lot when he'd had it whilst in hospital; yes, the one thing for sure McPeevish knew he disliked was Draconian cuts. Other kinds of cuts- such as the Brunoise, Julienne or Allumette- he wasn't too sure about, but couldn't say he actually disliked. Draconian was certainly not the way to cut bacon, that he was clear about.

-Remember to keep it turned on, the beloved one said.

McPeevish certainly would if he knew what she was talking about.

She was pointing to his ear- ah!

In his ear, his good left ear, nestled an ear-piece. For a while he'd thought he'd picked up a passenger, a small mammal that was looking for a lift down the road. He wasn't averse to giving small, furry creatures a lift, even if they nestled on the rim of his ear, just as long as they didn't fidget. But now McPeevish remembered: this was the means by which the beloved could keep in touch with him as he staggered along the route. She would be able to keep him up to date with all that was going on in the race, as well as whisper words of encouragement to him as he crawled around the circuit. If she played piped music he had asked her not to include the '*Ritt der Walküren*' (Ride of the Valkyries). At the best of times he found Wagner irritating; nowhere in a twenty odd mile run qualified even as second best of times.

- This is very brave of you, dear heart, she said as he flapped his arms to try to get some lift.

It is also the height of folly, McPeevish thought to himself. I may have knocked myself into some kind of shape by attending the gym. But there's shape and there's shape, let's be honest. My kind of shape, McPeevish thought, isn't the kind of shape which ought to be let loose on a public highway or woodland and hillside path. My kind of shape a chimpanzee would find difficult to slot into even a large round hole. Whilst it's true nothing really sags or bulges or drags along the ground, there are certain features which preclude me from success at any athletic activity more vigorous than opening a deckchair and sitting in it. Even that can be tricky if I'm not completely on the ball; and if I am on the ball my tendency is to slide off it.

As he ran McPeevish found himself thinking of many things. These ranged from 'My feet hurt', through ''I can't breathe' to 'Why doesn't somebody shoot me?' There were many subsidiary thoughts, thoughts which sprang from those primary thoughts and other thoughts. Amongst these could be classified 'Why am I doing this?' and 'Alien abduction about now would be welcome'. Some thoughts were uncategorizable; some could be slotted straight into the section headed 'Pain'. This was a large section, he recognised, and had many entries. The filing clerk who patrolled the reaches of his internal mechanism was extremely busy. In fact he hadn't had a second to himself for over five minutes, the length of time that the race had been going on. McPeevish had a fine view of so many backs that he felt privileged and entitled to receiving a diploma of some kind- a baccalaureate perhaps?

I have never, McPeevish thought, experienced delirium such as this, even when stranded in the Gobi- or was it the Kalahari? Sheer exhaustion, lack of sleep, the torments of a thousand demons, all these assail me as I struggle to master the ability to put one foot in front of the other. Left or right; right or left: both together or crawl? Sweat poured off his brow like the spume off the prow of a trireme.

In his preparation for this torment McPeevish had not been remiss in his reading. A well prepared body requires a well prepared mind, he knew. How he knew he didn't know. There was only one infallible guide he knew and that was good old Zen. You might need glucose; you might need water; but if you didn't have your Zen you were snookered.

The thing about Zen is that there is no rhythm to get into, no mode, no gear shift or rumble seat. The neatest thing of all, McPeevish thought as he passed the one mile marker, is that there's no Zen at all! It may look as though I'm plodding along a road behind a herd of antelopes which are getting further and further away; but just think of the old tortoise and the hare.

Okay, he thought, I'm thinking of them: so what?

Precisely: so what?

No good looking around for Jules Perceval, McPeevish thought; he wouldn't be seen dead in a vest and shorts. At this moment he'll be on the lounger in the back garden sipping a mint julep.

Now that would go down a treat, McPeevish thought as he took a swig of tepid water.

- You're looking majestic, sweetheart, the beloved's voice whispered into his ear; only twenty-three miles to go.

Poor demented creature, McPeevish thought. There she sits watching the television monitor trying to bring me comfort when all the evidence is that I'm not going to make it to the next clump of trees.

As any marathon runner will tell you, McPeevish thought, it's not the miles that matter but the pain.

But the Zen runner does not 'feel' pain; he uses it like a spur up the backside, recycles it into karmic energy.

Of course, dear old Philip whatsit, that bloke who ran all the way to Athens, he must have had a lot on his mind besides his helmet. Odd looking helmets they wore in those days, heavy lumps they were and some over seven pounds. Brad Pitt wore one in *'Troy'* and it gave a better performance than him. Now there was a movie that could have done with a Frankie Avalon *'How to Stuff a Wild Bikini'* kind of musical score.

In his more candid moments McPeevish would have been the first to acknowledge that he did not expect to win the marathon. As was usual with such events an impressive line-up of overseas and national professionals had turned out to scoop up the prize money. McPeevish's sole objective was to make it back to the lounger on the lawn. In his mind's eye he could see the lounger where he had left it. Others envisaged carrots, pots of gold, Kim Novak; for McPeevish it was the lounger.

Not for me the conquest of Everest, or the flight to Mars, or trekking through the Sahara. Those heady days of adventure are gone, McPeevish. You're a shell of the husk of the shadow of a shade such as flits through the lower reaches of the Underworld of the man you once were. Right now a bit of shade would go down a treat.

At the three mile marker McPeevish had one of those mystical experiences with which he was very familiar. Usually malt was involved and it would be late one night either in *'The Dirk'* or curled up in front of a fire with the beloved to hand. To experience such a moment whilst in plain view of the public and without recourse to malt was novel but not unwelcome. What would have been unwelcome was a ten ton block of Dolomite granite falling from the sky on to his head. Equally a pit of molten lava opening up beneath his drumming feet would have been unwelcome.

He saw the present embodied in a hexagram numbered twenty-two. The runner was just ahead of him, losing ground all the time and called Pye. He knew nobody by this name and had long ago given up dividing twenty-two by seven.

McPeevish moved smoothly past the fellow.

Another hexagram appeared to him, this one numbered twenty-seven. Another laggard, he thought. McPeevish munched on an energy bar.

Stillness and obstruction, movement and action: he followed the big arrow pointing the way and overtook another runner.

Third last now, McPeevish he thought. Good for the old morale that. Don't get cocky now. Hubris, old chap. The gods are watching with the piss pot to hand.

Another hundred yards gone, McPeevish thought.

All these habits- measurement, survival, thirst, despair, motion- limit you, McPeevish, the Zen voice within told him. Free yourself from them, recognise the futility of that which you see and fly like an eagle!

Well yes, McPeevish thought as he headed for some bushes; but right now I have to take a comfort break.

- They'll edit that bit out, beloved, the dear one's voice said.

The Zen runner frees himself from time, McPeevish thought.

First pain, then time; and then you disintegrate or are abducted by aliens. He wasn't sure which was preferable. The pain certainly had stopped, probably because he had stopped for a leak.

Once I am in motion again will the pain restart? McPeevish wondered as he stepped back on to the road.

You betcha, the pain said as it bit into his thighs.

At least the two I've passed haven't caught me up, McPeevish told himself. Resume the Zen, old chap. Best thing for it. Can't go wrong with Zen; just a question of finding the route in and then floating. This big black arrow pointing thataway looks promising.

McPeevish followed the big black arrow. Everyone was following the big black arrow. He noticed that there were big black arrows all over the course. Did Zen do big black arrows?

Free yourself from all shapes and colours, McPeevish, he instructed himself. The Zen is colourless, shapeless, lessless...

Oh dear; here's an uppy bit. Come on Zen; there shouldn't be uppy bits.

Free yourself from uppy bits, McPeevish, he advised himself.

Free yourself from the habit of freeing yourself, he thought, and you just might make Zen.

McPeevish freed himself from time; time freed itself from McPeevish- and good riddance too, it thought. He freed himself from pain; pain freed itself from him, reluctantly it must be acknowledged since there was nothing pain liked more than seeing someone squirming with it. He freed himself from distance; and distance sloughed him off gratefully as a snake might its old skin. He emptied his bladder and freed himself from bodily waste; bodily waste et cetera.

Non-mile followed non-mile followed non-mile to the non-numbered degree. He became as a zephyr, as a gust of wind, Zeno's ever flying arrow. His non-feet were like those of wingéd Mercury as he went about his Olympian postal duties.

Now and then into McPeevish's ear (which he had not freed himself from since it was part of him) would come the encouraging voice of the beloved one. Her voice was as an emollient, a stimulant, nectar from the heavens. He was poetry in motion; he was the Walrus...weeee!

He passed more and more sagging, lagging victims of the race...

And then he was running with Zen.

- G'day; how you doing, mate, Zen said.

An Australian accent, thought McPeevish.

He glanced at his companion's T-shirt. Wonder what that team is, McPeevish thought: Ubobo Flatfoot Organisation?

- Parked just by the standing stone, Zen said. Saw everybody down here jogging so I thought I'd drop in, have a chat.

Neighbourly sort of chap, McPeevish thought.

- Do this often, do you? Zen asked.

Once in a lifetime will do me, McPeevish thought as they rounded a corner.

- Who you talking to, my love? the dear one asked.

- That your lady on the ear'ole? Zen enquired.

McPeevish had never thought of the beloved one like that, but he supposed that, yes, she was 'his lady', as Zen put it.

- Mine's back in the vehicle looking after the tot.

A charming domestic scene, McPeevish thought.

- Everyone going the same place then? Zen asked.

In this particular instance McPeevish seriously hoped so since everyone seemed to be following everyone else.

- Where I come from we don't do things like this, Zen said.

McPeevish used some spare energy to raise an eyebrow enquiringly.

- Come in McPeevish, over, the dear one said.

-Not quite sure what the cocked eyebrow means, mate. Where I come from it's a rude gesture but seeing as how you're a friendly looking feller I'm guessing that it has another connotation down here. We leave this jogging business to the hoopitobs.

Hoopitobs? McPeevish thought.

- If you've got the hiccoughs you'd better stop for a moment, the dear one suggested.

-Yeah; they're like your sheep only bigger, less woolly and much faster. So fast you can't see them till they stop. One thing you can bet on: when they stop it'll be right behind you.

Sometimes McPeevish was convinced sheep were like that.

- Nah, they bah too much, mate. Hoopitobs make a soothing sound, a bit like your Om only much more soothing, Zen said.

This is most interesting, McPeevish thought, but I'd better push on.

- Sure thing, mate. You step up the pace; I'm turning off here anyhow. Gotta get back home for dinner. G'day.

Then McPeevish was running alone. He rather missed Zen. But then he remembered that Zen couldn't be particularised like that and maybe...

- I think he's hallucinating, McPeevish heard the dear one saying.

Off to his left McPeevish could see the craft rising rapidly from beside the standing stone.

Ye gods! he thought...

*

Suddenly McPeevish was a whirlwind of activity.

He raced from the lawn startling Shayla who had been happily curled in the shade beneath the lounger.

In the kitchen he sped around opening cupboards, pulling things out and spreading other things elsewhere. The oven was switched on and things shoved into it. Pots and pans were filled and put on the hob. Timers were set with the skill of a mad scientist priming a bomb to explode.

- This is awfully sweet of you, dear heart, the beloved said as she removed her gloves and considered the set table. But it's tomorrow night that Lucinda and Scuds are coming over.

Ah, McPeevish thought ruefully. Tomorrow was the word he had forgotten.

Gerran Manor

McPeevish had noticed the increased excitement around the town. It would soon be time for the Annual Summer Fair. Lord Gelding had scored quite a coup in securing a celebrity of some standing to open the event.

The Colonel, at the meeting planning the day, had argued long and hard for his friend Sir Hildebrand Hough (pronounced 'huff'), who held some portfolio in the Ministry of something or other. The Colonel was what is called a 'grinder' at committee meetings: he went on and on until every opponent was mince. Sir HH (as the Colonel affectionately referred to this nonentity) had a blank space quite by chance in his diary for that particular Saturday. He was taking time out from his onerous duties and would be staying with the Colonel and his wife that very weekend. The Colonel was sure that he could persuade his old army chum to officiate. His fee would be reasonable and could doubtlessly be claimed as tax deductible, given the nature of the good cause.

The committee were starting to despair, there seeming to be no other candidate, when his Lordship suggested that he might be able to persuade his friend to do the honours.

- David..., he started to say.

The Colonel sniffed. He was rather good at sniffing. His sniff had ruined many a subaltern's career prospects.

Eyes had turned hopefully towards Lord Gelding whose advocacy on behalf of the town had so far worked wonders on Dumfries council.

- I rather think that a Minister of the Crown is a far bigger attraction than a personal friend, the Colonel interrupted dismissively.

-...Tennant, Lord Gelding finished.

Local democracy, McPeevish had found, was at its best when the chips were down and the names of the contestants were in plain view. Sir HH's lineaments, personal habits and avoirdupois were unknown to those present; nor did they care a whit about his curriculum vita and old school tie collection. Neither money nor favour could sway men and women who could tell a winner when they smelt it. The vote was overwhelming and the Colonel was left to shuffle his papers as the other committee members took to the streets to proclaim the news: Doctor Who was coming!

The town had entertained diverse celebrities before, McPeevish knew.

In 1685 John Graham, Lord Claverhouse, had been billeted in the 'Black Bull Inn' when suppressing the local Covenanters who repudiated Episcopalianism. Boswell had come in 1766 as he remarked in his journal *'to wash off a few scurvy spots which the warmer climate of Europe had brought out on my skin'*. Robert Burns, an admirer of a Moffat beauty Deborah Davies, wrote *'O, Willie brewed a peck o'maut'* in the town and also the epigram *'An apology for Scrimpit Nature'* in the inn. David Hume the philosopher visited and dined exclusively with his fork. What part the spa played in forming the views he put forward in *'An Enquiry Concerning Human Understanding'* we do not know. Whether he was as sceptical about the waters as Dr. John Rogerson- at one time the court physician to Catherine the Great- who said their odour reminded him of a 'slightly putrescent egg', we do not know. But none of these had ridden in the Tardis and travelled the universe through time! None had battled the Daleks! The local presses of 'Torwen Printers' were printing handbills and posters before the Colonel had snapped shut his Tomacelli double-gusset leather briefcase. Sleepy old Moffat could move fast when put to the test.

*

Gearran Manor had a long and proud history. Their family motto *'Creatio ex Nihilo'* was carved in the very foundation stone. Within the current building were surviving parts of the original fortified L-plan tower house built in the fourteenth century by the first Lord Gelding, then 'Gee-l-ding'. The derivation of this name is unclear but it is as unlikely to be from the Dutch for 'yellow thing' as it is from the old Scots for 'pettish and unmanageable'. The current structure was designed in the eighteenth century by one 'Ramshackle' Dunface. The Borders are littered with examples of his work and he was derided for the rapidity with which his constructions collapsed. This was because most owners didn't pay him enough so he 'built in obsolescence' (as would be said nowadays). But the Geldings paid him handsomely and also held him and his entire family hostage for seven years after the building was finished.

Lady Gelding was worried. She feared that this summer's fair, traditionally held in the grounds of the Manor, would be the last.

Glenda- to her intimates in the stable and her other close friends; she had discreetly suppressed all trace of the 'Philippa' from her life- was not a mathematical genius. However, she didn't need an over-paid accountant or Mister Micawber to tell her that the family's finances were floundering. Her generosity to the tenants and various local charities (such as the 'Tangled ex-Wrestlers Benevolent Fund') was unstinted; but the Inland Revenue tax demands kept coming. Over the years, like many a stately home owner, she had quietly sold off pieces of junk which others valued highly. She had vowed to herself that she would never open the family home to the general public by handing it to the National Trust- they had a nasty habit of selling places off and building housing estates in the grounds. She did not wish to live in a converted stable since she believed that horses required their own living space. She had tried to shield her son from the realty of their plight; but once he was married she had laid it all out before him. Lord Gelding's new found sense of responsibility was evident in his response of 'Jiggs, Mother, something will turn up'. How unlike his father he is, Lady Gelding said to herself. His father, had he lived, would have 'consulted the claret' as the aristocracy say in their more sober and expansive moments. Lady Lavinia pitched in by learning to sew and knit, taking weekly lessons from Miss Potter (Maude).

All three were agreed that none of the servants would go, nor should they be alarmed by being told of the difficulties facing the family estate. However, Norrie Ramshoe the gardener (and his apprentice Galway), old Peacock the butler and her ladyship's maid Peahen, Molly Mutton and her daughter Mary who cleaned, as well as Daisy Dishwater the cook and Cathy Corriedale the kitchen helper, weren't daft. They could tell by the lack of banquets and ball-gowns that things were tight.

They had also not been unaware of the weighty letters arriving almost weekly bearing the stamp of HMG. Whenever anyone in Moffat saw the letters HMG they had an instinctive response which Pavlov's dogs would have recognised: they would bleat with alarm and send for Ratnick Radnor the local pest exterminator. There was little he could do with his fumigation machines but they always enjoyed a drink with him and a blether about how he hadn't paid tax for years. One of his little tricks was to claim the rodents as dependents.

Whenever Peacock handed the letters on a silver tray to his Lordship his Lordship would accept it the way an early Christian might have accepted a lashing from his Roman owner: with a grimace but a fervent prayer that the Lord (not him but the other One) would provide. His "Thank you, Peacock" would never evince a trace of unhappiness but only genuine pleasure at seeing the butler again, even if it was barely five minutes ago that he had brought in the morning coffee.

The Colonel had a keen nose for business opportunities. He was acquainted with a certain property speculator and developer called Maximilliamus Milkitt, MM for short. The Colonel knew a lot of people with double initials, and this was perhaps a bad thing. Mr. Milkitt was the kind of man who would have squeezed another half dozen persons into the Black Hole of Calcutta and doubled the rent. Having got wind of the financial difficulties facing the Geldings the Colonel had contacted MM. MM knew people in this department and that ministry and thus he turned up the heat on the Geldings with demands for immediate payment of their overdue taxes. It was a tactic he had used many times before with great success. At the appropriate moment MM would move in for the kill, his Rolls Royce arriving in the driveway at the Manor like a rescuing angel- or that was his hope.

Whether relative or tradesman one cannot just turn up at the door of a country mansion and expect to be afforded a welcome. At the precise moment MM's chauffeur Bundun was steering the Rolls into the driveway Lady Gelding was exercising her horses. They were in fine fettle. Some of the stallions were in heat. Seeing the Roller approaching they gave a glad whinny and leapt on it with passion and intent. It is difficult to detach a passionate stallion once it has committed itself. MM ordered Bundun to turn and beat a hasty retreat, pursued by several unsatisfied stallions. It was only Lady Gelding's sharp whistle which brought them to a halt and enabled the Roller to make its escape, though not unmarked.

*

- Finished with your writing, dear heart? the beloved asked.

McPeevish had come down early from the study to join her in the living room. She will have read me like a book, McPeevish thought as he plumped himself and his misery in his chair and glumly stared out into the twilight. Writer's block was the worst form of constipation. Being a writer was a dodgy business, he thought. Sometimes it flows like the Grey Mare's Tail and sometimes it's as dry as the Dead Sea.

- Never mind, dear, come and join me while I read this, she said.

McPeevish curled up beside her on the sofa. The artist must take comfort in what he can, he thought, feeling her warmth and vibrancy.

- It's a jolly exciting story, she said. A treasure hunt.

Could this be the moment for Jules Perceval to make an entrance? McPeevish wondered.

-When I started it the style seemed quite familiar. I thought it was one of yours, the dear one said.

She showed him the cover: 'The Lost Treasure of Salvaje Rodríguez, Pirate'.

Ah...

- You recognise it? she asked innocently feigning surprise.

Caught again, McPeevish, he told himself. Is there nothing you can keep from this wonderful woman?

- I would hope not, she smiled. Why isn't this on your 'He also wrote' list?

How to explain it? McPeevish thought. When one matures as a writer one can feel rather ashamed of one's juvenilia, he thought.

Who's this 'one' fellow? 'Fess up, McPeevish, since you've gone large with the sales you had rather hoped that this title wouldn't surface. Look what they did to Hemingway once he was dead: out come those unfinished and imperfect novels he wouldn't have wished to see the light of day: *'True at First Light'* and *'The Garden of Eden'*. For what they're worth Jane Austen's early works *'Henry and Eliza'* and *'Frederic and Elfrida'* have been published. Likewise Charlotte Bronte's *'Origins of Angria'* and Virginia Woolf's *'The Hyde Park Gate News'*. Would the Marquis de Sade have wished to have seen published *'Qui a tué M. Coq?'* that unscabrous collection of French nursery rhymes? It rather diluted his image as a whips and bondage man.

McPeevish wondered where she had found it.

- On one of the high shelves in the library, she said. It was rather dusty, undeservedly so, I might add.

McPeevish had to acknowledge that he felt a certain fondness for the book, though why he had used the pseudonym 'Pevensey Clapham' he could not now recall. Perhaps he had been going though a railway station rather than fish phase. Many of his early poems he had attributed to 'A. Carp' or 'C. Trout'.

- It would make a good game for the Fair, the dear one said. Hide and Seek and find the treasure all in one.

McPeevish conceded that it might be rather fun for the kiddies; but why hadn't he thought of it?

You're too wrapped up in your thoughts, McPeevish, he thought, wrapping himself up in deep thought. He could see that the beloved one was eyeing him speculatively.

What was it Mark Twain wrote...?

'With a bound' the lights were out and they moved smartly up the stairs.

*

In the library at the Manor McPeevish had been working for the past few weeks, preparing an information leaflet on the history of the Manor and the family.

The presence of Dr. Who at the Fair had generated considerable publicity.

If we're going to be that much in the public eye, the Geldings felt, then we should make sure that the facts are correct. Already tabloid journalists had run articles about 'the horse crazy, man-wrestling Lady of the Manor'. They had made up stories about ghosts and hauntings, being fed information about witchcraft in the hills and illicit stills by 'their special correspondent'. There were many who saw the hand of the Colonel in this. If his nose was any further out of joint it would have been around the back of his head.

The library, a small affair compared to that in the nearby Abbotsford, was somehow located in the heart of the Manor and had no windows. It wouldn't have surprised McPeevish if it had originally been a dungeon of some kind, or a cold cellar. There were piles and piles of ancient documents in boxes and cabinets which had not been polished for centuries. His sinuses had taken a terrible beating the first time he worked in the library. The dear one insisted he wore a protective air purifying face mask and goggles. The second morning he had been in the library young Cathy had brought him a cup of tea. She had promptly dropped it, screamed and fainted when he had looked up from the desk. This won't help the rumour mill, he thought as he held her head and she sipped some brandy. One of the tabloids was running a 'ghost-a-day' and 'Say-Boo-to-Dr. Who' competition and offering rewards for photographs of said ghosts. To help things along he sent them a grainy black and white photo of himself in his mask.

History is a funny thing, McPeevish thought. It should be what it is; but more often than not it was what we wanted it to be. Lenin and his cronies hadn't invented the 'airbrush' by making Trotsky vanish from photographs. The Romans after they had defeated the Carthaginians destroyed their city and ploughed salt into the land so as to obliterate it from both memory and history. Even today a cigarette is airbrushed from a photograph of Jean-Paul Sartre because smoking is frowned upon by some. Anyone can be a petty tyrant if they try, McPeevish concluded.

Many of the documents he browsed through were those typically dry legal documents recording sales and crops grown and rents paid and debts owed which historians love and the general public never read. His Latin was rusty, his Old French likewise, but say what you liked about McPeevish, McPeevish said, he was a stayer. When we McPeevishes say we're going to do something, McPeevish reminded himself each time his eyes watered and his head spun, we do it. Whether or not this was true generally he couldn't say, since he was the sole McPeevish that he was aware of. But being the sole McPeevish- unless there were unknown distant rich American McPeevishes- McPeevish felt it behoved him to persist. 'Behoving' was something he had had little experience of, but he quite liked the experience

as he behoved with the best of them in the dusty library. He became fond
of the tiny mouse which would sit on an empty candlestick and watch him
while he worked. Shayla, when he got home in the late afternoon, would
sniff him carefully and check his pockets hoping for a snack. It is hard
being human, McPeevish thought as he stroked Shayla. The thought of
feeding the wee mouse to her made him shudder. What was natural to her
is murderous to me, he thought. In other circumstances- exactly what they
might be need not be clarified, he thought- the presence of a mouse in a
room would have me calling for the cat. Perhaps it's because the mouse was
here first, McPeevish thought, and it has not chewn any of these documents,
that I feel fondness for it. Each morning he would bring in a biscuit and
leave it for the mouse and watch it nibbling before he began his research:
Gingerbread fresh from 'Crumbles' seemed to go down a treat.

One morning when McPeevish arrived he found a document lying on the
desk.

Now how did that get there? McPeevish thought.

I am a tidy chap. The beloved has marvelled at the neatness of my wardrobe
and dressing table drawers. I do not leave things lying around on desks. I
tidy things away. Sometimes I'm so tidy I tidy myself away, he thought.

The mouse sat watching him.

McPeevish, he told himself; don't be fanciful now and start wondering if
the mouse put the document there.

I wonder if the mouse had anything to do with this? McPeevish wondered
as he fed it crumbs.

Now don't go jumping to conclusions, McPeevish, he said as he jumped
to a conclusion; but I'd swear that the mouse winked at me. Hallucinating
so early in the day isn't a good sign, McPeevish.

-It was either blow my cover, the mouse said, or watch you spend the next
six months sorting through this lot and getting nowhere. Time is getting
short, McPeevish.

McPeevish was a firm believer in the belief that mice didn't talk. He
looked around for the ventriloquist.

Maybe this is my Walt Disney moment, McPeevish thought. Maybe these
cookies are laced.

Best make a start, McPeevish, he told himself.

It was the name 'Leonardo' which caught his eye.

There are Leonardos and there are Leonardos, McPeevish thought.

Personally, the only Leonardo I know is Lenny Lonk, the best darts player
in *'The Dirk',* McPeevish thought. I don't personally know that DiCaprio

film actor bloke and I don't know how good a darts player he is, but I know of him. I've never read Fibonacci's '*Liber abbaci*' or '*Practica geometriae*' but I appreciate his introduction of the Hindu-Arabic numbers to the West. I've never heard any of de Leo's baroque music and don't suppose I will, if my luck holds. The only other Leonardo I know of is that painter-inventor chap and I bet he could have given Lenny a good game with those Italian arrows he designed.

It took McPeevish all that day to read and translate the document. He wasn't sure whether he or the mouse turned the pages. He went through a whole packet of digestive biscuits, shared equally with the mouse. When Cathy brought him his tea he asked for a saucer of milk (with a touch of brandy in it) for the mouse (which had discreetly hidden itself so as to avoid another screaming and fainting fit).

When he got home later that evening McPeevish told the beloved one the story he had pieced together. In a sense it was simple but also unbelievable. Leonardo da Vinci had spent his last years in France, living in a manor house called *Château de Cloux* (now called *Clos Lucé*) in Amboise. This was near the royal château of Francis I his patron. It was there that Marguerite de Navarre, Francis's sister, wrote her erotic book '*L'Heptaméron*', a copy of which was in the Manor library. In 1517, with his apprentice Count Francesco Melzi, Leonardo travelled to Scotland at the invitation of John Stewart, the Duke of Albany, who was then Regent of the King of Scotland. Leonardo had been a guest at Gearran Manor and while visiting had sketched as a gift a portrait of the then Lady Gelding. According to the document he had studied the "Psalter of Saint Columba" which had then been in the family's possession. He had also left some sketches of designs for various implements which might come in handy for work on the surrounding grounds. Though he was elderly and needed the assistance of his travelling companion (who would sleep at the foot of his bed in case he needed help in the night reaching the gardez-loo), Leonardo had enjoyed his stay and had been much taken both with the local drink ('*malto fuoco-acqua*') and the inquisitiveness ('*curiosità*') of the sheep. What the sheep had made of dear old Leonardo wasn't recorded, though he had gone home wearing a woollen mantle specially woven for him by Lady Gelding. Maybe I'll have a word with Lachie about this, McPeevish said to himself. If anyone would know it was Lachie.

Over the years the Manor had been besieged, ransacked, rebuilt, besieged and ransacked, rebuilt and so on. During these ransackings, mentioned in the documents by chroniclers of the times, much was stolen, much was burnt or destroyed; but there was no mention of the fate of the portrait by da

Vinci or of the Psalter and his notes.

The assumption must be that they were among the items which were ransacked, McPeevish thought.

The mouse was shaking its head.

Did it want more biscuits or brandy?

- Come on, McPeevish, the mouse said; you're a published author; you can do better than that.

I suppose I can, McPeevish thought as he gazed around himself at the dusty shelves and cobwebs hanging high up.

- What a wonderful little creature, the beloved said.

Me? McPeevish thought.

- The mouse, the dear one said. You're wonderful too, of course. What's its name?

McPeevish had to confess that he hadn't thought to ask.

- Call me Kirkie, the mouse said.

- So what are we going to do about this? the dear one asked.

Jimmy will have to know, McPeevish thought.

- Of course, the dear one said; but what about the portrait and other goodies? Didn't the mouse say they were still around?

McPeevish wasn't sure the mouse had said anything. He took another stiff drink of malt.

- They have to have been hidden, the beloved said, frowning. Now where would you hide something like that?

Beats me, McPeevish thought.

- There must be a clue somewhere, the beloved mused.

When the beloved mused like that, McPeevish knew, there were consequences. The consequences weren't incalculable, but they did generally involve action and danger. When they had cleaned out the woodshed McPeevish had felt like a pioneer in New France hunting for his musket. He couldn't believe the stuff they hauled out of there. Once it was all on the lawn McPeevish did a quick calculation of the cubic capacity of the woodshed and decided that it had been impossible for even half of what was on the lawn to have been in the shed.

It reminded him very much of his mind: half of what was in there he didn't know was in there; and most of what he knew about that which was in there he wondered how it had got in. He also wondered why it had got in. Some of it he wondered when it would get out. When some came out he wondered why it had been in there in the first place, though he might understand why it had jumped ship. What might be left in there- his mind, not the woodshed, which was manifestly empty (apart from dust and long deserted bird nests) - he had no idea.

Having no idea didn't disturb him since he recognised that this was his usual state. McPeevish rejoiced whenever someone might ask him a question to which he could happily reply: I've no idea. He wasn't the kind of person, however, who waited about for such questions; sometimes he actively sought them out. Here was a perfect example:

Beloved's question: How on earth did all that stuff get into the woodshed?

McPeevish answer: I've no idea.

Beloved's question: Do you think it will all fit back in?

McPeevish answer: I've no idea.

Beloved's question: What shall we throw away?

McPeevish answer: I've no idea.

But to return to the problem of the missing treasure (the existence of which until that morning McPeevish could have honestly retorted 'I've no idea' had he been asked if it existed) McPeevish was clear: He had no idea where it was.

As to how they might find it- or (better) locate it and then find it- McPeevish could declare himself to be completely devoid of any idea. He could agree that they might dig, using a shovel, but he didn't know where, nor what kind of shovel. They might search, darting about hither and thither, but he didn't know where, nor whether thither was preferable to hither. There were too many places in the world- in the universe, if you were Dr. Who (which he wasn't, though he might wish he was)- for them to even chip the tip of the iceberg, or dent the side of the megalith, or...

He could see that the beloved had *that* look in here eyes. She had an idea.

- If you were being besieged, my love, the only place you could hide anything would be the place in which you were being besieged, would it not?

McPeevish could graciously concede that this was a reasonable hypothesis with which to start. But...

- Why not ask the mouse? If any of this lovely stuff has survived the Manor is the place to look; and since he pointed you to that document he must have a good idea of where the booty is, the dear one concluded.

McPeevish was in awe of her use of such classic jargon as 'booty' and swift resolution of what to him had seemed an intractable problem. Tractable problems he could handle with the same skill that Bertie Blackface handled the Manor's tractor at harvest time.

It's never as simple as asking a mouse, is it? McPeevish thought.

Here he was back in the library all primed to ask the mouse and...no mouse.

Perhaps I've dreamt the whole thing, he thought. That would be just like me. One minute I've got writer's block or composer's cramp, or some such complaint, and the next I'm like an overflowing cistern. What I need to do is keep a firm grip on reality.

McPeevish looked around for a handle or a piece of reality to grip. Everything looked quite tenuous and rather slippery, so he gave up the idea.

Let's go to the kitchen instead, he thought, and get a cup of tea.

*

The fair was a great success. The weather was as May-like as it could be. Dr. Who performed the opening ceremony with much élan and humour, charming the crowd with anecdotes about the filming of the show. Autographs were signed and photographs were taken with fans old and young. He delighted the crowd by mixing freely and even taking part in some of the events. Miss Potter (Mildred) was paired with him in the three-legged race and together they sailed down the course winning by a margin that impressed the onlookers who hadn't seen Mildred move so smartly- at least not since Rutledge Ronaldsay had proposed to her back in forty-five. McSwindel had miscalculated the odds and paid out with as much good grace- and cash- as he could muster. Dr. Who then judged the home made cakes and jam section in the food tent. His choice of the Dalek shaped jam tarts baked by twelve year old Patty Perendale was regarded as inevitable. McSwindel reached deep into his black bag and paid out again. In the Tug-of-War he had the gentlemen of '*The Dirk*', who tipped the scales together at something not short of a ton (old measure), as hot favourites against the five to ten year olds from Saint Soay's school, even though they were being anchored by Dr. Who. The gentlemen of '*The Dirk*' had over the course of the afternoon made frequent forays into the refreshment tent where Jim the barman was working the pumps in a Cyberman outfit. To the cry of "Aye ready! Aye ready!" the pull began. It was not clear afterwards whether this refreshment or the children's anchor tipped the scales, but McSwindel's face bore a fixed grin as he paid out on another upset. He was heard muttering about 'dark forces being at work'.

On either side of the grounds where the fair was taking place, on raised platforms were disposed the choir of the Episcopalians (the north side) and the choir of the Church of Scotland and United Presbyterians (south side). Throughout the afternoon their voices would waft across the lawns adding to the general gaiety. '*Dem bones, dem bones, dem dry bones*' came from the south and '*Joshua fit the battle of Jericho*' from the north. Both choirs joined in '*O, the old sheep know the road*' and '*Wonder where is good ole*

Daniel'. High-fives and alleluias rippled around the crowd like minnows scattering in a lake.

Ruby 'Gypsy' Rambouillet, who ran the 'Third Eye' boutique in the town, had a steady stream of customers to her tent. What she saw in her cards no one knew though all the men who emerged from her tent wore silly grins and looked rather cross-eyed. The ladies when they emerged seemed determined in their subsequent search of the grounds for whatever it was- or whoever it was- that they were seeking to find. The path to the boathouse seemed well trodden by the going down of the sun.

The raffle prize was won by teenage Tillie Teeswater and it took several minutes before her lips could be prised away from David Tennant's lips when he presented her with the complete collection of Dr. Who DVDs.

The children's hunt for the lost treasure of the blood-thirsty pirate 'Rotten' Rodriguez (played with verve and a cutlass between his teeth by Matty Dewspit) saw streams of squealing children dressed as Aggedors, Hoixes, Terileptils and Viperoxes hurtling around the grounds looking for clues hidden in bushes, wheelbarrows, potting sheds and outhouses. 'Romney' the confectioner had donated the prize of a specially made chocolate Dalek and tickets to see the latest 'Harry Potter' movie when it opened in London. Competition was fierce; mother's roared encouragement and stared narrow-eyed at each other. McSwindel was taking no bets on either human or alien.

The grounds of the Manor were spacious, which was just as well since also taking place were the archery, the axe-throwing, the clay pigeon shooting and tossing the caber events. Those who were surprised at Miss Bevel's win in the caber event didn't understand the muscle toning benefits of knitting.

Very popular too was the sheep herding contest, set in the maze. Sheep are good at mazes, as any shepherd knows, the sheep dogs less so. The sight of so many bewildered collies milling around in the maze while they grazed on the lawn had the sheep in stitches for days afterwards.

While the choirs took a break the pipes of the 'Oddfellows' Hall took over. *Hinda hindo, hinda hindo; Hindo, hindo, hinda, hinda...Hodroho hodroho, haninin hiechin; Hodroha, hodroho, hodroho hachin...*and the woodpeckers took up the beat. The strains of '*Wha'll be king but Charlie?*' and '*The maid of Islay*' swirled over the grounds causing fluttering flights of Pied Wagtails that soared vertically like the Red Arrows giving a display.

Though a time of general gaiety the day was also one of grim reality for Lord Gelding, for that morning the final demand pending court proceedings had been delivered by a doleful looking postman. For all the Gelding's attempts to keep their problems to themselves their predicament was common knowledge in the town. But like the family the townsfolk felt powerless to help.

A war council was being held late in the afternoon, in the Manor away from the celebration outside. Present were Jimmy, Lavinia, Lady Gelding, McPeevish himself and the dear one.

What a glum lot we are, McPeevish thought as he looked around the room. The only person who looks cheerful is the dear one.

- It's got to be in here somewhere, the beloved said. What we need is a map.

McPeevish could acknowledge that a map would be handy, but he could foresee problems. The main one was that they didn't have a map.

- Let's make one, the beloved said. We need a plan of the Manor first. Isn't there one in the library, dear heart?

McPeevish made his way to the library followed by the others. His tread was as heavy as his heart.

Come on, McPeevish, he urged himself. Would Hannay have given up before he found out what were the thirty-nine steps?

In the library the mouse was waiting for them. On the desk was a plan of the Manor.

- You see, the dear one smiled; Kirkie knows. What a clever mouse.

The mouse smoothed his whiskers and looked overcome with bashfulness. McPeevish instantly remembered the first time he and the dear one...

-A pity you can't come home with us, the dear one sighed.

- Have a look at the map, Binky, Lavinia said.

Binky? thought McPeevish. He noticed that Lord Gelding was becoming a shade embarrassed.

- Binky, how delightful, the beloved one said laughing lightly. Mine's Bonky!

Oh Lord, thought McPeevish feeling himself become embarrassed while the two ladies doubled up.

- This won't find the treasure, if there is any treasure, Lord Gelding said gruffly, the way men do when intimate details become public.

Quite, McPeevish concurred silently. He would have agreed but he thought that concurring was more in keeping with the solemnity of the situation.

The plan of the Manor hardly helps, McPeevish thought as he studied it with Binky- Jimmy. Mind on the business in hand, McPeevish, he urged himself. These are friends you're trying to help.

The dear one looked over his shoulder, resting her chin on it.

- Where's the X? she asked. There's always an X.

As far as McPeevish could see there was no X.

- Where would you put an X? the dear one asked.

McPeevish considered this from all sides- front, back, sideways, top, bottom up, the lot. He could see Lady Gelding, Jimmy and Lavinia looking at him hopefully.

The mouse- Kirkie- was drumming his fingers on the desk.

This is bizarre, McPeevish thought: a mouse with fingers.

- Get on with it, McPeevish, Kirkie said. You're the author; you can do what you want.

I'm the author, McPeevish thought. I've never looked at it that way.

- Where did you have 'Rotten' Rodriguez hide his treasure? the beloved asked.

If memory serves me, McPeevish thought, it was the usual place: buried on a deserted island in the Caribbean.

The dear one nudged him.

- Then just put a cross in the usual place, dear heart. Pretend it's the Pools. You can do it.

I can do it, McPeevish thought; I'm the author. What I say goes. Right then. McPeevish closed his eyes. He could hear the others draw in their breath.

This, he thought, was it.

He took a blind stab with the pencil at the plan.

*

"As the 'Tardis' slowly rose into the evening sky the crowd of merry-makers stood and waved good-bye to the Doctor."
A perfect end to a perfect day, McPeevish thought as, arm and arm with the dear one, he walked back through the town."

*

But a story can't end like this, he thought. There are too many loose ends! Where were the da Vinci portrait and his sketches? Where was Saint Columba's Psalter? What happened to the mouse? Why did Sergeant Sandpiper start to chase Gillie Gritstone around the Auction tent? Come on, any author worth his salt wouldn't leave it dangling like that, McPeevish!

- There's a cup of tea down here for you, dearest, the beloved one called up the stairs.

Whew! Thank goodness for that, McPeevish thought as he saved his work and switched off the computer. The dear one had a perfect sense of timing.

He raced Shayla down the stairs. The cat hurtled to the right, aiming for the fridge; McPeevish veered to the left, aiming for the cup of tea in the living-room.

He had only just raised the cup to his lips when he caught sight of Shayla sitting accusingly in the doorway.

- Oh dear, the beloved said. You had better tend to her first.

Once McPeevish had appeased Shayla's hurt feelings by filling her bowl with a surfeit of sprats, he resumed his armchair and the cup of tea.

- I thought Jimmy's speech at the National Gallery when they unveiled the portrait of his many-greats granny Gelding was lovely, the dear one said. The family resemblance was unmistakeable.

It had been, McPeevish thought a most agreeable conclusion to the matter. The National Gallery got the da Vinci drawing and his sketches of farming implements; the Museum got the colourful copy of the Psalter; and the Geldings would pay no tax for at least a generation.

Experts had fallen over themselves to authenticate the items. The moment McPeevish saw them, there where they had lain hidden for five hundred years or more, he had known that they were utterly genuine. Everyone started kissing everyone else in the small library as McPeevish's cry of success had echoed back to them. Lady Gelding- the mother- had rushed straight out to tell the horses (which celebrated in the usual fashion) while Jimmy- his Lordship or Binky- and Lavinia had rushed to tell the servants. When the word spread like the proverbial wild fire amongst the crowd who had stayed on for the country dancing after David Tennant had departed in his 'Tardis' designed balloon, the floor of the great hall shook so much it registered as a four scale earth tremor at the British Geological Survey centre in Edinburgh.

- You were very clever to work out where they were hidden, the beloved smiled. It was a perfect X, if ever I saw one. You wonder how all those ransackers could miss it.

People often overlook something that's right under their nose, McPeevish agreed. It was the old stand-by probably first described by Edgar Alan Poe in '*The Purloined Letter*'. Father Brown in '*The Broken Sword*' summed it up rather nicely: '*Where does a wise man hide a leaf? In the forest.*' There was even a nod in its direction in '*The Five Doctors*' episode of Dr. Who, McPeevish recalled. The musical code that unlocked Rassilon's secret chamber was on the pieces of music depicted in a nearby painting.

Mus ex machina indeed, he had thought when he opened his eyes and saw where the pencil had marked. All he had to do was to follow the dancing mouse and he was there.

McPeevish on Holiday

The maid with her lover the wild daisies pressed
On the banks of my own lovely Lee.

- And this is my mother.

At that precise moment McPeevish's eye had been drawn to the elderly person sitting on a stool whittling. With a slight bow McPeevish greeted her and kissed the gnarled hand which wasn't wielding the small knife.

- That is my father's hand you've just kissed, the dear one said. This is my mother.

Ah, thought McPeevish; *That* and *this* again. I must remember which is which.

The eyes which gazed into his were sparkling with humour.

- You've no need to kiss my hand, she said. You're lucky young man that he didn't slice your gizzard. So you're the daft stray our Caitlin's taken in. You'll be wanting a cup of tea, by the look of you. Sit down before the dog mounts you. Conbec, leave him alone.

- Who is that daft bugger? the old man said, as he inspected the line of the whistle he'd made.

- That's Caitlin's daft bugger, father, Mrs. O'Kelly shouted.

- What'd he kiss my hand for?

- He thought you was I, father.

The old man looked sharply at McPeevish.

- Daft and blind, eh.

- So what do I call you? the dear one's mother enquired as she busied herself with the kettle on the hob.

- Och just call him McPeevish, the dear one said. He'll answer to that. Otherwise he gets confused.

The dog, an Irish wolfhound of about twenty hands by McPeevish's estimation, stood on the floor in the centre of the kitchen. There did not appear to be any corner of the kitchen which a part of the dog didn't reach. A swish of its tail, as thick as a hawser, would have emptied the shelves of the dresser of cups and plates. Its head rested on McPeevish's knee and its eyes gazed happily into his.

- Don't let it hypnotise you, Mrs. O'Kelly said. Once it has done that it'll have you bouncing like a ball all round the garden.

McPeevish forced himself to blink. The dog sighed and moved away.

- We've put you up the top at the back, Mrs. O'Kelly said to her daughter. You'll have to shut the door to keep Conbec out.

- Conbec's used to sleeping on the bed there, the dear one explained.

McPeevish thought a door was a fine idea, though he rather suspected that Conbec could shoulder aside even the fortified gate of Blarney Castle.

- Take a cup to your father.

McPeevish watched the old man whittling another whistle. In the wicker basket by his side there were several newly whittled whistles.

- He's yet to tune them, the dear one whispered as she sat beside him with her cup of tea. We'd best be out when he starts that. Conbec helps him by howling. The finished whistle is fine; but the getting it finished is what can finish you.

It was a good job the house stood on its own, McPeevish thought.

- I'll take him for a walk by the river, the dear one said to her mother who was looking at the pair of them with some amusement.

- He's the quietest man I've never heard, Mrs. O'Kelly remarked.

- Oh don't be fooled, mother. He's just a bit shy to begin with. Taking it all in before he commits himself. Memorising the wallpaper and how the light falls. Once he starts there'll be no stopping him.

- He's a great one for the stories, you were saying in your letters.

Letters? McPeevish thought.

- Oh yes, he writes a lot.

- Don't let your father know that or your man won't have an ear left.

- Father, appearances to the contrary, is the reason there are so many three-legged donkeys in the county, the dear one whispered. Once he gets started on one of his stories, usually about hunting and wolves, you've had it for the evening. The best thing is to have a fit. I used to when I was little.

- Is he with Caitlin then, Mary? the old man called from the garden.

- Memory span of a slug, Mrs. O'Kelly smiled. No, he's with Conbec, father.

- What's the dog brought that one home for?

- He was fed up with your whistling.

- I've not whistled since Tuesday.

- You don't know when Tuesday is, father.

- What breed is he?

- Half Scots and half English, the dear one replied.

- Which half's which? her father asked.

The dear one eyed McPeevish carefully.

- It's hard to tell in this light, father.

- Can he do anything useful?

- Does anything as well as Cúchulain can whistle.

- I'll take him down the pub after supper then, the old man said.

- That kiss on the hand must have done the trick, the dear one said. You'll meet all his cronies.

- Tell him not to kiss anyone else's hand, mind, her father called. They're a bit peculiar about that sort of thing down "The Hounds of Banba".

McPeevish indicated that he fully understood. He was not to kiss any more hands.

- Tell him he's not to ask for a Black and Tan either. There are some got long memories, even if I haven't.

McPeevish caught the quick smile which flitted across the old man's lips.

- If you take Conbec with you he should be safe enough.

- Conbec's got his eye on the bitch O'Riordain brings in, so he'll be otherwise engaged.

McPeevish tried hard not to think about Conbec in that light.

- I'll take you to see the river now, the dear one said to McPeevish when they had finished their tea. It's much like any other river- fish, tadpoles, weeds, that kind of thing. But it does play a rather jolly tune.

- Supper's at six, Mrs. O'Kelly advised.

*

The *Neamh* is a gaily chattering stream not far from the Blarney River, which itself can spin a fair tale or two. The latter ran into the River *An Laoi* (Lee)- much celebrated in song- which, rising in the Shehy mountains to the West near Gauganberra emptied into the Celtic Sea at Cork City. It was said, so the dear one explained to McPeevish as they strolled by the Neamh with Conbec, that a young man who crossed all forty-two bridges over the Lee- twenty-nine of which were in the city itself- would never want for admirerers amongst the fairer sex. It seemed to McPeevish that there were many things a young man might have to do to be sure of winning the attention of Irish maidens and he was glad that he was in his maturity and spared all that, though he was sure there was still much fun to be had without scrambling over bridges, be they of brick, stone or wood. Crossing bridges was all very well, he thought, but forty-two was rather a lot, especially as they were spread along the fifty odd mile length of the Lee. A young man might run out of puff and pizzazz long before he met the maidens eager to admire him.

At times the stream seemed to be playing 'The Whistlin' Gypsy' and at other times 'The Juice of the Barley'. McPeevish had to concede that he had never heard such a melodic stream and the dear one assured him the trick was partly in the disposition of the stones and pebbles over which the water ran, partly in the early evening sunlight which shone upon the waters spreading warmth and pleasure which added tone to the play of the waters on the stones and partly to be sure was in the ear of the beholder. Many a courting couple, she smiled, had added their tune to that of the waters. An old fiddle, she said lightly, could often play a merry tune.

Had there been more bushes McPeevish felt he might have been at risk, but at that moment the dear one gave an unmaidenly whoop, leapt on to Conbec's back and was carried across the stream in a bound. Clinging to the hound she raced along the opposite bank and vanished from view. As McPeevish continued to follow the path on his side of the stream he could hear the hoots and cries as the dear one was carried through the undergrowth by the racing hound. Five minutes later he saw them leaping across the stream some yards ahead and waiting patiently for him to reach them. The dear one was carrying her shoes in her mouth and had her skirt bunched up into her undergarments. She was grinning down at McPeevish and looking like a ten year old.

- Sorry about that, dear heart, she said. Conbec and I always used to do that when I was a kid and it wouldn't be the same without a ride on him. Would you like to try?

McPeevish, despite the obviously eagerness in Conbec to comply, expressed the view that perhaps another day might be best for such an experiment since her parents might feel it a trifle odd should he return drenched and bedraggled. He had some social ground to make up, he felt, after kissing the father's hand. An act in Italy which might have gained him kudos with a Don, in Ireland perhaps simply marked him all the more as a 'daft bugger'. The hound seemed disappointed but happy for the dear one to remain perched on his back like Ériu as they began the return journey hungry for their supper.

*

Patrick, for that was Caitlin's father's name, as it was of virtually every other man he met in "The Hounds of Banba", had introduced McPeevish as 'Caitlin's daft bugger' to all and sundry. For some reason this seemed to stand McPeevish in good stead. Nobody asked him what he did or who his parents were. That he was 'Caitlin's daft bugger' seemed to explain his presence and state of being. Had he had two heads and a long tail being

'Caitlin's daft bugger' would have covered it all nicely.

When he tried to pay for a pint the old man gave him a look which was unmistakable and McPeevish stayed his hand.

Much of the conversation was about the upcoming races at Cork's course on the Killarney Road in Mallow. A local horse- *Dromoland Castle*- was running. It was felt she was well suited to the twelve furlong right-handed flat track with its eight fences. An odd number of fences might have altered the thing but never mind, all was well as all was even. There were some horses which could only jump the odd numbered fences and that was no good at all when there were even ones too, though much merriment could be caused should it be the afternoon of the *Cumann Matamaitice na hÉireann* (Irish Mathematical Society) outing. To see them with the calculus and the abacus, not to mention the quipus, never mind the pen and paper, was a hoot. Some horses became confused with the left and the right, as much as did many jockeys, who had the two reins and two stirrups to manage as well as the balance and the goggles. It was no help to look up and see which way the tricolour might be flying from the grandstand flag pole, nor which way the geese might be heading, should they bother flying. Following the first horse that shot beneath the tape could be folly. Patrick the barman was collecting the betting money which he'd be placing with his brother Seamus who had a shop in the city where one could do that sort of thing. The odds were 15/1 and sure that was a bit long but everybody in the village knew that it was a winner as long as the girl O'Callaghan was in the saddle and the nosebag was off. There was general agreement that the girl O'Callaghan was magic in the saddle. Fingers pointed to an old saddle mounted behind the bar assuring McPeevish that this was a famous *Tairise* saddle much sat upon by the tribe O'Callaghan, for her mother before her had been a grand lady in the saddle and had won many a cross-country race before she was caught by the man who was now her husband and that was him there in the corner winning at cards, despite the absence of one thumb which was lost during a harvest some years ago and though the hay was shifted by all and sundry not a trace of the thumb was to be seen. Her man was evermore thereafter of the opinion that a thumb on that hand had been an encumbrance and his hand slid more comfortably into his pocket without it. The mention of the lost thumb brought a pause in the conversation as it had in the harvesting all those years ago. It was agreed that Patrick O'Kelly's daughter had been a fine rider too though she was more a girl for the flat and the speed than the jumps and the bumps. 'Twas a pity she had left for the other place over the water there for they were sure she would have rivalled O'Callaghan in the saddle. It was wondered if she still visited the saddle and all the company looked politely to Mr. O' Kelly for the answer. He was lighting his pipe- it could have been a whistle which had gone wrong, McPeevish thought- and he considered the point for a puff or two. Then he looked inquisitively at McPeevish who assured him, and Mr. O'Kelly the company- for sometimes McPeevish knew his accent did not hang right in the air and he had caught the puzzled glances of the company a few times- that the dear one still rode in the local cross-country and was a fine horse-woman, which seemed to content them all. It was agreed that once you'd been in the saddle you should never stop and never forgot, much as riding a bicycle, once mastered, you never forgot, though the pedals might give problems depending on your footwear. It was asked if McPeevish himself rode but a glance at his legs was enough for the company to conclude that he did not. It was agreed that they were fine legs he had in his possession for standing on and that they would stand him in good stead and not be out of place at any bar in the land, and perhaps he might even cycle with them, for there were two of the fellows, which was the right and sufficient number for that kind of activity; but a horse-rider's legs they were not. If you were looking for the template of a horse-rider's legs you need look no further than that fellow Finnegan outside watching the grass grow while he waited for his glass to empty; which would happen sooner no one could rightly tell, since it often became dark before one or the other came to pass. A bowling ball- two side by side- would have passed through his legs without distressing the turn-ups. Patrick the shy was willing to bet that three bowling balls would fit but there were no takers, it being thought unseemly to bet on such an attribute. It was thought likely that the sun would set any time soon and those who then glanced out of the door would be spared the sight of those legs. If the sun did not set that might be a good thing for the wife, Patrick the bald said, since when he'd left the house the sheets were still hanging to dry and a few more hours would do no harm, even if it confused the bats in the church tower. For a while it was debated which might be the preferable, dried sheets or confused bats. There was no consensus, though they shifted a few stools and generally cast about for one before it became necessary to fill the glasses once more.

The church tower of Saint Saobhchaint's, McPeevish was informed, was the most unique tower in Christendom and certainly should have been more famous than that propped up telescope in Pisa. Had he been to Pisa? McPeevish indicated that he had not and the company acknowledged that neither had they for there were telescopes a plenty hereabouts for those who wanted to peep at anything beyond the reach of their eyesight, which was unusually keen, a result of the carrot crop which never failed. They kept quiet about the church tower because they did not want all those tourists coming with their digitalis cameras and curry vans and whatever next to disturb the bats which were very comfortable in the tower and had been for centuries since Patrick the saint had given them leave to enter and multiply. It had been bad enough when that fellow Achtenberg, the one with the brother who made those movies about dinosaurs- which had not been seen around thereabouts for some time, possibly on account of the wolfhounds which couldn't abide reptiles (at which word McPeevish noticed the recumbent Conbec prick up his ears) – when that feller had come around with his cameras and microphones wanting to record the bats beeping and farting. If there was one thing sure to scare the bats out of the tower it was a microphone, never mind a fellow whose brother made movies about reptiles running loose about the countryside. Patrick the limp had seen a microphone once when his cow Macha gave birth to pure white triplets with the bull not having been near her and someone from *Raidió Teilifís Éireann* had wanted to interview him. Patrick nodded and said they had interviewed the cow for five minutes but all she did was moo, which was convivial of her since she did not usually take to strangers. One of the company added that when they had interviewed Patrick himself all he did was moo too. Ah but there's mooing and there's mooing, it was agreed after much discussion of diphthongs, a topic which all were agreed seldom arose but, since it had, was well worth a good chewing over. The bats were very well educated and some Sundays should the sermon take a less than traditional turn you could hear their wings rustling unhappily above. The rustling wings kept the priest theologically right and the congregation awake. Once "The Hounds of Banba" closed its doors for the night- which it did though the key was often lost and those late repenting might still make their confession, as it were, past midnight- it was the custom of some of the unwed young men to make their way to the tower and count the bats, for it was thought that if you counted all the bats then you would meet your bride-to-be the very next day. There were others who thought that if you counted all the bats you became one of their number, which perhaps accounted for the disappearances of the likes of Murphy the shoe and Devlin the hat, though others held that it was on account of their debts that they had withdrawn from view. Those who fell in the river on the way might float for a while and count the stars, having lost their interest in the bats on account of being wet outside as well as inside. There was no consensus on the number of bats. One fervent priest- long gone and not missed in the least for his sermons had been as drawn out as the penance of Saint Culpoc's rosary, which was endless, and left you parched without hope of a drop of the necessary restorative until the Monday at noon

– had decided there were six hundred and sixty six of the fellows (though if this was by the infinitesimal calculus and its 'ghosts of departed quantities' criticised by Bishop Berkley in "*The Analyst*" it was not known, nor did it really matter since 'one two buckle my shoe' was as good as 'three four shut the door') and sought ecclesiastical permission to have the tower fumigated- or defumigated, whichever it was. The Bishop was particularly fond of bats, having grown up in the village himself, and was not minded to have any truck with this fumigation business; so the priest- was it Father Dander or Gander? – wrote to the Cardinal, a man who could flip zucchettos with the best of them. The Cardinal himself came down incognito arriving by the bicycle and visited the tower, where he meditated with the bats and before he left he visited "The Hounds" where he assured all the Patricks and others who had spotted him by the absence of cycle clips and the Gammarelli red hose over the trousers, that the bats would not be fumigated, excommunicated or anything-ated. It was Father Meander- or was he Philander? – who was shifted to another parish where there were neither bats nor tower, only flatness and as much peat as a man could possibly want to see in a lifetime. Before he left the village McPeevish was urged to visit the tower and see the bats, which were now a species protected by European law, which was a fine thing as long as it didn't interfere with the hurling. He was advised to wear some headgear and to have a clove of garlic in his pocket- it didn't matter which pocket since he looked like a man who had several pockets, though he wore them with discretion. Some people, it was agreed, flaunted their pockets and gave themselves airs because of them. It was something McPeevish might like to note, since they knew from Patrick O'Kelly that he was fond of employing the pencil, which was an honourable trade if ever there was one, that there once had been a time when within the parish there had not been five men with pockets- *Na cúig pócaí* as they were called by those who could count. Now pockets were commonplace and most of the villagers had one, though not all made use of the pocket for the want of what to put in one that would not sit just as sweetly in a sack.

McPeevish ventured ten Euros on *Dromoland Castle* and received his hand-written receipt with much ceremony. Patrick the post applied the stamp to make it all legal if barely legible thereafter. When invited to play some darts by one of the younger Patricks McPeevish stepped up to the oche with the confidence of the two pints of Guinness he had consumed. On the walk back the dear one's father complimented him on the way he had parted his opponent's hair with a dart. With practice he might become a barber had been the general verdict once his opponent had recovered his nerve.

When they reached the house the lights were on and Mrs. O'Kelly and the dear one in their chairs the one knitting and the other reading. The cheese board was on the table, with the bread knife and a half loaf, and the kettle was gently steaming on the hob. McPeevish felt content.

*

The dear one was out for the count and dreaming the moment her head hit the pillow. McPeevish had secured the door with the latch, as instructed, and had joined her. He was on the verge of throwing his arms around her and entering the sweet land of Lethe when a weight fell between him and the dear one. If someone had driven a steam-roller through the bed the divide could not have been clearer. Where the delicate curls of the dear one had spread on the pillow there now was a shaggy grey head the size of a well bucket.

- Conbec, shove over, he heard the beloved murmur.

McPeevish clung to the bed as the great dog rolled a few centimetres towards him. He had, he estimated, fifty centimetres if that which he could claim as his kingdom. Conbec licked his face with a tongue the size of a shovel's head and eased some wind from his fundament.

- Bad dog, the dear one murmured.

McPeevish thought of Alpine climbers clinging to the steep sides of the Eiger or peaks like K2. There was nothing for it: he threw an arm around Conbec and clung for dear life. On the other side of the great bulwark lay the dear one, as out of reach as any Princess in a fairy story.

This, thought McPeevish, is going to be a long night. It's hard to sleep with a dog the size of Conbec gazing devotedly into your eyes.

*

The *Scáil Theatre* in Cork looks over the River Lee between the Usarb and Tuinneamh pedestrian bridges. These are the oldest bridges in the city, older than the South Gate Bridge which was built in 1713. There are those who, superstition ruling their souls, will only cross these bridges from the north to the south side. Other bridges they will skip over willy-nilly, caring not a fig for the direction in which they may go. Countless others, male or female, be-hatted or bare-headed, cross the river in whichever direction they wish by these and any other bridges. There are no bye-laws to regulate the flow of pedestrians for such reasons. It is true that one cannot walk over the bridges of Cork stark naked and crossing a bridge whilst juggling-whether it be plates, swords or fruit- is frowned upon, though not expressly forbidden. Cork is not unusual in this respect. It is true that there are still laws which prohibit a trader from carrying any song-bird in a cage across bridges, or from peddling holy candles after midnight on a bridge; but these are anomalies which, were there more time, the town council would abolish. Time was one of those things which in the meetings of *Comhairle Cathrach Chorcaí* (Cork City Council) ran out sooner than it did should one be sitting on a bench beside the river watching the swans floating by. Time would flow past just as readily were they ducks rather than swans. You would often find the town clerk looking inside the old clock in the empty assembly room of the city chambers shaking his head and muttering 'Where has all the time gone?' To have received a reply would have been a shock; to receive no reply left him still perplexed and winding the clock. It took forty-nine turns to fully wind the spring: one more and it would have broken, though the town clerk did not know this.

McPeevish, with the dear one by his side, watched the ebb and flow of the early evening crowd over these bridges. Like some others they were waiting for the doors of the theatre to open at seven for the performance at eight of James Joyce's recently discovered second play 'Macroom'. His first- 'Exiles', completed in 1918- had been drawn from the story 'The Dead' in 'Dubliners'.

Ireland is a country of surprises, McPeevish thought. Unknown things are found in the most unusual places and the most unusual things are found in places nobody would dream of looking!

In 'A Portrait of the Artist as a Young Man' Joyce wrote:

> *'I am walking beside my father whose name is Simon Dedalus.*
> *We are in Cork, Ireland. Cork is a city. Our room is in the*
> *Victoria Hotel...'*

The hotel, built in 1810, is in St. Patrick's Street but had recently closed because of structural problems. During the work taking place in the rather twisted building an old suitcase was discovered in one of the unused coal cellars.

Few in Ireland have the instinct to just throw anything found away, be it history, memory or some artefact. In England perhaps given the national temperament and the state of disrepair of the old suitcase- it had mildew on the outside and the handle was twists of twine- it would have been pitched straight into the skip; and from there it would have found its way to the city tip, where it would have been ploughed in and served as landfill. Whatever might then have grown out of it would not have been what did grow out of it. But in Ireland the old is not automatically viewed as junk and treated unkindly. The workman who found the suitcase- Brian O'Nolan- was one of those curious fellows who liked to know what was inside things. It is true that, as a youngster, he had built up quite a record for the breaking and entering, but he was motivated only by the desire to see inside rather than to pilfer. Since he had been stepping out with his young lady he had been contented and had given up his burgling ways. But a suitcase found in such circumstances awoke his curiosity. During his lunch break, whilst his mates repaired to the near-by '*Tarcim*' bar, O'Nolan brushed the dust and dirt from the suitcase and read the still legible label:

Mr. James Joyce,
C/o the Victoria Hotel
Cork.

Well, well! O'Nolan thought and headed for the *Coláiste na hOllscoile Corcaigh* (University College Cork) on the bank of the south channel of the Lee.

James Joyce left Ireland in 1902. On his father's side his family came from Cork, where they had been merchants and owned property. From its contents it was clear that the suitcase had been left behind during his last visit to the city and had been put into storage and then forgotten about altogether. There was undoubtedly mild interest in Joyce's choice of shirts and ties and under-things, as well as the type of toothpaste and shaving soap he used. But the real excitement lay in the discovery of a typed and annotated manuscript of the play about to be performed for the first time ever.

Tickets were scarce and how the dear one had secured them McPeevish did not know. In Moffat he was used to the strangely effective way in which the dear one, with the minimum of fuss and personal derangement, could arrange things which seemed impossible and improbable. That she was able to do the same thing in her native land perhaps should not have surprised him. Favours may well have been called in. Blackmail of a sort may have been used. Nothing as indiscreet as a dead horse's head in the bed for her! A nod, a raised eyebrow, a wistful piece of reminiscence which delicately indicated that which the hearer did not wish to become general knowledge would become general knowledge- all these methods McPeevish had seen utilised in Moffat with remarkable effect. But here her father's name and that of his village had seemed to be the key. O'Kelly was a popular name, was it not, for there were pages devoted to O'Kellys in the local telephone book; but Patrick O'Kelly of Sonas- well now, was she sure that just the two tickets would be enough? And how was Patrick these days- still whittling? Now don't be foolish, no one would be charging the daughter of Patrick

O'Kelly for tickets I'm sure! Just tell him Fergal was asking after him and his good wife- and you'll still have a Conbec? Well that's a blessing I'm sure.

The dear one had smiled her thanks and bestowed upon McPeevish one of those innocent as an angel looks which told him beyond dispute that she had been *very* wicked indeed!

As the house lights dimmed, the curtain- a fine red velveteen affair that had hung with hardly a crease in it and had unveiled many a fine set in its time- went up to reveal a junkyard, around which was a high, wooden fence topped with barbed wire.

As the ghosts closed in McPeevish thought: Ye gods!

He hoped that the stage lights would fuse, but knew that the gods weren't listening. Why should they be? It was Saturday night and there was plenty of fun to be had in Cork- but unfortunately not here, McPeevish thought. If he could have sunk any further into his seat he would have replaced the cushion. He had the demeanour of a man who was haunted.

McPeevish, his ears pricked, leant against a pillar and affected a kinship therewith which he hoped would effectively discourage any stranger turning to him and asking him what he thought about it then. The dear one was circulating and talking to old friends she had not seen for a few years. This was the sort of thing she did best without the encumbrance of a McPeevish, though now and then she would point in his direction and he would raise his glass in acknowledgement as the eyes of her friends sized him up.

The discussions in the bar afterwards ebbed and flowed with passion and indiscretion. That the play was *avant garde* no one doubted. That it said 'ta ta' to Dada was beyond dispute. That it was absurd everyone concurred. Though it was surreal there was in it an element of *Noh*, if one may say so. What was the point of the rattle? Who was that figure in the wings that never entered? Were the noises off meant to be noises off or just noises off?

It was post-apocalyptical.

It was pre-mythical.

Only Joyce could have written it.

If only Joyce hadn't written it.

We'll have to rethink our complete approach to the evolution of the theatre. We'll have to evolve our theatre in order to approach a rethink.

We'll have to refill our glasses because they're empty and it's a free bar.

No wonder he left it in a suitcase in a cellar.

What kind of shirts did you say he wore?

If it's meaningless why are we even talking about it?

Well, McPeevish thought, it had certainly stirred up the mud at the bottom of the pool.

A sharp-eyed man, rather dandified and sporting a blue carnation approached McPeevish.

- I know you, don't I?

McPeevish thought not.

- You're here incognito- understood.

McPeevish looked over the man's shoulder trying to catch the dear one's eye. This could be tricky.

- *Entre nous*, the man said, sniffing his carnation; what did you think of it? Load of bollocks or what?

McPeevish coughed and took a liberal swallow of his drink.

- Personally I think it's a joke; you know, some university wind-up for April Fool's Day.

Was that the time? McPeevish thought desperately.

- Beckett's '*Eleutheria*' had the same effect on me, you know.

McPeevish had no idea things could be that bad.

- What I like is a plot, characters, a bit of meat to get your teeth into. Give me Synge, Shaw, Sheridan.

McPeevish felt the nails being driven in deeper and deeper.

- Where do they all come from, eh? Just look at them all. A night out with Joyce isn't what it used to be, mark my words. Couldn't hold his liquor, you know. Always singing dirty rugby songs in French and Italian. Fine voice? More like a mouse peeing through a pipette.

McPeevish decided it was time to head for the bar and get a refill. The gentleman with the blue carnation vanished as though he'd been a figment of McPeevish's imagination.

-Time to go? the dear one whispered materialising beside him.

McPeevish indicated in the simplest way possible that it was and together they lamped it out into the fresh night air.

- He thought you were *who*? the dear one asked.

She looked at the paper she was reading and quoted: 'Harold Pinter told me afterwards that he thought it was the most riveting play he'd seen in years. "A great boost for theatre" were his very words.'''

McPeevish tried to look sheepish and felt a clean breast of it was best before lunch.

- You did *what*? the dear one asked, incredulous as again she peered around the '*Irish Examiner*' in which she was reading Cormac Diblíghim's column on 'The Stage' with its glowing review of the play.

Having heard McPeevish explain once again the silly student prank he had pulled many years ago on his only previous visit to Ireland, the dear one put down the paper and helplessly began to howl with laughter.

Conbec, deciding this was for him, joined in, adding a balancing bass to the beloved's higher pitched tones. He wasn't sure about the tune but was all for a bit of scat.

Mrs. O'Kelly, busy making some bread, didn't miss a beat as she kneaded the dough.

- Will you just listen to the pair of them, father! she said.

Mr. O'Kelly whittled on without slicing off a finger.

- D'you think we should be calling out Father O'Brien to throw the holy water over them, Mary? he called from the back garden.

*

Conbec growled and dug his feet in.

At the opposite end of the tug-of-war was another wolfhound, differing only from Conbec in that it seemed twice as big and better groomed. Somehow McPeevish felt Conbec could not win. The other hound had almost double its body-weight and considerable more leverage in its lengthy limbs. Its jaws would have devoured a cannon ball and still have had room for dessert. The two hounds had been locked in battle for fifteen minutes. None of the spectators was saying a word. The kerchief tied in the middle of the taut rope fluttered like a butterfly anxious to be about its business but stuck on something sticky, like stretched toffee.

The larger hound's growl seemed louder, deeper, more menacing.

- Dad says you shouldn't groom a wolfhound, the dear one whispered in McPeevish's ear. It takes away the wolf in them.

He was enthralled by the spectacle as much as any of the several dozen onlookers. Between the two hounds the rope- a twenty-six millimetre hemp rope McPeevish thought, the kind used for very heavy industrial lifting and (he was given to understand) by those who dabbled in bondage- seemed to become thinner and thinner as they heaved backwards. McPeevish wondered at its approximate breaking strength. If it snapped he suspected the taller members of the front row of onlookers would be decapitated. Instinctively he let his head sink between his shoulders.

- It'll be over in a minute, the dear one whispered.

McPeevish wondered how she could tell. Neither of the monoliths, once they had snapped back into the 'heave' position had budged. The world beneath them may well have moved but, if so, neither of them had noticed it. A regiment of rabbits could have danced under their noses and they wouldn't have paid attention. They stared across the space between them with a fixity that a statue would have envied.

If he had blinked McPeevish would have missed it, the moment when it was all over.

Neart atá ar marthain fós (शक्ति मे ॔ है शा ंति)- 'strength is in stillness': a Zen hound? McPeevish marvelled.

One moment the two hounds were locked in immobility and the next the great hound opposing Conbec had flown over his head and into the crowd with a flip as fast and delicate as that used by the dear one to tickle trout in the Tweed!

Did he catch Conbec winking at them as they moved with him through the crowd taking in the stalls and displays? McPeevish could hear the locals discussing what they had just witnessed. It had been the same last year and the year before that, and as far back as you cared to go in the line of Conbecs. Once O'Riordain's bitch had her litter Patrick O'Kelly would have to choose the new Conbec-to-be. That was the marvel of the man: he could always pick the right one. There wasn't a man in the county with his eye for the hound that was agreed. McPeevish decided it was like replacing the Dalai Lama, except that the Great Spirit was implanted by more direct means.

-Neat, wasn't it? the dear one smiled.

McPeevish wondered how Conbec had known the exact moment to flick.

- It's in the eyes, the dear one said. Do you remember when we first met?

How could I not? McPeevish thought. A crowded tea room in Moffat one Saturday afternoon; he was mulling over a route map when the soft voice of a waitress asked if 'this lady' might sit at his table there being no room elsewhere. McPeevish had glanced up; his eyes had met those of this stranger- Snap!

- Exactly, the dear one said, squeezing his arm.

The village was like a bride decked out for her wedding. Colourful flowers curtsied in pots and boxes on window sills and stalls were set up on the village green.

It was the annual summer fair which involved displays of animals and craft, music and dance, and all kinds of competitions. Unlike the various festivals back in Moffat, which seemed to run throughout the year and to bring in visitors from far and wide, this fair was for the locals, their relatives who would come back from wherever they had moved to and one or two others who lived in the surrounding county and were competing. Any passers-by well they were welcome too but it was few who passed by this part of the county for there were plenty of roads with plenty of signs and arrows inviting and directing you elsewhere and elsewhere often seemed to have a more beguiling aspect, though once you reached Sonas well, who would want to take the road out? Today it was a day for walking about with your hands in or out of your pockets and shaking hands with each other and enjoying the air and the sunshine and the music and catching up on what had been happening since you had last met, even if that were only yesterday which- and here's no surprise- was only yesterday. Between yesterday and today much could happen, even if it was the changing of the cloth on the table or the hatching of the birds' eggs in the old guttering of the shed and the baking of a loaf or cake for the fair. The food was not to be missed either, though it was best to keep the dancing separate from the eating if you could since for some the mouth and the foot might become confused and the chewing and the tapping prove awkward in the extreme. 'The Hounds of Banba' decorated like Fingal's Cave was open all day, after the blessing by Father O'Brien who drew and drank the first pint which he pronounced to be as handsome as ever and this enabled the awaiting crowd to give free rein to their thirsts. The local Garda Siochána officer named Moriarty, whose freshly pressed uniform hung on a hook at home for the day, observed all with a kindly eye, giving directions to those who might be lost, their number increasing as the sun arched overhead and the water of life flowed.

All God's creatures seemed to be there- horses and cows and chickens and goats. There were animals McPeevish had never seen before, some sneaking around the back of 'The Hounds' and others boldly were entering through its open door. Someone had built an Ark- how closely modelled on Noah's original McPeevish could not say- and up and down its gangplank strolled the denizen of the village, showing off their plumage or coats and tails. Some had been eager to pull ploughs and draw straight furrows across the fields under the keen eye of Michael Lanigan who all were agreed had the straightest eye in the village. If you wanted your shelves level on the wall then Michael was the man for it, though carpentry was not his trade. For gauging the straightness of your furrow Lanigan was the man, though he did not till the soil himself, leaving that to others who had the feet for it. Other creatures clucked merrily or bleated with joy when their noses weren't in your pocket checking for sweeties or grain. The chickens had formed a choir, organised by the barnyard cats, and sat on the fences serenading all and sundry whilst rearranging their feathers. The cats' tails kept time. There was as much mud underfoot as you would wish and boots were the order of the day until you took the floor in the hall for the dancing later that evening.

On one side of the green- now, was it the north or the south, the left or the right?- the band were tuning up the melodeon, fiddle, guitar, whistle and Bodhrán, getting in the elbow and lung practice for the more vigorous events after twilight when the feet really got to work and the knees bent more freely. McPeevish had never seen elbows bending so fast and the music scattering like blown leaves to all corners of the village as they played 'Roger the weaver' and 'The Stonecutter's jig'. He was sure that the instruments carried on playing while the band- that would be Finbar, Eoin, Cianán and Niall (each with the collar and tie in the morning but bare-necked come the evening and not a bead of sweat on the brow) and Ethniu on the vocals, her voice like a fairy's kiss- were in 'The Hounds' reviving themselves for a while. Everything was thirsty work; even the thinking was thirst making. The secret was to maintain the balance, not just of the feet and body, but of the wetness and dryness, both inside and out. It was no good, no good at all, being dry outside and not wet inside; and likewise to be wet outside- though there was no fear of rain today because Ma Twomey's corns had given the sign that it would be dry for the fortnight of the harvest- being wet outside and dry inside, why that was unthinkable and needed to be put right before it became a permanent state. Was it not Rory O'Donnagaín, the one who went to Dublin University there and became one of those philosopher fellows who know what's what and why's why and how it fits and everything, wasn't it him who proposed that too wet and it hung limply and too dry and it would crack? Or something like that, it being better in the Latin if you had that tongue to be going on with, though if the man Agricola and his Roman cent-ur-ions got over here one couldn't be sure, there being none of your straight roads that they liked to plant about the place. But 'Wine can of their wits the wise beguile, make the sage frolic and the serious smile'; or 'wet is best' as one of those ancient Greek fellows said and the Greeks knew a thing or two about wet and dry, being the first to notice it, unless that was someone else.

Wherever you looked- and you could look wherever you liked, however you wished, whenever you could- there was something happening, or something about to be happening, or something just having happened, though not necessarily what you thought might happen. There was the sitting down or the standing up or the walking and talking, never mind the ploughing and milking of the cows to see which gave the most milk. Wrists were strong in Sonas, that was the truth, and fingers were nimble, which was as it should be. There were none of your mechanical contrivances for the milking and other activities. The electricity was fine for the light bulb and the *teileafóin* but not very clever if it needed a switch to get it going. Besides did a machine ever develop a *rapport* with an udder? It was a fine thing this rapport, which Padraig had been reading about in *Feasta*. If you whistled and Conbec came to you sure you had rapport. And when Hanlon the sheep-dog won the penning why there was another fine example of rapport. Brendan who'd been to Dublin just the other week there and had seen the TV was telling them at 'The Hounds' that the Japanese had invented a robot that shook hands and turned somersaults and played cards, which it was agreed was something to be wondered at though they'd had puppets at the fair for years. But Brendan was of the opinion that it would be bugger all use in the mud when the bull was loose among the cows. No rapport, it was agreed with much drawing on the pipes.

When Father O'Brien stripped off his soutane and other clerical attire and climbed through the ropes there were those who agreed that next Sunday's congregation would double in size as a result of the rapport he built up with a certain female section of the onlookers. It was easy to forget that he was a fine figure of a sixty and more years old man when he went around the parish wearing those dark clothes, which brought out the highlights in his ruddy visage it was true, but cloaked the rest of his physique in mystery. The fresh air of the countryside, unpolluted with the exhaust of all those motor cars you found in Dublin, and Misses Gregory's cooking of the fine food from the local soil, unpolluted with the *additives* and dyes and e-numbers you found in those packets and tins in the super-market; all that, together with the undoubted purity and restorative ingredients of Martyn and Moore's cask ale and the obligatory drop of Tyrconnell's single malt at the end of the evening, helped to keep Father O'Brien in good trim. The villagers liked their priest to be in good trim. Those who could remember him when he arrived forty years or so ago straight from *Coláiste Phádraig Ceatharlach* (St. Patrick's Carlow College) had known then that they would have to knock him into shape, for he had been on the skinny side what with all the mortifying of the flesh which they taught the poor things there, and there was no saintly glow to his face as there should be with a priest. He was good with the sermons, they had no cause for complaint there, and he did a good burial and sang like a lion with its tail up. There was none better when it came to consoling and he fair could put away the cake the ladies would bake for his consolation visits. But if he was going to handle the bull and the pig then he needed more brawn and beef else he'd be dragged through the mud like a broken halter. In those seminaries they didn't teach you about the bull and

the pig, nor about the consolation cake. If it was all mortification and more
mortification why the very light went out of a priest's eyes and he could
droop like a wildflower in a drought. A priest that couldn't catch Lorcán's
pig when it got loose- and it was a bugger for getting loose when you least
expected it- was little use to the congregation; so the Sunday the pig burst
into the church was the moment of truth for Father O'Brien. They don't
teach you in the seminary about pigs running loose in a church and it was
the view of those wise heads in 'The Hounds' that they should and that this
fundamental change would stop the decline in those young men seeking to
enter Holy Orders. The Bishop had said he would take note of the idea and
he would put it to the Cardinal when he was back from Rome where he had
gone for a sabbatical, though none in 'The Hounds' could understand why a
sabbatical in Cork wouldn't do the trick for anyone, Cardinal or otherwise.
Flynn described his sabbatical there and it was felt that that was the very
thing to loosen the clerical stress or whatever it was, without loosening the
agreed vows; and the Bishop sighed and said he would also mention that
to the Cardinal when he *et cetera*. Those in 'The Hounds' agreed that this
et cetera business required careful watching in case it became something
less agreeable, such as *quod erat demonstrandum*, which they'd all heard
about. When Lorcán's pig gets loose in the church it heads up the central
aisle and zigzags along the pews from left to right so that those knowing
its ways and having heard the cry go up from the back '*Seo chugainn go
muc beannaithe!*' (Here comes that blessed pig!) were already standing on
their pews as the pig went rooting amongst the kneelers, hoping for who
knows what. As one the congregations' eyes turned to the man at the altar.
It is not just any priest, especially one fresh from the seminary, who can
deal with such a contretemps. Father O'Brien did not falter. With a grace
and decisiveness some had only seen in those comic books featuring your
'man of steel, the priest hurled himself down the aisle and intercepted the
pig as it moved from left to right- or was that north to south? What the good
parishioners of Sonas did not know then, though they knew it thereafter,
was that Father O'Brien, when he had been plain Martin O'Brien, had been
a promising number 12 inside centre for Cork Constitution until the call
came for him to join the spiritual scrum. So it was that, as he had flattened
Conan Mulligan when the man was clear and heading for the line with
fifteen seconds to go and only a point in it, so Father O'Brien took out
Lorcán's pig with a cruncher that encouraged it to cease and desist from
straying that way evermore, for which Lorcán and the congregation were
grateful.

The less said about the bull the better.

For a Euro anyone could climb into the ring with Father O'Brien. Anyone who could throw him out of the ring won five of these harps. Anyone who could pin him for the count of two- three was thought one too far- would win two harps. All the proceeds were to go to the orphanage of Saint Gobnait in Ballyvourney. The likelihood of anyone getting out of the ring without having been pinned by   Father O'Brien or thrown out by him was reckoned to be as slim as Redmond O'Hanlon's body being knit together again. There were those every year who would try; oh yes there were always young fellows who, after a few mugs in 'The Hounds', felt it was time they sorted out the old man and were anxious to impress their lasses and mates. After an hour the apron of the ring was littered with the exhausted bodies of those who had tried and the Sisters of the orphanage were guaranteed a new roof and boiler. The wise old ones of 'The Hounds' noted that Father O'Brien's hair, still as flourishing as ever if more steely grey than black now, was hardly out of place and if he'd taken more than thirty seconds with any of them it would be a surprise. A pint was on the bar for the good Father when he was properly kitted out, someone murmured in his ear as he stepped out of the ring. The good Father said that his wrist was a little bit strained after all the twisting and flipping but that he thought he could manage to raise the glass if he was given the elbow room. There was always elbow room for Father O'Brien in 'The Hounds' and Pearse the stonemason had already carved the symbol of the bent elbow and hand on the stone which was to cover the Father's grave- may it be a long time coming!

There were those who thought the priest might be getting too old for the ring but he explained to them that... well see Conbec now. Conbec lifted his eyebrows and let his tail beat on the ground. There may be no rabbits to chase or dear one wanting a ride on his back but when Father O'Brien used him as an example, well, that made his tail wag with pleasure. All eyes turned to the hound which sat happily at Patrick O'Kelly's feet, as he sat beside the door in the sun with Father O'Brien and the other Patricks. Conbec was not the biggest wolfhound and they all agreed with the Father on that since Buckley's hound could only put its head through the door of 'The Hounds' its shoulder span being too great for its body to pass. Where Conbec scored, the Father said, was in the brain department and in the heart. There was wisdom in Conbec, more than brute force. In wrestling now it was more what you knew than how strong you were that mattered. That Danno O'Mahony from Ballydehob, now there was a *gleiceadóir*; and Con O'Kelly from Dunmanway- these were fine wrestling sons of Cork. Perhaps when he retired from the priesthood he might retire from the ring also- but they all smiled at that.

When the darkness of night-time drew over the village like a shawl over a babe in its cot, so the air outside was filled with the fluttering of the bats as, above the happy dancers who remained in the hall, they joined in the celebrations.

*

Johnny Cash had got it wrong. There were more than forty shades of green. There are as many as you liked within the wavelength of five hundred and twenty to five hundred and seventy nanometres; but 'forty' scans better in a song.

McPeevish could see green as far as his eyes could see. That was a lot of green. To describe it all you would need the vocabulary of a poet and Cézanne's paintbrush and palette. Emerald, chartreuse, teal, viridian, and asparagus- the shades multiplied even as his eye roved over them. It had nothing to do, McPeevish knew, with the fact that his eyes were green too.

In the desert, McPeevish thought, you probably faced the same difficulty describing sand with heat shimmering off it. A camel was lucky; all it had to do was plod on, not bothering about what all that sand looked like. Camels probably liked sand but he guessed they were fond of oases as well.

He couldn't quite imagine a camel amongst all this greenery. It would stand out like a haystack in a needle basket.

The dear one was consulting the map.

Maps, McPeevish thought, were a good thing. Ever since a nameless Babylonian living in Ga-Sur drew a map on a clay tablet depicting a river valley between two hills people had been producing maps to everywhere for any reason. Once someone had been there everyone wanted to go. Ptolemy's map featured a description of Ireland, though its shape was like a deflated bagpipe bladder. Every self-respecting cartographer thereafter carried around a copy of his 'Geographike Hyphygesis' for reference. Without this particular map- one of the Ordnance Survey kind- McPeevish guessed that they would be lost. Even with it he wasn't quite sure where they were, thought he believed that the dear one had an idea.

- It's over that way, the dear one said pointing in the direction of some of the green, perhaps a shade more jade than celadon.

In the Second World War, McPeevish had been given to understand at some point in his life (though he wasn't sure why), to confuse the invader – actual or potential- the French and British had removed or changed the road signs. The Visigoths and Hun had made it to Rome without the aid of signs, so McPeevish thought this ruse inadequate. Simpler, he felt, to have painted everything green. To his eye everywhere was *sin ar bhealach* (that way) in this green land. If you got lost- and none of those he had met so far who might be deemed to be lost by even the most general and flexible criteria seemed in the least bothered by this- then you knew that sooner or later you would come to some blue bits which would keep you right. There were blue bits sloshing around the green bits and blue bits peppered with white or grey bits hovering over the green and those sloshy blue bits: within such parameters even a child would be safe.

As the dear one set off in the direction she had indicated- *sin ar bhealach*- McPeevish faithfully followed. Where the dear one trod there trod he; unless she went up to her knee in bog, in which case McPeevish found a drier purchase for his feet. The wet boot was one of the prices you had to pay for exploring the green bits of this marvellous country, McPeevish knew. In that sense it was not dissimilar to the countryside around Moffat, though there it was more shades of brown and purple than green.

A pleasant breeze blew bringing with it the varied smells of the countryside. Some could be pleasant and some could have a nose wrinkling effect; but here, in the heart of the county, away from habitation and farmyards, the breeze was laden only with goodness. Bees were busy knitting invisible paths from here to there.

The spot where they were, so the dear one had told him as they dismounted from the car, was called *Cuímhne*. In past times it had been part of that territory in the county extending from Mallow westwards along the River Blackwater, now famous for its game and trout and salmon fishing. The land had been known as *Pobul I Cheallacha'in*, the ancient estate of the princely O'Callaghans, who had been dispossessed during Cromwell's time.

The art of the path, McPeevish had noticed, was sorely lacking in many parts of this county as it was in his adopted country. When in the countryside it was best to follow the sheep or the hare, who generally knew their way around. These hillsides, he concluded from their lack of paths, had never been trod by the sandals of the Romans, those past masters of the path and the road. Say what you like about the Romans they knew how to build roads. By their time the map had come on a bit. Dear old Anaximander was thought to have been the first Greek to have drawn a map of the known world. Whilst this doodle hadn't survived- although Indiana Jones might well have a shot at finding it- Hecataeus of Miletus had produced an improved version which did survive. Not that either would be much good here, thought McPeevish, as he stepped over tussock and bog, feeling the sinews and other bits or his ambulatory equipment stretch and protest.

When walking McPeevish found it best to contemplate whatever by chance tumbled into his consciousness. Looking too closely at what lay about him often led to contretemps such as collisions, tripping and general dishevelment. At such times his mind was best kept as a pleasant blank and he would simply gaze about himself and take in the scenery as it presented itself to him.

There was a tranquillity about this region, he thought, which translated itself into an inner sense of well-being and calmness. He envied the birds which he noticed besporting themselves overhead. '*I would I were a wide-winged hawk, beloved,*' he thought. To have been able to look down on it all that surely would have been a fine thing! But there was the imagination which could give him a ladder to the skies so that he too might gaze down on '*the fair hills of holy Ireland*' and catch the distant flash of silver which was a river and the white punctuation marks of the occasional sheep. Up ahead, making her way towards the ridge of the hill, was the dear one- what more could a man want on holiday?

The countryside was littered with ancient places- the gigantic grave mounds at Knowth, the portal tomb at Ahaglasin or the megalithic rings at Reanascreena. At *Temair* was the Neolithic site of Ireland's ancient kings, with several ring forts and standing stones.

Beyond the ridge they had climbed, as is often the case, lay another hollow and then, atop the next hill they could see the twelve standings stones which marked it, giving it the name *An coróin na dealga* (a crown of thorns).

As they approached the stones McPeevish imagined- or tried to imagine- all those thousands of years ago when this place had been a hot spot for whatever rituals occurred here. What to the modern visitor was a place for haunting photographs had been for them a place of magic and communing with whatever gods they worshipped. There were those who believed that such places around the country were linked by ley lines, or were navigational points for alien spaceships.

Cattle and sheep had grazed freely over the hillside thus keeping the site free from being overgrown by bracken. The twelve massive upright stones- locally called 'The Apostles' - stood in a circle, aligned to the sun and the moon. Like giants they were guarding the spot until who knows what point in time- perhaps the end of time itself. In the centre of the circle lay another massive stone, this one of a smooth, olivine hue. Most of these megaliths, McPeevish knew from having read the guide books, were made of river rolled boulders or quarried limestone and quartz. But this large central stone, an altar perhaps, was of a variety of rock not found in the country but in places such as France, Scandinavia or the Zagbargad Island off the coast of Egypt. How it had been brought to the site- and why- was another mystery.

Side by side McPeevish and the dear one lay on the slab and gazed dreamily up into the clear blue sky.

- They say, the dear one murmured, that buried under this stone is the *Claíomh Solais*, the Sword of Light, which belonged to Nuada Airgeadlámh.

McPeevish wondered what the significance was of sleeping on a sword. He knew the old Arthurian legends about swords in lakes but little about such Irish ones.

If I fall asleep here, McPeevish thought, I wonder what my dreams would be like. Wasn't it Jacob who used a rock as his pillow and saw angels ascending and descending from the heavens?

It was peaceful enough to fall asleep. From her breathing McPeevish thought that the dear one may already have done so.

He closed his eyes as he watched the two birds hovering high overhead.

*

On *Beckett's* bus, freshly washed outside and cleaned inside and hired specially for the outing to the race course, McPeevish and the dear one were accorded seats of honour behind the driver. These seats still had their springs, unlike all the others. The bus- proudly bearing the signage Number 1, though she sometimes sailed under Number 2- stopped at several points along the way either to pick up passengers or to permit those who had taken in more enlivened and fortified fluids than they could comfortably hold to relieve themselves discreetly by the side of the road. The Gaelic was much in evidence though for McPeevish's benefit there was always a translation to be had from the dear one, who slipped into her native tongue like a babe into her mother's arms. What was surprising was that there was no talk at all about the prospects of any of the horses or indeed of horse-racing as such. Much of the conversation was about the hurling and players such as Christy Ring of Cork who, from the reverence in which his name was mentioned, McPeevish at first had thought must have been a healer or priest of renown. The dear one explained that he was more than that and sixty thousand people had lined the streets of Cork for his funeral. The hurling, McPeevish was told, was akin to Shinty or Lacrosse but more poetic and significant in people's lives than even the Church. McPeevish sat back on the journey and listened to the flow of the voices all around him which seemed to be as melodic and mysterious as the scenery beyond the dusty window by which he sat.

The bus was a majestic contraption, an ex- *Coras Iompair Eireann* AEC Regal 4 from the mid-Thirties. Over the years she had been restored, rebuilt and repaired to the extent that all that may have remained of the original which came out of Hutton's in Dublin was the chassis and the body. The locals referred to her as the 'Ghost of Ballinlough' since it was in a scrap yard there that she had been found mouldering away. Despite the grating of the gears and the rattling of the windows and the bouncing and rolling as she cornered, the general opinion was that she was safe as houses. When not in use she was home to a variety of cats and dogs. Hooligan the driver, whose brother had one eye, held the wheel with his only hand and a serenity seldom seen outside a church carving. The curl of his cigarette's smoke gave his face a look reminiscent of Humphrey Bogart and didn't hinder his view of the road as much as the wild lock of hair which flopped down over his nose. He knew the road like the back of his hand, which was bumpy with knotted veins and mottled with freckles. The other hand was a plastic prosthesis which he left hooked to the window-frame. The speedometer was much influenced by the crosswind and the headwind and the wind in general. There were those who thought that the speedometer was, in truth, a weather vane, giving the direction of the wind. The polishing the bus had been given whilst in her barn overnight meant her resistance to the wind was less than it would have been had she not been polished. Hooligan's twin sons had used goose fat and cow-skin swabs to smooth it on. This perhaps accounted for the persistent pack of dogs which pursued the bus until they reached the village limits. These were not clearly shown on any map but were well known to the dogs. Beyond this point they had no licence to bark or to chase buses.

Arriving at the race course the crowd headed for the grandstand, where they took over a block of the terracing. Sandwiches were passed round and bottles uncorked. The bookmakers looked sad-eyed at the villagers from *Sonas* recognising many of them from previous years. Whilst other spectators were liberal with their money, betting freely on this horse or that, thus swelling the bags of the bookies, those from Sonas had come for one reason only and that was to see *Dromoland Castle* running with the O'Callaghan girl on its back. All their bets had been laid, so it was the craic, sandwiches and beer until the horses paraded.

McPeevish watched as the horses were circled in the paddock, lead by their stable lads. The girl O'Callaghan- wearing silks of an emerald green and beige checked body, with light green plain sleeves and an orange and light green striped cap- was pointed out to him by the dear one. She waved to her friend and hugged McPeevish in her excitement. It was an ancestor of the girl- one Cornelius O'Callaghan- who had in 1752 ridden the first steeplechase from Buttevant Church to St. Leger Church in Doneraile against an Edmund Burke. It is possible but unlikely, as are many things in Ireland, that this was the same Burke who wrote '*Reflections on the Revolution in France*'. The outcome was still a matter of light-hearted dispute between the two families. Pococke's '*Tour of Ireland*' (1752) makes no mention of this event, though he passed through both villages, being more interested in the churches and castles and dining than such matters as a horse race. The dear one pointed out that also running in the race was '*The Dullanhan*' a horse owned and trained by the Burkes. Thus was the traditional rivalry continued.

The time at which a race starts may have symbolic importance; then again it may not. At four o'clock the sun could be shining down brightly or a gale howling and the rain lashing. At two a mist may be forming or a tornado depositing frogs en masse anywhere or everywhere. However, at three forty-five, which was the declared time of 'the off' there were no particular inclemencies or heavenly hazards in the vicinity of Mallow. There may have been a light breeze blowing up the finishing straight, but not enough to disturb the grass which grew there. Worms were perhaps sunning themselves between the blades, ignoring the risk of trampling hooves soon to be dancing over the turf. There were those whose calculations took into account many factors, not least the weather or the state of the ground under-hoof, whether it was 'firm' or 'giving' or things of that sort. There were those who bothered about the weight upon the horse's back, whether it was too much or too little or not really worth a fig. There were those who viewed the silks- whether spotted, striped or plain- as guides to the outcome of the race. Many, perhaps disciples of Plato, paid close attention to 'the form'. Some closed their eyes and stuck pins in the card, often to the detriment of its re-sale value and sometimes drawing blood from a thumb or similar digit. Many and varied were the ways of the soothsayers who ventured to predict, for a small fee, the outcome. Nothing of this kind troubled the mind- corporate or individual- of the supporters of *Dromoland Castle* and the O'Callaghan girl. McPeevish, who candidly admitted to anyone who might ask about his racing experiences and competence as a pundit that he was hardly the person to predict whether grass would remain green, felt himself caught up in the simple and wholesale belief of the villagers that 'she was a winner'.

Thus it was when a bodiless voice announced 'They're off' heads snapped as one towards the distant starting point and eyes untrammelled by binoculars or telescopes from Pisa focussed upon the gaudy broken rainbow of colours which moved rhythmically along the far side of the course. It was *Lug Lámfada* who made the running until the first fence when it ran into the fence rather than jumped it. There was some dispute as to whether it could be said to have fallen when it was more the case that it had stalled, with its head through one side of the fence, grazing happily for all to see, and its rear on the other side the tail merrily waving as though at departing immigrants, while the jockey sat atop the fence with a fine view of the rest of the race and a wave for anyone who might see him. The other horses thundered on to the second obstacle. This much resembled the first, except it did not have a horse lodged in it. Horse after horse soared over the fence until *Angus Og*, well placed in the centre of the pack, managed to lodge itself firmly atop the fence. Its jockey completed the jump on his own and inspected the turf closely with his nose and forehead. Whatever he found of interest there held him rapt until the stretcher arrived and he was coaxed on to it with the aid of a medicinal bottle carried by the ambulance volunteers. The elixir therein was also suitable for rubbing the aching muscles of horses after their gallop. There are not many substances- to those who have read their Dr. Johnson oats comes to mind as another- which benefit both horse and man. At the third fence it was noted that *Dromoland Castle* rose and landed a length clear of *The Dullanhan*, while the favourite *Gabriel Conroy* decided that two was enough and three was a jump too far, refusing despite much encouragement from his jockey. There may well have been some things on this planet which would have induced *Gabriel Conroy* to continue his progress, but alas the jockey's repertoire was limited and he soon ran out of rousing songs and flagrant curses as his mount chewed reflectively at the fence and wondered what his nosebag would hold tonight. Somewhere between the third and the fourth fences *Gránne Ni Mháille*, hitherto well-behaved and galloping with the best of them, decided that the flora and fauna beyond the railing was much more interesting than chasing tails and bums and so she veered off and cleared the double rail barrier with a jump which, had it been executed by an Olympian gymnast of any nationality would have scored tens all round. All attempts by the jockey to call a halt proved futile and she was steaming full ahead for Connacht when even the keenest eye lost sight of the dot. Scholars of Shakespeare who perhaps had put their pension funds on *Macmorris* and *Rug-headed Kernes* would remember the fifth fence with something akin to the feeling Richard III had late on in his play, for inexplicably as the horses rose together the jockeys parted company with their rides and found themselves sitting in the wrong saddle before the indignant horses, being of independent and democratic minds, gave a swift imitation of their relatives in far Calgary throwing the interloper to the ground. They then wandered off together discussing the kinds of things horses do when at a loose end of a tether. Meanwhile all eyes from Sonas remained glued on the pair leading the rapidly diminishing parade: it was *Dromoland Castle* now by a couple of lengths, with the girl O'Callaghan stretched on to its neck whispering magic words in its back-pricked ears. Past the stand for the first time they came, stretched by the pace of the leading pair. Whilst three-quarters of the crowd were roaring encouragement the villagers of Sonas to a soul watched in reverent silence, biding their time with that patience which only those who have bats in the tower of their church will exhibit. It was as though the thirty or more souls who had made the journey in bus number 1 were there on the back of the horse with the girl O'Callaghan, riding like a fairy on her shoulder, no weight at all, just enjoying the view and the skill as the horse rose to meet each fence and landed with the grace of a ballerina. Strain though it might *The Dullanhan* could not draw level with *Dromoland Castle*, as her heels glinted like silver freshly forged hooves dancing as gay a jig as any ever seen. *Father Jack*, who had been gamely holding on to the coat tails on the remaining bunch, finally gave a derisive '*fek*' and tumbled happily into an open ditch, its rider having taken the parachute exit shortly before the wallow. From there, as happy as any rubber duck in a bath, the horse watched the disappearing rear ends of his fellows with some relief. The next to go, for reasons that were unclear to the punters but made good sense to the horse, was *Bagdemagus*. It was an unspectacular exit mid-way between two fences. A butterfly fluttered by and caught his eye. Why am I wasting my time going around in circles? the horse thought and it trotted off to follow its new found friend which meandered as butterflies do until it settled on some wildflower which offered the hope of pollen. Only four horses left now as they rounded the final turn and headed into the straight finish, the two at the front and the blinkered *Samson Agonistes* and *Telemachus* behind. 'A little onward lend thy guiding hand' might well have been the cry of the former for he wobbled and meandered over the course like a clockwork toy that was running down; and the latter also laboured like one at the end of a long quest. As the leading two horses cleared the final fence, with *Dromoland Castle* now five lengths clear and pulling away, with one voice that sent a shiver down McPeevish's spine and plucked a tear from his eye, the villagers began to sing:

> *Oh how oft do my thoughts in their fancy take flight*
> *To the home of my childhood away*
> *To the days when each patriot's vision seemed bright*

Ere I dreamed that those joys would decay...

As the O'Callaghan girl aboard the horse raised her arm in triumph and crossed the winning line 'The banks of my own lovely Lee' concluded and it seemed that everyone was embracing everyone else and cheering with a fervour that surely shook the sunbeams loose from the sky.

Dublin's fair city

'Oh, ye Dead! Oh, ye Dead!
Whom we know by the light you give
From your cold gleaming eye, though you move like
men who live.
Why leave you thus your grave?
(Thomas Moore)

It is said that wherever you stand in Dublin- or it could be Cork, for McPeevish who was having the thought was not sure; not sure, that is that he wasn't having the thought, for he was as sure of that as he was that he was in Dublin and not Cork, but not sure whether it had been said, this gnomic saying he was wrestling to comprehend, about Dublin or Cork. It could well have been said, he thought, about both cities or somewhere else entirely. But what it was that had been said about wherever it was about which it had been said, was that you could see a church spire, or a bridge, or a statue of some Republican hero or famous Irish writer or personage, wherever you stood.

It had also been said that there was always one in every crowd.

- You're that writer feller, aren't you?

McPeevish might have conceded that he might well be but he had to hold on to his hat- not of the Latin Quarter variety- with one hand as the tram rocked. His other hand held on to the overhead strap with the determination of a man sinking in quicksand.

- Saw you on that television show with whatchamacallim, the Irish writer with the glasses- you know the one. Always drinking he was.

McPeevish smiled the kind of smile a man with a wasp up his trouser leg might smile.

- How d'you do it, eh? I mean make up those stories?

McPeevish wished he was making up one now, one that involved alien abduction or the arrival of men in white suits with a strait-jacket.

- Myself, now, I haven't got a story in me. Not one story.

McPeevish thought this was evident from the type of nose the fellow had above the moustache which seemed poorly glued to his pale and intellectual face. It was the sort of nose McPeevish could see poking through newspapers held up to exclude it; a nose which had a life of its own, à la Gogol.

- My sister-in-law, now. She's good with the stories. Well, when I say 'good' I don't mean good I mean she makes 'em up. It drives my brother loopy. He gets home from his work at Buckley's the butcher and all he wants is his tea and a bit of peace and quiet and all she does, the sister-in-law, is tell him about her having done the ironing and what she chatted about with the neighbours and I don't know what else. Not married myself, you know; wouldn't dream of it now, too set in my ways, confirmed bachelor, like my own company.

McPeevish offered up a silent prayer that this particular line of humanity would end.

- Can't see that it helps, all these stories people tell. Just makes you confused. Facts are hard enough to slither round without all this fiction stuff getting in the way. Too much fiction gives you heartburn, that's what I've been told.

McPeevish wondered what material the window was made of. Would it shatter if he hurled himself through it or would he just bounce back? They usually tested windows with dummies and brick walls, didn't they? He looked around for a handy brick.

- Never told a story in my life. Well, that's a lie, I suppose. I was caught scrumping once and told a story to get away from the landowner. I was only ten. The sort of thing you do when you're ten, don't you? Didn't do any good; I still got my arse skelped. Not much of a story but there it is, for what it's worth.

McPeevish wished he was ten now and could slide between the assembled legs and escape.

- That building down there, behind you, some tall stories told in there, I bet you. Worth a visit if you want something to write about. You can still see the bullet holes in the masonry.

They had just passed the Four Courts down Inns Quay.

McPeevish wondered what sort of punishment would suit this chap who, having caught his ear, was now slowly chewing it off. Strappado seemed a bit of a stretch. Perhaps he should consult Gilbert and Sullivan, who knew a thing or two about making the punishment fit the crime. *My object all sublime I shall achieve in time, tra la!* For some Gilbert and Sullivan themselves *were* a punishment.

- My sister now (God! McPeevish thought; there are more of them!) she likes a good romance, you know, one of those Bilious and Swoons books, bodice rippers and what have you. Surprised you've not tried one of them. Make millions apparently. That Deborah Carthorse now, she writes a fine bodice ripper, not that I've read any. I've never seen a bodice either: not really into fashion, hate puce gloves and fancy silk throttlers. The sister-in-law now, she likes hats with feathers in them. I mean really big feathers, like ostrich feathers. You know the ostrich?

If I could bury my head in the sand I'd be happy too, McPeevish thought.

- Ostrich steaks, now, they sell them down Dunn's the poulterer in D'Olier Street. Any cut you like, thick, thin, diced, and square. I've never liked to eat a bird myself- something about the way they flap and squawk. I don't know how they catch ostriches: ever seen one running? Wicked fast: some legs on them fellers, like that Sonia O'Sullivan from Cobh.

The tram reached a stop. McPeevish couldn't read the sign and couldn't interpret the diagram of the line, which seemed to be printed in Ogham.

How could more people get on? McPeevish thought. His elbow, already up his nose, went in his ear as well. Either he was being groped or a briefcase had just wedged itself into a rather tender part of his essential being. And if that was his foot rather than someone else's, then it was in the wrong shoe. In fact, he thought, was I wearing these shoes when I boarded this tram?

- Tickets please.

How could anyone work in these conditions? McPeevish thought.

Now someone seemed to be going through his pockets!

No, it was his free hand- what a relief. He managed to find his ticket and held it out for the inspector to see.

- Like I was saying about stories...

He's still here, McPeevish thought despairingly.

- You might want to use this idea. I'm no good at that sort of thing, can't type. You need to type I suppose.

The mind, McPeevish thought, was both a marvellous thing and a curse. As the idea for a story was being poured into his mind via the one ear which hung in the air like a piece of guttering close to the man's mouth, McPeevish's mind was busy mopping up and baling out inside his skull. Short of thrusting his head into the chap's mouth, which may well have accommodated it, McPeevish could think of no way of stopping the flow. There was no spigot marked 'Off' to turn. There was no sign reading 'Press to Eject'. There were plenty of signs saying 'Exit' but he had no way of reaching them. He swivelled his eyes to and fro looking for help. Somehow those nearest to him- a few dozen, by his count, like bats on a wall- were impervious to the man's incessant blethering. Perhaps they had heard it all before. Perhaps they were all deaf.

- ...then there's another twist, you see...

The only twist I'd like to see, McPeevish thought, is my hands around your neck till your heads screwed the other way.

But should I feel like this? McPeevish chided himself. Isn't this a unique opportunity to capture the feel and buzz of this great city? Isn't this what I have come here for? What writer worth his salt wouldn't give his right ear to listen to the wisdom and wit of a Dubliner?

McPeevish tried to visualise all the one eared writers he'd seen over the years. It was a useless task, two ears being the common denominator in all those he reviewed in his mind, what was left of it.

The door was opening. Surely someone would get off?

McPeevish had no idea where he was but fought his way like a berserker to the door and hurled himself out on to the pavement. As the tram glided away he checked his person- all the necessary bits were there and his wallet (intact) and his shoes (correct as per that morning's donning).

- Day's the name, the familiar voice droned. Daniel Day, just in case you wanted to contact me for further details.

McPeevish fled heedless of the direction- Hell would do, for all he cared at that moment.

*

The *Ard-Mhúsaem na Feithiclí Leictreacha* (Museum of Electric Vehicles) in Merrion Square is a little known annex of *Ard-Mhúsaem na hÉireann* (the National Museum) in Benburb Street. The distance between the two is similar to that between fact and fantasy.

McPeevish had not sought out the 'Museum of Electric Vehicles' for reasons of self-improvement. If bound to a post trussed with faggots primed for the torching he had been asked to deny the existence of such vehicles then deny he would have done. Throughout his life he had not been filled with an unfulfilled desire to stroll amongst hundreds of preserved electric vehicles. Yet his frantic footsteps had brought him here, to this refuge, far away from trams and strangers telling him stories that were not stories and never had been stories.

It was almost with a sob of relief, like a penitent entering the confessional that McPeevish stumbled through the turnstile which ripped coinage from his palsied fingers.

Palsied fingers? McPeevish thought as he handed his hat in at the cloakroom. Clearly there had been damage done on the tram- and not just to the crease in his trousers and hang of his jacket.

His hat now hung amongst rows of similar hats and he wondered how he might tell it from the others. Some men, he supposed, would recognise their hat instantly; he suspected he might have to wait until closing time when his would be the only one left on a hook.

Before I avail myself of the transports of delight in here, he thought, I shall have a cup of tea and some kind of sticky bun.

A museum visit was not a museum visit without a sticky bun: this was something McPeevish had first learnt in the 'Victoria and Albert Museum' in London and it was a lesson he never wished to forget. Up and down his native island now across the water he had visited museums and their tea-rooms and would not be surprised if he hadn't become an 'urban myth': the man who always has a sticky bun. There might even be a story in this...No; he shook his head as though to dislodge something stuck in his ear.

He bought a guide book and headed for the tea-room. This was easy to find as there was a large arrow and sign reading *'An mbealach seo'* (This Way). Such arrows and signs, McPeevish had generally found in whatever language they were printed pointed the way to somewhere. It is true he had sometimes ended up in a boiler room or broom closet- and even on one occasion on a stage where his extemporary performance had drawn applause from an audience trying to make sense of an avant-garde play in the Edinburgh Fringe Festival- but this seemed a small price to pay for adhering to a general principle he was sure was sound. He strode happily along an otherwise anonymous corridor at the end of which were stairs leading downward. Had they lead upward he might have paused and doubt might have entered his mental apparat. Time enough, McPeevish thought, for 'onward and upward'; now was the time for downward and wherever-ward. The distant clinking of china and smell of foodstuffs told him he was on the right path- unless it was a trap, akin to the Venus-Fly-Trap which lures its victim in with welcoming odours.

The tea-room door snapped shut behind him.

Some museums were worth visiting mainly (or only) because of their menus and the decor of the tea-room. This one far excelled Barnham railway station's refreshment room but fell short- a considerable way short- of Joe Lyons' Corner House at Tottenham Park Road. Nevertheless- McPeevish quite liked 'nevertheless' this afternoon- it had all that he required: tea, comestibles, tables and chairs; and the ladies behind the counter were pleasant and helpful rather than decoratively indifferent.

Feeling peckish as well as dry McPeevish ordered some Coddle and then some Barmbrack all to be washed down with some tasty Barry's tea. Fortified and clutching his guide as Dante did the metaphorical hand of Virgil, he went forth to view the exhibits.

Should the curious wonder, McPeevish was 'killing' or 'passing' time. Once passed or killed there was always more of it, like dust in a room you've just vacuumed.

The beloved, who when she had kissed him good-bye that morning had a gleam in her eye, was 'doing the shops'. Dublin has a lot of shops. What she was doing to them he didn't dare to think. He called to mind the Vikings raiding and sacking the monastery in Raithlin Island. McPeevish supposed it would conclude in their suitcases being more bulging than they were when they had driven into the city. Her suitcases were like those of stage magicians: more and more went in and yet when opened they were empty save for a cooing dove or romping rabbit.

McPeevish always had good intentions once he'd bought a guide book. His intention was to work his way methodically from room to room, exhibit to exhibit, seeing everything there was to see in the order it was offered to him. But there was that about McPeevish- a true spirit of the chaos theory, if you will- which subverted his desire to be orderly in his dealings with the inanimate world. In the end he would inevitably meander from room to room, wondering where he was and whether he'd seen this item before and who that was reflected in the glass in front of which he stood, separated from the item in the case and unsure which was what.

Now this, he thought, is a 1902 Studebaker runabout electric car, one of which was purchased by Thomas Edison, who gave us the first commercially practical incandescent light, several examples of which depend from the ceiling. Edison was a bright kiddie, McPeevish thought, but he never seemed to have visited Ireland. Had he done so he may well have invented more things, for there is plenty of scope for that kind of imagination in the country.

Over there McPeevish saw was a Daimler electric mail van from 1899; and over there a 1905 Oppermann electric tonneau similar to the one bought by the King of Siam. And his eyes did not deceive him when he came across a 1938 Metro-Vick electric milk float beside a 1947 Brush Pony float. A generation that did not know milk bottles on a doorstep of a morning was deprived of one of the joys of life, McPeevish thought.

Ah! but this is the kind of thing I'm wanting to see, McPeevish thought as his feet took him not over there but somewhere else entirely.

He gazed upon the lineaments of the ten horse-power 1907 *Carpat*, the only truly Irish *ghluaisteáin*, built at Aitarbilk by Laég and Sons. In an unpublished letter to one of his friends in Dublin, Joyce regrets that he never had a chance to ride in what he calls '*Cúchulain's charabanc'*. There was a beauty to the vehicle, McPeevish could see and it was a pity that mass produced Fords had destroyed the small Irish industry.

- Ah yes, a familiar voice said beside him. Imagine the stories Joyce might have written had he sat in that beauty. 'Tis a fact that, as 'After the Race' shows, the man knew little about cars. Motion, that's what he needed to shake him out of all those word-salads he was so fond of. Beckett, now, there was a man who'd mastered the bicycle and look at the difference it made to him! You know my brother...

But McPeevish had moved with the speed of Uncas slipping through the forests of Lower Canada, or was it Upper Maine? In any event it was fast, despite the handicap of the luncheon he had so recently put below his belt.

It's a haunting, he thought as he peeked around the corner of the cubicle in the *Bhfear leithreas* (Gents lavatory) in which he had taken refuge. Dublin is famous for its ghosts leaching unsuspecting visitors and this one, perhaps escaped from *Príosún Chill Mhaighneann* (Kilmainham Gaol), has latched on to me.

It was hardly a dignified exit, McPeevish conceded as he dusted himself off after wriggling through the small window in the lavatory.

I shall make my way to South Lotts Road and Shelbourne Park on foot, he thought. The dear one will be there and we will dine in style as the greyhounds chase Patrick Smith's false hare around Paddy O'Donohue's track. Whatever you do, McPeevish told himself, don't bet on *Sceptre* in the Cup and forget *Zinfandel*: the winner will be *Throwaway*.

*

The hat is a mysterious thing indeed, McPeevish thought. His should have been on his head, of which he only had the one, the proper number perhaps but now naked to the world for his hat still hung on a hook in the lately exited museum.

On a bench near Oscar Wilde's statue- hatless but reclining smugly as befits the owner of a wide-brimmed fedora- McPeevish sat and fretted. To return for the hat was simple enough: the museum was but five minutes walk away. But the prospect of bumping into *that man* again, the man with his piping voice and squinting, watery, heavy-lidded eyes behind a pair of spectacles which might have been made out of chicken wire, was the cause of McPeevish's fretting.

I am not, by nature, he thought, a fretter; yet here I sit, in the middle of Dublin- or near enough the middle as makes no difference- and I fret. Were I a nail-biter I would be biting my nails. I could develop into a twitcher, the circumstances being what they are. I could pull my hair, were it not an endangered species, or pluck at my lip and gibber. But no, calmly and internally I fret. To the casual eye of the passer-by I must seem at ease on this bench in the late afternoon sunshine. No one would take me for a fretter. That man, they would say, these passers-by (who are not actually passing by at this moment, McPeevish assured himself, since he was alone with the pigeons in the square), that man is enjoying the sunshine and the fine view of another spire. He is hatless, that man. He does not seem discommoded by being hatless. Many might, though hats are not de rigueur in Dublin or any other city in this Republic. The statues of O'Connell and Parnell are hatless. Men may choose to wear a hat or not and a man could be hatless by choice as well as by reason of lack of the means to purchase a hat. The choice had been, McPeevish told himself, to stride back up the stairs to the lobby and claim his hat or to sneak out of the lavatory window and flee hatless. At the time the latter seemed preferable; but now his state of hatlessness was causing him untold internal fretting. Those who have not worn a hat may not comprehend how hatlessness could so distress the interior of the skull a hat was meant to cover.

A decision was called for.

If I turn up for dinner without my hat, McPeevish told himself, the dear one will raise an elegant eyebrow and enquire where it might be- my hat, not her eyebrow for that at all times remained attached to her head above her eye (hence the name).

McPeevish strode purposefully back to the museum. He approached the desk in the lobby with determination.

With the bravado of an arsonist at a firemen's ball, McPeevish offered his apologies but explained he had forgotten to collect his hat.

- Which one is it, sir? the young lady attendant asked.

McPeevish had anticipated this question. His mind had not been idle as he had sat on the bench. He had been visualising the act of the hat being hung on a hook earlier. Counting was the key. It had been the thirteenth from the left.

With a proprietorial flourish McPeevish pointed to the hat.

The first indication that something was wrong was when the hat slid comfortably down over his eyes and ears. McPeevish felt himself trapped in an immense pit of blackness- Yeats' Celtic hell minus the precious stone eating apes.

The girl giggled.

- I'm sorry old man, *that* familiar voice said seeming to come from *within* the hat; you've taken mine by mistake.

It is difficult to take evasive action with a hat so far down over your head that vision is impossible. The only thing to do was to disinter his head from the hat graciously and offer it to the bespectacled gentleman- the hat not his head, of which he still had need.

- I believe that one next to mine was yours, the gentleman said without rancour and pointing with his walking cane. Like a skilled planker he pulled his hat back into shape.

McPeevish placed the second hat upon his head and tried to settle it comfortably like a chicken on its perch on the knobs and furrows of his skull. With a dignified nod he strode back into the daylight and commending his soul to the gods, hoped that he would not be pursued.

*

The dear one was saluting him with her drink and a sweet smile of satisfaction as he made his way into the dining room overlooking the track.

In the distance the chimes were ringing out from church after church, lead by the sixteen bell peal of the 'Cathedral of the Holy Trinity'.

Upon her breast, pinned to her blouse, McPeevish noticed something that had not been there when they had parted that morning: it was a Celtic Arbutus berry brooch, made by Edmund Johnson if he wasn't much mistaken. Weirs and Sons of Grafton Street had taken a direct hit.

The beloved gave him a cool, appraising look as McPeevish settled the hat on a spare chair at their table and lightly kissed her cheek.

- What was that on your head just now, my love? she asked.

McPeevish over the months that he had known the beloved had become a connoisseur of her tone and phrasing. Words, after all, were the tools which he used to prise money from other people's wallets and piggy banks. In India, so he had been told, the tradesmen used specially designed "wallet tongs" (बट्आ चिमिटे) to extract money from tourists.

- Yes, that, the dear one smiled as McPeevish glanced at the hat on the chair. You weren't wearing a hat when you left me this morning. Have you been shopping as well?

He felt a slight tremor of uncertainty. He had a vague recollection of someone shouting '*Hóigh! Sin é mo hata!*' on the tram as he'd boarded it.

McPeevish pushed the seat on which smirked the unknown hat flush with the table. *Amach as radharc ar aigne* ('out of sight out of mind') as the *siabair* might say, McPeevish told himself.

McPeevish decided that the menu needed to be consulted closely.

A Day at Home

Today I twisted my ankle and had to take the day off from work.

It happened in a silly way, the kind of thing that you don't expect. I could just imagine something similar being contrived at the circus by a white-faced clown. I had been washing some socks and underpants in the sink before I had to leave for the office. I'd wrung them out and had hung them on the improvised clothesline in the kitchen. In order to speed their drying, I had climbed up on to a chair intending to open the window. It hadn't been opened for a long time and was well and truly stuck. In trying to work it free I overbalanced and fell. In fact, one of the chair legs was loose and that more than anything was what did for me. Fortunately, I didn't break anything, not even the cup I knocked off a shelf as I was reaching out to steady myself. But the washing came off the line and I had to soak all of it again.

I telephoned the office to let them know that I wouldn't be able to come in. I didn't have any keys or the safe code so that wouldn't be a problem for them. For a while I flirted with Jackie. She had come in early to get a bit of a start in balancing the weekly account. She's a cheerful person, always bubbling over with good humour and rather pretty. Harry's always grabbing her and pretending to drag her down to the boiler room "...for a spot of bagging". All the lads in the office fancy her something rotten. Some time ago they drew lots to see who should ask her out first. She has to be good natured to put up with their persistent attempts to make her. Everyone who has dated her says that they haven't got much change out of her, not even a feel; perhaps a goodnight kiss or a hug, nothing more.

Finally I forgot all about my injured ankle and plucked up enough courage to ask her out to the cinema this evening.

-What's on? she asked.

I read out the various shows listed in yesterday's evening paper. There was none that I particularly wanted to see so I left the choice up to her. She pretended either to have seen them all or to have heard from a friend that they were no good. She teased me so much that I said she was being impossible.

-And what about your bad ankle? she enquired pertly.

-It's really not that bad, I confessed to her.

Eventually she agreed to come out with me. I felt that she had been intending to do so all along. It was quite an achievement for me. I always feel that girls as attractive as her have so many admirerers that I'd never stand a chance.

When we'd fixed up where I was to meet her after work and what we were going to see, she put me through to the officer-in-charge. Naturally, he was far from pleased when he heard what had happened and that I wouldn't be coming in. He as good as accused me of being clumsy on purpose. The office is one clerk short as it is. The whole district is understaffed and the only reason things don't fall apart is that the postmen work all the overtime they can get. At the best of times we're pushed on the counter; but as annual holidays were starting to fall due any absence meant we'd be snowed under.

There was little he could do about it. He kept muttering to himself about how he, in all his thirty-five years in the post office (whenever he went on like that he always gave the exact number of years) had never had a day off on account of illness, nor had he ever been late. My attendance was excellent. Now and then I'd be late in the morning, but sometimes you can't help that, especially when the traffic gets snarled up. Like everyone else I would take the odd Whitley, but I didn't abuse that unwritten privilege. He hemmed and hawed and made all the standard disapproving noises; but finally he condescended to accept the inevitable.

I just managed to replace the receiver before I burst out laughing at his pomposity. Mr. Raven is one of the old school. With him things have to be just so. Nothing less will suffice. Things have to be done in such and such a manner, as laid down by the rules; and that is the only correct way to do them. I am sure he would allow no scope for improvisation in wiping one's backside. He rules the office like a petty tyrant. He hates anything smacking of the slapdash and is suspicious of the least untoward occurrence. His shield is not faith but routine.

-We've got to maintain a certain standard, he'll say over and over again. It's expected of us. We deal with the public. We can't afford to be lackadaisical or offhand.

Those are his favourite phrases, his little catechism. As soon as he starts to utter them- and once the first has been uttered you can be sure that the others will follow- those behind his back mime the words along with him. Half the time he probably doesn't even realise that he's repeating himself like that.

-He may be a raven by name, someone will mutter once he's safely out of earshot, but he's a right old parrot.

Mr. Raven disapproves of young people in general and of me in particular, probably because he envies the freedom which we have compared to when he was young.

-You lot don't know the meaning of the word hard work, he'll say. You've had a cushy time of it all your lives. The welfare state mollycoddles you from cradle to grave. You've little respect and less loyalty. When I was young I was glad to have a secure job because there were millions out of work and someone would soon enough replace me if I quit just because I might think the job didn't suit me. A pound a week, that's what I was getting when I started; and eighteen shillings of that went on my board and lodging. You lot throw money around as though it was confetti and then you're complaining that you haven't got enough of it. Hard work never hurt anybody but nobody nowadays takes any pride in what they do. Shoddy workmanship, that's all you see nowadays. And there's always someone who can come along and straighten out the mess you've made. Damn sight different in my time...

And so he'll go on.

Now and then, because he thinks I'm too flippant by half, he'll set little traps for me, hoping to get the opportunity for giving me a thorough dressing down. It irritates him no end when I manage to avoid falling for his traps. His face invariably wears such a hangdog expression that we refer to his private office as "the kennel". Some of the juniors are intimidated by his glower and manner, but not me.

Very occasionally, when he's in a relaxed mood and his ulcer isn't playing him up, he has invited me to step into his office for one of his fatherly little chats. When he's like that he's not such a bad chap. It's then that he concedes quite willingly that I'm a competent worker. He says that he relies on me to be a kind of mediator between the older members of the staff and the younger ones.

-You're almost their contemporary, he'll say. You've had enough experience... they can approach you with a problem more readily than Tom...And because you know your job and pull your weight people like Tom accept you. We're a team, you see, we have to work together as a unit, everyone is important, we can help each other...

And so he rabbits on. I've never known someone whose character is such a menagerie! Then he will go on about his butterfly collection:

-They're the least destructive and most beautiful of all the insects, you know.

And then it's his oboe playing and his wife. He has made the post office his life. He started out before the war as a messenger boy and worked his way up through the various grades until he became an office overseer. There his ambition and perhaps aptitude stopped. He no longer sought promotion. He understood and was comfortable in the little enclosed world over which he presided. The office was impeccably tidy; he knew every little rule and instruction; and his practised eye could spot an error in the office account at a glance. His honesty was almost legendary. Once, when a special issue of stamps had come out, he had discovered a sheet with a misprint on it. Instead of buying it for himself and selling it to a dealer for a profit, he returned it to the supplies division. Sometimes I feel quite sorry for him, especially when we hold our annual Christmas office party. Then, after his mandatory brief appearance upstairs in the dining room, when he'll sip a sherry and offer us all seasonal wishes, Mr. Raven will retreat to his office to escape the merriment. There comes a time when you're trapped by what you are almost in spite of yourself.

For six years now- no, eight years- I've been at the same branch office, doing the same job, seeing the same faces. You open at nine and start paying out pensions and giro cheques, selling stamps and weighing parcels, issuing money orders and cashing postal orders, selling saving certificates and government bonds, accepting telegrams and doing up registered mail bags, taking in savings bank deposits and giving out change for the telephone, issuing television licences and forwarding documents for stamping. You file pieces of paper- receipts, stamp lists, remittances received and so on. You make notations and abstracts. At the end of each week you count and balance your stock and cash and hope that you won't be out of pocket having made some silly mistake. It bores me. It would anyone. Even if they paid me double what I'm getting- which is enough for me to live comfortably anyhow, my needs being simple and few- even then the boredom wouldn't be alleviated one little bit. If I had to do it for, say, five or six more years, then I think that I might just be able to stomach it; but the thought of having to peg away at it for another thirty odd years and of steadily being pulped and degutted in the process, that appals me. The basic assumption of those who direct and rule us is that we all want the world to function smoothly, that we all want things to stay pretty much as they are (with certain adjustments for the sake of equity here and there); and that therefore we'll all pitch in and do our best to keep the wheels running smoothly. Personally, the more spanners I can throw into the works the happier I'll be. How Mr. Raven and others like him- those overseers who come to our office for their lunch, friends of his from the head office- how they can put up with it I don't know. Even the prospect of my being promoted to writing duties, or of getting a transfer to another type of job within the corporation, doesn't lessen the drudgery.

What makes it all bearable, up to a point, are the people I work with and the fact that through timetable fiddles you end up actually doing only about thirty-four hours a week instead of the forty-one you're supposed to do. The people I work with- most of them I only see at the office. When one retires, or goes out on reserve duty, or dies, you adjust to whoever takes their place.

Because they're fond of me, I occasionally go around to the home of Steve, our bagging postman, and Anne, his wife and our cook and cleaner. Stevie has problems with his nerves, a result of his having spent most of the war years in a Japanese concentration camp. Periodically, he has to spend a month or so at the postmen's convalescent home in Devon.

-The last time did it for me, Anne said once when I visited them. I told Steve no more overtime. He works too hard and they don't give you a thank you for it. D'you know this job's got the highest early death rate of any job? 'E was working Saturdays and Sundies on watching duties up at the D.O. or some B.O. they was working at, and it just weren't no good, Robert. They ask too much of you. So I put me foot down. You feel better too don't you love?

Steve will nod his head; but he'll also take on the next lot of overtime he's offered since they need the money to pay off the house.

He still has moments when his nerves give out. One morning recently when I was going through the stores in the basement looking for some old registered books, I found Steve in the boiler room. He was white as a sheet and sweating like a melting waxworks model. He had come down to stoke the furnace, to give Anne a hand, and the heat and the low ceiling had suddenly got to him, thrown him back to the P.O.W. camp. He couldn't move and I had to help him upstairs and outside so that he could get a breath of fresh air.

After balancing on Friday evenings and once we've locked up the office and set all the alarms, Harry and I usually go into the nearest pub for a jar or three. You need that after a Friday evening's session, especially if you've taken a chance and started to put your stock down on a 119 and someone comes in and wants a fistful of this and that; or someone wants to telegraph money to County Wicklow. You've got to grin and bear it. Harry can put a pint away faster than anyone I know. Every time I've tried to time him I've hardly been able to glance at my watch and his pint's gone.

-Time for a jimmy riddle, Harry will say, shortly thereafter.

Hand in hand with his blessing goes the curse of a weak bladder: an odd Achilles' heel, no doubt. I'd gladly sit and chat the entire evening away with him, but around half eight he has to leave as his wife's mother comes around for supper. If he misses that he's in the dog-house for weeks.

Only now and then does something unusual or exciting happen. A year or so ago I helped the Investigation Branch trap a bent clerk. He had approached me and offered to sell me a couple of lifts of low value stamps for twenty quid under their face value- that way we would both make on the deal. I reported it to Raven and the I.B. gave me some marked bills to make the buy with. When I paid him off in the market they were watching. As soon as I was clear they picked him up. For my honesty and cooperation I received a commendatory letter from the District Postmaster and five pounds reward.

Mostly, though, all you see is a succession of elderly men and women. For them the post office is a regular stop during their day's outing, and some of them queue ten minutes or more just to buy a book of stamps and have a chat with you. So many of them live alone in small bed-sitting rooms and their lives are governed by such things as whether or not they can muster the strength needed to clamber on to a bus, or to tug open the strongly sprung door of a shop.

Each of us in the office has his regular customers- like the old man whose neck is encircled by a metal brace and who is always slipping me sweets; or the old woman whose handbag is crammed full of fivers and who doesn't understand that it's her money and she should take care of it; or the old time gaiety girl who comes in all rouged-up and creases us by going into her routine of dancing and singing "When once I get hold of a good-looking He, with a balance at Coutt's sufficient for me!".

-Can't get me bleedin' legs up high enough no more, she'll swear, trying to do a high kick. Still, you don't want to see me drawers, do you boys?

There are so many of them that it's hard to listen to them all. So you get into the habit of nodding and mumbling platitudes as they ramble on. Sometimes I feel like a priest in a confessional booth as I lean forward to put my ear to the louvered guichet, except that I lack the power to absolve. All I can do is listen. And when on a Monday morning that is outwardly no different from a hundred other Monday mornings one of the pensioners doesn't come in to collect their pension and on Tuesday you receive a printed form from the D.H.S.S. to return their pension book, you know that they have died.

Really, my ankle wasn't all that bad. At first it did begin to swell and I had to take off my shoe. But the swelling soon eased and began to go down. I could hobble about without too much discomfort and after a couple of hours favouring it, resting it on a pouf, I no longer paid it any special attention.

I regretted that I had had to get out of bed. I like to walk to and from work;

it's about the only real exercise I get. In the mornings I get up round about six o'clock and leave the flat around seven thirty. That gives me plenty of time to stroll through Lombard Street with its row of seventeenth century houses, and around the defensive fortifications of the old town- the Tudor square tower, which served as an arsenal during Stuart times; the Saluting Platform; the Long Curtain battery and moat; Sally Port leading to the beach; and the Round Tower, the sole remainder of two towers which flanked the harbour entrance and between which was stretched a chain-boom.

As it now turned out had I wanted to I could have slept until mid-day, a luxury I can indulge in only on Sundays, when there is no compelling reason for me to get up early. Just recently I have been sleeping badly. I can never seem to get comfortable in any position- on my back, on either side, curled up, or stretched out on my face. I wake up aching all over, as though I'd received a savage beating during the night, and I feel internally dried out, boneless. I've even had nightmares at times, experiencing a sense of falling inwards and of being absolutely strengthless. My head appears to be the main weak point: it feels pulpy and at times there seems to be a growth inside it that expands and contracts, compressing the brain, so that I become quite dizzy when I first get up from lying down. Once or twice I've even blacked out, though not for long. So a lie-in would have been welcome. But after having dressed and shaved and washed my face there wasn't much point in getting back into bed.

While trying to decide how best to take advantage of this unexpected stroke of luck, I boiled the kettle and smoked a cigarette. I try to regulate that and other habits I am aware of having; but today I relaxed my normal stringent self-control and smoked whenever I felt like it. Later I even went so far as to buy a packet of expensive imported special blend king-sized cigarettes, probably unconsciously wanting to impress Jackie. Tomorrow things would be back to normal again; you can't expect such good luck every day, that would be too much to ask for.

I decided that I had better give my ankle a couple of hour's rest, just to be on the safe side. I didn't want to aggravate the sprain. If by mid-morning it felt all right then I decided I'd go out for the remainder of the day.

The sun was shining gloriously and the forecast on the radio was for the fine weather to continue throughout the day, although some coastal areas would have scattered thunderstorms towards the latter part of the day. A shower would be welcome then, as it had all the makings of a muggy day outside. If there was lightning so much the better, because then I'd go up on to the roof and watch the storm breaking over the island.

I plan my rest days carefully, so as to get the most out of them. Even so, it seems that I am conscious of less and less each day, no matter how much of an effort I make to assert myself. At the office we work a six day week, although on Saturdays we close at one. I don't like to be stuck in the flat longer than I can help it, otherwise I quickly become depressed and find myself walking from room to room, skirting the edge of the carpet, peering into the hall mirror, and drinking countless unwanted coffees until the taste in my mouth makes me sick. On days like that there seems to be no reasonable way of passing the time. There are times when I fancy that I'm leading a posthumous existence. I feel like some clockwork toy that has manoeuvred itself into a corner and can't back out or push its way through and all the while its mainspring is running down. On such days I'll lie on the couch and succumb to the senseless pointillism of the television's corroding silvery glow.

It amazes me that I automatically manage to navigate my way through some days. Previously I've never had much difficulty in passing the time. I'm a fairly well organised person. I like things to be neat and undemanding. In my youth (how silly that sounds, as though being twenty-eight made me a Methuselah!) I sporadically used to keep a diary. Every New Year I would be given a small desk diary by a relative. At the outset my intention was to keep a meticulous record of how I spent my time, as though the bare detailing of the facts would somehow justify my mode of existence. But that outburst of enthusiasm would seldom last more than a month. I'd soon be making only a brief cryptic daily précis and even that would peter out.

Nowadays, more and more, I have to keep myself from lapsing into a semi-comatose vacuity of mind. Some evenings, after I've returned from my meal, I'll sit staring endlessly out of the window. Across the road, in one of the flats in the facing terraced block, there is a girl who, on fine days, suns herself on her balcony. At night she sometimes forgets to draw the curtains when she's undressing. I'll hardly be conscious of playing the voyeur, but if she noticed me that would hardly make any difference. On occasion, she seems to be aware of her omission and to be teasing someone, taking elaborate pains to strip down to her bra and panties before pulling the curtains shut. Other times I'll sit in the armchair and release the handle and rock to and fro while I play through some masterpiece on my magnetic chess board.

There are all sorts of ruses which I can employ to pass the time, but I am wary of those which confine me to the flat. Saturday afternoons I'll have lunch in a pub after the office closes and then I'll either go to watch a football or cricket match. Or I'll wander through the shopping centres, browsing through the bookstalls and looking at the window displays. Even that simple pleasure can be hazardous. Once I was stopped by a store detective who thought that I was shoplifting. He took me to the manager's office and made me turn out my pockets. When nothing stolen was forthcoming he was reluctant to apologise and even in doing so he conveyed the impression that he thought I had been lucky that time.

In the evenings I'll go out to the cinema, even if there isn't a picture on that I might find interesting. The programmes are changed weekly and since there are the three cinemas that takes care of three out of the seven nights of the week. Best of all I like those old black and white gangster movies (like 'This Gun for Hire'), the kind in which the action and dialogue rattle along at a breakneck pace, thus paring down to a minimum the time for reflection and criticism and it all reaches a fitting climax- a shoot-out in a bar, or an alley way, or in the street after a thrilling roof-top chase.

There's one such film that I always go to see whenever it is being shown called 'Ferry to Algiers' and is a typical B feature by any standards. The celluloid is so worn that the frames jump frequently, enhancing the sense of dislocation which the pace of the film already conveys; and the soundtrack is fizzy, suggesting that a cataract of water is about to engulf everything. The scenery is quite obviously a contrived studio interior and the acting and production are stilted and absurd. Yet I am prepared to endure all that and even to join in the general laughter which greets any unintentional pun, just so that I can see the finale. Each time I see it I seem to notice some little detail, a gesture or shadow or word which I had overlooked previously.

I've kept a notebook in which I've written a précis of the plot. I can vividly call to mind the last sequence of images. Romain lures Verdou away from his 'legs', as the latter's bodyguards are called...the rainy striations of the worn celluloid are accompanied by the familiar susurrus of tyres on wet tarmac and the gurgling of water in a gutter.. The sleazy waterfront...A sea-mist wafting across the cobbled yard...Fragments of laughter...A couple embracing in the shadows...The man glancing up as Romain wheels Verdou past...Music from the bal musette...The Algiers's ferry being loaded...Romain seizing the handles of the wheelchair and pushing Verdou towards the edge of the quay... Sebastien's body falling into the water...His threshing arms...His soundlessly screaming mouth...Romain spitting on his submerging face... Bubbles...The oil-slicked surface of the harbour as the ferry's screw begins to churn...The empty upside-down wheelchair, its wheels slowly spinning to a halt...The mist drifting around the departing ferry...Romain gradually being drenched by the rain...He tries to light a cigarette but a stream of water running off the brim of his hat extinguishes the match...The camera slowly pulls back...Romain is walking towards the main gates...Headlamps flicker across the pock-marked surface of the puddles...The echoing sodden sound of his footsteps...The fading siren of the ferry as it whistles four times... Romain becoming an indistinct figure among the tendrils of mist and shadows...THE END in white capitals...

What is it, I wonder, that Romain whispers to Sebastien as he pushes him into the water? Despite the number of times that I have seen the film I've never been able to make out those words, although I've reconstructed practically all the other dialogue. On rainy days, when I'm trapped in the flat, I'll try to embroider the story, but I'm not very imaginative, especially where dialogue is concerned.

I decided to have a bath and to potter around the flat. While I was drawing the bath and waiting for the tub to be filled, I noticed that there was a mouse caught in one of the traps on the landing. Recently I've discovered that mice have been living in the bottom of the gas stove. Although I'd never actually seen one, in the mornings I would find their droppings on the floor in the kitchen. I got the pest control man to put down poison and traps and this was the first mouse that had been caught. I bent down to examine it more closely and discovered that it wasn't yet dead. Its eyes were watching me and the moment that my shadow fell across it the mouse tried to scramble out of sight, back into a hole in the skirting board. It gave me quite a start when it began to move, its front paws scratching at the linoleum. The spring of the trap had broken its back, near the tail, but its terror overrode the pain. I watched as its struggles became more and more frantic. I couldn't leave it there but I didn't relish the prospect of picking it up while still alive. I tried to push it with my toe towards the hole, but it began to emit funny little noises, like a rusty weathervane spinning in the wind. I couldn't stand it anymore and as it was the first thing that I thought of I stamped on it repeatedly until the squeaking stopped. I swept up the crushed body, keeping my eyes averted, and went downstairs to put it in the trash can out the back.

-What's that you've got? one of the delivery boys waiting outside the butcher's shop asked.

-A dead mouse, I said.

-'ere, don't chuck it away, his mate said. Give it us and we'll put it through the mincing machine. Ole Fred will sell it two bob a pound..

I felt rather sick at that thought and left them chuckling over the prospect of someone chewing minced mouse.

The tub was almost full when I got back upstairs, so I turned off the geyser, undressed, and clambered into the bath. I lay immersed up to my neck, soaking, keeping my eyes close. I try to take a bath every day, not because I'm a fanatic for cleanliness but because it relaxes tension. Before I learnt to swim I used to be petrified of water and even taking a bath was a harrowing experience. One of my most persistent childhood nightmares was of me hovering over a vast and fathomless expanse of water, beneath the surface of which lurked some vague and terrible monster which would seize me and drag me under the second that I touched the water. Apparently, when I was three or four, I was nearly drowned in the lido. I was playing about on a rubber dinghy and it overturned, trapping me beneath it. I can remember the darkness and airlessness as I threshed about. I was afraid to open my eyes or mouth, being too young to realise that there would be a small pocket of air beneath the dinghy. Nobody noticed what was happening. All around me, in the sunlight, other children were splashing happily about. The thought of anyone drowning in three feet of water wasn't even considered. In the end- it probably wasn't more than five seconds, although it seemed much longer- I managed to throw the dinghy aside and to reach the safety of the concrete apron.

After a good long soak I ran some more hot water into the bath and tried to work up a lather with the soap. The water is hard and it was like trying to toss off a gelding. As I soaked I found myself thinking about Jackie and that made me get a hard on, so I had to work that off. I might as well have been blowing my nose so perfunctory a gesture was it.

The bath only took half an hour. While I was drying myself, bumping my elbows against the walls because the bathroom is so small, I noticed how flabby I was becoming around the belly. I've never been a great physical specimen, but if there's one thing I dislike it's the thought of getting fat. I could pinch together the loose flab around my gut and, in side-view, my stomach sagged. A proper kangaroo's pouch, I thought. I'm always resolving mentally to do something about it, such as take up a vigorous course of exercises everyday, perhaps even go for a long run on the hill or around Tipner and past the greyhound track in Target Road where my grandfather used to take me. But I never seem to get around to it. I'm always telling myself that I'll start tomorrow, which is just another way of saying never.

To avoid that feeling of time coagulating and oppressing me, I seated myself at the open bay window and resting my elbows on the windowsill I gazed down into the street.

There's always a lot of activity there during the day because of the street market. It's a complete little world of its own. The people who live in and around the market need to go no further than the traffic lights at either end of the street for anything that they might need.

From my window I can observe practically the entire length of the street, in either direction. Opposite me is Rosedale Terrace, a series of flats above lock-up shops. There's a bakery (the bread is still baked on the premises and the early morning smell is particularly delightful), a hardware store, a Laundromat, Anthony's hairdressing salon, Jack's the newsagents and tobacconists, Jones's grocery and provision store, Timothy White's the chemists, the sub-post office, the bank, the 'Starlight' restaurant (run by a friendly Greek Cypriot family) and Dave's Camera Shop (in the basement of which he shows pornographic films). Even the dead are catered for in Flannery's air-conditioned funeral parlour, the window display of which hasn't been changed since I moved into the flat. About half way down the street to my right, on facing sides of the passageway (locally referred to as Vomit Alley because of the amount of puke which besplatters it in the evenings) are the local Co-op and an old church hall which is now used as a warehouse for an import-export antique furniture business. The remainder of the street is made up of similar terraces beneath which are florists, toy shops, and fish and chips shops. Stationed alongside the kerbs so that there's only room for a single line of traffic to pass, are dozens of fruit and vegetable stalls and bargain price clothing barrows.

Situated at either end of the market, like two ornate Victorian bookends, on opposite sides of the street, are the two local pubs: 'The Air Balloon' and 'The Gay Hussar'. Each pub has its contingent of regulars. Once a year the two pubs play a darts match against each other, the venue alternating. It's quite a social occasion, a real do, and the rivalry is intense, but never bitter. A reporter from the 'Evening News', usually a young journalist just learning the ropes, is there and the captain of the winning team is photographed being kissed by some local beauty queen. And, of course, after the match proper, which starts early in the evening while everyone is sober, there is the beer leg and general booze up. During the evenings an invalided accordionist plays outside one pub and his mate, a partially blinded banjo player, works the other. Every hour or so, just like the changing of the guard, they swap places and repertoires. They lodge together in a room off one of the alleys. I've visited them a few times because I find ordinary people like them fascinating. Despite their disabilities they play cheerful music, mostly from the thirties and forties eras. The tenement in which they lodge has been scheduled for demolition for years, but the landlord has avoided tearing it down because of this old widow who lives in the basement flat. She won't sell out and refuses to be relocated. She says it's her home and that she'd die if she moved. Her family once owned the entire house but they sold it and she has a lifetime lease on the basement. The working girls in the building call her Granny and one of them takes her pet mutt, a crossbreed collie, for walks on the common every morning and evening when she's picking up customers. They protect her ferociously. Once when a bailiff came around to try to shift her he was met with fusillade of abuse and the contents of gazunders.

It used to be quite a well-to-do neighbourhood: my paternal grandmother lived somewhere in the block. Now, the exterior stucco walls are decorated by a plexus of cracks; paving stones are either broken or missing; there are leprous patches of rust and damp on the walls; and the facades are still pockmarked from long-exploded war-time bombs. Only a year or so ago, while a site behind the Guildhall was being excavated, an unexploded five hundred pound bomb was uncovered. That caused quite a bit of excitement; all you could hear for days thereafter were stories about the big air-raids of nineteen forty.

It takes only a few years for buildings and people to be infused with the grime and general appearance of decay. The floorboards in those buildings which have stood empty for two or three years have been ripped up and used as firewood by tramps or those living thereabouts who couldn't afford to pay for coal. By the sides of the doors of many of the buildings there are cleaner rectangles where nameplates once had been. Guttering sags, windows are bricked up and doorways are boarded over. Rising from practically every basement area there is the smell of urine. The Fleur-de-Lys topped railings look like rows of decaying teeth; everywhere there are piles of discarded paper and garbage and empty cider bottles. At night winos squat on the stoops and pass around the bottle. Slate tiles lie shattered on the pavement and soot, like the refined essence of the past, has settled on the roofs. I've often thought how depressing the brickwork monstrosities in which we live our lives are. Far from being places of shelter, our self-made environment becomes in time the greatest threat to our sanity and the clearest reflection of our own decay and imperfections and debased values. I wish that those well-to-do landlords who live in comfort that is paid for by such hell-holes were obliged by law to endure such living conditions for at least half of every year.

I met Andy and Bill in the 'Air Balloon' one weekend lunch-time. They were playing for the amusement of the customers in between televised races and I sat down with them. I asked if they'd mind me playing the harmonica along with them. I don't play very well but I know a few of the tunes, so they let me join in. We hit it off together. They were quite pleased to have someone new to talk to and soon it was drinks all round. By closing time they were both well and truly slewed and I had to help them back to their place.

-Phew, what's that smell? I said.

-Bleedin' 'ore's rag stew, if you ask me, said Bill.

A naked light bulb, of the lowest wattage, illuminated a small section of the upper part of the stairwell.

The staircase had been shored up and several of the risers were missing. The newel leant precariously toward the wall.

While I supported Bill, Andy attempted to climb the stairs.

-One, two, three...bugger.

He fell through a missing step.

-Who put a bleedin' elevator in 'ere?

-Elevator be damned, said Bill. I think I've gone blind in me right eye.

-You are blind, Apus, said Andy.

-Ah, said Bill. That's a relief. I thought it was you was blind.

-No, said Andy, still struggling to extricate himself. I'm daft, remember? Someone get me out of 'ere.

-Hold the banister, I said.

-What banister? said Andy, groping about.

-Leave me, wailed Bill. I'm done for.

-If you sit there any longer, Andy said, someone'll think you're a pile of shit and step on you.

-I'm trying to fart meself upstairs, said Bill.

-Wish one uv them 'ores'd shine 'er cunt down 'ere so's we kin see where we is, said Andy.

The rooms around them are frequented by prostitutes, dead-beats and teenage runaways. The walls are so thin- where rats have gnawed their way through the skirting boards newspapers have been crumpled up and crammed into the holes- that you can hear the beds creaking and the foul obscenities mouthed by both customer and prostitute.

-Don't let it get to yer, mate, Andy said when my discomfort became obvious. Bill pounded on the dividing wall with a tin mug and shouted:

-Give 'er a rest, will yer? It'll end up size of the Blackwall tunnel.

Nobody paid any attention most of the time, or if they did it was to yell back something to the effect that they were a couple of old wankers.

-Wish I wus deaf an' dum' sometimes, Bill grumbled.

-Wut's the time? Andy asked.

I noticed that it was always he and never Bill who asked the time.

-All the same to us in this 'ole, Bill replied.

-Bit uv a paster, ole Bill, Andy said.

-Sell me soul fer a cuppa right now, Bill said.

-'salready in 'ock, Andy said.

I looked about for something resembling a stove. Beneath a pile of unwashed clothing I located a primus stove and a handleless saucepan.

-'Ave to get water from bathroom down the 'all, Andy said.

It was as filthy as the rest of the place. A ring of dirt encrusted the sides of the bath; the lavatory itself was clogged with shit and what looked like condoms; the walls bore the usual time-honoured graffiti and sketches of genitalia. I filled the saucepan as quickly as I could and hurried back.

Another door on the landing opened and a man came out doing up his flies. Behind him, leaning against the door jamb, was a woman wrapped in a kimono-style bath-robe.

-'Ello luv, she said, seeing me. Like ta cum in fer a while?

I declined. She shrugged and closed the door.

While I was brewing them a cup Andy was sitting on the bed and struggling to remove his metal legs.

-Gimme a 'and, Bill, he groaned. Me stumps are killing me.

-Must be goin' to rain, Bill said. Infallible sign, Andy's stumps. Met man swears by 'em, better'n kelp.

-Bill...

Bill squashed a cockroach beneath his thumb.

-Only time you kin kill 'em an' the bed bugs is when they're copoolatin', he said.

-Now don't embarrass the lad, Andy said.

-I'm not a lad, I said.

While they drank I sat back and listened to them talking. The walls of their twelve by fifteen room were plastered with old vaudeville posters, theatre bills on which they had appeared. It was practically all that remained outwardly of their past. Every time that a door in the building was opened or shut plaster would flake off the walls and ceiling and settle on my head. There were cockroaches and earwigs all over the place. Anything that lay on the floor for more than a day would either be carried off by the roaches or it would grow a covering of mould. The carpet itself looked like a culture of several kinds of lichen and in places it had become stuck to the floorboards.

-See this 'ere? Andy said, indicating a patch on his accordion. Jerry bullit went right through there...

-..An' out 'is arse'ole, Bill added.

They'd always end up talking about the war. It was the one great common experience of their generation.

-Remember ole Brown? Andy said. 'E got the clap from some bint in France. Got so screwed up by it 'e runs out in frunt uv a jerry machine gun. Weighed near on twenty stone frum all the lead in 'im.

-See this lad? Bill said to me. Ain't no Abyssinian medal, this 'ere's the George Cross. Got it on the north-west frontier fighting the Pathans. I wus on this ridge, someone 'ad to take a message to the other side uv the ridge. I volunteered, I wus that sick uv the other blokes' cowardice. I wanders out in full view of the enemy, who's all taking pot-shots et me. The sarge keeps yelling et me to get down but I stops an' shouts "They're spent!" The distance wus too great, you see. The bullits wouldn't 'ave 'ad the sting to tickle a fly...An' they give me a medal fer thet...Allus keep it with me. 'Andy fer takin' tops off bottles.

Andy belched and farted.

-...An' 'Oly Ghost, he said solemnly.

-Cheese an' crust! Thet's a cheeser! Bill complained.

They lay side by side on the large double bed, holding hands like newly-weds, gradually slipping into insensibility. When I left them they were snoring like a saw-mill and a dribble of sputum was trickling from Andy's mouth.

As the noise outside increased and dust and grime were churned up by the slow-moving traffic, I had to close the window. I like to revel in the sights and sounds and smells of the street, but there are times when the racket around me becomes unbearable. Late in the afternoon, after all the shops have closed and the barrows and stalls have ended their business for the day, the corporation dustcart goes slowly along the street, like a mechanical minotaur, its engine whining as it compresses the garbage being fed into it. That noise always grates on my ears. In the mornings it is the sound of that dustcart leaving the nearby depot, and the voices of the crew of roadsweepers, which wakens me.

Now and then someone would glance up from the street, as though they had suddenly become aware of my looking down on them. For some reason I don't like to be caught staring at people, so I'd pretend to be looking at a point just beyond them. I watched housewives going from shop to shop, their bags gradually getting fuller and fuller. They'd stop to chat with people they knew, talking about the weather, the prices, and their family troubles. They'd struggle along with young children in tow or in prams or with dogs on leads. They'd haggle with the stallholders over their selection and the price of tomatoes and cucumbers.

The barrow men each have their own distinctive line of patter. They'd vie for customers, sparking each other off with their remarks.

-'Ere you are, lady, only 'arf a nicker.

-Real bargain if yer one-legged, Alf. Don't mind 'im luv 'es soft in the 'ead.

-Can't tell you where 'e's soft, luv, but you jest feel them cukes.

I spotted Pépé, the pickpocket, plying his trade as he mingled with the crowds. Unlike other pickpockets he is neither vindictive nor greedy. He only steals enough to see himself through the day or the week. He loses most of what he steals in the bookies.

-The ponies, that's my trouble, mate, he'll say. Shoulda bin born a 'orse, but then I'd bet on 'oomans. Anythin' thet farts or pisses, I'd bet on goldfish if someone'd give me odds...Slow? Wus thet one slow? I've seen glue cumin quicker outa a toob.

Whenever Pépé wins, which is often enough to keep him hoping for the big win that will solve all his problems, then he'll treat all his cronies to a round of doubles and packets of fags. He'll even buy himself a night with an expensive prostitute.

-I'm going away in me cumin suit, he'll say. Even see me face in me shoes. 'Ow do I look, 'onest now.

-Seen cats eating worse.

-Me flies dun up?

-Might as well leave 'em undone, lotta traffic goin' thru there.

The next day he'll be back on the street, broke and on the lookout for his next windfall.

-Tell us abat it, Pépé.

-Wotta spread, mate, bettern bleedin' Marmite, he'll say. She couldn't 'arf gobble. Talk abat munch the trunch. Ain't 'ad me dinner yet, she says. Nothin' like a nice tossed salad, I says. Bleedin' 'ell.

I once asked him to teach me how to pick pockets. But after a few impromptu lessons he advised me to forget all about it. I was too nervous, he said. It's true, whenever I'm tense or excited my hands tremble. Pépé is a master of his art. He perfected it when he worked in the circus. When that livelihood was killed off by cheaper and easier forms of entertainment, he put his skill to work in the streets. Just before the winter sets in he contrives to get himself nicked so that he can spend a few months in a warm cell "at 'Er Goddam Majesty's Pleasure". He reckons it's just like being at a holiday camp, except the food's better.

Around half past nine I rang up Mick and told him that I had the day off. I was hoping, I suppose, that he'd invite me to come over to their house and we could wile away the day playing lightning chess or listening to records and talking. Before I could suggest it myself he said:

-Anthea wants me to shoot some photos of this end of term fashion show her group is putting on...

So that took care of that. He didn't sound too enthusiastic and I asked him why he was depressed.

-Oh Anthea's about to leave for a fortnight in Marrakech. She wants me to go but I'd hate the heat, I really would.

-It'd be a great chance to take some documentary pictures, I said.

-I know, but it's been done before and anyway I'm not into picture postcard stuff. I don't really want to shoot her fashion show, but there's a hundred quid in it and she thought I might as well have it rather than someone else...

Mick is one of the few close friends I've got. If I try to think of all the people I once knew while I was at school and college, people with whom I spent several years of my life, then I can come up with only a handful of names and even fewer faces. Whenever I read about them in the paper- for example, their engagement or wedding announcements- I may feel curious about them, but that soon passes. That they don't recall me I have no doubt. Anonymity suits me very well.

I met Mick when I was at the College of Arts and Technology; but in those days we only played chess and table tennis together. He went on to qualify as an art teacher. I've still got one of his paintings: it depicts a feminine face, probably Anthea, peering through what are either flames or the tattered remnants of a shroud, the tones of brown and burnt umber and sienna suggesting leprous flesh.

-Why do you keep that thing? Mick asks each time he calls. Every time I see it I want to tear it up.

He seldom keeps anything he has produced. As soon as he becomes dissatisfied with it, for whatever reason (and he will always find a reason) he will throw it away. Paintings, photographs, poems, even chess game scores, they all suffer the same fate. He seems to be intent on destroying himself, perhaps as an act of revenge on his father, whom he despises.

-I don't hate him, Mick says. What I feel isn't strong enough or harsh enough to be called hatred. He's a haberdasher, a successful business man and he's got no soul at all. He keeps referring to my photography as a hobby- a hobby! Unless what you're doing has a commercial or profitable application he thinks it's a hobby.

Anthea's success as a fashion designer has overshadowed Mick. Although she and I are quite friendly towards each other, she seems to tolerate me only because she can, through me, compare herself as she is now to as she was when she was a stenographer day dreaming about going to fashion school. When they moved to London, so that she could attend the Royal College of Art, I lost track of them. After a year working with a firm of furriers in New Bond Street, establishing contacts and learning the ropes, she went freelance and became the most sought after young designer in the country. A couple of years ago she returned in triumph to become the Head of the fashion department at the college we all had attended. Mick and I began seeing each other again and resumed our chess encounters, much to her disgust.

-It's such a futile game, she'd say. Grown men watching their lives tick away and pushing bits of wood around- ugh!

Anthea likes to play the role of a haughty grand dame and to luxuriate in the decadent elegance of the kind of society depicted in Scott Fitzgerald novels. It's a desperate attempt to disguise the insecurity she feels. Her father died during the war and she grew up knowing only her step-father. She was sent to a succession of boarding schools and always felt inferior to the other girls because she didn't have a real father. Mick once told me about a dream she had treasured since her childhood: there was a big tree in a fenced-off garden and all the children who tried to climb it fell out; but Anthea climbed it, all the way to the top and she didn't fall out.

Their marriage is in trouble, precisely because of her success and Mick's failure. They've already separated once and were having desultory, retaliatory affairs.

-I know she'll see that bloke in Morocco, Mick said, that Hungarian pilot. I walked in on them once. I was supposed to be away on an assignment for the weekend, but it rained and I came back Saturday night. I opened the door and he came wandering down the hall naked thinking it was a burglar. I nutted him, I could've killed him; I kept punching him in the face and beating his head against the wall. Anthea was screaming at me to stop. I broke his nose and his face was all covered in blood. I helped to wash him up and apologised and left them alone for the weekend.

Anthea had been trying to make him jealous, to shake him out of his lethargy. He took up with one of his models, a witch, who is married to a minor echelon aristocrat. She lives on a houseboat at Lee-on-Solent and their weekends he tells me were prodigies of debauched perversity.

When Anthea and he get back together again, after the initial erotic indulgence they discover that nothing has changed: they've merely starved themselves of each other for a while.

-You're so fucking lazy, Anthea snapped once. I base my success on your failure.

-Now you're beginning to sound like your mother, Mick retorted. She annoys me with her 'When are you going to do something with your life?' line. All I want to do is to take photographs; but that doesn't count in her book.

-Well it's a good job one of us tries to do something.

-You're so determined to succeed that you scare me.

-I want certain things out of life and the only way to get them is for me to succeed. You know what you are? You're a fucking leech. You could at least reconcile yourself to being purely decorative.

-Would destroying me make you happy?

-You won't face up to it, will you?

-Okay, so I'm lazy, call me Sordello if you will.

-You always try to disarm criticism like that, don't you? You appropriate it and make it all a game.

-I don't know how long we'll last like this. I've reached an emotional brick wall. Do you think I enjoy being dragged around by you like a pet Afghan, always being in your shadow? It isn't doing my male ego much good for you to be usurping my role as the bread winner. I don't particularly want to be a gigolo.

-Oh, I don't know, she smiled suddenly; you gigolo rather nicely sometimes.

They grinned at each other, like mischievous children, and the sparing session was over.

Mick looked at me, sitting across from them in the booth, where I was trying not to hear them tearing at each other.

-I don't know how Robert can bear to be with us, he said.

-You amaze me, the way you bludgeon each other, I said.

I've been the uncomfortable spectator of countless of their skirmishes, bickering and tantrum games. Once I had brought Mick home drunk and Anthea started in on him, so he took a swing at her. She easily dodged out of the way and he hit her dressmaker's dummy, which flew across the room.

-Oh Christ, Mick moaned, kneeling beside the toppled dummy. I've squashed one of your tits.

We all collapsed with laughter and another argument was defused.

For the remainder of the morning I read a library book. I'd had it out on loan for some weeks and it was overdue. As with most things I had begun it with great enthusiasm, but once I'd put it aside it lay unopened on the sideboard for several days. I couldn't recall the details of the plot so I started again from the beginning and read it all the way through. It didn't really hold me and I soon found myself skipping rapidly through the pages.

By the time I closed the book the ashtray on the carpet beside my chair was full of stubs. I was nearly out of cigarettes. While I had been reading the light had built up in the room like a glandular growth. The sun was streaming in through the window, probing the entrails of the room and encountering no real resistance. Only in the morning, before it rises too high, does the sun shine directly into the room. At night, a mercury street light substitutes for it.

I went back to the window, my eyes crinkled against the glare.

Beneath the sun's rays the road seemed to be liquefying, dissolving into ever widening whitish patches.

I watched the barely perceptible pincer movements of shadows as they annexed surfaces and erased solids.

A fly was buzzing around the room. It must have come in while I had had the window open, but I couldn't recall it passing me. I tried to locate it by following the drone of its flight, but it was too quick. Once the buzzing stopped I quartered the ceiling and walls for any speck that might be it. But still I couldn't spot it. I can't stand flies. As soon as it settled I'd swat it. More than likely it would be skulking behind the curtains, squatting on the windowpane, rubbing its forelegs together. Then the buzzing started up again and I could follow its erratic zigzagging across the room. It bumped into the window and swooped from corner to corner, keeping up its loud buzzing all the while. If it had only been quiet I couldn't have been bothered by it. Finally it settled on the ceiling and I cautiously climbed on to a chair to get at it. I didn't want another spill. I wondered what the room must have looked like to the fly, seen through hundreds of locellate eyes, a room that would be broken down into countless identical compartments in each of which a figure would be climbing on to a chair... and would be drawing back its arm... and striking.

I got it first time. It's always annoying if I miss and have to stalk it all over again.

Really, the flat could do with a complete redecoration. Everything- the curtains, the carpet, the couch, the armchair, even the coloured cushions which I bought to brighten up the flat- they all gave off little puffs of dust. The walls could do with repapering. My paternal grandfather was an interior decorator and from watching him I've picked up one or two hints, so I could do it myself. It's another thing I've never got around to. I've had plenty of practice at hanging wallpaper; we were always moving from one crummy house to another, doing it up and then moving out for some reason or other. The paint on the kitchen ceiling has begun to flake off. The gas oven and ascot and bathroom geyser all need cleaning. So do the windows. I tried cleaning them from the inside once. I sat on the sill and clung to the sash with one hand while trying to swab the pane with the chamois in the other. But I couldn't stretch up far enough and besides I've no head for heights. It's not more than fifteen feet to the ground, but it might as well be a hundred.

I could go on listing dozens of little chores which need to be done. I've a bundle of dirty bed linen which should be taken to the Laundromat. But there being no compelling reason why I should do anything like that today, I forgot about them.

Through the floor I could hear the heavy thudding of a meat cleaver as the butcher below chopped up joints. Funny that I, a vegetarian, should live over a butcher's shop. I could never chop up animals like that, although as a child I did have a cruel streak, mistreating animals and skewering frogs. Stamping on that mouse suggests that trait still persisted in me. It makes me sick just to see the carcases hanging up in the window. How anyone can work in a slaughterhouse I don't know. I suppose you get use to it. I had once seen a slaughterhouse-man at work- one firm blow of the cleaver on the medulla oblongata, or one quick practised slash of a blade across the carotids and death follows

A sudden flurry of rain had cleared the street of pedestrians. I hadn't been aware of the gradual darkening of the sky. The last time I had looked it had been virtually cloudless. The hue of the tarmac matched that of the sky. It was difficult to decide which was the reflection of the other.

The cambered roadway glistened like the unearthed shell of some burrowing insect.

The rain drummed down, strafing the street, being gusted against the windowpane. It rebounded from the metalised road like a thousand miniature flamingos taking wing.

Most of the shop doorways were crowded and people huddled together beneath the striped awnings, rather frightened I thought by the ferocity of the downpour. Fear of the elements is one of the few primitive feelings which living in cities hasn't eradicated. Only a few well-prepared people continued to walk through the downpour sheltering beneath their umbrellas. They walked without making a sound. The very possibility of sound in such darkness was inconceivable.

The glow from illuminated shop windows sparkled in shapeless puddles. The sewers couldn't cope with the sudden delude and the puddles spread out across the road. Debris from the barrows- cabbage leaves, coloured wrapping paper, bruised grapes, carrot tops, rotten apples and so on- was swept along the gutters in disorderly flotillas, adding to the choked sewer's difficulties.

In the darkness the coloured lights suspended above the barrows and stalls gleamed like a well-used rosary.

I played through some of my old chess games on my magnetic pocket set. Chess is a pastime which soothes me by its mathematical exactitude, its plethora of combinative possibilities and its almost clinical lack of emotional involvement. In my adolescence I had taken refuge in the chequered world of Palamedes' bones, sheltering happily therein from the onslaughts of reality. My prowess had never matched my obsession with the game. I had been the local up and coming hope, soon outstripping all my contemporaries. I still have all the cuttings from the local paper about my exploits in tournaments around the country. It was the only game which I enjoyed at school. I could never glory in any great athletic prowess. Chess was, I suppose, a psychological crutch which helped me to survive an emotionally unhappy but otherwise secure adolescence. It was something in which I could take pride, even though the then current social attitude towards the game was that it was a pursuit suited only for retired prelates, widower pensioners and snivelling onanistic juveniles. I've collected together and annotated my most interesting games in a small notebook. I am constantly playing through them, recreating the past in that act, revising and amending my analysis. Once I could replay them all by heart but now I have to keep referring to the game scores. One evening a week I used to attend a local chess club which met in a school hall. I'd play matches for them and for the county, when I could and for several consecutive years, until I left school and no longer had the time or desire, I'd play at the annual Christmas tournament down the coast. All my spare pocket money and that which I earned from my paper round, I spent on chess books. I bought collections of games, especially those about or by Alekhine, Lasker, Capablanca and Rubinstein; and endgame treatises, opening manuals and middle game text books. In all I have over a hundred books, including several scarce and valuable tournament pamphlets. I keep them in a suitcase beneath the couch. I seldom look at them now unless I'm feeling nostalgic or really at a loss. Despite the pleasure the game gave me in the past, it is little more than an antidote for my boredom. I would never have been good enough no matter how hard I had studied, no matter how often I had played.

Rain streamed off the rooftops. I could see faces at the windows opposite peering out.

I went into the kitchen to watch the rain gurgling down the broken gutter. The roof over my bedroom leaks. I had to have loose tiles replaced several times. Whenever there is a high wind they'll be blown into the yard.

The clock on the roof of the milk depot beyond the garden wall was showing quarter past eleven.

In the shed at the far end of the next door garden I could see the old man, marooned by the downpour. It took him all of half an hour on his walking sticks to shuffle the twenty yards or so to the hut from their conservatory. He'd sit there, spending the entire morning potting plants or sharpening knives or trying to weave baskets with his arthritic hands. At night I could hear him wheezing in the bedroom on the other side of my front room's wall.

*

I met Jackie outside the cinema as we'd arranged. It's the only one in town which I really like. The other two have been modernised and naturally they've jacked up their prices. The 'Galaxy' is the oldest of the three. Although inside it is rather cramped and several of the seats need to be resprung, I like the period decor, the ornate balconies and gilded friezes and imitation organ pipes over the pit. I used to go to the cinema a lot as a child, especially to Saturday morning matinees. I can vividly recall watching weekly serials about castaways on mysterious islands.

I was feeling light-headed again.

I bought a buttonhole for Jackie. A couple of Romany women were accosting passers-by and offering them sprigs of flowers.

I spent a quarter of an hour cooling my heels on the kerbside, beginning to wonder whether or not Jackie would turn up.

A youth was selling mimeographed copies of poems to people who were queuing for the cinema. He didn't say a word, just stood there holding out a sheaf of paper for whoever might care to take it. Out of curiosity I took a copy.

-How much? I asked him.

He still didn't say anything, just looked at me. I believe I could have walked off with it without paying a penny. The paper at least was worth sixpence, so I put a shilling in his hand.

When I saw her approaching and noticed the way that men's heads swivelled to follow her passage I felt quite excited and almost glowed with a kind of possessive pride. She's coming to meet me, I wanted to tell someone, but they'd all see soon enough.

I went into the foyer and bought our tickets and pretended to be checking my change when she touched my arm.

She was delighted with the spray of flowers.

-That was a kind thought, she said, squeezing my hand as she took them.

I helped her to pin them on to her lapel. I couldn't hide the way my hands were shaking.

-Have you been waiting long? she asked.

I said that I'd only just got there, which wasn't true because I had in reality been waiting all day.

There was still half an hour or so to wait before the film began so I suggested that we go into the 'Air Balloon' and have a drink. She agreed and slipped her hand through my arm as though it was the most natural gesture in the world.

The evening sky was filled with a murmuration of twittering sparrows. They seemed to have settled on every ledge and balustrade. They were so numerous you'd've thought that their weight would crush the buildings, or that had they wished to they could have carried them away.

A man was parading up and down in the gutter, quoting from Jeremiah and carrying a placard on a long pole. The sign condemned the eight deadly passions, which included sitting and eating protein and fish.

-What have you been doing with yourself all day? Jackie asked.

At that I pretended to remember my ankle and assumed an exaggerated limp. In as mournful a voice as I could muster I said that I had spent the entire day indoors playing countless hands of solitaire.

-You're an idiot, Jackie laughed and bumped her hip against mine.

It was crowded inside the pub. By luck a couple of seats near the window were just being vacated, so Jackie sat down.

-What would you like? I asked.

She said she'd have a gin and tonic. I shouldered my way through the press and reached the bar. Everyone wanted to be served at once. The rules of the scrum pertain in pubs; the queue is an unnatural offence in there. Pound notes and for greater emphasis fivers, were being waved around like flags at a parade. If you hesitate in the general rucking then someone else will bawl out their order and you'll have lost your chance.

-It's lucky this isn't the Sahara, someone said. I'd've died of thirst by now.

-You know, said another, I've stood here and had me balls tweaked so often that I don't think I'll have to wet my whistle after all.

-Just a second, please, gents, the landlord pleaded, lifting the counter hatch. Pint glasses, we're out of pint glasses.

-There's no tomorrow, the barman muttered wearily. Bugger tomorrow, there's no bleedin' today.

I managed to get my order in and carefully carried the drinks at arms length through the crowd. People edged out of the way to avoid having it spilt on their clothing. As I approached Jackie I saw that someone was making a determined attempt to pick her up. That made me angry and resentful. All day long I had been looking forward to the evening out and now I feared in case it all was going to be ruined. It's odd, but in such circumstances I'm totally unable to stand up for myself. What I should have done was to walk over and tell him to push off; instead I stood frozen watching the tableau develop. I remembered how out of place I would feel at parties to which I had been invited. So as not to betray myself I'd keep to the centre of the room, where the crowd would be the thickest, and on the fringes of several groups. I'd look as though I was enjoying myself; but I'd feel out of place and isolated even in the most crowded room. What would happen would be that, glass in hand, I'd slump in the furthest corner, gradually drinking myself sick. There I'd sit, out of the way, staring morosely at the floor, or my feet, or the ceiling, or a goldfish bowl, or a vase, or any other convenient inanimate target, just so long as I could avoid looking directly at anyone, gradually sinking into myself. And if somehow I did become embroiled in a conversation I'd soon become disgusted with the entire charade. Everyone, so it seems, has to be doing something or saying something. It would be too unbearable if they all fell silent and had to stare at each other and stew in their own thoughts. These people in the pub, so animated and caught up in themselves, so perfectly able to live, I wondered how they could do it.

- I'm sure I know you from somewhere, the bloke was saying. Are you sure we didn't meet at a party recently?

Jackie gave him the cold shoulder, which heartened me. I rejoined her, barging past him unceremoniously.

-Sorry to have been so long, I said.

-That's all right, I've been kept amused, Jackie said.

Although he hung around for several minutes hoping to catch her eye, Jackie ignored him. After a while, since she was offering him no encouragement and I was showing no intention of leaving her alone again, he wandered off, probably not a bit abashed. I know the type and somewhat envy his technique. I remember one occasion when at some youth club dance I'd asked a girl to dance and she had declined. I then proceeded down this row of half a dozen or so girls who were sitting the dance out, none as attractive as the first, asking each one the same question, unable to stop what I had begun, although they each refused and I felt more and more idiotic. At the end of the row, humiliated, at least in my own eyes, and convinced that everyone had witnessed it, I fled from the hall and never went back to the club. For weeks afterwards I tormented myself by trying to discover the reason for my failure. Was I really repulsive to look at? Was I really clumsy? Was it bad breath or acne?

-You're miles away, Jackie said.

-That bloke upset me. I'm sorry.

-It doesn't mean anything, she said. It happens all the time.

Her cheerfulness soon made me forget about the incident. We had another drink and then it was time to be getting back to the cinema.

As I'd already got our tickets we didn't have to queue up, which was fortunate as the queue now stretched around the corner. It was being worked by a young guitar-strumming busker. Strapped on his back was a large drum and fixed in front of his mouth on a wire frame were a kazoo and mouth-organ. He was singing: "...I'm a twentieth century boy living a life without any joy; I've got the urban disease; here I am on my knees: Look at this twentieth century boy..." His companion, a girl, moved along the queue with a bag collecting whatever was forthcoming.

First they showed a travelogue about Ascension Island.

'This small volcanic island with its harsh and stark landscape of clinker, slag, and cinders,' the narrator said, 'rises abruptly in the South Atlantic, part of the mid-Atlantic ridge. Only the persistent trade winds which sweep across it keep it from becoming intolerably hot. It is towards this tiny and unexpected island that the giant green turtles swim from Brazil, to mate and lay their eggs. It is here that Wideawakes, Black Noddies, Fairy Terns, Boobies and the cannibal Frigates nest in profusion. First occupied in Eighteen-Fifteen to ensure that no attempt was made to rescue Napoleon Bonaparte, then in exile at St. Helena, some eight hundred miles away, the island in the early days of this century was the exclusive province of the Cable and Wireless Company. Nowadays it forms an important link in the NASA manned flight Apollo programmes, with an earth-station recently having been built on Donkey Plain...'

Then, before the brief intermission, there was the Pathé news, with reports on events in Prague and a royal visit and the trouble in Ulster. During the interval I looked around to see if there was anybody there that I knew. The downstairs was about two-thirds full but the circle (which was nicknamed 'Fingerer's Row', because of the petting that went on there) was more thinly scattered with people. When the main feature started the picture kept going in and out of focus and that hurt my eyes. Eventually the projectionist got it right.

For a while after the house lights had been dimmed I felt awkward because Jackie and I had been sitting in silence for several minutes. What was it, I thought, which restrains me? The thought of precipitating any new situation always fills me with dread. I cannot approach people except by the most tortuous and torturing series of convolutions. My interior life, even from childhood, was for me a jealously guarded secret. In an attempt to break the impasse I offered her a cigarette.

The match flared off the dark brown of her irises.

We smoked in silence and my dejection deepened. After all, if I had simply wanted to see the film I could have come on my own.

It's hardening, I thought bitterly. It always seems to happen and there's nothing I can do about it.

I've no idea what might have come about- maybe I'd've excused myself and gone home- when something startling happened on the screen. Suddenly there were all kinds of flashes and bright burstings of light, punctuated by violent explosions. Several people shrieked. Jackie yelped in surprise and clutched at my arm. Then we both began to laugh, since it was only a film, and she leant against me, resting her head on my shoulder and everything was all right.

When the inevitable love scene arrived it was only natural that we should kiss. On the screen the starring actress was murmuring 'All over, I want you to kiss me all over...' and the leading man was doing just that. When his head sank out of sight and she started threshing about I felt uncomfortable because it was obvious what he was supposed to be doing and feeling Jackie against me accentuated my nervousness. But she didn't seem in the least bit bothered.

As we emerged from the stuffy cinema into the cool freshness of the night I overheard someone just ahead of us saying:

-...Quite preposterous really, pure escapism, that's what it was.

-...Every cliché in the book, someone else said.

-...Well, I liked it...

-You would...Come on, there's our bus. Quick!

-It was a bit of a cheat, really, another voice offered. That twist at the end: I thought I had it all figured out and then, well, I felt deceived. All my sympathies had been with the wrong person. It wasn't fair...

It was quite chilly and I had my arm around Jackie's shoulders.

-Have you got to go home just yet? I asked.

-Not really, she said. If I miss the last bus I can always walk it.

So I invited her to come back to my place for a coffee. It wasn't far out of her way. We sauntered along, looking in the shop windows of the High Street. The naval patrol was out, rounding up any drunken sailors.

Most of the buses were full as the cinemas and pubs turned out at about the same time.

On a corner, just by the level crossing, surrounded by a small fluid crowd, was an orator proclaiming the socialist millennium. We stopped to listen.

- Who benefits from the existing social and political system? he was saying. Not you or I, brothers. That's the truth. It's not the workers who benefit but the ruling classes, the pomaded elite who can afford to dine at the Ritz while we're hard pushed to pay for the crackers of the same name.

-Crackers? You're crackers, mate, someone heckled.

-Now it is true, he continued unabashed, that the lot of the working classes, you and I brothers, has been improved by advances in science and so on. But a rise in the standard of life and an alteration in our expectations doesn't necessitate any rise in real wages, any more equitable distribution of wealth, or any fundamental change in attitudes. The natural tendency of capitalism is to enlarge the middle-class so as to form a buffer between the workers and the upper classes. Superficially, you've never had it so good.

- If you'd've 'ad it mate you wouldn't be so anxious to git it agin, the heckler shouted.

-The outward trappings of power and affluence- the vote and status symbols- have been granted to the masses. No more wattle and woad...

-The man's drunk hofficer! the heckler protested to a watching policeman.

- Now the workers have got cars and colour teles and mortgaged semis and washing machines and all the usual paraphernalia. Nowadays the workers have apparently got everything to lose, not just their chains. The capitalist class is forming itself into vast corporations, faceless and formless masses which you can't see and consequently can't hang from a lamppost. Nowadays the fascist capitalist class may appear to be divesting itself of some of its privileges but it still retains power over the working class by involving the workers in its perfidity, tarring them with the same brush, so that their foibles and fetishes are our vices and thereby our bonds...

-Fetishist? Fascist? Whut's 'e on abaut?

-If you examine the facts, the real facts, you'll find that property and financial power still are concentrated in a few hands and that those hands aren't going to let go willingly of their grip on your...

-Balls!

-...Precisely! The ruling classes care nothing for the workers except in so far as they are able to assist in the preservation of their own standard of living. The only community of interests they have is with rich people elsewhere. Don't forget that it was Churchill, who we've all but sanctified, who would have used troops to quell the General Strike, as though Peterloo had meant nothing in our history; and it was Churchill who praised the rise of Mussolini in Italy in nineteen twenty-seven. The right to private property is decreed from above by our lords and masters and with it they assume the feudal right to exploit the masses. The masses are conned into identifying their interests with those of the propertied classes, whereas they are diametrically opposed. A revolution is necessary to purge the cancer of capitalism and greed from the organism of the state. Inherent in democracy are poverty, neglect, want, squalor and injustice. It is only through the existence of such blights that a capitalist society such as we live in can flourish. Democracy is a protracted mass suicide. As a people we are too willing to leave government and decision making in the hands of a bureaucracy of inepts. The trouble with the people is that they are inert...

-An' the trouble with you mate is you're fulla shit!

-If you sit on the fence long enough, brother, your balls will drop off.

- Hofficer! That's twice 'e's ad a go et me balls! That's han hoffence, ain't it?

-It is the social duty of man to rise up wherever he is oppressed, rather than to kowtow to the imposed strictures of a self-perpetuating and repressive social structure. A revolution doesn't mean red flags and barricades, brothers, but it does mean a fundamental shift of power from the hands of the privileged few into those of the workers. For centuries we have been enjoying in this country the advantages of a free society, or so we are told. Yet did you know that every one of our so-called natural rights and human privileges has had to be wrung from the ruling classes? Had they had their way we would still be illiterate, unwashed, starving and totally oppressed, our life expectancy suited to their economic designs. I can almost hear them stuttering over their Madeira: How dare you be so ungrateful! Look at all that has been done for you! Sops, I say, sops tossed to those they regard as swine. A fundamental question, brothers, is how do the moneyed classes spend the profits they amass through what they term business acumen? Ah yes, we have public lavatories but they have their private yachts and art collections and clubs. All that will be done away with by the new spirit of socialism that is sweeping the country . . .

-An' thet's all you're bleedin' good fer, mate, sweepin' the bleedin' country.

Even the policeman had to laugh at that.

-I'd rather be mocked at and damned and yet live in a just society, the speaker said, than to be fobbed off with the promise of eternal consolation; for consolation in heaven inevitably means deprivation on earth...

Nobody seemed to be converted by the speaker's diatribe, most of which was couched in self-defeating esoteric jargonese.

-You've got yer 'ead in the clowds, mate, the heckler shouted.

-Rather there than up the arses of the upper classes, came the retort.

Jackie and I eventually drifted away.

-What did you think of what he was saying? she asked

- He was standing on a box of rather poor quality oranges, I noticed, I said.

-Come on, what did you think?

-They'd've made a good vaudeville act, the heckler and him. I met a couple of tramps at lunch-time who made as much sense.

-I can see I'm not going to get anything serious out of you, she laughed.

Even when I can goad myself into offering an opinion I tend to reduce the conversation to some inane and laughable level. A slightly acerbic and spontaneous humour is one of my defences against being found out or too closely known. It's the only way in which I can defuse the hell in which I am. The more I try to live on the surface the more I fossilise within. More and more I have to rehearse the things I'm going to say to people.

What did I feel? Perhaps that the speaker and others like him (the students we'd seen in the pub, for example) were motivated less by altruism or a genuine love of social good and more by envy and a lust for power. If and when they seized the handle of the sword which guaranteed power it would be just as bloodied as it was at present.

As we passed the almshouses I noticed that only the porch light was on. All the inmates would be tucked up in their beds, their false teeth standing in glasses of water on bedside tables. The gate was padlocked. Anyone could have clambered over it but at least it kept stray dogs from wandering in and pissing on the flowers and shrubs.

-They've got a blind gardener in there, a Dutchman, I told Jackie as we passed. He can identify every flower by its scent and texture. Just think and I couldn't name half a dozen of them with all my sense available.

A couple of sailors came lurching towards us. They were too far gone to be more than harmless.

-Heave to, one of them said, trying to semaphore his request.

-'Avya gotta lite mate? the other asked.

I obliged and lit his fag.

- Where's mine? his mate asked.

He patted his pockets and ran a hand across his face.
-Your what?
-Do me dag.
-Look behind yer ear.
-Me what?
-Ear'ole.
-Oh. Ah.
He exhibited the butt, which I lit.
-Off to the Midlands tonight? he winked at me.
-C'mon, mate, his friend said tugging at his sleeve. Let's take our Daniel.
They lurched past us. As I rounded the corner I glanced back. They were weaving around a lamp post, one opposite the other, pissing with great vivacity and concentration and succeeding in wetting each other's bell-bottoms.

Back in my flat, while I put the kettle on to boil, Jackie looked through my record collection.
-What would you like me to put on? she asked.
-Anything you like.
-Haven't you got a favourite?
-Not really. I usually play whatever comes to hand first.
I brought the coffees in and offered her the sugar bowl.
-I don't know whether or not you take it.
She spooned some into the coffee.
-I like to see other people's rooms, she said.
-I'm sorry it's a bit of a mess. I tidy it once a week.
-What kind of things do you like doing? she asked, looking at me over the rim of her mug.
I always find it difficult answering direct questions like that, even the simplest ones. I don't like talking about myself or indulging in superfluous gestures. I'd much rather involve myself in a metaphysic of silences. At heart there is something mollusc-like about me, in my preference for silence and immobility. Yet I am aware of some vital part of myself which lies irretrievably beyond myself, which others see.
-Oh, the usual kind of things.
She looked around the room, taking in the various artefacts of my life.
-Is this the only room you have? she asked.
-No, there's a bedroom out the back, but the roof leaks, so I usually sleep in here on the couch.
She wandered over to the mantelpiece, looked at mother's picture which

needed dusting and fiddled with the trophies.

-What did you get these for?

-Chess tournaments I played in.

-Are you good at it?

-I used to be reasonable. I haven't played for some time.

-Could you teach me to play?

-Not just like that. You have to have a flair for it, otherwise it's just a case of woodpushing.

She asked me how long I'd lived here and whether I liked being on my own.

-It's all right. I do as I please.

-You're not a bit like you lead everyone at the office to believe you are, are you? she said.

-In what way?

-Oh, there you're very flamboyant and extrovert and you've got everyone laughing all the time.

It's easier to wear a mask, I thought. The nakedness you have to assume in any relationship can be too painful.

She turned over some of the pages I'd written earlier. I should have put them away, but I didn't think that she'd be coming back with me. She didn't say anything. I don't suppose she did more than scan the pages and none of it would have made sense anyhow.

Outside it had begun to rain. The sky's underbelly sagged like a cow blown out from eating too much fresh hay.

-Can you get up on to the roof? Jackie asked.

-Yes.

-Let's go up then.

I had to lower the ladder slung beneath the skylight.

-Mind you don't slip off the rungs, I cautioned her as she climbed up after me.

The air was very still and heavy. After the initial splattering of rain no more had fallen. Overhead the clouds wrestled and merged with the sound of missed gears. We gazed up at the vast black seam of the sky. It was as thick as a glass of stout, swirling. There were no stars to be seen, not even the winking navigation lights of an aircraft relieved the darkness.

-It looks so low you could almost reach out and touch it, Jackie said.

Lightning fizzled and then a great gust of wind charged through the treetops like a wild beast breaking cover. The accompanying downpour was so sudden that before we could make a move we had been soaked to the skin.

I started towards the open skylight, but Jackie pulled me back to the parapet.

-Isn't it beautiful? she exulted.

She skipped about in the downpour like a fantoccini, laughing and waving her hands in defiance at the elements.

The rain slanted down, prickling my face, an indelicate acupuncture.

Her hair was smeared to her head, like a close-fitting bathing cap. Her thin cotton dress was plastered to her slender body. Her laughter and complete sense of abandon were intoxicating. I felt that the storm was releasing all my pent-up emotions and I wanted her badly. She saw it at once and kissed me as the rain cascaded around us like a Chinese curtain. Her hair smelt of shampoo. She had to lift herself up to me. Her soft breast and hard pelvic bones all moved tantalisingly. She gave her hips a little upward heave and reached a hand down between our two bodies.

She led me back down into the flat. There was a large puddle on the floor. Even when the skylight was closed the cannonades of thunder outside sounded like the earth and the sky being ruptured.

Jackie kissed me again, biting my lower lip until it bled. I tasted my own blood mixed with the rainwater.

In the darkened room, lit only by erratic flashes of lightning, we peeled off our damp clothes.

Her naked body was a willowy waxen figurine, coslettized by the lightning. I couldn't move towards her. She took one of my hands and held it to one of her breasts. Her skin was almost scalding to my touch.

We warmed each other by making love on the couch, swathed in a skein of shadows. Her body unfolded beneath me like a flower's petals.

I felt increasingly dizzy. The room had become a cockpit of storms in which the veins and tendons stood out and every surface seemed to be impregnated with static. Whirling before my eyes were incandescent vortices, strange animalculi and eviscerating constellations.

At the last moment I bit on the jewelled crucifix that Jackie was wearing around her neck.

Afterwards I fetched a large bath towel so that we could dry each other. Wrapped in it she stood by the window, gazing down into the street.

-Come here, she called and I joined her.

In a doorway across the street she pointed out a couple who were embracing. -Stand still! Jackie laughed.

I squirmed under the rub of the coarse towel.

-Are you really trying to dry me? I asked.

She led me back to the couch and gently pushed me on to my back.

-Lie back, she said.

We made love again, she astride me, her hips giving slow jiving twitches, joggling like a houris devouring a votive offering. I felt I had become a mere appendage, an implement to be used by her. Flashes of lightning, fewer and less vivid as the storm moved inland over the hill, fleckered her body, imprinting weightless and shapeless chiaroscuro patches on her, just like a child's haphazardly daubed painting. Each time she moved the patterns shifted, as though a breeze was lightly ruffling a quilted pelt and she shook off a pleat or two of shadow. A strong plucked-bowstring pulsed in her neck. Delicate dark veins showed through the membranes of her half closed eyelids. Her hair fanned out like a sinuous oriflamme.

We lay side by side on the couch, she on her face and I on my back still. I could hear her gradually steadying breathing. I raised myself on to an elbow and inspected her body with a hesitancy she found both flattering and exciting.

-Haven't you seen a girl naked before? she asked.

-Not this close, not like this, I said.

I didn't elaborate about the girl in the flat across the street.

I kissed the bones of her left shoulder and traced a finger down the steps of her vertebrae. Across her behind was the concave spherical triangle of lighter flesh where she had worn a bikini whilst sunbathing. I found myself wanting to prise her open like a stubborn oyster and taste the saline pulpy flesh inside. I touched a mole on her shoulder, very lightly, as though playing some delicate instrument. It was like touching a keyboard of my own senses.

I felt horribly vulnerable, more than just naked. The proximity of any person always throws into stark contrast and doubt my own self.

She asked me what I wanted out of life. I couldn't think of anything offhand.

-Really? Nothing at all?

I asked her what she liked doing.

-Swimming, lying on the beach getting a tan, dancing, wearing new clothes, meeting people, making love. And you? she persisted. There must be something.

I couldn't answer. I am suspicious of ordinary pleasures. They deflect my gaze.

I remembered a line of a poem 1 had once read: *Je veux voir le monde de son coeur.* Perhaps that is as close to a longing as I can get.

I asked her how she got the scar on her lip. It wasn't really so pronounced as to be called a disfigurement, but it made her smile seem slightly self-conscious. Kissing her mouth and lingering on that scar, seemed a special form of intimacy.

-I fell from a swing, she said.

Then she wanted to know if I had any scars. When I said yes she wanted me to show her, so that she could kiss it. I felt embarrassed, but she laughed and nudged me with her knee.

-Show me, she insisted.

The scar is inside my right thigh, quite high up. It happened when I was nine. I was playing in the old folly on the hilltop and slipped as I was climbing an outer wall. I landed astride a sharp projecting piece of masonry, which fractured my pelvis and gouged deeply into my thigh.

-Let me kiss it, she said.

The touch of her lips was like a benediction. The tip of her tongue traced the scar's jagged length, matting the hairs on my thigh. She smiled knowingly up at me as I began to squirm and rested her cheek on my thigh.

-Tell me how you feel, she whispered, caressing me lightly with the tips of her fingers.

-I can't. It's impossible.

-Why? How is it impossible?

-There are no words.

I stared up at the ceiling.

-Look at me, she said.

-I'd rather not.

-I want to please you, she said. Look at me, please.

I looked down my body at her. Her eyes tangled mine into blind knots.

When she decided it was time for her to leave I gave her a dry pair of jeans and a sweater as her dress was still damp. I gave her my mother's sapphire ring. She didn't want to take it but I persuaded her.

-It doesn't mean anything, I said. It's just a gift. You don't even have to wear it if you don't want to really. I've no use for it.

I saw her down to the street.

-Will you he able to get home all right? I asked.

-It's not far, she said.

We kissed once more and I held her tight, not wanting to let go.

-See you tomorrow, she said and hurried down the street.

I stood on the pavement and watched until she turned the corner.

I shut the door and stood in the hallway looking at the stairs leading to my flat. I climbed them slowly, counting them carefully and closed the inner door after me.

A vivid ellipse of teeth marks stood out at the base of my thumb.

Now that Jackie had gone there was just that mark and the puddle on the floor and the tangled pile of our wet clothes to remind me of her.

I tidied the room and mopped up the puddle.

The record player was still playing. I hadn't been paying any attention to it.

> "...I've got those old coffee blues,
>   Old cup of coffee blues,
>   The brew another cup,
>   Then you drink it up,
> Make another cup of coffee blues..."

That's what was being sung. I switched it off.

I sat by the window and smoked a last cigarette.

Odd, I thought, how I somehow always seem to find myself marooned at the window.

The squat terraces opposite were breathing through their snorkel cranked chimneys.

The moon had long since reached the end of its tether and plunged out of sight.

My head kept tipping over to one side and I had to make a real effort to keep it upright.

The gleaming mercury filled globes of the street lamps looked like spectral decapitated heads in search of their bodies.

The street below was full of disembodied shapes and objects to which you dare not put a name. They seemed to be set on orbits that could never intersect, not even accidentally. I thought of that mythical place under the earth where the dead are supposed to wander ceaselessly through smoking acid mists, their cerements and flesh decomposing, becoming indistinguishable from each other. Even the memory of their ever having lived was effaced. That was what the street looked like.

The odd isolated figure slid past, gliding upon its reflection, hunched up against the rain, turned in upon itself.

It was pouring outside now, a real deluge. Nothing would survive it this time.

What else could you expect at the end of a day? I wondered.

I felt tired, really tired. That weariness should have been the culmination of a long journey; instead it was only another beginning. Tomorrow I would have to face the same old cul-de-sac. There was no way out of it.

It seemed so easy just to switch myself off, to relinquish all bar a minimal subsistence contact with reality. It was as though during those moments my brain was operating on a lower wattage than usual, by-passing all save the essential functions.

My eyes were smarting from peering out of the window. I couldn't retain in focus the images which I was seeing. The pain was dull and nagging, as though my head was overripe.

The street lights were burning little holes in the pith of the night, holes which were immediately sealed, reopened and sealed again.

Time passed.

Time was passing.

Nothing could halt its autophagous rampage.

That's how things were, how they are. You could go on year after year, without doing anything, without having to do anything, turning into a grey person. You never believe that it can happen to you, but that is a symptom that it is happening to you.

And in the end you die.

I thought how, when you die, you leave nothing behind, except perhaps children, who carry on the curse which has never been revoked and that soon nobody will know you, will know that you have lived and loved and felt and thought. They won't even know that you've died.

When you die all you will be is waste matter, a turd. All your life that's how you're treated tacitly, like a turd. Born and bred in a consumer society I am becoming one of the garbage cans; I have to consume and produce my proportioned quota.

I did not want to live such a scatophagous existence. I didn't want to be just a piece of residual excrement. But what could you do?

The only world in which I felt comfortable was that of my imagination. There are no moral reflexes in dreams, only given images. I thought of an epigramme I had read somewhere. How did it go? "A man caught up in his fantasies can satisfy his hunger from within, but it goes without saying that he will starve to death nevertheless".

I let my forehead rest against the pane. It was cold, like the snout of a glacier thrusting into the room.

Inside the pane there was the usual sort of blemish which distorts the images seen through it, no matter how you look at it. The outer surface of the window was speckled with haemorrhoidal clusters of droplets and stuck to it was an errant piece of thistledown. In the upper left-hand corner there was a spider's web and hung on it, in a grim mimicry of the crucifixion, was a cocooned fly. I had watched its death agony some days before. Now and then other insects collided with the glass and landed for a moment, their proboscises stabbing menacingly at me. Perhaps the heat of my body passed through the glass to them.

My nasal exhalations had misted part of the pane. I sketched a matchstick man. It's very simple really. The idea is to use the minimum number of strokes to complete the figure:

An ovoid head

Two jug handle ears

Two dots for the eyes

A horizontal gash for the mouth

A vertical line for the nose

Five straight lines for the torso, arms and legs

Sexless, of course.

I watched the figure fading away.

I felt like some rare tropical fish that was swimming to and fro inside a large, glass-walled tank, propelling itself by the absolute minimum of muscular contractions, hardly sufficient to ripple the water, breathing with the faintest feathering of prehensile gill-slits. Occasionally, in its being wafted to and fro by the unpredictable currents, it seemed to collide quite gently with the invisible and impenetrable barrier which confined it.

I experienced the absurd sensation of drowning in a non-existent ocean. I was treading water, becoming more and more tired, more and more saturated.

I found myself having to check frequently some nervous habit, such as twisting my fingers around each other or picking at my upper lip.

I heard a man walking by whistling the 'Irish Rover'. Nearly every night, at about the same time, he walks by whistling that same fragment, a few quavering notes that dissolve into a smoker's cough. I looked up and down the street but I couldn't spot him.

I heard the shattering of a bottle, the sound of others rolling in the gutter and then that too faded into silence.

The cigarette had burnt itself out between my fingers. I hadn't felt a thing. I sucked at the red marks.

Somewhere in the neighbourhood, probably St. Mary's, a clock tower chimed, each chime seeming to be louder than the last. I tried to keep count of them, as though my life depended on it, but I'd missed the first few.

I felt very still and very empty.

Empty of what? I wondered. The result of my empty hours lie within me, a spiritual form of pneumoconiosis, settling like lees in a closed bottle.

In novels it is within the realms of possibility that the hero will wake up; but in real life nothing of the kind occurs and slowly but surely you suffocate.

That's the only real death, suffocation. My own death I believe could only be of that kind. Gradually consciousness is being erased and in the end all that is left is the reflex to salivate and erect and excrete and spin and procreate and consume and decompose.

It was easy to doubt that I was alive anymore. Sometimes I feel that I am still enmeshed in the womb.

A corporation sanitation wagon, spraying disinfectant into the gutters, went past, wheezing like an ailing mole, its orange warning light flashing from atop the cab roof. It was on the last leg of its homeward journey to the depot down the road.

I felt too close to myself. But what was the distance which I had to establish?

In the back of the room, the gullet, a darkness as thick as roux had been accumulating, taking possession of everything.

The instant I switched off the light it surged through the breach to envelope me as well.

I lay on the couch and waited for sleep to come. Beneath me there was the damp imprint of Jackie's body and the rucked coverlet reminded me of her real presence. I smoothed the coverlet as though I was still caressing her warm and pliant flesh.

In the dark I reassembled her fictive presence.

I turned my face to the wall.

I could hear the alarm clock ticking for a long time, so loud that it might have been inside my skull.

Tic toc Tic toc Tic toc Tic toc Tic toc Tic toc Tic toc Tic toc Tic
toc Tic toc Tic toc Tic toc Tic toc Tic toc Tic toc Tic toc Tic toc
Tic toc Tic toc Tic toc Tic toc Tic toc Tic toc Tic toc Tic toc Tic
toc Tic toc Tic toc Tic toc Tic toc Tic toc Tic toc Tic toc Tic toc ...

It was easy to imagine, as I closed my eyes, the miniature flywheel mounted upon its spigot spinning out its invisible tippet.

TictocTictocTictocTictocTictocTictocTictocTictocTictocTictocTictoc...

The wall shuddered as my clenched fist pounded it.

In my mind I was entangled in the mysterious aumbry of her body.

Tic toc Tic toc Tic toc Tic toc Tic...

Each beat stretching me on the tensor of my delusions.

toc Tic toc Tic toc Tic toc Tic ...

Each beat winching me lower and lower.

toc Tic toc Tic toc Tic toc ...

Each beat measuring the silence, that longitude of my grief, as I lay as though waiting to be shriven, caught up in the flow of an unfathomed hour.

Tic toc Tic toc Tic toc

Tic toc Tic toc Tic

toc Tic toc Tic

toc Tic toc

Tic toc

Tic

toc

I pressed my face into the pillow. In my nostrils was the smell of perfume and hairdressing and perspiration and stale semen.

Tic

I didn't want to sleep.

toc

I rolled on to my back and stared at the ceiling.

Tic

Through the rain-speckled skylight I watched the liquid stars dissolving as the night was being decanted like some apothecaries concoction.

toc

In the distance I could hear the roaring of motor-cycle engines from the speedway and I wondered if Barry Briggs or Ivan Mauger were riding tonight.

Tic

What really matters in the end? I thought. Perhaps only that I should fabricate myself.

toc

I hated the thought of tomorrow, of the office, of all those tomorrows stretching into the endless future. The fixative of reality which conceals the rudimentary horror of having to daily take up my body and wash it and shave it and feed it and groom it and dress it and perambulate it and rest it: that fixative had been dissolved.

The miracle, I thought, is not that anyone would have to endure forty days and forty nights in the wilderness, but that they should endure even one ordinary day.

Tic

How had I spent my time today? I thought.

Already fragments of it had splintered off and been lost. Why this desire to fuse every single instant into the present moment's awareness and to hold it there, in the forefront of my mind, to contemplate it, as one does a fly trapped in amber?

toc

I yawned and turned back towards the wall.

Tic

What have I to confess? I have farted in confined spaces. I have eaten peas off a knife. I have worn dirty underwear. I have walked out on 'The Queen'. I have not washed behind my prepuce. I have not said my prayers. I have given myself enough rope.

toc

Funny that for twenty-eight years I have functioned quite adequately without having to think about it and that now I was desperately trying to dampen down the athenor in my skull.

Tic

I believe that I'd exist quite cheerfully in a wilderness of stones, playing with them, forming piles, banging them together just to hear their sounds, hurling them about haphazardly.

toc

Tic toc

Tic

I could feel her hands gliding over me, knotting and unknotting my flesh.

toc

I crumpled a fist to my mouth and tried not to moan.

Tic

There was a fetid stench about the room, like that when vegetation had been decaying for a long time.

toc

I listened to my heart beating.

Tic toc Tic toc Tic toc Tic toc

Tic

After a day is through with me I sometimes feel like one of those raw, frozen carcases hanging from hooks in the butcher's shop below me.

I thought that when a day ends, an ordinary day, one through which I have lived, then at the very least a death is to be expected. Death is the nearness with which you draw to yourself.

toc

Tic

toc

Tic

toc

Tic

I must have fallen asleep: there was no toc.
I do not know into what kind of silence I had fallen.

(*Written1974- Revised 2011*)

Aisling's Garden
"Touch lightly Nature's sweet guitar
Unless thou know'st the tune..."
Emily Dickinson

In the beginning it had been nothing special, the garden. A wilderness was too fine a term to use. At the rear of the house there was just this seemingly boundless space of tangled vegetation, none of it nameable.

It feels as though I have lived here forever, he thought.

That he had not done so he was sure of at times; that is, those times when he could recall a time before he had purchased the house.

That's too long ago to worry about now, he thought. This is home, whatever else it may have been, and I shall die here. There is nowhere else.

Does it matter who I am? he thought. Does it matter what kind of person I have been? What matters is *now*, not my antecedents, though they might be worth someone writing about.

He sits in his study by the bay window. His knees are covered with an old red, white and blue coloured blanket, patterned with alternating stripes of diamonds, triangles and wavy bands. On it is a closed book. It is Borges' *'Ficciones'* and he has just finished reading *'El Jardin de senderos que se bifurcan'*.

The sunlight of the morning warms him. From the bay window he can overlook the garden. He seldom goes out the front nowadays or gazes from those windows except from his bedroom on the second floor. The view there is of a road, hills and a distant stretch of water which might be the sea or a lake. He used to go for a drive that way, into the village or the hills. He used to cycle that way before he could drive and before he was driven.

I have forgotten the chauffeur's name, he thinks.

Each morning, once he has taken breakfast, he is brought from the dining room to the study. He eats little now, less than a mouse he thinks. It is just enough to keep the doctor at bay. When the doctor visits he asks about his diet and the manservant Ness shows him the notes he has made of the meals he has eaten.

He wishes that they would just leave him alone; but when he says he can manage they both smile at each other and pay no attention to him. Once that might have mattered; now it does not, not in the way it once used to matter. He smiles too.

Once I am here, in the study, I am left in peace, he thinks. It is enough that he knows Ness is there, that someone is there. Someone has always been there, he thinks.

Whatever Ness needs to be doing he will do out of his sight and without fuss. Sometimes he wonders what Ness finds to do all day long, that is when he is not tending to him. But there is the house and its grounds to maintain. That must keep him busy.

If he needs anything he will ring. That is the arrangement. Ness will leave him alone until eleven, when he will bring in some coffee, not in a cup but in a silver pot on a tray, leaving him to pour it as he wishes. The coffee pot is from the reign of George I and is of straight sided design. It was made by William Darker and is decorated with flowers, leaves and scrolls.

Ness will see that the blanket is tucked in securely and that the coffee on the stand is within his reach, and then he will leave him. He will sip some coffee, if he feels like it, and gaze out of the window as far as his sight can see. Some days he seems to see to the very horizon and some days his eyes can only see as far as the window and not beyond it.

He thinks of the places he has lived, or thinks he has lived. This will be the last. He cannot recall the first, though there will have been a first, the one where he was born. They are scattered everywhere, he thinks, the places I have lived. Some I was hardly there; others I seemed to start to settle. But I have never rooted, even here, where I am caught in this wheelchair and have to be waited on, put to bed, taken to the toilet.

This is no way to live, he thinks; and it certainly is no way to die.

Not that he can do anything about it. He is dependent upon others, where once he was dependent only upon himself- or so it must have seemed.

What did I make of my inheritance? Or was that one of my stories?
I become confused. I am confusing myself.
He blinked at the brightness of the day.

The coffee is still hot. Ness must have just poured it. I did not see him come in or go.

He drinks some coffee. He is careful not to let it dribble down his chin.

How many such windows have I looked out of? Have I ever seen what I have hoped to see, what I have wished to see? Have I always looked outward rather than inward?

There are no answers to these questions; he doesn't know why he asks himself them. Usually questions are asked with the hope- even expectation- that there will be an answer.

But I do not expect an answer, he thinks. I am asking these questions to hear myself think. I dare not ask them aloud. If I ask: Ness, what is the time? Ness will think I am even more forgetful. I *am* forgetful; but I have always been forgetful. That is how I have managed to last this long. Forgetting is an art; remembering is a burden- did I say that? I have said many things: perhaps I have said too much; perhaps I have said too little.

What name do I have today? he thinks. Should it be the same as the one I had yesterday? I have had many names. People have called me this and that and I have nodded or bowed as this or that. They were fine names, famous names, names printed on the covers of my books- but not my real name. Ness- does he know my real name? I cannot remember hearing him call me by it. It is always 'Sir' with him.

I look out the window and hope- what do I hope? That I will see my father or my mother or a ship come sailing into harbour? But that is not this window. This window looks out onto the land, the countryside, a wilderness I might once have described and explored with my imagination; a scene I can only gaze at now with as much understanding as one of those trees on the hills.

Everything I see in this landscape, he thinks, is older than I can imagine. In the distance are Neolithic mounds and standing stones where once perhaps ancient rituals were enacted. Somewhere nearer the building, beyond the lawn and the downward slope leading to the tangle of vegetation, are bee hives which once were tended but now cannot be seen for the shrubs and plants that have run wild.

Even the glass through which I am gazing is old, perhaps still original. Do you see things differently through old glass? he wonders. If someone were to look in, someone other than the birds which occasionally sit on the outside sill and peck at the insects in the corners and crevices, would that person see a different me to the one I think I am?

On the inside windowsill he sees a pack of playing cards and wonders in what order the cards lie. Perhaps, he thinks, they are not playing cards but

Tarot cards. There is also an ashtray, though no half-smoked cigarette with the smoke curling up from its glowing tip lies in it.

Do I smoke? he wonders. Have I ever smoked? Has someone just left the room, gone out of my sight and left the thought of a cigarette in the ashtray? What am I to make of the toy soldiers lying and standing there? Do I have children, grandchildren? Are they mine, those toy soldiers, relics of my childhood? I cannot recognise the uniforms they wear, perhaps Kitchener's 21st Lancers. Are they made by Britains, Charbens or Mignot?

Once all such speculation would have intrigued him. Once he would have sat with pen and paper and have written what he thought and what he saw. Now it all flits past him like the bird outside flying in search of nesting material.

Somewhere a radio station is giving out the weather forecast. The music that had been playing softly ceases and a masculine voice is saying that it will be fine and warm. A weather front will move in later in the week, bringing much needed rain. Somewhere there are small fires on the heath land of the peninsula. Local fire-fighters are containing the smouldering gorse. The temperature will be such and such and the wind is from this or that direction, the pollen count high or low- he cannot absorb it all.

A vase holding some dried flowers stands on a table near the window through which he has been looking. The flowers are carefully composed, or so he imagines- perhaps some Ikebana style? The vase is a pale green and has a curved shape below the narrower neck.

Why do I notice things? he thinks. Once perhaps I did so that I might tell the detail to another but now I only tell myself. Once you have seen is it not pointless to then say: there are dried flowers in that pale green vase.

In the light, this light, the vase seems to change colour, so that now he might call it a darker green. Gazing past it and through the window it seems to become one with what lies out there, though he knows it is in the room, this side of the window.

He sips the coffee.

I thought I had finished it, he thinks. Perhaps I have poured myself another cup, or Ness has come in and discreetly poured one for me as I've been distracted by what I see through the window.

I only drink coffee at this time of day, he tells himself. It is a habit I have had since I can't remember when. Some habits I can remember when I first started them, others are just habits- like tying my shoelaces. I no longer have to do that- or do I? I am wearing slippers so perhaps I never wear shoes these days.

These days: I do not know what day it is. It does not matter. I cannot remember when it ceased to matter. It used to matter, though I cannot recall why it used to matter. Now there is just today. Yesterday: that must lie somewhere behind me, like a shadow. I will have been doing what I am doing now, looking out of the window, wondering what I was doing the day before and noting what I see without changing anything.

Those clouds, he thinks; I once knew the name and shape of all the cloud formations. I can remember being taught that in school. I was sitting behind a desk and in the text book on the desk were black and white photographs of clouds with captions under each picture identifying this one as Cumulonimbus, that one as Altostratus and the other as Cirrus fibratus. The sky is like a constantly revised painting, or the palette from which paint is taken: how restful it can be just gazing up at its constant pageantry and silent unrolling!

Did I fall asleep? The coffee tray is gone. The clouds are still there, other clouds or the same I cannot say.

Now Ness is pouring me coffee. I do not know if it is made from Coffea arabica or Coffea canephora beans. I do not know if this matters. I taste it and it is as I like it. I say thank you; I hear myself saying thank you; I feel my tongue moving and my mouth opening. I watch his shadow on the carpet as he silently moves out of the room.

I did not ring for him but it must have been the time for him to come. There will be a clock in the kitchen. There will be clocks elsewhere. There is none in this room. One would serve no purpose in here. What could it tell me that I want to know or do not already know? Perhaps on the lawn there is a sundial. It would not surprise me if there was. Perhaps I once watched as the shadow slowly crept across its face. I was much given to that kind of thing, watching, as I am doing now.

On the wall to his left there is a large mirror with an ornate frame. In it he can see himself sitting in his chair with the cup raised to his lips. He wonders what his reflection would think of him sitting in this room, by this window, day after day. Does his reflection see what he sees?

Nonsense, of course, he thinks; but then I have been much given to that kind of speculation as well. I made my living from it. I am still making my living from it. And what then, he wonders; what then?

The music being played now on the radio is Manuel de Falla's '*Noches en los Jardines de España*'. It is the 1928 original recording by Aline Isabelle van Barentzen. He recognises this, one of Hemingway's favourite pieces found amongst the other over nine hundred records in the living room of 'Finca Vigia' in Cuba.

Why do I remember this, he thinks, and not the name of my chauffeur? He would drive me once a week to that headland where she was buried. He would wait while I walked to and from the grave. There was just a rough path through the grass leading to it. I would place the flowers- sometimes marigolds and sometimes zinnias- on her grave. Some days I would sit there with her and gaze out across the sea as we had done when she was alive. As I gazed out on my own I would sometimes imagine that I could see with her eyes and hear her murmuring as she sat beside me. We would speak seldom as we sat watching the waves and the birds, the clouds and the sun. Somehow words did not fit with the view. At the most one of us might say 'Look there' and point at something that had caught our eye. I looked without her and nothing would catch my eye; but sometimes I would hear her whispering 'Look there' and I would look and it was as though I had just glimpsed the coat-tails of an angel disappearing.

I do not believe in angels, he thinks. Or is that my reflection in the mirror thinking that? He stares at himself staring at himself, wondering. Somewhere between us is that thought, trapped by the glass, absorbed by the glass.

It is the second section, about the unidentified garden in which there is the exotic dance, that is being played now.

He reaches out to ring the bell for Ness to come to take away the coffee service. He sees that the table is bare.

If I ring the bell now, he thinks, will Ness appear with the coffee or will he wonder why I am calling him after he has taken it away?

He closes his eyes, feeling tired. Somewhere a piano is playing and he can hear flutes, oboes, a harp and trumpets.

This is not music to sleep by, he thinks, but to dance to. But he knows his dancing days are over. In his mind he imagines that he is dancing again with her. How she loved to dance, he thinks. He was a clumsy dancer, yet she had made him seem as nimble and agile as Astaire. 'I shall be the man,' she had said smiling that first time they had danced; and he had followed as she led. That was how it would always be: she would lead and he would follow.

*

The building- a mansion of some antiquity- stands on its own several miles from the nearest township on the coast. There is no sign that points to the building. If you wish to find it you have to stop in the town and ask. If you do not know its name then it may still be found for there is only one such building in the surrounding countryside. The day he came to view it he had the cutting from the paper and a letter from the solicitor, who had advised him to enquire at the local inn where he would be lodging overnight. Yes, he was told, the place is well known but it's off the beaten track. He was given directions, seemingly simple directions, but even then he had almost missed the turning.

The main road in and out of the town was itself a narrow road, for there was not much traffic came that way near the coast. The railway ran some distance to the north. The narrow road threaded its way through pleasant countryside- hills and valleys that seemed the same as each other as much as they differed in names and foliage. Even with the windows down and a fresh breeze blowing on his face he could feel the hypnotic rhythm of the scenery and motion of the car carrying him into a kind of trance. He decided to stop to break what seemed like a spell being cast over him; and it was then that he thought: I have come too far. He got out of the car and walked back along the road, more to shake himself awake and to loosen his cramped legs; and it was then that he noticed the turning to the right. There was no sign but from the description he had been given at the inn he knew that this had to be the road to the building. He returned to his car, reversed and began to drive carefully up the single track road. It was sunk somewhat deeply between wild hedgerows which hid from his view the fields to either side. The surface of the road was metalled and thankfully free of potholes.

After a moderate climb up the side of the hill the road levelled out swiftly and then ahead he could see the building. It had been designed by a Dutch architect in the second half of the 18th century. The walls were of rough stone covered with lime render. Dutch bricks surrounded the heavy sash windows and main door. It was set back from the road but the road more or less ended where the building was.

Even now I can see it, he thinks as he gazes out the window. That first sighting was enough to tell me that I had found what I was looking for here. I sit within the shelter of that mansion I once saw from a lofty rise after the drive. That morning I walked around the building, gazing at it not to find flaws- if there were any I did not see them- but just to familiarise myself with its lineaments. Perhaps that is how farmers look at livestock on a market day. All the while I was studying the building I thought that it was studying me: a strange thought but it felt true! I had already, on the very first sight as I crested the hill, decided that *this* was what I wanted; but was *I* what it wanted? I did not venture into the garden, designed by the Dutchman Johan van der Niemand, and grounds behind it. I merely took in the sweep of them at the back and the view to the coast from the front. Once I had circled the building I returned to my car and drove back to the town. I phoned the agent at once and told him I wished to buy the place. He sounded relieved- it had been on the market for some considerable time and there had been, so he told me later, no enquiries prior to mine.

Or has the house always been in the family and I have inherited it?

When it is time for lunch Ness will come to wheel me into the dining room. Two places are always set. A fresh rose in a small clear glass vase is always set beside her placement.

On a wall there is a portrait of a young woman. It is a three-quarter length portrait in the manner of Gainsborough. The young woman is half-turned in her high-backed seat and over her left shoulder is a view out of a window to a garden. The detail is very fine, not only of her dress and hair but of that section of the garden visible through the window. The colours of the painting are bright as though it has been cleaned recently. The young woman's head seems crowned with a neatly bunned riot of auburn hair, a long twisted tress of which hangs over her left shoulder and falls past her breast to her waist. Her features are sharp and clear, her skin light with just a sprinkling of freckles across her nose and on her half-bare forearms. Her hands are lightly clasped in her lap, the fingers interlaced and an emerald ring glitters on her wedding finger, matching the colour of her eyes. She is smiling slightly as though she is about to rise and embrace someone who is entering the room.

I remember how she would rise to embrace me, he thinks, whenever I came into the room. It would be as though I had been away for a long time, rather than for a few hours or the odd day or two. She would hold me as though she was reuniting herself with a part of her being she had mislaid.

Over the right shoulder of the young woman, along a wall is a bookcase full of books. It is possible to read the names along the spines of some of the books- '*Novum Organum*' and '*Essayes, or Counsels, Civill and Morall*' by

Sir Francis Bacon; *'Pinax Theatri Botanici'* by Gaspard Bauhin; *'Yuan Yeh'* by Chi Ch'eng; and *'Systema Horticulturae'* by John Woolridge. There are dozens of others but their titles are not so readily discerned.

*

He is frowning as he looks through the window.

My eyesight is getting worse, he thinks. His spectacles are on the table beside him. He cannot remember having taken them off and having put them back in their case. Perhaps he never put them on. Perhaps he took them off when he drank the coffee, to avoid them becoming steamed up. That would make sense, he thinks; but then why should things make sense?

He puts his glasses on and returns to his survey of the scene beyond the window. There are times, he thinks, when it could just as well be a screen, such as are to be found in cinemas, or a television screen. But what was it that had distracted him and caught his eye just then?

In those first weeks after her death he had wandered uselessly in the garden, already seeing those signs of neglect which he couldn't repair.

It is all a tangle of greens and browns, he thinks, like a tumble of sweaters in a chest. Some of this is because of my poor eyesight and some of this is because of the untamed growth in the garden.

It has been like that, he thinks, since she died. It was their garden but she was the one who tended it, as she tended him. He would do some of the more burdensome chores- shifting or wheeling things here and there at her behest, or mowing the lawn. He enjoyed the physicality of that, whilst she revelled in the creativity, the envisioning of the garden, the transformation of the wilderness into something more accessible.

What was it I would recite to myself from the "Dark Rose" as I worked beside her, he thinks? *'Shiubhalfainn féin an drúcht leat is fásaigh ghuirt, Mar shúil go bhfaighinn rún uait nó páirt dem thoil.'* Once the words would bind him to her like the invisible thread of freshly spun spider's webs in the avenue of trees. Now they weighed heavy as empty oil drums: they were unable to sink, jarring and echoing emptily as they floated on the surface in his memory.

If I turn my head, he thinks, on the wall behind me I would see her portrait. I can feel her gazing out with me on to the wilderness that has overtaken the work of her hands.

*

When he first turned the key and entered the inside of the house looked as though it was ready to be lived in.

The previous occupant had died suddenly; there were no relatives and so the contents of the house had been included in the sale. He had not wished to view inside before the purchase. He could not explain then or now why that was. Take it as it is, he told himself. Others might well have had all the contents carted away and disposed of; but he wanted to get a sense of the spirit of the place as it was, rather than impose on it his nature and tastes. Perhaps that was because then he was not quite sure of them, who he was and what he liked and disliked. Somehow he was incomplete and he felt that the puzzle he might find inside would propose answers to him- or at least insist on answers.

He told none of this to the agent, of course. The company were relieved to have the place off their books.

Once he had moved into the mansion he hired someone to look after the grounds. The fellow was named Josef Johann and though he lived locally, in the village, he was originally from Klosterneuburg near Vienna. Then Johann had mysteriously moved on. Some of the locals suggested he had been a Nazi spy and they swore that they had seen a U-boat surfacing in the bay one evening. But it was pub talk. He had been a good gardener- dependable and knowledgeable, someone who knew more than just that a tree was a tree.

That was before she came into his life.

It was the study where I now sit, he thinks, which welcomed me the most. Wherever I went that first day, into whichever room I strayed or was led, I felt settled; but it was here that I felt most at home. It was to this window that I was drawn.

The room had been bright, despite the mahogany bookshelves crammed with volumes all of which gleamed as though freshly dusted.

As I hurried to the window that morning, he thinks, I took in a few of the titles: '*Les Jardins de Samboursky*', '*Joyfull Newes out of the New Found Worlde*', '*Paradisi in Sole Paradisus Terrestris*' and '*Le Jardin de Mme Jeanne*'. Two leather chairs were drawn up either side of the bay window which looked northward into the heart of the countryside. I half expected two people to be standing to greet me, he thinks. The chairs are thrust back into the interior of the room now, so that there is space for the wheelchair in which I sit.

Have I taken any book down from the shelf? he wonders.

On his knees he turns over and over the copy of Wittgenstein's '*Tractatus Logico-Philosophicus*' he may have been reading. A sterile phrase lurks on the edge of his consciousness like a caterpillar in its chrysalis waiting to take the form of a butterfly. In the mirror he sees behind himself- himself in the mirror- a small vacant space on one of the shelves. It seems too high for him to have reached and perhaps Ness took the volume down for me, he thinks.

All of these books were here, he thinks, and I have added nothing to them. That first morning I had hurried to the bay window to gaze out of it, even though I had seen the view that day I had come to first see the mansion. It was exactly as I remembered it, the view. I had dreamt about it in the days and weeks following my visit. Now there it was, here it is, the view over the terrace with its skirting of lawn and then the wilderness which is the garden, and then the wilderness which is the wilderness.

I saw something then, he thinks, as I have seen something just now- or was it before I fell asleep? I may be asleep now.

He smiles at the thought.

*

He tells Ness there is someone in the garden.

That is what has been troubling me, he thinks. That is what I saw, or thought I saw, a moment ago as I was gazing out of the window.

Yes, he tells Ness, there was someone out there.

I shall investigate, sir, Ness says. But he can tell that Ness does not believe him. There is never anyone in the garden- birds, yes, wild animals, yes, but never anyone. The village is too far away, several miles of rugged hillside and heath-land, and why would anyone wander all the way out here?

Through the window he watches as Ness walks along the terrace, shading his eyes as he quarries the distant wilderness for a trace of this interloper.

Ness will know that I am watching, he thinks. He is a good servant; he will do his duty and look to see if someone is there. But I can tell that he does not believe he will find anything. Later he will tell the doctor and they will put it down to my declining state.

When Ness returns he tells him to ask the chauffeur to prepare the car as he wants to go to the headland to visit her grave. Ness says he will do so straight away and leaves the room. It has been some time since he has visited her grave. He cannot remember the last time he went. It was not last week- not that he can clearly recall last week. Maybe it was last month? He cannot say.

Why have I forgotten? he thinks. This at least I do not want to forget and now it seems that I have forgotten.

He looks at the painting on the study wall. It is the same woman as in the painting that hangs in the dining room. In this painting the young woman, perhaps a year or two older but perhaps not, is standing in a garden, most likely the garden that lies beyond the window.

It could be a mirror, he thinks, and if I were to turn suddenly I might see her at the window.

In her hands, held raised to her waist, is a bunch of flowers, a mixture of Daisies, Dahlias and Forget-me-Nots. He can see them in his minds eye in a bowl on the table in the sitting room at the front of the building, as fresh as when they had first been picked. If he were to look into that room now he would find those flowers still there, he was sure of it. Unlike the portrait in the dining room her hair is loose and cascades around her head and over her shoulders like some of the bushes and shrubs behind her. All around her flowers seem to be blooming, a riot of colours which make her figure stand out all the more. She is wearing a blue dress which is stirred slightly by an unseen breeze and perhaps some motion on her part as she moves slightly forward. On her lips there is that same smile, a hint of the sunrise which was her full smile, a smile which was sure to end in either a kiss or her rich laughter. Her laughter seemed to summon the creatures from the garden and if he looked closely he knows that he would see them peeking through leaves and branches, revelling in her joy.

It is not the chauffeur he remembers. This man is younger, he thinks, and his hair is cut differently. Perhaps he is the son of the chauffeur.

This is not the route that he remembers either. He feels as though he is being driven to an unknown assignation. He sits in the back of the car and watches the scenery as it scrolls past the windows. It might be a dreamscape. At any moment exotic creatures might appear. He hears some music from the car radio. It is Ravel's '*L'Enfant et les Sortilèges*' with its libretto by Colette.

When they stop he has to wait for the chauffeur to open the door and help him out. For a moment he looks around himself in bewilderment. Which way should he go? The chauffeur is busying himself with the car, rubbing some smear or mark from the long black bonnet.

I shall go this way, he decides.

The chauffeur makes no attempt to stop him. Why should he? It is none of his business. His job is to drive, to drive wherever he is told to drive. The route he may chose may vary- though hereabouts it cannot for there are few roads - but his orders are to go here or there, to wait or not to wait, to be prepared to leave at such and such a time. This is his job. His job is not to suggest that his employer is going the wrong way once he has left the car.

None of this is familiar to me, he thinks. Perhaps I was last here in a different season. It is summer now and there is new growth all around.

He looks at the grave, startled to find it so close, just over the ridge which shields it from the road.

The flowers in the small vase still look fresh. He replaces them with those he has brought today- Sunflowers set in a necklace of Queen Anne's Lace.

There is a mist over the headland as he gazes out to sea. It is barely possible to see the ocean and the boundary between it and the sky is obscured so that it is all one. He feels unsteady on his feet, untethered. He wonders why he has come today. It may be an anniversary of a kind but he does not think so. Perhaps, he thinks, I have come because I felt the need to come. Perhaps I have come out of habit.

When he returns to the house Ness carries him straight up to his bedroom as he has fallen asleep. The chauffeur will return the car- a 1931 Bentley 8 litre Saloon- to its garage after he has once more polished away the dust of the road and any other debris.

He lies in the large double bed with its canopy and gazes across the darkened room. The curtains are wide open so that the starry night can be seen. He has snuffed the candle which Ness always leaves burning on the table beside his bed.

It is odd, he thinks, that I insist on staying in this bedroom, with its view to the south. At night, when it is dark, when I can see only vague shapes in the darkness or the punctuation of the stars if there are no clouds, I lie here and gaze out of a higher window.

He cannot see the walls. In the darkness it is possible to believe that there are no walls and that he is laid out beneath the stars with this view towards the site of her grave.

She is still, he thinks, my compass.

When he dreams, if he dreams, he dreams of her, their life together. His life before her is closed off as though behind a wall.

Otherwise his dreams are empty, like a scooped out eggshell.

In the morning the candle will be alight beside him, as though his dreams have relit the wick.

When he dreams of her he wakes with a good appetite. When his dreams are absent he has no hunger in him and will only sip his tea of coffee, waving away the food he might be offered.

*

The mansion was built for a successful 18th century merchant named Diarmuid Fise. It was his marriage present to his wife-to-be. She saw it for the first time on the day of her marriage when he and his bride drew up outside the mansion in a landau. He could tell from her face that it was just the house she had seen in a dream she had once described to him.

In the library is an old leather bound volume of his diaries which he kept from the time of the clearing of the land to the death of his wife whilst in labour. He wrote no more after her burial in a grave which overlooks the bay where his ships would drop anchor before unloading their cargo. Her portraits- the only two pictures to be found in the mansion- were painted by Cornelia van der Mijn, sister of the better known Dutch painter George van der Mijn. Most of her works are lost, including a known self-portrait from the year 1780. Her only other surviving picture- of flowers- is to be found in the *Rijksmuseum*.

During the building of the mansion several local tradesmen were employed and some of their descendants still live in the village. In Fise's diary of the time- the work took two years all told- he notes the death of a couple of labourers who were buried under a collapsed wall. These deaths were thought to have brought bad luck to the site and for a while the workmen refused to continue building. Fise doubled their wages and this overcame their superstitious scruples. From the diaries it is clear that Fise was a daily visitor to the site when not elsewhere dealing with the calls of his business. Much material had to be imported, such as the bricks, and the mahogany used for the panelling in the hall, study and sitting rooms.

*

He tells Ness there is someone in the garden and Ness goes to investigate. When he returns he tells him that there was no one there and takes him to the red pine panelled dining room for lunch. He notices the solitary Provence rose in the small vase beside the second place at the table. Today the rose is red; was it a white Botzaris yesterday?

How she loved flowers, all kinds of flowers, the simple and the complex, those with scents and those without. Many of the original plants and seeds were brought from *Andrieux's* of Quai de la Mégisserie in Paris. It has now become *Vilmorin's* at Verrières-le-Buisson and was visited by Chekhov when building his garden in Yalta.

He would watch from the terrace as she cut those flowers she wanted to set around the house. He would feel an odd sense of excitement as she stood running her eye over the display. Would he have chosen the same flower, the same example of each flower? When she noticed the intensity of his gaze she would smile and then plunge her hand into the display to select one almost at random, although he knew that she must have already chosen.

Was that how it had been at the dance? he wondered. He had felt awkward as he watched the others moving on to the dance floor as the band began to play Paul Whiteman's *'Happy Feet'*. There had been no way to decline the invitation. He had told himself that he would go along for an hour, perhaps two, and then he would slide away discreetly. Then this young woman was asking him to dance. All his composure seemed to desert him. He mumbled something about not being much able to dance. She had smiled and said 'I shall be the man' and had held up her hands for him to hold and then he had been gently swept on to the dance floor.

He eats some cold meat with pickle. In the afternoon he requests that he be wheeled out on to the terrace so that he might enjoy the freshness of the air and the warm sun that the afternoon promises. Ness settles him beneath a large umbrella so that he has some shade. On a table beside him there is a book which he may read. The windows of the study are open so that he may hear Mozart's opera *'La finta giardiniera'* which is on the radio. Ness has left some lemonade in a pitcher on the table, in case he becomes thirsty.

He watches as the woman works amongst the beds overgrown with weeds.

Diarmuid Fise made his fortune transporting labourers from Ireland to Newfoundland and Labrador where there was a migratory fishing industry. He also supplied them with salt beef, pork and butter. He was a self-made man, hard-working and, like many of that time, devout without being a fanatic. Though he subscribed to the Protestant faith which was the dominate power at the time he was a Catholic but hid that fact so that he might trade and prosper and look after the family he hoped to raise. When his wife died he deserted the house, left his business in the hands of managers he trusted, and disappeared. Some thought he had gone into a monastery near Vienna; others thought he had become an adventurer, travelling to the Far East or the Americas both north and south. The truth is that nobody knows what happened to him. The house was eventually sold and over the years has had several owners. After their initial pleasure at owning such an estate the isolation becomes too much and the place is sold again.

Some of its owners over the years have revived the gardens and have installed lighting, gazebos and a Ha-ha. Over the years these improvements have decayed. The lighting no longer works and the gazebo and Ha-ha are as overgrown as the bee hives. There is no problem about things growing there. Whatever is planted thrives.

The only thing that does not thrive, he thinks as he sips some lemonade, are the occupants of the mansion.

Though he sees the woman he isn't sure if she sees him. Or if she does she must not care about his presence.

He looks at the words in the book he is holding. The letters seem to jiggle together in the sunlight, as though dancing. He cannot make sense of what he reads. Perhaps it does not make sense. Perhaps it is a foreign language, one that he cannot understand though he understands several. He turns the page and watches the letters dancing some more, leaving the pages and being carried away. Then a light breeze turns the page for him.

He looks up and sees that the woman has disappeared. He hears Ness approaching. Ness tells him that the doctor is here.

Has a week passed already? he thinks.

The doctor says it is good to see him out on the terrace. Doctors have this great belief in sunlight and fresh air. Doubtlessly they are right, he thinks, though he prefers the darker comforts of his study and the bedroom. He allows himself to be examined and blood to be drawn. Ness will have already told the doctor about what he has or hasn't eaten. They sit and chat for a while. The doctor enjoys some lemonade. He watches as the doctor runs his eye over the tangle that is the garden. Perhaps he is himself an amateur gardener like Chekhov and is imagining what he could do with such a place.

He does not tell the doctor about the woman he has seen. Some things I must keep for myself, he thinks. There is little enough that I have left.

When the doctor has said his goodbyes and gone he asks Ness to take him back inside. The opera has finished and he wants to read somewhere that the letters don't dance.

*

Cornelia van der Mijn did the painting in a studio in London. The background details in each of the portraits- the library and the garden- she improvised from the sitter's description. The garden had not been completed then, existing only in the recently wed young woman's mind. He is struck with how accurately the real garden, what can be made out beneath the tangle, matches the painting. Perhaps she had seen the library for those books are still there on the same shelves. Even curiosity has not made him remove them to glance through them. He wonders if he's fearful of what he may find in those pages.

She watches as the artist steps back to survey her. If the artist is conscious of her watching her paint she gives no sign of it, so absorbed is she in her task. She has chosen the blue dress especially for this sitting and the flowers that she holds at her waist. She has never sat for a portrait before and is excited by the occasion. Before he left Diarmuid had asked her if she might not become bored and perhaps a shorter sitting would be better; but she and the artist had waved him from the studio both excited at the prospect of the sitting. What he did not know then was that she was in the early stages of pregnancy; but the artist, being a woman, knew this at once. Though he was shooed from the room he is present in both their minds. The painter was thinking of the fine commission fee she has been promised; but once she began to put brush to canvas such thoughts had disappeared from her mind. The sitter was thinking of the pleasure the portrait would give to her husband; and the thought of him kept that expression on her face and that eagerness in her pose which excited the painter.

When he returned to the studio she was sitting downstairs in the lounge sipping tea with the artist who had changed from her smock and canvas trousers into a comfortable dress. He was surprised that it had taken less time than he thought it would. When he asked to see the painting she laughed and said he must wait until it was hung in their home and in the meantime he must make do with just her. The second painting, the one that hangs in the dining room, was done some months later by the artist from memory.

When she dies, the day that she dies, in his grief he wants to take a knife to the paintings; but he can not bring himself to deface what would be the only external image of her he is left with.

*

He wonders how the flowers come into the house. Only when he is going to visit the grave does he ask Ness to gather a few flowers for him to take. Ness will do that; but otherwise he has not seen Ness in the garden picking blossoms.

He does not select at random, though it may appear that way. She had made a list for him of flowers to collect while she was away visiting her sister in the north. She did not like to think of the house without their colours and scents. He had been diligent in collecting the flowers, though he could have asked the gardener or one of his boys to do it. He wanted to be close to her by doing what she would have done when she selected the flowers and cut them and arranged them. He knew that his eye was not as good as hers; but the results were not as bad as he feared they might be. Everyone would smile at 'the master's flowers' when they saw them on the tables and in the vases in all the rooms- and he would smile too, knowing that she would be smiling at the thought of what he was doing.

*

One day, with the aid of his walking stick, he manages to descend the steps from the terrace and stand in the garden. He sees the woman working some distance away. She pulls weeds from the beds and gives space and light to choked plants which are now flowering again. Wherever she moves in the garden she re-establishes order where there was wilderness. He watches her moving slowly through the beds of weeds. Her head is uncovered and her hair is plaited down her back. She is well tanned by the sun and wind. He cannot guess at her age. There is a determined air about her as she works, her arms and hands never still or empty. He wonders how long she has been working in the garden. Was it yesterday he first noticed her? But Ness said he saw nothing then and today. But there she is, crouched down on her knees and intent on her work.

He would call out to her but he does not want to startle her. She does not look up.

Motionless, leaning on his stick, he stands at the edge of the garden almost afraid to venture into it. He glances around at the vastness of the garden and when he tries to locate her again he cannot see her.

He manages to climb back up to the terrace and return to his wheelchair under the umbrella.

In the book he has been trying to read the words seem to have settled down.

It is '*El Jardin de los Sueños Perdidos*' a story by an obscure Spanish Basque poet and novelist Javier Galera. They have never met. He has read the story many times before. It is one he translated for an anthology many years ago, before Galera achieved fame and notoriety. Like many who fought on the Republican side during the Civil War in Spain he was murdered by Franco's Nationalists during the *Represión Franquista*. His body, along with others shot beside him, was buried in an overgrown garden in the town of Badajoz. The site is now marked with a bed of carnations.

Is this really the story of Galera, he thinks, or one I have written but forgotten? He closes the book and the words disappear, leaving only an echo of some indescribable feeling.

He wonders what it would be like to fight against fascism and to be put against a wall and shot. There are all kinds of walls against which all kinds of people have been shot, he thinks.

*

Ness will find me, he writes, where I have collapsed in the garden.

He will pick me up and carry me up to my bedroom and will lay me on the bed. He will summon the doctor but will know already that I am dead.

As I lie on the bed I will see the painting on the ceiling, the painting of a garden; and in it I will see a woman working. The palm of one hand is bloodied where she has pricked it on a thorn.

Each time I see the painting the garden becomes more and more vivid. I recognise it and am smiling when the doctor comes to pronounce me dead.

On his cheek is a smear of blood.

A Crystal in Darkness

It had been raining most of his three hour journey.

From his window he could see a strong wind lashing the foliage around the border of the enclosed triangular garden. Rosary-like beads of rain raced down the glass to reach the corners and edges of the panes. Over the drenched valley through which he had driven a short while ago a clamp of greyness was pressing down. The wind whistled like the ghosts of departed brothers whose graves he had passed as he'd been escorted to the building.

The room- in the Abbey's guesthouse they did not have numbers but names and this one was 'Saint Dominic'- was well appointed. It had its own private bathroom and shower. It was simple in design: the walls were of bare brick and the ceiling was roughly plastered. The red tiled floor had under-floor heating.

There was a simple wooden desk, on which stood a lamp, and a wooden chair tucked close to it. Otherwise there was just the single bed (which had felt solid but acceptable when he had sat on it) and a comfortable looking armchair, beside which was a small table with another lamp on it.

A built-in wall closet was where he could hang his clothes.

On the inside of the main door were a list on rules: you were to keep silence in the corridors and the area of the front door; an absolute silence was to be kept when going to and from the Abbey church; you should only speak in the general sitting room if the door was closed; you should not wander unaccompanied through the monastery and the church; only go through the monastery to the church when the guest-master rings the bell- the guest chapels may be accessed at any time; there is always coffee available in the pantry next to the dining room; a meal will be placed on the dining table for each guest; guests should only go into the kitchen to wash up after meals; the guest-master should be informed if you are going to be absent from any meal as this avoided waste.

Although there was a schedule based around the Hours, in many ways you were left to your own devices, he thought. There was no compulsion for you to join in any of the services.

On the wall above the head of the bed was a simple wooden crucifix on which hung an alabaster Christ.

A young monk dressed in faded blue denims and a white cotton shirt had come in to swab out the already meticulously clean bathroom with disinfectant; other than that he was left alone.

His arrival had been accomplished with the minimum of words. Brother Aelred had greeted him, conducted him to this room and told him that supper was at five. As soon as he was in the room and had been shown where everything was, the brother had left with a smile and slight nod.

Apart from the noise of the storm outside everything here reflects and represents silence, he thought. The bricks laid and bound so tightly together were like so many sealed mouths.

He felt cut off from the world and interred within the silence.

No wonder the wind was raging outside, he thought. No wonder the storm is spewing its fury down upon the hill-top cluster of buildings. No wonder that all the way here the twisting back country roads were like a slick-backed serpent trying to shake him off. He had had to concentrate so much, to see through the rain-sheeted windscreen whose wipers could barely cope with the downpour that his head had been pounding with a migraine when he arrived.

No sooner had Aelred closed the door than he had hurried to the bathroom and thrown up in the toilet.

*

He came late to supper at five o'clock. There were nine others he counted. All the places were taken and there was no plate of liverwurst and mustard sandwiches for him. One of the brothers went into the kitchen to see what was available but came back empty-handed except for some chocolate mousse. One of the other guests pushed a plate containing half of his sandwiches to him. He smiled his thanks for that simple gesture of sharing. As they ate they listened to readings from the beginning of St. John's Gospel.

He was curious to know who the others were, where they came from and why they were here; but the silence was obligatory. Perhaps it's enough, he thought, that I know who I am; but that might also be the question, he thought smiling to himself.

Once the light meal and coffee were finished they went into the church for Vespers. There seemed to be no more than a couple of dozen brothers in the choir stalls, looking like pure white flames. At one point he thought he recognised a few of them from elsewhere but he knew that this was hardly likely. As best he could he played 'follow-my-leader', bowing when others bowed and crossing himself likewise.

As they returned from Vespers the Garth beyond the plexi-glass enclosure of the cloister was a well of darkness into which the interminable rain kept falling. He half imagined fish swimming in the murk, but it was only their reflections as they made their way to the kitchen to do the washing up.

At half seven the hand-bell was rung for Compline which was sung in the darkened church as the cantor strummed a guitar.

Darkness and light seemed inter-changeable. He stood with the others in the darkened nave, aware of this vast emptiness inside himself and he wondered how he had become so empty and detached. He kept his eyes closed while the melodious voices of the brothers filled the cavernous body of the church like dancing butterflies. The chanting seemed to bind the empty space between the ceiling and walls and floor together into something more tangible than the darkness.

At the *Salve Regina* a solitary light lit up the stained glass window over the high altar. It picked out that part of the window which depicted the Virgin and the Child Jesus.

He could hear the rain falling heavily. Three bells were rung thrice, marking the end of Compline. The guests filed towards the altar where a brother sprinkled holy water over them with a goupillon.

In the greater silence back in his room as he sat in the armchair he was filled with chaotic, unrefined and unsayable thoughts. He felt like a cracked and warped piece of metal being struck with a hammer.

*

He slept badly. The mattress had been lumpy and there was no position on it in which he felt comfortable.

Someone knocked on the door to let him know that the morning Vigil was due but he was unable to rouse himself and get up.

I always sleep poorly in a strange bed, he thought as he rose at six the next morning to prepare for Lauds and the morning Mass.

He was washed and dressed when the hand-bell was sounded and he joined the others out in the corridor.

The morning service was simple and moving. The brothers, all in their white habits, flitted like moths as they made their way into the church. They seemed to provide flesh to the skeleton of the nave. After Lauds the celebrant wearing a gorgeous red cope over his habit conducted the service. A priest brought the elements to the guests at the rear of the church.

After the Mass the sweet smell of baking bread filled the corridor as they made their way to the dining-room.

The breakfast of porridge and raisins, two slices of brown toast with jam and then coffee was welcome. As they ate the reading from John's Gospel continued.

Afterwards there was a short time to himself before the Conference at ten. The brother leading the session told a story about a man who lived in a cave. He tried to understand who he was, why he was where he was and what he ought to do by sifting through all the contents of the cave. There came a point, however, when he had to stand up and quit the cave; to set off without a backward glance; to step out into the daylight in all his ignorance and fear, trusting that all would be made clear.

*

Outside it was a sunny but blustery start to the day. The clouds were shredded like the torn banners of warring regiments. Wherever he looked things were in flight- birds revelled in the wind, soaring and plunging; branches strained on the maple, oak and pine trees trying to take flight themselves; he imagined the still rising sun itself being blown around the heavens like some ping-pong ball. He walked outside for a while, keeping to the gravelled paths though the buffeting wind seemed determined to shove him on to the damp grassy surrounds. Long skirted spruce trees trembled like spinning tops set in motion but unable to dance as freely as they longed to do. His hair was being tugged as though by an invisible wrestler. He looked back frequently to the building perhaps wondering if it might not be in danger of being blown away. The cross over the church seemed to pin it down. He wondered if he was seeing things any clearer that morning than he had when he arrived in the deepening darkness of the previous evening.

*

The Abbey was completely self-supporting. It had its own telephone network (linked into the national one), its own petrol and electricity systems for power, a fully automated jam factory and the small farm and orchards which provided grain, fruit and eggs. The water supply was drawn from an artesian well.

The main building had been designed by a local female architect who had also designed various Hilton hotels. In her will she had donated to the Abbey the two priceless paintings by Piero della Francesca- '*Il Seminatore e la Zizzania*' and '*Cristo cammina sulle acque*'- which adorned the otherwise bare walls of the conference room. It was built in 1950 by the brothers themselves after they had been burnt out of their previous monastery. They lived then in old tin huts and semi-ruined farm buildings. Locals thought them foolish to have chosen a site on top of a thousand foot high hill where the winds could reach almost a hundred miles an hour. But they were well away from the river below that flooded and damaged property in the town. They were also, someone had said, nearer heaven.

A little way down the hill was what was called the 'dynamite' house. That was where the explosives used to blast the rock so that foundations could be laid were kept during the building work. It was now used as a workshop where the brothers made copes and other ecclesiastical garments. Further down the hill was a wood-fired kiln for making the pottery that was sold in the shop.

Hermitages dotted the surrounding woods which several eremitic monks shared with the wildlife therein. In the winter trees were felled and sold as firewood to the townspeople. All told there were over sixty brothers attached to the Abbey, although they seldom seemed to be all together.

Before lunch he walked down to the shop by the main gate. He bought a couple of books of poetry and a few jars of blueberry conserve. He also bought a rosary for his mother.

I have not thought of anyone except myself until this moment, he thought as he paid for his purchases.

On the way back up to the Abbey he stopped by the stream that runs down the hill. He peered into the wooded valley littered with pine needles, dead leaves and large boulders which looked like the muscular backs of slumbering giants. They seemed highly polished, both by the waters which must rush over them when the stream was in full spate and the wind which had not let up since his arrival. Many of the greying branches of the trees had been stripped of their finery, like slaves being prepared for servitude. Beneath his feet the waterlogged ground squelched. High up in one tree he could see a bird's nest balanced exquisitely. The berries of the Hobblebush clinging to the wall of one of the old farmhouses where aspirants lodged were like splatterings of blood.

Further away was the stubbly cheek of a ploughed corn or hay field. In the distance he made out two low white buildings beside which was parked a tractor and a beat-up pick-up truck.

The twin bells in the bell-tower above uttered their metallic summons for those working in the fields and outbuildings. Solar heat panels on the roofs of the attached guest houses looked like camp arched eyebrows. He studied the crazy stonework of the church as, breathing hard and his ears stung by the cold, he climbed back up towards the Abbey. Below him two silent black cowled brothers drift up the hill like foraging crows blown by the wind.

In quarter of an hour it will be time for lunch, he thought. Having such simple thoughts pleased him enormously.

Lunch was a bowl of meat broth and vegetables. For dessert there was a jam-soaked cake and strong tea. The reading of John's Gospel continued and familiar though it was he found himself listening with unexpected eagerness to the story. Words were a precious currency in this silence.

In the afternoon he continued his wandering around the grounds, finding it pleasant to have the thoughts he had feared or expected being swept from his mind by the strength of the wind. Not to be constantly spitted by thought was a relief. The life he had been living was one of gestures; all he had seemed to be doing was to tie knots in himself and drive himself into a corner. When a brief cloud-burst raked the ground he did not dash for shelter but continued his walk despite it, thinking only of the hot shower he could have once he had returned to his room.

After Vespers as he was washing the dishes one of the others whisperingly asked him what he did for a living; or did he just go around showing off his refined English accent? They were the first words he had heard outside of the Offices and meal-time readings. It was an attempt at humour, he supposed, though it also had an edge to it. His questioner admitted that he was dying for a cigarette and found the silence oppressive. He smiled sympathetically but did not reply.

*

That last night he lay thinking that tomorrow he would be leaving the Abbey. He wondered what he would be leaving behind and what he would be taking away. Was he still bedded in the silence or it in him?

He fell asleep hearing the rain tapping on the window.

The Tunnel

1.

Hunter closed his eyes as the fine spray of hot water raked the dirt and sweat from his up-turned face and naked body. The tiny needles tattooed on his eyelids causing exotic blooms of light to explode inside his skull. The grime was peeled from his body like a false skin. It lay at his feet in foamy mounds before disappearing down the drainage hole.

On either side in the other cubicles Hunter could hear, above the sound of the music, the horseplay and laughter of the others in his work squad.

- Christ, Tabb, you should've used that on the rock face! It'd be better than a pick any day, man!

-Pass the fucking soap, Ghant.

- Catch.

- Some rock fall, eh?

- Had to fucking happen on our shift, eh? We'll get a rookie now to replace Dyne. Stupid bastard should've moved faster. That's our bonus down the pan for another week.

- What's the game plan, boys?

- Me, I'm for a few beers.

- A few beers? Christ, man that filth has given me a thirst a geyser couldn't quench. I'm for jumping in a lake of the stuff.

- What I want is one of those Comforters to give me the works.

- Split her in two with that pick, Tabb.

- Hey Hunter what about you? Fancy a beer and a bit of Comfort?

Hunter lowered his face from the spray and opened his eyes. The others, wanting to make the most of their time off, were already towelling themselves dry.

- I'll meet up with you all somewhere, Hunter said. I need a bit of space first.

He could still see Dyne's body being pulled from under the rock fall.

Hunter turned back into the curtain of water which shut out the voices of the others as they left the cleansing room. Only when his hands slid over his body without encountering any resistance from the clinging dust did he step out of the shower. Once his weight was no longer on the ribbed tray the shower jet automatically stopped.

Hunter dried himself with slow, methodical movements, examining each limb and part of his body. He studied his muscular back in the wall mirrors. Unlike Tabb and Knebb who had been below the surface working in the tunnel for more than a thousand shifts, Hunter's eyes were still blue and clear. The eyes of old-timers like those two had already acquired that opaqueness which had an inevitable result. As yet Hunter could see that his skin hadn't begun to show the mottling signs of corrosion commonplace among the squad. Despite their masks and the skin-tight suits the dust infiltrated. The extractors and ventilators succeeded only in drawing away the coarser, visible dust particles. Even the most advanced purification showers and body cosmetics only delayed that corrosion. Once the tell-tale signs were noticed medical check-ups became more regular and more rigorous. Once the corrosion could no longer be disguised by the cosmetics and the itching became intolerable then you would be withdrawn from the shift. If you were lucky- so the rumours had it- you might be surfaced. In any event you would be moved from the face of the tunnel, sent back down the line to the pleasure complex.

It was the supervisor Quex's job to keep a tally of the shifts they worked. He calculated the time they took and the men lost and the distance covered. Those who had contributed the most were rewarded with a fortnight at the complex where your every need was catered for. Food, drink, sex, visuals: whatever you wanted you could have.

Few of Hunter's squad had logged even half of the qualifying time. The accident to Dyne would set them back several hours. The most any of them could hope for in the immediate future was a visit to the Comforters for a few hours of caressing and stimulation to take their minds off their exertions at the rock face.

When he was dressed Hunter closed his locker and left the cleansing area. He stepped past the green light at the discharge gate and entered the conduit which lead away from the forward work area. Through the window at the embarkation area he could see another work squad- their uniforms blue as opposed to the yellow of his squad- handing in their tools. Even as that squad was filing past Quex into the cleansing area another squad was being disgorged by the monorail which ferried the work force to and from the rock face. The entire area was full of activity- squads coming and going; others repairing machinery or realigning the huge lamps which burnt ceaselessly above in the vaulted roof of the excavation. Nowhere was there a hint of a shadow, just the brilliant blaze of those lights, the gaudy coloured uniforms of the work squads and the dull grey walls of the excavation.

Stepping on to the central travelator, Hunter allowed himself to be swept along the conduit until he reached the numbered exit which lead to his quarters. He stepped off the moving floor and entered the lift which would take him up to his apartment.

Ever since he had come off duty he had been silent except for that brief reply to Tabb whilst in the shower. He knew it would have been impossible to join his workmates. He felt too flooded by the noise and chaos and his exertions at the rock face, as well as by the sight of Dyne's crushed body. They had been riding in the cab behind the Mole, watching as its grooved bit bored into the solid rock. Now and then he and the squad would leap out of the cab and smooth the sides of the tunnel, digging out recesses and laying tracks and scaffolding for the follow-up squads, who would do the finer work.

Hunter had been tidying the debris which hadn't been pulverised when the Mole struck a softer vein. It sped forward rapidly and cracks appeared in the roof. The automatic warning siren had sounded and the squad had either jumped back into the cab or scurried into the recesses. That is all but Dyne. He had forgotten his training- that's what happened, they said, when you were twenty per cent corroded- and had stood in the middle of the Tunnel staring upwards as part of the unshored roof sagged and fell towards him. None of them could do a thing about it.

It was that sense of uselessness which numbed Hunter now. Not that he really knew Dyne; but then who knew anybody in the tunnel? You worked alongside them, took Comfort before or after them, played cards and ate and drank with them; but that didn't mean you knew them, just that you were with them.

The door of the apartment slid soundlessly shut behind Hunter.

He eased his weary body into the chair, pushed the button on its arm and felt himself being tilted backwards. The room's lighting dimmed and changed to a softer, mistier colour. A soothing noise gradually filled the room. On the walls and the ceiling he could see a blue vastness and then all around him, as he seemed to float, there were open fields and vast forests and endless oceans being stirred by gentle breezes. Like a bird he seemed to swoop and soar, catching sight of a carp breaking the surface of a lake and the sun setting majestically behind a range of snow-capped mountains. All around there were clouds and the sound of beating wings, the flashing of light upon moving waters. He could see flocks of furry-maned beasts galloping across a grassy plain.

Hunter lay on the tilted chair until the machine registered that his pulse rate had dropped below the alarm level it had been registering. The thoughts of despair at Dyne's accident had been washed away. The lights in the room gradually returned and the chair gently resumed the upright.

Hunter rose, stretched and yawned. He felt ravenously hungry. Part of the circular wall slid open to reveal a kitchen. He went in to make himself something to eat in the wave oven. Only the dull pain at the very back of his head caused him to frown as he watched the package in the oven gradually assuming the shape and texture he required.

2.

- I'd like to discuss Hunter with you, sir.

With a slight gesture of irritation Dr. Frinck took the file which Dr. Aann held out to him.

- Well? What about Hunter? Who is he?

Dr. Frinck was always surly when one of his assistants- especially one of the younger females like Dr. Aann- sought to engage him in conversation about the squaddies. Although he was responsible for monitoring the health of this, the most forward section of the Tunnel's workforce, Dr. Frinck had long ago lost interest in the clinically predictable effects of the corrosive dust on their tissues. His conclusive findings had been put in a paper which he'd presented to his colleagues at Level Five. They had unanimously assured Dr. Frinck that his paper would secure him promotion to one of the upper levels, where the air was purer and still drawn from the surface. As the weeks and months passed so Dr. Frinck had become more moody and restless, there being no notification regarding his transfer Up. His work remained as precise and analytical, but his temper did not improve. He began to harbour the suspicion that a more illustrious colleague had taken his findings and used them to secure his own promotion. There was no way of checking his suspicion, only the hope that his further researches might see him chance upon some unexpected complication, some further ramification of the corrosive effect. If ever he got the chance to present another paper Dr. Frinck promised himself that he would be less naïve, less willing to surrender all the data to the head of Level Five's medical unit.

-Hunter, Dr. Aann was saying, has reached the stage when he's due for a complete check-up. I'd like to call him in and interview him myself.

- Yes, yes, Dr. Frinck said, noting the date on the file. There are thousands like him. Why not let one of the Subs collect the information?

- Hunter has been tagged, Dr. Aann said.

- Tagged?

Just for a moment Dr. Frinck's irritation disappeared.

-Yes. Surface have tagged him as being of special interest. This is the first opportunity since his orientation phase to examine him thoroughly.

- Well, Dr. Aann, you know the procedures for a special category like this. I suggest you start immediately and keep me informed of developments.

He watched as Dr. Aann left the office with Hunter's file.

She is competent that one, he thought; competent and eager.

He sensed danger. It was always the same with the new ones, Dr. Frinck thought. They come down here to make themselves a name, to get back to the Surface as quickly as possible. Well, it's a long, hard route, not as easy as getting into a lift and pushing a button and riding up to Level Five. He had found that out. Most of them end up elsewhere in the Tunnel, perhaps further back in one of the maintenance stations, but always on this level. They might end up specialising in the diseases which affect the young or the old and worn out; or working with the Comforters. But someone like Dr. Aann, still wet behind the ears, still labouring under the illusion that she can better herself and the lot of those to whom she ministers, she was dangerous to Dr. Frinck. She might just get lucky! She might just chance upon that part of the conundrum which he, despite all his experience, was overlooking.

Yes, thought Dr. Frinck; she bears watching, even though she, like all the others he had overseen, might discover nothing of note.

He had before encountered three or four individuals like Hunter who had been tagged by the surface. At the beginning of his service in the Tunnel Dr. Frinck had been intrigued by those individuals. He had sent back to the Surface the required data expecting momentous things to occur. But nothing had happened, nothing at all; and so his interest had waned.

Let her waste her time, he thought, as he reached for his stimulator. But keep an eye on developments just in case. If there is a way up to Level Five then he didn't want to miss it through negligence.

3.

The bar was crowded and full of smoke and music. Overhead bright lights pulsated and flashed. Hunter spotted Tabb, Knebb and the others sitting at one of the tables. He made his way through the throng to them. A chair had been kept for him. He nodded to the others as he sat down and glanced enquiringly at the strange face.

- This is Beel, Hunter, Tabb said. He's Dyne's replacement.

- Hullo, Hunter said shaking the new man's hand.

The hand was pure and white. Tabb laughed as he caught Hunter's glance.

- Yes, he's fresh from the battery, Tabb said.

- So, it's a wake and a baptism we're having then, Hunter said.

Beel seemed confused by the bantering mockery of his new workmates.

- Hope your back's strong, Beel, Knebb said. Old Dyne could carry two hundred weights but a ton stove him in- splat!

- Same again, lads? one of the others called and gestured to the bar.

Hunter had forgotten what it had been like to arrive as Beel had just done. The squad had been together for so long that they had begun to think that they'd grow old together and finish the Tunnel together. It was a frame of mind you got into. Other squads seemed always to be changing. Hunter would look around the bar sometimes and, apart from those at his table, would not recognise a face. Maybe the others did the same. The shifts never overlapped regularly and then the dust corroded some faster than others. Who would have thought that Dyne wouldn't be here today?

Hunter looked at the large clock behind the bar. It simply showed the total number of hours that had passed since the Tunnel had begun. There was nobody here from point zero or one. Whenever a comfort hour was due a hooter would sound.

- You with us Hunter?

Hunter shook himself out of his reverie and lifted his glass.

- Here's to Dyne, he said. He can't drink it so I will.

They watched as, in one gulp, Hunter swallowed the liquid.

- Dyne, they all said in harmony, including Beel who had never met the man he was replacing. Beel had difficulty in swallowing in one gulp like the others had done. The drink dribbled down his chin and he spluttered.

- Never mind, Beel, Knebb said. We'll knock you into shape lad.

4.

- Come in, a woman's voice invited and Hunter entered.

He was in an office but not the kind he was used to. Those at the work base were full of sweating men drinking stale coffee and cursing as the squad managers haggled over their assignments. This office, unlike those steely grey ones with their utilitarian furniture and strip lights, was comfortable and soothing on the eye. The furniture was solid but homely; there were bookcases lining some of the walls; a large fish tank stood in one corner; and shaded light from hidden points caressed rather than daggered the eye.

Behind a wooden desk, just rising from her chair, was a woman in a neat brown suit.

Hunter felt alarmed, the way he did when he might smell that gas which could suddenly hiss out from cracks in the rock face. It could asphyxiate you within seconds if you weren't quick with your mask. This room seemed redolent with strange odours. They confused his senses and heightened his wariness. He was also unused to the sight of a woman such as the one approaching him with an outstretched hand and warm smile on her face.

Hunter involuntarily took a backward step, only to encounter the solidity of the sliding door which had closed behind him.

- I'm Dr. Aann, the woman said as she took his hand. You're Hunter?

He nodded and, as though recalling some long forgotten gesture, returned the pressure of her hand and shook it.

A jolt ran up his arm at the softness of her palm.

- Please, Dr. Aann said, turning and indicating a large chair beside the desk. Do sit down.

She returned to her seat. Hunter watched her walk and quickly sat where she had indicated.

- Would you like something to drink? she asked.

He shook his head.

- Why am I here? Hunter asked.

Dr. Aann smiled.

- Straight to the point. Very refreshing. Do you know where you are?

- I was told to report to the Centre. This is where I was directed to. I assume it's the Centre.

- You are in the Centre.

- But why am I here?

- I don't wish to seem to not be reciprocating your directness, Hunter, but before I answer that question what I need to do is get some idea of your thoughts as they are now. Could you just tell me how you feel?

- Confused. I shouldn't be here.

- Shouldn't? Where should you be?

- With my squad at the rock face.

- Why?

- That's my job.

- How long have you been doing this job?

Hunter frowned.

- Since I came down to this level- almost a thousand shifts.

- What were you doing before?

- Before?

Again Hunter frowned. He took some time.

- I suppose I was on the Surface.

- Can't you remember?

- Not really. Not clearly in any case. Sometimes...

Hunter's voice faded away, uncertain, puzzled.

- Sometimes what? Dr. Aann prompted, unable to suppress the excitement which entered her voice.

She regretted that at once. She could see that Hunter who had been reluctant to enter and then uneasy at sitting in the comfortable chair, was now quite alarmed.

- I don't know. Look, can't I just go back now?

- Go back where?

- Damn it, to my squad! Where else?

- Are you worried about them?

- They're one short already and with a rookie replacing Dyne we'll lose our rating bonus for sure.

- That's all been taken care of, Hunter. While you're here someone is there in your place and the bonus won't be affected. Really, you can relax. Please, let me get you a drink.

Dr. Aann opened a drawer in the desk and took out two glasses and a bottle of syrupy essence. Hunter had never seen it before, though he knew that those who had been to the leisure complex spoke of it as though it was magical. He watched as she poured two large measures, leaving the bottle unstoppered on the desk top as she passed one glass to him.

- Cheers, she said and swallowed half of her drink.

Her teeth where white and clean. Her tongue was pink.

Hunter took the glass and stared at the contents. Then he knocked it back in one swallow, the way you did in the bar. He felt a not unpleasant tingling in his chest as the liquid went down.

- Help yourself when you want more, Dr. Aann said, indicating the open bottle as she sipped at her drink.

She studied him carefully all the while, her trained eye taking in his every movement, tic and gesture.

He is a handsome man, she thought, and showed no visible signs of corrosion. He was naturally ill-at-ease in this strange, clinical environment. She watched as his clear eyes glanced alertly, perhaps warily, around the room. He was taking in everything but also, she felt, noting avenues of escape, even potential dangers – and weapons?

- Why am I here? he asked again.

His tone indicated greater curiosity now than his earlier anxiety. She was glad that he had taken the drink. Her system was immune to its relaxing effect, but his would not be so highly tolerant.

- In a moment, she said. But first, do you know who you are?

- I'm Hunter.

It was clear from his expression that he found the question ridiculous but politely held back from saying so.

- Have you been asked that before?

- Who I am?

- Yes.

- No.

- But you know you are Hunter.

- Yes.

- How do you know?

- I have always been Hunter.

- What is always?

Now he laughed.

- Really, Doctor Aann! I don't mean to be rude but, well, ask yourself that question about yourself and see if you don't laugh!

She smiled.

- Yes, it is an interesting question, Hunter, isn't it? You are Hunter because you have always been so; and I am Dr. Aann perhaps for the same reason. But indulge me if you will, Hunter: where were you born?

Now he frowned.

- You'd have to check the records for that, I'm afraid.

- You don't know?

- Not offhand.

- What records shall I check?

- The ones Head Office keeps, I suppose. We all have them.

- Let me now answer your question as to why you are here, Hunter.

Dr. Aann pressed an unseen button and, to Hunter's left, a Visi-screen appeared on the wall.

- You've seen one of these before?

- A computerised display screen, yes.

- Watch- I enter my coding and look...

On the screen a mass of details appeared. They were interspersed with photographs of a baby, a young girl and a grown-up woman who was clearly Dr. Aann.

- That's my record, Hunter. It tells where I was born, who my parents were, where I was schooled, details of my career, my personal history, all up to date. Now, I'll enter your coding.

The screen was virtually blank. Hunter seemed to flinch as he recognised the one photograph of himself when a youngster.

- You see, Hunter; you are an enigma. That you are here and have been in the Tunnel since- well, you can read the date for yourself: it's hardly just over a year- is beyond dispute. But before that, well! There seems to be nothing. Just the words- you can read them yourself- "From the Surface". Nothing more.

- What does this mean? Hunter asked.

He seemed bewildered, out of his depth.

- What it means, Hunter, is that nobody- and that seems to include yourself- knows who you are or where you are from, apart from 'the Surface'.

Hunter reached for the bottle and refilled his glass.

- Are there many like that?

It was interesting that he asked that question, Dr. Aann thought. He might have asked so many others.

- Well, I can't give you the exact figure but since the Tunnel has been in operation there have been a few others.

She could have told him that there had been no others but she chose to tell him the truth, as much of it as she knew.

- Who were they?

Dr. Aann pushed the button again and one the screen there appeared another figure of a man. Facially he was not dissimilar to Hunter. Then a second figure appeared beside that one and a third. Ranged beside Hunter's image they might all have been brothers.

- All I can show you are the images of a few, Dr. Aann explained.

- Where are they?

- That, Hunter, is the perplexing thing. Just like you their details are very limited. As to where they are now, well, your guess is as good as mine. We simply don't know.

- That's impossible, surely, Hunter said. We either die down here, like Dyne did on my last shift, or we're retired back to the Surface.

- Generally that is the case, Hunter; but there's not a trace of those three and the others anywhere in the records. The last one disappeared a generation or so ago. Since then the company has kept a closer check on all its employees in   anticipation of another such case occurring.

- And I'm it?

- Yes, Hunter, you're it. That's why you're here. We're all very excited. I've been assigned to the case to try to make sense of it all. My job is to find out where you've come from and to find out where you might go if, like these others, you're to disappear.

The idea of disappearing was evidently incomprehensible to Hunter. He had seen Dyne die, and before him several others in the squad had died. They had all heard about those who were too badly corroded to work being sent back to the Surface. He, like all his squad, believed that the corroded must eventually be returned to the Surface. 'Fresh air's the only cure' was what they all said once your sight grew so poor that even the bright glare of the lamps to guide you failed to register.

- Do you think I'm going to disappear?

- If what seems to have happened to those others is anything to go by then yes I do.

- But where? Where else is there? It's either here in the Tunnel or the Surface, surely?

- Logically, yes that's true Hunter. But there's no trace of those others on the Surface and they're certainly not down here.

- Maybe they've been buried by a cave-n, Hunter suggested. We only just managed to dig Dyne out.

- We're all equipped with those in-built bleepers, Hunter. You know that. Look.

Dr. Aann pressed another button. Now the screen was displaying graphically segmented views of the Tunnel, interspersed with visuals from the observation cameras.

- There's your squad, Hunter. That's us. There's Dyne- his body has been vapourised but the bleeper is indestructible, as you know. If you wish I can display the signals of everyone who has been in the Tunnel. They're either at work now, or in the leisure complex, or on the Surface, or in the Terminated zone like Dyne. There's nowhere else.

Hunter swallowed the remainder of his drink and unthinkingly poured himself another one. He felt light-headed, but not because of the drink. It will have had its maximum effect, Dr. Aann knew. It was all this unexplained and novel information which was detaching him from the certainty of the reality he had become so attached to.

- Okay, okay, Hunter said. I'm sure you could show me any damned thing you wanted to. I have no way of knowing that all you've shown me isn't a sham, have I? I mean, that's just a screen isn't it? We've got games like that back in the comfort zone of the leisure complex. They can make you think you're tracking a tiger or fucking a whore or any damn thing you like; but they're just games, nothing more than games. This all could be some game on your part for all I know.

- Why would I do something like that?

- How the hell should I know! I'm just a worker in the Tunnel. I just dig. All I want to do is get the damned thing completed and get the hell out of here and back to the Surface.

- What's so attractive about the Surface?

- It's not the Tunnel for one thing!

Did he realise he was shouting now? Dr. Aann wondered.

- You don't like the Tunnel? she asked.

- I neither like it nor dislike it. I'm here, I'm in it, like you, like all the rest of us down here. I came here to do a job, to make a living, and then to get out, back to the Surface. That was the Contract.

- What Contract, Hunter?

- We've all made a Contract. It's in the records.

- There's no record of you having made a Contract, Hunter. Look at your file again.

- You can't do this to me!

Hunter felt a surge of anger and started to rise; but then he checked himself.

- What were you going to do? Dr. Aann asked.

- Do?

He was looking around himself as though bewildered.

- You were angry when I said you had no Contract.

- If I've got no Contract then why am I here in the Tunnel?

- That is precisely the point, Hunter, Dr. Aann said. Let's stop there for now, shall we?

She stood up to indicate that the interview was at an end.

- What am I meant to do now? Hunter asked.

- Return to your quarters and re-join your squad on the next shift. We'll meet again, Hunter, tomorrow at the same time. I'm sorry if it seems confusing. Please don't be too alarmed. If I were you I would use the dream machine and get a good sleep. I'm confident we'll make sense of it all eventually.

Hunter stood somewhat unsteadily. Dr. Aann held him lightly by his elbow and guided him to the door; had she not done so she wondered if he would have found his way out.

*

I don't know what to think, Hunter was telling himself as he lay in his room. I don't want to think anything and yet I can't stop myself remembering what Dr. Aann told me. Was it true? Why would she lie? He did not believe that she would lie or that she had lied; but he couldn't make sense of it.

He found he had no memory of having signed a Contract. So why then did he believe that he had? Would he be down here without a Contract? Would anyone? Look what happened to you- corrosion, blindness, for some sudden death. Who'd give up the Surface for this, he thought, unless there was a Contract which made it all worthwhile.

After twisting about for some time Hunter did what she had suggested and turned on the dream machine. He lay back and closed his eyes and within seconds he was dreaming.

5.

The Director waited until the initial murmuring died down. All eyes were now on him and he waited a few more moments while he gazed around the group.

- I have called this special meeting because there may be a problem. I'll ask Cromell to explain. Cromell?

The Director sat back and watched their faces as Cromell quickly went through the facts. He wondered if anyone in the group had known about this beforehand. This kind of problem could hardly have simply happened. There was wilfulness and planning behind it, subtlety too. It was only by the merest chance that Cromell, during his normal over-viewing of the data and flow charts had noticed the anomaly. Someone less skilled would have overlooked it. It had taken him a while to make the Director see the implications. Whilst the Director was thankful that Cromell had brought the matter to his attention he had secretly resolved to shift the man to another section. It was one thing to be diligent and committed to the company; quite another to uncover something which could be seen to make the Director out to be negligent or less than competent. He would soften the blow by making sure that Cromell's remuneration was considerably enhanced; not that Cromell would be fooled by that largesse.

When Cromell had finished and resumed his seat the Director waited and watched their expressions. He saw nothing out of place. If there was anyone at the table who had known about this that person was expert at keeping control of their face. He had suspected Rafel, an ambitious type and clever with it. His career trajectory was aimed at the very top; but the Director had already put in place those controls which would frustrate the man and, hopefully, see him moved sideways or on to a competitor. Once outside the company he would be no trouble at all. Nobody outside the company mattered, despite how hard they might try.

- You can all see how serious this is, I trust, he finally said.
- How did it happen? Quell asked.

Typical of the man, the Director thought. He wants to waste time dredging through the past when we should be plugging the holes now.

- This meeting isn't about raking through the ashes, Quell, he said sharply.

What I'm looking for is advice and thoughts on how we deal with the matter now that we're all aware of it. The rest can be gone into once we've got things back under control.

- Why don't we just nullify? Stenth suggested.

Precisely my thought, the Director said to himself; but let's find out the temper of these others. If they know what I've already set in motion you can bet there's some here who'll want to rock the boat just to be bloody awkward.

- Is that necessary? Vorder asked.

You could bank on him asking that question, the Director thought. If nobody else asked it he would. Of course it had to be asked but the answer was glaringly obvious: they had no other choice.

- How do you suggest we re-programme? Wicke asked Vorder.

The only other reasonable possibility, the Director knew. But that would involve too many people knowing and raise the possibility of attrition to his status.

- What has been done when this happened before? Rafel asked.

There it was, the Director thought. Rafel *knew* and if he knew he might have initiated it.

- What do you mean, Rafel? the Director asked in his most pleasant voice.

- The archives mention a few similar cases, I believe, Rafel said. I've been looking through them. It was before my time, of course.

But not before mine, is what you mean, the Director thought.

- In the archives, you say? Quell asked.

Now Rafel's got someone else interested, the Director thought.

- As you know each individual and each incident is unique and it is misleading to extrapolate from one such to another, the Director said with a smile. What happened before, regrettable though it may have been and outwardly similar though it may appear, is really not a good guide. The archives are helpful as a history of what has been achieved, rather like that painting on the wall. We who are here now need to deal with this current situation. If whatever we decide can be generalised and help to avoid any similar future incident then all well and good. It serves little purpose to look to the past for solutions in the present.

He could see that Rafel didn't accept any of that but Quell had sat back in that posture which indicated that he felt too much in the line of fire. They all knew about Rafel's ambitions; after all one by one he had risen above them, although hypothetically they were all on the same level. Quell had taken the hint and Rafel was on his own. The Director wondered if he would push the matter. Was this the moment when his ambition over-rode his desire to survive?

- Have we got anyone down there? Stenth asked.

The Director noticed the pointed look Rafel briefly gave Stenth. He had been going to go for it! There was something more, the Director thought, but Rafel wasn't able to show his hand nakedly now because of Stenth's question. These things were all a matter of timing and opportunity. Rafel might just be willing to risk giving it another go today, the Director thought. Best not give him a chance to recoup ground

- Cromell, can you answer that? the Director asked.

- Yes Director we have someone down there.

- Good. That shows forethought, Cromell.

The Director watched as Cromell glowed and Rafel simmered.

- My own view, gentlemen, is that we should nullify, the Director said gravely. It is not an option I would recommend lightly but in a situation such as this when contamination may spread swiftly, we need to act surgically. We can hold   a post mortem at our leisure and perhaps you, Quell, could convene that.

That brought Quell upright in his seat and now Rafel knew he was isolated.

- Your votes, gentlemen? the Director asked. Those in favour of nullification?

It was unanimous. Rafel wouldn't let himself be seen to be the only one opposing not just the Director but the entire board.

- You'll see to that Cromell, the Director said. Let me know when it's done- and tell Quell so he can arrange the meeting. That's it, gentlemen. Thank you.

As the board members began to rise and depart the Director signalled silently to Deth to return. Had he simply remained Rafel would have picked up on that and, given the frame of mind he had been in, doubtlessly he would have drawn the correct conclusion and might well have taken a pre-emptive counter-action. Deth had been one of the silent ones during the meeting. Some were silent because they had nothing to contribute, or because they were afraid of the power of someone like Rafel. He had risen quickly and though he had not made enemies as such during his rise he certainly had not made any friends. To challenge the Director, which was obviously the next step up for him, he would have to have a perfect argument, one which would convince the others and disarm the Director. Today he must have felt he was ready and that he had the ammunition. He would feel frustrated at having been foiled by a chance remark from another member of the board, especially one like Stenth whom he seemed to despise as a mediocre time-server. What would rankle would be the fact that that person had been blithely unaware of the power struggle that was going on. But the Director knew that someone like Deth- in fact, Deth especially- would have been aware of the undercurrent of challenge. After all, that was what Deth had been put there for.

When Deth entered the room several minutes later the Director spoke briefly to him and Deth nodded. Rafel was no longer going to be a problem.

6.

When the shift had ended and he had showered Hunter made his way to the Centre where Dr. Aann was waiting for him.

- How do you feel today, Hunter? she asked once they'd settled.

- All right.

Normally she would have pursued such a generalisation, tried to make him break it down, but she smiled and waited. Finally, as the silence grew, Hunter could stand it no more.

- What do you want of me?

- Please understand that I don't wish to harm you, Hunter. I can understand that it is bewildering at the moment. You just want to be doing your job and here I am raising all kinds of awkward questions and feelings. But I want to help.

- Can't you do that by leaving me alone?

- I'm sorry, I can't. I've got my job to do, just like you.

- What if I don't cooperate?

- You could do that, but I don't think you're the kind of man who would do that. If you did then, yes, it would all stop; I'd put in my report and those who've asked for it would make whatever decision they felt best. I've no idea what that would be, by the way.

She watched as Hunter considered this. Despite what she had said she had a good idea of what the decision would be: Hunter would be pulled out from the squad and would vanish up to Level 5 where a further assessment would be made. That would be more intrusive and non-cooperation would not be an option. She watched the struggle inside him being won on his face by his curiosity.

- Okay. Where do we go next?

Dr. Aann suppressed her desire to breathe a sigh of relief. She had spooked him once the first time they'd met and didn't want to do so again.

- At this stage, Hunter, all I'm trying to do is find out a bit more about you and to get you to look in a different way at things you maybe take for granted. Let's try this: What do you remember of your first day in the Tunnel?

Hunter frowned.

- I don't know that I can remember anything in particular, he said hesitantly.
- Does that surprise you?
- I can't say. I've never really thought about something like that.
- Do you remember the photograph being taken?

She flashed his record on the screen and Hunter stared at himself as he had been.

- Is that really me?
- It's in your record.
- I can't remember it being taken.
- Can you remember those who were in your first squad? You'll've been the rookie just like Beel is now with your squad.
- Sorry, there's not even a blur.

She wondered if he was stalling her; but the frown on his face seemed utterly genuine.

- Does it worry you not knowing who they were?
- It didn't; but maybe it does now. I mean, I worked with them and now I can't recall them.
- Try something closer in time. Beel's replaced Dyne, yes? Who did Dyne replace?

Again that look of concentration on Hunter's face and then the puzzled admission of defeat.

- I can't remember.
- Look at the screen.

Hunter did so. On it he saw a list of names.

- This is the record of the squad before Dyne joined you.

Hunter read the names. They were all familiar except one.

- Lucé? he said hesitantly. But I don't remember him.

-Yes, Dr. Aann said; it was Lucé and this is his picture.

Hunter stared at the strange face and shook his head. He looked anxiously at Dr. Aann.

- What's wrong with me?
- Why do you think there's something wrong with you, Hunter?
- I can't remember someone who I worked beside. Does that mean I'll forget Dyne and the others if they go first?
- I can't say, Hunter. Let's try another tack. What did you have to eat yesterday?
- The same as I always have, I guess, Hunter said.
- And what's that?

Now Hunter was frowning.

- I'd know it if I saw the selector and oven.
- But can you name it?
- Not at the moment, no.
- What did your father do for a living?
- I can't remember.
- Can you remember your father?

Hunter was shaking his head in frustration.

- No, no I can't. This is bad, isn't it?
- Why do you make that judgement, Hunter?
- I should remember someone like that, shouldn't I?
- Have you heard anyone in the Tunnel talking about their father?

Again Hunter shook his head.

- We just talk about the job, maybe what we plan on doing in our rest time, what we did in the leisure complex, that sort of thing.
- How did Dyne die?
- The roof caved in.
- How will you die?
- I don't think I will.

Hunter stopped and stared at her.

- You sound very certain, Dr. Aann said.
- I don't know why I said it like that. I think I meant that I hope that I won't die, in a cave-in I mean.
- But you said that you didn't think you would die.
- I wasn't thinking what I said.

She studied him for some time. He didn't seem especially distressed and he didn't seem as though he was trying to back-track and hide something he'd inadvertently revealed. He was waiting patiently for her to continue. His powers of attention and patience were highly developed for a man who preferred physical activity.

- I want you to do something for me between now and the next time we meet, she said.

He was quite accepting now of the fact that they would meet again.

- I am going to give you a note-tablet and writer. I want you to write down what you do between now and when we meet. Keep it simple. Bring the note-tablet tomorrow when you come so I can discuss it with you. But now I want to do some simple basic tests on you before you go.

After Hunter had left Dr. Aann recorded her thoughts about their meeting. She made two copies. The official record was entered into the computerised recording of the meeting. She had not told Hunter the meeting was being recorded and this was in keeping with the directives for those who were tagged. If he knew he was being recorded he might act so as to confuse the record. Then again he might not.

The second copy she made once she was out of her office, away from the monitoring and recording equipment. She wrote in the old way in the notebook she had in her private quarters. What she wrote in this notebook differed considerably to what she had recorded for the official record. She was aware of Dr. Frinck's interest and his tendency to poach the research and ideas of his juniors. Let him feed back her public account to Level 5 if he wished but there was nothing in there which would further his career.

7.

Hunter found himself wondering why Beel had done it.

He lay in his room trying to keep his mind focussed on the incident in the Tunnel. Accidents happened, he knew that. A rookie could be careless and that was why they were usually confined to the cab of the Mole until they had built up enough experience- ten digs at least.

I was like that once, Hunter told himself. But was I? I must have been. We all were like that- cautious, hesitant, anxious, eager to please, willing but frustrated by being held back and treated like a child amongst men.

When the fall had started Hunter had been on the far side of the Mole working on a recess. Sometimes you can hear the cracking as the collapse starts; sometimes your first warning is the alarm going off. However you pick it up the response had to be the same: if you were near a usable recess you sheltered there and would be dug out if the rubble blocked your way out once the fall had ended. Your signal would be picked up by the recovery team so you just had to wait. But if you were near the Mole then you returned to the cab. That's what Hunter had done. But he had found the door locked and Beel was on the other side of the Mole helping Ghant and Tabb clamber in. Rock was already cascading down around them. Hunter pulled at the door, which should have been hinged open as per the standing safety instructions for when the Mole was in operation. That's the first thing the driver did once in the cab: make sure the doors were open and readily accessible.

It was a matter of seconds between life and death. Looking back Hunter marvelled at the speed of his reaction made without thought: he had hurled himself beneath the Mole until the fall was over. He would have crawled out sooner but something told him to lie there for a moment.

- Hunter must have bought it, Tabb was saying.

- I didn't see him, Beel said.

- We'll have to call up the recovery team. They'll find him, Ghant said.

Of course Beel didn't know him, Hunter told himself; but there was something in the tone of his voice which worried Hunter. Tabb and Ghant sounded sorrowful, whereas Beel's voice struck a discordant note. Hunter told himself that Beel would be in shock. When you were in shock anything could happen. Hunter remembered seeing some men start to dance with joy in situations which should have seen them being solemn-faced and silent. Others wouldn't be able to talk or work for days.

He rolled out from under the Mole as the trio in the cab clambered out to look for him.

It's a pity I didn't see Beel's expression then, Hunter told himself. Both Tabb and Ghant had looked relieved and delighted, slapping him on the back and joshing him to cover up their embarrassment. Beel, when Hunter saw his face, was smiling, but it was a strained smile, as though forced. While the others examined the extent of the fall Hunter had said he'd call back to cancel the recovery team. In the cab he found that the door on the side he had tried to enter was fixed open as per regulations. Was Beel trying to cover his mistake or had Hunter in his scramble for safety somehow tried to open the door the wrong way? But that wasn't possible, not if the door was openable as it should have been.

But why would Beel do such a thing? This was only his third shift with the squad.

Hunter found himself trying to remember the assessment he had been through on the Surface. Would the shock bring it back? Before you were offered the Contract, Hunter thought, they must have run all kinds of tests on you, physical and psychological. Nobody could go down the Tunnel without passing those tests: that must be the case surely?

Do I write this down for Dr. Aann? he thought. He didn't want to get Beel into trouble, not so early in his Contract.

When they'd met up after the cleansing Hunter noticed that Beel wasn't there. The others didn't seem bothered by this. Maybe Beel was experiencing delayed shock. It had been his first cave-in after all and they'd thought for a few minutes that they'd lost Hunter to it.

8.

- This is interesting, Hunter, Dr. Aann said, looking up from the note-tablet.

What he'd written was: Could you turn off the recording equipment; there's something I need to tell you privately.

She pushed the pause button on her desk's hidden console and nodded at Hunter.

- I'm sorry I didn't tell you the sessions were being recorded, she said.

Hunter smiled.

- I assumed they would be since this was official.

- It's good of you not to make waves about it.

- There was a cave-in yesterday.

She felt slightly disappointed.

- Is that all?

- I think someone was trying to kill me. But I'm not sure and I don't want him to get into trouble.

Dr. Aann looked at Hunter closely.

- Why do you think that?

Hunter described the incident to her.

- I've thought about it since. I didn't want to write anything down other than that there was a cave-in. The more I've thought about it the more I've felt Beel deliberately made sure the door was locked and then opened it once the fall was over.

- Why do you think he would do that?

- Haven't a clue.

- Did you consider asking him what he was up to?

- There's the funny thing, Dr. Aann; Beel hasn't been around since then. He's off our shift. We've got another rookie.

- Maybe Quex thought...

- I haven't reported anything. Quex just knows there was a cave-in and nobody was hurt. I wondered if you could find out where Beel was, but discreetly.

Dr. Aann found herself wondering at Hunter suggesting 'discretion'. Did he know that any search she made via the Visi-screen would be logged and potentially she might be asked why she'd made such a search? If he did know then how did he know? Is Hunter's paranoia, if that's what it is, rubbing off on me? she thought.

Dr. Aann went to her desk and took out her personal miniputer. This did not have the in-built identifier in it and she could use it to access the Visi-screen anonymously. All medics were able to do this since they may be away from their offices and in need of information. All that would be logged was that a trace had been requested. She entered the basic request data and Beel's numerical tag.

- Nothing there, she said in puzzlement.

- Disappeared? Hunter asked quietly.

- Apparently, yes.
- Should that have been me? he asked.
- I've no idea what any of this means, Hunter.
- I don't know what to do about it.
- Neither do I, Hunter. This sort of thing isn't supposed to happen.

*

Once the session with Hunter was over- she had switched back on the recording machines and they had discussed the other entries in his note-tablet – Dr. Aann thought about what she should do. Strictly speaking she should raise the matter with Dr. Frinck, but she felt reluctant to do this. What had happened to Beel was not her concern; but since Hunter had raised the possibility of Beel having tried to kill him she should have noted this in her record (but had not) and she should have sought advice from Dr. Frinck (but did not). Concentrate on Hunter, she told herself. You've made a private note of what Hunter has said about Beel and should anything further develop from this then perhaps take action.

But inevitably she wondered about Beel's disappearance. People did not disappear unless, like Hunter, they were tagged. Beel had not been tagged- or at least that's what his record indicated. He had come down from the Surface a day before Dyne's death and had been at one of the holding posts at the beginning of the Tunnel. Nothing unusual about that and neither was there anything unusual about his being assigned to Hunter's crew to replace Dyne. No, the only unusual thing was that Beel had simply disappeared and nobody seemed to be bothered by this. This was not a clinical problem. Those responsible for the selection, allocation and distribution of the workforce should deal with a matter like this, Dr. Aann thought, though she was unaware of any precedent.

9.

The archives were seldom consulted. Those who sought permission to consult them needed to be very specific about what it was that they wanted. One couldn't just walk in off the street and ask to look through the archives. There were channels to go through, different levels of permission and authorisation to be sought. The Director viewed all requests in summary usually after they had been granted or refused. More were refused than granted. Fewer and fewer requests were made, even as more and more information accumulated in the archive.

All of which made the Director curious as to how Rafel had managed to 'consult the archives' without him being made aware of it. Could there be someone collaborating with Rafel? The fact that Deth was dealing with Rafel didn't do away with the Director's concern. If there was a collaborator, someone who had willingly or unwillingly assisted Rafel then that person had to be nullified as well.

It was not forbidden that those on the board should access the archive. Indeed, those who wished to get on and improve matters in their division would fairly frequently consult the archive. But in the record of accesses for the past count of time the Director could find no reference to Rafel. The fact that Rafel had openly spoken about the archive suggested that it was general knowledge that he had accessed it and in preceding counts Rafel's name did occasionally occur. More than likely then that he had been quietly gathering information with a view to using it at a time when it seemed likely to do the most harm. But even if that were the case the type of information he had consulted on previous accesses didn't include the anomalous individuals identified by Cromell. It is likely then, the Director thought, that Rafel searched more widely than he is recorded as having done; and to do that he must have used a device which over-rode the in-built identifier. Who knows what else he might have trawled through!

*

- He's on to you.
- Exactly what I wanted to happen!
- He'll try to nullify you.
- Of course. That's what I'm waiting for, for him to try.
- Are you sure of your ground?
- I wouldn't have taken the chance to prod him during the meeting if I wasn't sure.
- I don't know that you can count on any of the others.
- Perhaps, but neither can he. They'll swing behind anyone who seems to be offering them what they want.
- What's your next move?
- It's best that you don't know.
- You're right, of course. But I just thought I'd warn you.
- Thanks. I won't forget that.
- You'll've heard about Beel?
- It's all over the place by now.
- Clumsy.

- Another sign he's losing his grip.
- Or setting a trap?
- Yes, that's possible. We mustn't take anything for granted.
- Any ripples from below about that?
- None so far, which makes me suspicious.
- You'd've thought he would have tried to keep the lid on something like that.
- All the more reason to wonder about why he's not done so.
- There'll have to be some kind of enquiry.
- He'll put Cromell on that, I expect, since he's incompetent enough.
- Well, I don't want to take up too much of your time and we don't want to be seen together too often.
- Contact me if there are any further developments.
- Of course.

*

- I've started to dream, Hunter said.
- Why is that unusual? Dr. Aann asked.

She knew from the reports in Hunter's file and her recent medical assessment that he used the dream machine regularly, as did virtually everyone else in the Tunnel.

Including me, she thought with some surprise.

- I'm not using the machine.
- When did this start to happen?
- The night after the cave-in and Beel's disappearance.
- You're connecting these occurrences with your dreaming?
- I guess; but maybe it's just a coincidence.
- Do you believe in coincidences?

Hunter pondered.

- I don't know if I'd know a coincidence if I saw one, now that I think about it. Things just happen, don't they?
- What do you think, Hunter?
- Well, it seems to me that things just happen.
- Without rhyme or reason?
- Maybe we stick that on later, once other things have happened. I don't know.
- But your dreams, what are they about?
- Mostly it's shadowy figures moving about just out of sight, as though I'm waking up and just starting to see things again.

- Different from the dream machine?

- Very much so.

- Any thoughts as to why that might be?

- I'm no expert on the machine but maybe that stuff's in there and what I'm starting to dream now is in me?

- That sounds reasonable enough. But even though you're not using the machine what you could be experiencing might have been imprinted by the machine during those times when you were using it.

- And it's coming out now? But why?

- The trouble with 'why' is that it can stop you from exploring, Hunter. It's understandable that you ask that question- we all do about all kinds of things- but sometimes it's helpful to keep it up your sleeve and wait until you've seen more.

- Or dreamt more?

- Or dreamt more indeed.

*

- Well, Beel, you failed.

- Wasn't I supposed to?

- Of course; but only we know that.

- Will they find anything?

- Only what they're meant to find.

10.

The rock they were drilling through now seemed quite different to anything Hunter had seen before. He checked the level. For some time they had been drilling at a slight incline downwards. The planners would have studied the rock in front of them to as great a depth as they could with the scanner. They would have adjusted the level to take into account any possible obstacles they might have identified. Any kind of liquid had to be gone around. In the distant past, or so went the rumours Hunter had heard, the Tunnel had been flooded and many men and equipment lost. The drilling had to begin again. Now, even though the Tunnel had special dividers built in which could be closed off in case of such a calamity happening again, the Tunnel would be routed around any hazards. All Hunter and his team knew was that they were drilling through the rock-face that lay directly in front of them. What lay beyond it was more of the same; and beyond that more of the same.

But here they were and Hunter could see that this rock was different. He wondered if any of his comrades noticed. Perhaps only he did because he was not corroded and they were. The rookie Angu wouldn't notice since he'd not seen enough rock.

Once again Hunter experienced a sense of foreboding. He held up his warning light which pulsed and glowed red. At once the Mole stopped. At least the rookie knew what to do when he saw that signal, Hunter thought.

- What's up, Hunter? Tabb called as he and Ghant made their way to his side.

- I'm not sure but there's something wrong. This rock we've just hit, it bothers me.

He could see the two men peering at the rock ahead.

- Can't really say, Hunter, Ghant said. It all looks the same to me nowadays.

- Let's get in the cab for a minute and consult the Control room back there, Hunter said.

Once they were all in the cab Hunter spoke to the supervisor. It wasn't Quex but someone called Yadl, a new man brought in while Quex had an extended comfort break.

- What's the hold up? Yadl asked aggressively.

These stand-ins, Hunter thought. They're anxious to make a name for themselves and get a regular shift, which paid more and had more perks- like longer comfort breaks. So they want to drive you as hard as they can.

- We've hit a seam of rock which looks odd, Hunter said.

- The scanner showed no problems. Dig on.

- I think we need to rescan, Hunter said.

- We don't need this kind of delay, Yadl said angrily. Dig on, Hunter.

- I don't think that's wise without a rescan, sir, Hunter replied.

- A rescan will take up time, Hunter, and you're behind schedule as it is.

That comes as news to me, Hunter thought, glancing at his comrades.

- The sheet shows we're well ahead of our schedule, sir, he said. I'm requesting a rescan as a matter of safety.

- Damn you, Hunter, Yadl said and broke the connection.

- Guess we sit and wait, Tabb said.

- What's wrong with the rock? Angu asked.

- It's hard to describe, Hunter said. It's something about the texture and the colour. I've not seen anything like it before and we've done a thousand or so shifts. Anything like that it's best to report it and get it checked.

- You'd've thought the scanner would have noticed if there was any problem, Ghant said.

- You would have thought that, Hunter agreed.

- What was that rubbish about us being behind schedule? Tabb asked.

- We'll clear that up once the shift's over, Hunter said. You all saw the chart at the end of our last shift: we were well in credit. Maybe this Yadl guy can't read charts properly.

It was just under ten minutes before the mobile scanner drew up beside the Mole. There were two men operating it, both well known to the squad.

- You boys have got the supervisor jumping back there! one of them said. Lucky you called in; you're way off track.

Hunter stared at the man.

- Off track?

- Yep. This is the path you should have been on and this is what you've been doing for the last hundred measures or so.

They all stared at the chart and saw the discrepancy. Angu went pale.

- I'm sorry, guys.

Hunter put his hand on Angu's arm.

- It's not your fault, Angu. The Mole's path is programmed in automatically to avoid driver error. You're steering it but not deciding the path it follows for the Tunnel. Someone has cocked up back at Control.

- Have a look at this Hunter, the man operating the scanner called.

The squad joined the two men by the scanner.

- You're damned lucky you stopped when you did, Hunter. You're five minutes away from a glue pit.

If they'd drilled into the glue pit unlike a rock fall which would have crushed them the glue pit would simply have swallowed them like a swamp on the Surface.

- Right, Hunter said. We back up, fill in and then do a controlled fall to seal the drilling. I'll call back to Control and they'll have to check where the tracking error occurred.

- Hunter, old son, Tabb said warmly; thank goodness you noticed. I've been called for a Med and I think they're going to retire me as I'm twenty-five per cent gone, you know. I want to see that Surface again, not the bottom of some glue pit.

11.

...We wait and watch. That is all we can do. It is what we have been given to do. When our time comes then we will act as we must.

Hunter sat bolt upright in his sleeping podule. He felt himself shaking. There was sweat all over his naked body. Someone was coming for him, he was sure of it.

He got up and went into the shower room and let the cold then hot then cold again water sluice the dream from him. He dried off under the warm air blower and then pulled on a light gown.

Whatever was happening to him he did not like it.

In the dream 'we' had broken through the rock and were trapped in the glue pit. 'We' did not include anyone he recognised- not Tabb, not Ghant, not Angu or himself. Yet there was a 'we'.

Am I going crazy? Hunter quizzed himself as he sipped some E-liquid. He looked at the time-piece: he had been dreaming for just over an hour, hardly any time at all. He was wide awake.

Don't bother with the chair, he told himself. There is something you have to be wide-awake for.

The door was firmly shut. It opened only to his touch or voice command. Attempts to duplicate either would set off an alarm and spring security partitions in the corridor which would trap anyone trying to force entry.

All the same Hunter kept an eye on the door. Strange things had been happening, that was for sure.

When the squad had returned to Control Quex had been there, fuming- but not at them. 'That bastard' Yadl had upped and disappeared and nobody knew where he'd gotten to. They'd traced the alteration to the Mole's track: it had been entered shortly before the crew had left Control. It must have been entered manually. Yadl perhaps? Hunter thought. Quex had been called back by the second operative when he realised that Yadl wasn't in the Control room with him. There had to be two supervisors on duty at all times. Security was searching the vicinity but the bastard was nowhere to be found. What the hell was going on? Quex demanded of nobody in particular. He confirmed that Hunter's crew were ahead of their schedule despite the error in tracking. That wouldn't count against them. What had happened could have happened to anyone.

But could it? Hunter thought.

A slight 'ding' told him that there was a message for him on the Vu-screen. It was from Dr. Aann. She was asking him to report to her office before his next shift, not after it. He wondered if she had heard about this latest incident.

I won't sleep any more, Hunter told himself. I'll take a pill and get a boost.

*

- But Dr. Aann sent me a message saying I was to see *her* this morning, Hunter said as he studied the man sitting behind her desk.

Unlike Dr. Aann he hadn't risen to greet Hunter when he entered.

- Well it's me you have to see, the man said. Sit down.

Hunter reached behind and pressed the door opener. As the door slid open he stepped smartly back out into the corridor before the man behind the desk could protest. Hunter hurried to the administrative offices a short distance away.

- I need to speak to Dr. Aann, he said. It's urgent.

- She's not on duty until fourteen hours, the secretary told him.

- I'm due to see her then, I know, Hunter explained. But I received a message last night to attend now. When I went to her room there was a strange doctor in there.

- I'll call security, the secretary said. There should be nobody in her office.

Within a minute three Securimen appeared and Hunter followed them back down the corridor to Dr. Aann's office. The door slid open: there was nobody there. The Securimen looked quizzically at Hunter.

- He was behind the desk, Hunter said. Is there another way out of here?

- That's the only door.

- Check the recording machine, Hunter suggested. See what it replays.

No luck there either, Hunter saw. The Securimen were clearly of the opinion that he was one of Dr. Aann's more corroded patients. No point in arguing with them, Hunter thought.

- Well, he was there, behind the desk and he must have slipped out when I went to the administrative office.

- Yes sir, the leader of the Securimen said in a neutral tone.

Rather than return to his room Hunter decided to go to the Inter-lounge where you could relax and read rather than drink and sing. I need to be in company, he told himself. I'll feel safer there.

Dr. Aann listened to his strange story. She had already received a report from the secretary and also an Inci-message from Security. Their opinion was clear: Hunter was deluded; the room had been empty.

- Can you describe him to me? Dr. Aann asked.

As he did so Hunter could visualise the man sitting behind her desk.

- That's a pretty thorough description, Hunter, she smiled. However, there's no doctor down here who answers to that description.

- I thought he was a fake as soon as I saw him, Hunter said. This is all part of the craziness that has been happening to me.

- What made you think he was a fake?

- I thought it was odd that you would send me a Vu-screen message. No reason why you shouldn't send one, I guess, but you haven't done before so I wondered why so late at night. You'd've heard about the Mole being set on the wrong track and our close escape. I reckoned that if you'd wanted to see me you would have done so immediately I was off the shift, as you have before. When I came in the room and saw this man there the alarm bells went off at once. I know we've only met a few times but I didn't get the impression that you would hand me over to someone else without having told me or asked me. In uncertain situations like that I play it safe- that's how we avoided drilling into the glue pit.

- You've got a highly developed sense of danger, Hunter.
- You need it at the rock-face.
- It's more than that, I think. Do you feel that you're on guard all the time?
- I am now!
- Before you started to see me, were you like this then?
- Maybe not as watchful but I guess I've always had a keen sense of danger.
- What about when you came down into the Tunnel? Did you feel that was dangerous?

Now Hunter was frowning again. Each time she asked him to reach back beyond a relatively recent point- a few shifts ago, for example- he clearly had trouble summoning up any memory.

- I guess I didn't, but I can't recall. Somehow I don't think I would have taken the job if I'd thought it would put me in danger.
- But it puts you in danger! In the Contract- and I know there's no record of one for you- it distinctly states what the dangers may be: cave-in, gas escape, corrosion. Even if you haven't got a Contract your daily work highlights those dangers to you. The men you work with are heavily corroded...but you're not. So there's danger but you seem...immune to it?
- When I sense it I circumvent it, that's for sure.
- As you did when the Mole went off track and as you did when you found a stranger in my office.
- Where could he have gone?
- Is that the most important question?
- I don't know. I'd guess that he didn't intend me any good since if he was genuine then why vanish? There's been too much disappearing going on recently! I'm the one who you think is going to vanish and yet all these others are disappearing and nobody seems bothered!
- Yes, that puzzles me too, Hunter. But we've both reported such incidents to those we have to report to and there's little to be gained by speculating further- do you agree?
- Okay, let me tell you about last night's dream then.

She had listened intently as Hunter described the 'Watchers' who waited for whatever the moment was when they would act, or perhaps be able to act. As Hunter recounted the dream- a fragment really- she was aware of how different he was in his feelings about it now to those he described having when it had woken him. Now he seemed relaxed but then from his description he had been in a state of high alarm. Was this change because internally he had made sense of things or because, having avoided the 'doctor' in her office he had dealt with the danger?

- You say these 'incidents' are happening regularly now? Dr. Frinck asked her sharply.
- That seems to be the case, Dr. Aann replied.
- You should have come to me at once.
- With what, sir? Like everyone else you would have dismissed each of them as just one of those unfortunate things that can happen in the Tunnel. But it's clear after this fake doctor in my office that something significant is happening.

Dr. Frinck didn't like trouble. Dr. Frinck didn't like Dr. Aann for bringing him trouble. Dr. Frinck didn't like the fact that, having received a summons to ascend to the fourth Level- the fourth and not the fifth, mind! – he was being faced with a potential crisis which might detain him. When the order had come through yesterday he had been ecstatic. Not for one moment did he ask himself why he was being promoted; his only thought was that now he would be out of this excremental pit and able to breathe purer air again. He would be able to take comfort trips to the Surface. He would be able to do some real work rather than this mindlessly mundane checking of corrosion.

- Just ignore it, Dr. Frinck snapped at her. Your remit is the clinical aspect of Harper's life, nothing else.
- Hunter, sir; his name is Hunter.
- Harper- Hunter: they're all the same, aren't they?
- He has been tagged, sir.
- Does that really make any difference, Dr. Aann? All it means is that there's more work to be done, more tests and more reports. Don't bother me with all this non-clinical nonsense. Discuss it with Security. Now, if you'll excuse me, I've things to attend to before I leave.

He looked down and she was dismissed.

*

- I'm not sure what you feel we can do, Dr. Aann, Officer Gabber, the

Head of Security, said.

- This man's life is in danger, Dr. Aann replied.

- So are the lives of every other man- and woman- down here.

- Generally speaking, yes; but can't you see that this man is being targeted?

- Even if I was convinced of that, Dr. Aann, the only sure way to keep him safe is to move him to the Surface; and I don't have the authority top do that. Nobody down here has that authority.

She came away from their brief meeting feeling frustrated. Everyone was so busy, so caught up in the routine of their job, so limited in what they would or could see. So what if another of the numberless work-force died in an accident? It happened all the time. There were plenty on the Surface who could be recruited to come down and replace those who became corroded or were killed by a cave-in. Was she letting herself become a bit too attached to this Hunter?

*

"The Tunnel is our greatest achievement yet also our greatest conundrum. Although the Archives refer to its beginnings it is by no means clear to scholars and scientists who have studied its origins, that these details aren't pure myth rather than indisputable historical and scientific fact. That the Tunnel was begun we cannot doubt for here it is."

Here the lecturer pressed his remote and the next slide appeared on the screen.

For some of the students in the auditorium this was their first view of the vastness and complexity of the Tunnel; for others it was all old hat and several yawns were stifled. The lecturer was not unaware of this mixed reaction among the students. It was always the same. This part of the course was compulsory but it wasn't to everyone's taste or interest. Nowadays jokes were made about the Tunnel; misbehaving children were threatened with being 'sent down the Tunnel' (though this had little effect on those inclined to delinquency); popular songs were written about it. Once it had been discussed in reverential tones. None of those in the auditorium would ever go down the Tunnel, unless they fell on such hard times that it became their only choice. The closest they might come to the Tunnel was either this lecture- which he had given for the past decade and, in truth, was becoming rather bored with himself- or some display in the local museum. Few if any would actually see the site of the entrance to the Tunnel; and if they did they would pass it by without the slightest idea that it was the entrance.

"We have only these drawings and the conjectures of scholars since its beginnings to give us an idea as to the Tunnel's basic design. You will see that there is even dispute over this. The more radical theorists prefer this model (another change of slide) whilst the conservatives prefer this (slide). You will notice the similarities and the differences. It's hard to believe now that wars were fought over such details before the general opinion favoured this compromise (slide)."

He wondered how many of them had actually fallen asleep. Perhaps they all were. Perhaps he was. It didn't matter. Once the half hour lecture was over they would file out, their cards would be stamped and that would be it until the next intake. They would forget about the Tunnel which would have no significance in their lives. In the end it would become as important to them as the answer to a simple crossword clue or a button lost from a jacket.

He didn't tell them (as he could have done) that it was all nonsense, that there was no Tunnel and never had been a Tunnel and never could be a Tunnel. Let them work that out for themselves. Let them justify the money their parents were expending for them to attend the academy.

"This is thought to be the person credited with the original idea of the Tunnel..."

But the only person who was paying attention at this point was someone who was not meant to be in the auditorium.

*

The Director looked down from his office window. From here he could see everything there was to see outside. Not that there generally seemed to be the time for him to stop and gaze out of the window. Yet his subordinates would have been surprised at the amount of time he did so spend. This was not idle time-killing; he was deep in thought. Not for him those charts and brainstorming sessions. In this office he would not be disturbed. There was no Visi-screen or Voice connection in the room. Once the door was closed behind him nobody else could enter. The door would only open again when he decided to exit. Messages would be taken in the meantime.

He was seldom in the room for long. Often all he needed was a few moments to get away from those who fawned on him or sought his decision or ruling on some project or case. It was usually enough for him just to gaze out at the sky and clouds, or the waters that stretched like a mirror beneath the sky. Down there, out of sight most of the time because of the height of the tower, there would be throngs of people going about their business quite unaware of his scrutiny.

The room was circular and he moved around its circumference slowly. By the time he had reached the door leading out he had made a decision. It was not one he was prepared to divulge to the board yet. He needed to run it past Deth first. He trusted Deth. There had been a time when he had wondered about the wisdom of this; but then Deth had no ambition. He just wanted to serve, to do whatever the Director required him to do. He had been on the board for so long the Director almost felt him to be his twin. Unlike the more obvious hatchet-men the various board members employed in their dealings with those below Deth had never become redundant or so powerful as to have to be replaced.

Not that the Director took Deth for granted. One of his golden rules was never to take anyone for granted. Never turn your back and never relax your vigilance. As he had gazed out of the window where all had seemed so tranquil he had witnessed a sudden storm break out on the waters and twisters dance across the land. That was how unexpectedly trouble could arise. That was why someone like Rafel had to be neutralised.

With a last glance around the Director touched the pad to open the door.

Nothing happened.

*

...We dance in the storm on the lake and over the land we skate. We tread down the waves and the hills. We seek our prey wherever he is. None can escape us, none can withstand us...

I am not dreaming this, Hunter thought as he sat at his table eating. However it is I am *seeing* this as it happens.

12.

- We need to stop this now. Things are getting too complicated.

- We must hold our nerve.

- He's right; we've come too far now to back off.

- I've got a bad feeling about this.

- You've always been too cautious.

- The stakes are high.

- We all know that. We knew that when we took this on. Let's not go through all that again.

- But look at what's happened so far. It's hardly been an endorsement of your plan.

- Of *our* plan. We've agreed everything each step of the way.

- I just feel we need to be very careful at this stage.

- There's no question about that. But it's been the same at every stage before.

- I think he's scared of success.

- No, I want us to succeed. I'm scared of failure.

- We will only fail if we waste our energies squabbling amongst ourselves.

- All right, all right. I know we've gone too far to stop now; I'm just advising caution.

- That's your valuable role. You are the voice of caution and we need that. But we also need to keep focussed on the goal, on what we are doing.

- So, what about this latest development? Has it alerted and alarmed too much?

- The response seems to have been as we expected.

- This meeting he's called...

- We expected that. We know he's worried about what's happening in the Tunnel as much as up here.

- It's what's happening in the Tunnel which concerns me most.

- Yes, the subject has been lucky so far.

- Luck has nothing to do with it. I think we've underestimated his abilities.

- Perhaps; but remember we are in control, in control of everything.

- Except him?

- Let's not build him up to be something that he's not.

- I'll be happier once he's out of the way.

- Why not just surface him and then deal with him?

- We've discussed the problems in that. It would be too obvious and there would be an immediate counter-measure. I doubt that he would reach the Surface at all in those circumstances; but much of our hand would have been exposed. We have come a long way, but we need a bit more cohesion. Remember, we're up against someone who has been in control for longer than all of our experience put together. The Archives reveal previous incidents which he's dealt with ruthlessly. We know he's on the alert- we've set that up so that he's looking in the wrong places...

- Or we think he's looking in the wrong places. What if he's on too us and is playing us along?

- The voice of caution and now the voice of panic? If he was on to us, as you fear, he would not 'play us along'; he would have pounced by now, on one or all, and we wouldn't be meeting like this but languishing elsewhere.

- I'm not panicking; I'm merely voicing what I feel may happen if circumstances turn against us.

- We've taken sufficient precautions every step of the way. I am confident we have not been breached and all our stratagems so far have worked exactly as we predicted they would.

- Except...

- Except below- yes, that is true. But it is rectifiable. You heard the order being given for nullification. We've all agreed to that. The problem is the incompetence with which the order is being executed. I half suspected something like this might happen.

- You could have voted against...

- Any of us could. But it was the best, most obvious solution and was not proposed directly by any of us.

- Why don't we take our own steps to ensure the subject is nullified?

- I can report that we already are doing so.

- Without having sought our agreement?

- It was agreed, if you remember, that I had the authority of the group to take whatever steps I felt were consistent with our objective should the circumstances arise.

- I only meant...

- We can reverse that decision now, if you like?

- No, no- I mean, there's a process such things should go through.

- Quite right; but when circumstances arise which mean that instant decisions have to be taken this group did agree that I could taken such decisions. Do we wish to change *that* decision?

- Of course not. Look, we need to move on. What about this meeting he's called?

- Yes; we need to be clear how we are going to handle the matter.

- Usually he's already got an idea in mind.

- We must be prepared for the usual and the unusual at this stage.

- We don't want it to be obvious that we're following your lead.

- Our plan should be to do as we have been doing. We can challenge each other but we need to get some idea first of what he is proposing. If it fits with our overall plan then, even if we bicker over it for show, we can agree it.

- And if it doesn't fit with our plan?

- The time may well be ripe. We've all agreed that we need to act soon and that the moment may not be perfect.

- We need to be ending now, gentlemen.

*

- Thank you for taking the time to attend, gentlemen, the Director said.

'As if we had any choice' more than one thought.

- What I have to tell you will doubtlessly be unexpected but believe me it is utterly essential. You will be aware of the problems we have had in the past few days regarding the nullification. To deal with the matter I have decided that I shall go myself to attend to this, to avoid any further mistakes.

Several of the board members gasped. That pleased the Director. They hadn't expected that.

- I shall be leaving matters in the capable hands of Rafel, he added.

That certainly made one or two- Rafel included- sit up!

- I would not expect to be in the Tunnel zone more that one complete time count. I have already set matters in motion for my journey and arrival and will be leaving immediately after this meeting ends. There will be various items which need attending to but I believe Rafel, in consultation with yourselves- all of whom have considerable experience- will be able to make such decisions as are necessary. In the event of anything unexpected occurring- unlikely but possible, as we know only too well- you will have to fend as best you can. I have prepared a brief for you Rafel and Deth, my secretary, will be able to fill you in on any details not clear. Now, are there any questions?

The one question they would not be asking is 'Why?' the Director thought. They may be suspicious and they may not believe their luck, but they're not going to give me a chance to reconsider.

- I appreciate your faith in me, Director, Rafel said.

The Director nodded absent-mindedly as though already en route.

- As there are no questions I'll be on my way. Thank you all.

As the door closed behind the Director all eyes turned to Rafel.

- I think it best if we adjourn for a short while so that I can read the Director's brief and consult with Deth, Rafel said.

He felt as much at sea as any of them, the Director's announcement and rapid exit having taken him aback. Why, he thought, is the Director playing into my hands like this? Once he's in the Tunnel there's nothing he can do to stop us. Or is there? Rafel had always envisaged a full-blooded confrontation with the Director not this meek stepping aside. That it was merely temporary wasn't the point; the point was the Director was out of the way and all the power was in this room, in Rafel's hands. They were all gazing at him for guidance.

- Deth, if you would join me in the Director's office; and the rest of you shall we meet back here at one? Perhaps two- that will give us time for lunch and then we can take our time if we need to.

As his colleagues headed for the door Rafel fought down a surge of triumph, cautioning himself that nothing was secure yet and that Deth was still to be dealt with. He watched as Deth closed the door behind the others and turned expectantly to Rafel.

- Shall I open the door for you, sir, Deth asked politely.

Of course, thought Rafel; it would need the Director's palm-print and voice tone to open it.

- Can you do that? Rafel asked.

- Of course, sir, Deth replied holding up a small audio-visu device. The Director has left this so that we can enter and also so that any decisions can be properly authorised, should that be necessary.

The keys of the kingdom! Rafel couldn't help himself thinking. It was not just the door of the Director's personal office such a device could unlock! There had to be a catch. Had to be- but he couldn't think of what it might be. Caution was still called for, but the end might be closer than they had anticipated.

13.

- Are you sure these are all your current cases, Dr. Aann? the Assessor asked.

- There's the tagged one as well, sir, she answered politely.

- The file please.

Dr. Aann produced it and passed it across the desk to him. Why did I hold it back? she thought.

No sooner had Dr. Frinck left for the fourth Level than Dr. Aann had received the summons to attend the Assessor. She knew that above the likes of Dr. Frinck and his senior colleagues there were others who kept an overview of the medical work on behalf of the Tunnel administrators. However, the sudden appearance of the Assessor puzzled her. Were they concerned about Dr. Frinck's work or hers? None of her colleagues had been so summoned as far as she was aware.

She dutifully sat and watched as the Assessor turned slowly through the pages of Hunter's file. He had not bothered to look at the others. He knew, she thought; he knew about the tagged case, about Hunter. That's why he's here.

- Tell me about this man.

She gave a concise summary of Hunter and her several meetings with him. She suspected that he had already reviewed the recordings. I am on trial here a bit, she thought. There is more going on than a simple review of my cases. This has nothing to do with Dr. Frinck. They've got him out of the way, that's the reason he's gone up to Level four. Not that he would have been any protection.

Do I need protection? she thought.

- What is your prognosis? Is he a risk?

- To whom, sir? Dr. Aann asked surprised.

- These others who have died or vanished, the Assessor said; being around him seems dangerous, perhaps a threat to the Tunnel's completion.

Dr. Aann urged herself to be calm. It would have been easy to have jumped to Hunter's defence and commented on the utter unfairness of that suggestion. She did not know what the Assessor's remit was so maintained outwardly her best professional and dispassionate appearance. If he wanted to provoke her to reveal some sort of sympathy for Hunter beyond that normal to her role, then he wasn't going to succeed.

- No sir, he's no threat, either to himself or to others.

- Could he have caused the cave-in that killed Dyne?

- That's a non-medical matter, sir.

- I know that. I'm asking for your opinion.

- On the basis of what I know about the situation and Hunter I would say no, he couldn't have caused the cave-in.

- The replacement Beel, what has happened to him?

- That's another non-medical matter, sir.

- I am interested in all aspects of this case, Dr. Aann. I'd appreciate your candid opinion.

I bet you would, Dr. Aann thought.

- I've no idea what has happened to Beel... or Yadl.

- That's your opinion?

- Yes sir.

- Could Hunter have disposed of them?

Again she resisted the temptation to challenge such a thought.

- No sir.

- On what do you base that opinion?

- On my study of Hunter, sir. He is not a killer. He has no reason to kill any of these men. Dyne was a workmate, as was Beel. Yadl he had never met.

- What about Hunter's hallucinations?

- What hallucinations, sir?

- He sees a man in your office- Security say the office was empty and there was no sign of a man in the recording tape.

- I believe there was someone there, sir.

- On what do you base that opinion, Dr. Aann?

- I believe Hunter, sir.

- Perhaps you believe what he wants you to believe.

- What is this about, sir?

She'd had enough of this inference and hinting.

- Do you know why Hunter is tagged?

- No sir. We're not given that information down here. We're simply told to assess such cases regularly and thoroughly.

- And would you say that you have done that?

- I am *doing* it, sir.

- How much longer do you think you will be before you are able to give your conclusions to the Surface?

- The normal requirement is for a dozen sessions including two medical and psychological evaluations. I'm about half way through that, sir.

- Surface require a conclusion sooner than that, Dr. Aann.

- Any assessment I give now, or before the required twelve sessions, will be deemed invalid under administrations own guidelines, sir.

Dr. Aann was keenly aware that there was a battle going on. The Assessor wanted her to pick up his hints and develop her conclusions accordingly.

- Do you regard yourself as a loyal person, Dr. Aann?

- Loyal to whom, sir?

- Precisely.

He gave her a thin smile which was chilling.

- That will be all for the moment, Dr. Aann. I may need to see you again after I've read through all of your files. I will try not to interfere with your scheduled work if I do need to see you.

*

- This is Professor Null, Hunter.

Hunter felt no inclination to offer his hand to the stranger and the Professor didn't offer his.

- Professor Null is assessing medical cases and practice for the Surface, Hunter, and he has expressed an interest in your case.

Dr. Aann could tell by the way that Hunter was sitting that he was uneasy.

- If I may Dr. Aann, Professor Null took over, not bothering with any further formalities. Things have been happening to you, Hunter.

Hunter didn't respond. There was hardly any point. It had been a statement not a question.

- There are concerns about your influence on progress in the Tunnel as a result of these incidents. Not to put too fine a point on it, Hunter, there is some concern that you might be trying to sabotage the effort. What do you think of that?

Dr. Aann could tell that the Null was being deliberately brusque and confrontational. She felt that she had to intervene but there was something about Hunter which told her not to. It wasn't anything as obvious as a glance or any movement, just...something.

- I think, Hunter said, that you are an asshole.

Null gave his thin smile.

- It is hardly sensible to insult someone who controls whether or not you stay here or are removed.

- You're still an asshole and whatever you think you can do to me doesn't alter that.

- People perish or disappear around you, Hunter.

- People perish or disappear in the Tunnel, professor, Hunter replied.

- You accept no responsibility?

- Do you?

- What are your plans?

- No different from yours.

- You do not know what my plans are.

- That is what I have said.

- You like playing games?

- Professor Null, I have no wish to spend any more time in your company.

Hunter rose.

- Dr. Aann, my apologies and goodbye.

Hunter left the room.

Again Dr. Aann found herself refraining from any comment. Whatever Professor Null's object was she sensed that for her own safety she had to avoid giving him cause to criticise her for identifying too closely with a tagged individual. He had been intent on being provocative that was for sure and hadn't cared whether she or Hunter found it objectionable. Whether he found Hunter's response equally objectionable he gave no hint; but once Hunter had left he himself got up and left her office without a word.

What has happened? she thought. She re-ran the recording and found to her surprise that there was nothing on the monitor. She had not switched the machine off. Had Professor Null done so? He had entered the office after her and had been nowhere near the controls. She hadn't checked them on entry, that was true. There was no need. The mechanism was automatically activated and recorded everything. It was clearly not broken for there she was seated at her desk starting the process of checking things. So why had it malfunctioned? Whatever the reason was the indisputable fact was that there was no record of Null's interaction with Hunter and she had no doubt that this was deliberate.

Could the Assessor be another one of those inexplicable people who sought to do Hunter harm? What did she know about him? When someone appears 'from the Surface' with an air of authority and knowledge of the Tunnel who would question them?

Dr. Aann left her office and went in search of the Assessor. There was no trace of him. She went to Security and requested that they put out a general call for him to contact her at once. There was no response.

- Can you locate him for me? Dr. Aann asked the head of Security.

- He may have returned to the Surface.

- If he came from there.

- Why do you say that, Doctor?

- Do people from the Surface normally just vanish? Aren't there checks on who arrives down here and who leaves?

- Of course. You know the Access station which leads to the upper Levels and Surface.

- Can you check with them to see when Professor Null arrived and if he has returned?

- Let's have a look.

There was no record of his arrival or any departure.

- What is going on, Doctor?

- I've no idea, none at all. Is there any way of checking with the Surface as to whether this Professor Null actually comes from there?

- I can check, but he can't have come from anywhere else, can he, Doctor?

- One would have thought not. But please check for me.

The head of Security spoke with the Surface while Dr. Aann waited patiently.

- This is bizarre, he said finally. Surface have no record of any Professor Null as an Assessor or otherwise. No official has descended from the Surface in the last full time passage. Looks like we've got intruders.

*

Hunter waited for the Mole to complete its forward roll and then he went into action clearing the debris and shoring up. When he had reported for the shift he had found that neither Ghant nor Tabb were there. Angu was in the cab but the other two crew members were new. They had introduced themselves as Spen and Kale but otherwise had been quiet. Hunter had explained their duties and positions once out of the cab and so far they had worked effectively and quickly. He was used to the joking and joshing of his erstwhile colleagues; but as long as the new crew members were productive and safe he set his questions regarding Tabb and Ghant aside.

There was time enough to think about them once the shift was over.

Hunter had made a side sortie to strengthen a recess when he realised that he was alone. He looked for the Mole, expecting it to be either just ahead of the recess or outside it. The Mole was nowhere in sight. He looked back along the track and saw that there was a solid wall of rock where the Tunnel should have been. For a moment he felt bewildered: the raw rock-face to his left and another rock-face to his right: he was walled in. He spoke into his Vox-link but found that there was no signal. He was walled in and unable to communicate!

He had no doubt that what had happened was deliberate. He had heard nothing   as he was wearing ear mufflers to protect him against the noise from the Mole. The in-built speakers had remained silent, so there had been no attempt to communicate with him from the Mole, to warn him of a sudden cave-in.

*

- I'm sorry about what happened, Hunter, Dr. Aann said.

- So this guy's vanished as well, you say? Hunter said.

- It would appear so.

- And you reckon he wasn't an official Assessor?

- That seems to be confirmed. I should have been more careful.

- Can't see as it's your fault, Dr. Aann, Hunter said. It seems that everyone was taken in.

- I should have asked for some authorisation.

- Would that be normal?

- Well, no. If someone's in the Tunnel you take it that they have authority and reason to be there. But after all the odd things that have been happening...

- Yeah, like this latest dream.

- How did you escape?

- I woke up. I was covered in sweat again.

- You thought it was real?

- It *was* real! I mean, I know I was in my room when I woke up but though it was a dream it was as real as me being in my room.

- A premonition?

- I've had those warning feelings, but this was quite different. It was as though I was in two places at once- well, not quite at once but one after the other.

- And Tabb and Ghant?

- They're still around- around here, that is.

- So where else is there?

- It certainly wasn't the surface. It was the Tunnel. It was our Mole, solid as the one sitting on the track waiting for us to start our shift on it.

- I have to be honest with you, Hunter...

- You've always have been that, Dr. Aann.

-Thank you, Hunter. What I mean to say is that this assessment I started doing on you is taking on a shape and significance which I'm not sure I can deal with. I don't mean that I want to hand it over to someone else; I want to finish it. But all these accidents and incidents baffle me and I'm not sure how relevant they are to the kind of assessment I've been asked to undertake.

- I can appreciate that, Doctor. If someone is determined to kill me, or at least make me fail the assessment- whatever that will mean- then for my part I don't want that person to succeed.

- I suppose I'm trying to give you the opportunity to disengage, Hunter.

- I guessed that; but wouldn't that be to give in to whoever is making all this trouble?

- Yes, it would.

- I'm not someone who gives in.

- Neither am I, Hunter.

They smiled at each other.

- So we continue?

- We continue, Hunter.

14.

...We welcome you. It was time. There is still much to see and to do. Don't lose heart...

Who are they? Hunter wondered. They are no shadows down here in the Tunnel- somehow he had a vague memory now of shadows on the Surface. He wondered at the absence of shadows in the Tunnel. Even in the dreams he had- not those created by the machine but his own dreams, which were more numerous now and more welcome- there were no shadows. It was all the glare of the overhead lights, or the blackness of sleep. There was no in-between, no shadowland.

*

- We can't locate Rafel anywhere.

- Nobody has seen Deth either.

- We have to decide what to do.
- Are we all present?
- Yes.
- Someone will have to take the chair as acting-Director.
- Do we go by seniority or vote on it?
- I suggest we write out nominations on a paper and then see who have the most votes. I for one don't wish to be nominated.
- Nor do I.
- Me neither.
- Let's vote then, shall we? Perhaps one of those who doesn't want to be nominated will do the count and someone else can check it?

After the first round of voting there were only two names with more than one vote: Dreer and Moud.

- We'll vote again for one or the other. Everyone agreeable?

Heads nodded and once again they all made their selection. The count was made and checked.

- Moud it is. Moud, over to you.
- We'll need some sort of minute of all this given that Deth isn't with us. Dreer would you be good enough to transcribe the recording once we've finished? Thanks.

The discussion began and it went on for some time.

The Watcher paid close attention. He was altering the recording even as it recorded.

*

"The Archives are silent on this point. We would not expect them to offer anything on such matters, though historians are not in agreement as to why this should be. Some take the view- impossible to prove or disprove- that the Archives have been altered, not only in this respect but in other ways as well. Others believe that the Archives preserve a full and true record and that nothing else ever existed. There are still others who believe that the Archives are a total fabrication, made up by some unknown person or group whose wish was either to confuse or to consolidate power for themselves. Since no such group currently exists- or seems to ever have existed- this view is dismissed by all manner of historians, even those who differ amongst themselves. There are those who wish the Archive to be openly available so that its integrity and contents are no longer a matter of dispute or the preserve of factions vying for supremacy. Others feel the

Archive should be ignored and treated as any other artefact from the past. Whichever view one espouses the reality is that the Archive exists and that its interpretation affects the lives of all."

*

Hunter closed his eyes as the fine spray of hot water raked the dirt and sweat from his up-turned face and naked body...

As he read the Director drummed his fingers on the desk. Those who knew him well- and there were few indeed who knew him as well as Deth did- would have recognised the sign. It was not that the Director was not happy. Happiness or unhappiness did not enter into his being. It was that he was wondering what to do.

It was possible to end it all now. A mere nod to Deth would have been enough. Deth already knew his mind, knew what he required and waited only for the external indication which a nod of the head would have been.

With Rafel out of the way down in the Tunnel- Deth had seen to that with his usual efficiency and despatch- there was no urgency about this minor irritation. For the moment it was contained. Cromell had been reprimanded, as had always been the Director's intention, and would be happy with his extra income, even if the sheer boredom he would now face would destroy his inner life.

But ending it all now did not have that feel about it which the Director had felt as he dealt decisively with Rafel. There were signs, the Director felt, that things were more complicated than they superficially seemed. It is true that Cromell's bungling attempts to deal with the problem had failed and resulted in queries from Security to the surface. It was also true that Rafel's attempt to complete the nullification had come to nothing. Rafel, for all his scheming and ambition, the Director knew was not a bungler. His attempted coup had been doomed from the start- the fault lay not in the attempt but in Rafel's character. But that Rafel failed suggested that this man Hunter was resourceful. He had also been alerted and any further attempt to nullify the problem would be more difficult because of this.

The Director studied Deth, who sat motionless across from him. What a boon Deth had been! A most loyal and faithful servant, the Director thought. Perhaps there was a way to simplify the situation in the Tunnel and conclude the nullification successfully.

- Deth, the Director said, careful with his thoughts; I have a little chore for you. It involves more than mere deception, at which I know you are adept. Let me tell you what I have in mind and give me your opinion on it, whether or not you think it will work.

But what the Director told Deth was not what he had in mind.

Even if Deth had known what the Director's true intention was perhaps his response would have been the same. There was no sign in Deth's eyes that he disbelieved the Director's explanation.

- Yes, Deth said; that will work.

- Do it, the Director said.

*

- *Welcome...this way. We have been waiting for you. Now is the time...*

Hunter woke. He did not recognise where he was. This is not my room, he thought as he looked around himself.

Strangely, he did not feel any sense of foreboding. Somehow, although he knew he had never seen such a room before- all white and luminous- he felt he had been here before.

I am Hunter, he thought.

- *You are the Director.*

I am Hunter, he thought with more force, as though he could make his very thoughts burst out into the white room.

- *As you wish, so it shall be.*

He found he could sit up and looking down saw that he was lying on nothing visible.

I cannot be suspended in mid-air, he thought.

The space he was in- he could not call it a room, although that was how he had first thought of it- seemed to have no shape. There were no corners, no doorways, no ceiling or floor. Yet he felt contained as though in a room and he felt certain that if he should move that some aperture would open and allow him egress.

- *This way...*

*

- Hunter has disappeared? Dr. Aann said as she tried to take in the news.

Dr. Frinck's replacement nodded. He seemed unconcerned by the disappearance.

- Send your report to the Surface as it is, Dr. Aann, he said.

- But surely we should do something, sir.

- Other than report it what do you suggest? There are things within our remit and others that are no concern of ours. Just send in your report with such conclusions as you can make. There's plenty of other work pressing-this new case, Rafel for example. Surface wants a close scrutiny of his behaviour.

Dr. Aann took the new file and returned to her office.

Hunter was there waiting, smiling.

Curiosity

- 'And these?' the visitor asked.

He paused in his tour of the building and indicated with a casual flick of his hand the row of low, arched doorways which his guide had been hurrying past. That long, ill-lit corridor stretched away to their left. It seemed to end with a worn flight of stone steps barely visible through the gloom and the smoke from the torches set in wall sockets.

The visitor fluttered a lace kerchief to his nose, inhaling the sweet perfume which masked the dank odour seeping from the walls. The guide offered no explanation and seemed ill at ease, eager to press on towards the stables outside. From there, once they had viewed the horses- a fine collection of Arabians- they could return to the hall, where the master awaited his honoured guest.

The visitor turned aside from the main corridor and stepped into that silent side passage. At once he felt a chill which seemed more intense in that subterranean corridor. He drew his cloak tightly around his shoulders as he looked at the locked doors along the passage.

The guide had become quite agitated. The visitor did not concern himself with this for he was used to having his own way.

- 'And what are these used for?' he asked, indicating the locked doorways.

He glanced compellingly at the guide who was unable to meet his eyes. You could almost hear the poor fellow cursing his luck at having been allotted the task of showing the visitor around the castle. He silently berated himself for having chosen this, the most direct route to the stables instead of walking across the courtyard. The visitor would have known no different. But now his interest and curiosity were stimulated by the sight of the dungeons.

The visitor was in good humour after the fine meal he had shared with his host. He decided to overlook the obstinacy being displayed by his guide. With a slight smile he continued to stroll along the forbidden corridor. He ignored the servant suddenly rushing after him and the fellow's timorous plucking at his cloak.

- 'Please, sire, these are only disused wine cellars. They've long been emptied and boarded up.'

The explanation was so patently false that the visitor glared at his guide.

- 'For such an obvious lie were you in my service I would have your tongue cut out, you wretch' he said.

The guide paled and began to shake with fear.

- 'But Excellency, I only obey the orders given by my master.'

- 'Your master commanded you to show me his castle. Is this how you interpret his instructions?'

- 'But the master allows no one to enter this corridor, sire.'

How intriguing, the visitor thought. He felt in no mood to bandy words with the guide, who was scampering beside him like a rat and whimpering entreaties to 'come away, sire'. Instead he walked deliberately to the end of the corridor, studying the solid stone walls and the grey, metallic doors.

There were six such doors along either side of the corridor. They were each set in a shallow recess and were smooth and devoid of decoration, window or spy-hole. They bore only a lock socket and four wide hinges, which suggested the doors were heavy and needed much support.

It was clear to the visitor that such doors would not hide mere wine cellars. The undisturbed dust on the flagstones indicated that the corridor was seldom used. This too was inconsistent with the regular too-ing and fro-ing which went on around wine cellars.

For all the flickering light that the torches gave you might have imagined that you were in the very bowels of the earth, the visitor thought. No gusts of air or draughts disturbed the flames from which smoke rose straight up to mark the ceiling with a thick encrustation of soot like heavy cobwebs.

The visitor felt slightly piqued at his host's having invited him to view the castle but having debarred him and others from seeing this corridor. His curiosity was heightened and it was because of this that he chose to linger in this oppressive and clammy atmosphere. He wondered what treasure the host might be hiding.

- 'Open one of these doors!' he commanded.

The effect of this order was to throw the servant into an even greater fit of trembling.

- 'But sire, it is forbidden!'

This further insolence angered the visitor. Up to this moment he had been prepared to tolerate the fellow's hesitancy; but now his good humour evaporated. He assumed the daunting pose of someone who was obeyed without question.

- 'This door, open it!'

He pointed indifferently at one of the doors.

- 'Open it, or your master will be informed of your disobedience.'

One can imagine the dilemma the guide had: to obey one was to disobey the other. However he acted he would earn the displeasure and condemnation of someone. Which choice was the least unpleasant?

The compelling, imperious presence of the visitor won the day. It was just possible, the guide might have thought, that his master would never find out about his disobedience. Perhaps, if he did find out, he would be understanding of his servant's dilemma and commend him for obeying the visitor.

While the servant searched for the key the visitor became aware that the corridor was not as silent as he had first thought. He could hear a vague moaning sound, as though a draught was finding its way through cracks in one of the doorways. The enigmatic nature of the sound, and his inability to precisely locate from where it was coming, made the visitor begin to wish that he had not been so keen to explore the side corridor. Perhaps he had hoped to discover some family secret which might have given him some advantage over the proud figure of his host. But now he began to wonder if there was something less pleasant to be found behind the door he had chosen. He swallowed nervously and stepped quickly back, hoping his apprehensiveness would not communicate itself to the servant.

The guide hurried towards the visitor waving the key ring he had found hung outside one of the doors. Had he possessed a sense of humour the visitor might have been amused by the unstated reversal in their roles: now he was eager to by-pass the corridor while the guide was eager to show him whatever lay beyond the door. If he were to say that he had changed his mind he feared that the servant would secretly sneer at this, perhaps suspecting cowardice. To back away now and belittle himself in front of a servant was unthinkable.

The guide held out the key ring to him. He snatched it and turned to the door. Clumsily and hastily the visitor tried several keys attempting to find the one which would engage the lock. Exasperated he flung the keys at the guide ordering him to open the door. While the servant was doing so the visitor stood to one side, his arms folded across his chest, trying to affect a casual and commanding air. As he waited he began to wish fervently that the fellow would never be done with his fumbling and fiddling.

- 'Isn't the key there?' he demanded, hoping to keep from his voice his earnest desire that the key wouldn't be on the ring.

- 'There are still three or four that I haven't tried, Excellency,' the servant replied, his head bent over the keys as he thrust them one at a time into the lock.

Just as he was praying that the last key would not work the visitor heard a loud click as the lock opened. The servant gave a relieved sigh and began to pull the heavy door open, stepping aside to permit the visitor entry.

The visitor seized one of the burning torches from a wall socket. His nostrils were assailed by a fetid, disgusting odour and he held his perfumed kerchief to his face. The torch flame flickered and the visitor staggered slightly as a draught of putrid air rushed into the corridor. Nauseated despite his kerchief the visitor wondered if he had unleashed the fiends of hell.

He thrust the torch inside to illuminate the darkness of what seemed to be a cavernous emptiness. The glow of the torch hardly lit more than the space it filled. Beyond lay a vast chasm of darkness. Stepping barely over the threshold the visitor peered in all directions hoping to see something, anything. Then he seemed to catch sight of an emaciated being shackled against a far wall. As he moved the torch to and fro the visitor seemed to see another skeletal figure, then another and another until he thought there were countless figures ranged around the walls.

Terrified, as the torch went out, the visitor stumbled backwards and his shoulders encountered the smoothness of a closed door.

(February 1970- Revised 2011)

Under the Hood

It was only later- when there seemed to be nothing but time rather than no time at all- that he was able to reconstruct what had happened so swiftly and unexpectedly. He had at first taken it as a bad dream.

*

Something woke him but the tape was already being stuck over his mouth and the hood pulled over his head. His wrists were being tied in front and then he was being pulled from his bed and pushed across the room. How many there were he did not know. No one had spoken a word. Beneath the slippers someone had put on his feet he felt the gravel of the drive. It was cold outside as they left the house and he felt the dampness of a recent rainfall. He was shoved into the back of a van, scraping his knees through the thin pyjamas. What felt like burlap bags were thrown over him. He heard the doors being shut. Someone got into the front and started the engine. Then they were driving out of the yard and on to the small country road which wound down to the river. He heard the sound of a match being struck and then smelt the smoke of a cigarette through the fabric of the hood. After that it was just the jolting of the floor under him and the catarrhal sound of the engine as they drove.

When they arrived wherever they were going he was pulled out of the van and pushed and lead across a patch of damp grass. He stumbled as he was guided clumsily through a door and then down some stairs and through another door. This room felt colder than the outside air had been. He was forced on to a mattress and felt his feet being tied to what might have been the foot of a bed. Then he felt a head close to his and a harsh voice whispering to him.

'Not a sound from you or you're dead, understand?'

He had no doubt that the voice meant what it said.

Then he heard footsteps- two maybe three or more men- and a door was shut. He heard muffled footsteps climbing back up the stairs and then fading as they made their way to another part of the house.

How long he lay there he could not tell. He certainly fell asleep for the next thing he remembered was feeling himself being shaken awake.

He opened his eyes and could see. They had taken the hood off his head. A man wearing a balaclava was sitting on the side of the bed shaking him. Somehow he would have preferred the hood rather than to be seeing what he was seeing. Once he was awake the man took his hand from his shoulder.

'Just listen and don't say anything, Mister Paynter. You'll be getting something to eat in a moment and there's a pail over there you can pee in. I'll be untying your feet but advise you not to try to get out of here. Here's the plan: we'll be in touch with your agent and will be asking for one hundred thousand pounds. We're not unreasonable, you see: it could have been a million we were wanting but who can raise that kind of cash at the snapping of fingers? We'll be telling her any contact with the police and you're a dead man. I hope for your sake she's a sensible woman. If we get the money then we'll leave you by the roadside somewhere and let her know so you can be collected. She'll have forty-eight hours. It was twenty-four the others were wanting but I've persuaded them a little longer makes it more likely we'll be paid. What you have to do, besides pray, is keep quiet, give no trouble and do as you're told. Understand?'

He had nodded and the man grunted, patted his arm and untied his feet. Then he left the room, turning a key outside in the lock.

I have either got forty-eight hours left to live, he thought, or in a couple of days' time I will be telling what I can recall to the police.

It would be hypocritical to start to pray now, he told himself. Whatever I believe I don't believe in the 7th Calvary version of God. I can keep quiet- they'll not hear a peep out of me unless they ask for a reply- but it's what's going on in my brainbox which could be the problem.

He did not doubt that his agent, Melinda, would do as she was instructed. She would want him alive and well and writing. He was surprised at the smallness of the sum being demanded. Was that a good or a bad sign? If they received it would they ask for more? Were these kidnappers 'honourable' men or greedy villains?

He had never thought of himself as vulnerable to this kind of happening. He had lived here happily for more than ten years, despite being a 'foreigner'. His neighbours were friendly and he had entered into the social life of the nearby town. He donated to local charities. He could not imagine who could want to do something like this.

There are no guidelines on how to think in this kind of situation, he thought. You can't go into a local bookshop and buy a self-help manual on how to survive a kidnapping. Perhaps it was no help to recall what had happened to other victims- Aldo Moro killed by the *'Brigate Rosse';* Patty

Hearst joining the *Symbionese Liberation Army*; Frank Sinatra Junior being freed once a ransom was paid by his father. That kind of thinking didn't help. The only thing to do is to empty the mind, the way that mystics must do, and to observe, to wait in silence.

*

The worst thing, he told himself when it was all over, were the questions from the police. When the man wearing the balaclava had come back into the room, which now stank with the smell from the unemptied pail, he had momentarily felt fear. Until that moment it had been as though all feeling other than the basic feeling of coldness or warmth had vanished from him. It had been when the hood was pulled back over his head that he had felt flooded with relief. Perhaps it had been silly to imagine that he would simply have been shot where he lay on the bed; but he believed when the hood went back on that the ransom had been paid and he would be released.

He had been helped up the stairs and taken back outside. He was pushed into the back of the van again and once more covered with bags. He sensed that there were fewer men now- the driver and one man sitting in the back watching him. He could imagine the others, however many there were, making good their escape. After what might have been an hour the van stopped and he was bundled out of it. They left the hood on his head after pushing him into a ditch beside the road. He heard the van driving away. By wriggling his shoulders and pulling with his hands he was able to remove the hood. It was the dead of night and he had no idea where he was. He dragged himself from the ditch and sat by the empty road. Above him the stars were a welcome sight. If he had been like his brother, he thought, he might have been able to read them and draw further comfort.

It had just started to turn from darkness to dawn when he saw far off the lights of several cars.

That, he thought, will be the police and it was.

He was wrapped in blankets and someone gave him a cigarette. They drove at speed to the city where Melinda waited to greet him and then the questions began.

No, he had no idea at all where he had been held other than that it was in a basement room. What direction they'd gone in? Well he had soon lost track of the turns they took and the ups and downs there had been. Only at the end had there been a longish straight stretch before they pulled up to the house where he'd been held. For all he knew it could have been his own, except for the basement. He had heard no noises nearby as he'd been bundled from the van into the house. He had no idea how big it might be. No, he had no real idea of how many men there had been. At least three, he could say with some certainty, but possibly four if there had been someone in the front with the driver. The van could have been any make; he was no good at that kind of identification. It was an oldish panel van, perhaps the kind the mail was delivered with in the countryside. Whether there had been anyone awaiting them in the house he couldn't say. The only person who had spoken- and that very briefly- had been the one man who had woken him and then returned to the room with the meal: his eyes had been green and he had been six foot tall and solidly built. Yes, he'd recognise his voice if he ever heard it again. He had been reasonably treated, once you discounted the fact that he'd been kidnapped and told that he'd be shot if no ransom was paid! The food they'd given him was a stew, but probably from a can, like that *Fray Bentos* stuff you could buy in any supermarket. The cigarette that had been smoked in the van he thought had been a *Sweet Afton* as requested in Godard's film 'Tous les garçons s'appellent Patrick'. But what good was such a minor detail as that to them?

He had not wanted to appear before the press and television cameras but Melinda had said it would be a good idea. Get it out of the way now, she said, and then you won't be pestered by them afterwards, you know what they're like. Don't bother shaving; I'll be beside you and so will the policeman leading the enquiry. So he had submitted to that after he had told the police all that he could. Did he think it was the IRA? Were they just after the money? Was it a stunt? Would he use this in his next book? What did he feel when told that he could be shot?

God, he thought looking out at the flashing cameras and microphones and camcorders: it was like being faced with a group of piranha, only their morality was more understandable as they just wanted to dine.

Melinda was excellent, fielding most of the stupid questions and making it clear when they'd asked enough. He wanted to go home but the police advised him not to do that. Melinda had arranged for him to stay with her and her husband. He needed to be with people he knew, she said, rather than on his own. Who was to say that the kidnappers might not do it again?

In the weeks that followed he went back to England and eventually sold his cottage in Ireland. He thought about it often. He would sit in his Cotswold garden and remember the beauty of the hills and valleys in which the cottage had been set. When he was at a low pitch- and that was the one remaining sign of that time- he would imagine that the place he had been held was one of those he had seen during his many walks around that lovely countryside.

For some time afterwards he had been unable to continue the work he had been writing at the time of his being kidnapped. It was Melinda's opinion that he should finish and publish it. When he did start to write again a few years later he produced the short novel based on his experience. It won several major prizes in Canada, the States and Europe. He was much in demand on the talk and book festival circuit. Melinda beamed whenever they met.

*

In the years that followed much happened to him. He got married and then his wife was killed in a freak driving accident during a storm. Each year on the anniversary of the kidnapping he made sure he was either staying with friends or booked into a hotel in a large city somewhere. That was how he had met Ann. She had been attending a conference and they had shared a table one evening when the dining room had been crowded. He successfully underwent treatment for prostate cancer. The story he had been writing then abandoned was eventually finished and proved to be another best seller. He was reluctant to stay on the celebrity circuit and spent most of his time in the Cotswold cottage declining invitations to speak at this or that festival. He didn't become a recluse- he loved the countryside too much for that- but he severely limited his contact with people. Melinda he would see in London whenever there was a new manuscript for her. His work, she said, got better and better. His own private verdict was that he was saying less and less and worse and worse, much as Beckett might have felt. The compulsion to write was rampant in him, though he offered Melinda only a fraction of what he wrote. The rest he was sure would be disinterred from the boxes containing it which he stored in the attic. What would be thought of it he did not much care.

He returned again and again to the time he had been under the hood and threatened with death.

It's an odd thing, he thought, each time he wrote about that experience; I believed I'd exorcised this years ago and yet here I am approaching it from another angle. What had my captors been thinking as they waited for the ransom? He could imagine them upstairs playing cards, passing the time as he had to pass the time until the ransom was paid or refused. What might they be doing now? Each time he read about a soldier being kidnapped in Iraq or Afghanistan it was as though he was undergoing afresh those forty-eight hours of uncertainty. How long it had been in reality he found out was just over twenty-four hours. He had had no watch- he always placed it on the bedside cabinet when retiring for the night- so time was measured by how often he filled the pail and how far he could count while holding his breath. There was pleasure in losing count rather than frustration, since that meant he just began once more from 'one'. There was something satisfying about 'one' rather than 'thirty'. Sometimes the strategies he had invented to pass the time felt like the games he would play as a child when he roamed over the hills behind the town where he was born. His favourite book as a child had been '*Kidnapped*' by Stevenson; but of course reading it now (and he never did) would be different to reading it when he was ten.

He tried to recall what he had been doing the day he had been kidnapped, what time he'd   risen and what time he had retired. Would they have been watching and waiting until they saw the light going out in his bedroom? He had once kept a diary but that time was one of those periods in which he had let it lapse because he was so engrossed in the story he was writing. In the aftermath of his release he had not thought about what he had done that day; but now he assumed it would have been much like he did any other day. He would have been writing. There may have been telephone calls, which he would leave the answering machine to handle. Had he listened to them once he was free? He had not been back to the cottage so clearly he hadn't. Not that it mattered, he thought. Nor did it matter what I had to eat and drink. Everything that happened that day, every trite little detail has been wiped away by the kidnapping; all that remains is the memory of being woken up and gagged and hooded. The loss of Ann, my wife, was more agonising but I do not turn that over and over in my mind like I do the kidnapping. Some have compared such an event to being raped but I felt I had been violated in a much more fundamental way. Physically, yes, I was made to feel that I was an object rather than a person. I was at the mercy of these unknown people. They could do what they wished with me. What I wanted and who I was didn't matter. The fact that they were 'honourable' and did not kill me once the ransom had been paid doesn't matter. They had been prepared to kill me if they didn't get what they wanted. I have survived and lived the rest of my life as a result of someone else's decision not to kill me. When I underwent chemotherapy for cancer I was not so close to death and all the efforts of those involved then were directed at keeping me alive, not using me as a bargaining chip.

He found himself wanting to give his captors names- Sean, Brendan, Padraig, James- so as to humanise them and render them less threatening. Then he would take the names away, leaving them as anonymous and menacing as they had been. Not knowing how many there had been, whether the house had been near to his cottage or miles away from it, details like that swirled around his brain at such times. He would wake up in the bedroom and be thankful that the bedside light was on: he could no longer sleep in a totally darkened room.

Of course he had taken up the offer of counselling and he would still attend the occasional session when he felt the need to do so. Why had he felt more comfortable under the hood than when he could see the man whose face was masked by the balaclava? Whenever I see someone wearing a balaclava I shudder, he told his therapist. Understanding the association doesn't lessen the fear.

In one of his novels he wrote about a man who could only get sexual gratification whilst wearing a hood. It's completely made up, he told himself; but what if it wasn't? He and Ann had enjoyed a perfectly normal sexual life. Since her death he had not wished to have any intimate, although Melinda kept trying to introduce him to this or that female acquaintance of hers.

*

'I'll have to wear a suit, I suppose', he said.

'And shave,' Melinda said down the phone. He could imagine her running her eyes over him. 'You've let yourself go.'

'I walk the dog every day,' he said.

'You haven't got a dog, Laurence.'

In all these years she's never called me Larry, he thought. Not that I like or dislike being called Larry. How did I introduce myself to Ann that night in the hotel dining room? Laurence, I think.

'Do I have to attend?'

'It's a lifetime achievement award, Laurence. It's only for a few hours and you'll be staying with us afterwards. The publicity will help your sales. You've not given me anything for a couple of years now.'

'I don't need the money. What would I do with more money?'

'Give it away to one of those charities you support. You know you're going to go, dear, so don't be awkward with me.'

'I don't know what to say to them.'

'Laurence, you have the most fluent tongue I've ever known. A few words of thanks, an anecdote about the long road you've travelled, anything will do as long as you turn up, have shaved and your zipper's done up. What time will your train be arriving? I'll meet you and check you over. We can drive to our place and have a snifter beforehand.'

Yes, I'm going to go, he thought as he replaced the receiver. I need an airing. I'll catch the train up to London and let Melinda take me to this swish hotel where the ceremony is being held. I'll be on my best behaviour, humbly say the right things and make good my escape the next day.

Melinda had been right, he thought; once I'm in it I'm a natural social swimmer. All these people, writers and others I've known or heard about, are here because of me. The only uncomfortable thing is reading those 'Famous kidnapped author honoured' articles. It's like having been branded; no matter what you do afterwards the brand is still there. He could see the eventual obituaries: 'Famous kidnapped author dies.' Thank goodness Ann and I got married abroad, he thought. They only found out about the marriage when she was killed and then it had been 'Wife of famous kidnapped author killed in accident'.

Melinda kept close to him, protective as always. They were seated together with her husband and his publisher and his wife. As usual there were drinks and snacks beforehand. Occasionally someone would come over to say hello and exchange a few pleasantries.

Then the speeches began. Well-known critics, friends and fellow writers spoke amusingly, movingly and briefly about the honoured guest's work. A comedian ('famous comedian' it would undoubtedly read in the morning paper's write-up) described how reading one of Laurence Paynter's books had inspired him to pursue his career. Then the event's compère introduced the individual who was to present the prize the Ambasadóir na hÉireann.

He recognised the voice as the hood descended.

Sunday Sonata

-That's a nuisance, I thought; my seat is taken.

I had climbed the thirty-nine steps from the station road. I was early for the Low Mass. I like to get that obligation out of the way so that I've got the rest of the day to myself. Today it is sunny, gloriously so. After all the rainfall of the past few weeks the prospect of a hill-walk was to be relished. So I had parked the car in my usual spot near the railway station. In the boot was my back-pack containing sandwiches, bottles of water, map and camera. Once the Mass was over I'd drive straight out of the city and into the hills to the south.

When I saw that my usual seat was taken- it is four rows back from the front in the small Lady Chapel and beside the alabaster crucifix with its missing toe- I felt slightly irritated. Two strangers- an elderly lady and a rather corpulent Franciscan friar- were firmly anchored in that row of three seats. I found myself wondering why they had decided to sit there.

As I walk past the side chapel to see what weekly leaflets there are on the piano at the rear of the nave, I am trying to decide where I should sit. I cannot bear to sit on the right-hand side in any church, don't ask me why. I could say it's because of my poor hearing- I'm virtually deaf in my right ear- but I've avoided the right-hand side long before my hearing went. Sitting on the left-hand side means that I have to twist my head slightly to the right in order to hear the short sermon the priest will give mid-way through the service. I often come away from Mass with a slight crick in my neck.

I am always curious as to what the priest will say to us. Sometimes I wonder what _I_ would say if I was there behind the lectern. I like short sermons; they're like a quick brush and scrub up before heading out into public. Those long, tedious Protestant affairs which roll on endlessly like boulders flung by Sisyphus numb my backside. Give me any day a quick shake of the pepper pot, a poke with the fork and let's get on with it!

I could sit behind the pair, I think. But then I surmise that the bulk of the friar would blot out everything in front. I like to look at the Fra Angelico triptych of the Annunciation behind the altar in which the angels seem to be wearing saucers on their heads. I don't fancy staring at his pate while the priest is going through the ritual. When I'm stuck like that- and it happens sometimes when there's a rush of summer-time visitors to the church- I find myself studying the shape of ears and hairlines and dandruff on collars, or ear-rings and the smell of perfume. I also had olfactory memories of the malodorous and silent farts Brother Taubars used to loose during the Hours when I was on retreat once. His face would be glowing with concentration as he meditated while those kneeling to his rear were gagging. I was convinced he was doing that deliberately; others held the more charitable view that he couldn't help himself; 'the wind bloweth where it listeth, and thou hearest the sound thereof, but canst not tell whence it cometh' and all that.

If I can't sit behind them, I think, then it will have to be in front. I can't sit immediately in front of them since I'd be all too conscious of their presence looming behind me. So it will have to be two rows in front. That's one row from the very front of the seats; but at least I can lean against the wall to my left.

Once I'm there I feel dreadfully exposed. That's one reason why I like to be further back, lost in the crowd as it were, just one of the passengers on the bus waiting for it to start. As a child I hated being seated at the front of the class. I didn't want to sit right at the back because that's where the miscreants would hide themselves. I'm sure I would have made a good galley slave, down there in the lower decks pulling on an oar rather than striding dominantly on the quarterdeck.

I've been worshipping here ever since I came to the city over thirty years ago. The first Sunday after I had arrived I went to a large church at the top of the main street leading down to the old docks. The church- a vast, stark hanger-like affair- had been virtually empty. I felt as though I was in the belly of some large, toothless beast. The liturgy was the 1929 order with all its 'thees' and 'thous'. Afterwards I felt as though I was an extra escaping from a bad mediaeval epic filmed by Ealing Studios and lacking an Olivier to spice it up. I wouldn't have been surprised to hear the cry 'An 'orse! An 'orse! My kingdom for an 'orse!'

Slowly worshippers are arriving for the Mass. Of course nobody chooses to sit in the row ahead of me, or even in either of the seats beside me; they all tuck themselves in behind me, where they can see but not be seen. I sense that there are more people than the four or five other regulars who attend. It's not a special feast day, just one of those ordinary Sundays during the year, after Pentecost and before Advent. I guess that some of them are visitors for the festival who are staying at one of the local hotels.

The old retired priest hobbles on his canes to the statuette of the Virgin and Child. He lights a candle and sticks it in one of the seven branches of the Menorah standing beside Her. A clump of freshly cut flowers stands in a vase at the base of the statuette. I recall the time an artificial bunch, too close to the flames, caught fire as the priest gave his sermon, which happened to be on 'the Burning Bush'.

When the bell sounds it's eyes down for a full house. I remember services when I was a youngster and it seemed to me that many of the adults were competing to see who could get on their knees the quickest! There are all kinds of techniques for doing so, some dictated by age and rheumatic joints, others pure showmanship like the high jump's Fosbury Flop. There's the straight drop; there's the gradual bend and wind; there's the crouch and collapse; there's the weary wilt- oh I've seen them all! How far down you sink is also a matter of style. Some prefer the L with a slight head droop topping it off; others go for the full crumple so that you end up like a Z. I've never seen the full prostration though I know it's rife amongst Higher Church breeds. Nowadays I just lower myself gently a knee at a time on to the cushion and cling to the ladderback chair in front, my balance not being what it was. Some of the chairs have uneven legs and wobble when you sit on them. The cleaner must move them around for they never seem to be in the same spot two weeks running.

It's the Rector today assisted by the diminutive female server. I don't know either of them outside the service. I like to keep myself to myself. It's much the same when I take my car to Charlie for its MOT or check-up. We'll chat briefly, I'll pay the bill, and that's the end of that until next time. I've heard that the Rector's marriage has broken down. We all have our problems and these things happen, I suppose. It can't be easy working the hours they do and being more or less constantly on call. There are difficulties for both married and unmarried priests. Myself, I've kept my head down and my nose clean all my working life in the civil service. The only call I've heard is for 'last orders please'.

Sorry, I missed that, I think as the motor starts to run.

I look at the order of service card I've collected from the back of the chapel and can't make sense of it. 'What on earth is the priest saying?' I wonder as I hear words which don't seem to make sense either. There's no *Gloria*, no *Creed* and no *Prayer of Humble Access*, Cranmer's masterpiece, printed on the card. But it's too late to change it. I am reminded of the time I sat in a Catholic church in Paris and heard a Tridentine Mass being said in Latin while I was struggling to make sense of it all in French. Now and then I catch a familiar phrase coming over the priest's shoulder and I squeak out a response; but the voices behind me are churning out something completely different. Thank goodness we're on our knees, I mutter feeling ridiculous.

We all sit when it's time for the readings. I'm still at a loss as the server reads what should be the epistle.

'Aliquam nec ante non lectus facilisis feugiat eu sit amet nibh.'

That can't be right, I tell myself. I don't recall Paul saying that, certainly not in *Romans*.

'Sed interdum fermentum massa at hendrerit.'

Maybe her dental plate is giving her trouble.

'Integer mauris lacus, eleifend non tincidunt nec, bibendum ut tortor.'

It could be the acoustics or my ears. I've been having trouble with them again recently. They fill with wax quickly. It was only a couple of months ago that I had them syringed. That was an oddly erotic experience at the time. When I told the nurse that she laughed and patted me on the shoulder in a motherly way. Not that I particularly wanted such an experience- it's been years since that tickle has nibbled at me; the snake's hiss of tinnitus has been more troubling.

'Nunc quis magna nibh.'

'Thanks be to God', I concur. Thank goodness that seems to that.

The server steps away from the lectern and stands to one side. Maybe we'll get some sense from the Rector. But he also seems to be having similar problems with enunciation. The Gospel is supposed to be about parables but instead it seems to me to be about puddles or poodles.

After a general zippering-north south east west (and some tap the sternum)- it's take your seats for the ten minute pep talk.

'Τέλειοι εργαλείων στη μα, προκύπτουν επεξεργασία συνεντεύξεις ναι ώς.'

Oh Lord, I think, this really isn't going very well.

'Φράση εργασίας προγραμματιστές να όρο, μέσης έστελνε κι λες, μη για νιρβάνα προσπάθεια εργαζόμενοι.'

He likes making eye-contact; they must teach you that at Cuddesdon. That way you can see when they're coming to get you.

'Αναφορά απαραίτητο λες τι, αν λες σελίδων επιδιόρθωσης μεταγλωτίσει.'

I must be missing something here, I think, as I hear the Franciscan chuckling behind me. It's a deep chuckle, the kind which comes from the belly. Thin Franciscans tend to giggle, I've found. I don't mind priests making jokes- in fact one of the best sermons I've heard was made by Rowan Atkinson in his one-man show some years ago- but I've always found erudite academic humour as dry as German gumboots- or it could be gunboats.

The service runs its course. The bits I can recognise I grab hold of with the fervour of a drowning man; the bits- and there are lots of them- which I don't understand (and not just theologically) I watch float past like an untethered astronaut outside the Shuttle.

I avoid the general skirmish around the Rector at the end by slipping rapidly out at the altar end of the chapel.

*

From my vantage point I can see hills and valleys in all directions. I've eaten my sandwiches and lie in the sun reading some Tabucchi short stories. Throughout my walk and the gradual climb of the shoulder of the hills I've observed all kinds of wildlife, all kinds of growing things. There are times when I wish I could nail them all with names more specific than bird or bush or flower. But I don't have that kind of mind. I enjoy the not knowing as much as others might enjoy the knowing. As a child- and such memories float about within me like the wispy clouds that decorate the blue sky above me- I would give new things I came across my own names. Those names I have forgotten, of course, but they would do just as well as the Latinised tags we use for flowers and animal or insect species.

It has been a while since I have climbed this particular hill. My health has not been good. Up here I feel refreshed as I look down on what were ancient kingdoms. Dotted about the landscape, invisible to my untrained eye but there nevertheless are ancient camp sites, tumuli, burial grounds and hill forts. The Romans, the Selgovae, Votadini and others meandered over this land, following the ridges or the valleys. Every so often someone with a metal detector will discover a treasure trove. As a child I remember playing hookey on the hill that overlooked the town where I grew up. I would imagine that I was an explorer, someone discovering that place for the first time. Behind me would be the overgrown redoubts built centuries ago and out at sea I would faintly make out the forts built to guard the harbour against invasion. Nowadays they are either abandoned or have been turned into luxury restaurants to which diners are taken by helicopter.

Up here I seldom think. I like to observe and up here I seem to become a pure observer. What I see does not change, or so it seems. There is a givenness about this landscape, which an age ago was under thick layers of ice. In my mind's eye I can see this as I lie daydreaming in the sunlight. What others may see may well differ. To me this high point has become necessary. The views from my windows in the city are restricted and what they reveal must be compensated by such natural beauty if I am to remain at peace and intact- or so I've come to believe. Looking back I cannot countenance growing up without those times I spent upon the hill. Nobody ever knew about them, those days I'd feign sickness and miss school.

*

At home in the evening after my shower I try to continue working on the story I'm attempting to squeeze from information I've found about Arletty, the French actress famous for her appearances in '*Hôtel du Nord*' and '*Les Enfants du Paradis*'. She fell in love with a younger man, a German Luftwaffe officer Hans Soehring and had an affair with him during the nineteen forties. After France was liberated she was arrested in October 1944, interrogated and imprisoned for two months in Drancy internment camp. Like many other women who had collaborated she had her hair shorn. When she was released she spent eighteen months exiled to the Château de la Houssaye-en-Brie outside Paris, which she could not enter. Her film career was effectively over although she appeared in minor roles later and also acted on the stage.

I wondered why a writer such as de Beauvoir didn't write about her and turn her into some kind of 'existential heroine' the way that Sartre turned Jean Genet into a 'saint'. Perhaps it's easier to write about a thief than it is about a collaboratist. Perhaps it's easier to silence someone who writes (which is effectively what Sartre did to Genet with his book) than it is to vanish someone who acts. Arletty on the screen or stage was never less than Arletty in real life. There was an androgynous amoral boldness about her, an indifference to opinion proclaimed in the title of her autobiography '*Je suis que je suis*'. It is therein that she contradicts the popular version of what she said during her interrogation, maintaining that she had been talking about her 'soeur' and her 'culottes'.

The one role she was most suited to was that of Joan of Arc. She appeared at the *Théâtre Guignard* in Montmartre in this role in the 1953 production of Genet's 'Jeanne Jaune', based on St. Thérèse of Lisieux's plays '*The Mission of Joan of Arc*' and '*Joan of Arc accomplishes her Mission*'. Interwoven were extracts from Arletty's own trial and auto-erotic dream scenes based upon Genet's prison memoirs. The opening night (May 30th) was a 'succès de scandale' and a 'cause célèbre' in the great tradition of Jarry's 'Ubu Roi'. Those who had packed into the small theatre to boo Arletty ended up cheering her; while those who had come to cheer ended up weeping. Arletty really did bare her backside for the burning at the stake scene. The play was banned- Genet was said to have overstepped the bounds of decency and to have offended the hierarchy of the church; the theatre was closed for breaching non-existent fire regulations; and reputations were made or destroyed, sometimes both at the same time. Posters were ripped from the walls and sold almost as religious relics. All copies of the script were confiscated and ceremonially burnt under the direct orders of the President. Only a few survive in the hands of private collectors who prefer to remain anonymous. The play has never been staged since though it was rumoured that Godard wished to make a film of it with Deneuve in the title role.

Late at night, as I'm falling asleep I wonder about that missing toe. It strikes me as less than coincidental that all the images in that little chapel have bits missing. The statue of the Virgin Mary is minus a pinkie and the Baby is missing an ear. The large crucifix affixed to a ceiling crossbeam above the lectern is missing a different toe. The wall carving of one of the Stations of the Cross depicts the Saviour with only one eye.

I fall asleep imagining myself on a hill-top watching a pyre being built in the valley below.

A Straightforward Assignment

'We need to check out this information,' the Section Head said to his depute. 'It's really not worth sending someone like Wiggins. He's too valuable. We may need him if things deteriorate further in Karachi. Who's available?'

Denton opened the file he had placed on his side of the desk at the beginning of the meeting. He really didn't need to look at its contents since he had already made his choice. But the Head didn't like to be anticipated- guided and informed, yes but not anticipated. So Denton made a show of leafing through the papers, each of which bore a photograph at the top of the page and a summary underneath that. He took out the one he had already mentally ear-marked after a few moments of apparent consideration.

'There's Albyn, sir,'

'Albyn? Tell me about him.'

'He's relatively new, sir. Finished his training with excellent marks. He's clever and unobtrusive. He knows several languages, including Turkish I see. He's a promising addition to the strength but has had no field experience so far.'

'Nobody else more experienced?'

'There's one or two, sir; but this strikes me as a good opportunity to see how Albyn handles things. As you say it's not a high risk job but a straightforward check on information received. Ideal, I'd say, for someone like Albyn.'

The Section Head held out a hand to take the sheet of paper Denton was passing to him.

'Not the kind who stands out in a crowd, you say.'

'He knows how to listen, sir, how to sort out the important from the unimportant. He follows orders. A clean pair of hands and not over eager to shine.'

'All right, Denton. You're right; this doesn't require the kind of experience the others have got. If he's successful then we've got another agent with some field experience. Brief him personally and stress that it's purely an information checking operation. He's to report directly to you. Keep me up to date, will you? I'll need to brief the Minister once we're clear about this whisper.'

'Of course, sir. I'll see to it at once.'

Well that went smoothly, Denton thought satisfied as he made his way back to his office on a lower floor. There was no reason why it shouldn't have, of course. There was nothing the Section Head liked better than easy decisions. If he ran true to form, Denton thought, he would be off for the remainder of the day 'networking' with Civil Servants and Ministers in pursuit of the step after his recent O.B.E.

'Get hold of Albyn for me, would you?' Denton called out to his secretary Suzanne as he hurried across her office towards his door. 'Schedule a meeting for us as soon as is possible-tomorrow, if there's space.'

Denton smiled as he pulled the door shut behind himself and he strode to the window, tossing the folder on to his desk set beside it. He stared down into the busy thoroughfare several storeys below his vantage point. Yes, he told himself again; that went surprisingly well.

*

Well, here I am, Moore thought as he turned another page of Cordwainer Smith's *A Planet named Shayol* in 'Rediscovery of Man', the book he was reading. In the hotel room behind him much of the bulk of the contents in his suitcase was made up of paperbacks brought for the holiday. As was often the case it had all been a last minute thing packing and letting those few people know who he wanted to know. He'd put a hold on the mail, paid the gas and electricity bills well in advance, told his neighbours and phoned to book the taxi the day before he was due to depart. In fact it had arrived the day before his actual departure and he had sent it away to return the following day, paying the driver handsomely for his trouble. Always keep in with taxi drivers and barmen that was the kind of wisdom he valued. He'd just finished a bowl of bran flakes that morning- *this* morning he corrected himself as he turned another page- when he remembered that he hadn't packed a bag. Lucky the office can't see me now, he had thought as he ran his eyes over the shelves of books and pulled this one and that down at random. Of course he had forgotten stuff- his toothbrush, for example. As soon as he'd dumped his bag on the bed and tipped the porter, he'd decided to head out to the nearest shopping centre and buy all that he needed.

Once he had taken in the sights and sounds of the street below his balcony he took a shower, put on cooler clothes and headed over to the 'Good Luck Club' and casino. Watching others gamble helped him not to. His father had gambled. Like many working class men of his father's generation it had been the dogs. He'd backed the dogs and had gone to the dogs, which is why James' mother took the four year old boy and left with him. All that he remembered of his father was the smell of tobacco smoke which clung to a flat cap. Moore had never liked dogs particularly. The working kind of dog, that was useful; but the others which ponced about on the heels of their master or mistress and yapped, crapped and piddled indiscriminately, those he thought little better than vermin. In Korea, he understood, they ate dogs, which he thought was going a bit too far. If he ever went to Korea he would stick strictly to a vegetarian diet, he told himself.

The '*Iyi şanslar*' Club and Casino in Ankara was noted for its opulence once you were through the rather unprepossessing entrance. Moore having nothing to compare it with withheld judgement on his surroundings. However the barman had made a fine cocktail for him and he sipped it with pleasure as he took in his surroundings. Up the stairs and through what looked like a wide decorated double marble archway was the main gambling room. He'd check that later. In the meantime he found an out of the way table and sank into one of the numerous leather armchairs scattered around this ground floor room. In a far corner of the room a small quartet were playing music. Overhead fans turned like sultry dancers; but the real cooled air was being discreetly circulated by the hidden air-conditioning vents. Evening was only marginally cooler than daytime outside; inside there was some relief from the heat. One thing you could guarantee about Turkey was that you'd sweat, Moore thought.

Whenever he found himself in a new place- not so much found as put himself in such a place- Moore would take his time to familiarise himself with his surroundings: the people, the lavatories, the entrances and exits, the closed doors and windows. Even when he went into a church or mosque he would do the same. One ex-girl-friend's mother had once commented on the way he gave their Chiltern home the once-over every time he visited. He couldn't believe their awful taste and the barbaric effects they chose to call landscaping.

Those who noticed him sitting with his eyes closed might think he was just another tired businessman; but inside he was reconstructing what he could not now see, so that should the lights suddenly fail he would know exactly who stood where and how to make his way to the nearest exit. As a child he had been the one in the family who would lead them out of the maze in the grounds of many an historic mansion. He never got lost, even when he wished that he would.

'May I join you?'

When he opened his eyes- without hurry, as he did most things- he recognised the young woman who had preceded him into the club.

'Please do.'

There were dozens of empty tables around but he had never had any doubt that she would come to sit at his.

'I thought I recognised a kindred new spirit,' she smiled. 'I've just arrived and came along to check the place out. You looked as though you were doing the same.'

'Arrived late this afternoon,' he smiled in return.

'My name's Katerina Burton.'

'James Moore,' he said, offering his hand. 'From London.'

'I've just come in from Athens. Doing the tour while it's still possible. Home's in the Isle of Man.'

'Never been there.'

'If you get the chance do visit; it's delightful.'

After the brief introductions came the pause. Without appearing to do so he watched as she gazed around at the club, her eyes wide as though to soak it all in: the glitter, the sparkle, the laughter, the posturing and the background reek of money, money being spent and money being won. There was a certain intoxicating odour in the air.

'Not quite Southend,' he said dryly.

'Southend?'

'Used to go there with my mates when I was at Poly,' he said. 'Big thing in those days when you were a student was to get into a club and play the wheel. We'd put all our cash together and one of us would play for the others. We'd each keep just enough for a couple of drinks. Never had any luck; who does? The House always wins.'

'Fancy going upstairs for a look see?'

'Why not?' he replied.

He wasn't sure if he'd been picked up or not. Maybe she just wanted company for a few hours until she'd found her holiday legs, as it were. He decided there was no harm in it. She was a pleasant young woman-attractive, inquisitive, ready to smile and certainly not pushy. He doubted that he'd see her after tonight. He followed her up the stairway, deciding that her legs were just fine as they were.

The upper floor was several smaller rooms joined by ornately decorated arches. In each room some kind of card or dice game- Baccarat, blackjack, poker, - was going on. At the far end of the series of rooms, in the largest open area was the roulette wheel. Monkey-jacketed waiters wearing fezes moved around discreetly bringing drinks from the bar area to the left. There you could sit while watching the swirl of players and onlookers at the tables. Around the walls were frescos of historic incidents and scenery. The main ceiling- a swirling pattern of floral and Kufic calligraphic mosaic tiling in turquoise, cobalt blue and violet- seemed to catch and hold shadows. The lighting over the tables was bright; elsewhere it was dimmed.

He followed her to the bar where they freshened their drinks. He noted that she didn't hesitate as though inviting him to pay but was opening her purse and offering payment for her own. He liked that show of independence. They might be together but so far that meant nothing significant. As he paid for his drink she was moving across to the nearest gaming table. He could follow her or drift off in his own direction. With a smile Moore followed her.

All the male players were wearing cuff-links, Moore noticed. His own shirt had button down cuffs. He studied the fingers and hand movements of the players. Faces would only tell you so much. Nobody at the table wore spectacles but one man had contact lenses, he was sure of it. There were two women, both in their fifties he'd say, also playing. They each had vividly sparkling rings on their fingers and heavy gold necklaces around their necks. From the chips in front of them he'd say that they were winning. Neither of them was sweating, though all the men would occasionally mop their forehead or cheeks with crisp white handkerchiefs. Why weren't the two ladies sweating? Were they adherents of some obscure yoga regime which gave you control over your sweat glands?

Katerina Burton had made her slow, measured circuit of the table and was now by his right hand side.

'Utah and Nevada,' she whispered.

'I had them down as Montana and Oregon', he whispered back.

'Easy mistake to make.'

A couple of players rose to cash in their chips.

'Shall we play?' she whispered.

'I never do,' he replied.

'Mind if I have a flutter?'

'Be my guest.'

As she took a seat Moore stood behind her chair and watched the play unfold. At least in this game you had a chance to win, he thought. The cards were dealt and that was all the House seemed to do. Somewhere amongst the players, though, Moore was prepared to bet that there was a plant, someone who played 'for' the House. If he stayed around long enough he was sure that he'd be able to spot the plant, a professional whose job was simply to help the House. A percentage of what that player won would go to the House; and whatever excitement he or she generated would bring more punters to the table. As he watched he could see the glances of the other players checking her out and then him. He let himself drift around the table as she had done so that he could study each of the players in turn. At each of the other women he paused to work out why she made it Utah or Nevada rather than Montana or Oregon. He caught her amused glance as he made the connection and smiled silently applauding back at her. Clearly there were advantages to being from the Isle of Man.

'Would you like me to freshen that for you, sir?' a voice asked him.

'Actually a sparkling water with ice and a touch of fresh lime would do the trick,' he replied as he handed the glass to the waiter. 'And perhaps you could ask the young lady over there if she'd like anything.'

'Certainly sir.'

She didn't look up from her cards as the waiter leant close to her and whispered; but he caught her nod and the movement of her lips as she made her request to the waiter. When the waiter returned he took the drink first to her at the table and then brought a frosted glass to Moore, who put a note on the tray. Wordlessly he indicated that the waiter could keep the change and received an equally wordless blink of gratitude. She still had not looked up from the table. Moore had to admit that he was intrigued. He moved to a position behind her chair and watched the flow of the game while sipping his drink. He could not have made it any better if he'd made it himself.

In half an hour Katerina Burton from the Isle of Man had amassed a tidy sum in winnings. The ladies from Utah and Nevada were not taking kindly to this. He wasn't sure whether they objected more to her having no rings, necklace or other visible bodily adornments than to the fact that she was cutting into their pie. When she stood up indicating she was leaving the game the look in Utah's eyes was one of suspicion while in that of Nevada it was relief.

'That went well', she said as they moved further into the room.

'You seemed to know what you were doing,' he replied.

'Bad upbringing,' she said. 'Father was a stage magician; mother was a university professor in mathematics. Quite unlikely that with those genes I'd turn out to be a gardener. My brother, the jockey, he's the bad apple I'm afraid. Why don't you play? You've got a good eye for what's going on.'

'My father used to bet on the dogs,' Moore said. 'I remember what that did to him, to us. Not a lesson you want to forget or repeat.'

'Sensible man. Shall we move further in? The stakes get higher, I'm told, and the excitement becomes positively Byzantine!'

'Definitely not Southend, then.'

'Definitely not.'

'Albyn's report is rather concerning, sir.'

'Oh? I thought everything was straightforward?'

'It is, sir; or rather was. It's just that there seem to be elements we weren't able to anticipate.'

'Give me the details, Denton.'

Denton settled himself to relay Albyn's recent summary. On his face he kept a slightly worried look, although inside he was smiling at how well things were starting to turn out. He had thought that it might take a few days- a week perhaps- before Albyn's report told him what he wanted to hear; but Albyn had proved himself to be more than capable. He had done nothing but observe, just as he had been instructed to do. He had not doubted himself or waited unnecessarily to confirm what he first noticed, but had immediately communicated his findings. Denton had to admit that he had some misgivings in returning so quickly to the Section Head with this news; but he knew that his hesitancy was unnecessary. He had known that this would happen and the only   potential problem was whether or not Albyn, given his rank rawness in the field, would make the connections quickly or slowly. The fact that he had done so almost at once would endorse Denton's faith in him. Clearly the acuteness of the situation was not something for which he could be held responsible.

The Section Head listened as Denton presented his summary. Denton sat back and watched as his superior gazed out of the window. He won't know what to do, Denton thought; but he won't want me to know that.

'He's your man,' the Section Head said. 'What do you think of it? Can we leave it up to him to sort out?'

'At this stage I think so, sir.'

' "At this stage..."; does that mean you think things might deteriorate?'

'Not at all, sir. It's just that, having received this rather surprising piece of information we'd best be aware that there may be other revelations further down the line. Had everything been as we'd hoped it might be Albyn would be on the next plane home and we'd be looking at something else entirely. How things play out now will be a further test of Albyn's ability, which I've every confidence in given the way he has responded to this unexpected development. But we are in the happy position of knowing that if- and I repeat it's *if*- things do take a further twist we've got the likes of Halford and Hoben returning from leave and therefore available.'

'So you suggest what?'

'Leave it with Albyn for the time being and re-assess the situation in the light of his daily reports.'

'He'll be making daily reports?'

'Yes sir; I've instructed him to do so already.'

'Well done, Denton. The Minister will be pleased even though things are a little more complicated than we had hoped. I'm available to you on a daily basis should that be necessary, understood? We want to keep on top of things given what's happening in Somalia.'

*

Albyn sat outside the small café opposite Gençlik Park watching the world going by. Large yellow umbrellas with tasselled fringes offered shade at the tables for those who wanted it. Like any other tourist he was dressed casually- open-necked linen shirt, linen jacket draped over the back of his chair, casual trousers and loafers on his feet. Occasionally he would fan his face with his lightweight fedora which otherwise lay upturned beside him on the metalwork table. He wore prescription sunglasses and behind the dark lenses his eyes were constantly scanning the street. When a waiter passed he ordered another sweet black coffee and some tahini halva. Now and then he would pick up one of the papers- the *Hürriyet* and *Cumhuriyet*- which lay near his elbow as it rested on the table. He would read an article with some deliberation and light another 'Helmar' cigarette as he neatly folded and laid the paper back on top of its sister. Had you asked him what he had just read he would have been able to repeat it verbatim and to provide a passable English translation. Although he had read the papers completely through once already each time he picked one up it was as though he was reading the article he choose for the first time. Between his eyebrows was just the merest of vee-shaped creases as he concentrated.

A pick-pocket or mugger would have been disappointed on several counts had one tried his luck with Albyn. His wallet was not where a wallet should be for a start; and Albyn was adept at disabling any assailant. Those who had seen him responding to such an attack swore that all he seemed to do was brush the assailant with a few patting motions, the resulting collapse of such an attacker easily being attributed to the heat rather than physical force. Not that Albyn expected to be attacked. There was an assured litheness about him when he walked which usually made potential muggers look elsewhere. The Turkish language newspapers were also a good defence against those beggars who might be working the street where he was sitting having his morning coffee. The beggars and robbers tended to target those more obviously visiting the city; whilst he had the air of a tourist- the light skin for one thing- Albyn also could easily have been a national.

There were two things on his mind as he sat and smoke contentedly. Well three if you counted the delightful young lady staying by the purest chance in the same hotel as him. He was awaiting a reply to his message of yesterday evening to his Aunt Josephine in London, to whom he had described his safe arrival and some of the sights he had already seen. He was also wondering who had been through his belongings in the suite while he had been enjoying himself at the Casino the previous evening. They would have found nothing other than a list of addresses to which postcards were to be sent and a collection of photographs of a lovely old lady and others in the back garden of a fine looking Sussex mansion. The burglars had been very careful, so he doubted it was the normal run of the mill hotel burglar checking out a new arrival. He had reported the intrusion discreetly to the hotel management and they had been mortified. Hotel security was alerted and steps would be taken, he was assured. He was also offered a fifty per cent discount on his bill which, since Her Majesty's Government was slightly strapped for cash these days, Albyn happily accepted.

The great thing about Albyn, one of his trainers had said, was the way he detaches himself from things- his past, people, his surroundings, whatever it is necessary for him to shed in order to be who he has to be. Maybe it had to do with his ability on the amateur stage to inhabit any role and make it so believable that even those who knew him well seemed bewildered by the person he became. That was how he had been talent-spotted whilst at Cambridge taking part in an Edinburgh Fringe festival production of Pirandello's plays. At that point in his life- about to graduate with honours and wondering if he was really cut out for life in a financial firm in the City which is where his step-father saw his future- Albyn would have welcomed the opportunity to join a travelling circus. It was a well-known and floridly bisexual Knight of the stage and screen who had approached him after one show and suggested a few drinks together while they discussed 'the future'. Albyn knew he was not an unattractive fellow, though he also knew he was thoroughly heterosexual, if he was sexual at all. His comrades in the cast had hooted with derision when he told them Sir Whatshisname had invited him to meet for drinks in 'The Gay Hussar'. 'If you're not back by midnight we'll send a search party,' his comrades warned.

'I've been following your career with some interest, Charles- I may call you Charles, mayn't I? Charlie is not quite you and Chas is rather toadish,' Sir Whatshisname said as he unwrapped the scarf from his neck. Whatever the weather- and here it was the height of summer- he was always to be seen wearing a long, multi-coloured scarf. Fans would dispute how long the scarf was and whether or not there were several similar scarves marginally longer or shorter than each other. It was a secret, he had once told a television chat-show host, which would only be solved once he was in his grave. 'Don't worry, dear boy, I'm not after your virtue. Tell me, how do you see your future?'

Albyn, fortified with a good Islay malt, had told Tom- 'just call me Tom, dear boy and forget all the Sir rubbish: it looks good on the billboards and puts bums on the seats, that's all it's worth really'- that whilst his mother and step-father wished him to go into merchant banking or something like that in the City, his heart was not in that kind of future. He would do it, to keep them happy, as he was sure that he would marry one or other of the daughters of family friends who were constantly being brought to his attention. He knew that he was not destined to be a great actor like Tom-'dear boy, flattery is not your style; I'm well past me prime and they just bring me in for gravitas and that kind of thing these days'- he had no illusions in that direction. But he wished he could do something with the acting ability he knew he had. Tom had studied him for some minutes and Albyn returned his gaze.

'I know people in London,' Tom said. 'I'm a bit of a talent scout for them. I'm sure they'd be interested in meeting with you to discuss…possibilities which don't entail working in banks. In fact I've already mentioned you as a possible recruit and they've given me carte blanche to contact you. They humour me these days but I like to think they trust my judgment.'

'It sounds…mysterious,' Albyn replied already hooked on the prospect of a career which offered more than a bank could. 'What does it entail?'

'That I'll leave up to them to tell you,' Tom said. 'If you give me your mobile number I'll get them to call you and arrange an interview. Would that suit?'

Of course, Albyn said enthusiastically. Albyn had another malt and then Tom sent him back to his comrades, encouraging him to blandish them with tales of outrageous and failed seduction. 'It's what they'd expect, dear boy, and won't do my reputation an ounce of harm. Besides, I've got my eye on someone at the bar and it's best if you're not around to queer my pitch, as it were.

*

Denton considered his socks. There were a multitude of them in his sock drawer, which was below his underwear drawer, likewise below his shirt drawer. In the very top drawer were his ties. He could hear his wife downstairs on the phone. She had one of those voices which penetrated walls. In a submarine she would have caused a mutiny within hours of any plunge below the surface. It was fortunate that he had always been slightly deaf; it was thus that he had avoided over the thirty odd years of their marriage the worst excesses of her decibel level. The surprising thing was Denton told himself as he pulled on his navy blue hose, that in company his wife's voice level became quite normal, indeed almost a whisper. He had never told her he was slightly deaf for the same reason that he had never told her that he was sleeping with his long-term secretary: he didn't want her to know anything more than she already knew the morning after their first night together as a married couple. The marriage had been his mother's idea, and not one of her better ones. True, his wife came from a wealthy background and had roots in the country going back to the Normans, which combination of factors helped his career no end. It was also true that his wife had quickly born fruit and produced three male off-spring within four years, thus taking care of his mother's need to be a grandmother. She did not enjoy that status long, dropping dead within a month of the birth of the third child. Perhaps I could have stopped at two, Denton thought; but then it had been a relief to see her put in the ground. The continuous dialogue she and his wife had had over Denton's head wherever they were- opera, dinner table, or the back of the Rolls- at least had come to a full stop. He now only got an ache in one ear.

'Do hurry up, Godfrey,' she bellowed from the foot of the stairs.

The fact that he was tardy in getting dressed she in no way attributed to her having lingered in the bath for as long as she had while he waited to be able to shave. They may have separate bedrooms but the bathroom remained a shared facility. His wife had laid it down as an immutable rule that when she was soaking in the bath nothing short of the house burning down was to disturb her or occasion anyone- that could only mean him- intruding upon her privacy. She lived such a public life, she maintained, that her only inviolable personal space was the bathroom. Frankly, he was pleased to be able to comply with her wish and sincerely hoped that any lover she might take up with would show the same concern. Not that anyone had attempted to pass under her portcullis, as it were. The knowledge that her husband was 'something in the security services' tended to cool the interest of most men, had she not already done that by hosing them down with a volley from her larynx.

With a last look at himself in the mirror Denton moved out of the bedroom and began to descend the staircase. His wife gave him a steady overall appraisal as he reached the foot of the stairs and turned on her heels to head for the door. It was going to be, Denton decided, one of *those* nights at the opera.

The phone rang right on cue as he reached the open door and saw her poised to get into the back of the Rolls as Bradley held the door for her.

'Do leave that, Godfrey. We already should have been on our way.'

'Sorry, my dear, have to take it. Might be nothing in any case.'

He knew that it wouldn't be and she, as a result of many such last minute calls, likewise knew that it was unlikely to be anyone except his office.

'Something's come up, sir,' Suzanne said with just the right amount of concern in her voice in case it had been his wife who had answered.

Denton called out to Bradley to take his wife on and that he'd follow as soon as he could. With the phone to his ear he watched as the Rolls noiselessly pulled away from the house and disappeared up the curving driveway to the gate.

'She's just left,' he said. ' I'll be with you within half an hour.'

By taking the alternative route in the MG Denton, who had enjoyed rally-cross racing in his younger years (before his mother and new wife decided it was too dangerous for a man with responsibilties such as he now had to continue doing), reached the city's outskirts before the Rolls and was making love to his secretary half an hour before the curtain rose at Covent Garden. Their mutual needs satisfied Suzanne drove him to the opera house and he arrived just as the lights were dimming and the curtain rising.

'Crisis sorted,' he said as he sank into his seat.

He only then noticed that he had put back on the wrong pair of socks. Throughout the first act of 'Manon Lescault' Denton found himself wondering whose socks the pair he now had on were.

*

'This is a very pleasant idea,' Katerina said as they sipped Boza and strolled around Ankara Citadel, admiring the marble and red stone of the inner castle walls.

Moore thought so as well. It was one thing to walk through the neighbourhood pazars and streets yourself, another to be doing it in the company of a young woman such as she.

It was how it had come about that he found interesting and suggestive.

In the casino the previous evening he had watched for a while as she had gambled on the roulette wheel. Her cheeks had been flushed and she had become more and more caught up in the game. Moore found himself having sudden visions of his father returning from the greyhound track. He thought he had long since discarded those from his interior world. His father had looked so pathetic and apologetic as he came in, his pockets empty and his eyes those of a beaten dog. It was not something he was supposed to have seen: his mother would have long ago put him to bed and crooned to him until he was asleep. But he always woke up when he heard his father's faltering, dragging footsteps in the lane outside. His father would never come directly in but would wander past the house, up the lane and back again, screwing up his courage to come in. For James that was the worst part. He would sneak from his room and hide on the landing. When the back door finally opened- always the back door never the front door for those moments of humiliation- James would be able to just see his father's sorrowful face and downcast eyes. What excuses or promises to change he made James would never hear as his mother would always close the kitchen door before she brought her husband his now cold meal to eat. Every Friday the same scene would be enacted. They all coalesced into one in James' memory as he watched Katerina's fascinated eyes following the ball as it bounced around the spinning wheel. When seemed to hypnotise her and all those others at the table bored and sickened him, so that he found himself slipping quietly away and down into the lower room. He doubted that she noticed him leaving. I shall have a last drink, he told himself and then I shall walk back to the hotel and read a few more chapters of my book.

He was surprised when he saw her coming down from the upper level a few moments later, clearly looking about for him and waving when she saw him. 'Lucky again!' she said with delight as she showed him the bagful of notes. As she sat down to join him in a last drink she caught his mood. 'Why so solemn?' she asked and he explained how the scene upstairs had brought back those unpleasant memories. She apologised but he told her it wasn't her fault. He hadn't expected it, that was all. He'd not had those memories churned up for years. She said she would make it up to him (though there was nothing to 'make up' he felt) and suggested that they spent the following day seeing the sights, since for both it was their first time in Ankara. James agreed to that and offered to walk her back to her hotel, given the amount of money she had won. Why had he not been surprised to find that she was staying at the same hotel as him? There were those who believed in coincidence but James Moore was not one of those. Nor did he believe in luck where gambling was concerned.

*

The *Hayal Dünyası* cinema on the Konor Sok left much to be desired, Albyn thought as he took his seat. He had his choice of seats, the cinema being virtually empty as it was the first show of the day. He counted the seventh row from the front and the seventh seat in from the aisle. Once he had taken his seat his hand swiftly felt under it, found the small package and quickly transferred it into his trouser pocket. When the house lights dimmed Albyn moved across the aisle to another seat. According to the handbook at headquarters he should have exited at once, job done; but he decided to watch the film, there being little else to do once he'd made the collection.

The advent of television had destroyed many small cinemas. Albyn was one of those who regretted this change. He also missed milk bottles on doorsteps. You can't halt progress but you can miss what the bulldozer knocks over. He lit a cigarette and sat back as he used to do as a teenager in the local 'Roxy', his knees drawn up and jammed against the seat in front. A flickering beam of light began to paint black and white images on the rather grubby screen and a scratchy soundtrack of noise- music, voices, street sounds- filled the cinema. The film began with a chase and arrest in a crowded street, all happening as the credits rolled in English, with Turkish subtitles along the bottom edge of the screen.

*

The story he was reading might well have been written by Graham Greene, Moore thought as he put the paperback to one side. He had been unable to sleep, his thoughts troubled by the incident he had witnessed with Katerina that afternoon. There had been a chase by plain-clothed police- or he assumed they were the police- an arrest and some man had been bundled into a car to be driven away at top speed. It had happened suddenly and quickly. It was almost like a scene in a movie being made on location. Moore had found himself wondering what the man might have done. He seemed a perfectly respectable looking fellow and had been sitting at a table reading a newspaper. Then several burly men came hurtling out of a series of black cars which screeched to a halt by the café. The man had leapt up and made a run for it- was this a sign that he was guilty of something? Although it had been all over in a matter of minutes Moore had found himself trembling. What if that had been me? A quite preposterous idea, he tried to reassure himself, since he was simply a tourist enjoying a week's holiday in Turkey. He wasn't doing anything illegal such as smuggling drugs.

The thought wouldn't go away as he lay there on the bed, the window open and the ceiling fan slicing the warm night air. He could only read a few lines of the book and then would set it aside to gaze thoughtfully into the darkness of the night outside. Even when he put out the light and tried to make himself sleep he couldn't get rid of the image of that man being hurried away to face who knew what. He certainly wasn't getting first prize in the weekly lottery, that was for sure. What Moore also recalled vividly was Katerina's blasé reaction-'Nothing to do with us,' she had said and carried on with their sightseeing walk.

*

Albyn watched as the man who had been shadowing him was taken away by the police. He'd spotted the tail before he'd gone into the cinema. He didn't wonder how long the man had been tailing him but he did wonder why. It could just be a mugger staking him out; but Albyn felt certain this was one of the opposition. The locals would have politely asked him to get into a car and questioned him at their headquarters. But why should anyone look at him twice? I'm an unknown face and here a mere twenty-four hours on a simple job and somehow I've got a tail. Something has leaked somewhere. Then just as unexpectedly, while Albyn was having some refreshment and trying to decide how to drop his tail without that appearing too obvious, the dog-catchers turn up and net the chap! Who arranged that and why? He would have felt thankful except that it all stank of leaks everywhere. Should he abort his trip to the cinema? No, he had told himself; let's brass neck this out. Even if it's what someone wants me to do let's do it and see what happens.

He wrote three or four postcards, to his aunt and a couple of friends. In these the message was basically the same, though in his haste as he scrawled the words he made one or two mistakes on each card. Nothing serious, just the odd spelling mistake, some of which he corrected by striking through the errant letter and some of which he left. Not even a native English speaker would have made anything of this. The message was what would be expected from a single man on holiday abroad. He told his aunt that he was 'off to the race track tomorrow' and that he 'rather fancied' certain named horses (the names having been taken from the cards printed in the daily papers). He reassured his aunt that he 'wasn't gambling heavily' and that he was 'having a great time'. There was 'lots to see', 'the food was good' and 'the weather was fine, if a trifle sultry' for his liking.

Albyn dropped the cards off at the hotel reception desk asking that they be stamped and sent with the next post. They would be quietly removed from the other outgoing post, he knew, and swiftly conveyed to wherever it was that the coded messages were sent from.

*

The racetrack was built on the drained site of former marshland which had been the source of many feverish epidemics in the city's past. Once there had been a fine view across to the fortified hills of Ulus, the old town, but nowadays there were buildings obscuring most of that view.

Katerina stood out among the crowds of elegant and well-dressed women with the sheer simplicity of her clothes. The hat she wore contrasted sharply with the more exotic attire of the wealthy wives and companions in the members enclosure. Her one-piece cotton dress showed off her slim figure admirably. Moore felt rather out of his depth as he escorted her to their seats in the box. She continued to surprise him. How on earth had she managed to get them tickets to such a swank box, he wondered. When she had suggested that they go to the racetrack he had been torn between wanting to accompany her and not wanting to put himself in another gambling situation. His internal debate had been short and one-sided. Moore was aware that he had become quite fond of her- two days in her company and he knew he was smitten. She was behaving like the slightly older sister he had never had but had often imagined. She seemed oblivious to the effect that she was having on him and that was part of her charm. He told himself just to enjoy it, the holiday and this unexpected friendship. She was doing his ego the world of good in any case. When had he last had an attractive woman wanting to spend so much time in his company? He had told her more about himself in the short time they had known each other than he had told anyone else ever. In contrast, apart from those brief details she gave him in the casino, he knew virtually nothing else substantial about her. He knew what he saw- and liked very much- but what job she did, where she lived, and other details about her life were still a mystery to him. Maybe she was the sort of person who when on holiday simply dropped all that and lived within the flow of the moment. One thing was certain and that was all Katerina had to do was to smile at him (as she was doing now) and all those thoughts fled from his mind.

'I know you don't approve, James, but I'm going to have a little flutter.'

'It's more the case that I don't indulge, Kat, than that I disapprove,' he replied. 'Flutter away. That's what we're here for, I guess.'

Moore watched as she went off to place a bet.

He thought he caught sight of a familiar figure in the crowd but it was too fleeting a glimpse to make any real impact on him. Hightly unlikely, James old boy, he told himself, that you'd encounter someone from the office out here! Throughout the afternoon, however, each time Katerina left his side to 'have another flutter' Moore felt uneasily that there was someone familiar out there in the crowd, someone watching them.

This is nonsense, he told himself. There are several thousand people in the crowd and there's no reason in the world why any one of them should be taking a special interest in me- or her. Then he corrected himself: Well, me undoubtedly, but do I really know that someone wouldn't be watching Katerina? What about 'white slavery'? Come on, James, you dolt; keep a grip on things. For some reason your imagination is starting to take off; maybe it's the books your reading when you fall asleep. Which story was it last night, *I Married a Dead Man* by Cornell Woolrich? Maybe you should try some *Blandings Castle* he advised himself.

Albyn watched the woman making her way to the window to place a bet. He wondered what horse she was putting the money on- Kafkasli, Geçimsizik, Yikim or Malikan? He had manouevred himself so that he was standing directly behind her. He could smell her perfume, an orange flower kolonya- very nice, he thought. When someone bumped him from behind it was only natural that he should bump into her slightly.

'I do apologise,' he said as he took her elbow to steady her. 'Someone behind...'

They both looked back but all they could see was a rather portly man scurrying away.

'That's all right. I'm surprised there hasn't been more shoving and pushing,' she smiled.

'You've dropped your betting slip,' he said stooping and picking up the paper on which she'd printed a horse's name.

As Albyn handed it back to her he shook his head.

'A bit of a long shot, that one.'

'I rather like long shots.'

'The word around the stables is that Ciragan is going to walk it.'

'Never did trust rumours,' she beamed. 'Only trust my nose and that seldom leads me astray.'

'Good luck with your nose then,' he said.

Once she had placed her bet and hurried away Albyn passed a note to the man behind the window. He read it, nodded and closed the hatch as Albyn headed back to the grandstand.

'That's peculiar', Katerina was saying beside Moore as the runners returned to the unsaddling enclosure.

'What is?'

'Someone's put a note in me pocket.'

She showed him. On an otherwise blank piece of paper was printed : Last race- bet on Olomaz.

'There was a man behind me...He bumped into me when someone bumped into him. Maybe he put it there.'

'Did he say anything?'

'He apologised- in English. He was English, well-spoken, thirties. He said Ciragan was going to win that race...'

'Shows what he knew then,' James smiled. 'Your pick romped home.'

'I'm sure I've seen him somewhere before as well.'

'Lots of Brits around,' he said. 'But you know, I didn't want to mention this but I've had the feeling that someone has been watching us. I thought I saw someone I knew, or at least recognised, earlier, when you went off to place that bet.'

She looked dubiously at him.

'I know, I know- it's probably my imagination.'

'What about this then?' she asked waving the note.

'Throw it away?'

'Why the tip though?'

'If it was meant for you.'

'You think it was put there by mistake?'

'No idea- but you didn't know the bloke did you?'

'But I'm sure I've seen him...That was it!'

She clapped her hands with excitment.

'What was what?'

'Yesterday when there was that police chase and arrest- remember? That man was sitting at one of the tables having a coffee.'

'Are you sure?'

'Positive.'

'But why remember him, Katerina? There were dozens of people round about. I can't remember one of them.'

'I've got a good memory like that,' she said. 'Runs in the family. I'm sure it was him.'

'Well, so what? Why shouldn't he be at the races like us?'

Suddenly the excitement went out of her face.

'Yeah, I suppose so. It must be coincidence. But then why the note?'

Moore had preferred it when she was illuminated by excitement so he found himself saying:

'Why don't you back the horse like the note says and see what happens?'

'Why James I do believe you're becoming hooked!' she laughed.

'Not at all. Look, there's just the one more race isn't there? You've done all right so far, haven't you?'

'Four winners out of four,' she said proudly.

'You're a worry to me, Katerina,' he said with mock sternness. 'I've never known anyone with such luck.'

'Luck my foot,' Katerina snorted. 'I'm a fine judge of horse flesh and of...'

She abruptly cut her sentence short and looked quickly away. Moore didn't notice her slight confusion.

'All you've got to do is place the same bet as you've been doing so far. That will still leave you well ahead for the day, won't it?'

'Mmm,' she replied. 'But what's the point of that? If I lose that's not going to hurt my pocket and if I win that'll hardly break the bank. There has to be something else to this.'

'Blowed if I know what it could be. We could always just forget it and you bet on whatever you were fancying anyhow.'

'We'll never know then, will we.'

'Know what?'

'I don't know!' she laughed and James laughed with her.

*

Denton read the latest report and sat back to contemplate the ceiling. He knew it well, every curlicule and swirl of the ornate rose in the centre of the ceiling. He was as familiar with it as he was with the mirror on the ceiling over Suzanne's bed. That there was a camera recording behind the mirror up there he had no doubt. The question was: why hadn't someone put the bite on him so far? Were the films being kept for Suzanne's own purposes? He knew that she had a lesbian lover and wondered if they viewed the tapes together, laughing at his mediocre performance.

What Albyn said was interesting- unexpected but interesting. The question was whether to abort or take advantage of these new circumstances. Albyn's action in the cinema, what about that? All right, Denton thought, it had been unauthorised and against handbook practice, but then look at the results. The other question in his mind was whether or not to run these developments past the Section Head in his daily briefing. He couldn't imagine him initiating any action, not with all that was going on elsewhere. It wasn't that Denton wanted to exclude him from the process- far from it; Denton wanted him to be as thoroughly embedded in it as possible. But there were ways of handling such situations. It was a bit like fishing, Denton imagined. That's all he could do 'imagine' since he was no angler. If he had been he wouldn't have thought of it as 'fishing'. The process by which a piece of fish made its way from the ocean's depths or the Tweed to his plate at 'Cheyne's' restaurant in Mayfair wasn't something which exercised his mind at all. Nevertheless he knew that a good *angler* would have to play the fish into his net; a brisk jerk on the line wouldn't do as the hook might be ripped from the fish's mouth. What they were 'angling' for was much more difficult to land than some rainbow trout. So- softly softly then, Denton told himself, practising steepling his fingers and looking immersed in thought.

*

'Someone's been through my room,' Katerina said.

They were meeting in the hotel bar to plan something for the evening. Moore quite liked the way it had been unstated that, while the holiday lasted- and a week seemed an incredibly short time as the third evening came- they would spend the time together.

'Are you sure?'

'Positive. Nothing was taken. Well, there's nothing to take really. I keep my purse with me and the hotel safe has my passport and other cash.'

'You know, I had the feeling the other day that someone had been in my room, but I just thought it was the cleaning maid.'

'Should I report it?'

'Probably best. It'll give the hotel detective something to do.'

'You've spotted him as well?'

'Chap over there reading the paper.'

'He's a bit obvious, isn't he.'

'Probably deliberately so. Put any burglars off.'

'If I was a burglar I'd be glad to see him there. Give me a free hand upstairs.'

'He may just be the lobby man, part of a highly trained team.'

'Hmmm. Let's go see the manager. You can tell him about your suspicions.'

By now, Albyn thought as he entered the room, she will have found out that someone had been searching her belongings. He had been deliberately clumsy, a hard thing for him to be. His instinct had been to be as careful as possible. However, because it was an act he did it perfectly, leaving this drawer slightly ajar, the mirror tilted to the left rather than to the right, the fringe of a nightgown poking out from under a pillow and other things rather untidy.

What he had noticed before he began his prying and planted the object, was that someone seemed to have been there before him. Now that was interesting! A tail the other day and now someone ahead of him with the subject under surveillance. Hmmm. Was it the locals or a stray? A hotel like this attracted burglars the way a cat did fleas. Some hotels even employed their own burglars. Whoever had been through her things had been remarkably clumsy. By the time Albyn left her room for the second time he had done more tidying up than probing. The main thing was that the package had been discreetly put in place. Now all he had to do was wait. He knew her departure time and that of the man she had linked up with. No need to worry about him, Albyn thought.

*

Moore took his time over composing his postcards home. Katerina had cried off for the afternoon, pleading a migraine as it was 'that time of the month'. Rather than venture out on his own Moore had decided to sit on his balcony, write his cards home and daydream.

Daydreaming had been the way he had survived his childhood. An essentially solitary individual he spent hours in his own head making up stories. He devoured books and his mother used to say that he spent more time in the local library than he did at home. It wasn't true, of course, but not far off the truth! Unlike other children he hadn't dreamt about becoming an astronaut or great hero, a train driver or heart surgeon. For most of his teenage years and early twenties he had no real idea what he'd like to do for a career. His teachers and tutors gave up asking and suggesting. Whatever he would end up doing- and Moore had no doubt that he'd eventually find his niche- he knew it would   have something to do with books and libraries and daydreaming. He wondered what dreams his father might have had, that is if someone of his generation was allowed to daydream. Perhaps daydreaming wasn't a working man's privilege. You needed energy to daydream and his father, what little he remembered of him, had always seemed exhausted and beaten down. His mother, on the other hand, had had the resilience of a willow. She worked hard to ensure that he was well fed, well clothed and well educated. Sometimes Moore felt guilty at the fact that it had taken so long to find what it was that he was meant to be doing. What had allowed him to live his life that way was his mother's attidude: *As long as you are happy, Jimmy*, she would say, *that's all I want*. Well, she had seen that he was happy and in her retirement could take some pride in his success.

He wondered what the burglar- he was sure now since what had happened to Katerina that it had been a burglar and not a clumsy chamber maid- would have made of his reading material. If the burglar would have been disappointed at not finding anything worth taking- no Rolex, no golden cigarette case, no platinum cuff links, no leather wallet bursting with credit cards and cash- would he have been puzzled by those well-thumbed paperbacks scattered on virtually every surface in the room? Moore remembered the completely random fashion in which he had selected books and had thrown them into his suitcase. Had he thought about it would he have selected these books- *Ice* by Anna Kavan, *Ubik* by Philip K. Dick, *The Shadow Laughs!* by Maxwell Grant or *Les Paletots sans Manches* by Léo Malet? He could envisage all those bulging blockbusters on the shelves in the airport shop as he waited to board his flight. Why had he not simply made do with a couple of them? He wondered if his friendly burglar had flicked through the paperbacks, inspecting the print for microsdots or coded messages! Wasn't it a standard cliché that inside the cover of a book you might find something other than that book? Well, Mister Burglar, Moore thought as he sipped a glass of iced water and twiddled his Biro, I hope you've had better luck elsewhere.

He composed four postcards, taking great care over them all and making no spelling mistakes. Some people scrawl the first thing that comes into their head- 'Having a great time; Wish you were here and I was there', that sort of thing- just to have done with it. But if there was one thing that Moore really cared about it was what he said and how he might say it. The first card was to his mother. A second was to his university friend in Leeds. The third was to the gang at the office of his publisher. The last one was to Morwen.

Moore told his mother that he was enjoying his holiday and that he'd met a nice girl named Katerina from the Isle of Man. His mother liked to hear about any women in his life. They had been few and far between; the fingers of one hand were more than enough to list them. The one thing now that would give her great joy was to see him settled down and married. She understood his caution, recognising that the memories of his childhood would have had an impact on his idea of marriage. She had always been truthful with him and though she had sought to shield him from the sadness of her marriage she had not lied to him or hidden anything. But as with his life's work Moore's approach to the state of marriage was that if it was meant to be it would happen in due course; otherwise he was happy as he was. His mother would be interested in hearing about Katerina, he knew, just as she had been about Naomi, Carla and Bridget. She had never met any of them, of course, because Moore had not proved to be quite what they wished him to be and had soon been dropped.

What do you tell your mother about your holiday within the limited space permitted on a four inch by six postcard? He wouldn't mention the burglary or the police chase they had witnessed, nor did he think he should mention the visit to the casino. His mother would have worried about any of those incidents. The thought that he might be gambling would have brought a stern rebuke from her on his return. Instead he found himself telling her that Katerina was the nicest woman he had ever met and that he hoped they could keep seeing each other once the holiday was over. They would be flying back on the same airplane.

The postcard was one he had had made specially. While he and Katerina had been seeing the sights a street photographer had snapped them. The deal was that your photograph could be printed on a postcard for you to send back to your friends. The idea struck Moore as better than buying those standard sights of the city cards which hung on racks outside every tobacconist and newsagent's shop they passed. So while they waited the photographer had popped into his small kiosk and printed out on a laptop the half dozen cards they each requested. There they were, smiling as though ridiculously pleased with themselves and standing closer than he had realised. In the background was the Seljuq Sultan Alaaddin mosque.

The messages to his friend in Leeds and the people at the office were more general. He did not name Katerina but simply referred to her as 'a fellow Brit' staying at the same hotel with whom he'd 'done the sights'. He knew that when he got back home the office would quiz him closely about this woman but he'd deal with that when the time came.

The card to Morwen was different. For one thing it was a standard postcard bought from the rack in the hotel lobby. He had been using it and several others as bookmarks. With this message Moore took extreme care. He wrote it out in his notebook, the one he always carried around in a pocket so that he could jot down ideas which occurred to him as he strolled about the city. Katerina had noticed him doing this but hadn't asked him what he was writing. Once he had got the wording right he carefully transcribed it to the message space on the postcard. It was in a mixture of English, French and Turkish and made as much sense as *La Blanche Neige* or any part of *Alcools*. He took particular care over the punctuation. Then he tore up the draft and flushed the pieces away.

*

When the postcard to Morwen was copied and the interceptors attempted to decipher it this is what they came up with:

Castle Handicap Hurdle Race (2 miles)
For 4 year olds and upwards
1st Ballinaborey (at 10/1) ridden by T. O'Brien (10st-12lb)
2nd West of the Moon (at 8/1) ridden by C. Kinane
3rd Connkeheley (at 4/1) ridden by S.Patton
9 runners. The favourite was Brighter Sovereign at 2/1 on.

'What the hell is this all about?' Harris, the head man in the decoding section asked.

'We're still trying to crack it, sir,' Porter his main underling said apologetically.

'Do we have any location on the recipient?'

'The address seems to be somewhere in rural Ireland, sir.'

'Can we please get someone over there without causing a diplomatic incident,' Harris ordered.

But what they found was that the location was a deserted old farm house that had not been inhabited for years. There were a few owls about, some rabbits, and lots of weeds, but no sign of anyone having lived there for many years. Not a milk churn, cartwheel or rusting harrow to be seen. The agent with his Boston accent took plenty of photographs of the site. He had a pleasant stay in the local hostelry where his 'search for his roots' involved him in much conversation with the likes of the landlord Mr. Rafferty (father and son) and O'Connor and countless others who came and went as the evening drew its skirts around them all. None of them could recall anyone by the name of Morwen living in the place, but they appreciated Tom Murphy's liberality with his purse and tongue.

*

Moore became concerned when Katerina was not to be found anywhere the next morning. At the reception desk they were only able to tell him that 'someone had called' on her early that morning and she had gone out of the hotel quite willingly with the man. No, they had no idea who he was other than that he had given the name Bünyamin Özdemir. No, the man was not familiar to them.

There was little that Moore could do. She had gone out with this man and Moore did not have an exclusive call on her time and person. Deprived of her company he slouched around the city in a haphazard fashion, using his camera to take both standard tourist pictures and other images which caught his eye. One of his passions was the photography of people such as Lartigue and Bresson whose vision he found refreshing. 'We think we are seeing but we do not really see until we have seen what we have not seen'- he could not recall who had made that gnomic statement (whatever it meant).

He stopped at small restaurants and cafés frequently, both to get out of the heat- it was one of those days when the heat simply sat on everything like a giant, invisible toad- and to rest his feet, which seemed to be drawing up the heat from the pavements.

This is the sort of holiday I would have been having had I not met Katerina that first evening, he told himself. Without her he felt he was merely going through the old routine of passing time as pleasantly as he could rather than branching out and having fun. He remembered the holidays he and his mother would take, down to the south coast or across to Wales to visit some obscure relative. He could always entertain himself and script something in his head if he was left alone while the adults talked. His holidays as an adult tended to be like the excursions of some timid creature, quite a contrast to the daydreams he would have whilst on holiday. Here he was sitting in a nameless café surrounded by Turks chattering away to themselves like so many exotic birds in a cage. Outwardly he was someone like them sitting sipping his sweet coffee and eating a sugary pastry while browsing through the daily paper. Inside, however, he was imaging all kinds of things- for example, what if Katerina had been kidnapped?

'Excuse me- are you Mr. Moore, Mr. James Moore?' someone asked in English.

He looked up and found himself gazing at a stranger.

'Yes,' he replied hesitantly.

'May I join you?'

Moore made a gesture towards the empty chair across from him and the man sat down. A waiter scurried over with what seemed to be more than usual haste. The stranger gave his order in fluent Turkish and the waiter hurried away. The man smiled easily at Moore and offered him a cigarette.

'Who are you?' Moore asked shaking his head at the offer.

'Of course. Forgive me. I am Inspector Atalik of the Ankara police'

He flipped open a wallet and Moore caught sight of what he took to be a warrant card. For all he knew it could be a bus pass. But there had been something about the way the waiter had moved which made Moore believe that the man across the table really was from the local police.

'Has something happened to Miss Burton?'

That was the first thought to cross his mind.

'No, the delightful Miss Burton is back at the hotel quite unharmed.'

'How did you know I was here?'

'Unfortunately we have had someone following you and Miss Burton, discreetly of course.'

'Why on earth are you doing that?'

'It was thought, wrongly I am happy to say, that you- either one or both of you- were engaged in an activity which was contrary to the interests of our state.'

'Good lord! Whatever gave you that idea? I'm simply here on holiday.'

'Crossed wires, I believe you might say. Information received which was rather tarnished. It didn't help that you looked somewhat like the man we were asked to watch. He had a female accomplice and unfortunately Miss Burton fitted that   role. I've been asked to extend our apologies to you.'

'If you don't mind I'll have one of those cigarettes now.'

'Of course.'

Moore studied the hands which offered the cupped match to him as he put the cigartette to his lips. The knuckles sprouted dark hairs; the cuticles and nails were well looked after.

'A bit of a shock all this,' he said once he'd inhaled.

'Yes, I understand that. When one world intrudes into another it can shake one's certainties.'

'Are you responsible for going through our hotel rooms?'

'Not personally but, alas yes.'

'May I go back to the hotel to see Katerina?'

'Of course, Mr. Moore. You are free to enjoy the remainder of your holiday which I hope has not been made too unplesant by my disclosure.'

'Not at all, Inspector. It was kind of you to inform me in person.'

'The English are a fine race, very correct- apart from the football hooligans; but we have them as well.'

Moore rose and started to leave payment but Inspector Atalik stayed his hand.

'Please, let me take care of that. A token of apology.'

'That's kind of you. I'll nip back and see Katerina.'

'My regards, Mr. Moore.'

*

Albyn had sent his final report and had received the order to return as 'his mother was ill'. There had been no trouble at the check-in and the flight home had been smooth and incident free. When he'd stretched his legs and had walked back from first class through economy he had seen the couple from the hotel sitting together. The young woman was asleep and had her head resting on the man's shoulder. He was happily gazing out of the oval window watching the clouds below the aircraft. Back in his seat Albyn asked for some iced water and he continued to read the paperback he had brough along for the flight, *I married a Dead Man* by William Irish. The landing at Heathrow was non-eventful. Both the man and the woman from the hotel went through the 'Green Channel' at customs and neither was stopped. They shared a taxi into the city. The agent who was hiding in the space under the back seat on which they sat quietly retrieved from the young woman's luggage the package which Albyn had hidden there some days earlier. That bag was not the original one she had flown out with but a subsitute with a hidden compartment under the false bottom.

*

Of course, that's not *quite* what happened, is it?

Lakeside

The cottage was built on a narrow wooded point projecting into the lake. It divided what was called North Pond from the two, smaller southern lakes. A deeply rutted dirt-track wound uphill through the woods from the black-top road to the cottage.

There were three other cottages spaced irregularly around the point. Each had its own stretch of water-front with a wooden jetty. Moored at these was either a small motor boat or a canoe.

Once Labor Day had passed the visitors who rented summer cottages around the lake went home. Everything became peaceful once more, apart from any late night noise filtering up from the 'Lakeview Inn', the local drinking spot. It was situated on the main road at the narrow neck of the promontory giving its name to 'Gooseneck Island'.

I spent much of that summer recovering by reclining on a lounger on the roof of the boat-house. As hard as I tried I didn't get a deep tan. My chest, arms and legs would go a light brown, my shoulders and back would be covered in freckles, but otherwise I barely changed colour at all. Being fair-haired I reckoned I had a pigment deficiency.

Shading part of the boathouse were tall pines and oaks, from which might fall the caterpillars of gypsy moths. Higher up the slope were hickory, beech and butternut trees, a vermillion berried sumac, cedar and yew shrubs and a honeysuckle. I had always loved trees- not gloomy trees but happily coloured trees, especially maples and birches. As a child I had been fascinated to watch syrup being tapped from maples

Like everything else about the cottage the boat-house needed repairing. At some point, before we bought it, vandals had broken through the roof. Inside there was a cluttering of old tyres, wooden planks, beer cans and other rubbish. Muskrats occasionally tried to nest in the boat-house.

The vandals had also dismantled part of our shore stone wall and broke part of the jetty. Each day I would tidy something up or make a repair here and there. At night the occasional stray drunk or couple might come stumbling up the drive. The cottage having been unoccupied for so long they still thought they could mess around the place. I'd switch on the floodlight and sometimes fire the shotgun into the air and they got the idea fast that they weren't welcome.

In those days because I couldn't sleep too well and my back would begin to ache, I'd get up early, often before sun-up, and wander barefoot down to the jetty to watch the dawn breaking. A flight of thirty-six steps led down from the cottage to the water. When the early morning mist evaporated a clammy feeling would be left in the air. Now and then a lone fisherman in a canoe rented from 'Elmer's Supplies and Bait' might be out trolling in the shallows across the other side of the lake.

Breakfast time was always the time when my mother talked to me, wondering what I was going to do once I was better. When she did that I'd keep my eyes fixed on the cereal packet and read the information on it about vitamins which played an essential part in the conditioning of my skin. I seldom spoke except about inconsequentials like how the Red Sox were doing and whether she wanted me to drive over to the 'Big Y' for anything. We were both reticent by nature, I suppose, and one conversation a day seemed enough for us. She'd spend her day drinking. She would start as she watched re-runs of 'The Lucy Show' or 'The New Price is Right' on day-time television. Sometimes she'd make it through to 'As the World Turns' or 'All My Children' before taking a snooze. I'd see her with a perplexed look on her face some days as she struggled to pick up the thread of the storyline. Maybe it made sense and maybe it didn't, whether you fell asleep or not. I'd be sunning myself while reading whatever books I'd managed to find in the library that week.

Once I got the job as a part-time janitor in the paper mill there was a lull in that kind of morning conversation. After a few weeks however she was asking me if I'd given any thought to going back to college to complete my qualification. I didn't mind the job I was doing, I'd reply whilst reading how those vitamins strengthened my nerves, aided my digestion and maintained my vision. It didn't demand much of me, the job, apart from physical effort which suited me fine. I was able to save some money and I was happy enough. The conversation would usually end with mother at the sink washing the breakfast plates and dishes. I'd slip away to my room where I'd read a book or listen to something on the radio. At some point I'd work out with the barbells or go for a jog through the woods. By the time I got back mother would be watching 'General Hospital' or 'The Edge of Night' and be well into the bottle.

Of course I'd given thought to what I might do. Every day seemed to take the same spiralling course mentally, bringing me back to the same inescapable impasse. I could never see straight ahead in any direction far enough for me to decide I'll do this as opposed to that. I knew the kind of job mother wished me to be doing- something like working in a bank: something clean, something with reasonable prospects, something with challenge and responsibilities. To me that felt like putting on a strait-jacket.

In the past year thousands of soldiers and ex-POWs had returned from Vietnam, just like me. The patience and sympathy extended to them had seemed practically unlimited until you started to read about ex-vets going crazy and slaughtering people. I was relatively lucky compared to others. I wasn't missing a limb or otherwise physically damaged. I was only 'psychologically traumatised' by some internal rupture to a psychic ligament. Looking in the mirror I had no way of knowing how dislocated inside I had become, how much my emotional metabolism had been damaged. At times I didn't feel that changed at all; at other times, usually at night as I struggled to sleep, I felt as though a storm was about to break within me. I felt as though over the previous eighteen months I had been transformed into a totally different person against my will.

I spent my time, when not sunning myself and daydreaming, walking through the surrounding woods. You could reach a clearing atop one of the surrounding peaks from which you could catch sight of the twisting, silvery river which split the township in two. The river had twice overflowed its banks and the town council had on their agenda permanently various schemes for strengthening dikes and building larger reservoirs. The spruce and pine trees had once been valuable natural assets before logging became unprofitable. But pulp was still supplied to the paper mill where I worked.

Occasionally I'd walk all the way to the nearby township Whip City. The great days of that whip making industry were long past and you might as well have renamed the place 'Vacant Lot City'. The town was spread over nearly fifty square miles of countryside, although Main Street was the commercial backbone of the place. Thereon you found the library, the post office, all the various stores there were, the town hall and the small police station. The fire station was tucked away off a side street.

Once in town- whether I'd driven there to shop for us or walked- I'd spend an hour or so in the 'Athenaeum' reading the daily papers in a side room. That summer there was a numismatic exhibition in one of the rooms and another of Indian folk lore after that. I became fascinated by a false face Iroquois mask carved out of basswood that was supposed to have magical properties. Then I'd wander up and down the side streets looking in shop windows or at whatever caught my eye. Pedestrians were few as the streets were usually long and the heat wave seemed continuous. The first day I'd gone for a stroll I'd been quizzed by a patrolman who pulled up beside me and asked me what I was doing. He couldn't believe that I was just strolling around.

The Indians had called the area Woronoco, which means 'the winding country'. There were none of the original Algonquin speaking Pocumtus and Wampanoags left. The largely Congregationalist early settlers- pious folk, simple folk, practical farmers- had massacred and obliterated the indigenous native population.

Many of the once numerous graceful elms which lined the older side streets were diseased. But it was still beautiful and I loved to walk those streets remembering when I had played in them as a child.

At the weekend I'd take mother out for a drive and a picnic somewhere. She'd prepare sandwiches and hot dogs and there'd be coffee in the thermos flask and cold drinks packed in the ice box. In the old Chevy I'd avoid the busier highway and drive along the rural routes which wound through the green and purple hills. The trees of the silent and motionless forests seemed like tufts of anemones thrown up from the bottom of the ocean. We passed under power lines and over their shadows as though skipping a rope.

Beside me mother would be gazing at it all as though seeing it for the first time, which in a way she was.

'And where are you taking me today, Jimmy?' she'd ask as we set off.

'Wait and see, Mom,' I'd say; 'It's a surprise.'

'I love a surprise,' she'd say.

'That's a surprise,' I'd say and we'd look at each other and smile.

Once she had known the area like the back of her hand; but she'd forgotten it as a result of the drinking which she'd started after Dad died. That had been when I was ten; before that she never touched a drop. She hadn't watched much TV either as she and Dad had loved scooting into the hills to walk and spot birds. When she started drinking it never seemed that heavy; but she was a slightly built woman and it didn't take much to leave her bemused.

We'd stop now and then and get out and walk a bit. I needed to do that so my back would settle. Mother would point out and name the various flowers- purple columbine, white anemone, blue bugloss and red devil's paintbrush. Some parts of her memory seemed perfectly intact. Over the fields of spatula grass, which were peppered with white daisies like dandruff on a collar, would fly red-winged blackbirds or orioles. Crows sat on roadside power lines looking like crotchets on a musical score. In a distant field a tractor might be trailing a hay-baler which would spit out like cuds neatly wired bundles of hay.

In places the roads had been blasted through the solid rock. You could still see the dynamite scars and bore holes in the exposed swathes of basalt, gneisses and schists. At some places signs warned of falling rocks. In winter suspended from those sheer faces of exposed rock hung udder-like pendules of ice, more like bleached and bloodless organic tissue than chandeliers or lace frills.

I would drive slowly through the small villages so that mother could look at the old brick buildings and white-painted clapboard houses with their porches and verandas and trellising overgrown with Virginia creepers. Bread-bin shaped mail boxes stood guard at the foot of each driveway. On the outskirts of many such towns were net-covered tobacco fields.

Mother's favourite picnicking spot was beside the reservoir. There were rough-hewn tables with benches, outdoor charcoal grills and oil drum rubbish bins. Once we'd had our picnic mother would snooze in the folding chair I'd brought for her while I wandered around the reservoir. Feeding into it was a small stream which had its source near an abandoned quarry. The stream gushed out between angular blocks of black lichen covered stones. Ferns choked part of the gully through which the stream ran. I could cross it by a fallen tree. On the other side of the stream I'd reach a sphagnum swamp fringed with arrow weeds and cattails. The bright pink flowers of knotweed floated above a web of stems like the multiple eyes of some alien monster. Speckled throughout the swamp were the red rosettes of pitcher plants. Everywhere there was a profusion of colours- white hellebore, skunk cabbage, marsh marigold.

What I liked most of all was looking out across the lake now that it was no longer swarming with water skiers and holiday makers riding around with outboard motors at full throttle. That was all I felt like doing most days, or felt capable of doing. You adapted to the season and circumstances, I guess, like the animals head for cover and plants head for the light. Each day seemed increasingly unreal, as though I was on the other side of the television screen which mother stared at unrelentingly as though it held the key to the future. I wondered at what precise moment whatever it was that had gone out of me had done so. I wondered what it was that was still seeping out of me, like a slow puncture.

Some days I'd go swimming in the lake along with the trout and pike. Despite the heat of the day the water would be cold. For hours, centuries even, the sun had been pouring its warmth into this lake and still the water was cold. Glaciers had reached this far south. The post-glacial clay deposits had provided the foundation for the pre-Civil War local brick industry. Gliding out on my stomach I'd hang face down in the water doing the dead-man's float. Turning on my back I would gaze up into a pure blue sky. I'd be comforted if I could locate in it no fissure, no superfluous blemish, no point of stress and no points of egress or access. It was just a flat, opaque and bland membrane that much later would turn black and blind us all. After several minutes of aimlessly floating I broke into a slow crawl and swam towards the distant shore, not straining myself but keeping up a steady rhythm and pausing now and then to tread water and look around.

Once in a while Kimberly, the sixteen year old daughter of our nearest neighbours on the point, might paddle her canoe beside me and chat. She was always offering herself to me sexually- a shag, a blow-job, whatever I wanted. She seemed puzzled by the polite way I would reject her advances, so used was she to having them taken up by the various teenage youths who hung around her. She wanted to know if I was impotent, or gay, or had been injured in the "gentials" during my tour of duty in Vietnam. She seemed totally bewildered by the response that I really wasn't interested in sex with her or anybody else at the moment. She'd paddle away and look back at me strangely, as though I was some peculiar fish that had drifted into the lake.

Eventually I'd swim back to our shore and towel myself dry. I'd sun myself some more on the jetty and listen to the empty oil drums being knocked together beneath me by a gentle tongue of water. The surface of the lake would eventually settle and become a frosted glass panel which could hold no image. Everything would be being pulled gently apart on its surface.

*

Around three o'clock I'd drive to the paper mill. The company had been formed just before the beginning of the First World War and had its headquarters in Pennsylvania. It was the largest single employer in the area with over a thousand people- many semi-skilled Puerto Ricans- on its payroll. I was the part-time janitor, my shift running from four until ten at night. I could clock off three minutes before my time without jeopardising my pay's calculation. I drew two dollars fifty an hour.

Inside the old factory, even with all the doors and windows wide open, it was a hothouse. Overhead pipes and tap brackets hissed steam. Condensation pooled on the floor. I was fortunate since I moved around the various floor levels and wings. Others had to sweat over the conveyor belts and cutters. On the top floor Tom (who had for some reason befriended me) sat in his underpants, sipping innumerable cold drinks as he regulated the steam output conditioning the various papers.

I wore a special pair of overalls with the company's insignia- a thistle-printed on the back. Before I donned the overalls I would strip off my outer clothes and wear only my underpants. Even so I would lose three pounds weight in a week. My first chore, after I'd collected all my mops and brooms and buckets from the store cupboard, was to swab down the tables, clean the ashtrays and sweep the floor in the cafeteria.

Next I'd sweep the steps down to the ground floor and the basement. I'd head along to the packing room office and sweep that, tidying the bins and ashtrays and cleaning the windows. On the office wall was a calendar each day of which was marked by some historical event, great or small. I wondered sometimes if there was one day on which nothing of any significance happened.

Then using a mobile propane vacuum I would sweep along the aisles of the ground floor packing, storing and trimming rooms. Where the wooden floors of the older part of the building weren't protected by metal sheeting they were badly gouged and broken, so that the vacuum sometimes got stuck.

Battery operated fork lift trucks and hand-pulled trolleys moved skids stacked with paper into the various rooms. A roller conveyor belt carried the bundles of trimmed paper from the mechanical guillotines to be packaged. The packages were then moved into the newer storage room, where the floor was concrete.

After this I would sweep the remaining stairwells leading to the basement before sweeping the rear stairs from the second floor conditioning room. By this time, having paced myself the way I did when swimming across the lake, it would be six o'clock. The women's and then the men's separate quarter of an hour coffee breaks began. I would sit out the whole half an hour before going into the only air-conditioned room in the mill, the General Finishing Office where the factory manager was located during the day.

At seven o'clock precisely, bearing disinfectant, toilet paper refills, scrubbing brush and paper towels as well as my mop and bucket, I would stand on the threshold of the women's toilet off the first floor sorting room. I would always pause, rattle the mop against the bucket and call out 'Anyone home?' Though some of the younger women teased me by dashing out of cubicles shrieking they soon got over doing that when I took no offence and screamed in mock horror back. I had an hour in which to clean the sinks and toilet bowls, the mirrors and the walls, and to empty the sanitary bins in cubicles two, four and six. Finally I'd mop the floor and exit shouting 'All yours, ladies!'

When I had swept out the foreman's office on the same floor I had an hour to kill before the nine o'clock coffee break. I'd re-mop the cafeteria floor and wipe the tables and make a couple of circuits of the ground floor again. I'd chat to one of the office girls who always worked late and the lame security guard who sat by the clocking-out cards.

Eventually I'd make my way back up to the top floor to chat with Tom, who had a ten hour shift and was the highest paid employee outside the office staff. At nine we'd go down to the cafeteria together and drink cold grape juice. The women would come in and sit at the far end of the room, while the men when they came in sat near the automatic vending machines. I couldn't decide if this was 'company policy' or an agreed form of 'segregation of the sexes'. Certainly the women had to walk a little further to get their snacks and drinks (unless they had lunch-boxes with them) and this gave some of the men more time to watch them moving. Some of the women, knowing this was happening, wiggled more than was necessary for normal locomotion. One woman-Maxine- a tight breasted and petite woman was fancied by many of the younger men and I'd often hear them describing what they'd do to her if they got her into one of the service lifts. Nobody ever did.

Sammy and Guy, two of the box stitchers, joined us and invited us to a party at their place after work. They were vets just like me but dope-heads who often spent their breaks in the parking lot smoking a reefer in their car. Tom and I declined the invite. They shrugged and wandered away together.

Once everyone had finished I'd mop the floor again, empty the waste bins and clean the tables one more time. Then I'd rinse out the mop head in a hand-trough downstairs in the men's lavatory. I'd drag the full bag of rubbish I'd collected out to the mechanical compressor at the rear loading bay.

Finally I'd wash myself, put my street clothes back on and amble to the clocking out board to punch my card dead on 9.57 pm.

I'd drive slowly home, listening to the cicadas sounding like dozens of rusty lawnmowers in the still night air. All kinds of malevolent looking insects flew across the bright headlights and splattered against the windscreen. As I approached the gully leading up to the point I would hear a bullfrog sending out its stentorian croak from amongst the unseen reeds. Every evening as I passed the inn a dog ran out and barked at me.

When I got home I would find mother in her dressing-gown sprawled on the settee fast asleep with some dumb programme still showing. I'd carry her to her room- she weighed nothing at all, it seemed- and put her in her bed. I'd locate the empty bottle and throw it in the bin, then wash out her drinking glass. I'd take a shower after I'd had a glass of cold milk and the sandwich she usually left for me in the fridge.

I wouldn't go straight to sleep. When there was a night game at Fenway I'd listen to the exploits of Fisk, Yastrzemski, Petrocelli and Smith on the radio. I'd thumb through some old magazines, flicking the pages like I had done dozens of times before. I had read all the magazines but I liked to go through them again and again because most of the stuff in them I'd missed while I was in Vietnam. Somewhere in those pages maybe I thought there was something I had to know. When my eyes started to lose focus I'd switch off the bedside lamp and lie in the dark listening to my breathing.

Sometimes a dog would howl until its owners let it in; or the noise of a rock band playing at the inn would drift up to the lake.

I would lie and wonder if there was anything remotely human about me. Sometimes I felt as though I was wearing that Indian mask.

I thought about my mother and wished that somehow we could escape from here.

I thought about my Dad and the day we hauled the stump of a lightning shattered old beech tree from the ground. I had loved to work beside my Dad. When he was papering a room I'd mix the paste. The day after we'd removed that stump he had the heart attack and died.

I thought of the long stretch of days that lay ahead of me and those that I had somehow survived.

I thought of the mobile vacuum which had become jammed as I wheeled it through the paper mill and how it had taken three of us to dislodge it. I wondered if something similar had happened to me and how I would get going again.

I would fall asleep when I had become sufficiently disgusted with all my self-pity and worrying. My dreams would engulf me as though I was slowly sinking into the lake.

(1973, revised 2011)